Katerina's Wish

Katerina's Wish

Jeannie Mobley

MARGARET K. MCELDERRY BOOKS
New York   London   Toronto   Sydney   New Delhi

MARGARET K. McELDERRY BOOKS

An imprint of Simon & Schuster Children's Publishing Division

1230 Avenue of the Americas, New York, New York 10020

This book is a work of fiction. Any references to historical events, real people, or real places are used fictitiously. Other names, characters, places, and events are products of the author's imagination, and any resemblance to actual events or places or persons, living or dead, is entirely coincidental.

MARGARET K. McELDERRY BOOKS is a trademark of Simon & Schuster, Inc.

For information about special discounts for bulk purchases, please contact Simon & Schuster Special Sales at 1-866-506-1949 or business@simonandschuster.com.

The Simon & Schuster Speakers Bureau can bring authors to your live event. For more information or to book an event, contact the Simon & Schuster Speakers Bureau at 1-866-248-3049 or visit our website at www.simonspeakers.com.

Also available in a Margaret K. McElderry Books hardcover edition.

Book design by Debra Sfetsios-Conover

The text for this book is set in Cochin LT Std.

Manufactured in the United States of America

0214 OFF

First Margaret K. McElderry Books paperback edition March 2014

10 9 8 7 6 5 4 3 2 1

The Library of Congress has cataloged the hardcover edition as follows:

Mobley, Jeannie.

Katerina's wish / Jeannie Mobley. — 1st ed.

p. cm.

Summary: Thirteen-year-old Trina's family left Bohemia for a Colorado coal town to earn money to buy a farm, but by 1901 she doubts that either hard work or hoping will be enough, even after a strange fish seems to grant her sisters' wishes.

ISBN 978-1-4424-3343-4 (hardcover)

ISBN 978-1-4424-3345-8 (eBook)

[1. Family life — Colorado — Fiction. 2. Coal mines and mining — Fiction. 3. Immigrants — Fiction. 4. Czech Americans — Fiction. 5. Colorado — History — 1876-1950 — Fiction.] I. Title.

PZ7.M71275Kat 2012

[Fic] — dc23

2011044392

ISBN 978-1-4424-3344-1 (pbk)

In memory of my father, whose dreams took us
so many places,

And to my mother, whose belief in me helped make
this wish come true.

Chapter 1

MY PAPA'S DREAM brought us to America. Momma said only a fool believed in dreams, but she knew Papa, so she packed our trunks. And whether she believed or not, that dream swept us out of Bohemia and across the ocean. We'd arrived, in the autumn of 1900 in "a new land for the new century," as Papa put it. By May of 1901, neither the dream nor the country felt new. They both felt old and worn out. As I stood behind our house, staring at a dozen bundles of filthy laundry, I couldn't help but think Momma had been right.

Papa had dreamed of a thriving farm where we would live well. He had imagined acres of green fields, not the dry, barren hills of southern Colorado. He had imagined fresh air and sunshine, the bounty of the fertile land filling our larder and our pockets. Instead, he spent long days underground, toiling in the unwholesome air of a coal mine. And even with all this laundry Momma took on, our pockets stayed empty and our larder was never full. Now that my sisters and I were out of school for the summer, Momma had determined to take on as much washing as we could from the bachelors in town. But it still wasn't likely to mean much money.

"This is too much wash to do in the kitchen," Momma observed from the back door.

"It's too much to do at all," I grumbled.

"If you want to be going back to school in the fall, you'll be needing a new dress," she said. "And the money's got to come from somewhere."

The new term would not start until October, when the schoolmaster returned from one of the other coal camps in the area. But saving money wasn't easy. When we left Bohemia, Papa had thought a year in the coal mines would earn us enough for a farm. We had been here nine months already and had saved almost nothing.

"At least Trina will get a new dress," Aneshka said. She was sitting on the back step, kicking at the dust. "I'll just get her old dress cut down to my size, and Holena will get mine that used to be hers."

"I don't mind," Holena said quietly from her seat beside Aneshka. She would be starting school for the first time in the fall.

"Mind or not, it can't be helped," Momma said, her mouth setting into a thin, tight line. It was almost the only expression she had worn since coming to America. "And you do have to go to school." School was important. Momma had had few chances to learn English. She relied on my sisters and me to translate for her.

Momma sighed, looking again at the big piles of coal-blackened laundry. "We'll take this load down by the creek. That way we don't have to haul water. Trina, you carry it there, and we'll all join you when chores here are done."

I began hauling tubs and bundles of filthy clothes across camp and down the steep slope to the little creek to the west. It took me four trips back and forth across the shabby town, and each time I returned to the house it seemed Aneshka was working slower and slower at her easy jobs. Holena, who was too little to help carry anyway, was watching Momma knead the week's bread dough. I glared at Aneshka as I gathered the bundles, but she ignored me.

In the creek bottom, I found a wide, grassy spot and built a fire, then arranged stones to balance a tub over the flames. Then I filled the tub with water from the creek. By the time I was done, my sweat-soaked dress clung to my shoulders. My mother and sisters had still not arrived. I wiped the sweat from my forehead with the corner of my apron. Was this all there was to my father's dreams — sweat and coal dust and endless hours of work?

I stretched and looked around. If I was going to spend the day scrubbing filthy clothes, I wasn't going to stay here while I waited for the water to boil. I deserved these few minutes to myself. I wandered along the water's edge, listening to the birds chirp in the low bushes and trying to forget the drudgery of the day ahead.

A short distance downstream, the valley narrowed and turned. The slopes of the valley became steeper, blocking the view of anything around the bend. I had never gone there. For months, I had come only to the creek to draw water. My pace quickened as a flutter of adventure stirred in my heart. I glanced back toward the laundry. My mother and sisters still weren't there. I had time to see what lay beyond the shoulder of land.

Around the bend, I stopped in amazement. The creek spread out into a still pool. At its edge, an ancient cottonwood tree leaned out, its massive branches reaching across until they shaded the creek bottom from slope to slope. For a moment I thought I might be dreaming. I had never seen this tree before.

As I approached the tree, the high slopes of the valley shut out all sounds from the mine. For the first time in months, I couldn't hear the clank and screech of the cables in the hoist. The only sounds were the gurgle of the stream as it entered the pool and the sighing breath of breezes in the leaves overhead. Unexpectedly, tears filled my eyes. How often I had taken those sounds for granted in Bohemia. How foolishly we had left that behind to come here.

I pressed my hand against the rough bark to assure myself the tree was real. The trunk was so thick, I could not have reached even halfway around it if I'd tried. Two massive roots, each as thick as a mule's haunch, ran from the trunk to the water's edge, enclosing a triangle of soft grass between water and tree. I stepped over the closer root and sat down, my back against the massive trunk. The roots encircled me like my father's arms had when I was a child, making me feel safe. In the stillness, the constant ache for our home in Bohemia welled up inside me.

I watched a small leaf spinning lazily across the surface of the water, feeling like I was in a secret place. The mine, the washing, the endless chores had disappeared. There was only me, and the soothing stillness of this place. But as the leaf drifted out over the deepest part of the pool, I realized that I was not alone. A movement beneath the surface created a ripple that caught the leaf and spun it faster. I sat up to see better. With a flash of silver, the thing disappeared under the bank. I crawled forward and leaned out over the pool. The water was clear, and I could see the pebbles on the bottom in the shifting green light beneath the tree. I lay still and watched. After a long moment, a fish emerged from beneath the bank. It was not a large fish, but

4

larger than I had expected in a creek that size. It watched me, just as I watched it.

A story stirred in my memory. Back in Bohemia, my grandmother had told stories as we helped her stuff sausages. One had been about a fish—but I couldn't quite remember.

The fish began to rise toward me with slow sweeps of its tail. I leaned closer, until my face almost touched the water. I could clearly see its flat, broad head and the whiskerlike feelers protruding from either side of its mouth and chin. It was a carp, a fish we had considered lucky back in Bohemia. Only a few inches and the surface of the water separated us as it watched me with one shiny black eye. I held my breath, waiting to see what it would do.

"Katerina!"

A shout from upstream shattered the moment. I jerked my head up and the fish darted away. Aneshka was standing at the bend, her hands cupped around her mouth, getting ready to yell again. I scrambled quickly to my feet and stepped out from the shade.

"Coming!" I called, and hurried toward her. I didn't want Aneshka here. This place felt special—magical—in a way Aneshka couldn't understand. She was too much like our mother.

"Where have you been?" she said, her hands going to her hips.

"Nowhere," I said, and brushed past her without another word. She was five years younger than me; I didn't have to answer to her. But as I approached the washtubs, I knew I would have to answer to Momma.

"Where have you been, Katerina! I sent you down here to start the washing."

"The water was heating; it wasn't ready," I protested. I hadn't been gone very long.

5

"But it isn't hot, because while you went off daydreaming, the fire went out."

I looked at the washtub. Weak wisps of smoke and bits of half-burned wood were all that remained of the fire I had started. No steam rose off the water.

"I'm sorry." I began stuffing fresh wood beneath the tub. Soon the fire was lit again, but Momma wasn't satisfied.

"Trina, the family needs your help, not your daydreams. You are thirteen, practically a woman, but you act like a child. Honestly, Holena is more help than you some days."

"I am sorry, Momma," I said again. What else could I say? I couldn't talk back to her. And there was no point in saying how I ached with homesickness, not just for what we had left behind, but for what we were supposed to have here in America. That was not the sort of thing I could say to my mother.

I wasn't sorry I had left the laundry and found that peaceful place beneath the tree, either. It had been worth a scolding to feel still and secure for those few moments.

We boiled and scrubbed laundry until dusk that day, stopping only briefly to eat a lunch of bread and pickles while a fresh tub of water heated. In the afternoon, Momma left us to finish while she returned to the house to form the week's bread into loaves and begin preparing our supper.

"You are in charge, Trina, so don't go wandering off again," she said before she left, proving she hadn't forgotten my mistake. I hadn't forgotten either. I had worked extra hard to make it up to her, but I was still thinking about the fish and trying to remember the story.

As soon as Momma left, Aneshka started complaining, but I wasn't listening. Every time I bent over the boiling tub, I saw the fish in my mind, just beneath the surface. As I scrubbed the clothes on the washboard, I searched my memory for the story that I couldn't quite recall.

We carried load after load of heavy, wet laundry to the house, and hung it to dry. When we finally heaped the last pile into the washtub and struggled up the slope into camp, the whistle had blown at the mine and the shift was changing. Aneshka and I were still hanging shirts on the lines when my father arrived, trudging silently, his shoulders slumped by exhaustion. In Bohemia, he had always whistled or sung when he walked. Here, he was just too tired.

I was relieved when Momma said nothing over dinner about my absence that morning. I didn't want to tell them about the tree or the fish. It would sound childish, like something out of a fairy tale. Besides, my mother's accusation of daydreaming still stung. I hadn't been daydreaming. What I had seen was strange, but real.

When supper was over, Papa went out to sit on the porch in the cool evening, and Momma took out her mending basket and sat with him. Before she went, she turned to me.

"Trina, you will wash the dishes tonight. Holena and Aneshka may do as they like."

I opened my mouth to protest, but closed it again when my mother gave me a sharp look. "They worked all day without complaint—you ran off and left your work undone, which slowed us all down. So this evening, you will make it up to them by doing the dishes alone."

I bit back my reply as I stacked the plates and carried them to the counter. Couldn't she tell that Aneshka had dallied at her morning chores while I did the hard work? And, she had done nothing but complain after Momma left us at the creek. Still, I couldn't talk back to my mother. Soon I was alone in the kitchen, scrubbing plates while my sisters giggled and played outside.

Our neighbor Old Jan arrived just as I finished. Like us, he was Czechy, or "Bohemian," as we were called in this country. He and his two sons had lived in the coal camp longer than we had, but had fallen on hard times shortly after our arrival. Old Jan's leg had been crushed in a cave-in at the mine and had been amputated just below the knee. The old man had not worked since, nor would he again. As they were our neighbors and our countrymen, we had stuck by them, and they had become like family to us. His younger son, Marek, was a year and a half older than me and had gone to school with me at first. After his father's accident, however, he had lied about his age to get a job in the mine.

Since both sons worked the night shift, Old Jan was alone in the evening, so my parents welcomed him, no matter how tired they were. Momma got out of her chair and scooted it forward for Old Jan, while Papa filled a pipe with tobacco for him.

"Trina," Momma said, "go put the coffee on for our guest."

I turned back into the hot kitchen and set the pot on the stove to heat. By the time I returned, Old Jan was comfortably settled. Holena and Aneshka were sitting cross-legged on the porch in front of him, begging for a story. In Bohemia, Papa or our grandfather had often told us stories after supper, but since starting work at the mine, Papa was always too tired. My sisters had discovered, however, that Old Jan was more obliging.

"Come on, Trina." Aneshka patted the porch beside her. "Old Jan is going to tell a story."

I was too angry to sit by Aneshka. I gave cups of coffee to my parents and their guest and sat down on the porch steps a few feet away.

"What story would you like?" Old Jan asked.

"A story about a princess!" Aneshka cried.

"And what kind of story would you like, Holena?" Old Jan asked, leaning forward and patting her round cheek lightly with his gnarled fingers.

"I would like a story about animals," Holena said quietly.

"Animals and a princess, eh?" Old Jan said with a chuckle. "And what about you, Trina? What story would you like to hear?"

"My grandmother told a story about a fish. I've been trying to remember it all day."

"A fish. Hmmm." He considered for a long moment. "Was it 'The Magic Carp,' perhaps?"

I sat up straighter, feeling the same tug of excitement I had felt that morning when I saw the tree. "Yes, that's it! Can you tell it? Please?"

He smiled. "That is a good story, and it has animals. Very well, then. 'The Magic Carp.'"

Aneshka scowled at me, but Old Jan didn't seem to notice as he began the tale.

"There was once an old fisherman and his wife, so poor they had only fish broth for supper and went to bed hungry. One day the old man had caught nothing all day long. He was about to give up when he saw a flash of movement in the deepest pool in the river, so he cast his line one more time. When he did, he hooked a carp with whiskers on its chin. This carp was hardly big enough to eat, but it was all the old fisherman had, so he prepared to kill it.

"'Stop!' the little fish pleaded." Old Jan spoke in a high-pitched voice that made Aneshka and Holena giggle. "'If you let me go, I shall grant you three wishes.'

"'Three wishes?' the fisherman asked, amazed.

"'Three wishes,' the fish assured him. 'Spare me and your dreams could come true!'

"Well, the fisherman couldn't believe his luck! Dreaming of what he might wish for, he unhooked the fish and let the little fish slip back into the water before he knew what he was doing. He thought he had lost his chance, but the carp poked its head up above the surface of the pool. It twitched its whiskers three times and said, 'Three wishes are yours, before the summer's end.' Then, with a slippery white flash, it disappeared into the depths of the pool.

"The fisherman hurried home to his wife and told her of the wishes, but she merely grumbled that he was a fool to fall for the trick. She gave him his bowl of fish broth, even thinner than usual. The fisherman looked into the bowl, and with a sigh he said, 'I wish just once I had a nice, fat sausage for my supper.'

"And what do you know, just like that, a nice fat sausage appeared on his plate. Well, the old couple was amazed, but immediately the old woman began scolding, 'Now look what you've done! You could have had anything and you've wasted a wish on a silly sausage!'

"The old man tried to calm his wife, but she kept scolding until he got angry. 'Quiet, woman!' he shouted. 'I've heard enough about this sausage! I wish it were stuck to your nose!'"

Old Jan paused while Aneshka giggled. Holena clapped her hand over her nose, her eyes wide. "Sure enough, that sausage stuck itself to the old woman's nose. Well, they tugged and pulled, and pulled and tugged, but they couldn't get that sausage off! So in the end, they had to use their last wish to wish the sausage away, and they ended up no better off than they were before." Old Jan paused and turned to me. "Is that the story your grandmother told?"

"Yes. Grandmother always asked us what we'd wish for if we had three wishes." I ached remembering how we would laugh at our wishes as we worked.

Papa smiled. "So she did. Very well, my girls, what do you wish for?"

"All the plum dumplings I could ever eat!" Aneshka cried, clapping her hands in delight.

"I would wish for blue hair ribbons," Holena said dreamily.

I couldn't believe what I was hearing. Hadn't they learned anything at all from the story? Holena was only five, but Aneshka was old enough to understand the moral.

"You're as foolish as the fisherman and his wife," I said. "You would waste your wishes on simple things!"

"Well then, wise Katerina, what would you wish for?" Papa asked, smiling.

I frowned, wishing I hadn't started the game. "There's no such thing as wishes."

"You sound like the fisherman's wife," Aneshka said. Then she giggled and added, "Trina's going to end up with a sausage stuck to her nose!"

"It's only a game, Trina. What would you wish for?" Old Jan asked.

"It's a stupid game," I insisted.

"Just say what it is you want, Trina. Please?" Holena asked, but even her sweetness couldn't soothe my annoyance.

"I want to go back to Bohemia!" I said, bitterness sharpening my words more than I intended. I could see in my father's eyes that my words hurt him, but before I could take them back, he gave an answer I hadn't expected.

"And I would wish us right back to America and onto a farm. So you see, Trina, your wish would be wasted too."

"But why?" I asked. "It's horrible here!"

"Perhaps for now it is, but here in America, we will have a better future," he said.

"That's right," Old Jan said. "In America, our children's dreams can come true."

"Dreams don't come true! Especially not here!" I knew better than to talk back to my elders, but now that I had given voice to my anger, I couldn't seem to stop it.

"They do if you know what to wish for," Old Jan said. "And if you find a magic carp."

I opened my mouth to answer, but I couldn't. *Had I found a magic carp?* I was staring at him with my mouth open when my mother stood abruptly. "Enough of this nonsense. It is time the children were off to bed," she said.

Aneshka protested, but I did not. Old Jan's words had made me uncomfortable, and besides, I was tired from a day of scrubbing clothes. I thanked Old Jan for the story. Taking Holena's hand, I retreated into the house. I helped her into her nightdress before changing into my own, and the three of us lay down on the mattress we shared. Through the thin walls, I could hear my mother apologizing for my outburst to Old Jan, and my cheeks burned.

"Never mind, Mrs. Prochazkova," Old Jan said in his kindly way. "She is just homesick. She's very young yet, after all."

"She is old enough to know better," Momma said.

"But she is still a child inside," Old Jan replied.

His tone had been kind, but I squeezed my eyes shut in shame and turned toward the wall so I could not hear what else they might say. I did not want to be talked about as a child—I didn't want to be talked about at all. I wanted to go to sleep and forget the day, and, slowly, I did.

I woke in the cool moonlight, lying on the thick cottonwood root, leaning out over the water. A flash of white deep in the pool caught my attention. I leaned farther, watching and waiting, my nose almost against the surface of the dark water. The gleaming carp slipped out into the moonlight and rose to the surface. It thrust its flat head up through the glassy surface and its whiskers twitched—one, two, three times.

"Three wishes before the summer's end," it said in a voice that bubbled like washwater. "Wise Katerina, what do you wish for?"

Suddenly I was aware of Aneshka beside me. "Plum dumplings!" she squealed, clapping her hands. "I wish for all the plum dumplings I can eat!"

"And blue hair ribbons!" added shy little Holena from my other side.

"Stop! Stop!" I cried, leaping to my feet. "You're wasting my wishes!" But it was too late; the dumplings and ribbons had already appeared.

Only one wish was left! I had to formulate it carefully. Before I could speak, Momma appeared from over the hill with bundles of laundry, calling my name and scolding me for dreaming.

I woke with a start, my heart thumping in my throat. I was back on the thin mattress, Aneshka and Holena pressed up against me, breathing evenly. It had only been a dream, but it had seemed so real—just as being beneath the cottonwood that morning had seemed like a dream. Momma was right; I was too old to believe in fairy tales. But if there really was a magic carp in the creek by the coal camp . . . I smiled to myself and snuggled deeper under the covers, comforted by the idea. Soon I had fallen back into a dreamless, forgetful sleep.

Chapter 2

I HAD NEARLY forgotten the dream the next morning, but I had not forgotten my mother's disappointment in me, or my own embarrassment at being thought of as a child. I determined to do my chores quickly and allow nothing to distract me. When the kitchen was clean, I heated the irons on the stove and carried in the mounds of stiff, wrinkled clothes that had dried on the lines overnight.

Ironing was hot, tedious work, with the stove burning all day. The piles of clothing never seemed to get any smaller, and by midmorning, I could not keep the cool, shady pool of the creek out of my mind. I tried to push it away, but it lapped back in, and I found myself ironing the same spot on a shirt long after the iron had cooled. I jerked my attention back to my work with a guilty glance toward Momma. She hadn't noticed, so I folded the shirt and quickly took the next one from the pile, trying harder to keep my mind on my work.

The ironing took all day, Momma and I pressing clothes

while Aneshka and Holena carried each neatly folded pile back to the house of its owner. The men were all at work in the mine, of course, but no one locked their doors in camp.

It was late afternoon when we folded the last shirt and sent Aneshka off with the last pile. Momma poured herself a cup of coffee from the pot on the back of the stove and slumped into a chair at the table. She mopped her brow with her sleeve.

"It'll be time to be getting your papa's supper soon," she said. She nodded toward the tobacco can on the shelf behind the stove. "I need you to run to the store, Trina. Take the money from the washing."

I took the can down from the shelf, my heart sinking. Momma often sent me on this chore, since I had learned enough English to speak with the storekeeper, Mr. Johnson. I didn't mind the chore so much, but I hated the idea of spending the money we had just worked so hard to earn. We would never save money at this rate.

"Shouldn't we save some for new dresses?" I asked.

Momma shook her head. "Shame on you, Trina. Think of your papa. Think of how hard he works! He needs a few good meals a week."

That was true enough, but I left a little in the money can anyway, hoping I had enough. If I didn't, I would just have to put it on credit. Mr. Johnson kept a ledger book under his counter for such occasions, and was happy to let us use it if we needed to.

I was glad to be outside at last. I was grateful for the breeze that dried the sweat along my hairline. The street we lived on — in fact, the whole camp — ran in rows of drab houses up a hill, with the mine at the top. At the bottom stood the only fine buildings in the town, a few two-story houses with picket fences and neat yards for the mine officials, a school, and a community meeting house that served as Saturday night dance hall and Sunday morning church. The largest building in the group, a long, low building with a covered porch, housed the store and company offices.

I had never been in those offices, but I came to the store at least once a week. It was jammed with an assortment of goods, from buckets and brooms to coffee, flour, and fresh meat two days each week. As I approached, I noticed a team of horses and a wagon tied up at the rail beside the steps. The front door was open and I could hear voices inside, but it wasn't until I had stepped through the doorway that I realized the voices were raised in anger.

I paused uncertainly. Mr. Johnson was behind his counter, and facing him from my side was a tall, dark-haired man I didn't recognize. He was holding a piece of paper under Mr. Johnson's nose. Beside him on the floor were two wooden crates. A third crate was open on the counter.

"But you ordered them!" the dark-haired stranger was saying. He had an Italian accent, but his English was better than my own. He gave the paper a little shake. "It says so right here on the invoice. Twenty crates. Right here on the invoice."

"That's not my invoice," Mr. Johnson said without looking at it.

"It's your company. It came from the head office in Pueblo, like always."

Mr. Johnson pushed the paper away from his face impatiently. "Well, I didn't order them, I can't sell them, and I won't take them!"

The man with the invoice clenched his free hand. I backed out of the doorway, afraid a fight was about to start. My movement caught Mr. Johnson's eye.

"Now, look, you're scaring my customers," he said. He turned his gaze to me and smiled. "Come in, missy, and tell me what I can do for you."

Both men's eyes were on me then, and I felt foolish as I stepped forward into the store once again. I swallowed hard and spoke, just wanting to get my purchase and get out before their argument resumed. "I need a pound of coffee and four chops, if they aren't too much."

Mr. Johnson turned back to the other man. "'If they aren't too much.' You see what I'm dealing with here? Miserly Greeks and tight-fisted Irishmen, all day long."

Anger warmed my cheeks, but I held my tongue. The Italian man was still looking my way. His mouth turned downward into a frown under his bushy mustache. "She's just a kid, Johnson."

Mr. Johnson was wrapping the chops in paper. "Yeah, well, kid or not, they won't buy that lot around here, so you might as well haul it back out to your wagon."

The Italian's frown deepened, and he turned back toward Mr. Johnson. But before he could say anything, Mr. Johnson slapped the chops onto the counter beside a tin of coffee and looked back at me, still rooted beside the doorway.

"Well, come on, missy. You can't very well pay for these from over there, can you? Torentino here won't bite."

I hurried to the counter, pulling the handful of coins from my pocket. "How much?"

"Seventy cents for the coffee and two fifty for the chops." He gave a sudden, insincere smile and reached into the open crate on the counter. "Say, missy, how about a special treat for your family, huh? A nickel a can."

I looked at the can. Across the top it read EMPSON'S FANCY. Below that was a picture of ripe, purple plums on a branch. It would have been a treat, he was right. I thought briefly about Aneshka and her love of plum dumplings, but I only had enough money for the coffee and meat. "No, thank you, sir," I said, and handed him the money for my order.

"Don't you like plums, miss?" Mr. Torentino said.

"Yes, sir, but I have no more money."

"You can put them on credit on your father's account," Mr. Johnson said, reaching under the counter for his credit ledger.

I shook my head. "No, thank you."

Mr. Johnson tossed the can of plums back into the crate. "You see, Torentino? I can't sell them, and I won't take them. Send them back. Tell the head office they made a mistake."

"I can't send them back; I'll lose too much money. The order—"

"Damn the order—get those crates out of my store!" Mr. Johnson said.

More uncomfortable than ever, I scooped up my packages and hurried for the door. Behind me I heard the scrape of the crates being picked up and the heavy step of Mr. Torentino as he lugged them toward the door. Though I longed to escape, he was coming behind me, so I held the door for him. He carried the crates out onto the porch and set them down.

"Thank you, miss," he said. "Do you buy all your food from Johnson?"

"Yes, sir," I said. "There's nowhere else to buy it."

Mr. Torentino glanced over my shoulder, back through the open doorway toward Mr. Johnson's counter. "And he's getting plenty fat off you folks at those prices. Send back all twenty crates! We'll see about that!"

He seemed to be talking more to himself than to me. I tried to go around his crates and down the stairs, but he called out to me, plenty loud enough for Mr. Johnson to hear him.

"Hold up there a minute, miss."

I paused.

"You say you like plums, and I'd guess you got a family from that package of chops."

I nodded, edging a little closer to the steps. I could see Mr. Johnson watching suspiciously through the open door.

"Here," Mr. Torentino said. He took a can from the top crate and held it out to me. I shook my head.

"Take it, it's free. Here, take a couple more, too."

"Free?" I said. I couldn't believe it—it had to be a trick.

"If he won't take them, I have to do something with them. Take these for free and tell everyone you see that I'll be selling the rest for a penny a can."

"Hey!" Mr. Johnson yelled from inside the store. "Hey, you can't do that!"

Mr. Torentino put the three cans in my arms and grinned. "You'd best run along now."

I was happy to oblige. I went down the stairs two at a time. Behind me I heard Mr. Johnson burst out onto the porch, shouting at Mr. Torentino.

I kept my head down and ran! I was panting by the time I burst into the kitchen. Momma looked up in alarm, but her expression shifted quickly to annoyance when she saw me cradling the cans of plums.

"Trina! We don't have money for such things!" she scolded. As soon as I could catch my breath, the whole story tumbled out of me.

"He said he'd be selling them for a penny a can, if Mr. Johnson hasn't run him off yet."

"A penny a can!" Momma exclaimed. "That's cheaper than anything else we can eat. Do you have any change left?"

"I left a little in the money can," I said. Momma reached for the can and got out the dime still there.

"Go back and get as many cans as you can carry. Aneshka, you can start mixing the dough. We'll have plum dumplings tonight after all."

Aneshka gave a little hop of delight and giggled. "Trina must have seen a magic carp in the washwater while she was daydreaming yesterday, Momma."

That's when I remembered my dream. It flooded back into my mind with brilliant clarity: Aneshka wishing for plum dumplings at the pool by the tree. And here they were, exactly as she had said, all the plum dumplings she could eat. The first wish. But it had only been a dream, I was sure of that. This was only a coincidence.

"Come on, Trina, don't just stand there," Momma prodded. "Go back and get more before they are all sold. Take Holena with you; she can help you carry."

I set out for the store again, Holena's hand in mine and the money in my pocket, and I pushed the dream out of my mind. As I passed neighbors and houses with their doors open, I called out Mr. Torentino's offer. Soon word was spreading and other women were hurrying down the hill with us. I was glad for their company, in case Mr. Johnson was still there, still shouting.

At my side, Holena trotted to keep up. "Did you really see a magic carp in the washwater, Trina?" she asked. "Really?"

"Of course not," I said. I was annoyed that Aneshka had made such a joke in front of Holena. And I was annoyed that it felt true, even though I was too old to believe it.

"But Aneshka got her dumplings," Holena said. "Do you think I will get my hair ribbons, too?" Her eyes were round and shining with hope. I hated telling her that her hope was for nothing, but how could I tell her otherwise? I turned my eyes back to the dusty road ahead of us.

"We had better hurry or there won't be any plums left for us," I said. I felt her hand slacken in mine and knew she was disappointed, but I didn't look at her. I just kept walking.

Mr. Torentino had moved his wagon across the street from Mr. Johnson's store. Though the storekeeper was standing on his porch, glaring at the growing crowd of women around the wagon, there seemed to be nothing he could do about it. Mr. Torentino was in the back of the wagon, prying open crates and handing the cans to the women who were holding money up to him. I tried to blend into the crowd, but Mr. Torentino noticed me.

"Well done, girl!" he called out over the heads of the gathering women. "Well done! And will you have more?"

"Yes, sir," I said and held up my dime. He took it and handed down ten cans of plums, which I cradled in my apron as I worked my way out of the crowd. I could not help noticing Mr. Johnson watching with narrowed eyes. He hadn't missed Mr. Torentino's words, I was sure of it.

"Papa will be surprised, won't he?" Holena said.

"He will," I agreed. Despite Mr. Johnson, I couldn't help smiling to myself. Plum dumplings! We hadn't had such a treat since arriving in America.

"You know what, Holena?"

"What?"

"We should make it a special night for Momma, too."

Holena's eyes glowed at the thought. "How?"

I thought for a moment, not sure how, but then I saw a patch of dandelions blooming alongside the road. "Flowers for the table?" I suggested.

Holena's smile nearly split her face. All the way home, she

skipped along the edge of the road and picked dandelions. They were only weeds, but they were bright and cheerful clenched in her little fist. When we got home, we put them in a can of water and onto the table while Momma's back was turned. When she saw them, she smiled—the first smile I could remember seeing on her face in a long time.

We busied ourselves in the kitchen, full of anticipation and excitement as we swept and washed and set the table with great care. Momma disappeared into the bedroom and came back holding a tablecloth, embroidered on the corners with flowers. She only brought it out on Christmas and Easter, so we were all surprised when she spread it on the table. She saw us watching and gave a little shrug.

"The Lord knows we have few enough things to celebrate here. We'd best use it while we can." She turned back to the stove, but I had seen the smile crinkling the corners of her eyes. I felt a pang, almost like homesickness. She had been quick to celebrate when I was little, but not since we had left Bohemia.

My thoughts were interrupted by the whistle at the mine. The shift was changing and Papa would be on the way home soon. I hurried to straighten the silverware Aneshka had laid on the table.

Papa always washed off the coal dust and dirt in a tub at the back door. It wasn't until he was drying his face that he stopped and sniffed the air.

"What is that smell?" he asked with a smile.

Holena tried to tell him, but Aneshka shushed her.

"It's supposed to be a surprise," she insisted.

Papa smiled at them both. "She doesn't have to tell me a thing, Aneshka," Papa said. "I know plum dumplings when I smell them. But how? Did your wish come true after all?"

"So it would seem," Momma said from the doorway behind me. "Now come inside. Supper's all ready."

Supper that night felt like a grand affair, although the food was much the same as always—gristly meat, boiled potatoes, and bread spread with salted lard. But the tablecloth, the flowers, and the plates of plum dumplings made it festive. I recounted for Papa all that had happened at the store. When I told him of Mr. Torentino's selling from his wagon while Mr. Johnson glared at him from the porch, he laughed.

"Serves the swindler right," Papa said.

Momma looked stricken. "Hush, Tomas! Don't say such things!"

"They can't hear us here, Ivana. Besides, this is America, isn't it? A man can say what he thinks here."

"They'll fire you for saying such things," she said.

"Not tonight," Papa said, unbothered by her warning. "Tonight we have plum dumplings and all the luck in the world, right, Aneshka?"

Momma frowned at Papa before rising from the table to fetch more of the dumplings still steaming on the stove. They were the best things I had tasted since we had left Bohemia. Aneshka ate so many we all thought she would be sick, and Momma made her stop.

We were still at the table when we heard the familiar clop of Old Jan's crutches on the porch steps. Papa went out to greet him while Momma dished up a bowl of plum dumplings and took it out to him. That left my sisters and me to tidy the kitchen.

For once Aneshka was cooperative and cheerful, and the job went quickly. I was soon stacking away the last plates on the shelf while Aneshka and Holena folded Momma's lovely tablecloth. Holena carried it into the bedroom to put away while Aneshka and I took coffee to the adults.

I had just settled myself comfortably on the porch steps when Holena appeared in the doorway. Rather than skipping out like usual, she seemed frozen, staring at us as if we were strangers. In her hand she held two long, sky-blue ribbons. Her eyes met mine.

"They were in the trunk," she said. "I found them."

Momma turned to look. "Why, so they were! I had forgotten I had such things; it's been so long!" she said.

"You wore them at our wedding, Ivana, remember?" Papa said.

Holena's face fell a little, but Momma smiled.

"So I did, but I have no use for such things now. And they are just the right color for your hair, Holena. Would you like to have them?"

Holena's little hand clenched the ribbons and she threw herself into Momma's arms with a dozen thank-yous.

Everyone was smiling. Everyone but me—I was still staring in disbelief. The second wish! My ears seemed to be buzzing with the shock of it.

What would you wish for, Wise Katerina?

I felt someone looking at me and glanced up into Old Jan's face. He, too, was smiling, but he was watching me. "You see, Trina, dreams can come true," he said.

I didn't know about dreams or about wishes—didn't know if they could come true or if they were even real. But maybe it was time I found out.

Chapter 3

I LAY AWAKE THAT NIGHT, feeling my sisters breathing in the bed beside me, as I tried to sort out what was real. In the months we had been in America, very little in our lives had been good. Momma and Papa worked to exhaustion every day. My sisters and I had gone to school, but we had so many chores to do to help Momma that we had little time for fun. We hadn't had money or time for anything new or nice until today. Today, there had been plums for dumplings, and hair ribbons—exactly what my sisters had wished for!

We had had so few truly happy days here in America, and none that I would have called lucky. It seemed lucky to have so much good happen in one day, but not impossible. It seemed impossible, though, that those things appeared the day after Aneshka and Holena had made wishes. How could an order have been mistakenly placed for plums and I *just happened* to be the one to discover it, and it *just happened* to be the day after my sister had made a wish for plum dumplings? Things didn't just happen like that. But if it wasn't just chance, that would mean I had discovered a magic fish in the creek by the coal camp and it had granted me three wishes. And it had spoken to me in a dream. It seemed that I was faced with choosing between a wish that had come true or an impossible coincidence. It was not a question of which was possible so much as which was less *im*possible.

Aneshka stirred and sighed, her breath still smelling of plums. A little smile curled at the corners of her mouth and I knew she was dreaming. I closed my eyes too, hoping to fall into a dream, but I could not. The day's events were too fresh in my mind, and I kept hearing that voice, prompting me for my wish.

My wish, of course, was to return to Bohemia, to the small village where my grandfather and uncle were still the clockmakers, and winter evenings were filled with family and laughter and the stories that had taught us to dream. I wanted to go back to how it had been before my papa's dreams had become too big for that village. Of course, I would not say that out loud again, not in front of my father. I didn't know why he would wish us back to America, but I knew that it was not a subject for discussion. Besides, we didn't have the money for the fare back to Europe. A wish was the only way we could return, and I'd have to make the wish in secret.

I caught myself. It was all nonsense. Fish did not grant wishes except in stories, and even in stories the wishes didn't fix people's lives, they only proved them foolish. I shifted in bed, trying to get comfortable enough to forget the day and go to sleep, but I only disturbed Aneshka, who muttered a complaint without waking. Eventually I must have drifted off, because the next thing I knew, Aneshka was poking me to wake me up. It was still dark out, but I could hear Momma in the kitchen frying the last chop for Papa's lunch bucket, and I could smell the coffee.

I rubbed the sleep from my eyes and sat up. Holena was still asleep, and I slipped out carefully so as not to wake her. In the kitchen, Papa was at the table, scooping oat porridge into his mouth as quickly as he could. In Bohemia he had taken his time over his breakfast, reading the papers and discussing politics with my grandfather, but here there was no time for that. If he was not in line to ride the hoist down into the mine when the shift whistle blew, he could miss a whole day's work—and a whole day's wages. So, I had learned to stay quiet and out of his way in the morning.

When he had eaten, he took the lunch bucket from Momma, kissed her cheek, and set off for the mine. Once he was gone, Momma filled a bowl of porridge for each of us and we sat down to our own breakfasts.

"I told Old Jan we would come give his floors a good scrub today," Momma said. "He can't do it himself with his leg as it is." She paused and looked at me, and I knew what she was waiting for.

"I'll do it, Momma," I said.

Her eyebrows raised a little. "There's a good girl." She was surprised. Though we had both known it was my duty to volunteer, she had not expected me to do so as quickly or cheerfully as I had. In truth, I was a little surprised myself—I had never liked cleaning for Old Jan and his sons. Marek and Karel worked the night shift at the mine, so they slept all morning. That meant I couldn't start cleaning until the afternoon, when the work was hotter and I was already tired. Today, though, I had been quick to volunteer because I wanted to talk to Old Jan. I was curious to know what he thought about dreams coming true.

The whistle blew at the mine, and a moment later Holena appeared in the doorway between our two rooms, still in her nightgown. Her hair was still messy from sleep, but she had tied the ribbons to the ends of her braids.

Momma smiled at her. "Perhaps we should save those for special days."

"Today is a special day," Holena said, her large eyes sparkling.

"Is it? What day is it, then?" Momma asked.

"Today we get our third wish," Holena said.

"What third wish?" Momma said.

"From the fish Trina saw in the washwater."

Aneshka giggled. I looked at her.

"Have you been filling her head with nonsense?" I asked accusingly.

"No." Aneshka's tone was defensive, but I could see the mischief in her eyes. "Wishes always come in threes. Everyone knows that. It's not nonsense."

"Of course it is," I said.

"It is," Momma said in a matter-of-fact tone that put the issue to rest. "And it is time we got dressed and started our chores. Trina, you get Holena her breakfast." She ushered Aneshka into the other room while I filled a bowl of oat porridge for Holena. I set the bowl on the table in front of her, but she didn't begin eating. Instead she looked up at me, her expression troubled.

"But you did see a magic fish, Trina. You must have."

"There's no such thing, Holena. Not really."

"But Aneshka and I both got our wishes," she insisted.

"That was just luck," I said. I could see she wasn't convinced, so I offered proof. "After all, I haven't gotten my wish, have I?"

"You didn't make your wish," Holena said.

I looked at her, confused. Had she had the same dream I had? We had all said our wishes after Old Jan's story. "Yes I did," I said.

She shook her head, her little brow still wrinkled. "You said it was a stupid game and that you didn't believe. You said what you wanted, but you didn't make it a wish. You have to say '*I wish*.'"

I thought about it. I couldn't exactly remember what I had said. I shrugged. "You should eat your porridge."

"You have to believe and make your wish. Then we can go back to Bohemia, just like you wanted."

Back to Bohemia! She said it with such conviction that it sounded almost possible. And it was the third wish, so Papa couldn't wish us back! I thought of our village, nestled among the dense forests I had loved, of the rolling hills, and of my grandmother's kitchen.

"Trina, go get dressed. Holena, get that porridge eaten; we have chores to do."

My mother's voice from the doorway jarred me out of my daydream, back to the bleak reality of our new life. I went into the bedroom, where Aneshka was braiding her hair, and I dressed quickly, still thinking of home and feeling a trickle of hope. That hope carried me through the morning chores. After lunch I gathered our buckets and rags and set out up the hill to do as I had promised and clean for Old Jan.

Old Jan was sitting out on his front porch, whittling a piece of wood with his pen knife. He paused and smiled up at me in greeting. "I'm afraid my boys are still sleeping," he said. "Would you sit here a bit with me while we wait for them?"

I sat down on the porch steps, happy enough to take a break

from work. I wanted to ask him about the night before, but I didn't know how. Every question I shaped in my mind felt foolish. So instead I asked him what he was making. He turned the block of wood over in his hands and considered it.

"I think it is going to be a horse," he said. "The horse is a noble creature. When I was a boy on my father's farm, we boasted the strongest team in all Bohemia. Those horses could pull a thousand pounds if they could pull one! And at the spring festival, we would tie ribbons and garlands on one of them. My mother would ride into the village, all dressed up, looking like a queen."

I nodded. "I miss the spring festival. There is nothing like that here, though. There's nothing but work here."

Old Jan looked up at me from the carving and smiled. "I've heard of a girl whose life was all work and never anything pretty. She was pretty, though, and her stepmother and stepsister were jealous, so they made her work very hard. But she was still pretty. So they tried to get rid of her."

I leaned back against the porch rail. I had heard the story before, but I was content to listen.

"'Marushka,' they said to her, for that was her name, 'Marushka, go up the mountain and pick us some violets.' It was the dead of winter and Marushka knew there would be no violets on the mountain, but they pushed her out of the house and forbid her to return without them. Crying bitterly, the poor girl set off up the mountain in search of the flowers.

"On the mountaintop she met the seasons of the year, sitting around a fire, and when she spoke kindly to them, they took pity on her. Spring rose up, waved his wand, and the violets sprung into bloom.

"Well, you can imagine the stepmother's surprise when she saw the violets. She wove them into her daughter's hair and thought, 'With Marushka's help, my daughter might become beautiful enough to marry a prince!' So she ordered Marushka back up the mountain for fresh strawberries to give the girl's complexion a rosy glow.

"Marushka went, more distraught than before, for where would she get strawberries in January? But once again, she met the seasons, and once again they took pity on her because she was good and gentle and wanted nothing for herself. So Summer rose up and waved his wand, and fields of strawberries glistened before her, plump and red and waiting to be picked.

"Marushka gathered all the strawberries she could carry and took them down the mountain. Well, of course, the stepmother was surprised and delighted. She and her daughter gobbled up every last strawberry, and the stepmother thought to herself, 'Now all my daughter needs are apples to polish her teeth, and she will be the most beautiful maid in the kingdom. So she ordered Marushka back up the mountain for apples.

"Marushka went, knowing there would be no apples but hoping against hope that there might be a way. Once again, the seasons saw how good and gentle she was, and when she told them she was looking for apples, Autumn rose up, waved his wand, and ripe, sweet apples burst forth on the trees.

"'Shake the tree once and take what it gives you,' Autumn told her. Two apples fell from the tree, and Marushka hurried home with them. Well, of course, the stepmother was amazed, but she was angry, too, because they were the best apples she had ever eaten, and she wanted more. She ordered Marushka back up the mountain, but her greedy daughter said, 'Marushka ate them all; that's why she only brought two. She's cheating us. This time we will go, Mother, and we will get everything we deserve!' And what do you think happened?"

"They got just what they deserved?" I guessed with a smile.

Old Jan nodded. "When they met the seasons, they were rude and selfish. So angry old Winter rose up and waved his wand, and a great blizzard blew over the mountain, and they were never seen again."

"And what became of Marushka?" I asked.

"The farm became hers from that day forward. The seasons blessed her with fine crops, and she made the house and everything around her beautiful. So you see, Trina, things can get better for a good, hard-working girl."

"It's a nice story," I said, "but I don't think anyone is going to rise up, wave a wand, and make the coal mine go away."

Old Jan laughed a wheezing, coughing laugh. "No, I suppose not. But if you are a good girl who works hard to help your mother, just maybe things will get better."

"Maybe," I said, "but it is harder for those of us without magic wands."

Old Jan smiled, his eyes twinkling. "Aneshka says she got her dumplings because you saw a magic carp. That is just as good as a wand."

I frowned. Aneshka must have told everyone her idea last night after dinner. At this rate she would have told everyone in the camp in no time. Everyone would be laughing at me. "I don't believe in such nonsense."

"Ah, but believing is never nonsense," Old Jan said. "You have to believe something can happen before it will, you know."

"Marushka didn't believe she would find her violets or strawberries or apples, though."

"So she didn't, but she tried to find them anyway, trusting for something to happen, even when she didn't know what it might be."

"My father's like that. That's how we ended up here. Momma says only a fool believes such things."

"Some would say Marushka was wise, and others that she was foolish, I suppose. You have to decide for yourself which you think she was."

Though I had heard the story before, I had never thought of it that way. I was still pondering Old Jan's story when Marek stepped out onto the porch, pulling his suspenders up over his shoulders as he came. When he saw me, he quickly combed down his rumpled hair with his fingers. He smiled at me. I smiled back and then quickly looked elsewhere to hide the discomfort I always felt in his presence.

"Good morning, Papa. Good morning, Trina."

"Good morning, Mark," I said, careful to pronounce his name the American way, which he had used since going to work in the mine. He said foreigners didn't have as good a chance as Americans at getting good jobs, so he no longer wanted a foreign-sounding name. Since his father's injury, getting and keeping a job had been his biggest concern.

"Good afternoon, you mean," Old Jan said.

"To you it's afternoon. To me it's morning," Mark said. He sat down beside me to put on his boots. I watched his hands as he laced and tied each one. When I had first arrived here and started attending school, I had shared a desk with him, and those same hands had guided me through lessons. They were entirely different hands now. He had lied about his age to work in the mine, since he hadn't been quite fifteen, and I had marveled that the coal company had believed he was sixteen. Now, looking at his hands, it seemed believable. When they had helped me at school, they had been like everyone else's in the schoolhouse. But now the fingernails and the creases at the knuckles bore the permanent stain of coal, and red scars and nicks showed where the chips of rock had cut them as he hammered and drilled underground.

Everything else about him seemed older too, and that's what made me so uncomfortable. He no longer joked and smiled like he had back then, no longer teased me or pulled on my braids for a lark. When his family spent time with mine, his concerns were all those of my father—wages, rumors of unions, paying off debts. It was like he had grown up and I hadn't, and I didn't know what to say around him that he would want to hear.

"I've come to clean. Is Karel up?" I asked.

Mark nodded. "He's just finishing his breakfast."

"Then Trina will want to be getting her work done," Old Jan said. "Be a good lad, Marek, and fetch Trina some water in her buckets."

"Glad to," he said, still grinning, and he picked up my buckets. "Will you come with me, Trina?"

"I should get started here," I said, jumping to my feet a little too eagerly. Mark looked disappointed as he set off with the buckets alone.

I got to work sweeping and beating the rugs. When Mark returned with the buckets filled, I scrubbed the counter and table in the kitchen, then scrubbed the floors, starting in the bedroom and working forward through the kitchen until I finished at the front door. I straightened, stretched my back, and heaved the buckets of now dirty water over the porch rail out into the yard. Old Jan and his sons were on the porch, and they invited me to sit down and rest with them, but I declined. I knew my mother would not be expecting me back right away, and there was something I wanted to do in the few free minutes I had.

"Let us pay you," Mark said, as he did every week, and as always, I shook my head no. My mother would not allow it, not when they were neighbors and friends and had been through hard times.

I said good-bye and hurried to the creek, where I set down my buckets on the bank. I walked downstream, but I paused as I neared the bend in the bank. Were the tree and the pool really there? It all felt too much like a dream, and I was suddenly nervous that it wasn't real. I stepped around the bend and breathed a sigh of relief. There stood the tree, its leaves moving gently in the breeze. Below it the shaded pool looked cool and inviting, just as before.

I paused in the shade of the tree and looked at the water, but I saw no sign of the fish. Suddenly I felt very silly. What had I been expecting to see? Had I really thought I could come make a wish and be back in Bohemia for supper?

I stepped over the tree's root, into the quiet space and sat down, my back against the tree. The shade was pleasantly cool and the soft sounds of the leaves and the water relaxed me. I leaned back and closed my eyes, thinking about magic fish and wishes, and about Marushka. She was wise, I decided. Certainly she had gone looking for something impossible, like my papa had done when he came to America. But she had been modest and good and sought nothing for herself, and so she had made friends instead of enemies. That was why she had received what she needed. In the stories with magic fish or fairies or rings that granted wishes, it was the selfish ones who were harmed rather than helped by their wishes. They were the fools. I smiled to myself at a new thought. If Marushka saw a magic carp, she would make the most of her wish.

What would you wish for, Wise Katerina?

My eyes flew open as I jerked upright, the voice ringing clearly in my mind. A perfect ring of ripples was widening in the pool before me. I leaned forward, my heart in my throat. There, just under the surface, I could see the carp, its tail waving slightly in the current. I was sure it could see me, too. Had it spoken, or had I been drifting off? What would I wish for, if I had a wish? My mind flashed to our village in Bohemia, but there was only one thing I could wish for if I were going to be Wise Katerina. I took a deep breath to quell the pang of homesickness at my heart, and I spoke.

"I wish for a farm where my family can be happy and live well—the farm my papa wants. I wish for a farm here in America."

Chapter 4

AS SOON AS THE wish was spoken, the fish darted off under the bank and disappeared. I waited. Nothing happened. Everything felt very ordinary, and once again I realized how foolish it was. I got to my feet, glad no one had seen me. I walked back to where I had left my buckets and I filled them, then climbed the slope and walked home. Nothing there was different either. Not one thing all evening. The feeling of foolishness grew, along with bitter disappointment. I had actually been hoping, I realized. Hoping to be saved by a magic fish! I was almost fourteen, too old for fairy tales or wishes. I could not stop myself from dreaming entirely, though. All that night, I found myself in fields of ripening wheat.

With the laundry behind us for the week, we had other chores, but we had a little free time in the afternoons, too. Out in the street, kids gathered for games of kick the can, hopscotch, and skipping rope. I went along to watch my sisters, but I was too old to play. The girls my age gossiped over knitting or mending. I sometimes joined their conversations, but too often it turned to talk of boys. It made me think of Mark, and right away my feelings got tangled up inside me. I would send my thoughts off instead to the pool by the creek.

I felt strange, like a part of me was still waiting for something to happen, hoping it would. I suppose that part of me wanted to be like Marushka, or like my father, able to believe in the impossible. But as the week passed uneventfully, my hope dwindled. Even my sisters stopped talking about wishes, and things seemed to go back to normal.

Sundays were the only day of the week that the mine closed down and Papa stayed home. Momma, my sisters, and I got up quietly and went to church while Papa slept late. When we returned home on the Sunday after I made my wish, Papa was sitting on the porch reading the newspaper, his legs stretched out comfortably before him.

Momma sat down beside him with a contented sigh. "You girls can run along and play today," she said.

At once Aneshka was clamoring to go play in the creek.

"If Trina will go with you, to keep an eye on you," Momma said.

I agreed, so we changed out of our Sunday best and set off. Momma needn't have worried about the water. There were already several families spending the afternoon on the broad, grassy bank where we had done laundry. The creek was filled with laughing, splashing children, shouting in a mixture of languages, but playing together as if they understood one another.

I sat down on the grass and watched my sisters. Aneshka ran out into the middle at once so she could splash her classmates who were already there. Holena stayed close to the bank, looking for pretty pebbles and gathering them into her apron. Before long her quiet amusement was interrupted as a wild game of tag broke out. The older children, Aneshka among them, raced past her, splashing water and mud in all directions. A flailing arm caught Holena square in the back and she toppled forward, landing facedown in the icy water, soaked from head to toe.

I hurried to her, scolding the older children as I went. I helped her to her feet and up onto the grassy bank.

"Are you all right?" I asked her.

She nodded, but her teeth were chattering from the cold water and she was blinking back tears. I wrung the water from her skirt and invited her to sit with me in the sun to warm up. We watched the game continue for some time, Holena chewing her lip uncertainly. A big Welsh family had arrived, and the Welsh children were especially wild. We were always wary of the Welsh, who lived on the other side of camp. There were plenty of rumors that the careless Welsh miners had caused more than one deadly accident in the mine. Their children seemed just as troublesome as they went splashing and shouting into the creek. Aneshka wasn't bothered by them, and I knew she could hold her own. Holena, though, wasn't one for so much rough-and-tumble play. I stood and held my hand out to her.

"Let's take a walk," I said. "I know a quieter place I think you'll like better."

With a sudden, bright smile, she jumped up and took my hand. We set off downstream. I felt a little uncertain as we walked. I hadn't, until that moment, considered sharing my special place with anyone. I certainly didn't want to share it with Aneshka, but Holena was different. She appreciated quiet and beauty and wouldn't disrupt it with mindless prattle.

Holena was still holding my hand as we rounded the bend. At once the high slope shut out the sound of the children splashing and shouting. We could hear the burble of water and the chirping of birds. I could hear another sound, too—one I hadn't expected. Someone was whistling a tune. And not just any tune, but a Bohemian folk song.

I shaded my eyes with my hand and looked to the tree. A man was reclining in the shade with his feet propped up on one of the roots. It was silly of me to think a place so close to the camp was a secret, but I was disappointed to learn it wasn't.

"It's Mark!" Holena said. She let go of my hand and skipped toward him.

He heard her voice and sat up, the sun lighting his face. He smiled, looking glad to see us.

"Trina! Hello. Come sit in the shade," he said.

Holena was already sitting on the big root of the cottonwood, leaning out over the pool and trailing her fingers on the surface of the water. I stepped over the root, into the narrow wedge of grass, and hesitated. It was too small a space to share with another person, though Mark seemed to be expecting me to sit down there beside him. He saw my hesitation and his smile faltered.

"What's the matter, Trina?" he asked.

"It's just that it's awfully crowded here," I said.

He shook his head. "Not just here. You don't want to talk to me at my house, either, or anywhere else. What have I done?"

The heat of embarrassment filled my cheeks. I wanted to flee, but I could not. I sat down on the root of the tree, trying to decide what to say.

"It's always like this now," he continued. "You hurry to get away from me. You won't even look me in the eye."

I had kept my eyes on Holena, but I could hear the hurt in his voice. I forced my eyes up to meet his.

"You haven't done anything wrong, Mark."

"Then why are you avoiding me?"

"I'm not. It's just—" I thought hard, trying to untangle my feelings. "We used to talk about school, and what we wanted to do afterward. Now that you're working, things have changed."

"I'm still the same," he said.

I studied his face. It was the same—blue eyes with pale lashes, the soft beginnings of whiskers, and a mop of blond hair that wanted to flop across his forehead toward his left eye. Something else was there too, though. A new seriousness, perhaps, or more worries. Things that had aged him faster than me. I wanted him to still be the same, but like everything else in America, what I wanted made little difference.

He reached his hard, coal-stained hand out and took mine. "Trina, I still want to talk about school and our friends there. Just because I had to go to work doesn't mean I wanted to give up everything else."

"I'm sorry," I said, "I just thought—" I was still searching for the right words when I was saved by Holena.

"What's this?" She held up a fishing pole that had been lying in the grass next to Mark.

"I bought that with my paycheck last week," Mark said with a smile.

I jerked my hand out of his. "You're fishing? Here?"

"I thought if I could catch a meal or two it might stretch our income, but I'm not having much luck."

"Maybe there are no fish in this creek," I said.

"You're probably right. There's another stream over that ridge." Mark pointed toward the hill that rose on the other side of the water. "Johnson at the store says there's good fishing there, but I thought I'd try here first. I'm tired, and this is my only day off."

I shaded my eyes and surveyed the slope, my thoughts on the fish in the pool that I did not want him to catch. "It's not too bad of a climb. It might be worth the trouble to have fresh fish for supper, don't you think?"

"If it is worth the trouble, you are welcome to use my pole. I've got a can of worms you can take with you, too." He grinned and held the pole out to me.

"But—" I looked at the pole and the water before turning back to Mark. "But I don't know how—and I'm supposed to be watching my sisters."

"Holena can stay here with me. This is all you have to do," he said, and he explained how to cast the line into the water and how to reel it back in. Uncertainly, I took it and tried casting as he had said, only to whip the hook into the grass practically at my feet. Holena giggled.

"No," Mark said. "Like this."

He got to his feet and stood behind me. Then he wrapped his arms around me, his hands on mine to show me how to hold the pole. He pulled it back gently and cast. Though my hands and arms followed obediently through the motion, I could not concentrate on the lesson. His encircling arms felt strong and safe, and his body was warm and solid. It felt nice. My heart began to hammer unexpectedly. I hoped he couldn't hear it.

"Now you try it," he said, stepping away from me. I forced my thoughts back to the fishing pole again. This time the hook landed in the middle of the pool. I reeled it back in quickly.

"That's it," he said. "Now let me show you how to bait the hook and you're all set. You're not squeamish about worms, I hope." He dangled one in front of me. Then he deftly threaded it onto the hook and held the pole out to me.

"But—" I looked at Holena. I wasn't as eager to get away from Mark as I had been before.

"I will stay with Mark," Holena promised. "I don't mind. And Papa loves fish."

That was true, and fresh fish for supper did sound good. I looked back up at the ridge, then at Mark. My face flushed unexpectedly.

"Okay," I agreed, and set off quickly before I could change my mind.

The ridge was both steeper and higher than it had appeared. When I reached the top, I paused to catch my breath. From this height I could see beyond the mine and the nearby hills to the snow-capped peaks of the Rocky Mountains, cool and white against the sky. Below me on the other side of the ridge ran a green valley with a stream somewhat larger than our own. I looked back the way I had come. I could see the lone cottonwood. Mark and Holena stood in the sunshine beside it, looking up and waving. I waved back and set off down the opposite slope.

Mark had been right about fish in this stream. I caught one almost immediately after casting my line into the water. After catching a fish in one pool, I walked along the water to the next, and I soon learned which places were likely to have fish and which were not. I worked my way upstream for some time, until at last I had twelve trout—one each for me, my sisters, and mother, and two for each of the men. The sun's rays were slanting from the western horizon, and I knew it was time to get home. I gathered the fish into my apron and I tied it into a bundle with the apron strings. Swinging the bundle over my shoulder, I began to walk back toward the ridge. I had been moving upstream all afternoon, and wasn't sure how far I had come. I had planned to climb to the top of the ridge and use the view from there to find my way back home.

The bottom of the valley was choked with willow bushes and shrubs, and I had to fight my way through them to get away from the stream. I burst out into a plowed field and almost into the farmer. A tanned, squarely built man, with thick black hair and a large mustache blinked at me in surprise, as did the two barefoot children beside him.

"Excuse me," I said, taking a quick step back. "I was fishing. I didn't know—" I was afraid I was on his land and he'd take my catch. He only stared at me. His little girl giggled, reminding me of Aneshka.

"*Buenas tardes,*" she said to me, but her papa shushed her.

I recognized the language as Spanish. I had heard it at school, spoken by the children of Mexican miners. At least, the schoolteacher called them Mexican, but I knew some of them had grown up on farms in the area. Farms like the one I had apparently stumbled onto. Now that my surprise was wearing off, I saw that they were planting a field. Each carried a canvas bag of seeds and a sturdy, pointed stick to form the holes for the seeds. I felt a pang of longing—this was exactly the life my father had wanted us to have.

Suddenly I had an idea. I swung my bundle of fish off my shoulder and opened it. "Will you trade?" I asked. "Half my fish for some seeds?"

The man held his hands up and shrugged. "*No hablo inglés, señorita,*" he said.

I took six fish from the apron and held them out. "For seeds?" I repeated, pointing at his canvas bag.

The children and the farmer spoke for a moment in Spanish, then the man smiled at me. He took a handful of seeds from the bag and held it out, pointing between me and the seeds. I nodded and he poured corn kernels into my open hand, saying something to his son. The boy took a handful of beans and added them to the seeds I already held. I accepted them with thanks and poured them carefully into my pocket before gathering the fish and giving them to the man.

"*Muchas gracias*," he said. He handed the fish to his son, who ran off with them toward the low buildings on the far edge of the field. I retied the apron bundle and hurried away. The load was considerably lighter. There would not even be a whole fish for each of us now, but I was happy with my trade. I planned to plant a garden behind our house and grow some of our food. That way, we could save some of the money that we usually spent at the company store.

The sun had nearly set when I got back to the creek, and everyone had gone home. I found both Mark's family and my own waiting for me at my house.

"Well?" Mark asked when I arrived. "Did you bring us supper?"

I untied my apron so they could see the six fish. With so many expectant people gathered around, the fish seemed smaller than they had before.

"We'll have to share," I said.

"That's not even one apiece!" Aneshka complained.

"Hush, Aneshka," Momma said. "I'll put them in a stew with vegetables and there will be enough for everyone."

"And enough is as good as a feast," Old Jan said, tweaking Aneshka's cheek gently.

"I'd rather have a feast," Aneshka grumbled, but I ignored her.

"I think it will be a fine meal," Mark said, grinning at me.

"I had more," I said, "but I traded some to a farmer for these." I pulled the seeds from my pocket and spread them gently on the porch.

"That's not enough for a feast either," Aneshka said.

"They're not to eat," I told her. "They are for planting a garden behind the house. We can grow fresh vegetables and we won't have to spend our money at the store."

"That's a fine idea, Trina," Papa said, smiling.

"Indeed it is!" said Old Jan. "Fresh vegetables for your table will be very nice to have."

"And, we'll save money," I pointed out again.

"And that means Holena and I can have new dresses for school!" said Aneshka, finally growing excited. "I want yellow calico with blue flowers! What do you want, Holena?"

As my sisters prattled on about new dresses, I glanced at my mother. To my surprise, she was frowning at me, and my heart sank a little.

"What's wrong?" I asked.

She shook her head. "Put those away and come help me get supper now. Everyone is hungry."

I did as she said, confused. I had thought she would be happy and proud that I had made the trade. In the kitchen I chopped vegetables while she cleaned the fish. When they were all bubbling together in the pot, I asked her again what was wrong.

"Trina, I asked you to stay with your sisters. I need to be able to count on your help."

Her words surprised and stung me. Didn't she realize I was trying to help with the fish and the seeds? Couldn't she see the opportunity here? "Mark was watching them," I said.

"I thought you'd be pleased. Aren't you glad to have the fish?"

She sighed, wiping her hands on her apron. Her brow drew down and her lips tightened. "I don't want you to get hurt, Trina."

"It was safe, Momma. Really."

She shook her head, and I knew I had mistaken her meaning. "I know it was safe. But a garden, Trina? What do you know about growing a garden?"

"I know I have to—"

"It's another dream that won't work out!" she said. "And now you've got your sisters and your father all excited. And you're already dreaming of the money we'll save and what we'll do with it. But the seeds won't sprout or the crop will be eaten by locusts, and then what?"

"But they might—"

"Then more disappointment! More heartbreak!" she burst out.

I stared at her. How could she be so upset over such a simple plan? She couldn't really believe that we would break our hearts over something so small.

"It's only a garden, Momma," I said quietly.

Momma took a deep breath and returned to her usual resolute expression. "You should have done as you were told and stayed with your sisters. Now set the table."

The matter was closed. She left the kitchen and I obediently set the table, biting back my disappointment.

Momma said nothing more about it for the remainder of the evening, but Papa and Old Jan couldn't stop planning. Old Jan had a shovel I could use to turn the soil, and Papa had a plan for where we should lay out the garden. Aneshka was telling Holena of all the lovely bolts of fabric she'd seen at the

47

store, and the new dresses we would all have. Momma only sat in silence and chewed hard on her food.

"Will you have a garden too?" Holena asked Old Jan. "It was Mark's fishing pole, so half the seeds should be yours."

Old Jan patted her head affectionately. "I had once thought of planting a garden, but I can't till the soil with only one leg. But you've given me an idea. Excuse me for a moment."

He rose from the crowded table and thumped out of the house and up the road. When he returned, he had a bulging paper envelope. He handed it to me with a smile.

Gently I poured the contents out onto the table. A variety of seeds spilled out.

Old Jan leaned over the pile and began sorting them with his finger. "I was saving these when I thought I might plant a garden. I have squash here, and cucumbers. These are tomatoes, and this—" he paused as he picked up a fuzzy gray pod, and his expression softened. "This I brought with me from the old country. My wife always had poppies by the front door."

"Then we will plant them by your door here," I said.

"And yours," he said, smiling. He cracked the pod open with his gnarled fingers and showed me the hundreds of tiny black seeds inside. "There are plenty to go around."

"We're going to have a big garden, aren't we?" Aneshka said.

Momma stood abruptly and began gathering our empty bowls. "And who's going to weed and water and tend this garden? That's what I want to know. Lord knows, we have little enough time for our chores as it is now."

"It won't be a chore, it will be a garden," Holena said.

"Your mother's right—it will be more work," Old Jan said. "I can't till the soil, but I can do other things. I can weed and harvest. I can build trellises for your beans. I'll help out all I can, so it won't be a burden."

"And it will be worth it, Ivana, you will see," Papa said.

Momma only tightened her mouth and set the dishes on the counter.

As I washed the dishes that evening, I thought about the garden and all the plans that had been made at the table as we feasted on fresh fish and plum dumplings. I was excited to get started, proud to be helping my family, and determined to overcome my mother's disapproval. We'd soon have a thriving garden and fresh vegetables, and she'd see that it had been the right thing to do. After all, what harm could possibly come from planting a garden?

Chapter 5

ON MONDAY EVENING, after the washing was done and supper was eaten, I took Old Jan's spade out behind the house and began turning the hard, rocky soil. Old Jan offered advice. Aneshka and Holena picked out the biggest rocks and arranged them in neat borders on the edge of the plot. Momma did not help, but she sat at the back door with her mending and watched our progress. I could see fear in her eyes when she did not know I was looking. It only pushed me to work harder. When she saw our hopes turning into success, she would be pleased. I fell into bed exhausted that night, but happy.

When we had finished planting the patch behind the house, we turned a bit of soil by the front porch steps and planted some of the poppy seeds. The rest we took to Old Jan's house and planted along the porch there, while he instructed us on their placement. He wanted them to be just as his wife had had them in the Old Country. We had just finished planting them when Karel and Mark emerged.

"They won't grow," Karel said. "The seeds are too old. It's been four years since we left Bohemia."

Mark shrugged. "Who knows, it's worth a try."

"A lot of trouble for nothing, if you ask me," Karel said.

"Anything worth having is worth the trouble of getting it, isn't it, Trina," Old Jan said.

I agreed it was, although privately I had to think about my papa and his farm. He had come to America willing to work the coal to get it, but it wasn't enough. There was no promise that hard work got you anywhere—it could just as easily come to nothing. Still, we had to try. So I pretended I agreed with Old Jan.

After the planting was done, we waited. Old Jan came by to pull weeds. On hot days I hauled buckets of water from the creek and he spread them along the rows. Every morning Holena rushed out into the backyard to check for growth, though both Old Jan and I told her it would take time. At last, a week later, she was rewarded with the discovery of thick sprouts in the bean row, pushing their bowed heads up through the soil. Holena came dashing into the kitchen before she had even eaten breakfast. We followed her to the garden, where she showed us her discovery. Aneshka, after some scrutiny, reported the first sign of grassy corn sprouts as well.

I secretly glanced at Momma as my sisters padded barefoot along the rows, squealing with delight at each new discovery. Her face had softened and she was almost smiling, but then she saw me looking her way and her expression tightened again.

"I am glad things are sprouting, Trina, but don't get your hopes up that anything will come of it."

"I know it may not, Momma. But maybe it will. Old Jan says that anything worth having is worth working for."

"So it is," she said. "And we have plenty of work to do today, so enough nonsense. Go start heating the irons and I'll get the clothes from the line."

When the ironing was done that afternoon, Momma took the majority of our laundry earnings from the can on the shelf and sent me to the store for meat, as she did every Tuesday. Since the day Mr. Torentino had sold his plums, I had hated this chore. Mr. Johnson still gave me his usual salesman smile, but his eyes were hard. The previous week I had sent Aneshka in to make our purchases while I waited outside, but Mr. Johnson had tempted her into spending all the change on sweets, and I had gotten a scolding for it. So today I was by myself, with strict instructions to buy only what was on the list.

Mr. Torentino's wagon was just rumbling away from the store. I waited a few minutes before I entered, in case they had had another argument. I didn't want to do anything to offend Mr. Johnson again. Inside, he was stacking canned goods on the shelf behind the counter. I waited in silence for him to finish and notice me. When he did, he glared at me for a moment before pasting on his salesman smile. I knew my week's absence had done nothing to soften him.

Clenching my money nervously, I told him what I wanted. Without comment he set the goods on the counter in front of me. He totaled the amount and I handed him my money.

"Well," he said, looking at the cash in his hand, "you have three cents extra here. That will get you a piece of licorice, three lemon drops, or a stick of horehound." He gestured toward the jars of candy lined up on the counter. "What will it be?"

I swallowed hard and spoke. "I'd like my change, please, sir."

His salesman smile remained on his face, but stiffened. "It's just a few pennies, and I bet you've worked hard all day. You deserve a treat."

"No, thank you, sir. I'd like my change, please," I repeated, holding out my hand.

"What's the matter—you were happy enough to spend your money on Torentino's plums. Isn't my stock good enough for you?"

I did not know what to say to that, so I just waited silently for my change. With a shake of his head, he opened the cash register drawer, dropped my money inside, and took out the pennies he owed me.

My money safely in my pocket, I quickly gathered my purchases. "Thank you," I said, and hurried toward the door.

Mr. Johnson had already turned back to his shelves, but I heard him mutter something about "tightfisted Greeks." I could have kept walking, but I did not. I straightened my shoulders and raised my chin a little.

"Czechy," I said.

"Hmm?" he said, turning from his work. He didn't know I had heard him.

"We are Czechy," I said. "Not Greek."

He waved an impatient hand and went back to his work. "Bohunks, huh? You all look the same to me," he said. "Just like sheep."

My cheeks were flushed as I left the store, but I vowed to keep it to myself at home. My father would be angered by the insult, and my mother would scold me for talking back to Mr. Johnson. And since there was nowhere else for us to buy the things we needed, we couldn't afford to offend him.

When I arrived at our house, Holena was sitting on the front steps, her chin on her knees, staring at the place where we had planted the poppies. I followed her gaze, expecting to see sprouts breaking through the ground, but there was nothing there.

"What are you looking at?" I asked.

"Why haven't the poppies sprouted, Trina?"

"Maybe they just need a little longer," I said.

"Do you think Karel was right?"

"I don't know. We will have to wait and see."

Over the next few days, I went out to the garden in the back each morning to see the progress, but Holena went to look for the poppies. I knew they hadn't sprouted by the look on her face when she sat down at the table for her breakfast.

"I don't know why you're in a bother about them," Aneshka said. "They're only flowers. We can't eat them."

"None of it may come to anything, anyway," Momma reminded us all as she set our usual bowls of porridge on the table.

"But it might," I said. "And then maybe we won't have to spend so much money at the store and we can save a little."

Momma shook her head. "We'll still have to buy all the same things as we do now. Unless you can grow meat or coffee or flour in that garden of yours."

Despite myself, my heart sank. She was right; we couldn't live on the kinds of vegetables growing in my garden. There were just too many things that we needed that weren't in my little garden.

Momma looked at my face, and hers softened a little. "It's a good thing you are doing, Trina, and I am sure our meals will be better if anything comes to fruit. But you have to be realistic."

I nodded and ate, then started my chores, still thinking

about what she had said. Our biggest weekly expense at the store was meat. After wash day and Papa's payday, we had enough money for fresh meat from the store, and we certainly couldn't go without—at least, Papa couldn't. As hard as he worked, he needed something to sustain him. And Momma was right that I couldn't grow meat. I didn't have a cow or a pig, and even if I did, we had no way to feed it or to keep the meat if we butchered it. But I could fish. If I could bring fish home from time to time, even just once a week, I could save us a little money—maybe two or three dollars a week. And that could be one hundred dollars or more in a year!

The thought sent a tingle up my spine. One hundred dollars was an awful lot of money. I thought about it until I was finished with the last of my chores. When my sisters went outside to play, I went along, with one of Papa's old newspapers. I sat down on the porch steps and flipped through it, looking for the pages of advertisements. I knew they were in there, because when we had first arrived in America, Papa had used what little English he had to translate them for us each night—ads for land and farms here in America. I wasn't sure if he still read them or not, but he never read them out loud anymore.

I found the page and flattened it on my lap. A long list of ads in small print offered everything from horses and buggies to the services of laundresses and dress makers. Mixed in were the ads I wanted to read. Most of them were for established farms. My favorites were the ones that had fruit trees. I liked the idea of acres of apples or cherries or plums, so I looked for those first, and I found one right off that sounded perfect. A black border highlighted the ad. Inside the border, large block letters declared LAND! LAND! LAND! and below that ORCHARDS! PLENTY OF WATER! MOUNTAIN VIEWS! I could see it in my mind—at least, until I read the price: $2,500.00! I could never save that kind of money! Still, we didn't need mountain views; we just wanted a farm of our own. I read on, refusing to let my hope collapse, but just as the passing months had worn away at my father's dream, reading these ads wore away at mine, too. Even undeveloped land was selling for two or three hundred dollars, and it would cost much more to turn it into a farm. I couldn't see that we would get out of the coal camp with a penny less than five hundred dollars. Catching fish for one meal a week wouldn't be enough — but if there were other things I could do to save us money, maybe it was a start.

What we needed was a better source of meat — someone who could provide it at a better price than the company store. I remembered the farm where I had traded for seeds, and I had an idea, but I didn't share it with anyone. If my plans didn't work out, it would disappoint my sisters.

The next time I went to the store was on Saturday, after Papa got paid. As usual, there was a bit of change from my purchases, but I didn't return it to the can behind the stove when I got home. I felt guilty and wondered if I was stealing, but I planned to use it to help my family, so I did not see how I could be. After all, when Aneshka had bought candy with the change, she had not been stealing.

That afternoon, I asked Momma's permission to go fishing again, and she agreed. She had enjoyed the fish as much as the rest of us. I walked to Old Jan's house, where he sat on the front porch whittling. I borrowed the fishing pole, promising to bring fish for his supper as well as ours. Then I set off over the ridge.

As before, I caught fish in the stream, and as before I worked my way upstream, but this time I was not surprised to find the farm. This time, I had been looking for it. I left my string of fish and my pole in the bushes and walked to the cluster of buildings, carefully stepping in the space between the rows of young corn in the fields.

The buildings were bigger than they had appeared from across the field and for a moment my courage failed me. The structure was not just a single house, but many. The low adobe buildings formed three sides of a rectangle around an open courtyard. Each flat-roofed building had several doors, all facing into the courtyard, all painted a cheerful, bright blue. The open courtyard was bare dirt and busy with children playing. Their mothers kept a watchful eye from their shaded doorsteps where they worked.

A chorus of barking dogs announced my arrival, and several mongrels ran toward me. I froze until one of the older women came off the porch and called to them. They retreated, wagging their tales, and I let out my breath.

"Hello," I called to her. "Do you speak English?"

She shook her head, then with a quick word in Spanish, she sent a boy running to the cluster of low barns and buildings behind the houses. She smiled at me, and I felt my nerves relax a little. It was a warm smile that formed deep crinkles at the corners of her eyes, as if she had been smiling for most of her life. I smiled back and gave a little curtsy, which only widened her smile.

I took the money from my pocket, and gesturing as I spoke, I said, "I was wondering if I could buy—"

The woman held up a hand and gestured for me to wait, so I closed my hand around the money and stopped speaking. A moment later the boy returned from the barn with three men and several older boys. One of the adult men said something in Spanish to the others, and I recognized him as the man I had met in the fields. I hoped he was telling the others that he recognized me, but I couldn't be sure.

"*Buenas tardes, señorita.* You come here before, no?" another man said, and I quickly nodded. I held the money out to him.

"I—I wanted to buy a chicken, please, sir."

His eyebrows raised and he looked at my money. It was only forty-five cents, less than half what I would have paid at the company store, but I knew Mr. Johnson's prices were high. I held my breath and waited while he translated my request and the men discussed it. Finally, the man nodded.

"Come," he said, and the group walked back toward the barn. I followed with rising excitement. My mother would be so pleased to get a whole chicken for so little—we often could only afford a part of one to put in the pot.

Chickens were everywhere around the barns, scratching and pecking the bare dirt. Several hens had little broods of chicks scurrying around their feet, and young chickens with new pinfeathers in their wings were flapping and chasing each other like school children. The man to whom I had spoken singled out a hen without a brood and snatched her up, deftly catching her legs with one hand and binding them together with a strip of twine with the other. He held the squawking, flapping bird out to me.

I stared. It hadn't occurred to me that the bird would be alive. Of course, I knew it would be alive, but I hadn't thought about carrying it home that way. In my mind I had seen it much like buying a chicken from Mr. Johnson's store, where they hung already dead and plucked over his counters.

The farmer must have seen the uncertain expression on my face. He calmed the bird and turned her for my inspection. "Don't worry, she is strong, a good layer, no? She gives you many eggs."

My mouth fell open and I snapped it shut again. Eggs! I had only been thinking about buying a chicken for the pot, but eggs! If I had hens that could lay eggs, maybe I *could* grow meat! There was enough room behind our house for chickens. But one hen could not lay enough eggs for my family to eat well, or to hatch a brood large enough to fill a henhouse — at least, not soon.

"How much for two or three of those?" I asked, pointing at the young chickens chasing each other in and out around an old cart. "I have a large family; one hen won't give enough eggs for all of us."

"How big is your family?" the man asked.

"There are five of us, plus Old Jan and his two sons."

The man laughed. "Five is not so big," he said, unwinding the twine from the hen's legs and letting her go. He spoke to the other men in the group again, and after a time turned back to me.

"Three pullets," he said, pointing to the young chickens.

"All hens?" I asked.

"*Sí*, pullets," he said.

I nodded and smiled. "Thank you. Thank you very much." I handed him the money and he sent one of the boys into the barn for an old sack made of gray, hand-spun wool. The farmer collected three squawking chickens and put them into the bag, which he handed to me.

"Thank you," I said again. "How long until they lay eggs?"

"A few weeks, *más o menos*," he said.

Carefully holding the squirming bag, I set off back to where I had left my fish and my pole, then over the ridge toward home. I was thinking happily about the fresh eggs we would have when the chicks got old enough to lay. It would not be much at first, but if these were successful, maybe we could hatch more, and have meat. My mouth watered as I imagined roasted chicken for our Sunday dinners.

From the top of the ridge, I looked down into the drab coal camp and my thoughts returned to the present. What would my mother say when I came in with live chickens? And what would she say when she found out I spent the change from the store without her permission? My plan had been to bring a chicken for the pot—there was no foolish dream in that. But my bag filled with squirming chicks was full of dreams. And that was the last thing my mother was going to let me bring into the house! How was I going to explain this? More important, what on earth was my mother going to do when I tried?

Chapter 6

I SAT DOWN on the ridge and looked into my bag. The three little chickens looked up at me with their glossy black eyes and peeped their uncertainty. I stared back the same way. I knew nothing about raising chickens. Maybe I should take them back to the farmer and get my money back rather than try to explain it all to my mother. The farmers would laugh at my foolishness, and I hated that idea. I hated even more the thought that it was foolishness; I wanted my plan to work. I wanted the chickens, and I wanted fresh eggs and meat. Mostly I wanted to prove we didn't have to rely on Mr. Johnson and his awful store.

It was a good plan; I just had to find a way to convince my mother, and that wouldn't be easy. She had protested a garden. I didn't like to think what she would say about chickens. I closed the bag again and got slowly back to my feet. I descended the ridge and entered camp on the west end, so I could pass Old Jan's house before going to my own.

"Ah, here's our fisherman now," Old Jan said as he saw me coming. "Did you have any luck?"

I climbed the porch steps and sat down beside him. "I caught plenty of fish," I said. "And I have something else, too. But I need your advice." I told him of my idea to buy a single chicken for meat and how it had changed, and I showed him the three pullets in the bag.

"That is very serious, Trina, taking money without asking," he said, his tone sober but still gentle. "You shouldn't have done so."

"I was afraid my mother would not let me try."

"Your mother only wants what is best for you," he said.

Frustration welled up inside me again, just as it had the night I brought home the seeds. "How is it best for me—for any of us—to be stuck here, working and working and never getting ahead? If she wanted what is best for me, she'd let me try to make things better. That is all I'm doing—where's the harm in trying?"

Old Jan patted my knee. "You are a brave girl, Trina, and a good girl. How many fish did you catch?"

I held up the string. "Enough for everyone to have a whole one this time. But what about the chickens?"

"Do you think your momma would cook all the fish for us? I will bring potato soup. I have it simmering on the stove already, but your momma's a better cook with fish."

I nodded. "She is always happy to have you."

"Then leave the chickens with me and take the fish to your momma. I'll work something out."

I did as he said and set off for home with the fish. Momma was pleased to get them, and pleased, too, that I had invited Old Jan and his sons to supper.

"It's the neighborly thing to do," she said, "and the least we can do, since they are kind enough to lend you the fishing pole."

I helped Momma prepare supper and filled the tub of wash-water for Papa, as I did every evening. My mind, however, was not on my work. I hoped Momma wouldn't notice. I needed her to be pleased with me, to be in a good mood. I had no idea what Old Jan was planning to do when he arrived. I did not see any way he could bring the pullets to our house without brooking my mother's opposition.

My stomach swirled with butterflies when I saw Old Jan approaching with Papa. They were discussing something in earnest tones, so I slipped back inside the house before they saw me. Old Jan did not appear to have the chickens with him, and I was afraid my expression would reveal that I had a secret.

Papa washed the coal dust and dirt from his face and hands in the tub by the back door as usual before the two of them entered. I watched as Momma greeted Papa, then welcomed Old Jan. Neither gave any hint that anything was out of the ordinary.

"Where are your sons?" Momma asked Old Jan.

"They will be along shortly with the soup," Old Jan said. "I wanted to talk to your husband, so I came along when I saw him passing my house."

Momma looked between the two men, her eyes registering surprise. "Is something wrong?"

Papa glanced at Old Jan, then back at Momma. "There's talk of layoffs at the mine," he said. "Just not as much demand for coal now that summer is here."

Momma's jaw clenched. "Talk? When will we know?"

"They say some people will get their slip with their pay next week," Papa said. "And, they are going to start giving out scrip payments for the summer."

63

"Scrip?" I asked. I had never heard of such a thing.

"It's not real money," Old Jan explained. "It's like a voucher that you can use to buy things at the store. But you can't buy things anywhere but the company store with it."

"That doesn't worry me. Where else are we going to spend it, anyway? But the layoffs. I don't know what we will do if you're laid off, Tomas," Momma said.

Old Jan put a hand on Papa's shoulder. "Don't worry, Mrs. Prochazkova. I have been here for four years and I have seen this many times. Your husband is a hard worker and a family man. They will keep him on. It will be the lazy ones and the bachelors that will go."

"Let us hope so," Momma said.

"It's a good thing Trina's such a good fisherman," Old Jan said with a wink in my direction. "You won't have to worry about going hungry with her in the family, no matter what."

Momma smiled in my direction, but the creases of worry between her eyes did not go away. "Supper is almost ready," she said. "Sit down and relax while the girls and I finish up in the kitchen."

I understood her worry, and I shared it silently as we finished preparing supper. If Papa lost his job, I didn't know what we would do. I felt a surge of guilt for having spent our money without permission. We would need every last cent we had if there were layoffs at the mine. I was glad that Old Jan hadn't brought the chickens right away—maybe I could still return them and get my money back. My heart fell when I looked out through the open kitchen door and saw Karel and Mark approaching. Mark was carrying a wooden crate, and I had a good idea what was inside it.

He set the crate down outside the back door, putting a rock

on the lid to prevent escape, then came inside just as Momma called everyone to supper. Holena skipped up to Mark and greeted him with a hug.

"Trina caught more fish for us with your pole," she said happily. Her mood, at least, had not been smothered by the news from the mine.

Karel laughed. "So she did. Trina has out-fished you again, Mark."

I shrugged. "I'm sure if you had more time, you'd be the better fisherman," I said to make him feel better. I'd only just started to be able to talk to him again. I didn't need Karel making things more awkward between us.

Papa smiled at me. "Trina has many talents that she's only just discovering," he said, making me wonder if Old Jan had already told him of the hens. Embarrassed, I retrieved the skillet from the stove and put a fried trout on each plate. Luckily, the conversation among the adults turned back to the topic of the mine, and I could breathe more freely. Maybe the chickens would be forgotten.

Karel was especially worried about the possibility of layoffs. He and Mark were bachelors, even though they had an injured father to support. And bachelors were always laid off before men with families.

"If they let one of us go, we could still get by, I suppose," he said. "But I don't know what we'll do if we are both laid off. All the other mines are laying workers off too; there won't be any jobs anywhere."

"I'm good with my hands. I might find some odd jobs," Mark said. "I'm sure they'll take us back once fall comes and the demand for coal goes up again."

"If we can make it through to fall," Karel said.

"We'll help you, Karel, won't we, Papa," Holena said. "We have the garden, and money from washing clothes."

"Of course we will," Papa said, patting Holena's hair. "We are family now, aren't we? That garden will be a big help."

"Well, we will cross that bridge when it comes. No point worrying," Momma said, but I could see she was. If the bachelors in camp were laid off, they wouldn't be paying us to do their laundry anymore, and it would be some time yet before the garden produced any food. Of course we had to help Old Jan's family, but how would we do it? I understood why the lines of worry across Momma's forehead never quite went away anymore.

"What we need," Old Jan said, "is something to see us through the good times and the bad. Something to fall back on."

Papa nodded.

"In the Old Country, I remember we had a cow," Mark said. He glanced in my direction and gave a little grin. "She grazed up on the commons and we had milk, whether we had money or not."

"Can we get a cow, Papa?" Aneshka asked.

"Where would we keep a cow?" Momma said.

"Yes, a cow is much too big, but I have something smaller in mind that might help," Old Jan said.

"If it's small, it's not going to be much help," Aneshka said. "I want a cow."

"Well, I don't know." Old Jan pushed away his empty plate and leaned back in his chair. "Sometimes you have to start with small things to get the big things you really want. Do you know the story of the three brothers who inherited their father's farm?"

"Tell us," Aneshka said, bouncing in her chair and clapping her hands.

"Please tell us," Holena added more politely.

"The oldest son took the biggest and best share, and the second son took almost all the rest. For the youngest son all that was left was a good, sturdy rope. Now, a rope, that is not much, is it?"

"No, his brothers should have given him more," Holena said.

"Perhaps. So all he had was one small thing when he set out to make his way in the world. When he came to a forest he made snares from some of that rope, and he caught a squirrel and a hare."

"What did he want those for?" Holena asked.

"Don't interrupt," Aneshka said.

"He put the squirrel and the hare in his basket and continued on until he came to a lake. Beside the lake was a cave and in the cave was a bear, snoring away.

"The boy sat down beside the lake to make a bigger snare to catch the bear, but before he finished, a water sprite that lived in the lake saw him. It was just a small sprite, and very curious, so it rose to the surface and said to the boy, 'What are you doing with that rope?'

"Well, the boy was a clever lad, so he said, 'I plan to tie up the lake so no one can get out.'

"The sprite dropped to the bottom of the lake and told the king of the sprites what he had heard.

"'Go back up and challenge the boy to a race. When he is tired from running, catch him and drag him into the deep water, and we will be rid of him,' said the king.

"So the little sprite rose to the surface again and challenged the boy to a race.

"'I can't right now,' the boy said, still shaping his snare. 'But my younger brother will race you, though he's very small.'

"The sprite accepted the challenge. So the boy let the squirrel out of his bag and the creature zipped away so quickly it was half-way around the lake before the sprite started. Of course, it won. When the sprite told the king what had happened, the king sent him back to try again.

"'I can't. I'm still too busy, but you can race my other brother,' the boy said.

"The sprite agreed, and the boy set the hare loose. Well, what do you know, that hare was even faster than the squirrel had been."

"And the sprite lost again!" Aneshka said with a delighted squeal.

"Yes. So when the sprite returned to the king, it was clear that racing wasn't going to work.

"'Go back up and tell the boy you will wrestle him, and when you have a good grip on him, drag him into the lake and we'll be rid of him for good.'

"So the sprite returned to the surface, and he challenged the boy to a wrestling match.

"'Oh, I am much too busy,' said the boy, 'but my old grand-father is sleeping in that cave, and if you'll wake him up, he might be willing to wrestle with you.'

"'If I win,' said the sprite, 'will you leave our lake alone and not tie it up?'

"'Certainly,' agreed the boy. So the sprite went into the dark cave and saw the sleeping figure.

"'Grandfather, come wrestle with me,' he said, but the figure went on sleeping.

"'Come on, old man,' the little sprite said impatiently, and he slapped the bear hard on the nose.

"Well, that bear came awake with a huge growl and swatted the little sprite so hard he flew backward and landed with a big splash in the middle of the lake. When the king saw that, he knew he had to do something to protect the lake from such a strong, clever, fast family. So he rose to the surface and asked the boy, 'What do you want to leave our lake alone?'

"'Just enough of your gold to fill my hat,' the boy answered.

"'Agreed,' said the king. And while he was at the bottom of the lake gathering the gold, the boy dug a pit in the ground and cut a hole in the top of his hat. So when the king poured his coins into the boy's hat, he kept filling and filling, and the hat did not fill until the boy had nearly all the sprite king's gold.

"And that is how, with nearly nothing, the boy ended up the richest of all the brothers," Old Jan finished.

"We have nearly nothing—maybe we are going to be rich too," Aneshka said, and giggled.

Momma gave her a reproachful look, but Old Jan smiled. "As I said, I have a small thing that may help."

"What is this 'small thing' you have?" Momma asked, her voice skeptical.

"Well," Old Jan said quietly, looking at me, "they are not really mine. But maybe Trina would like to tell this story."

All around the table eyes turned to me. I looked desperately at Old Jan and he gave me an encouraging smile, but nothing more. I was on my own from here; he had done all he planned to do. I had made the choice to take the money and buy the chickens, and I was going to have to tell my parents on my own. I swallowed hard and spoke up.

"I bought chickens," I said simply.

"You what?" Momma said.

"Chickens?" Papa said.

I nodded and hurried to explain everything before I lost my courage. When I finished, there was silence at the table for a long moment. I kept my eyes on my empty plate, not daring to look at my parents.

"Well, where are they?" Papa said at last.

Mark rose from the table and returned a moment later with the crate. He set it on the floor and everyone gathered around as he lifted off the lid.

All of a sudden, Papa began to laugh.

Momma frowned at him. "What is the matter with you?" she said, but he only laughed harder. It was a long moment before the laughter quieted enough for him to speak.

"You remember, Trina, when your sisters made wishes and you would not?"

"I wished for plum dumplings," Aneshka said.

"And I wished for hair ribbons," Holena said.

Papa nodded, still chuckling, "And Trina wouldn't wish, but I did, remember? I said I'd wish for a farm. And here it is—a garden and livestock of our very own. Our little farm here in America. You should have wished, Trina, but since you wouldn't, it looks like I got the third wish instead!"

Chapter 7

I GAPED AT my father in disbelief. Had my wish come true, only to leave us stuck in the mining camp?

"You and your foolish nonsense," Momma snapped at Papa. Then she turned to me. "What were you thinking, Trina? Chickens? Where on earth are we going to keep them?"

"I thought we could keep them behind the house," I said. "They will be old enough to start laying eggs in a few weeks. I just wanted to help us save money to get our farm," I said.

"And just how are we supposed to fence or house them?"

"I hadn't thought of that," I admitted. The truth was, I hadn't really thought of any of it.

"There is always scrap wood in the mine dump," Mark said, surprising everyone. "We could probably dig up enough to make a chicken coop."

"And when will you have time for that?" Momma asked. "You boys work too hard now as it is."

"But we are going to need the extra food if we get laid off

at the mine," Mark pointed out. "I think it's a lucky thing that Trina found that farm and got these chickens." He smiled at me, and I blushed so suddenly I could not hide it. All I could do was smile back, grateful for his support. Then I caught my mother's eye and my smile quickly faded.

"I know I shouldn't have spent the money without permission, Momma. But please let me try. If it doesn't work out, we could still butcher and eat these chickens. I got all three for less than a whole chicken from Mr. Johnson's store."

Momma was watching the little hens scrabble and peck around the crate as Aneshka dropped bits of bread in to them. She sighed. "You do have an eye for a bargain, I suppose, but your head is so full of dreams. You get that from your father."

"Can we keep them then?" Aneshka asked.

Momma looked to Papa for his decision.

"If you can house them and feed them, Trina, you can keep them," Papa said.

I nodded. "They can eat kitchen scraps. And grasshoppers down by the creek."

"But do not do such a thing again without permission," Papa warned.

"I won't. I promise."

"And the first time they start costing us money instead of saving it, they go in the pot," Momma added.

That evening Aneshka and Holena herded the chickens around the small yard, but since we had no house for them, the chickens spent the night in the kitchen in their crate.

The next morning I woke to someone quietly calling my name through the open window. The rest of my family was still asleep, so I slipped outside to see Mark measuring out space and writing down his measurements on a scrap of wood.

"What are you doing?" I asked.

"Good morning, sleepyhead. I'm getting started on your henhouse."

"So early?"

"I only have today off, and I'll have to sleep this afternoon before going back on the night shift tonight, so I thought I'd better get started. It shouldn't take long."

"Really? I wouldn't know where to begin," I admitted.

"Then you're lucky you have me," he said, grinning. He looked like his old self, with his hair flopping over his forehead, and I couldn't help grinning back.

"So I am," I said. "What are we doing first?"

He picked up a stick and scratched out a square on the ground. "This is where we will build it," he said. "And here is what we'll need." He took a scrap of newspaper from his pocket, on which he had written a list of materials.

"Can we really get all this from the mine dump?" It wasn't a long list, but it was more than I imagined we could get for free. As far as I could tell, the stingy mine owners wouldn't let anything go for free if they could charge us for it.

"Let's go find out," Mark said.

"But—won't we get in trouble?"

Mark shook his head. "It's trash. No one will even notice. It all gets buried and forgotten under the mine tailings in a matter of days."

My family was still asleep, so I set off with Mark, up the hill toward the mine.

The slanting rays of the rising sun softened and brightened the drab houses and dirt lanes of the camp, but they could do nothing to alter the ugliness of the mine. As we approached, the hoist and the gaping shaft stood out as starkly as ever, surrounded by tangles of steel cable and grimy coal cars. I could never shake the sense of dread that came over me near the shaft. The thought of descending into the darkness, with all those tons of earth looming over me, made my insides knot. I stepped closer to Mark, glad for the warmth of his presence.

"Over there," he said, pointing. An enormous pile of dirt and crushed rock trailed down the slope toward the creek. The pile was streaked gray, brown, and sulfur yellow from loads brought up from different levels of the mine, and the entire mass seemed to be creeping relentlessly down the slope. On the front edge of the pile, trash and debris had been dumped and was being swallowed up by the advance of the dirt and rock.

We climbed down the slope to inspect the tangled debris. Splintered beams and boards, frayed loops of rusting cable, broken gears, and empty liquor bottles lay scattered on the ground or sticking out of the loose tailings. The whole pile smelled of coal, engine grease, and rot. I couldn't help wrinkling my nose, but Mark was grinning cheerfully.

"It may take us some time, but there's a lot here, if we don't mind getting our hands dirty. And the more we find, the less we have to buy."

"Then let's get started," I said.

Searching through the rubbish was hard work, and my hands were soon scratched and bruised, but with every new discovery of something useful, my spirits soared. It was like a treasure hunt, even if our treasure was really just trash. We soon had a pile of wood in a variety of ragtag sizes and shapes, but all were serviceable. After all, the chickens didn't care if they had a fancy house or not, as long as they had a place to roost.

"We need a fence, too," Mark said as we worked. "That will be the most difficult part."

"I didn't think of that when I got them," I admitted. "Is there any way we could make do without a fence?"

"Well, I suppose if you want them visiting your neighbors and roosting wherever they please," he said. "But if you want them to set in your henhouse, you better keep them there. Besides, there are too many stray dogs in camp to let them wander."

"How do you know so much about chickens?" I asked.

"When we were in Bohemia we had chickens. Collecting the eggs was one of my chores, so I got to know our biddies pretty well."

"You had a cow and chickens in Bohemia? Were you farmers?"

"More or less," he said, prying a board loose from the soil and throwing it onto the pile.

"And you gave that up to come here? To work in a mine?"

"We didn't really give up much. We didn't own the land or the crops. It was more like they owned us. And Papa was already a miner. More than once he left home for the mines all winter when the harvest was poor. So, after my mother died, Papa heard about the better wages here and we came. He believed Karel and I would have a better future."

I knew that land was scarce in Bohemia, and most of it was owned by wealthy families. The peasants who worked the estates were often no better off than beggars, but I couldn't see how working the coal mines here was any better. I said as much, but Mark laughed.

"You weren't farmers in Bohemia, were you."

"What does that have to do with it?"

"Farming's hard, miserable work, Trina. You spend your

days out in the heat all summer and in the cold all winter. And you never get paid. When a crop fails, the farmer goes hungry. When you run out of money here, the store will extend you credit so you can still eat."

"But you'll never get out of here that way. You're always in debt to the company," I protested.

Mark shrugged. "Where is there to go? We've got jobs here, and a house."

"But you don't own anything. It's not yours."

"You bought chickens. And you'll own your chicken coop, and your garden."

"But don't you want more?"

He shrugged again and tossed a board onto our growing pile. "Sure I do. But a farm isn't more. I never want to go back to farming. What about you?"

"My father wants a farm, and I think that would be a fine place for Aneshka and Holena to grow up. I think it would be better for you, too. Your papa doesn't mind farming, I think. He's been happy working in my garden."

Mark laughed. "There's a lot more to having a farm than a little kitchen garden. My papa can't swing a scythe anymore, and I don't ever want to either."

"Better than swinging a pick," I insisted.

He shook his head. "The way I see it, the biggest difference between farming and mining is just in what you're shoveling. And at least in the mine, you're getting paid to shovel it."

Mark was turned away from me, tugging at a timber that was stuck fast, so I scowled at his back. I was annoyed by his opinions, but he was doing me a big favor building my hen-house, so I held my tongue. I began gathering nails that we could reuse.

"Help me with this, will you? Something is holding it down," he said a few minutes later. He was still trying to pull the same timber out of the tailings. Using a bent piece of tin roofing, I scooped away at the dirt that held the end of the beam. Soon we could see why it would not come free. A crossbeam was still nailed to its end at right angles, and the second beam jutted downward into the heap of tailings and trash.

"Get at the corner and pull," Mark said, pointing toward the intersection where the two timbers formed an L. I did as he instructed, and together we heaved and pulled but they still would not come free.

"Maybe we should leave this one," I said.

"No, these are good, sturdy beams. They will be worth the trouble. I wonder what is still holding them." He lifted and pulled on his end again.

"Look," I said, pointing at what I had seen as he pulled. The timber he held was not the only thing that had moved. The dirt and trash around it had lifted and flexed as well. "Do that again," I said. Once again, the ground shifted across a wide area. I stepped into the L of the boards and cleared away the dirt in the area that had moved. Strands of wire appeared in the ground, but I couldn't tell what they were. Once some of the dirt was removed from the wire, I took hold of the wood again.

"Let's try it again now," I said.

Together we heaved and tugged, and suddenly the soil gave way and the wood came free. I staggered back a few steps and sat down hard. Mark looked at me, his eyes glinting with mischief.

"Are you okay?" he asked.

I nodded. "It just caught me by surprise, that's all."

He turned back to the timbers, his shoulders shaking.

"Are you laughing at me?" I demanded, getting to my feet. I tried to sound indignant, but my own laughter was starting to rise as well.

He shook his head, but a little chuckle broke out of him as he did.

"Yes, you are!" I said.

He shook his head again. "I'm not. I'm laughing because — look at what was holding us back."

I looked to where he was pointing. Attached to the L of timbers were strips of wire mesh fencing, the kind the mine used to hold back loose rock, but also the kind used to fence in chickens! I stared, open-mouthed. We had pulled loose about four feet of it, and more had disappeared under the tailings.

"How much do you think there is?" I asked.

"Let's dig it out and see, shall we?" he said.

We set to digging and pulling on the rusty fencing. When at last we had it free, we had enough to enclose a small chicken yard.

"I can't believe it!" I said, looking at it after we had it neatly rolled and added to our pile.

"I can," Mark said, grinning at me.

"You can?"

He nodded. "Because I think you, Trina Prochazkova, are the luckiest person alive. All you have to do is wish for something and it appears."

Chapter 8

MY MOUTH FELL open as what he said washed over me. Lucky things were still happening to me! If he was right, my wish wasn't complete. Hope filled me—the chickens and garden weren't the fulfillment of my wish—finding this wire proved that! And that meant we were still on our way to a real farm. I just had to keep trying and hoping and believing! I smiled at Mark, feeling happier than ever.

He smiled back. "We should get these things back to your house," he said, and I agreed.

By the time we arrived at my house with our first load of supplies, my family was awake. A work crew was soon assembled to bring the remaining boards and timbers to the house and start building. Old Jan and Karel joined us with hammers and saws, ready to start construction. I was eager to help build, but Momma called me inside.

"If you are going to have all these men working for you through their day off, you are going to have to feed them," she said.

"But I want to help them build," I protested. After all, the coop was for my chickens.

Momma shook her head. "You can help by making sure these men are taken care of," she said, and ushered me into the kitchen. We set to work cooking and baking as if it were a holiday. I supposed it was only fair. I did need to show my appreciation. But I still could not resist sneaking to the back door whenever I had a moment, just to take a peek at the progress. At first not much seemed to be happening, but when I stepped outside at noon to announce that dinner was ready, I was amazed to see a little square house there, lacking only part of the roof and a door. It was an odd-looking structure, made as it was from ramshackle bits of wood, the grime of mine tailings still clinging to some of them. To me, though, it was as good as a palace—or at least a palace for chickens.

"What do you think?" Mark said, pushing his hair back off his forehead as we inspected his morning's work.

"I think it's wonderful!" I said. "I am lucky to have such good friends!"

He grinned wider. "Come look." He grasped my hand and pulled me toward the little building. Standing on tiptoe, I could look over the wall through the missing portion of the roof. He stood beside me and pointed.

"You see, I put in five nesting boxes, in case you get more chickens."

"Oh, I plan to!" I said. "I'm going to let some of the eggs hatch so that I will have a whole flock!"

He gave me a quizzical look, then burst out laughing.

"What?" I asked, already feeling the color in my cheeks, though I didn't know why.

"You may have your farm, Trina, but that hasn't made you

a farmer just yet. If you plan to hatch chicks, you're going to need a rooster."

I stared at him for a long moment. When I finally realized what he meant, the blood flooded into my cheeks.

Mark tried to straighten his mouth into a serious expression, but the laughter kept bubbling out, despite his efforts.

I turned abruptly back to the house, feeling every inch the fool. "Dinner is ready," I said, a little more shrilly than I had intended. "I have to go put it on the table."

"But you do like my nesting boxes, don't you?" he called after me.

I nodded, too embarrassed to look at him.

"Come inside when you've washed up," I said, and fled into the kitchen.

Momma and I had outdone ourselves cooking, or so the men said as they took big helpings of stew, dumplings, and potatoes.

"Trina should get a cow, too," Karel said, as he spread a knife-full of lard on a thick slice of bread. "A little butter and this meal would be a perfect feast."

"Don't go putting any more ideas in that girl's head," Momma said, but she didn't sound angry. In fact, she sounded a little amused, and that gave me hope. If my chickens supplied us with fresh eggs and saved us money, maybe I could find a way to get a rooster, or at least a few more hens. But since I couldn't take more money, I needed to gain Momma's approval first so I could do it with permission.

My hope rose even higher at the end of the meal when the men finished their coffee to go back to work. Momma smiled in my direction. "You may go out and help them finish, Trina. Aneshka and Holena can wash the dishes."

I went outside with my heart singing. Papa and Old Jan

were fashioning a roof for the henhouse, so I helped Mark dig holes and place the mismatched posts for the short fence. When the posts were in place, we stretched the precious chicken wire across them, and I held it tight while Mark nailed it to the posts. I was intent on my work and did not notice that Papa and Old Jan had finished and left us alone in the back until we had the last bit of wire nailed into place. I stepped back and looked at our work, then exclaimed in surprise.

"What?" Mark asked.

"We haven't made a gate—there's no way to get out," I said. We had stretched the wire in a complete square, connecting it on either side to the chicken house with no openings at all—Mark on the outside and me on the inside.

"But the fence is only waist high," Mark pointed out. "You can step over it."

I might have done so if I were alone, but the thought of hiking my skirts and clambering over in front of Mark made me feel suddenly shy. I gazed at the fence uncertainly.

"Come here," he said. I stepped to him, with only the fence between us. He bent forward, caught me behind the back and legs, and swung me up and over the fence. I gave a little shriek of surprise and clung to him for support, noticing again the hard muscles of his arms and back. He set me down beside him on the right side of the fence, his eyes gleaming with mischief. "Next Sunday we can go get more wood and I will build you a gate," he said.

"Thank you," I said, a little breathless, still thinking about those strong muscles. I took time to brush myself off and straighten my skirts while my heart settled back into its beat. Mark had never had this effect on me when he'd sat next to me in the schoolhouse.

"Let's introduce your chickens to their new home, shall we?" he said.

We retrieved the chickens from where they were pecking and scratching along the roadside. Holena and Aneshka had been watching them and shooing off the occasional stray dog. Mark and I carried the hens, flapping and squawking, to the newly fenced yard. Then we stood and watched as they explored, pecking at the ground, testing the barrier of the fence, and darting in and out of the little house.

"Trina, do you remember this morning, when you asked if I wanted something more?" Mark's voice was unexpectedly nervous, and I turned to look at him. His nervousness made him look like the schoolboy once again, instead of the miner.

"Yes."

"What I want is for you to go with me to the dance at the community hall on Saturday. Would you?"

My heart skipped a beat. The older girls all talked excitedly about the community hall dances they went to with the bachelors in camp, but I had not looked for an invitation to one yet. The idea of it made me giddy.

"I have to ask my parents," I said.

Mark smiled, and I noticed how handsome his smile was. "Go ask, then. I'll wait here," he said.

I nodded and slipped inside, feeling like I was walking in a dream. So many things were going right so quickly it couldn't be real—and yet it was! I found Momma alone in the kitchen, putting away the last stack of plates. Through the open front door, I could see Papa, Jan, and Karel on the porch in conversation. My sisters were playing hopscotch in the dust beyond. I cleared my throat and spoke.

"Momma, Mark—Marek—" I added, remembering my parents'

preference for his Bohemian name. I didn't want to give any reason for her to say no. "Marek has asked me to the community dance on Saturday. May I go with him?"

Momma's face burst into a wide smile. "The community dance? That's a fine idea, Trina. Marek is a good boy — a fine young man, that is."

"I may go, then?"

"Of course you may go. We must find you something nice to wear. You should look your best. I'm glad to see you thinking about practical things and not just dreams. Marek is a good match for you. He's almost family already, and he's a practical boy. And you and Marek are very fond of each other, I think."

"A good match! It's only a community dance," I protested.

Momma smiled. "Don't act so surprised, Trina. You're almost a woman. It's time we started thinking of these things. Marek is handsome, and he already makes a good living. Go tell him you would be glad to go."

She smiled at me again and went out onto the porch to sit with Papa and Old Jan, leaving me in the kitchen, my mind reeling. I liked Mark, but I couldn't see myself marrying him. I hadn't thought of marrying anyone yet, but especially not someone who was content to stay forever working at the coal mine. I couldn't bear being trapped here forever, no matter how kind or handsome a husband I had. I'd made other plans. Of course, it would be years yet before I was ready to marry, but as I stood in the kitchen, I could hear my mother suggesting the idea to Old Jan and Papa on the porch. I did not want to make promises to Mark, or to Momma, that I couldn't keep if we got our farm.

Slowly I returned to the backyard. Mark was waiting. He pushed his hair away from his face and smiled when he saw me coming. I felt a pang in my heart, but it couldn't be helped.

"Well?" he asked.

I bit my lip, my eyes on the ground. "I'm sorry, Mark. I'm not ready," I said softly.

He frowned. "You'll be fourteen soon. Will your parents let you go then?"

"Maybe," I said, trying to decide whether it was wrong to let him think my mother had said no. Before I could decide, Karel came around the house to remind Mark that they had a night shift at the mine and should go home for a few hours' rest. I watched them go, already regretting my answer.

Holena suddenly came running around the corner of the house, bursting with so much excitement that I couldn't make out what she was telling me. She tugged at my sleeve. I took one last glance toward Mark and let her pull me away. She stopped by the front porch and pointed excitedly.

"See, Trina, see? The poppies! They've sprouted at last!"

There where she pointed, gray-green sprouts were curling up out of the ground.

"Well, I'll be," Old Jan said quietly from his seat above us on the porch. "And to think I had nearly given up on them! Tereza's poppies!" The faint tremor in his voice made us all look up at him. The corners of his eyes glistened with tears. Holena climbed the steps to him and took his gnarled hand in hers.

"Don't cry, Jan," she said gently. "Be happy. They will be beautiful when they bloom."

Old Jan smiled and patted her soft cheek. "You are a wise child, Holena. I was caught up in thoughts of what was, but you . . . You are right to hope for the future. After all, that is why we came to America, isn't it? To grow our hopes for the future. You are a wise child, indeed."

And with that, I knew I had done the right thing too.

Chapter 9

IT DID NOT take long for everyone in the coal camp to hear about my chickens, and at least half of them came by to catch a glimpse for themselves. The children came eagerly to the backyard to stare over the fence while their mothers walked slowly by on the road, trying to slyly glance past the house to the chicken yard. I could tell how far the news had spread each day by the changing nationalities of my visitors. We all had our own neighborhoods and we didn't mix much. The coal company preferred it that way—if we didn't mix, we couldn't organize against them. My chickens, however, managed what the union leaders could not. In no time Polish, Greek, Italian, Mexican, and Bohemian children were all mixed together, talking and laughing. By the end of the week, even Mr. Johnson knew of my chickens, as I discovered on my next trip to the store.

"Ah, it's the not-Greek girl," he said. I gave him a polite smile and listed the things I needed. He set each item dutifully on the counter in front of me.

"No eggs for you today?" he asked, smirking as if he knew a secret.

I could not help but stiffen, but I only said, "No, thank you."

"What about chicken feed?" he asked.

I hesitated. Was he merely trying to confirm the rumor? Something sinister in his manner made me afraid to tell him anything, though I could think of no reason not to. There was no law against keeping chickens, as far as I knew.

"No, thank you, sir," I said again and held out my money to him, wanting to get away from him more than ever. He did not take my money but continued to look at me with the same cold smirk. My outstretched hand began to tremble, but I said nothing. What was there to say?

Finally he took my money and made change. I hurried out of the store, relieved to get away.

"Never mind him," someone said as I stepped out onto the porch. I nearly jumped out of my skin—I'd had no idea anyone had been watching or listening. I turned to see one of the other Bohemian girls in the camp, sitting in one of the chairs on the porch. Her name was Martina, and she was three or four years older than me. She'd been in school with me when I had first arrived, but soon after she left school to marry. She had no children to come watch my chickens, but still I had seen her walking by our house, glancing curiously toward the backyard. I nodded a greeting in her direction. She rose and began to walk with me.

"My Charlie is on the same crew as your papa," she said as we began down the steps together. "Don't worry about Mr. Johnson. He's just afraid of the competition, that's all."

"Competition?" The idea surprised me—how could my three chickens be competition for Mr. Johnson?

"He's afraid you'll be selling eggs," she said.

"Oh."

"Will you be?" There was an eagerness behind her question that made me think she would be a ready customer if I had eggs to sell.

"I haven't really thought about it," I admitted. "I only have three hens, and they won't start laying for at least two more weeks."

Martina's face fell a little. "I see. But if you did have any to sell, I wouldn't require many. It's only my Charlie and me, and he'd sure be delighted to taste a really fresh egg now and then. You will let me know, won't you?"

I nodded. "I will let you know."

We had been walking as we talked and had come to her house. I thought she would say good-bye and go inside, but she hesitated.

"You have a garden too? And cucumbers?" she asked.

"Yes."

"Mr. Johnson never has cucumbers fresh enough to make a crisp pickle," she said. "Do you think —"

My mother called me from up the street. I could see her on the porch of our house, shielding her eyes from the sun, trying to see who I was talking to.

"Coming, Momma!" I called to her, then turned back to Martina. "You would buy cucumbers, too?" I asked.

She nodded eagerly.

"I'll let you know when they are ripe," I said. When I got home, Momma asked who I'd been talking to. I told her what Martina wanted.

"I said we probably wouldn't have anything to sell," I said. "But if we did have anything extra, from the garden or the chickens, she would like to know."

Momma gave a little snort and went back to work in the kitchen. "You've got everyone in town caught up in this nonsense. You'd be much better off to let Marek court you, and to forget your grand plans."

I did not reply, only put away the tins of food I'd brought and returned the change to the money can. Then I went out to the backyard and looked at my garden. The squash and cucumber vines were sprawling out from their hills, their wide, shady leaves sheltering the blossoms that would soon turn to fruit. The beans were climbing the simple trellises Old Jan had made from sticks and twine, and the corn was almost knee high.

What if there was enough here to sell? We were still going to have to purchase the necessities at the store. The garden would only produce a few extra things that would make my family happier. But Martina had given me something to think about. If these fresh vegetables would be a luxury to my family, they would be to others, as well. And people would pay money for a luxury, even if they could only get a little of it! All this time I had only been thinking of *saving* money—but maybe with my garden, I could be *making* money! And it must be possible, otherwise Mr. Johnson would not be so suspicious. It made me laugh to think that Mr. Johnson's suspicion had led to this discovery, but it gave me an odd feeling, too. It was yet another lucky coincidence—another unexpected occurrence that opened an opportunity. How could I account for so many lucky coincidences?

Holena and Aneshka came skipping out of the house, having finished their chores for the day as well. They each carried an empty plum can.

"We are going down by the creek to catch grasshoppers for the chickens," Aneshka said. "Do you want to come?"

I nodded and found a can for myself, and we set off for the creek. It probably would have been more efficient to bring the chickens to the creek to catch their own meal, but my sisters enjoyed chasing grasshoppers and trying to trap them in tin cans. As for me, I had been so busy with the garden, the chickens, and my regular chores, I had spent little time at the creek lately. So when my sisters tired of catching bugs, I sent them home, and I wandered alone around the bend to where the high bank silenced the mine. I needed the silence and the solitude to think.

I settled myself in the space between the tree's roots and waited, wondering if I would see the fish again, wondering if it really was a magic fish. I knew it couldn't be, but how else could I explain what was happening? I heard a noise behind me and turned to see Holena. She was watching me, her eyes uncertain. I smiled at her and patted the tree root beside me. She sat down on it, still looking at me with questioning eyes.

"What is it?" I asked.

"I like this place," she said. "It feels special."

"I think so too," I said.

Her face brightened. "You do?"

I nodded.

She chewed her lip, looking at the pool. I waited and soon her question spilled out. "You didn't see a magic fish in the washwater like Aneshka said, did you?"

"No, I didn't," I said.

"You saw it here, didn't you?"

I was so surprised by the question, I could only gape at her.

"I saw it too, the day I was here with Mark."

"You did? How do you know it was a magic fish?"

90

"I knew it was because you didn't want Mark to catch it. Why else did you make him stop fishing here?"

I couldn't help but smile. She had seen through everything.

Holena sighed and hugged her knees. "I wish you had made a wish, Trina," she said.

"Why is that?"

"Aneshka and I used our wishes on little things, just like you said. You would have wished for something smarter."

"Do you regret your wish, then?" I asked. People in the stories always did.

Holena shook her head. "But you would have wished for something wonderful and you'd be happy."

We sat in silence for a long moment before she spoke again. "If we see it now, Trina, will you make a wish? Please?"

I hesitated. I hadn't told anyone about my wish. It had seemed like an embarrassing secret all these weeks, but Holena was different. I took a deep breath. "I already have."

She looked at me, her eyes round with surprise. "You have?"

I nodded. "After your wishes came true, I came here and saw the fish, so I made a wish."

"What did you wish for?" Holena asked.

"I wished for a farm here in America, where we could all be together and happy."

"That was Papa's wish too! And that's why you got your farm!"

"That may be why we got the garden and chickens," I said slowly, "but I don't think that's the farm. Things are still happening. Lucky things. And we've never been lucky before. Not in America, anyway."

"You mean we're going to get a *real* farm? And Papa won't have to work in the mine anymore?"

It sounded so big when she said it—I couldn't promise such a thing to sweet Holena. I couldn't bear to disappoint her, despite my own hope.

"I don't know, Holena. But I do know things are getting better for us. And I have a new idea, to help make a little extra money, to help even more." I told her we might sell extra eggs or produce. "Maybe I'll make enough money to buy a rooster, and then our flock can grow. With more chickens, we could sell more eggs, too. What do you think?"

Her eyes gleamed happily. "I think your wish is coming true, Trina!"

"Don't tell anyone, please?"

"Not even Aneshka?"

"For now, not even Aneshka," I said. I stood and brushed the dirt off my skirt. "We should get back home."

I offered her my hand. As she took it, she glanced back at the pool. "I'm glad you believe in the wishes."

I followed her gaze. I had come here alone to decide what I believed, but I hadn't decided. At least, I thought I hadn't. Now, as I thought about it, I couldn't explain away our luck any other way. Slowly, I nodded.

"Yes," I said, "I suppose I do believe."

We turned and started toward home. Behind me in the water, I heard a soft plop and, looking back, saw ripples. Holena, it seemed, was not the only one who had heard me, and I had a feeling that I had made a commitment to more than just myself.

Chapter 10

I TENDED MY backyard empire with extra care after that, watching eagerly for our first harvest. I fished, too, and as I'd hoped, the free fish one day a week saved a few dollars at the store. Unfortunately, the layoffs at the mine had sent many of the bachelors away. As they left, they took their laundry—and their laundry money—with them, so the money can on the shelf stayed as empty as ever. I didn't worry, though. Opportunities had come along ever since I had made my wish. All I had to do was watch for them and snatch them up when they appeared. And although I had discouraged Holena from hoping for too much, I was once again reading the advertisements for land and daydreaming of shady orchards and fields of ripening wheat to the horizon.

Right on schedule, my hens began laying eggs, enough for us each to have one with our breakfast porridge several times a week. Even Momma agreed they were a treat.

The next opportunity came one morning in mid-June as I

worked in my garden. I was searching among the broad squash leaves for the first of the bright yellow vegetables when I saw a pair of unfamiliar shoes in front of me on the edge of the vegetable patch. I looked up to see Martina holding her pocketbook before her.

"Good morning," I said, and straightened to face her. I couldn't help a curious glance at her pocketbook as I waited for her to speak.

She shifted uncomfortably and gave me a shy smile. "It's my Charlie's birthday today."

"That's nice."

"And I want to bake him a cake. But I have no eggs. I was wondering if I could buy two from you."

I knew we had eggs in the house that we were saving up to make a meal's worth, but I suspected Momma wouldn't let me sell those. But I hadn't checked my henhouse yet today. My young hens didn't lay every day anyway, so two fewer eggs could be explained away easily enough.

"Let me see what I can do." I crossed to the chicken yard and entered through the fine new gate that Mark had made me. As luck would have it—especially the kind of luck I'd been having—there were three eggs in the nesting boxes. I removed them carefully and gave two to Martina. She gave me a nickel. I thanked her and slipped the nickel into my pocket, intending to put it in the can when Momma wasn't looking so I wouldn't have to explain what I had done. But as I continued to work in the garden, I started thinking again about a rooster. If I was going to get one, this nickel could be the first step. Then once I had a rooster, we could have more chickens, and more eggs, and even meat from time to time. And, more important, there would be more to sell—we'd be saving *and* making money.

This was the next opportunity I'd been waiting for. The money didn't have to go into the can.

Later that same day, another neighbor showed up in the yard. "I hear Mrs. Pearsonova bought eggs from you," she said. I smiled and nodded. Martina had married an American, but in the Bohemian district, the older women couldn't resist adding the "-ova" ending to the name of a married woman, whether her married name was Bohemian or not.

"I sold her two," I said, "but my hens don't lay many yet."

"What else do you have? Do you have cucumbers?" she asked, sounding as if she were inquiring across Mr. Johnson's counter.

"I do," I said. "They are small yet, though."

She strode into my garden and bent over my plants. To my surprise, she plucked a tiny cucumber off the vine without even asking permission. She put three cents into my hand, thanked me, and marched away. I stared after her, unable to say a word.

Once again, rumor spread quickly among our neighbors. Within the week, I had more requests than I could fill. Those I could, however, brought in a few cents here, a few there, until my apron pocket jingled when I walked. By the end of the week I had enough to buy a rooster. That I could not do without my mother's permission, so I waited until the chores were done and my mother sat down for a few minutes before starting supper. Then I showed her the money and told her where it had come from.

"Forty-eight cents this week, Momma, and that's with our garden barely starting to produce. When everything is growing and if we had more chickens —"

Momma sighed heavily and held up her hand to stop me. "What is it you want, Trina?"

95

"I want to buy a rooster. Then we could get more chickens, more eggs. We need a rooster if we want enough for eggs every day and some to sell as well."

"The eggs are nice to have, but it worries me that you always want more, Trina."

"Please, Momma? A rooster will make things even better."

She sighed again, but there was an unexpected gleam of humor in her eyes. "Roosters are trouble, Trina. Haven't you heard the story of Kuratko the Terrible?"

I looked at her in surprise. I had not heard my mother tell a story since I was a little girl in Bohemia. "Who was Kuratko the Terrible?" I asked.

"He was a rooster, of course," she said, and began the story. "There was once an old woman who wanted a baby, but she had never been able to have one. So she got a chick from a neighbor's chicken, and she babied it and cared for it like a real child.

"'Don't do that,' her husband warned her, but she wouldn't listen. She named that silly little rooster Kuratko, and it grew bigger and more spoiled every day. It ate and ate, and grew and grew until it was bigger than the dog."

"A rooster bigger than a dog?" I smiled at the ridiculous thought.

"Yes. And as it grew it got greedier and greedier until it had eaten up nearly everything in the house.

"'Put it out!' said the husband, but that silly old woman refused, saying, 'It's my baby!'

"But when that rooster had eaten up all the food and the old woman had nothing left to feed it, Kuratko gobbled up the old woman, all in one peck. Then it ate the old man and the dog, too."

"That's not a very happy ending," I observed.

"That isn't the ending. After eating the old man and the dog, the rooster was still hungry, so it went out in the yard, where it swallowed up the pig and the cat. But the cat used its sharp claw to cut the rooster's craw as it was swallowed, and when Kuratko went to crow at sunrise the next morning, his craw split open and he fell over dead. And the cat jumped out, followed by the pig, the dog, the man, and the old woman, who promised never to be so silly again. And that is the story of Kuratko the Terrible."

I laughed. "I don't think I will let my rooster grow that big."

"But you've let your dreams," Momma said. "And just like the old woman's, they may swallow you up if you aren't careful."

"But the garden hasn't, and neither have the chickens. You said yourself they are a help."

Momma nodded. "So they are. Very well, Trina, get your rooster. But don't look to me for help if it gobbles you up."

I climbed the ridge that afternoon, feeling light and happy. Momma's opposition had been the only thing wrong with my plans for the future, and now even that was beginning to give way. And when she saw how much money we could make — as well as save, once we had eggs to sell — it would disappear entirely!

I acquired a rooster easily enough, a cocky little red fellow who had most likely been headed for the pot at the other farm. He strutted around as king of his own kingdom in my little chicken yard. Momma christened him Kuratko, and Papa and Old Jan, who related the story to my sisters, agreed the name fit his character. And this time, we didn't have to wait for rumors of his arrival to spread. He announced it gleefully at the crack of dawn the very first morning, and every morning thereafter.

Chapter 11

WITH KURATKO making his presence known, my house once again drew visitors, the children bringing gifts of worms and grasshoppers so they could watch him strut and crow. I even saw Mr. Johnson pass by once, craning his neck toward my backyard. I stayed out of sight, but afterward when I thought about it, I felt a small satisfaction that he was worried enough to come take a look for himself.

For the next two weeks, everything went back to normal, but with more anticipation than usual, for we had one hen brooding on eggs. Mark said it would take about three weeks before they would hatch. Counting down the days in my head, I wished it would all go a bit faster. I was so eager for the new arrivals to my flock that it was nearly all I thought about, even as I washed and ironed clothes, kneaded bread dough, or endured Mr. Johnson's glares and insults at the store.

July arrived. There were only two or three days left in my reckoning, and I had started checking regularly to see if the eggs had hatched. I was in the garden with my sisters, thinking as always about my new chicks and planning for how I would feed them, when the air was split by a long, loud screech of metal on metal that raked along my spine like fingernails on slate.

Momma appeared in the back doorway. "What on earth?"

Our eyes locked in the horror of recognition as a muffled boom shook the earth. The mine!

I dropped my hoe and began running, my mother and sisters beside me. We weren't the only ones. Within minutes the streets were filled with other wives, mothers, daughters, and sisters, all running for the mine, all wearing the same expressions of dread.

A choking cloud of dust and smoke was roiling out of the open shaft and enveloping the gathering crowd. It smelled of coal and dirt, burning rubber, and hot metal. We joined a crowd of women gathering near the great framework of the hoist. The thick cables that hauled the mesh cage of the lift into and out of the shaft had snapped, and raw-edged tangles of wire jammed the huge gears of the hoist. Ropes of cable dangled from the framework, sweeping in slowing arcs over the shaft. Beside the shaft, which should have been obscured by the lift but now gaped open, was a small booth where the lift operator manned the levers to raise and lower the lift. It was considered to be a better job than blasting through rock in the deep tunnels below, and the man who held the job was considered lucky. Today that luck had run out. The body of the hoist operator lay crumpled over his levers, his neck twisted back into an impossible position, his body gouged and scored where the broken cables had whipped him as they ripped loose. Four or five other men were sprawled on the ground nearby, gashed and bloodied by the cables, one of them screaming in pain.

My hand went to my mouth to hold back the rising fear and nausea. Crowds were gathering around the bodies, including women crying out their husbands' names. As the man's screams sank to moans, I wrenched my eyes away. Death, I thought, should not be a public spectacle.

My mother had drawn my sisters' faces into her skirts so they couldn't see the carnage. I wished I was small enough for someone to do the same for me. Momma's face was gray and her lips were pressed so tightly together that they were turning blue. I stepped to her and put my arm around her waist, though I'm not sure who I was trying to comfort. She caught my hand in hers and squeezed, her own fear turning her grip into a vise.

"He wasn't on it. He wasn't on it," she said, as if trying to reassure me, but I knew it was really a prayer.

I looked again at the broken hoist cables and let the same prayer run through my mind. The lift, a mesh cage that lowered men into the mine and brought them back to the surface when their shifts ended, must have dropped when the cables snapped. How far had it dropped, and who had been on it? Or beneath it? I remembered the muffled boom somewhere far underground, and knew that more bodies would be coming out of the mine.

Indifferent to the scene, the mine's automatic whistle blew, reminding all of us that the shift had been changing. All the men were either entering or leaving the mine at this hour. Anyone could have been on or near the lift. Anyone. Papa, or Karel, or Mark.

I looked desperately through the men still on the surface. They were mostly clean—men on the night shift, reporting for duty and not yet into the mine. Already their wives and families were finding them, hugging and crying with relief, but there was no such relief for me. None of the faces I loved could be found.

Old Jan hobbled up beside us.

"Where are Karel and Mark?" I blurted out, hoping against hope they were late to work today and still at home.

He shook his head, then tipped it toward the mine. Around us, a grim silence was spreading through the crowd, though I could hear women whispering "trapped" or "no other way out." I could hear men's names, too, names of husbands, brothers, and fathers, spoken like prayers.

I said nothing. My lips were tightening down just like my mother's, and my own determination was all channeling into that one, fervent hope. Papa wasn't on it. None of them were on it!

An alarm bell was clanging now, and mine officials were arriving from their fine houses and offices at the bottom of the hill. They kept well away from the open shaft and the settling dust that might soil their fine black jackets and waistcoats. Workers were gathering around the open shaft, looking down it, and men were climbing into the mangled gear housings of the hoist to examine the damage. Without the hoist, they wouldn't be bringing anyone out of the mine. The crowd of women continued to grow.

We stood for some time, watching and waiting. Finally an official came and pushed us back to a safe distance. He said they were doing all they could, that we would be taken care of, and that we should go home. I did my best to translate his words into Czech for my mother, just as other daughters were doing in Welsh, Polish, Greek, and Spanish. Despite so many tongues, we all wore a universal expression of fear. Questions were thrown back at the man in many languages, but he had no answers. We refused to go home, so we were left once again to our silent vigil.

"Trina," Momma said, her words stiff and tight in her throat, "take your sisters home and feed them. Then get them to bed. There is no need for them to be here."

Although I wanted to stay, I did not protest. I understood her meaning. This was no place for children. They deserved to keep whatever bit of innocence life here still left them. I wanted to be useful in whatever small way I could, so I gently pulled their hands loose from my mother's skirts and began walking toward home.

The town seemed deserted—the houses mostly empty and unlit. I could smell burned food and coffee from more than one house we passed—many wives had been preparing supper and left it, forgotten on their stoves. Whether we knew the families or not, we went inside and removed the scorched pots from the stove tops. I was glad to do something to fight off the helplessness I felt.

Our own supper had been on the warmer when the accident had happened and so was fit to eat, but we were not fit to eat it. I filled three bowls with stew and put them on the table, but we only picked at it, and in the end it went back into the pot. Without our usual bickering, we washed our bowls and put them away. Afterward we sat briefly on the porch in the cool air, but the unnatural silence of the camp weighed too heavily upon us.

"Perhaps we should get ready for bed," I said.

"When will Papa be home, Trina?" Holena asked.

"I don't know."

"Will he be here when we wake up?"

"I don't know, Holena," I said, putting my arm around her

and pulling her to me. It was all the comfort I could offer, and yet it was so little.

Aneshka burrowed her hand into mine. "Say he will," she begged in a small voice, her usual sassiness gone. I did not know what to say.

"Come on, let's get ready for bed. Fretting won't do any good," I said.

I helped my sisters into their nightgowns and together we said our prayers with extra fervor. We lay down on top of the covers, for the summer evening was hot. I stared at the ceiling as the room grew dim, afraid to close my eyes and see again the bloody body of the hoist operator, or the dying man on the ground. Neither of my sisters were sleeping either. I turned and looked at Aneshka. She was curled into a tight ball, her eyes squeezed shut. Holena pressed her small body up against me.

"Will you tell us a story?" she asked.

I thought for a moment, but I couldn't make my mind focus, so I told her the first story that I could think of. "Once upon a time, there was a poor fisherman and his wife," I began. Holena closed her eyes as I told the story, and by the time I finished, she was breathing in soft, steady breaths. As for Aneshka, she hadn't moved at all, but when I came to the end, she whispered something. I tilted my head closer to hear.

"I would wish for Papa to be all right," she said.

"Me too," I answered softly.

Tears squeezed from between her closed eyelids and slid down her cheeks. Then suddenly she was convulsing with sobs.

I rubbed her back and told her to be brave, but she only sobbed harder until she at last cried herself into a shuddering sleep.

When both girls were peaceful, I rose silently from the bed

and dressed again. I took the pot of stew, the bowls from the kitchen, and blankets from my mother's bed, and I returned to the mine.

Bright gaslights illuminated the area around the open shaft, and a crowd of men was gathered around the hoist, but I could not tell what they were doing. I could not keep my eyes from trailing back to the hoist controls, so I was relieved that the mangled body of the operator had been removed.

On the edge of the bright light the crowd of women still waited. Among them, I found Momma and Old Jan.

"You must sit down, Momma," I said. "You must save your strength." It was the sort of thing I had heard people say in a crisis, though I didn't know what she had to save her strength for. I didn't want to think about that.

I coaxed the two of them away from the crowd a bit and they sat. For each, I filled a bowl of stew, but they had no more appetite than my sisters or me.

"Is there any news?" I asked Old Jan. He shook his head. "The hoist is ruined and the lift cage is gone. They won't be getting anyone out without it. They're trying to get men out of the top levels with ropes and pulleys, but most of the men are in the deeper levels. The top played out years ago."

"But they have to get them out!" I said.

"They've telegraphed the head office to get a new lift down here, but it will take some time. The gears in the hoist are stripped, too. It will take three or four days to get the parts here and installed, I think."

"Four days!" I said.

Old Jan squeezed my hand. "Now listen, your papa is a strong man and a hard worker; he'll be all right. He wasn't one to leave his shift before the whistle blew. He wasn't one to crowd by the lift to get out at the first chance, either. He's probably got some food and water left in his lunch bucket. I imagine he's already bunked down for the night and is sound asleep."

I smiled weakly at Old Jan. I appreciated his effort, but no matter how much I wanted to believe, I knew this was just another one of his stories—he couldn't know for sure.

"And Karel and Mark," I said. "Their dinner buckets were full, so they will be fine too, right?"

"That's a good girl. That is how we must think," Old Jan said, but I saw the pain of uncertainty in his eyes. I looked at Momma. She gave a little warning shake of her head that I knew meant I shouldn't ask, and I pieced together the rest. The lift must have been taking men into the shaft when the cable broke. That meant Papa would not have been on it, but Karel or Mark might have been. And no one on it could have survived. I fought back my tears, but they were coming all the same.

"There, there," Old Jan said. "We know nothing for certain yet. We have to keep hoping. Keep believing."

I nodded and wiped my eyes, but not even I could stretch hope that far. This was a far cry from wishing for a few chickens.

Old Jan gave a thankful smile and wrapped one of the blankets I had brought around my mother's shoulders. She clasped it there with one hand, but she said nothing. We sat with her in silence for a long time. Finally, Old Jan patted my hand.

"Go back and get some sleep, Trina. Your sisters may need you. Nothing more is going to happen here tonight."

"Then we should all go home," I said.

"I'm not leaving," Momma said, her tone fierce.

"I'll stay here with her, Trina, until she is ready to go home."

I didn't want to leave Momma there, but I finally returned alone to our dark house. It felt empty, even as I lay between my two sisters and listened to their steady breathing. The absence of my parents seemed to fill the house.

I did not sleep much that night. I woke before dawn, at the time Papa usually set off for work. I lay half asleep and waited for the automatic whistle at the mine. It blew, jerking me awake to an empty house, no cooking smells coming from the kitchen. I remembered then, and fear overwhelmed me again, just like it had the first time. I turned to see my parents' bed still empty and unused.

I rose quietly and went to the kitchen. It felt strange to be doing normal chores—lighting the stove, making coffee, measuring out oats—in a world that was no longer normal. And yet, what else could I do?

When my sisters were dressed and fed, I left them to do the morning chores and I took my pan of oatmeal and the coffee pot to Momma and Old Jan at the mine. All was quiet there. No one was working near the shaft or the hoist. The mine officials had declared that nothing more could be done until a new lift was installed, and the workers who were not trapped in the mine had all been sent home. The only people there now were the small clusters of women who had settled into camps on the margins of the scene. In the full daylight I could see just how many there were. The accident, happening as it did when the new shift was entering and the old had not all come out, had trapped more than a hundred men in the mine.

"If nothing is happening here, why not come home?" I said when Old Jan had explained everything to me.

"We will wait here for our husbands," Momma said. "We will not go home and let them forget the urgency of the situation."

I looked around and saw the grim determination on the face of not only my mother, but of the other women scattered across the hillside. It was an expression all too common to miners' wives. I could feel it settling onto my own features as well. "Then let me stay today, Momma. I want to help."

Momma smiled at me, one small flash, before her face turned hard again. "You are a big help, Trina, but I need you most to take care of your sisters."

I would rather have stayed, but this was not the time to argue with my mother. Once the meager breakfast had been eaten, I returned home.

For two long days, the routine was the same. If Momma and Old Jan slept at all, they did so beside the mine. Holena and Aneshka wanted to help as well, so we started each day with our chores. Then we gathered all the food we could from our garden, our henhouse, and our kitchen. We baked and cooked meals enough to feed not just Momma and Old Jan, but other women, too, who were holding their vigil at the mine. They opened their larders to us so we could prepare pots of food and coffee for ten or fifteen of the women from the Bohemian part of town. Under other circumstances such gatherings would have felt festive, but nothing could dispel the oppressive quiet.

The afternoon of the third day, my sisters and I were in the kitchen shaping dumplings when we heard the whistle of a train approaching camp. With the mine shut down, the train that transported the coal had been silent too. I paused and listened to be sure of what I had heard. It blew again and now I could also hear the chug of the engine. My heart pounded with urgent excitement. This would be the new lift! At last! I dropped the dough and, not even taking time to clean the flour from my hands, I ran to the mine. I was not the only one. Aneshka and Holena came with me, and the streets were once again filling with people—not just women, but men, too, pulling up suspenders or putting on work gloves as they went.

At the mine, men and boys were assembled into a work crew before the train came to a stop. They got to work at once, unloading the new cables and gears for the hoist, and the parts for a new lift. A mine official came to the hillside where the women were camped and told them to go home, but they refused. In the end, the officials set up a rope barrier that we were required to stay behind.

The grim silence of the past two days was now replaced by urgent action, as every able-bodied man in camp went to work getting the hoist operating and the mine open. Wives and daughters, including me, took turns carrying water and coffee to the work crews so the usual water boys could be put to other tasks. Lights were again set up, and work continued through the night. No one quit when their shift was over. Every man there knew that it could have been him trapped below—that it could be him next time.

The new lift was in place by sunrise, and a cheer went up when the lever was pulled and the hoist gears jolted into action, pulling the cables tight. Still, the ordeal was far from over. The shaft had been damaged or blocked in places by the erratic course of the falling lift, so the descent of the new lift into the mine was gradual. At each level men got off the lift to clear a section of the shaft below before it could descend farther.

It was past noon before they raised the twisted wreckage of the original lift to the surface, and with it, the first of the dead. Like the lift, those who had been on it were crushed beyond recognition. They were laid out by the train track, where ashen-faced women filed by, looking for a familiar patched boot or shirtsleeve to know for certain. The lucky ones came away having recognized nothing; the unlucky collapsed in despair.

Momma ordered me to stay at the rope with my sisters while she and Old Jan joined the line. I was glad to be spared a closer view of the dead, but I could not help watching as Old Jan and Momma moved slowly past them. I did not breathe until I saw Old Jan shake his head and turn away. My hopes that Karel and Mark had not been on the lift rose, and I told myself again that they were all right. They had to be. They were with Papa now, cheering at the sight of the new lift arriving to bring them home!

My anticipation was not to be satisfied so quickly, though. As the afternoon passed and the day grew hotter, we remained in the crowd, watching. Men had been working on three levels in the mine, and it was being cleared of both the living and the dead from the top down. As the day progressed, the line of bodies by the train track grew, and the crowd of waiting women dwindled. Some slipped under the rope and ran, screaming with joy to embrace a man as he emerged, blinking and squinting into the daylight. Others crouched, weeping, beside the tracks, their shawls or aprons over their heads. Those of us still behind the rope waited in tense silence.

By dusk, only a handful of women remained behind the rope, but we were still among them. The lift rose to the surface once again, and the gates opened to pour out more men. One of them carried a body toward the train track. I saw Martina — who had baked a cake for her Charlie just a few short weeks ago — gasp and go white. She seemed to shrink as she watched. Then, with a soundless sob, she pulled her shawl over her head and walked slowly toward the tracks. The knot of fear tightened around my heart, squeezing out my breath. Charlie had been on Papa's crew.

I turned my eyes back to the lift, now descending smoothly

into the shaft. The gears of the hoist stopped turning, indicating the lift had stopped somewhere far below. We waited in silence. A wagon clattered up the street and stopped by the train, driven by Mr. Johnson. Inside it were stacked coffins, their pine boards still fresh and smelling of sap. Mr. Johnson jumped down from his seat and approached the mourning wives and mothers, his sales ledger in his hand. His face was composed in a respectful expression, but it looked too practiced to be sincere. I turned away feeling sick, unsure I could bear one thing more.

Just then, the hoist clanked into action and the cables began to move. The handful of us still behind the rope drew in a collective breath and held it as the lift came into view and stopped, the cage filled with more grimy men. More women slipped under the rope as the men staggered out. The last to come out were Papa and Karel, carrying between them a limp and bloodied body.

Mark.

Chapter 12

MOMMA, ANESHKA, and Holena were under the rope in an instant, but Old Jan stood frozen, staring at the still form of his youngest son. The same shock and fear rooted me beside him. I took his hand, and together we tried to go forward, but it was like trudging through deep water.

Momma and my sisters were already with the men, Momma taking the tragic burden from Papa while my sisters clung to his legs. At once Papa collapsed to his knees, holding the little girls to him.

Momma turned, and I knew she was looking for me.

"Quickly, Trina, go to Jan's and prepare hot water and bandages. Quickly!"

The desperation in her voice broke me from my trance. Water and bandages? Surely it was too late for that. Then I saw Papa on his knees and all the fear came back—he must be hurt too! I let go of Old Jan's hand. I turned and ran, as my Momma had told me to. I wanted to run forever—run from the pain and

111

from my regret that I had never told Mark how I felt. But I had a job to do, and the living still needed me. Old Jan's house was not far.

Once inside, I lit the stove and began heating water. Then I found clean rags and tore them into strips. I had a mound of them ready when Momma and Karel came through the door with Mark between them, Papa and Old Jan hobbling behind. I saw now that Karel wore no shirt or suspenders. He had fastened his own shirt as a bandage across his brother's chest and secured it there with his suspenders to stanch the bleeding. The makeshift bandage was now brown and stiff with dried blood.

They laid Mark on his bed before collapsing themselves into chairs. I ventured a glance into Mark's face, and to my amazement I saw him wince with pain as they settled him onto the mattress.

"He's alive!" I gasped.

Momma gave me a surprised look. "Of course he's alive—why did you think we needed bandages?"

"I thought— Oh, Papa!" I cried, and like a child threw myself into his arms, sobbing with relief.

Papa held me, patting my hair. "There's my good girl," he said. "Now get me a drink of water—I'm parched!"

I dried my eyes and hurried to fill and refill cups of water for Karel and Papa as they drank deeply. Old Jan, meantime, was feeling his younger son's forehead and cutting the suspender straps to remove the bandage.

"We were the last group off the lift before the cable broke," Karel explained. "We were still signing out tools with the foreman when the lift came crashing down. A piece of flying metal caught him across the chest. Something hit his leg, too. He's lost a lot of blood, Papa."

I went to the bedroom doorway and watched while old Jan peeled back the bloody bandage. Mark groaned and clenched the sheets as the stiff bandage pulled the scab from the wound. New blood bubbled up through the ragged gash that ran for eight inches across his chest.

Papa staggered to his feet. "I'll fetch the doctor," he said.

"Nonsense, Tomas," Old Jan said. "You're hardly fit to be standing yourself, and the doctor has worse than this to attend to." Old Jan turned back to his son and probed the edges of the gash with his fingers before speaking again. "You are lucky, Marek. If it had caught you two inches lower, it would have torn your stomach and we'd have lost you. This is only skin and muscle. Trina, bring me the water and those rags."

Together we bathed Mark's wounds. Then I did what I could to soothe away the sweat from his brow while Old Jan stitched the edges of the gash shut with a length of thread and a sewing needle that he had heated in a candle flame. I might have emptied my stomach at the sight of the needle pulling through Mark's skin had I eaten anything that day. As it was, I swallowed my nausea and tried to find comforting words for Mark until he passed out from the pain.

When the wound was sewn up, we smeared it with a salve my mother provided and wrapped it with the clean rag bandages. Then Old Jan inspected Mark's leg, which was swollen and blue at the ankle. Another deep gash cut to the bone across the front of his leg, just above his boot. Mark jerked back to consciousness as his father removed the boot, torn beyond repair by whatever had cut his leg.

"Lucky again," Old Jan said with a look of relief. "If it hadn't been for your sturdy boot, you might have lost this foot. As it is, it's just a deep cut, not even a broken bone."

I stayed beside Mark until he slept, then I went to the kitchen, where our families were eating supper. I could barely keep my eyes open long enough to finish my meal. My sisters, mother, and I cleared the dishes while my father staggered off to home. When the dishes were all washed, Momma, Aneshka, and Holena followed. I looked in on Mark once again. I thought a bit of color had returned to his face, but I couldn't be sure.

"He'll be all right," Old Jan said.

I jumped in surprise. I hadn't realized he was standing at my shoulder.

"Are you sure?"

"I've seen men survive worse, and he's as strong as a horse. The only danger now is infection, but we'll take good care of him. Now go on home and get some rest yourself."

Reassured by his calm, I agreed. It was well past dark as I walked the short distance from Old Jan's house to my own. With each step my weariness grew heavier until I was stumbling across the threshold. I stepped into the bedroom and breathed in the fullness of my family, all of them here and asleep. With a simple, silent prayer of thanks, I settled myself beside my sisters and slipped at once into a dreamless peace.

I slept until the sun was high in the eastern sky and the air was becoming warm and stale. My sisters were still asleep, so I slipped quietly out of bed and padded barefoot into the kitchen. Momma was sitting at the table, drinking a cup of coffee and darning stockings.

"Where is Papa?" I asked, after glancing around and seeing no sign of him.

"He's gone to work," Momma said.

"At the mine?"

"Of course at the mine."

"But—" I stared, paralyzed with fear. How could he go back down that lift after all that had happened? "But he can't!"

"And what are we going to live on if he doesn't?" Momma said, but the lines of worry were deeply furrowed on her forehead. She was afraid but, as usual, the practical needs were foremost in her mind. "He has already lost three days' pay this week."

"But he was trapped! The mine surely owes him something for all he's been through!"

"We have much to be thankful for; we must remember that," Momma said, not looking up from her work. "Many families were not as fortunate as us."

I remembered again Martina's Charlie, and I knew she was right. Still, all I could think about was how we had to get out of here so that Papa would never go through such a thing again. I vowed to myself that I would work extra hard in my garden so that we could buy our farm.

"Thank you, Trina," Momma said.

I looked at her in surprise. I had no idea what she was thanking me for.

"You worked hard these past few days to look after everyone. I don't know how I would have gotten through it without you. I am proud of you."

I hurried to dress after that, eager to work in my garden. I wanted to do the things that would earn the money to get us away from the mine.

I swept the kitchen and the porch, and as I did I remembered for the first time in days that I had a brooding hen. I put away the broom and took up my basket with rising excitement, hoping to see a nest full of cheeping chicks in the henhouse. It wasn't until I stepped out the back door and saw the gate swinging crookedly on torn hinges that I realized I hadn't heard Kuratko crow that morning. I looked around, hopeful that the chickens were simply loose in the yard and garden, but they were not. There was no sign of life in the yard at all — but there were signs of death everywhere. Feathers littered the ground, and a smear of blood ran across the chicken coop wall near the door. I hurried through the open gate, searching the ground. The tracks of large dogs were everywhere in the yard among the chaos of feathers. The limp body of one of my hens lay in the corner of the yard, tossed against the fence and forgotten. Everyone in town had been at the mine; no one had been in the neighborhood to hear stray dogs in the chickens.

I remembered the brooding hen and hurried to the henhouse, hoping against hope. It was no use. The brood had hatched, but without their mother's care the bald hatchlings had all died in their nest.

I backed out of the henhouse, anger and grief stinging my eyes. Then I saw my garden. The battle of dogs and chickens had ranged beyond the broken gate. Row after row of vegetables were trampled flat. The bean trellis had been torn down and had uprooted most of the stalks when it toppled. The remains of bold little Kuratko were tangled in its strands of twine.

I looked for one long moment of despair, then collapsed on the back step in tears. Every grief and fear of the past week tore from my throat in racking sobs. My mother found me there sometime later, still weeping uncontrollably.

"Trina, what on earth . . . ?" Then she stopped and looked around at the carnage. "Oh, Trina. I'm so sorry," she said, her voice mixing sympathy with resignation. I knew that tone too well. She had to be thinking she had told me so.

"No, you're not!" I blurted out before I could stop myself. "You never wanted me to succeed!"

"What we want and what life gives us are seldom the same thing, Trina."

A new burst of sobs kept me from answering. She stood silently beside me for a long moment before she said, "Hush now, Trina. We have work to do."

I wanted to stop crying, but I couldn't. It was all too much.

"Hush now," Momma said again. "How can you carry on like this for a few chickens? Men died in that mine and all you can think about are your silly chickens?"

"No, Momma! Don't you see, the chickens were to be our way out! So Papa would never have to go back into that mine."

"It was a dream, Trina. You're crying for the loss of something you never had to start with."

"And you don't believe in dreams," I said bitterly. "You don't believe in anything but staying stuck here."

Momma sighed heavily and sat down on the stoop beside me. "Trina, dreams aren't real. You can't eat them; you can't keep your papa safe with them. And believe me, you'll never feed your children with them. We only have what life has given us, and dreams . . ." She paused, fumbling for the words. "Dreams get you hurt, just like this one's hurt you. Just like your papa's dream put him in that horrible mine."

"So you'd have us never try to make our lives better," I said. "To have something more."

"Believing I could have something more made me what I am today," she said. "I could have been a tailor's wife, living in a comfortable cottage in Bohemia, but instead I married the man who filled my head with dreams. And look where it got me!"

I looked at her in surprise. For the briefest moment, I saw her not as the resilient mother I had always known, but as a

117

young, vulnerable dreamer herself. Her usual hard expression quickly returned when she saw me looking.

"But—you love Papa, don't you?" I asked.

"Of course. I love all of you. But these dreams! Dreams only crush the things you love!"

She turned her face away from me, and for the first time I understood. I ached from the loss of a few chickens and a garden. What pain must she feel from the weight of years of disappointments? No wonder she had warned me against this dream. I put my hand on her shoulder. She straightened, strong again.

"We have other things to keep us busy now, Trina. Put this behind you and look to all you still have. Papa still has a job, we still have our family and friends, and you have a handsome young man who wants to court you. That should be enough for anyone. To want more than what you need is a vanity."

I wiped my eyes and nodded.

"Now, see if there is anything you can salvage in your garden."

I took a basket to the vegetable patch and began searching through the trampled and wilted leaves. A few squash clung to the torn vines, and I picked those. The corn was all ruined, without a single ear having ever formed, and only about one-fourth of the bean plants could be saved. The cucumbers at the very edge of the garden were the only crop that had been spared. The few surviving beanstalks might produce enough for a meal now and then, but my hopes of selling anything more were gone.

The disappointment was a steady ache in my chest that wouldn't go away, though I tried not to think of it. And I could see now that a few eggs and vegetables would never have earned us enough money to get out of here. The dream had clouded my judgment. I had wanted far more than I could ever have. I told myself it was best that it should come apart now while it was still only a small thing. I thought again of Martina and others who had lost someone in the mine, and I felt ashamed.

I was putting the trellis back in place along the few bean plants when I noticed a bootprint in the soil. I had seen the tracks of the dogs everywhere, but this surprised me. Had someone been in my garden while we were at the mine? I couldn't imagine that anyone had taken any vegetables. Maybe someone had seen the dogs and tried to chase them off. Surely no one would steal anything at such a time—everyone in town was connected to the disaster; no one would be thinking of robbing a garden.

I looked again at the bootprint. A pawprint partially obscured it—it was from before the dogs had done their mischief. It must have been Old Jan's, I decided, from before the accident. I put the question out of my head and finished collecting vegetables.

When I finished, I had more than enough for a meal. I set aside a few, but most of them wouldn't keep. They were bruised and had been withering on the ground for too long. I looked again at the two chicken carcasses. They hadn't been chewed by the dogs, and were still fresh enough to use, and that gave me an idea. I wanted to make up for my foolishness, so with Momma's help, I plucked and cleaned the chickens and put them into a big kettle of soup with the trampled vegetables from the garden. When it was done, I put some into two pans and set out.

I went first to Martina's house. Charlie was laid out in the bedroom and a small group was gathered around him, sobbing or fidgeting uncomfortably with the hats they had removed

119

upon entering. Martina sat at the kitchen table, staring into a cup of tea, her face like marble.

I knocked at the open door and held up the soup pot. "For you," I said.

She raised her eyes to mine. They glinted with a look of panic. I entered and set the pan of soup on the table beside her.

"What am I going to do?" she whispered. "The mine says I can only stay through the end of the month now that there's no worker living here. Where am I going to go?"

Rage rose in me again at the mine owners, but I bit it back. "What about your papa?" I said. Her family had been at the mine before she'd married.

She shook her head. "They've moved to the mine at Cokedale. They don't know about any of this yet. But there are seven kids in that house. I couldn't burden them by going back."

"You'll think of something," I said.

A loud sob rose from the other room and Martina choked back one of her own. Her face was so white I thought she might faint. "They've been here all day," she whispered. I looked past her to the woman keening at the bedside and the silent men that surrounded her like a queen's attendants.

"Who are they?"

"Charlie's mother and brothers. They arrived from Pueblo on the train this morning. She hates me. She didn't want Charlie to marry a foreigner. She won't let me near him."

Martina clung to my hand now, as if I were the only solid thing in her world. I had only intended to pay my respects and be gone, but I couldn't leave her like this.

"Walk with me," I said. "You need some fresh air."

"And leave Charlie?" She glanced guiltily toward the back room.

Leave his mother, I thought, but instead I only said, "You have to think of your own health, too." I coaxed her to the front door and through it. She stepped out into the sunlight and blinked, like a dazed creature pulled from its burrow.

We walked slowly up the road, past my house and toward Old Jan's, where I intended to leave my second pot of soup. The fresh air did bring a little color to her pale face. When we reached Old Jan's, I paused.

"I have another errand here, Martina. Do you mind?"

She shook her head, so we walked to the front door. The door was open in the hot afternoon, but Old Jan was not sitting on the porch. I called in a greeting and he called back from the bedroom, inviting us in. I stepped inside, but Martina only hovered in the kitchen.

Mark was propped up in bed, though he was leaning far back to ease his chest. His face wore an expression of pain.

"How are you feeling?" I asked him, scrutinizing his face for any sign of fever. I was relieved to see none, but frightened by how pale he looked.

"Sore," he admitted with a twitch of a grin. His voice was weak, but at least he had tried to smile.

"He's resting easy. That's the best thing for him now," Old Jan said.

"I brought you some soup," I said. "I thought it might help."

As they thanked me, Karel came in through the back door, carrying two buckets of water. I supposed that, like Papa, he was expected to return to work for his regular shift. He started to say something, then he caught sight of Martina, standing uncertainly near the kitchen door. A look of tender sadness came over his face and he set down his buckets.

"I am sorry about Charlie," he said to her. "He was a good

man and a hard worker. He was near us there, waiting to get on the lift, to get home to you." He shook his head regretfully.

I looked at Martina. Tears were welling from her eyes. Karel took a handkerchief from his pocket and carried it to her. They were speaking in hushed tones when I turned back to Mark.

"They are evicting her," I said, trying to control the outrage in my voice. "And they're docking your pay for the time you were trapped in the mine. How could they!"

"They can do as they please," Mark said.

"But it's wrong!"

Mark sighed, and I immediately regretted my anger. He didn't have the strength for it. I laid my hand softly on his.

"You should sleep," I told him. "It will help you get your strength back."

"I'd rather have a bowl of your soup," he said, this time managing a small smile at me.

I filled a bowl and, sitting beside him, spooned soup carefully into his mouth.

"It is delicious," he said. "Are the vegetables from your garden?"

I nodded. "It is all there will be, though." I told him what had happened to my chickens and the garden, struggling to hold back my grief. It was silly to cry over such a small thing, and I could not explain that my tears were for something so much larger.

"There, there," Old Jan said, patting my hand. "It's a blow to be sure, but we survived without it, and we will again. You can plant again next summer."

He was right, of course, and so was my mother. Survival was the most we could expect in this world. I looked at Mark and knew that survival itself was a blessing.

Karel reappeared in the kitchen to collect the dinner bucket his father had prepared for him. "I'm off to work. Enjoy lying about while I'm laboring away," he said to Mark with a grin.

"I should get back to Martina," I said when Karel had gone. "And you should rest."

"Thank you, Trina," Mark said. He clasped my hand in thanks, but he did not let go when I tried to leave, so I turned back to him. "Trina, I'll be laid up here for a short while, but I'll heal fast. I'll be back on my feet before the next dance." He squeezed my hand and looked into my eyes. "Will you go with me?"

Before, when I had refused him, I had thought I'd had a future—that I'd be leaving the coal camp soon. Now, I saw otherwise. I saw the foolishness in believing in anything other than what was real right now. And in the four days the men had been trapped in the mine, I had also learned how fragile my real world could be. I hadn't appreciated what I had, and I had almost lost it. I'd almost lost Mark.

I looked into his pale, sick face, waiting eagerly for my answer. I could not know what the future held for either of us. All I could do was make the most of each moment that I had, whatever or wherever it was. And where it was—where it would always be—was here. But at least it could be with Mark.

"I would be honored," I said.

Chapter 13

THE NEXT WEEK did not start with dancing. It started with funerals. In all, twenty-seven men had died and countless more were injured in the disaster at the mine, and no family in our community was untouched. The mine closed on Tuesday, and everyone in town crowded into one service or another. There were so many services held in so many different languages that they took place wherever space could be made. Afterward, the wagons full of coffins converged in the hilltop cemetery to the south of the mine. The whole community watched as one after another was lowered into the long row of open graves. Final prayers were said before the first shovelfuls of dirt were thrown onto the pine boxes. Then we united, no matter what our religion or language, in grief for our shared loss.

Mark insisted on going to the funerals, though we all begged him to stay home in bed. He could not walk on his injured foot, and the stitches across his chest made leaning on crutches unbearable. Papa and Karel carried him much of the way, though they were still pale and wrung out by the ordeal. It took all their strength to get Mark to the hilltop cemetery, and all Mark's strength to stand through the prayers and scriptures read there.

It was past noon when the mourners dispersed from the hill. The mine officials shooed us all away from the graves, telling us to go home and mourn in private. Rumors had spread that union organizers would be at the funerals, so wakes and public gatherings had been forbidden.

Papa and Karel started back down the hill with Mark, struggling to keep their footing on the loose, gravely slope. Fortunately, other men came to their aid, healthy men who had not been trapped underground. Two bachelors took over and carried Mark down the hill and all the way back to his house. Old Jan was beside himself with gratitude for the men and, since they had no families to spend the afternoon with them, he invited them to stay for dinner.

Amid the commotion, it took several minutes for us to realize that Karel had stayed behind to assist Martina from the cemetery. Still snubbed by her mother- and brothers-in-law, she had stood alone at the funeral. She had collapsed, wailing with grief as the first shovelful of dirt was thrown on Charlie's coffin, and Karel had gone to her aid. Now, as they approached down the road, she moved like a sleepwalker, relying on Karel's strong but gentle arm to guide her. As they arrived at the house, Old Jan took one look at her and declared that she would not go home alone either.

Momma looked around at everyone—Mark, propped in a chair, his face tight with pain; the lonely bachelors; the desolate Martina. She squared her shoulders.

"Yes, Jan, you are right. We must all have a meal together. We must keep up our strength and support each other through these times."

"I'm not hungry," Martina protested weakly.

"Come now. The living must live," Momma said.

Old Jan nodded and gently guided Martina to a chair. "Life goes on, my dear. Even at times like these."

"Trina, go to the store and get us enough meat for a decent stew. We've got potatoes and a few vegetables left from the garden," Momma said.

"The superintendent forbade gatherings," Karel reminded us.

Momma made an impatient, dismissive gesture. "This is no gathering. It is family, and a few people who need family. They can't deny us that. Besides, we've no interest in the union. Trina, run along. We must get started."

I did as she said. Old Jan came along too, insisting that the bachelors had helped his son, so he intended to pay. Mr. Johnson's store was open, but he had no customers, so Mr. Johnson was sitting outside on the porch. I stopped and stared when I saw him. He was leaning back in his chair, a bottle of soda pop in one hand while his other hand scratched a big yellow dog behind the ear. A second dog, equally large, lay at his feet, its tongue lolling out of its mouth in the summer heat. I stood staring until he looked up and saw me. His eyes tracked my gaze to his dogs before returning to my face. Then his lips curled into a slow smile.

"Do you like dogs?" he asked with mock innocence. "These are a special breed. They're *bird* dogs." His smile widened even more as anger flooded my face with color. "I believe you have pets too, don't you? Tell me, how are your chickens these days?"

I couldn't answer. I was seeing in my mind all that had really happened. It made sense now. Stray dogs couldn't have broken through the gate or done so much damage by themselves, and hungry mongrels wouldn't have left carcasses uneaten. And there had been that bootprint in the garden. I clamped my mouth shut, unwilling to respond to his taunt. I smiled back, though my insides were boiling, and walked into his store as if nothing was wrong, refusing to let him get the better of me. Mr. Johnson followed. I could feel him still smirking behind me.

Inside the store, Old Jan got busy selecting meat and a few other items. I wasn't sure just what. My head was pounding with anger, and I could barely see.

"Looks like you're having a little party," Johnson observed as Old Jan counted out his money.

"Only a family supper," Old Jan said.

Mr. Johnson shot me a suspicious look. "Didn't know she was part of your family."

I said nothing. I hoped Mr. Johnson would soon forget this encounter. I did not want his hatred of me to harm Old Jan and his sons, especially now that I knew what Mr. Johnson was capable of.

At home I helped my mother prepare a hearty meal and tried to forget the encounter myself. When dinner was ready, we carried it to Old Jan's house, where we ate on the porch, as it was too hot inside. The men had dragged a mattress outside for Mark, and I sat beside him and helped him eat. He had little appetite, but could at least eat some of the gravy from the stew, and a few bites of the chewy meat.

As the afternoon wore on, his color grew worse. His sweaty face looked like a wax doll, with a high flush of pink in his cheeks. I left his side again only when I had to wash the dishes. When I returned, I was more alarmed than ever. He was leaning against the wall, his eyes closed and his lips slightly parted. Flies were crawling on his face and shirt. For a moment I thought he was dead, and I gasped. My gasp awakened him, as well as drawing the attention of the others. He stirred and brushed at the flies on his face, grimacing with pain as he did so.

"I think it's time you were back in bed, Marek," Old Jan said.

"And time we went home and gave you some peace and quiet," Momma added.

Taking her meaning, the two bachelors thanked my mother and Old Jan and set out for their own home. Karel offered his arm to Martina, who stood to leave as well.

"Perhaps Trina might stay long enough to help me get Marek settled," Old Jan suggested.

Mark protested, insisting that he didn't need help. By the time we got his mattress back on his bed and moved him, however, his jaw was clenched with pain. He leaned heavily on me and hopped the short distance to his bed. Once there, he collapsed, spent. I tucked a pillow under his head.

"Holena told me today that you made a wish for a farm," he said, managing a brief, teasing smile. "No wonder you've had so much good luck. It's magic!"

I scowled. She had promised to keep it a secret. "I don't feel very lucky."

"But you are," he insisted. "You got your little farm— chickens, garden, chicken coop."

"That wasn't a farm. And anyway, it's all gone now."

He sighed as I gently tucked his bare feet under the sheets. "Maybe that's my good luck."

"What do you mean by that?" I asked.

"With your chickens and garden, you were too busy for me. Now we are going to the dance."

I did not reply to that, only busied myself arranging the sheets comfortably around his feet, then helped him out of his shirt. His skin felt warm, and I looked again with concern at his face. Sweat stood out on his brow, but it had been a warm day, and he had exerted himself. I hoped desperately there was nothing more to it.

"We are going to dance all night," he murmured, shutting his eyes and settling back comfortably once his shirt was off him. I looked at the bandages on his chest. There were a few dark spots of blood, but not enough to give alarm.

I smoothed his damp hair back off his forehead. "Rest," I whispered, but needlessly—he was already asleep.

The next day Papa was back at work once again. Old Jan arrived at our house midmorning.

"How is Mark this morning?" I asked. My concern had only grown in the night, but Old Jan did not look worried.

"He is still sleeping," he said. "He was worn out from yesterday, so I did not wake him for breakfast. Sleep is the best thing for him. I came to see if there is something I might do for the garden."

I did not want to think about the garden or see the ruined chicken yard, so I stayed inside to help my mother with the mending while Old Jan and my sisters worked outside. Still, I was fidgety and my mind was not on my work. The third time I had to remove a big tangle from my thread, Momma asked me what was the matter.

"If you want to go out to your garden, go on," she said. "Heaven knows you're not very useful here as you are."

I dropped my hands to my lap and sighed. "I'm worried about Mark. He felt warm last night when I helped him to bed."

Momma's needle stopped in midair.

"A fever?"

"I—I don't know. It was a warm day. Maybe he was just worn out, like Old Jan said."

"There's broth for our lunch on the stove," Momma said. "Perhaps you should take some and look in on him."

"Old Jan said he's resting."

"But you won't be easy till you're sure he's all right, and I won't either, now. Go on. If all's well with him, you can come right back."

I already felt better just to be checking on him myself. I poured some of the broth into a small pan and set off at once up the hill to Mark's house.

Inside, the house was still and quiet. I set the pan of broth on the stove and tiptoed through to the bedroom. The curtain was closed, so the room was dim. Karel was snoring in one corner. In the other corner, Mark lay still on his back in Old Jan's bed, his face turned toward the wall. I stood in the doorway and watched him, his chest rising and falling with each breath. At first, I felt a rush of relief at how peacefully he slept, but as I stood watching, I realized something was wrong. His breaths were not the slow, deep breaths of a restful sleep. They were too quick and shallow.

I crossed the few steps to his bedside and leaned over him, trying to see his face. His hair was plastered to his neck with sweat. Dread filled me. I reached out and put a hand on his forehead. Even before I touched him, I could feel the heat of fever.

He stirred at my touch and turned his head. The flush in his cheeks and, his hair, curling with sweat, made him look so young. His eyes fluttered open and swept past my face before closing again. He mumbled something about dancing.

I bit my lip hard to hold back the sob of fear that lurched up from my gut. I didn't know what to do. Should I wake him? Feed him? Let him sleep? I did nothing—only stood staring at his burning face, thinking how young he was. Thinking he was too young to die.

Chapter 14

I DON'T KNOW how long I stood there before my mother called my name from the front porch.

"Trina? When you didn't come back, I—" She stopped talking when she stepped through the bedroom door and saw me there.

"He's burning up with fever!" My voice cracked with desperation.

She whisked past me and pushed the curtain aside, flooding the room with light. Karel groaned and turned over, his face to the wall. Momma bent over Mark and felt his forehead.

"Get cool water and a cloth to bathe his face," she said, her voice calm but serious. I hurried to do as she said—of course it was what you did for fever. I felt foolish for not thinking of it myself. When I returned from the kitchen with the water, Momma had peeled back the damp sheet and was cutting away the bandages on Mark's chest. I began to bathe his face with the cool damp cloth, but stopped dead when my mother removed the bandages and I saw the gash in his chest. The wound was still mostly closed, but the skin around the scab was red and puffy. Near his shoulder, the stitches had torn loose, and the gash had split open. My mother pressed her fingers along it, and thick, bloody pus oozed out, giving off a foul smell.

Momma sucked in air through clenched teeth. Her expression was as grim and pinched as it had been during those nights and days of waiting at the mine.

"Momma—"

"Go fetch Old Jan," she said.

I ran, tears blinding me along the way.

"It's Mark," I told him when I reached the garden plot. "He's— Fever."

Old Jan dropped the hoe he had been using and grabbed his crutches. Together we headed up the road as fast as the old man could go. Back inside his house we met up with Momma in the kitchen, where she was heating water at the stove. Old Jan looked at her inquiringly.

"Infection," my mother said through tight lips. Old Jan paled and clomped past her into the bedroom.

I stood tentatively in the doorway, watching as he bent over his son, feeling his forehead and examining the gash on his chest. My mother nudged my arm, her hands full with a wash-basin of warm water and clean rags.

"We must open the wound again to clean out the infection. It will be very painful for Mark. Perhaps you should go home."

I straightened my shoulders. "I want to help," I said. "Maybe I could be a comfort to him."

Momma nodded. "Then bring those towels," she said, indicating a stack on the kitchen table. "And that new block of lye soap."

While I hurried to get those things, Momma woke Karel

and sent him to our house to sleep. She knew there would be no sleeping with us tending to Mark.

In the bedroom, Old Jan was holding his son's hand and calling his name. Mark woke and looked at his father, his eyes glassy.

"Time to go to work already?" he said, and tried to sit up. Old Jan pushed him back down and gently shushed him.

"No work for you today, son. You have to rest, get your strength back."

Mark sighed, and I could see he remembered now, all that had happened and why he wasn't working. A hard shiver racked though him.

"Your wound's infected, Mark; we're going to have to clean it out," Momma said in her matter-of-fact way. "It's going to hurt, I'm afraid, but it can't be helped."

Mark's eyes traveled from my mother to his father to me. He reached for my hand.

Lancing and cleaning the infected gash was horrible, and the worst of it was Mark's pain. Where the wound had torn open, cleaning it was easiest. Along the rest of the gash Momma cut away all the stitches Mark had suffered through a few days before, and lanced the tender scab that had formed. Then she squeezed the stinking puss and blood from the wound, wiping it away with towels before using rags and the harsh soap to wash it again.

At first Mark gritted his teeth and squeezed my hand to resist making a sound, but before long he gave in to the misery, crying out as my mother cut and squeezed and wiped. I held his hand, though my own was soon bruised and aching from his grip, and mopped his burning face with the cool rag I'd brought in earlier.

When my mother at last finished, she laid a clean towel gently over his chest and examined his ankle. The cut there looked angry and red as well, though not oozing pus like the wound on his chest. She left it alone, though she looked worried.

"Stay with him until he's resting again, Trina," she said. She motioned Old Jan toward the kitchen with her.

I stayed where I was, holding Mark's hand. Gradually his grip loosened and his jaw unclenched.

"It's bad, isn't it?" he said after a time.

I cupped his hand between my own. "Just rest now," I said.

"Am I going to die?"

I swallowed hard. "Shh. Just rest," I said.

"Will you stay with me, Trina?"

"I'll stay as long as you like."

He closed his eyes and sighed. "Forever?"

"As long as you like," I repeated. "Now get some sleep, if you can."

"I'd like forever," he murmured.

I said nothing, just held his hand and watched him drift toward sleep. My mother and Old Jan were talking in low tones in the kitchen. I strained to hear them over Mark's shallow, panting breath.

"I don't know where the money will come from," Old Jan was saying.

"Wait until tomorrow and we will see, but if he doesn't improve quickly, we will have to find the money," my mother said. "Trina made a little selling eggs. It may not all be gone."

They were speaking of the doctor. I knew my mother would not suggest it if it wasn't serious. I looked again at Mark's face and blinked back my tears. They were welcome to all the money I had left.

I stayed at Old Jan's house all the rest of that day, mopping Mark's brow with a cool cloth to try to ease the fever. In the evening my mother returned with a kettle of soup and tended Mark while Old Jan and I ate. I took my bowl to the porch, eager for some fresh air after the long hours in the still, stale air of the bedroom. When I finished my supper, I asked my mother if I might stay the night.

"I can tend to Mark if he needs anything, and that way Old Jan can get some rest too."

Momma nodded. "I think that is a very good idea, Trina. If you need anything, we are just down the hill, and you can come get me."

She went home and returned with blankets to make a bed for me on the kitchen floor. I slept poorly that night in that strange room. Mark moaned and mumbled as he sank deeper into the delirium of fever. He thrashed and tangled himself in his sheets. The next morning when he jerked awake, he did not know us.

The doctor wouldn't take the scrip the mine was issuing, so we had to scrape together every last bit of cash we had to get him to come. He restitched the wound, using a bit of whiskey to numb the skin as he did so, and he left a small bottle of opium syrup to help Mark rest. As for the infection and the fever, we would just have to wait and see. I stayed on, taking turns sitting with Mark so that Old Jan could rest himself, but the old man would not go far from his son's side.

On the fourth day the fever subsided gradually. I wasn't sure, at first, but by midday, Mark was resting peacefully for an hour at a time without the aid of the syrup. Toward evening, he opened his eyes and looked at me as I mopped his brow, and he was sensible of who I was. I smiled with relief and called

Old Jan to the bedside, but by the time he arrived, Mark had slipped back into sleep.

Old Jan and I stood together and watched him sleeping peacefully.

"He's been improving all day," I said. "I'm sure the fever is down."

Old Jan said nothing at first, only stood leaning on his crutches, looking down at his son. At last he gave a deep sigh. "He is so young," he said. "Too young to be throwing his life away in that mine."

A knot tangled up inside me and all I could do was nod.

"Do you know, in the Old Country, my wife and I had five children."

"Five?" I didn't know. While Old Jan had told us many stories, this had never been among them.

He nodded, sighing again. "Five. Karel and Marek were my youngest. The first three are all dead now, just like my beloved Tereza."

"What happened to them?"

"It was long ago, child; it doesn't matter now. I came to America for these last two—so they might have a better future. And they would have, too, if I hadn't lost my leg."

I tried to push down the lump in my throat, but it was stuck fast. Old Jan brushed a gnarled hand across the top of my head, smoothing the hair that had pulled loose from my braids.

"If he recovers, Trina—"

"He will, Jan! I'm sure he's better tonight!" I knew not to interrupt my elders, but I could not bear the thought that Mark might die.

"He is better," Jan agreed. "And I have you to thank for that, Trina. You have taken good care of him."

I shrugged, embarrassed, but pleased, too.

"I think you are more fond of my Marek than you have admitted," he continued.

"I am fond of him," I said. "I'm fond of all of you."

"But with Marek, I think there is something more. When he recovers, Trina, go to the dance with him. He likes you very much, and it would make us all happy, don't you think?"

I wasn't sure who he meant when he said "all," but I knew it would make Momma happy, as well as Old Jan and Mark. I supposed it would make me happy too. I saw that more now than I had before. Now that I had come so close to losing him.

I nodded. "I've told him I will, if he's well enough," I said.

Old Jan smiled at me and patted my cheek. "You are a good girl, Trina. You take such good care of my boy. You will keep taking care of him, won't you?"

"Of course! He isn't better yet. Of course I will tend him, as long as he needs me."

"He will need you for a long time, my dear. A long, long time. You know what your mother wants, and I think Marek wants it too. You and Marek are a good match. With you, I think my dreams for him could grow again. I think he could build a good life here in America."

I listened to him while I watched Mark sleep, his cheeks still flushed but his breathing deeper and quieter than it had been in days. I was suddenly aware of the ache at my heart. It had been there for days, but I realized that now it was different. Watching over Mark, fearing for him, being by his side every day, I realized how fond of him I had grown.

My plans to get the farm had been crushed, and with them, my hope. But I hadn't lost Mark. Before, I had felt like I had to choose, but that choice had been taken from me. All that was left was Mark, and as I looked at him, my heart swelled within me. Slowly, I nodded.

"I will take care of him, Jan. For as long as he needs me. I promise," I said.

Old Jan smiled and hugged me. Before the day was out, my mother knew of my promise and couldn't wait to tell my father of the match. The whole family was excited and spoke of nothing else that evening. Everyone except Aneshka. She glared at me, stomped her feet everywhere she went, and wouldn't speak a word to me. I simply ignored her and tried to enjoy the happiness the rest of my family shared.

Mark's fever broke at last the next day, and the wounds at his chest and foot began to heal in earnest. His strength had been sorely taxed, though, and he did not get out of bed for some time. I returned to my own house at night and to help with chores, but whenever I had free time, I was at Mark's bedside. Momma, delighted with my promise, released me from my chores as often as she could spare me, so that I could help Old Jan and Mark.

When I was with Mark, I could almost forget the empty feeling inside me from my lost dreams. I cooked and cleaned for them, thinking that this is what it would be like to someday marry Mark. I was glad to have work that kept me from my wrecked dreams in the backyard at home.

Unfortunately, the more time I spent with Mark, the angrier Aneshka seemed to be about it all. Whenever we made beds or washed dishes or scrubbed laundry together, she was surly and uncooperative. I tried to ignore her, thinking it would pass. But after several weeks, I lost my temper one afternoon, when she threw an armload of shirts into the washkettle, nearly splashing the scalding water over the edge and onto me.

"What is the matter with you?" I shouted, feeling almost as close to the boiling point as the washwater.

"What do you care what's the matter!" she shouted back. "You don't care about us anymore. You just care about Mark!"

"Mark's been very sick! He needed me," I protested.

"But he doesn't need you anymore. I think it's that you *like* Mark," she said, making the word *like* into a taunt. Then she puckered up her lips and made kissing sounds.

My cheeks flamed with anger and embarrassment. "Stop it, Aneshka!"

"Well, you're always with him! It's not fair!"

"What's not fair?" my mother said, arriving with a bundle of laundry from Old Jan's house.

Aneshka crossed her arms and glared at me. "It's not fair that Trina's always with Mark when she's supposed to be getting us a farm."

Momma gave an exasperated little sigh and began vigorously stirring the shirts in the tub. "Don't be silly, Aneshka. Trina can't get us a farm. Whatever put such an idea into your head?"

Aneshka only glared harder. "Trina knows what I'm talking about," she said.

"I don't," I said stoutly. At least I didn't know how she had pried the secret of my wish out of Holena. "Besides, Mark has nothing to do with it."

Aneshka scowled and stomped her foot. "It's not fair!" she said again.

"Stop that, Aneshka," Momma said. "We have work to do."

Aneshka did as she was told, but she was surly for the rest of the afternoon. I was too. I could not explain the truth to her. The wish had not failed because I was with Mark. The truth was, I was with Mark because the wish had failed.

Chapter 15

SOON MARK was up, doing his own chores and walking to help rebuild his strength. He went striding by our house, up and down the road, farther and farther each day. Though his strength was coming back, his gait was still awkward. He could not seem to flex his foot upward properly, causing it to drag when he walked, and it did not improve with practice.

Old Jan wanted to consult the doctor about it, but Mark refused. They were out of money and a month behind on their rent as it was. The mine had extended them credit; however, rumors were spreading of another round of layoffs. Karel was one of the few bachelors left at the mine, and the family feared he would lose his job as well, and Mark would have no job to go to even when he recovered. Everyone in town was struggling and praying their jobs would last. Martina, who could not bear to return to her parents' home, had resolved to sell Charlie's clothing and whatever of her own possessions she could spare. She hoped to pay off her debts to the mining company and have enough left over for train fare to Denver, or perhaps Kansas City. There she hoped to find a factory job. I did not dare ask what she might do if there were no jobs to be had. The thought of being alone in a big city was too terrible for me to imagine.

When Karel and Mark heard of Martina's plan, they went to her house, though they themselves were in debt. Mark came back up the road a short time later with Charlie's old boots. They were worn, but he needed something to replace the boot that had been ruined in the accident, he said. He could not go back into the mine without boots.

"Where is Karel?" I asked.

Mark sat down on the porch step. "It's Saturday, his night off, so he's taking his time coming home. He stayed to visit with Martina."

I thought nothing more of Karel's absence that evening, or the next day when Old Jan and Mark came to our house to share our Sunday dinner. We were just about to sit down to eat when Karel and Martina came walking up the road toward us. They stopped and stood before the porch, Karel looking up uncertainly at his father while Martina's eyes stayed shyly on the dirt before her.

Karel took a deep breath and cleared his throat. "We've gotten married, Papa."

We all stared, our mouths hanging open stupidly. When there was no response, Karel continued.

"The priest was here, and he won't be back for two weeks. This is best for everyone. I'm not a bachelor now, so the mine will keep me on. And Charlie would have wanted Martina taken care of. I'll do that."

Momma was the first to recover her composure. She stood

and beckoned to them. "Come in, come in. You are family here now."

Karel took Martina's hand and led her up onto the porch. Momma clasped her and gave her a kiss on either cheek in congratulations. Old Jan leaped up to do the same, and the rest of us followed. I did not know what to think as I kissed her blushing cheek. It had been barely two weeks since she had wailed at Charlie's funeral. Perhaps it should have been shocking, but all I felt was relief that she would not be alone and penniless in a distant town.

"Dinner is almost ready," Momma said. "It will serve for a wedding feast, I think."

We all went into a flurry of activity at that. Papa and Karel carried the table and chairs out into the yard. I spread Momma's fine linen tablecloth on the table. In the kitchen Momma mixed up batter and used the last can of plums to make dumplings. She had been saving it for a special occasion, she said, and this was it.

We did not have time for many wedding traditions, since the marriage had already occurred, but Mark did tie two spoons together with a ribbon. As we sat down to eat, Mark brought a bowl of potato soup out for the newlyweds to share. We all watched as they struggled to eat it with their joined spoons. It was supposed to bring good luck, but mostly it was good fun. We laughed as they spilled, and yet I thought they did very well for two people joined on a moment's notice as a practical necessity. There was a careful, tender courtesy between them that seemed very comforting. It occurred to me as I watched them that there was a certain wisdom to my mother's views — that accepting what life gave you and being grateful for it could bring a comfortable life.

Mark was seated across the table from me, and I couldn't resist a glance at him. He was looking at me, too, and when our eyes met he smiled. I smiled back.

After dinner was complete, Momma and Aneshka took the broom and mop and marched off to Martina's house to prepare it for the new couple. Holena and I stayed behind to wash the dishes and though it was her wedding feast, Martina insisted on helping.

"I'll not have Karel thinking I'm a lazy wife," she said.

We began working in silence, but soon she spoke. "Do you think poorly of me for marrying now, with Charlie barely in the grave?" She kept her eyes on her work, but I could see tears welling in her eyes. "I loved Charlie, and I wouldn't do anything to dishonor his memory. But I was afraid, Trina. And Karel is a good man. He was Charlie's friend."

I stopped her flow of words with a hand on her arm. "You haven't done anything wrong," I reassured her. "Charlie would not have wanted you alone in the city. And Karel *is* a good man; he'll be good to you."

"He was Charlie's friend," she said again. "He was afraid of being laid off. With his father and brother unable to work, he had to keep his job somehow. And I had nowhere to go. Maybe that's not a good reason to marry, but I swear I'll take good care of him, Trina."

I nodded. "We are glad to have you in the family," I said. Not that Karel and Mark were my family yet, but we spent so much time together it felt like it.

I heard a noise from the doorway and turned to see Mark.

"Your groom awaits you, Mrs. Kocekova." He gave a stiff little bow and swept his arm toward the porch.

Martina startled a little at the sound of her new title, but then she smiled and went outside. Everyone was gathered there and applauded her. Aneshka gave her a little bouquet of flowers, mostly dandelions and grass, and the family paraded the couple to Martina's house. Karel swept Martina up and carried her through the doorway, and the rest of us returned home. We all settled comfortably into the shade on the porch.

"Do you think they will be happy?" Mark asked, to no one in particular.

Aneshka gave a little snort. "How can they be when they are so poor? Martina shouldn't have sold her things."

"Aneshka," Momma said sharply.

"They will have a hard time of it in that respect, I'm afraid," Old Jan said. "They are at her house for now, but she can only keep it through the end of the month. I'm afraid until Marek is back to work, they will have to crowd in with us, and that is not pleasant for newlyweds."

"It can't be helped," Momma said. "Some things in life we simply must accept, and the sooner we do that, the better off we are."

I had worked hard to believe that view of things in recent weeks. Still, it didn't seem the same as being happy.

"What do you think, Trina?" Mark asked. "Do you think they will be happy together?"

I thought again about the gentle courtesy I had seen that day between Martina and Karel. I sighed. I wasn't sure I knew what happiness was anymore.

"I think they are kind to each other, and that is a good start," I said.

"A very good start, indeed," Old Jan said. "Kindness and respect are more important than all the riches in the world."

Aneshka, sensing that Old Jan had a story to prove his

point, scooted closer to him. Holena watched him eagerly as well. He smiled at them obligingly.

"Let's see. There once was a shepherd who was cheated by his rich neighbor. For his work, the shepherd was to receive a fine heifer, but when the work was done, the neighbor refused. So the shepherd and the neighbor went before the burgomaster, a young man, new to his position. The burgomaster did not know who was in the right, so he decided the case by saying, 'Each of you go home. Return tomorrow with the answer to this riddle: Of all things in the world, tell me, what is the swiftest? What is the sweetest? And what is the richest? Whichever of you answers best shall have the heifer.'

"So the two men went home with their questions. The rich neighbor consulted his wife, who was as greedy as he was. The poor shepherd had only his clever, gentle daughter at home, but he told her the riddle too.

"In the morning, the two men returned to the burgomaster, who put his question to them again. 'What is the swiftest thing in the world? What is the sweetest? And what is the richest?'

"The rich neighbor gave his wife's answer. 'It is simple, sir. The swiftest thing is my fine gray mare, for no one passes me on the road. The sweetest is the honey from my hives, for they are the best in the world. The richest is my sack of gold ducats, for I have been saving them away for years.'

"'Hmm,' said the burgomaster. Then he turned to the humble shepherd and asked him. And thanks to his clever daughter, the shepherd answered, 'I believe the swiftest thing in the world is a kind thought, for a kind thought comforts a loved one in no time at all. The sweetest thing is another's love, for it can soothe any suffering. The richest thing is the earth itself, from which honest labor brings forth all other riches.'

145

"At once the burgomaster saw the shepherd had answered most wisely, and so he gave the man the heifer and sent the rich neighbor home to quarrel with his wife. But to the shepherd he said, 'I must know who gave you this answer.'

"'My clever daughter, Manka, told me these things,' the shepherd replied.

"Now, the burgomaster had been thinking of taking a wife for some time, and at once he was intrigued by such a clever girl. So he gave the shepherd six eggs to take to Manka and said, 'Tell your clever daughter that if she will hatch these eggs into chicks and bring them to me tomorrow, I will marry her.'"

"That's not fair," Aneshka interrupted. "You can't hatch eggs overnight."

"They would need their momma to hatch," Holena said. I knew she was thinking of my chicks, dead in their nest. I wished Old Jan had picked a different story.

Old Jan smiled at my sisters and nodded. "The shepherd thought the same thing, and he was sorry, for he thought the burgomaster would make a fine son-in-law. But he took the eggs to his daughter and told her of the man's request.

"Manka only laughed. The next morning she gave her father a handful of grain and said, 'Take this to the burgomaster and tell him that if he will grow a field of wheat for me and bring it to me tomorrow, I will know he is my equal and I will consent to be his wife.'

"When the burgomaster received this reply, he mounted his horse at once and rode to the shepherd's home, where on one knee, he asked the clever girl to marry him. She consented and they were wed. That night, after the wedding feast, he said to her, 'You have proved to me that you will be a kind and honest wife, and so we will be happy. But you must never use your cleverness against me or I will turn you out of my home.'

"They lived together for some time in happiness, for they lived by the principles of kindness and fairness that Manka had shown in her answers. But as the burgomaster grew older he grew lazy and eager for gain in his duties. One day, a dispute was brought to him from the marketplace. A farmer's mare had given birth to a foal, but a loud noise had scared the foal under a merchant's wagon, so the merchant claimed the foal was his. Now, the burgomaster knew the farmer was a poor man, while the merchant was wealthy and powerful, capable of giving many gifts and favors. So without much thought, the burgomaster gave the foal to the merchant, and the poor farmer went home with nothing for his trouble. When Manka saw the sad farmer leaving, she asked what was wrong and he told her. Manka at once told the farmer what to do.

"The next morning, the burgomaster stepped out his front door to see a fishnet strung across the road. The farmer was sitting nearby, watching it eagerly.

"'What are you doing?' the burgomaster asked.

"'Why, I am fishing,' replied the farmer."

"Fishing in the road?" Aneshka said with a shriek of laughter.

"That is exactly what the burgomaster said. And the farmer replied, 'Why, yes, for if a wagon can foal in this town, I would suppose that fish could be caught in its streets.'

"At once the burgomaster saw the wrong judgment he had made. But he also saw Manka's hand in the farmer's clever act, and so he went back inside and said to her, 'I warned you never to use your cleverness against me. Now you must leave my house, as I said. But I am not hard-hearted. Take with you whatever you like best from our home, and return to your father.'

147

"'Very well,' Manka said. 'But please, husband, let us sup together one last time before I go.'

"The burgomaster agreed to this, so that evening Manka served him a fine, heavy supper and many tankards of good, strong beer, and before long, the burgomaster was snoring in his chair at the table. When he was asleep, Manka did as she had been told. She took her favorite thing and returned to her father's house.

"The next morning the burgomaster woke, confused, for he was in a shepherd's hut on the edge of the forest. He looked around, and there was Manka, preparing breakfast at the humble hearth.

"'Where am I?' the burgomaster asked. 'And how did I get here?'

"'You are in my father's house,' Manka said, 'for you said I could take with me my favorite thing in the house, and that, dear husband, is you.'

"When the burgomaster saw that she had once again outwitted him, he might have been angry, but he was not. For he saw what she said was true—she was his favorite thing too. He had married her for her cleverness, but he found that as they had given each other the kind thoughts, sweet love, and honest labor over the years, she had become his greatest treasure. And so he returned the foal to its rightful owner, apologized to his wife, and took her home, promising to never behave so badly again. And from that day on, when a particularly difficult case came before him, he always consulted his clever wife before he made his judgment. And with kindness and respect, they lived out their days in happiness."

Aneshka clapped her hands in delight at the end of the story. I think she liked best that Manka had outsmarted her husband.

But Holena seemed to better understand Old Jan's meaning.

"I think Karel and Martina will be kind to each other too. I think they will be happy, even if they don't have much," she said.

"I do too," Mark said. "I think if you care about someone, you don't need much else to make you happy. What do you think, Trina?"

I had a hard time answering. As Old Jan had told the story, Mark's hand had found mine and closed around it. Now all I could think about was the feel of that hand and the happiness that eased the ache in my heart at its touch.

"It's the last Saturday of July this week. That means the community dance," Mark said. "I think dancing with you is the last thing I need to completely heal me, Trina."

I looked up to see Momma smiling and Aneshka glaring at me. I ignored them both and turned to Mark with a smile of my own. "I'll be ready at six," I said.

Chapter 16

MARK'S UNEVEN gait did not improve much over the coming week, but he was determined to keep walking and gaining his strength. The day of the dance he stopped by our house in the morning and danced me around our porch in front of Momma and my sisters, just to prove he was well enough to go.

That afternoon, Momma helped me prepare. I bathed, and she brushed out my hair. I would wear it in a bun rather than my usual girlish braids. From her own trunk, she found her best dress, the one she had married in. She had not worn it since we left the Old Country. Now she offered it to me.

It felt good to put on a dress that reached to the floor, like an elegant lady. I was not yet a lady, though, as the loose bodice proved. My mother only smiled at the way the shapely dress fit my mostly shapeless frame.

"Soon, Trina. Don't worry," she said, and she pinned the bodice under the arms where a few tucks would create a serviceable fit. She made the alterations without cutting the fabric. There was no point in making the dress fit a girl's body now, when mine was on the verge of becoming a woman, she said.

My mother hummed happily as she worked, and it made me happy to see her so cheerful. It didn't even bother me when Aneshka came into the kitchen, scowled at us, and then stomped off to the backyard with an angry snort. She stayed in the back all afternoon, though I couldn't imagine why. The ruined chicken yard and garden had been such painful reminders of our failed dreams that I spent as little time as possible behind the house. How Aneshka could spend hours at a time with those reminders was beyond me.

By suppertime, I was ready for the dance, wearing my mother's fine dress and with my hair pinned neatly at the nape of my neck. My father smiled with pride when he saw me.

"My little Trina is becoming a woman," he said, kissing me on the forehead. "And a beautiful woman, at that. Marek is a lucky fellow."

My family sat down to supper, but I hardly ate a bite. I was afraid of spoiling my dress and I was feeling nervous. Even though I'd seen Mark every day since the accident, going to a dance with him was different.

Mark was in high spirits when he arrived to escort me to the dance. He, too, was clean and polished, in a suit that probably belonged to his father. His hair was trimmed and slicked down smoothly. He smiled hugely when he saw me, which made me blush. He complimented me politely and greeted my parents even more politely.

"You are looking well, Marek," Papa said. "Why, to look at you now, no one would know you've been sick."

"I am much better, thanks to your daughter. I am going back to work on Monday!" he announced.

He had meant this as good news, but the knot of fear I'd carried since the accident twisted tighter inside me. He wasn't yet well enough for the long hours of hard labor. He showed no sign of pain that evening as we danced or visited with the other young couples, though. In fact, he was so merry that I buried my misgivings. By the end of the evening I, too, was merry, and I was sorry when the fiddlers announced the last song.

Afterward, as Mark and I walked up the road toward home we could hear other couples whispering and giggling in the darkness. Mark's hand found mine and they clasped together. Our pace slowed, neither of us eager to end the evening. It was very romantic, at least until Mark broke the silence between us.

"Will we be getting more chickens?" he asked.

I was surprised by the question. My chickens were the last thing I'd been thinking about—or wanted to think about. "No. We haven't got the money, and besides, it all came to nothing last time."

"That's not to say that it would come to nothing again, though, is it?"

I frowned, thinking that Mr. Johnson would not let me succeed, but I didn't say it. Mark had enough to worry about. "I was just thinking," he said, "that the chickens would be a good idea for us now. With me having been out of work, it would be good if we had some means of food that costs no money at the store."

"Maybe we should get chickens for you and your papa," I said. "If you can bear to be a farmer."

"The chicken house and fence is in your yard, but perhaps we could share the cost of the chickens. My papa can come and help you care for them. I don't mind that much farming for a good meal now and then."

"What about the dogs?"

"We have to be more careful, that's all. That happened because no one was home. But if my papa came to look after them, that couldn't happen."

"I don't know. It didn't work last time."

"You aren't going to give up that easily, are you? It's just a minor setback," he said a little impatiently.

"Minor? I lost everything."

We were in front of my house now, and we had stopped walking. In the darkness Mark pulled me to him and wrapped his arms around my waist. "Not everything," he breathed into my hair. "You didn't lose me."

I leaned my head against his chest, my chin just above the still-tender scar that had nearly killed him. I felt lucky to be wrapped in his arms, and I felt safe, too.

He bent forward and kissed me lightly on the forehead. I wanted to stay there like that, but he spoke again. "I think we can make the chickens work, and the garden. In a few more years we'll be the envy of the camp."

I pressed my cheek in tighter against his chest, listening to his heartbeat. I tried not to think about the future when we would still be here, doing the same things, forever. He squeezed me to him in his strong arms for a long moment before finally bidding me good night and releasing me. I climbed the steps to my house and went inside alone. In the darkness, I changed into my nightdress and lay down on the bed. Aneshka rolled over immediately to face me.

"Did you set a date to marry him?" she whispered.

"Of course not! He's barely sixteen. That won't be for years yet."

Aneshka slipped her hand into mine, much as she had the first horrible night after the mine accident. "Please, Trina. You can't give up on your wish—you just can't. I know I was selfish with my wish, but I'll work extra hard for yours to make up for it, if you will just try too."

I sighed. "Aneshka, I didn't give up on the wish. Everything was ruined, remember? Besides, wishes aren't real. It was just a game."

"But you said you saw the fish," whispered Holena from my other side. I hadn't even known she was awake. "You said you believed!"

"That was before, when there was something to believe in."

"Before you gave up," Aneshka insisted.

"What else am I supposed to do?" I said, my whisper sharp as annoyance rose in me. "There's nothing left!"

"Yes, there is," Holena whispered.

Suddenly Aneshka was out of bed and pulling me up as well. "There is," she said. "Come on, I'll show you."

"Aneshka, go to sleep," I said, but now Holena was up too, so I got out of bed myself before they woke our parents. Quietly we slipped out the front door and around the house to the back.

"See?" Aneshka said, pointing.

Across the garden, which should have been only bare earth or weeds, I could see a dark mass of leaves in the moonlight. Not the neat, orderly rows I had originally planted, but a sprawling expanse of luxurious growth. I stepped closer, to the very edge of the garden, but it was too dark to see properly.

"What is it?" I asked.

"It's your cucumbers," Aneshka said.

"We've been tending them for you," Holena said.

"Because you won't," Aneshka added.

I stared in disbelief. The tiny corner of cucumber plants that had been spared by Mr. Johnson seemed to have magically expanded to fill the desolation of the destroyed garden.

The ugly emptiness of the ruined rows had been replaced by a carpet of wide leaves and curling tendrils of vine. I bent over the plants and raked through the leaves with my fingers. I could feel several hard fruits sheltered beneath them.

"I don't believe it," I said. "How could they have grown so much in such a short time?" I thought about it. "I suppose we have had some good rains."

"It's not the rain; it's the *wish*," Holena said, as if my suggestion was the silliest thing she'd ever heard.

I straightened. "It's not the wish. No matter how many cucumbers we get, they aren't going to get us a farm."

"You could sell them."

"We'd have to have acres of cucumbers to earn enough money for a farm," I said, still looking at the patch before me. "But maybe we have enough to make pickles. Papa likes pickles with his meat. We'll have another look in the morning."

I took both of my sisters by the hand and walked them back the way we'd come and into the house. I got them into bed, then slipped in beside them. Someone stirred across the room.

"Trina, is that you?" came my mother's sleepy voice.

"Yes, Momma."

"How was the dance? Did you have a nice time?"

"Yes."

"You are happy, then?"

"Yes, Momma," I said softly. "Yes, I'm very happy." It was true. I had had a wonderful evening with Mark, but there was more to it than that. My discovery of the unexpected cucumber plants seemed to have delighted me like nothing had in weeks.

"Good. Good night, then," Momma said. The bedsprings squeaked as she settled back into her bed.

I lay still, listening to the soft breathing of my family and looking up at the ceiling. Why had those plants made such a difference? I had told my sisters it wouldn't, and I had believed that when I said it. So why was I feeling so happy? I couldn't explain it, but I knew if I asked Holena, she would easily do so. She would say it was the wish, and she would be content in her innocent trust.

I closed my eyes, refusing to slip back into the foolishness. *It's not the wish*, I told myself. *Wishes and dreams are for fools.* But though I repeated it several times before falling asleep, I dreamed once again that night of fields of ripening wheat.

Chapter 17

THE NEXT MORNING was Sunday, so we had no chores. I got up early before church, and taking my basket with me, I went out to the garden to inspect it in the daylight, half expecting the sprawling cucumber vines to have been a dream. They were not, and by the time my mother called me in, I brought with me a full basket.

Momma looked at the basket in surprise. "Where on earth did you get those?"

"The garden, and there are more on the vine," I said. I couldn't keep from grinning. "Do you think it's enough to make pickles?"

"Enough?" Momma said with a laugh. "I think we'll have enough pickles for the year."

We went to church that morning, but all I was thinking about through the hot, airless service was getting home to the cucumbers.

After church I walked back up the hill toward home with

Mark and his father, going slowly so that Old Jan could keep up on his crutches. I told them of the cucumber vines as we walked.

"You see," Mark said, "I told you it was only a minor setback. Your farm is back on its feet already."

"A cucumber patch is hardly a farm!" I pointed out.

"But you can turn it into one," he said. "As you get more chickens or other seeds, we can expand into our backyard, too. Maybe we could get a goat—or maybe even a cow, like Aneshka wanted. We'll be the richest folks in the coal camp."

"But we'll still be in the coal camp," I said.

"For now," Old Jan said. "But you have your whole lives ahead of you to build your dreams. You've got to have dreams."

I did not contradict him, but I knew better. It was better not to have dreams, and I wasn't going to be pulled into them again by a few cucumbers. Besides, I couldn't see how being the richest family in the coal camp was much to believe in anyway.

Back at the house, Mark and Old Jan talked with Papa while Momma and I prepared Sunday dinner. Karel and Martina arrived with a pot of soup and dumplings. We dined outside, as if we were all one big family. Afterward the women gathered in the kitchen to talk of pickles while the men moved Martina's sparse possessions to Old Jan's house.

"The first thing we must do is make a brine," Momma said. "We can do that today and get started in the washtub. In Bohemia, I had a pickle crock, but we will have to get a new one here, or jars. Here in America they use jars. See?" She flipped through the paper and showed me the advertisement for Mason jars at the mercantile in Trinidad. Momma did not know enough English to read the paper, but she was learning a little about America from the pictures in the ads and stories.

"With jars they can be shared more easily," Martina said, a little nervously. "I would pay half on the jars and provide sugar and spices, in exchange for some of the pickles."

"That's a fine idea," Momma said.

We were a cheerful party that afternoon. The first stage of making the pickles only required a brine of hot water, salt, and a chunk of alum, all of which we had without a trip to the store. We could get sugar and jars later; the store was closed on Sunday. I enjoyed starting the pickles, but I dreaded the prospect of a trip to the store for jars. If Mr. Johnson really had been the one to destroy my garden and kill my chickens—and I was sure he was—what would he do when he found out that something had survived and that we were making pickles? Would we come home from a day of doing laundry to find our jars of pickles all smashed in the backyard?

I tried to convince Momma that Martina should buy the jars. But the next day was Monday, laundry day, and Martina was washing Old Jan's and Mark's clothes as well as Karel's these days. Momma admonished me and sent me off to the store. I couldn't explain why I didn't want to go, because I had not told Momma of Mr. Johnson's hatred for me. So I had no choice but to go obediently, though my dread grew with every step. To make matters worse, a wagon was hitched in front of the store. As I drew nearer, I saw that it was Mr. Torentino's supply wagon, the same one that had brought the plums. I had liked Mr. Torentino, and everyone had been happy to get his plums. But I didn't need another reminder of why Mr. Johnson had a grudge against me. My steps faltered and I considered coming back later.

"Trina!" The call came from the shaded porch, and I looked up to see Mark sitting there. "Come join me."

Though his invitation was warm, his expression and the sag of his shoulders gave off heavy melancholy. I climbed the steps and sat down beside him. "I thought you were going back to work today," I said.

He nodded. "So did I, but when I reported for my shift last night, they said they couldn't use me. They don't have much work, and what they have they aren't giving to a fellow with a bad foot."

"Your foot's getting better," I said, trying to sound hopeful for his sake.

He looked down at it and shook his head. "I don't think so. I don't think it will ever be right again."

I didn't know what to say. I understood his desire to work and his fears about the future, but I felt relieved that he wouldn't be returning to the mine just yet. I sat beside him in a heavy silence for a long moment, searching for the right words.

The door swung open, and Mr. Torentino stomped across the porch to his wagon. I remembered then why I was there. Eager to end the awkward silence between us, I excused myself and hurried into the store, momentarily forgetting my fear of Mr. Johnson.

"I need jars," I blurted out when he acknowledged me.

"Jars?"

"Pickle jars," I swallowed, my fear coming back to me. "For making pickles."

Several women in the store raised their eyes to me, curious.

"You're making pickles, are you? I suppose you'll be needing cucumbers, too, then," Mr. Johnson said.

"No, thank you, sir."

His eyes narrowed, and I felt a stab of satisfaction. He thought he had destroyed me, and now he was wondering. *Let him wonder*, I thought. *Better yet, let him know he hasn't beaten me entirely.*

I raised my chin and my voice, so everyone in the store could hear. "They're from my garden."

"Are they now," he said, and there was a dangerous quiet in his voice that caused my defiance to wither as quickly as it had risen. "Well, I don't see any jars here, do you?"

I glanced around. "Can I order them, then?"

"Certainly." He pulled a dog-eared Sears and Roebuck catalog from under the counter. "It will cost extra, of course. Postage is expensive way out here, and someone has to haul it up from Trinidad." He was flipping through the catalog as he spoke, until he came to a page filled with pictures of jars of various sizes and shapes. I could see the price beside the picture of pickle jars—eighty-five cents a dozen.

"That will be four dollars," Mr. Johnson said. "Paid in advance."

"But—it says right there eighty-five cents," I said, pointing at the picture.

He shrugged and slapped the catalog shut. "Shipping is expensive."

"That's not a fair price!"

"Take it or leave it," he said with a nasty smile.

I didn't want to do either. If I didn't buy jars, we couldn't preserve the cucumbers we had already begun pickling. If I did place the order, I was agreeing to a price that we both knew was highway robbery. He had gotten the best of me once before, and I couldn't let him do it again.

Then I remembered the picture in the newspaper that Momma had seen. If she had seen jars in the paper, that meant someone in Trinidad had them for sale. And that gave me an idea.

"Never mind," I said to Mr. Johnson, "excuse me," and I hurried out of the store.

Mark was still on the porch, and out of the corner of my eye I saw his mouth open to speak, but I hurried past and down the steps. Mr. Torentino's wagon was disappearing down the road in a cloud of dust and I had to hurry to catch it. I gathered my skirts into my hands and I ran. I had to shout several times before he heard me over the creak and clatter of his wagon. He pulled up on the reins and looked down at me, breathing too hard to speak.

"Yes, missy? What is it?" he said in his musical Italian accent.

"Do you have a store in Trinidad?" I asked.

"Yes, ma'am. Torentino and Sons, on Main Street."

"I need pickle jars, but Mr. Johnson doesn't carry them. Could I get them from your store?"

"Sure. We have plenty. With so many farms around, there's ready demand at this time of year. Come in the next time you're in Trinidad."

"But we don't go to Trinidad," I said. It was too far, and with Papa off work only one day a week and always needing to rest on that day, we hadn't left the camp since we'd arrived. I took a deep breath before venturing further on my idea. "If I paid you for them now, would you bring them with you on your next trip back up here?"

Mr. Torentino stroked his mustache as he considered it. "I don't usually make deliveries outside of town, but since I bring the supply wagon up here every Monday anyway, I don't see why not. Do you have the money?"

"How much are they?" I asked, praying he wouldn't add too much for delivering them so far from his store.

"Eighty-five cents a dozen," he said.

"That's so much cheaper than what Mr. Johnson's asking. Could you bring two dozen?"

Torentino glanced back toward Johnson's store. "I imagine everything seems cheap to you after dealing with Johnson," he said. "All right. Two dozen, next Monday at this same time."

"Thank you, sir!" I counted out the money and handed it up to him, then stepped back so he could be on his way again. I remembered Mark then, and how he'd probably been about to say something to me when I had run past him and after Torentino. I walked back to the store to apologize and explain, but when I got there, Mark had gone.

I walked home again, hoping I had done the right thing. What if Mr. Torentino forgot, or what if he had taken my money with no real intention of bringing me the jars? I realized he hadn't given me any receipt or anything to prove the deal. In my heart, though, I had a good feeling about the man. He had granted Aneshka's wish—not that he had known anything about the wish itself—and he'd been polite and kind.

Since I wasn't sure whether or not I'd done the right thing, I only told my mother that I had had to order the jars. Things had been so much better between us since I had stopped dreaming of a farm and agreed to a match with Mark. I didn't want to tell her that I was scheming again. Besides, I didn't want to worry her by telling her of Mr. Johnson's grudge against me.

I was finishing the ironing the next afternoon when I heard Old Jan call a greeting to my mother from the street. I stepped outside behind Momma, hoping Mark would be with him, but he was not. Old Jan was standing in the road, grinning from ear to ear, and I saw why right off. He had no crutches. His leg stump was neatly cradled in a wooden leg.

"My heavens," Momma said.

He grinned and waved at us with both hands.

"What do you think? My hands are free now—no more crutches for me!"

"It's wonderful! Where did you get it?" I asked. I couldn't imagine how they had come up with the money for it now, with all their other troubles.

"My Marek made it for me," he said, "from a post he found in the mine dump."

I looked again at the leg, and I could see now that it was homemade, but made well, shaped and smoothed with care. The cup at the top that cradled Old Jan's leg stump was padded with rags, and the strap that secured the wooden leg to the real one was an old leather belt.

"He's always been clever at making things," Old Jan said.

"Where is he?" I asked.

Old Jan sighed heavily. "Down at the creek, I think. I suppose you've heard they wouldn't take him back at the mine. Frankly, I don't think he is ready either, but it's certain now that we'll have to rely on Karel until the fall. That means we can't start catching up on the doctor bills or the rent, and that Karel and his bride will have to suffer the company of me and Marek for a while still. Marek blames himself, though I told him it couldn't be helped. If you'd go find him, Trina, I'm sure you could cheer him up."

Momma gave me permission to go even before I asked, so I set off for the creek, taking with me the buckets for Papa's washwater. I knew where Mark would be—exactly the place I would be if I were upset.

As I expected, Mark was sitting under the tree by the pool. He was throwing pebbles into the water. I called his name and he glanced up, then returned to glumly tossing pebbles without so much as a greeting. Though he didn't invite me to join him, I stepped under the tree and sat down on its raised root. He shifted, keeping his back to me.

"Mark, what is the matter?" I asked.

He shrugged and said nothing. I waited. I knew he would speak when he was ready.

"I could have been something, you know. If things had been different. If Papa hadn't gotten hurt, I could have gone to high school. If I hadn't gotten hurt, I'd have a job."

"You'll have a job again," I said. "You just need time to heal."

"But it's not good enough, is it? I'll never walk right. I don't blame you. I can see why you don't want a lame husband."

"What are you talking about? I never said—"

"When you found out I couldn't work yesterday, you couldn't wait to get away from me. You ran off into the store, and then when you'd finished with Mr. Johnson you left without even looking at me."

"No, Mark! I ran after the supply wagon to buy jars," I said.

"Jars?"

Quickly I explained to him what had happened at the store. "He's bringing them, and for much less than Mr. Johnson wanted to charge me."

"It's still true, though, isn't it. I'm not worth much to anyone anymore—a cripple who can't get a job."

"You're hardly a cripple!" I insisted. "You'll get a job again, and in the meantime you can do other things. Look at the leg you made for your father. It's beautiful! How can you say you're of no use?"

He shrugged, but I could see he was proud of the leg and pleased by the compliment, so I went on.

"The mine isn't the only job in the world. There must be other things you could do."

"If you're trying to talk me into farming, forget it."

"It wouldn't have to be farming. There are all kinds of jobs in town."

"Not for me. We owe the mine owners here, two months' back rent on the house, and all that credit at the store. We'd have to pay it back if we left here, and we don't have the money."

"But you'll never have the money if you stay here," I said. It was so unfair the way the mine trapped us all with debt. "Karel is still working in the mine. He could take care of things here and you could look for work in town. Surely you could find work there where your foot wouldn't matter."

Mark looked at me, his eyes reflecting both hope and fear. "You want me to go? To leave here?"

"I want to get out of here, don't you? And if they don't hire you back soon, the debt is only going to grow. There must be something you could do in town, but you won't know if you never try."

His face had been brightening as we talked, the hope slowly overpowering the fear. "I wish you could come with me, Trina."

I nodded, wishing I could too, but we both knew that was impossible. Mark reached over and took my hand.

"You will wait for me, won't you? Promise me you will," he said.

"I promise," I said, my heart swelling until I could barely speak. Suddenly I regretted encouraging him. Life would be so dreary here with him gone, and what if he never came back? What were the chances he would still even want me after he'd been away, meeting the pretty, sophisticated girls in town?

"I promise to come back, Trina," he said, as if he had read my fear. Perhaps he had. "The mines always need more men by

September or October. That's just two months away. And by then I'll be stronger; surely they will hire me. When I'm back and our debts are paid, I promise we will get on with all our other plans, Trina."

"If you get out of here, Mark—" I began, but he suddenly clutched me in a tight hug and repeated his words.

"I'll come back, Trina. I promise. And I'll think about you every minute that I'm gone."

I wrapped my arms around him and shut my eyes. I wanted my whole world to be him for a moment—his warmth, his smell, and the strong muscles of his chest against my cheek. I breathed in the mingled scents of shaving soap, sweat, and coal dust, with the faintest perfume of Old Jan's pipe tobacco. For just a moment, I wanted to let the warmth and strength of his embrace push away any thoughts of the future. I didn't want to think about the dreams or plans or problems before us. *Dreams only hurt us*, I reminded myself, and I held him tighter while I still could.

Too soon Mark released me from the embrace and I opened my eyes. He was fishing around in his pocket. He drew out a piece of copper wire and began twisting it around itself into a single braid. Then he curled it into a ring, knotting the ends together to finish it. Smiling, he slipped the band onto my finger.

"This is so you will remember my promise, okay?"

I nodded, my heart thumping as I looked at the simple wire ring on my finger.

I had nothing to offer in return, so I bent to the edge of the pool where pebbles glinted colorfully from under the water, and I picked a pretty red-and-yellow-speckled stone, smooth and wet and glistening.

"So you will remember too," I said, placing it in his hand and curling his fingers around it.

He grinned, a little mischievously, then quickly leaned forward and stole a kiss, right on my lips. He pulled back and looked at me, and when I gave no objection he leaned in again. This time, I kissed him back—at least, until we were interrupted by the whistle from the mine.

"Oh—Papa's washwater!" I said, remembering the buckets I had abandoned just upstream.

"I'll help you," he said.

He stepped over the tree root awkwardly, holding the trunk for support as he swung his bad foot over. Despite his own difficulty, he turned and held his hand out to assist me once he was on the other side. I had stepped over the root many times without help, but it was a gentlemanly gesture, so I took his hand. But as I stepped over to his side, I saw his gaze was falling somewhere behind me.

"Look," he said, pointing toward the pool. Even before I turned, I knew what I would see. The fish was there, waving softly in the current in the center of the pool.

"I've seen that fish before, but I can never catch it," Mark said. "I guess it can see us, too."

And it had seen me accept Mark's ring and give him my promise. "Holena says it's a lucky fish," I said. "Like in your papa's stories."

"Maybe it is," Mark said, encircling my waist with his arm and pulling me toward him. "Maybe we can make a wish for our future, and it will all come true."

I shook my head and pulled him away from the pool. Wishes and dreams were for fools; that was what I had learned. That was the moral of all the stories, including my own. I felt the twist of copper wire around my finger. Whatever my future would be, I refused to make a magic fish a part of it again.

Chapter 18

ANESHKA WENT into a fit when she saw the copper band on my finger, then refused to talk to me for the rest of the evening. I didn't care. Mark had decided to look for work in town, so it was my last evening with him for a while. I was just as glad to have Aneshka leaving us alone. Her silence didn't last, however. In the morning, I woke to her glaring at me.

"What about the pickles, Trina?" she said accusingly.

"What about them?"

"You're planning to marry Mark, but you promised to finish the pickles with us."

"I'm promised to Mark is all. Momma and Old Jan have agreed on the match, so it's none of your business."

"What about the wish?" she demanded.

I groaned and flopped onto my back, shielding my eyes with my arm. "Why did you tell her, Holena? It was supposed to be a secret."

"She was sad," Holena whispered from my other side. "I thought if she knew, she wouldn't be so sad."

"Well, it was my wish, so it's mine to do with as I please, isn't it? Maybe Mark is going to get a job on a farm and take me there," I said.

"But the farm was supposed to be for all of us," Aneshka said.

I got out of bed, angry now. We were all disappointed; it didn't help to have Aneshka always bringing it up and accusing me with it. "Well, it didn't work out that way, did it? What am I supposed to do about it?"

"You're supposed to make it work out!" Aneshka screamed, throwing her pillow at me.

"What is going on?" Momma said, looking in from the kitchen. "Aneshka, pick that up."

"It's not fair!" Aneshka said, tears now welling from her eyes. "Trina's going to leave us here and go somewhere nice with Mark, and she promised she wouldn't. She promised—"

"Hush, Aneshka!" Momma's words were firm, but she sat down on the edge of the bed and wrapped her arms around the girl, who was fighting back angry sobs. "Trina's growing up, that's all. Things change when you grow up. Marek will probably get another job at the mine in no time, and we will all be here together, just like before."

Momma had meant her words as comfort, but they were not. I wished that I was still young enough to be able to pour out my disappointment as Aneshka did, in sobs and rages and thrown pillows. Instead, I said good-bye to Mark an hour later and, as the week progressed, I had only chores to distract me from my loneliness and my broken dreams.

* * *

Aneshka was still sulking on Monday when Mr. Torentino was to return with my jars, so I asked Martina to help me retrieve them. I couldn't carry them all myself, and I didn't want to listen to any more of Aneshka's scolding. We skirted around the store so we could meet Mr. Torentino where I did not think Mr. Johnson could see us, then we sat down to wait.

"Why did you arrange this, rather than just buying the jars from Mr. Johnson?" Martina asked as we watched for the wagon.

"You remember how Mr. Johnson doesn't like me much," I said, and told her the story.

"You mean, you're getting the jars for eighty-five cents a dozen? The same price he charges in town?"

"I think so."

"Do you think he'd sell me boots at his town rates, too?" Martina asked. "Karel's boots have worn through, and we gave Charlie's boots to Mark."

"You could ask," I said.

The wagon came into view, climbing the dirt road to the mine, kicking up a cloud of dust into the dry summer air. Our wait wasn't over, however, because Mr. Torentino wanted to conduct his business at the store first. We watched from a short distance away as Mr. Torentino carried crates into the store, then carried some of the same crates back out. When he returned to us, he was angry.

"That man," he said, glancing over his shoulder toward the store, "is a robber baron!"

I did not know what that meant, but I could tell Mr. Torentino shared my view of the storekeeper, so I agreed with a nod. "Did you bring the jars?"

"I've got them right here." He climbed over the seat and into the bed of the wagon. He handed the crates down to me one at a time, and I thanked him. Martina nudged me with her elbow.

"Mr. Torentino, Martina is newly married and her husband needs new boots, but she can't afford them at Mr. Johnson's store. Could she buy them from you, like I did the jars?"

Mr. Torentino's eyebrows raised. "Well, I hadn't thought to do this more than once, but I do sell boots." He told Martina what he had, and she was soon paying him and thanking him.

"Karel will be so pleased!" she said as we walked back toward home. "I am going to surprise him with the boots when they come!" Her face glowed with the idea, and I felt a pang of envy. I was missing Mark.

Finally the next Saturday afternoon I saw him returning up the street toward our house. Though his shoulders still sagged, his gait was stronger and more even than it had been when he had left almost two weeks before. I rushed to him and threw my arms around him, right in the middle of the street. He hugged me back and told me he was happy to see me, but there was no enthusiasm in the greeting. I pulled back and looked him in the eye.

"What's the matter?" I asked.

He sighed heavily. "I couldn't find work. Too many other coal miners are looking for jobs too. No one wants a cripple like me."

"You're not a cripple, Mark! You're walking much better than when you left."

"I should be, after all the useless miles I've walked looking for work. I'm sorry, Trina. I didn't want to disappoint you."

"The mine will be hiring again come fall, and you'll be better by then," I said, trying to sound hopeful. Trying not to let my disappointment show.

"But what about our plans? Our dreams?" He brushed his fingers tenderly along my cheek.

His plans had never been my dreams, but I couldn't tell him that. I shrugged. "My momma says dreams just make you unhappy, that to be happy, you have to appreciate the things you have. When I thought I had lost you, I saw she was right."

"She's not right!" came an angry shout from behind me. It was Aneshka. I hadn't known she had followed me out into the street to greet Mark. Now her hands were firmly planted on her hips and she was glaring at us both. "You can't give up on the farm, Trina! It's not fair!"

I was fuming mad at her for eavesdropping, but Mark tousled her hair.

"You're right, Aneshka. We won't give up," Mark said. "We'll get those chickens back, and the garden, too. Maybe even buy some goats. We have time yet."

"That's not a farm, and Trina knows it!" Aneshka said.

"Stop it, Aneshka," I said. "Mark only just got home. Stop being so selfish."

Aneshka thrust out her bottom lip in a pout, but I ignored her and turned to Mark.

"Go greet your papa and bring him back to our house. Karel and Martina, as well," I said, squeezing Mark with the arm I still had wrapped around his waist. "We will have a welcome-home feast for you!"

Momma and I prepared supper, and everyone was there, but we weren't very cheerful. Our money was already stretched thin, and Mark still without work was bad news for us all.

"I'll keep asking every day at the mine," Mark said. "Sooner or later they will have something for me."

Old Jan looked at his son and shook his head. "It's no wonder you couldn't find work in town. Look at those trousers—you've got patches on your patches, and your elbow's coming through your shirt. You're too poor to get a job."

I could see Old Jan's point. How could Mark convince folks in town that he was a hard worker when he looked like a ragged beggar? That thought stayed with me that night, along with the general sense of desperation that had run through the whole evening. There had to be something we could do.

"Is it true that Mark didn't get a job because of his trousers?" Holena asked from beside me in the bed.

I hesitated. "I don't know. Maybe partly."

"That nice man could get him new trousers, I bet," she said.

Aneshka reached across me and gave her a little push. "We don't want Mark to get a job, remember?" she hissed. "We want Trina to get us a farm like she's supposed to."

"I wish I'd never told you about her wish," Holena murmured. Silently I agreed.

Momma hushed us from her bed across the room and our conversation ended, but I thought about what Holena had said. Mr. Torentino had been willing to bring jars and boots; why not new pants for Mark? Then again, Mark didn't have the money for them, not even at Mr. Torentino's prices. But what if Old Jan was right? What if Mark could get a job—a better job, in town, if he had new clothes and looked a little neater? I could patch the elbows of his shirt so the patches would barely show.

By the next morning I had hit upon an idea. I walked to church with Mark and explained it to him. We could catch fish after church and sell them to our neighbors. I was sure there were plenty of folks around camp who would buy fresh fish from us. We could make enough money to buy him new trousers and he could try again to find work in town.

He shook his head. "It wasn't my pants, Trina. It was my limp, my lack of education, and my foreign accent."

"But you need money. We could still sell fish, even if you don't want new trousers. Can we at least try?" I asked.

Mark smiled. "Why not? We can take a picnic. And if we can't sell the fish, we can always eat them."

The plan worked better than I had expected, though it angered Aneshka. She glared at me the whole time I was packing the picnic, and I could still feel her eyes boring into my back as I set out with Mark to go fishing. It was a pleasant afternoon, and the fish were biting. Soon we had two long strings of trout. It was late afternoon when we returned to the coal camp, and all through town, parents were relaxing on their porches while their children played in the streets.

"How do we sell them?" I asked Mark.

He grinned at me. "That's easy enough." He cleared his throat and called out, "Fish! Fresh fish! Caught today, nice and fresh!"

I had to laugh. He sounded exactly like the hawkers in the village square on market day back in Bohemia. In no time at all we had a crowd of women around us. We hadn't discussed a price, but it didn't matter. The women seemed to know what was fair and were eagerly pressing their payment into Mark's hand to ensure that they got the fish before others beat them to it. In no time the fish were all gone, and Mark had three dollars and seventy-five cents, nearly as much as he got for a day of work in the mine. It was almost entirely in scrip, only good at the company store, but his family owed so much there, they could certainly use it.

"We should have thought of this sooner," Mark said as he counted his money. "If I can make this much money fishing each day, we just might get by until the mine's hiring again."

"Maybe you shouldn't go back to the mine. Maybe you should become a fisherman," I suggested.

He shook his head. "I don't think there are enough fish in that creek to keep this up. But maybe I could keep it up for a few months. It's good to have something like this to fall back on."

I couldn't help thinking sadly about my chickens and garden. They had been my hope for a bit extra to fall back on. I pushed away the sadness and tried to feel joy for Mark's success. Maybe eventually he'd get paid in real money instead of scrip, and I could still talk him into buying new trousers and looking for work again. I would at least ask Mr. Torentino if he'd be willing to do me one more favor.

The next afternoon, Martina was busy, so I was alone as I waited for Mr. Torentino. Once again, I met him a short distance from the store, where Mr. Johnson wouldn't see me. Once again, I saw Mr. Torentino's disgruntled expression as he left the store and came in my direction. He smiled, however, when he saw me at the side of the road and pulled the horses to a stop.

"Where is your friend?" he asked.

"She couldn't come, but I can take the boots to her," I said. He nodded and handed me a sturdy new pair of work boots.

"I was also wondering what it might cost to get us a pair of trousers. For a friend."

Mr. Torentino considered me for a long moment. "This seems to be turning into a habit, doesn't it?"

"I didn't mean for it to. But—" An idea was sparking to life in my mind, and as it formed, I let it come tumbling out. "But would it be a problem if it did?"

"Depends on who you're asking," he said with a glance up toward the store. Of course I knew what he meant. I had already experienced firsthand what Mr. Johnson did to competitors.

"But would there be anything wrong with it? I mean, it isn't illegal or anything, right?"

He smiled. "It's a free country, as they say. No, it's not illegal. What are you thinking of, anyway?"

I swallowed and told him, even though I knew the risk. "I was thinking that there are a lot of other people in camp who need things and can't afford them at Mr. Johnson's store. If I brought a list each week of what was wanted, would you bring the goods?"

"Johnson won't like that," he said, stroking his mustache, but he sounded more amused than concerned.

"It wouldn't really be competing with Mr. Johnson. If they don't buy them from you, they'll just be doing without. They can't afford to buy them from the store."

"I don't know that he'd see it that way."

"Mr. Johnson is cheating us," I said in a sudden flare of anger. "He's cheating you, too—I see how angry you are when you come out of there each week."

Mr. Torentino nodded. "That's true—some weeks I barely break even, hauling up so much that he sends back without paying for it. But what's in this for you?"

"Well, I was thinking I could add a little to the price for my services: taking orders, picking up the goods from you, and delivering them to people. It would still be cheaper than buying things at Mr. Johnson's store."

"A sound plan. If you added ten percent on everything, that would add up for you."

I nodded. "That's what I was thinking."

Mr. Torentino's bushy mustache twitched as his mouth curled into a grin. "How old are you?"

I bit my lip. Perhaps I should lie about my age, as Mark had done to get a job in the mine. But I didn't like the idea of lying when Mr. Torentino had been so good to me, so I told the truth. "Nearly fourteen, sir," I said, hoping that he wouldn't back out when he heard how young I was.

"And this was your idea?"

"Yes, sir."

"You have a good head for business. I never really considered taking on a girl as a business partner before."

I drew in a breath. I hadn't thought of it in those terms. Business partner! It sounded exciting when he put it that way.

"I'd want the money in advance," Mr. Torentino said. "I don't want to be hauling things up here for folks that have changed their minds. I already do too much of that. And it has to be cash. I can't use that worthless scrip."

"I could get the money in advance if I knew your prices."

Mr. Torentino took a pencil and a little booklet out of his pocket. "It will have to stay to the things folks aren't buying from the robber baron," he said with a nod in the direction of the store. "What goods would that be?"

"Dry goods, mostly. Buckets, washtubs, pots and pans. And school's starting soon, so plenty of mothers will be needing dress material," I said, painfully aware of my own bare legs showing below my skirt hem.

As I listed these things and more, Mr. Torentino scribbled down prices. When I finished, he handed the booklet to me.

"There are your prices. You can write down your orders in that and give it to me with the money next week."

I nodded excitedly. "Thank you!"

"Good luck, partner," Mr. Torentino called as he climbed up to his seat and started his horses with a slap of the reins.

I felt triumphant as I climbed the hill back to town. I didn't know what would come of my scheme. Maybe I could make a few dollars, maybe replace our chickens, or maybe— I stopped myself. I wasn't going to dream—I had promised myself. I wasn't going to be disappointed again.

The next day I set out to visit the neighbors I knew best. I explained that they could order things through me, that the goods would arrive a week after I put in the order and the prices would be reasonable. Everyone was interested, though many had no cash. A few people placed orders with me, however. Most families had hoarded away a little cash for emergencies, and they were willing to use it to get a bargain. Gradually over the week, my list grew. By the following Monday, I had a list of twenty items. I met Mr. Torentino and gave him my list and eighteen dollars, keeping one dollar and eighty cents for myself on my first order.

Mr. Torentino looked over the list, and I could see he was impressed. "This is a good start," he said. "Bring someone with you next week, so you can carry it all."

He tipped his hat and drove away, and I walked home jingling my money in my pocket. I hadn't told my plan to anyone in my family—I didn't want to disappoint them again—but Aneshka caught me putting my money in the can on the kitchen shelf.

"Where did you get that?" she demanded.

"Um—it's the change from going to the store this afternoon," I said. But I had hesitated too long in coming up with an explanation, and she knew it. She glared at me, demanding the truth. Holena stood in the doorway behind her.

"Let's go out to the garden," I said. I picked up a basket and we walked out to the sprawling patch of cucumbers. I bent and started picking.

"Well?" Aneshka said, her hands on her hips.

I explained the plan to her. "But you can't tell anyone!" I said as I finished.

"But we have to tell people," she protested. "How else will they know to buy from you?"

She had a point. "Mostly don't tell Momma or Mr. Johnson."

"Momma's going to notice the extra money in the can," Holena said.

"We won't put it in the can," Aneshka said. She ran into the house and returned carrying an old cigar box that she kept under our bed. It was where she kept her treasures, but she had dumped those things out and the box was empty. "We will keep it in here, and when we have enough to buy a farm, we will surprise Momma and Papa with it."

"Aneshka." I wanted to stop her before she got her hopes up again, but it was already too late for that. Hope was shining out from both girls' eyes. "This won't get us a farm. I won't be making that much money."

Aneshka wasn't listening; she was already headed back into the house to get the money from the can. I looked at Holena, hoping she would understand. She only grasped me in a hug.

"Thank you, Trina," she said.

"For what?"

"For believing in your wish again so it can finally come true."

I held her to me, filled with fear for her. What a huge responsibility my wish had become.

Chapter 19

MY NEW PLAN was the worst-kept secret in the world, thanks to Aneshka. She made sure everyone had a chance to order from me, and I think that she nagged a few of them into doing so. Nearly every day, someone would come looking for me, and I would take my little booklet and my pencil from my pocket to record his or her order. Momma could not be kept in the dark under such circumstances, but I was vague on the details of the arrangement. After all, I wasn't that sure of the plan myself. I made a few dollars the first few weeks, but since we had agreed to sell only dry goods, I doubted business would continue. After all, how often did a family need a new bucket? Besides, since I could only take cash, and the mine had been paying mainly in scrip all summer, it couldn't hold out much longer.

I tried to explain this to Aneshka so she wouldn't be disappointed, but she only accused me of giving up, so I left her alone. She and Holena would accompany me to pick up the goods and deliver them, and I let Aneshka take charge of the money, since she had designated her treasure box as our bank. She and Holena had even cut pictures of farms and advertisements for land out of Papa's newspapers and pasted them onto the box. I paid little attention. I helped them add up the total each week and determine our portion, and I kept the money that had to go to Mr. Torentino, but I left the rest to my sisters. The temptation to dream of a farm crept into my head occasionally. To resist it, I spent as much time with Mark as I could. He was at the mine asking for work every day, and occasionally they did have odd jobs for him. When they did not, he fished.

As he predicted, his catch steadily dwindled, but even so, he was doing better business than I was, since he was willing to take payment in scrip. His family was gradually paying off some of their debt and he was once again talking of all the things we would do in the future. I listened and tried to smile at his dreams, even though none of them were big enough to get us out of the coal camp. I knew he was being practical. I knew, too, that I should be — his modest plans would not hurt anyone, and yet I couldn't get rid of a growing dissatisfaction. I loved Mark as much as ever, but a hollow feeling inside me would not go away when I thought of our future together in the coal camp.

The new school term was quickly approaching, and the question of dresses plagued my mother. One Tuesday afternoon, after Momma and I had finished the ironing, Momma took down the money can and dumped its contents out on the kitchen table. She counted through it and shook her head.

"I don't know how we'll manage school dresses, with Holena starting this year."

"Mr. Torentino can sell us the cloth for less than the company store," Aneshka said.

"That may be," Momma said, "but even so . . ." She went to the small pantry cupboard and took out the stack of flour sacks she'd been saving. They were a thin cotton, but printed with pretty flower patterns. Momma sorted out those that were enough alike to go together.

"We can make Aneshka a new dress from these, and Holena can have Aneshka's school dress, with a little mending. But Trina's bursting out of that dress everywhere, and we don't have enough flour sacks for that," Momma said. "We will just have to buy fabric on credit, I suppose. I don't know what else to do."

I looked meaningfully at Aneshka, but she refused to meet my eyes, so I spoke up. "We have some money, Momma. From working for Mr. Torentino. It's in Aneshka's box."

"But that's for our farm!" Aneshka protested.

Momma raised her eyebrows and looked at me. "For a farm?"

I shook my head. "It wasn't my idea," I said.

"Yes it was! It was your wish!" Aneshka said.

"We need the money now," I insisted.

"Why, just so you can get a new dress?" Aneshka scowled at me.

"Show me this money," Momma broke in.

Aneshka could not disobey Momma, so she retrieved the box. She set it on the table and Momma opened it. I gasped at the same time Momma did when we saw the contents. I knew the money had been accumulating, but seeing it all together startled me.

Momma counted it, laying it out on the table in neat rows.

"Fourteen dollars!" she said when she finished. She looked from the money to me and back to the money with an expression of bewilderment. "How on earth did you get so much money?"

"I told you, we've been delivering goods for Mr. Torentino. From his store in Trinidad."

She frowned. "Yes, that's what you told me, but delivery girls don't make this much money. What is really going on, Trina?"

I told her the details of the business, omitting any mention of Mr. Johnson's anger that had inspired it. I had been careful to avoid him since we had started the deliveries, but word of my business had spread around camp. I was pretty sure Mr. Johnson had heard, or at least suspected. I had never told my parents of his role in destroying my previous plans, or even that he harbored a grudge against me. I saw no point in bringing that up now. Especially since I expected my mother to be angry enough with us as it was. Nervously I tried to read her mood as I explained, but her expression remained closed. She kept staring at the pile of money.

"How long have you been doing this?" she asked at last.

"Four weeks," I said.

"Four weeks," she repeated thoughtfully. "You have saved fourteen dollars in only four weeks?"

"It's been going up every week, too," Aneshka said proudly. "This week we made almost six dollars, and Trina's already taken two orders for next week."

"I had no idea," Momma said. "Who orders from you?"

"Mostly our neighbors," I said quickly. "And sometimes people find me after church."

"If we went across the tracks, we could make a lot more," Aneshka said.

I shot her a warning glance. Momma had a strict rule that my sisters and I were never to cross the tracks that ran through the middle of the coal town. The houses on the other side were exactly like our own, but we didn't mix with the Welsh and Scottish families who lived there. Even at school we avoided those children. Rumor had it, the Scots collaborated with the mine officials. They would betray union organizers or trouble-makers to the bosses. And Papa said a Welshman was at fault in the accident that had crushed Old Jan's leg, as they so often were. Even if they could be trusted, we had a hard time under-standing their English, and they ours, so it seemed best for everyone if we didn't mix.

"You mean you have made all this from only this side of town?" Momma asked.

"Mostly. It's enough for dresses, isn't it?" I said, trying to return the conversation to the safety of our original topic.

"Yes, it's certainly enough for that," Momma said, but the tone in her voice was one I didn't recognize. She turned to Aneshka with a smile. "Run along and play," she said. "We will work on dresses later. You too, Holena."

It was all too clear that, though my sisters were being dis-missed, I was not. Aneshka noticed too, and she gave me one more hard glare before taking Holena's hand and leaving the kitchen.

"Does Marek know of these plans?" Momma asked when we were alone.

"Momma, I didn't tell Aneshka to save for a farm. I haven't said anything about it—it's her idea."

"But the orders, the deal with Mr. Torentino, that was all your doing."

"Mark knows of all that. In fact, he gave me the idea," I said. "But I wasn't really doing it for the farm. I've learned my lesson about those kinds of dreams."

Momma wasn't looking at me. Her eyes were on Aneshka's box and the advertisements my sisters had pasted there. Momma couldn't read the English text, but she could certainly read the prices. When she spoke, it wasn't directed at me so much as thinking out loud.

"Fourteen dollars in just four weeks, and just on this side of town, when the mine isn't even at full production —" She paused and seemed to be adding in her head. "If we can save this much now, by the end of the year . . ."

I stared at her, my mouth open. "Do you mean — Momma, do you think by the end of the year we would have enough for something big?"

"Everyone here needs more than they can name, but we're all scrimping to get by. Come fall, when work picks up again, people will be buying more. Everyone in town is counting the days till the mine is in full production and giving out cash payments again to get what we are doing without for now. And the bachelors will be back, and they are looser with their money than families are. In another month or two your business will boom, I think."

"Enough to buy a farm?"

Momma's eyes snapped up to my face, as if the mention of a farm had startled her awake. Her expression hardened.

"You have to tell Marek of this. You know he has no interest in being a farmer. You shouldn't be thinking of a farm, either. You should be setting a share of these earnings aside to set up a household when you marry. Whatever plans you are making, you should be making them with him."

"But —" I felt a knot tightening in my gut again, the same knot that had been there ever since the accident at the mine. I swallowed hard.

"But what? What's the matter, Trina? You should be happy to share this with Marek. He has so many good, solid ideas you can start working on together. Go on and tell him now, why don't you."

I nodded and stepped outside into the street. I couldn't tell her what I was thinking—that I had only promised myself to Mark because I thought a farm was impossible. I hated myself now for even thinking it. I loved Mark. But I had seen my mother's expression as she looked at those ads and calculated. I had seen hope. And if even Momma thought we might be able to get out of the coal camp, how could I turn my back on that? How could I bear spending money to build something here with Mark when it could have been enough for my family to get our farm?

At Mark's house, Old Jan was stumping around the kitchen, helping Martina wash and put away dishes. He smiled at me, offering a cup of coffee from the pot simmering on the back of the stove.

"Is Mark here?" I asked.

"He's out walking. He's determined to have that foot strong by the time the mine's hiring again." He set the cup of coffee on the table before me, but I stood chewing my lip, trying to decide if I should go after him.

Old Jan raised his eyebrows. "You look like you have heavy matters on your shoulders, child."

I nodded. "I have a lot to think about."

"Can I help?"

I sighed and sat down at the table. How could I explain it to him? "Have you ever wanted something so much that even after you know you can't have it, you still can't stop thinking about it?"

He smiled and nodded. "Once hope has a hold on you, it doesn't want to let go. I think that's for the best, don't you? Where would any of us be if hope abandoned us?"

"Hope did abandon me," I said, remembering the terrible weeks after the accident when I had lost so much.

"Did it?" he asked. "Or did you abandon it?"

"I don't know what you mean."

He smiled. "Do you know the story of the boy betrothed to the frog?"

"I'm a little too old for such stories," I pointed out. My problems were real-world matters now; I didn't need more fairy tales in my head. "I'm almost a woman."

"So you are," Jan said. "But no one's ever too old for the lessons. We are always still young enough to learn."

Martina poured herself a cup of coffee, and one for Jan, and sat down beside us. "And I'm not too old to want to listen, if it means sitting down for a few minutes," she said. So Old Jan began his story.

"There once was a man with one small farm and three sons, and he did not know which of them should get his farm. So he sent his sons into the world to find a bride.

"'Whoever returns with the finest betrothal ring, he shall have the farm,' the father decreed.

"So the three sons set out, each in a different direction. The two older brothers traveled the road, and it was left to the youngest to clamber through the forest. The boy traveled a full day without meeting another person, and he was about to give up entirely when an ugly toad jumped onto a log in front of him and spoke.

"'What are you doing so deep in the forest, boy?' the toad asked.

"'I am seeking a bride who will make me the betrothal gift of a ring,' the boy answered.

"'I have a daughter who will gladly marry you, and she has a fine betrothal ring for you,' the toad said.

"The boy was too kind to reject the ugly creature, so he followed her to her home, a rough cave, and the toad called in to her daughter to come out. The creature that emerged from the cave was the ugliest thing the boy had ever seen. Splay legged, bulgy eyed, and covered in crusty warts."

I couldn't resist a little shiver, and Old Jan smiled.

"But the ugly creature had with her a small chest and told the boy, 'If you will accept a betrothal gift from me, you may choose it yourself from these.'

"She opened the chest to reveal the most costly and beautiful rings the boy had ever seen! Not wishing to be greedy, the boy took the least valuable, but the toad mother protested and insisted he take the finest ring in the box—a perfect diamond the size of a robin's egg.

"Well, of course the boy had high hopes of getting the farm, as you once did, Trina. When the boy returned home with his gift, his brothers were already there, so his father called them all to show the rings they had received. The first brother had a small copper ring, worth only a few pennies. The second had a ring of poor silver, worth only a bit more. But when the father saw the fine ring the youngest son brought, he was sure the boy had stolen it. So he beat the boy and told him he must return it to its owner. Then he set a new challenge to his sons: They must each find a girl who would give them a fine embroidered handkerchief. The brother who brought back the finest would inherit the farm.

"Once again, the youngest son set out through the woods,

this time in a different direction, but once again, he encountered the toad. Though he tried to get around it, he was soon on his way to meet her daughter, who produced the finest silk handkerchief he had ever seen.

"Once again, the boy returned home hopeful, and once again, though he had the finest gift, he received a punishment instead of the farm."

"So the moral is, no matter how you try, you cannot succeed?" I asked bitterly.

"So it might seem," Old Jan said. "But let me finish, because the father sent the three boys out a third time. 'Produce the girls who have given you these gifts and whoever has the loveliest bride shall inherit the farm,' he said.

"Now the youngest son was truly wretched. For while his bride had fine gifts for him, he could not bear to bring the ugly toad before his father. So he chose once again to go in a different direction, hoping against hope to avoid the toads. But much to his dismay, the mother toad found him and begged him to come to her house. So the boy went, and told them what his father had decreed. Still the boy hoped to save himself, and to spare their feelings. So he said, 'I am too tired to return tonight. Let me sleep the night here, and tomorrow we will venture to my father's house,' for he planned to sneak away in the night.

"He lay down to sleep on the stone floor of the cave, and surprisingly enough, fell into a deep, dreamless sleep. It was full light when he woke the next day, and he looked around amazed, for he was no longer in a cave, but in a stately palace. He left his room and wandered to the great hall, where a graceful queen awaited him.

"'You have broken the enchantment!' she told him. 'I am the queen of this land, laid under a curse by a jealous sorcerer.

We were doomed to be toads until a good man would promise to marry my daughter and stay the night to seal the pact. And now, behold your bride.'

"The most beautiful princess ever seen—who, of course, had been the ugliest toad—stepped forward from the shadows and took the boy's hand, and they were married right then and there. And though the boy did return to his father with the most beautiful bride, he did not need his father's farm. For he was now prince of a fine kingdom, where he ruled happily for many a long year."

"It is a fine story," I said. "And what is the lesson?"

"Well, the lesson is whatever you take from it. But it seems to me that the boy was much like you. He thought his efforts had failed again and again, but he didn't give up. And because things once started had a course of their own, good came of it all in the end, even when the end wasn't the one he'd expected. He set out in a different direction each day, but the important thing is that he kept setting out."

"The problem is, I set out in a different direction, and now I don't know which direction is the right one," I said.

"No one can tell you which is right for you, child," Old Jan said, patting me on the back kindly. "But maybe you'll have the luck of the boy in the story and discover that all directions lead to success. Sometimes things have a way of working themselves out."

I nodded and sighed. "I hope you are right."

He looked past me out the open kitchen door and smiled. "Here is my Marek. I'll leave the two of you to talk, shall I?" He picked up a bucket and set off toward the creek.

I greeted Mark on the porch so we could talk and wouldn't be in Martina's way in the cramped kitchen. He smiled when he saw me, and the smile warmed me deep inside. It felt good to be near him, and to know I could make him happy just by being here.

"I'm glad to see you, Trina. I've got good news!"

"Tell me," I said, happy enough not to have to say what I had come for.

"On my walk today I passed by the mine office and the superintendent was there. He noticed how much better I was walking, and he said he thought they could hire me back on, come fall."

"That is good news," I said.

He nodded, still grinning. "And they'll be hiring again soon. Once I'm back to work, Martina and Karel can move back to their own place. And once we've paid off some of our debt, maybe Papa and I can move to a better house, plant a garden, buy some new chickens. What do you think?"

I hugged him and told him it was a good plan, and then I let him talk about all his plans and hopes. I couldn't bear to tell him I had money now to start building that dream. And I certainly didn't want to undermine his happiness by bringing up the possibility of getting a farm.

When I left his house a short time later, my feet took me to the quiet pool by the creek seemingly on their own. I settled myself in the shade under the tree to think. I thought back over recent months and my new business plan. Old Jan was right. Hope for a farm had never really died in my heart. It had always been there, compelling me to set out once again. I had tried to deny it—had denied it to Holena and Aneshka—but it had lingered all the same. My heart was still looking for the other path. But I loved Mark, too, and I didn't want to break my promise to him. And so many things could still stand between us and the farm. I was scared to hope—but scared not to.

"You tell me what to do," I said to the pool, but I saw no sign of the fish. I was apparently on my own for the hard decisions. I thought again about the box under Aneshka's bed and my mother's reaction to our savings. Of everything that had happened, that seemed the most magical of all. It seemed I had made a wish that would come to fruition whether I was still trying or not—it was going to keep jumping out in front of me like that toad in the story. The question was, was that a blessing or a curse? A chance, or another disappointment? And what was I going to tell Mark? It was mid-September. If the schoolmaster wasn't coming until October, we had two weeks yet before school started, and probably about two weeks before the mine would be hiring again.

"All right," I said to the pool. "All right, I will give this two more weeks. I will try selling on the other side of the tracks. If it doesn't work out, I'm done with you and your wish."

A leaf fluttered down to the surface of the pool and I watched, strangely expectant, as it spun slowly across the surface. I saw no sign of the fish.

It didn't matter, I decided, as I climbed the slope and walked home. I had made a decision, whether the fish had heard my bargain or not. Two weeks. I couldn't wait forever for a dream— not when I seemed to have promised that same forever to Mark, and I was going to have to choose.

Chapter 20

THE NEXT DAY, I asked my mother if I could go across the tracks and take orders in the Welsh and Scottish districts. Momma consented, as long as my sisters and I went together and stayed together. She needn't have worried. After having been warned to stay on our own side for so long, it felt strange and daring to step across the tracks and walk down the streets that had for so long been forbidden.

In truth, this part of town looked no different from ours, with ragged children and tired women on the streets and doorsteps. But the refrains of Welsh and Scottish and the flashes of red hair among the children made it all feel foreign.

My sisters and I were too shy to knock on doors. We only approached women in the street or called out to those on their porches. We had little luck. Several old women who were mending together on one porch just stared at us and spoke secretively to each other in Welsh. Another shooed us away, mistaking us for beggars. My heart sank. My mother had reawakened my hope for nothing.

We were about to give up when we saw several young women in the street ahead of us. They were a cheerful group, laughing over their gossip, so we decided to give it one more try.

"Are you in need of anything I could order for you, ladies? I can get things delivered for much lower prices than the store," I said politely.

The tallest, and apparently oldest, of the women looked suspiciously at me. "Can you?"

"Oh, she's that Polish lass we've heard about," said a second, younger woman. Her curly hair was escaping from her loose bun and playing in ringlets around her face.

"Czechy, actually," I said, taking my order book from my pocket. "Is there anything you need?"

"Are your prices really that good? How much for, say, a bag of flour?"

"I only sell dry goods, I'm afraid."

"A yard of dress fabric, then?"

"Three cents a yard," I answered.

"That is much better than the store," the first woman said, considering.

"How many yards do you need, then? And I will need payment in advance."

"Actually, I was thinking of the Llewellyns. They need all the help they can get right now," said the curly-haired one.

"Oh, aye, Glenys," agreed the older woman. "His old parents— eleven children, including a wee babe, and she's laid up with the gout. And there's something wrong with that poor baby. Oh, aye, they need all the help they can get. Go see them, lass, last house down that way."

"Here, I'll show you," said curly-haired Glenys. She led the way down the street to the very last house. It was a decrepit structure, the yard cluttered with old cans and slats from a broken-down picket fence. Two little boys were shouting and chasing a skinny yellow dog through the yard. The steps creaked threateningly as our new guide climbed onto the porch and knocked on the door. A small, pale, blue-eyed child opened it. Though she was about Aneshka's age, I could not recall ever seeing her in school.

Holena gripped my hand tightly as we entered the dimly lit kitchen. Aneshka crowded close as well, and I couldn't blame her. The smells of dirty laundry and urine were overpowering, and I fought the urge to pinch my nose. At the stove an old woman stirred a pot while a thin, naked toddler pulled on her skirts and whimpered. Dirty dishes were piled on the table, crawling with flies. From the bedroom came the high, sharp wail of a baby.

Glenys said something in Welsh to the old woman at the stove. She smiled toothlessly at us and waved her spoon toward the bedroom. There we met the lady of the house, a woman about the same age as our mother, but far more worn. Her blond hair was streaked with gray. Strands of it had escaped her bun and hung limp in her face, as if even they had given up hope. She was trying to get the fussy baby to nurse, but the baby kept throwing his head back and wailing.

"Nancy, I've brought some girls here to help you out," said Glenys.

The mother frowned. She turned the baby up over her shoulder and started thumping its back.

"I can't afford to hire help," she said.

"This is that Polish—er, sorry—Bohemian lass that gets goods for cheap."

Nancy looked at me again, a bit of hope in her eyes. "Can you now? Can you get me flour, oats, and potatoes to feed me wee ones? I'd be grateful."

"I'm sorry, I can't get food, only dry goods. But I can get shoes or clothes for your children."

"What good are shoes for them if I can't feed them," she said.

I could see her point. "Maybe I could get you flour or oats," I said. Mr. Johnson wouldn't be hurt if we broke that rule just once. "I think it would be about fifteen cents for a sack of flour, and about the same for oats. I have to have the money in advance, though."

Nancy's face fell. "Could you give me credit? Come fall when the mine's back to full production, I could pay you then."

Before I could answer, Aneshka spoke up.

"No credit," she said firmly. "The man who brings it demands his pay in advance."

Nancy bit her lip and shifted the still-crying baby. "We could pay you next week in scrip. Just as soon as my husband and son collect their pay."

I frowned. I was thinking that perhaps we could take scrip, just this once, but Aneshka shook her head and said "Cash only!" before I could respond.

Nancy nodded, her face grimly resigned. "Thank you anyway."

She laid the squalling baby in a worn cradle and limped into the front room of the house, where the old lady was dishing up bowls of thin gruel and handing them to the crowd of children.

Seeing we'd make no sale here, we retreated quickly. We walked in silence up the street with Glenys.

"What's wrong with that baby?" Aneshka asked.

Glenys shrugged and shook her head. "The doctor can't say. He won't nurse proper. He can eat a little gruel made real thin, is all. Poor wee thing." She shook her head again.

"I am sorry," I said. "I wish there was something I could do."

"I don't think you're that sorry, lass," Glenys said. "It's the same with everyone in America. Money first; nothing else matters much here." She turned and walked up the path to her own front door, not saying good-bye to us. I felt a rush of shame.

"Maybe we should give her goods on credit," I said. "Just this once."

Aneshka scowled at me. "If we start giving people things they haven't paid for, how are we going to save enough for a farm?"

"But they will pay later," I said.

Aneshka snorted. "They are never going to have the money. You saw that house."

"I wish there was some way to help them," Holena said quietly, slipping her hand into mine again at the memory of the house.

I wished it too, but I could see Aneshka's point. Since I had surrendered control of the money to her, I would have to convince her otherwise if I wanted to spend any money from the box.

We walked on in silence, crossing the railroad tracks and continuing toward home. There we helped Momma with supper. Aneshka and Holena laid the table while I rolled the dumplings and sliced cucumbers. I was quiet as I worked. I was still thinking of the poor family, but there was more to consider. We had made no sales on our trip across town, and we weren't likely to, even if we went back. Momma had been wrong; my business wasn't going to grow. I was glad now that I hadn't said anything about the money or the new plans for a farm to Mark, glad I hadn't disappointed him for nothing. Glad I had his happiness as a refuge.

Old Jan, Mark, and Martina arrived after supper, just as we finished washing up. We went out onto the porch, where a hint of breeze cooled the sweat on my brow. Mark smiled at me and I smiled back, despite the tangle of feelings inside me. He still had a dream, at least, and I felt lucky that he had made room in it for me. After seeing the poor Llewellyn family, I could see just how lucky we all were, despite our disappointments. I watched my sisters, fed and clothed, settling on the porch at Old Jan's feet, and an idea came to me.

"Old Jan, would you tell us a story?" I said. At once Aneshka and Holena added their voices to the request, as I knew they would.

Old Jan looked at me, his eyebrows raised. "Aren't you getting a little old for stories, Trina? After all, you're nearly a woman."

I smiled back. "We're never too old for the lessons," I said.

Papa smiled. "My Trina's becoming a philosopher," he said.

"What story would you like?" Old Jan said.

"A princess story!" Aneshka said, as she always did.

"I like animals," Holena said.

"How about the one about the boy betrothed to a toad?" I suggested. "It has a princess and animals."

"Ewww!" Aneshka said, and both my sisters giggled. "Who would want to marry a toad?"

"Exactly what the boy thought," Old Jan said, and he began the story.

"That's a fine story," Momma said when he finished.

"And what is the lesson?" Mark asked, smiling at me. "Am I your ugly toad, Trina?"

"Of course not," I said. "The lesson is, goodness will be rewarded. If the boy hadn't been so kind and charitable toward the toads, he would have ended up with nothing. But his charity brought a great reward in the end."

"That is a good lesson, indeed," Old Jan said. "Trina *is* becoming a philosopher."

I glanced at Aneshka. She was chewing on her lip thoughtfully. I took the opportunity to raise an idea to my mother. I told her of our visit that day, of the squalid house, the poor family, and the thin gruel they ate for their dinner.

"May we take them some cucumbers?" I suggested. "I don't think they had anything good to eat. And I was thinking that tomorrow if you don't need the tubs, we could go do some washing for them. With that baby, I don't think the mother has been able to keep up. Plus, she's got the gout."

Momma's eyebrows raised. "And what do you plan to charge them for your help?"

"Nothing. They can't afford it. I just want to be charitable."

Aneshka gave a little "hmph" in her throat, but Momma smiled.

"Of course you may help them. I am glad to see there is charity in your heart, Trina, and not just the desire for money," she said. "You will find that good deeds are their own reward."

"And I'll help," Holena said. "Will you help too, Aneshka?"

Everyone looked at Aneshka. She scowled at me, but agreed.

Old Jan smiled. "And good will come of it, too. Wait and see. Good always comes from good, one way or another."

The next morning, when our chores were finished, we set out once again across the tracks, carrying our washtubs between us.

When we reached the Welsh district, Glenys was outside, sweeping her porch.

"Where are you going with that?" she called out.

I told her of our plan.

"Bless you! Wait a minute," she said, and disappeared into her house. She reappeared a moment later with a tub of her own and a loaf of bread. She accompanied us through the streets, calling out to her neighbors in Welsh when she saw them. By the time we arrived at the Llewellyn house, we had two women with us and others collecting their things to come along.

I had never imagined that laundry could be as fun as it was that day. We built fires and heated tubs of water in the yard behind the house. The women who knew the family best worked together to carry the laundry out of the house. They laughed and joked as they scrubbed and rinsed and hung the clothes in the sunshine. Soon Aneshka, Holena, and I had joined in their jokes, just like family. Nancy's children helped by toting water or keeping their little siblings out from underfoot. We had the laundry done in no time, so we washed the dishes and swept out the house. When the work was finally done and the women were all leaving in chatty groups, I gave Nancy the cucumbers I had picked that morning.

"For your family," I said.

Tears rose in Nancy's eyes. "How can I thank you?" she said.

"No need," I replied.

"And about your order," Aneshka suddenly said, surprising me. "We could do a little on credit. A bag of potatoes, maybe? Or a bag of flour?"

"Potatoes," Nancy said at once. I wrote it down on my pad, feeling so proud of my little sister I thought I'd burst.

I delivered the week's orders to Mr. Torentino, including the sack of potatoes for Nancy. I was nervous that he might not agree to bring them, but I explained the situation to him. My new partner was a good man with a good heart. He agreed to bring the potatoes, suggesting that he might be able to throw in a sack of flour, as well.

I walked home, content in my heart. Momma had been right; good deeds were their own reward.

Chapter 21

I HAD ASKED Old Jan to tell the story of the boy and the toad to convince Aneshka that we should help the poor family we had met. I had not expected a rich reward for doing so. After all, Nancy Llewellyn was a miner's wife, not an enchanted princess. But perhaps the old stories had more magic in them than I realized, or perhaps their wisdom was eternal, because right away good things began to happen.

Good news came just after supper on the very next evening, when Old Jan arrived for his usual visit. Since Mark had been hurt and Karel had married, he was often accompanied by Martina and Mark when he arrived, but this evening, Mark was not with him. Old Jan was grinning from ear to ear, so we did not have to wait long to learn where Mark was.

"Our worries are over!" Old Jan announced. "The steel mill in Pueblo got a contract for a new rail line, and they are firing up the smelters. The mine's going back into full production!"

"Already?" Momma said.

"Several weeks early," Old Jan said. "No more worries about layoffs. They're looking for men to hire. They've already put my Marek on the night shift. He's at work right now. We'll all soon be back on our feet again, and Karel and Martina can get a proper place of their own."

"That is good news," Momma agreed.

"I hope that means they'll be paying with cash again soon," Papa said.

"And that the bachelors will be coming back to the camp too," Momma said with a smile. "With their laundry."

"And their orders," Aneshka said, her eyes glowing with an ambition bordering on greed.

Papa laughed and tousled her hair. "You see? Our worries are over!"

I couldn't quite see it as Papa did, although I knew I should. Hard times were easing up, but it also meant one more person I loved in the mine. In harm's way.

News spread fast through camp, and the very next day, I began to see its effect in another bit of luck. I was in the hot kitchen with a hot iron, trying to press the wrinkles from Papa's collars, when someone knocked on the open kitchen door. I looked up to see Glenys and her friend who had first sent us to the Llewellyn house. They were both smiling.

"How much did you say for a yard of fabric?" Glenys asked.

I told her again, and she pulled money from her pocket at once. "I have two girls in school this year," she said, "and at that price they can both have new dresses."

"Mine too," agreed her companion. "I could use a new coffee-pot. What else do you sell?"

Before they had gone, I had taken down orders and collected money for a long list of goods, and my new customers left chatting cheerfully in Welsh. Half an hour later it happened again—and again. In fact, for an hour or so in the early afternoon, I had a small crowd of women waiting with their money in hand to place their orders. Some of them I had met at the wash party, but many I had not. Word of my good deed or my good prices had spread through the other side of town. Now that the mine had announced more work and, as my father had hoped, cash payment, purse strings were loosening. It was just as Momma had predicted; people had been waiting for better times. With those times in sight, they weren't waiting another minute. They were spending the money they had, knowing more was on the way, and they were getting the things they had been doing without. And because of my good deed in the Welsh district, they were trusting me to get those things for them. By the time I had a break and could empty my pockets into Aneshka's eager hands, my apron was sagging under the weight of the coins I carried. That evening, Aneshka piled the day's earnings on the kitchen table and counted it out as my whole family watched.

"One hundred and twenty-one dollars!" she announced in an awed whisper.

"And twenty-seven cents," Holena added.

We gathered around it, my sisters stroking the coins lovingly. None of us, except perhaps Papa, had seen so much money in one place before.

"That's twelve dollars for us," I said, "in one day!"

"It's a miracle," Momma whispered.

None of us slept well that night. We had tied the money in a sack and placed it under the mattress for safekeeping, but the excitement of it was enough to keep us all awake.

The excitement was not over, however. The next morning, the wife of a Scottish crew foreman appeared on our doorstep with money in hand. Through her husband, who supervised a crew of Italians and Greeks, word spread to the remaining corners of camp. Our house was a hub of activity for the rest of the week. By the following Monday, I had more than eight hundred dollars to give Mr. Torentino, and an answer to my two-week bargain with my wish. One hundred dollars was tucked away at home. A farm of our own seemed possible once again.

My sisters and I were eager to see Mr. Torentino that afternoon, anxious to hand over the large sum of money I had for him. When he arrived at last, I quickly thrust the orders and the money at him.

His eyes grew wide when he saw how much I had. "All this is from this camp?"

I had expected him to be as pleased as I was with all the business, but he looked worried.

"What's wrong?" I asked.

"It's so much. I don't know if I can fit it into my wagon with all that I have to bring to the store. I would have to raise the prices if I had to bring up a second wagon. But never mind." He brightened and smiled at me. "You're quite a salesman. Maybe someday you'll have his job," he said, pointing over his shoulder toward the store. "And believe me, there's none of us who wouldn't be glad to see him go. Now, let's get these things unloaded."

Together we took all the goods from the previous week's order out of the wagon. It was nearly more than we could carry.

"It's too heavy," Aneshka complained as I handed her a crate.

"Well, we have to get it home—we can't leave half of it sitting here to make two trips."

"You better get a plan in place for next week," Mr. Torentino said. "You'll have to have plenty of help for that order!"

He was right, of course, but at the moment I could think only of getting our current load home. We usually cut through an open field of weeds to avoid passing Mr. Johnson's store. But the ground there was uneven and the tangles of tansy and bindweed made tripping easier than walking. Since we had so much to carry, we decided to stay on the road and walk past the store, just this once. And though we had had exceptional luck that summer, it did not seem to be with us then. While we were passing the store, Mr. Johnson stepped out onto his porch. His face registered surprise, then malice when he saw us.

"Where did you get all that?" he demanded.

"It's ours," I said, and picked up the pace.

Mr. Johnson said nothing more, but Holena looked back just before his store disappeared from view. "He's still watching us," she said.

"He can't do anything. Mr. Torentino says everything we're doing is legal." I tried to sound more confident than I actually felt. I did not want to alarm my sisters. I waited until they were out playing that afternoon before I found a better hiding place for our savings. Afterward, I told them it was hidden, but didn't tell them where. The fewer people who knew, the safer it was. I figured if Mr. Johnson could not find our money, he could not hurt us.

Orders were still pouring in that next week, and I turned my attention away from Mr. Johnson and toward the problem of delivering so much. Even if I got the help of my mother and Martina, we could not carry it all up the hill in one load. We could have asked another neighbor, but I was hesitant to introduce more people to Mr. Torentino. I didn't want anyone else to see how the business worked or to negotiate with Mr. Torentino directly. He had called me his partner, but I wasn't sure that he had any particular loyalty to me. If people found out they could buy directly from Mr. Torentino without paying my ten percent, they would surely do so.

I decided the best way to handle the larger delivery of the next week was to ask those who had placed orders to come directly to the field where I unloaded from the wagon, but not until after Mr. Torentino had gone. Then they could each carry their own order up the hill. Aneshka and Holena agreed it was a good plan. We each took a portion of the names on our order list and spread the word to meet us Monday afternoon at the designated place.

By Saturday afternoon, I thought that nothing could ever go wrong again. Our lives seemed charmed at last. I did not hesitate for a minute when Mark asked me to take a walk with him that evening. He said he had something to show me. My heart sang as we set off up the road, hand in hand.

We walked past his house and on toward the edge of town. We were out of the Bohemian area now, into a group of houses occupied almost entirely by Greeks. I was increasingly curious of what he might be planning to show me that required us to come here. At last we came to an empty house on the very edge of the camp, its back door opening out onto a steep, treeless ridge.

"We will rent this," he announced proudly. I looked at the house, then at him. He had an expectant look on his face, as if I was supposed to understand something. I turned back to the house, looking again, trying to see what was special about it. As far as I could tell, it was just like every other house in town.

"Why here?" I said at last.

"Don't you see?" he said, wrapping an arm around my waist

as we looked together at the little house. "There's a whole empty hillside behind it. We could move the chicken coop here and plant a garden twice the size of what you had. When we have the money, we can buy a goat or even a cow. There's plenty of hillside where we can keep it. With his new leg, Papa could take a goat or a cow up the hill each day to pasture. It would be good for him."

"That's a nice idea, Mark, but that's all still years away. I'm not old enough to get married yet, and you don't have the money to do any of this now. This house will be rented to someone else long before we are ready for any of that."

"It doesn't have to be, Trina. We can start before we are married. Karel and Martina want to be on their own anyway, so they are going to stay in our house, and Papa and I are going to move here. We can move the chicken coop and get chickens right away. We can't plant the garden until next spring, but you can come over and help Papa start preparing the ground for the garden patch. We can go by the mine dump on Sundays and look for more fencing, to keep the dogs and the goat out of the garden, but if we can't find any, we can always buy that, too. I've seen it in the Sears and Roebuck catalog. What do you think? I'll go tomorrow to the mine office and rent this place."

"But how are you going to do all this now? You've only been back to work for a week, and you have back rent to pay off first."

"We'll do it with the money you've saved. Everyone knows you've been making money on your deliveries. Why should we wait? This is exactly the opportunity that we need!"

I pulled out of his embrace. "My money! But it's not my money—it's my family's. We can't spend it on this."

"But your mother told me you were setting it aside for us,

for our future. After all, it's your delivery business; you do all the work. Your momma's very proud of you for building such a good dowry."

"Mark, it's not my dowry. It's for—" I stopped myself.

"For what?"

I took a deep breath. "It's for my family. Don't you see? We came to America so my father could own land."

"A farm, you mean," Mark said, his voice hardening.

I nodded. "A farm. And this is the first time we've saved any money at all since we came here. This is our chance to get what we really want—what we came to America for. This is our chance to get out of the coal camp for good!"

"Not we. You. You know I want nothing to do with a farm."

"Aneshka and Holena are counting on a farm," I said.

"And what about me? About us? You made a promise to me, and I've been counting on that."

"I can't crush their dreams, and my father's dreams, by spending that money on anything that would trap us here in the coal camp."

"Is that how you see your promise to me? As a trap?"

I hesitated, unable to look him in the eye.

"You said you would stay forever," he said, his voice full of bitterness.

"I can't, Mark."

"Can't? Or won't?"

I bit my lip. I wasn't sure myself.

"You lied to me," he said.

I shook my head. "I didn't. But when I promised myself to you, I thought there was no chance of a farm. Things have changed."

"Nothing's changed for me."

"Don't you want to get out of here? Come with us! Come help my papa on our farm—a real farm away from here. Your papa can come too!"

"I won't be a farmer."

"Just to get out of here. Then you can go to high school, or get a job in town, or—"

He shook his head. "I've got a job now, a real job, to support *us* like *we* planned, you and me. Like we promised each other."

"Try to understand, Mark. You know this has always been my dream."

"If this has always been your dream, Trina," Mark said, his voice shaking with anger, "what have I been to you?"

I hesitated, trying to sort out the confusion of disappointment, hope, and pain in my heart.

He took another step away, misinterpreting my silence. "Never mind. I think I'd rather not know. Go on, then. Get your farm. Find yourself a nice farm boy." He spat out the last words with such anger that it seemed to scorch the air between us.

"I don't want a farm boy!" I insisted.

"But you sure don't want a coal miner."

I put my hand on his arm, trying to stop the widening gap between us. "But don't you see? You don't have to be a coal miner. I want you, Mark, but I want to get out of here too. This is our chance! What about your dreams?"

At that he jerked back and pulled his arm from my grasp, as if I had been a wasp and stung him. "This is my dream, having all this with you. But you never wanted any of it, did you? You never wanted me. So, I know it's not much more than a piece of trash, but if you'll give me back my ring, I'll be out of your way."

"Mark—"

"My ring, please," he said, holding out his hand.

Tears were stinging my eyes, but I blinked them away angrily and pulled the copper band from my finger. He put it in his pocket and pulled out the smooth pebble I had given him. I refused to take it back, so he dropped it in the dirt before me. I stared at it as he walked away. No longer shining with the creek's water, it looked dull and worthless, just the way I felt.

Chapter 22

I FORCED my thoughts back to the farm that was nearly within reach. That was what I had really wanted all along, I told myself. But inside I felt my heart going as dry and dull as the pebble in the dust.

I did not tell my mother what had happened, but it wasn't long before she knew. Her anger and disappointment were thick in the air at home all the next week as I went about my chores and my orders. By the end of the workweek on Saturday, my sales were nearly equal to the week before. I set off to church on Sunday, hoping to push my total a little higher. Sure enough, women found me in the crowd outside after church, their money in hand. I wanted to keep my attention diverted from Mark, so I paid no attention to anything but the orders. I was surprised by my mother's question at the dinner table a short time later.

"How long has Mr. Johnson been watching you like that, Trina?" she asked.

I stiffened. "Mr. Johnson was watching me?"

"After church, when you were taking orders."

I felt a chill go through me, but I tried to hide it. "Mr. Johnson is afraid of competition," I said. "That is why I have to be careful and only sell dry goods. Most of his business is in food."

Momma frowned. "I don't like it. Don't cross him, Trina. He's trouble."

"I haven't. There's nothing wrong with what I'm doing. It's perfectly legal, and I've been careful to keep away from him."

"You worry too much, Ivana," Papa said to Momma, casting a quick smile to me. "What harm can Mr. Johnson do us? Trina's making so much money now, we'll be out of here in a few months' time. It won't matter one whit what some shopkeeper thinks of her."

I felt a pang of guilt. I wanted to agree with Papa, but I knew that Mr. Johnson could cause us harm, that he had already done so. When dinner was over, I went as soon as I could and checked our hidden money. I would have to be careful no one knew where it was. And I would be more careful to take and deliver orders out of Mr. Johnson's sight.

I didn't have to deliver orders forever. As Papa had said, only a few more months and we would have enough money saved. We could leave here for good, and never worry about Mr. Johnson again. I reminded myself, too, that he had known of my garden and chickens for weeks before he had found a way to destroy them. I had time.

The following day was laundry day, but since we only had our own to do, I carried water from the creek, and we did the job at home. That way, we did not leave the house unguarded. I was hanging the last basket of clothes on the line beside the house when I looked up to see my father approaching, though it was only midmorning. The only reason I knew why a miner would be home so early was because he was hurt — but though my heart skipped a beat at the thought, I knew immediately it could not be true. Papa wasn't even dirty; he didn't appear to have been in the mine at all that day.

Curious, I went in the back door, just as he went in the front. Momma and my sisters were in the kitchen, kneading bread dough. Momma looked up in alarm when Papa stepped in and set his lunch pail, still full, on the counter by the sink.

"What on earth? Are you hurt?" Momma asked, echoing our constant fear as she hurriedly pulled out a chair for him.

Papa flopped down into the chair. "I've been fired, Ivana," he said quietly.

There was a moment of silence as we all stared open-mouthed at him. Momma shooed my sisters outside to play before she spoke again.

"I thought they were going to full production. I thought they were hiring more men," Momma said.

Papa nodded. "I've been fired. Not laid off, but fired."

"But — why?"

Papa glanced up at me and I knew I had misjudged Mr. Johnson's malice, and his power.

"When I arrived at work this morning the foreman told me the bosses wanted to talk to me. I was to go to the superintendent's office. The superintendent was waiting for me with two Pinkerton detectives, as well as the mine officials. They asked me all kinds of questions about the union — was I an organizer, had I been talking to the other men? Where were we holding our secret meetings?"

"But you're not involved in any of that!" Momma said.

"I'm not, but I couldn't convince them of that," Papa said. "They said they knew I had been organizing, that I had a gathering after the funerals that they figure was a union meeting. And they said I had organized a network to smuggle goods into camp. They've seen people from all over camp coming in and out of our house, even the Welsh and Scottish from across the tracks. They figure the only reason we would mingle is to unionize. They said they wouldn't tolerate such 'subversive labor practices.' That's when they gave me my back pay and told me I would have to leave."

Momma looked at Papa, then at me, then back at Papa. Papa nodded.

"But what I'm doing isn't illegal!" I insisted again. "They can't do this!"

Papa shook his head. "It doesn't matter whether it's legal or not to them. They can fire or hire as they see fit. They don't have to put up with anyone who does something they don't like."

"But it has nothing to do with the unions or with your job," I said. "This was Mr. Johnson's doing. He's hated me since we bought those plums. He killed my chickens, and now he's lied to get you fired. It's not fair!"

"What do you mean, he killed your chickens?" Papa asked. Shamefaced, I told them everything I knew.

Anger flared in Momma's eyes. "Why didn't you say any of this before, Trina? You knew he could be dangerous. Why haven't you been more careful?"

"She couldn't have known, Ivana. She couldn't know he would go to the superintendent with lies."

"Well, know or not, you still have to make this right, Trina. You will go to the superintendent and apologize to the company.

Tell them your father had nothing to do with it so they will take him back! Promise to stop your little business right here and now!"

"I can't do that," I said. "My biggest order yet is coming this afternoon, and people have already paid for it. I have to pick up and make these deliveries. But Papa, with this week's orders we have nearly one hundred and eighty dollars saved! We don't need their job, right?"

Papa smiled at me, but it was a sad smile. "That's not enough for a farm, Trina. And with autumn already upon us, we wouldn't have a cent left come spring to buy seed, even if we did get a farm for so little. But it is a good cushion while I find other work, and that's a lucky thing. Run on about your business now, and let your momma and me sort out what we are going to do."

My heart was heavy as I walked down the hill with my sisters to meet Mr. Torentino that afternoon. Though Aneshka and Holena didn't know everything, they knew enough to be quiet on our walk. They each walked close, burrowing their hands into mine. At least I would have this one last order to deliver, and maybe Mr. Torentino would know of someplace that would have work for my papa. Or maybe Papa was wrong, and we *could* somehow get a farm with the money that we had. I could not bear the crushing disappointment of failure now, so I pretended to myself that all would become right when I saw Mr. Torentino.

I arrived at our usual meeting place a little early. I wanted to be sure to get there while he was still unloading Mr. Johnson's goods. But when I squinted up the road toward the store, I did not see his wagon. A hint of foreboding stirred within me. Mr. Torentino should have already been there, unloading or wrangling with Mr. Johnson about unkept promises, as he did every week.

Perhaps, because my order was so large this week, Mr. Torentino ran late loading it in Trinidad. Or maybe his team plodded up the hills toward our town more slowly than usual because of the extra weight in the wagon. I looked down the road in the other direction, but saw no sign of him coming. I began to pace nervously.

I was so unnerved by Mr. Torentino's absence that I forgot that I had arranged for the ladies who had placed orders to meet me, until the first of them appeared. I should have been completely unloaded and had their goods waiting for them long since. When I saw them and realized how late it was, hope died in my heart.

"I'm afraid my partner from town is running late today," I said as they gathered around me with questions. What else could I say? "But I'm sure he will be along. He's usually very punctual."

We waited there for another half an hour. With each minute that ticked by, more women arrived, more suspicious comments were whispered, and I grew more desperate. Something was very wrong, and I was going to have to face it alone.

"You haven't cheated us, have you?" said an impatient Welsh woman. Though it was a question, it was stated more as an accusation.

"No, of course not. Perhaps his wagon broke down."

"Or maybe his horse went lame," Aneshka suggested.

"Maybe we should get our money back," came another voice from the crowd.

"Please, you have to believe me. He always comes!"

A stir went through the crowd of women, and their

attention turned away from me. Women at the edges of the crowd scurried away. I turned to look where everyone else was looking. Mr. Johnson was approaching with three men in dark suits. Two of the men carried shotguns and wore badges. I couldn't read the badges, but I didn't have to. I knew they were the Pinkerton detectives my father had mentioned—the private police force of the mining camps. I had heard plenty of rumors about Pinkertons in our year in America, and none of them were good. The sight of the detectives now sent a bolt of fear through me. I whispered to Aneshka to run home with Holena, and I pushed them both away from me. The little girls slipped out of the crowd through the legs of the women. There was no such simple escape for me. I knew it from the look on Mr. Johnson's face when his eyes met mine.

Chapter 23

"WHAT'S GOING on here?" One of the detectives called out as he approached. "Who's in charge here?"

I glanced around at the women, every one of them struggling to get by. None of them could afford trouble with the mine.

"I am, sir," I said, stepping forward on trembling knees.

"You," the man said, surprised.

"She's the one, all right," Mr. Johnson said. "She's been nothing but trouble. She's a union rabble-rouser if there ever was one. Her and her pa, too."

The detective gave Mr. Johnson a doubtful look, and his shotgun sagged a little. "Hardly Mother Jones, is she? She's just a kid!" He looked back at me, a sarcastic smile on his face. "You a union organizer, miss?"

"No, sir," I said, trying to look as young and innocent as possible. "I am only thirteen."

"Then what's going on here?" Mr. Johnson demanded. "What are all these women doing here?"

The crowd had continued to scatter, but there were still women around me who had not been able to slip away. My mind raced for an answer, but I couldn't think of anything that would save us all.

"Sewing circle," said a bold voice behind me. I turned, and was surprised to see Nancy Llewellyn.

"Sewing circle?" asked one of the detectives.

"My oldest girl's getting married," Nancy said, "and we've fallen on hard times, a bit."

"So Trina, here, organized a sewing circle so the lass will have some pretty things to take with her," added Glenys.

"Is that so?" said the second Pinkerton, looking at me. "Friend of yours, is she?"

"Yes, sir," I said, trying to keep my voice steady.

"What's her name, then?"

"Mary." Half the girls in school were named Mary, so it was as good a guess as any. "We're schoolmates."

"So then let's see this sewing you're doing," Mr. Johnson said, trying to trap us in our lie.

I suppressed a smile as all the women around me pulled bits of sewing, mending, knitting, or crocheting from apron pockets. These were the sorts of things women carried with them to fill idle moments.

The detectives looked at each other, their shotguns now hanging casually at their sides. Mr. Johnson shouted at them to arrest me, but they only shook their heads and rolled their eyes. They did not seem to have any better opinion of the storekeeper than anyone else.

"You've got quite an imagination, Johnson," said one of the detectives. He turned back toward the store. The other clapped a hand on Mr. Johnson's shoulder to walk him back the same way, but Mr. Johnson jerked loose. He glared at me, practically purple with rage and humiliation.

"You think you're so clever, pulling the wool over their eyes, missy, but think again. You haven't got any of the things you sold. I'd say you better pay the money back or you could be finding yourself in jail. It's theft to take the money and not deliver the goods." He gave one last nasty smirk in my direction and turned to follow the Pinkertons back to his store.

The women dispersed quickly, but not without giving me looks of warning.

"We've got to have our goods or our money back," Glenys said before slipping away herself. "I'm sorry, lass, but that's just the way it is."

I nodded and fled to the one place I could be alone, the cottonwood by the creek. Once again, my family's hopes and dreams had been snatched away. I did not have the goods or the money to return to the women. Even if I paid them back with the money we had saved, it wasn't nearly enough. And besides, that money was all my family had now.

I simply had to get the goods, but it was impossible. Mr. Torentino must have been run off by the Pinkertons, and I had no way of bringing the delivery up from Trinidad myself. I had lost everything—Mark, our money, my business. And all for having believed once again in a foolish dream. I sunk down in my shady refuge, and gave in to my misery.

I don't know how long I cried beside the pool before Papa found me. Holena was with him, and of course she had known where to look. Papa sat down on the raised root of the tree and gently caressed my hair.

"There now, Trina. Things aren't so bad; you've just had a fright, that's all," he said.

I shook my head. "I'm sorry, Papa. I've ruined us. I didn't mean to." I could not go on. Fresh tears spilled down my cheeks.

"Trina, you are taking this too hard. I will find another job. Come to think of it, this is probably a lucky turn."

"But Papa, there's more that you don't know." Shakily I told him of the delivery that hadn't come. "People want their money or their goods, and I don't have either. Papa, it was eight hundred dollars! We can't even begin to repay them."

Papa's face looked grim and he sat silent for a long moment.

"I'm scared, Papa. What if they send me to jail? Mr. Johnson says—"

"Where does this Mr. Torentino come from?"

Papa's sudden question surprised me. "His store is in Trinidad. I have the address." I pulled the order book from my pocket and showed Papa the first page with the prices. Mr. Torentino had written the name and address of his store across the top.

"Then we will have to go find him. Come on."

"Today? Now?"

"We haven't got time to waste."

We returned home only long enough to tell Momma we were going and to gather a few things for our trip, including a substantial portion of our money. I wasn't sure that Mr. Johnson wouldn't concoct some reason for the Pinkertons to raid our home, and I couldn't bear to lose the money we had to them!

"If anyone comes for their order, tell them there has been a delay and I have gone to town to sort it out," I instructed Aneshka. She nodded seriously, a fierce look on her face, and I knew she was adequate to the task.

Momma frowned. "But Tomas, we are already in enough trouble. Let's just pack and go."

"We can't." Papa said. "Trina and I will be back tomorrow."

We set out on foot, carrying supper in Papa's lunch pail since we could not expect to reach Trinidad before nightfall. A shred of luck remained with us, for we encountered a farmer with a wagon headed to town. We hitched a ride for almost half our journey, but it was still past dark before we arrived in Trinidad, and all the businesses were closed. We walked the main streets, until we found Mr. Torentino's store. It occupied a brick storefront with a large glass window along the front. The words TORENTINO AND SONS MERCANTILE AND EXCHANGE were painted in large gold letters across the window. We stood outside and peered through the glass, looking for all the world like country yokels who had never seen a store before. It looked much like Mr. Johnson's store inside, the narrow interior crammed with everything under the sun. It was dark and silent, and there was no sign of Mr. Torentino.

"We'll come back in the morning," Papa said. We walked on, past the closed businesses around Mr. Torentino's store, pausing briefly in front of the land office, looking at the advertisements pasted on the board just inside the window. Everything cost more money than we had, and once again my hope failed me. Papa, though, smiled and pointed at listings for acres of fruit trees or prime river-bottom land for vegetables, pretending we could afford them. I let out a deep sigh of sadness, but Papa patted my hand where it nestled in his.

"Someday, Trina. You'll see," he said.

Turning from the land office, we crossed the street to the hotel, where we took a room with two narrow, squeaky beds.

Despite my exhaustion, it was hard to sleep in the strange room without my whole family around me. I was worried about Momma and my sisters, alone in our house. I was praying that Mr. Johnson and his Pinkerton detectives would not give them any trouble. I could hear Papa stirring in the next bed, and I knew he could not sleep either.

I squeezed my eyes shut, but a sense of shame washed over me. How had I gotten my family into this? I thought I had learned my lesson when the chickens were killed. How had I gone back to my foolish dreams, and made matters even worse?

"I'm sorry, Papa," I said into the darkness. "I didn't mean for this to happen."

"Nothing's happened yet, Trina. In fact"—Papa paused, but I could hear the mischief that had slipped into his voice—"I think it is just my wish going according to plan."

"Your wish?"

"Remember? I wished for a farm, and I thought it was the garden and chickens, but now I think I was wrong. This must be it—I got fired so I could get my farm."

"Papa, be serious," I said. I appreciated his attempt to make me feel better, but it didn't help. He didn't know that I really had, for a time, believed there was magic in those wishes.

"What good is being serious?" Papa said. "Besides, maybe I am serious. We don't any of us know what's going to happen, do we? So where's the harm in expecting the best instead of the worst?"

"Because it's like Momma says—dreams like that only lead to disappointment."

"And you were disappointed when your chickens died, weren't you."

"Yes," I said, feeling a lump rising again in my throat as I remembered that awful day.

"But was it really the loss of the chickens that hurt you, Trina?"

"No," I admitted. "It was so much more."

"Right. It hurt so much because you lost your dream that day. You gave up on all your hopes and plans."

I lay in silence, surprised that Papa understood all that so well, when I hadn't been able to make Momma understand. "So," I said, "that's my point. Dreams just set you up for disappointment."

"No, *giving up* sets you up for disappointment. That's the big difference," Papa said. "That's why I say we are on our way to getting that farm. I refuse to give up."

His logic was tugging at my heart, tempting me back into the dream. But fear and remembered pain held me back.

"Momma says only a fool believes in dreams," I said.

"Your Momma's afraid," he said quietly. "That is why we have to do her dreaming for her." I heard him shift in the bed. "But for now we had better get on with some real dreaming of our own, don't you think?"

I rolled over onto my side and realized I could sleep now. Papa had made me feel better. "Good night, Papa," I said.

The next morning we were up early. Papa waited patiently at Mr. Torentino's storefront door, but I couldn't hold still. My stomach was knotting with nerves. I paced the length of the block until he arrived to open.

"Mr. Torentino!" I cried from nearly a block away when I saw him putting his key into the lock. Two boys were with him, both somewhat younger than me. I assumed they were the sons referred to on his window.

He turned, looking surprised, then broke into a warm smile. "Miss Trina!"

"Mr. Torentino, I have to have those orders, or else the money back!" I blurted out, without even a "good morning."

226

He unlocked the door and ushered us inside, glancing around nervously as he did. When we were all in the cool, dusty interior of the store, he spoke again. "I am glad to see you safe, Trina. I was worried! Did they give you any trouble?"

"A little," I said. I introduced my father to Mr. Torentino and told him what had happened.

"They accused us of trying to organize a labor union, but I don't think Mr. Johnson really believes that. I think he just wanted to be rid of competition," I said.

Mr. Torentino nodded and smiled at Papa. "Your girl's got quite a head for business. When she first came up with this idea, I didn't think it would amount to much. This week I've gotten more business from her than from the coal company. That's what's got them scared."

"What happened to you?" I said. "Why didn't you come yesterday?"

"Well, I was up at the store at my usual time. My wagon was half-full of produce and canned goods for the store, and half-full of your orders. But I never unloaded a thing. When I stopped my wagon in front of the store, old Johnson steps out with three Pinkertons. One of them had a shotgun. I didn't even get down from my wagon seat before Johnson says, 'You been cheating me right under my nose.' I says, 'I don't know what you're talking about.' And he says, 'You've been supplying them union organizers, haven't you? I've seen all the extra goods that you don't unload here. And then next thing I know, there goes that Greek girl with a load of goods, up to camp. I know what you're up to.'

"And then, two of the Pinkerton men came up to my wagon and started pawing through everything, spoiling the vegetables while they were at it. I couldn't do a thing to stop them, as the one with the gun was keeping his eye on me every minute."

"Did they confiscate your merchandise?" Papa asked.

"Did they hurt you?" I added.

"No, but they made me plenty mad, that's for sure. I guess they were looking for guns or something illegal. I says to them, 'There's no law that says I can't deliver supplies to my customers here.' And old Johnson, he just laughs and says, 'No, but this is private property; this whole town belongs to CF&I. If you come up here again, we'll have you fined for trespassing. And no need to make other deliveries to me, either. I'll be doing business elsewhere.'

"Then his Pinkertons escorted me back down the road to the edge of the company land and told me to go on back home. I hated to leave without letting you know what had happened, Trina, but what else could I do? That man with the shotgun just kept standing in the road watching me. So I kept going, right back here with everything still loaded in my wagon."

"Were you scared?" I asked. Chills were creeping up my spine just listening to him.

"Mostly I was mad, but I'll admit it gave me a prickle on my neck to have that fellow with the shotgun watching at my back. I'd have been a lot more scared if you had been waiting for me. I've been worrying about you ever since. I'm awful sorry to hear what this has done to your family."

Papa nodded. "They say we've got to be out of our house and out of camp by tomorrow. You can see that we have a real problem if Trina doesn't have the money to give back to the people in the camp. They are going to demand it before we go."

"But I don't have it either. It's all in the merchandise on the wagon," Mr. Torentino said, "and I can't take my wagon back up there. If your customers will come to Trinidad, I'll be happy to give them their goods."

I shook my head. "It is fifteen miles or more," I said. "And no one in camp owns a horse or wagon. But—" I paused and thought. An idea was starting to form in my mind. "How much space does the merchandise take up in the wagon?"

"Without the delivery that went to the store, about half the bed."

"So if it was all spread out on the bottom, no one could see it without actually coming up and looking in."

"If you are thinking that I could sneak it in, forget it. I can't go back up there whether I have anything in my wagon or not. I'm sorry, Trina, but it's not worth the risk. The coal companies have so much power around here, they could put me right out of business if they wanted to."

"You can't go back up there, but we can, until tomorrow. In fact, we have to. So, I was wondering if Papa could borrow your wagon for my family to move our household into town," I said with an innocent smile.

Both Papa and Mr. Torentino stared at me.

"If they knew it was his wagon, they still might stop us," Papa said. "They will likely recognize his team."

"But if we wait until this evening to go into camp, after the store is closed we could get by. Besides, they admitted to Mr. Torentino that there was nothing illegal in his deliveries, just trespassing. And until tomorrow, we still live there, so we won't be trespassing."

"I don't know, Trina. There could still be trouble. They pretty much make the law up there," Mr. Torentino said.

"But if we don't do it, all those people will lose their money.

Mr. Johnson said I could be arrested for stealing. Please, Mr. Torentino? Papa?"

Papa nodded slowly. "I'll try it, if Mr. Torentino would be willing to loan us his wagon and team."

"It's the least I can do," Mr. Torentino said.

"Oh, thank you!" I exclaimed, feeling relieved and nervous all at the same time. I had to deliver the orders; I knew that. Still, the thought of getting caught by the Pinkertons sent another shiver along my spine.

"I wish I could do something more," Mr. Torentino said with a kind smile. "If you'll be staying here in town, I could offer Trina a few hours of work here in the store. It wouldn't be much, but I hate to see such a good head for business go to waste."

"What I was hoping is that I might find work on a farm," Papa said. "You know of any that need help?"

"I'm sure there's plenty that need help with the harvest," Mr. Torentino said. "But that won't keep you through the winter."

"We came to America to have a farm," I said. "If I had been able to take orders in camp for just a few more months, we might have been able to buy one."

Mr. Torentino's eyebrows raised. "You mean you have been saving your money all this time for your family?"

I nodded. "But it hasn't been enough."

Mr. Torentino laughed. "I figured you and your sisters were spending it on lemonade and candy and new dresses to impress the boys."

"No, sir."

"I should have known better. Like I said, a good head for business. So how much money have you saved up?"

"Not enough for a farm," I said. "I'll have one hundred and eighty dollars if I could fill this week's order."

"And I collected fifteen from the mine yesterday," Papa said. "They had to pay it all out in cash since they were firing me."

"Well, I have a few connections, but I have to get opened up here first," Mr. Torentino said. "Then, Trina, if you'll stay here with my boys and run the store, your papa and I can go talk to the folks at the land office."

Eagerly I agreed to the arrangement. While Papa and Mr. Torentino were gone, I waited on customers for him. When there were no customers, I gathered the necessary goods for my remaining orders. Mr. Torentino's sons, Antonio and Vincenzo, though younger than me, were very helpful. I better understood his willingness to work with me despite my young age.

When all the goods were gathered, I watched for Papa's return. With each passing hour I felt a little more nervous about my plan, and I knew that Momma must be beside herself with worry by now. Finally I saw Papa and Mr. Torentino approaching. They both looked pleased, which I hoped was good news. I wanted to ask the moment they came through the door, but I didn't get the chance. Before I could say a word, Papa had swept me off my feet and spun me around in a big hug.

"What did I tell you, Trina! Didn't I tell you? We've got a farm!"

I gasped. I couldn't help it; it was too much to believe. "A farm! A real farm?"

"On the Arkansas River," Mr. Torentino said with a smile. "Sixty acres of vegetables and another thirty of apple trees."

I pulled away from Papa. "So much? But we don't have the money for that!"

"Not to buy," Papa said, "but enough to lease. Turns out there's a fellow looking to move into town, but he hasn't been able to sell his farm, so he's willing to lease it."

"Lease it?" Such an idea had never occurred to me before.

Papa nodded, grinning wildly. "The papers are already drawn up. There'll be no real profit this year, since we didn't plant or tend the crops there now. But after that, we can use our profits toward buying it. And I think, Trina, that in just one good year, we could make the money to buy it. What do you think?"

I smiled. Papa was off and dreaming again, and he'd never looked happier. I was feeling pretty happy myself. Who would have thought so much good could come from so much trouble? I stepped back into Papa's embrace and let his big dreams and big arms catch me up.

"Why not, Papa. It's a new country and a whole new century," I said. And it was America—a land for dreamers—where lucky coincidences made those dreams come true. Or at least it had been for me, since I had seen a fish and made a wish.

Chapter 24

ALL THE WAY back to camp in the wagon, Papa was whistling Bohemian folk songs or talking about what we'd plant in the spring. I shared his happiness at first, but as we got closer to camp I felt increasingly nervous. We still had the load of goods to deliver. I had no choice but to deliver it, for Papa had already committed our saved money to the lease of the farm. Refunding so much as a penny to my customers was no longer an option.

One other fact weighed on me as well, marring my happiness. Leaving the mining camp meant saying good-bye to people I loved. Saying good-bye to Mark. The fear and excitement of the previous day had kept me from thinking about him or the little ring of copper wire I had returned to him. I wanted him to come away from the coal camp, but how was I to convince him? He'd made it plenty clear he had no desire to farm.

As we came nearer the camp, Papa's whistling quieted, then stopped altogether. I could see his expression through the dim light and knew that he was worried about trouble too.

"Do you think they'll be waiting for us?" I asked into a silence that was already filled with the question. We could see the mine hoist in the distance now, haloed by the setting sun.

Papa shaded his eyes with his hand. "Well, we'll know soon, won't we?" he said. I shaded my eyes too, and looked where his gaze was fixed. Someone was standing on the road ahead of us, just this side of the store. I felt my chest tighten and I forced in a deep breath. *It might not be anyone connected to us at all*, I reminded myself. But as we drew closer, I could see the man was watching our approach. With the sun behind him, I could not tell who it was, though he could probably recognize us.

"Should we keep going?" I asked uncertainly.

Papa shrugged, but his grip tightened on the reins. "What else can we do?"

We continued forward, now almost to within shouting distance of the man in the road. He could have easily called out a greeting to us, but instead he turned and ran back toward the camp.

"Well!" Papa said. "I do believe that's your Marek."

He was right. We could see Mark's uneven gait. As we watched, he ran past the store, which was closed at this hour, and on up the road until he was out of sight.

I felt relieved, but also confused. Why hadn't he greeted us or waited long enough to tell us whether or not the Pinkertons were watching for us?

"Perhaps he's gone to let Momma know we are coming," Papa said. "She's probably worried sick with us being so late."

"You are probably right," I agreed, but my nerves only tightened.

"Well," Papa said, "he gave no warning, so the road must be clear."

I nodded, but I gripped the seat tightly with both hands as we came into town, passing the company store first. The doors were closed and the lights were out in all the buildings, but I could not keep my eyes from turning toward them as we passed. I saw no movement in any window and no one stepped out any door. Once past the store, we were climbing the hill, passing the houses of our neighbors. Many of them were on their front porches and watched us pass. I looked back and saw several of them, those who had orders to be filled, rise from their chairs and follow us up the road. By the time Papa reined in the team in front of our house, it would have looked like a welcome-home parade if not for their silent, nervous expressions. They wanted their goods, but they didn't want trouble with the mine officials.

Momma was on the front porch, drying her hands on a towel as Papa stopped the wagon and we both jumped down. Papa hurried up the steps and grabbed her in a hug like he had done to me as he announced the good news. Momma gave a quick, girlish squeal of surprise that set both of my sisters giggling, but over the din of it all, Papa was telling Momma of the farm.

I looked around. "Where's Mark?" I asked. He should have been here after the way he had run ahead of us.

Old Jan, who had been sitting on the porch with my sisters, put his arm around my shoulders and walked me back off the porch and toward the wagon, where women were congregating. His face wore a worried, strained expression.

"Do you have those purchases you went for?" he asked.

"I do."

"Then you better get on with your deliveries as quick as you can."

"But where's Mark?" I asked again.

Old Jan glanced around before he spoke in a low voice. "He's at the superintendent's office."

My heart froze. Had Mark been stopped by the Pinkertons when he had run ahead of us?

"He's not going to get fired too, is he?"

"Just get your deliveries taken care of," Old Jan said. "Quickly."

I nodded and climbed up into the wagon, calling Aneshka and Holena to help, and we were soon handing down goods to the women who had followed us. I had expected to be done with that quickly, as only a handful of women had seen our wagon coming into camp, but soon I noticed that the line was not getting any shorter, and I was handing out goods to women who lived several streets away. Word was apparently spreading fast. Within an hour, I had dispersed nearly everything.

Aneshka and Momma set off to deliver the few orders that remained so that Papa and I could eat our supper. We were just walking up the porch steps when someone shouted behind us.

"There they are—and that's Torentino's wagon. I recognize his team! I knew it!"

We turned back to see Mr. Johnson walking toward us, Mark beside him. He didn't look like he had been dragged in by the Pinkertons. No one was forcing him to walk with Mr. Johnson. I threw a questioning glance at him, but he looked away.

"If you've brought contraband goods to this town, I'll have you arrested!" Mr. Johnson shouted, running to the wagon to look inside. When he saw that the bed was empty, he didn't seem to know whether to puff up indignantly or slink away shamefaced.

"We rented the team and wagon to move to town," Papa said. "So we can get out of our house by the deadline."

Mr. Johnson squinted at us, angry he hadn't caught us red-handed. Then he wagged a finger at my father. "You think you're so smart, do you? Well, don't. We know all about you—this boy has told us everything about your secret union meetings."

"But that's a lie!" I said, looking angrily at Mark. "There were no secret meetings here."

Mr. Johnson gave a snorting laugh, his arrogance returning in force. "We know all about you now, and word's gone out to every other mine in the state. You won't find work anywhere. You're finished in the mines. You might as well pack up your bags and go back to where you came from."

Papa and I looked at each other for a brief moment, then Papa burst out laughing.

"You're right, Mr. Johnson," Papa said. "We are finished in the mines. Good-bye."

We went inside and shut the door behind us, but not before seeing Mr. Johnson's shocked expression. My father was still laughing.

I watched through the window to make sure he did no harm to the team or the wagon. It was probably the sort of thing he would gladly have done if he'd thought of it. As it was, he was so surprised by Papa's reaction that he did nothing but walk away. I might have laughed too, but through the gathering darkness, I could see someone else turn away.

Tears sprang to my eyes. I knew Mark was angry with me, but I never thought he would be spiteful toward my whole family. The pain of his betrayal was sinking in now that the confrontation with Mr. Johnson was over. I skipped the supper my papa was piling on a plate for me and went straight to bed, where I cried myself to sleep before my sisters got home.

* * *

The next morning we were all up early. We ate a hasty breakfast of oat porridge and coffee. Momma, who had been up before any of us, packed a cold lunch of bread, pickles, and cheese. When breakfast was done, we cleaned everything in the kitchen and arranged it all in the washtubs or crates, using towels and blankets to cushion the few fine things Momma had brought with her from Bohemia. Packing was not a difficult task; after a year in America we had little more than what we had come with. Yet our hearts and minds were all filled to bursting with the realization of Papa's dream, and that gave a new richness to our labors.

Of our neighbors, only Old Jan and Martina came to help us. She brought plum kolaces for our dinner on the road and stayed to help Momma fold the sheets and blankets so they would come out crisp and ready to use. Old Jan helped lift our goods up into the bed of the wagon. I avoided him, still too angry about his son's lies to want to face him.

When nearly everything was in the wagon, Old Jan and my sisters took the team to the creek to drink and eat a few mouthfuls of grass before we hitched them up. I stayed behind to help Momma with the last few chores. Papa found me out back a short time later, beating the dirt from the last rag rug.

"That will do, Trina. Don't you have any good-byes you want to say before you go?" he said, jabbing his thumb over his shoulder toward Mark's house. "He's working the night shift again, so he should be home."

Bitter anger surged in me again. "He betrayed us, Papa! He lied to the superintendent about you just to get us in trouble. I never want to see him again!"

Papa's eyebrows shot up. "Is that what's been bothering you all this time? Trina, it was a trick."

"A trick?"

"The superintendent and his detectives will listen for hours to anyone willing to squeal on union organizers. Marek knew we were going to need time to unload goods if we had them. When he saw us coming, he ran to the superintendent and told them the kind of stories they wanted to hear so we had time to unload. Old Jan explained it all last night."

"Why did he say you'd had meetings, then?" I said, still angry.

"Well, what harm could the mine do to me? He didn't want to get anyone else in trouble who still needed the job here."

"What about them?" I asked. "If he said he'd been at these meetings, couldn't he have been in trouble too?"

Papa's face grew serious and he nodded. "It was certainly a big risk for him. We can only hope that it doesn't come back to hurt them. He did it for you, Trina. Now go say good-bye."

Tears burned my eyes as I realized the size of my mistake. Mark had risked his own job to help me get a dream, even though that dream stood in the way of what he wanted. I put down my broom and hurried to Mark's house.

He was not home, so I knew where he had to be. If he had things on his mind, he had always gone to the same place I went, so I set off for the creek. At the creek bottom I found the horses tethered in a patch of dry grass where they were chewing contentedly. But my sisters and Old Jan were not with them. It seemed all our paths led to the same place in this last hour before we left the camp for good. That felt right to me. Whether there was any magic in that quiet pool or not, it was forever linked to our dream in America. I was glad to get the chance to say good-bye to Mark and his father there, where so many good things had happened. And I hoped that the spot might have one more bit of magic left for Mark and me.

When I rounded the bend, I saw what I had expected to see. The cottonwood leaves were turning autumn gold, and Old Jan, Mark, and my sisters were all together in their golden shade. I had thought that perhaps my sisters had taken Old Jan there so he could tell them one last story, but the telling seemed to be the other way around. Aneshka was talking up a storm, her hands gesturing wildly. Holena was nodding in agreement and throwing bits of bread into the pool. Mark was sitting by himself a short distance from the others with his back toward them and his shoulders hunched. A painful tug at my heart stilled my breath when I saw him.

Aneshka glanced up from her storytelling and saw me approaching. A huge smile spread across her face and she gave a quick bounce of excitement.

"Trina's here! Now he will come for sure!" she called excitedly. She ran to me and grabbed my hand, to pull me to the tree.

"What? Who will come?" I asked. Everyone I expected to see was already there.

"The magic carp, of course," Aneshka said.

Old Jan smiled up at me from his seat on the tree root. "Your sisters have been telling me the whole story of your wishes, and how they have all come true. They brought me here so I could see the carp and make a wish too."

Holena turned to me. "Please help us find him, Trina. We want Old Jan to get a farm too."

"And he could wish to have his leg back," Aneshka said.

"And Mark could marry you," Holena added quietly.

"Holena!" I said, glancing, mortified, at Mark's back. He gave no sign that he had heard, but I knew he had.

Old Jan laughed. "That's an awful lot to wish for," he said.

"But we got all our wishes," Aneshka pointed out.

"But you have to see the fish first," said Holena, "and we've been down here a long time. I don't think he's going to come."

"Well, never mind, girls," said Old Jan. "Magic carp can be finicky things. They don't show themselves until they're good and ready."

The twinkle of pleasure in his eyes warmed me. "That's true," I agreed. "But Old Jan will still be here, Aneshka. He can come look for it, and sooner or later, he's bound to see it. Then he can make whatever wish he wants to."

"Will you, Old Jan?" asked Aneshka. "Promise you will come down here every day until you see the carp and make your wishes."

"Please?" Holena said.

"Well, I don't know if I can promise every day," said Old Jan, "but I'll try, for you girls."

"Oh, but it's not for us," Aneshka said. "It's for you."

"This is all such nonsense!" Mark said suddenly, jumping to his feet. "Enough of your magic and your wishes and your dreams, Papa! It all comes to nothing!"

"But it hasn't," I said. "My family has their farm, and we are going there right at harvest. Come with us, Mark. Please."

"We've been through this before, Trina."

"But it would just be for a little while. You could look for work in town. Maybe you could even go to high school. You told me once you had planned to do that before your papa's accident."

"It wouldn't make a difference! I'm a coal miner, and I'll always be a coal miner, and that's not good enough for you."

"But what about your dreams for the future?" I begged.

"My dream for the future was you. I don't think I believe in dreams anymore."

I stepped forward and took his hand. "Mark, I love you. If you would just try again, I promise I will wait for you, and I'll go anywhere with you."

"Anywhere but here," he said.

Slowly I nodded. "Anywhere but here."

"And with this foot, I can't work anywhere else."

"But you can, if you just try! If you would just believe—"

Mark shook his head and pulled his hand out of mine. "It's all dreams, Trina. And for a while you had me believing, but life isn't like that. Life isn't one of Papa's fairy tales, full of dreams and wishes and magic fish." He paused and took a deep breath. When he spoke again, he was pleading with me, his eyes desperate. "I have something here, Trina. It may not be much, but it's real. Stay with me, like you promised."

"I can't, even if I wanted to. Mr. Johnson would just have you fired too, to get rid of me."

"And, you don't want to."

I dropped my eyes and shook my head again.

"Good-bye, then," he said, bitter and defeated. He stepped out of the shade and walked away without looking back. I wanted to run after him and beg him to change his mind, but I knew it was no use. I sat down on the root, trying to fight back tears, but without success. Holena sat down beside me and slipped her hand into mine.

"He'll change his mind, Trina, when he hears how nice our farm is," she said. "You will write him every day. He'll see how much he misses you, and he'll come join us and marry you, and you'll be happy. Okay?"

Despite my sadness, I couldn't help smiling at her innocent faith. "You are just like Papa," I said, hugging her to me.

She squeezed my hand and nestled against me. "So are you."

"Come on, we're wasting time!" Aneshka said. "Trina, help us make the fish come out."

The pool had shrunk over the summer to little more than a wide spot in the creek. I could see no sign of the fish. I couldn't even be sure it was still there now that the water was so low. With noisy Aneshka there and the water no longer lapping at the roots of the tree, the magical feel of the place was gone. Or maybe the magical feeling was gone because all the wishes had been granted.

I shook my head to clear it of the idea. Though it had only been a few months since I'd first come here, I felt much more grown up. I planned to face the future with a clear head. No more magic fish for me.

"Aneshka," I said, "seeing the fish won't make any difference. Everyone has to do what they will in their own time."

Aneshka stamped her foot. "But it will! The fish is magic! You saw it, and we got three wishes."

"It's true we got our wishes," I said, thinking back over all that had happened that summer, "but we've worked hard for them too, haven't we. The fish didn't send me to the Llewellyns' house to do their washing, or to Mr. Torentino for jars." I laughed at a new thought. "In fact, you might say it was Mr. Johnson who granted our wishes. He's the one who sent away the plums, overcharged me for the jars, and made Papa and me go to Trinidad for the order. Why don't you go ask Mr. Johnson for three more wishes, Aneshka."

She glared at me. "You said you believed, Trina. You said so yourself!"

I nodded. "I did believe, and that's when things really started getting better. I think—" I paused and chose my words carefully, wanting to get it right. "I think the magic was in the believing, and not the other way around."

Aneshka looked confused, but Old Jan smiled and nodded. "Believing can be powerful magic, indeed."

"But if there's no magic fish, what is there to believe in?" Aneshka said.

"Your dreams," I said. "Don't you see? Once we believed we could get our dream, we all started working harder for it and didn't give up. Well, *you* didn't give up, Aneshka, even when I did, and you pulled me back when I strayed. Hard work and believing is what got us our farm."

"That's not true!" Aneshka said. "How do you explain the plums? How do you explain that Mr. Torentino just happened to know someone with a farm for us? That wasn't our hard work; that was magic!"

"Well, let's think about that," Old Jan said slowly, considering. "The plums were certainly lucky. But as for the farm, what does Mr. Torentino do for a living?"

"He owns a store," Aneshka said.

"More than that. He brings all kinds of goods to the mining camps like ours, right? He buys produce from farmers and sells it to Mr. Johnson. He probably knows a hundred farmers, and farming's hard work for low pay. Some of them are bound to be as desperate to get out as you are here. I think opportunities are probably around us all the time, but we have to be looking for them before we see them. What do you think?"

Aneshka frowned, but before she could answer, Papa appeared from upstream with the horses and called to us. Holena and Aneshka both got to their feet. Aneshka gave Old Jan a hug. "I still think it's magic," she insisted before flouncing off to where Papa was waiting.

"Maybe when Mark sees it like Trina does, his dreams will come true too," Holena said to Old Jan as she hugged him.

He patted her cheek and smiled. "Perhaps."

He chuckled as he watched her skip away. "With her wisdom, Holena will always have magic," he said.

"And Aneshka?" I asked. We watched as she took the reins from Papa and started bullying the horses up the path.

"That one won't need magic. She'll make things happen all on her own."

"And Mark?" I asked quietly after a moment. "What about Mark?"

Old Jan sighed. "My little Marek has let magic slip through his fingers, and not for the first time."

"Do you think Holena is right? Do you think he might still change his mind if I write?"

Old Jan gave a sad sigh. "Marek gave up on his dreams when I lost my leg. That was my fault, I suppose, because I quit believing. He tried to revive his dreams this summer, but they are so fragile, Trina. Maybe, when his heart is not so full, he'll find the strength to try again.

"As for me, watching you this summer has me believing again. I think you may be leaving behind just enough magic for the two of us."

I brushed tears from my cheeks and gave Old Jan a hug. "I'll miss you," I said.

"Write when you can, child," he said.

I started back up the path, toward where Papa and my sisters had disappeared around the bend. Just enough magic, he had said, but I was leaving behind more than that. I was leaving behind good people, the hardest thing of all to leave. But just maybe I was leaving behind enough hope for a wish, and of course, there was still the magic carp.

No sooner than I had the thought, I heard the familiar soft

plop in the water. I turned to look back. Ripples were forming on the surface of the pool, and the fish's nose was just breaking the surface as it nibbled on a bit of Holena's bread. Old Jan turned toward it, and I could see his lips move.

Smiling to myself, I turned and climbed the bank to join my family as we set out once again, chasing the dream that had brought us to America.

Author's Note

WHILE I have not specified the coal camp in which this story takes place, I have tried to make the setting of this novel typical of the coal camps of southern Colorado around the year 1900. Though they were called "camps," these were permanent communities where many mining families spent their entire lives. The coal companies owned all the houses, stores, saloons, and gathering places in the towns, and since they were somewhat isolated from other communities, there were few options for residents other than those the coal company provided.

The many nationalities of miners that I have presented are accurate to those found in turn-of-the-century coal camps. Prior to 1900, the Welsh and Scottish were recruited heavily, and they were established in some of the better-paying jobs by the time my story starts. After 1900, the mines recruited heavily from eastern and southern Europe. They believed that by maintaining a large population of diverse foreigners who spoke many different languages, they could keep their labor force from unionizing, since the immigrants could not communicate well.

Of course, the difficulties in communication also led to more accidents in the mines, which increased the distrust among ethnic groups. And mining accidents were common. In 1900, half of all workers' deaths in the United States occurred in two industries: coal mining and railroading.

To create authentic details for the family life of miners, I relied heavily on the book *Coal People: Life in Southern Colorado's Company Towns 1890–1930* by Rick J. Clyne (Colorado Historical

Society, 2000), which not only describes the social life of the camps but contains numerous firsthand accounts of what life was like. Many of the background details of my story are based on the anecdotes recorded in those accounts. I also drew upon visits to the area and historic photos in the Western History Archives of the Denver Public Library, which can be accessed by the general public online at photoswest.org. Prices for goods were taken from newspaper ads of the era, and inflated, as they would have been in the coal company stores.

The Eastern European fairy tales told by Old Jan are all traditional stories, although I allowed Old Jan to tell them in his own style, as all traditional storytellers do. Versions of some of these stories can be found in the Favorite Fairy Tales series, retold by Virginia Haviland and published by Little, Brown and Company. For variety, other versions of the same or similar stories were found on the Internet.

Acknowledgments

I OWE heartfelt thanks to a number of people. My mother Betty and daughter Leah have always been my first and best readers. I have benefited from the advice, encouragement, and at times much needed nagging, from excellent critique partners: Mike, Megan, Kiersten, Jenn, Victoria, Lisa, and Rebecca. My son Greg has been my go-to idea man and keeps me laughing, and I suspect my husband Ken has stayed in bed longer than he really wanted to some Saturday mornings to give me quiet time to write. In addition, thank you to my young beta readers, Holland and Graham, who helped me see it through middle-grade eyes.

Once my little manuscript got past all of them, it benefited from the wisdom, insight, and professionalism of my brilliant agent, Erin Murphy, and my wonderful editor at McElderry, Karen Wojtyla. And to her patient assistant Emily Fabre and all the behind-the-scenes folks at Simon & Schuster who take a stack of pages and turn it into a beautiful book, thank you.

Turn the page for
a first look at

Searching for
SILVERHEELS

JEANNIE MOBLEY

I T'S STRANGE HOW SOMETIMES, even though the whole world is changing around you, everything can feel so much the same. President Wilson had declared war on Germany just two months ago, and everyone was stepping up to do their part. My father had gone up onto the mountain to mine zinc for the war effort, folks were planting victory gardens, and young men were talking of enlisting. Yet here I was, same as always, working every day in the Silverheels Café. The old timers were at their table in the corner, just like always, talking at length about nothing in particular. My best friend Imogene was at the counter, trying to flirt with my big brother Willie, who only had eyes for his breakfast. And I was refilling cup after cup of coffee and facing a long day of taking orders and hauling plates without much chance of escape.

"Order, Pearl!" Mother called from the kitchen. I went to retrieve the plates of eggs and bacon for the old timers. Mother fed them nearly every morning, come rain or shine, whether or not they had money to cover their bills. Neighbors do for neighbors, she always said, and it seemed to be true. Those who never had the cash always seemed to find other ways to pay—fresh fish or game for the kitchen, or a load of firewood for the stove. And with father away at the mine this summer, there'd likely be plenty of chores needing doing. Father had left Willie to be the man around the house, but so far, he'd made himself scarce most days, and keeping the café going had fallen to Mother and me.

I stepped from the kitchen back out into the café just as George Crawford and his mother stepped through the front door. Imogene glanced at them, then turned a pointed stare at me, her eyebrows bobbing. I tried to ignore her and offer a polite good morning to George and his mother, but I'm sure George noticed the rush of blood that flooded my cheeks.

"Good morning, Pearl," he said with a smile. George had the most stunning smile in all of Park County. Even girls who had no interest in him said so, not that there were many of those. Possibly the only girl who claimed no interest was Imogene, and that was mainly because she was my best friend and knew how I felt. Besides, she was sweet on Willie.

Mrs. Crawford directed George to the table in the opposite corner from the old timers and began to peel off her kidskin gloves. Why she bothered to put them on at all mystified me; the Crawford General Store was only just across the street and a block down, but Mrs. Crawford was always a lady. At least, in her appearance.

"Coffee, please, Pearl," she called, even before she sat

down. I hurried with my load of plates to the old timers' table, then I went behind the counter to retrieve the coffee pot from its warmer. Imogene leaned across the counter toward me and whispered, "George is watching you."

"Shh!" I said.

She sat back and spoke in a voice loud enough for everyone in the café to hear. "We have some tourists at the hotel, Pearl. They came in last night and reserved a room for four nights."

I paused, waiting for her to go on. This was good news. Tourism was likely to be down this summer with the war on, and that meant less business for our café as well as Imogene's family that ran the hotel.

"They look like the type that might want a tour, too," Imogene continued. Most years this would have been good news, too. My father and I made a few extra dollars in the summer taking folks on excursions. This year, though, with Father away, I wasn't sure if I'd be able to do that, no matter how much I wanted to.

Oblivious to my dilemma, Imogene kept talking. "There are three of them. A fashionable young couple, Mr. and Mrs. Robert Fischer, and a fellow about our age named Frank. Frank is *mightily* handsome!" She said the last with a hopeful glance at Willie, but he showed no sign of jealousy. Imogene sighed.

"Where's that coffee, Pearl? And George might want a cinnamon roll, when you are done with your little chat," said Mrs. Crawford.

"Yes, ma'am. Sorry," I said, snatching up a cup and the pot and hurrying to her table. George did want a roll, so I hurried to the kitchen and cut the very biggest one from the pan, as I always did when it was for George. I don't know if he ever noticed, but he always gave me that stunning smile when I placed it before him, which was worth more than the biggest cinnamon roll in the world.

I reluctantly turned from George's smile when the bell on the door clattered. Everyone in the café turned to see the three tourists step inside.

Imogene was right when she had called them fashionable. The lady's skin was lily white, her fingers long and delicate, and her corset was cinched so tight, her waist was as thin as a wasp's. No one in Como had hands so soft, a waist so thin, or clothes so fine, not Mrs. Crawford or even Mrs. Engel who ran the millinery and yard goods shop. The lady's hat angled jauntily on her smooth dark hair, the ostrich plume sweeping elegantly behind her. She wore a starched white shirtwaist, all ruffled up the front, and a blue skirt that reached just to the tops of her pearl-buttoned boots, according to the latest fashion. She was exactly what I imagined the ladies in my dime novels looked like. I could easily see her in distress, being rescued by a brave hero.

The man who escorted her, however, struck me as more of a dandy than a brave hero. He wore his hair parted neatly in the center and slicked down tight against his head. From his crisp, pin-striped traveling suit and polished leather shoes, I could tell he hadn't stepped off pavement very often in his life. Nor did he want to, judging from the sneer on his face as he took in the locals in their work clothes and sturdy boots.

The boy Frank tagged along behind the couple. He was close to my age or a little older, perhaps fourteen. Though he looked good natured, Imogene had exaggerated when she called him mightily good looking. Unlike his companions, he hadn't bothered much with his clothes, and was a little disheveled. His hair needed a cut and a comb. The top button was missing from his shirt, and his collar, where it rubbed his neck, was brown with dirt. He walked with his hands crammed into his pockets and glanced around him as if he was eager to see new things. I gave him a warm smile of welcome. *Exactly the sort of person who would want a tour*, I thought. Surely I could do it on my own if we didn't go far.

As soon as they were seated, I fetched the coffee pot to their table. The young lady smiled up at me. She was not old enough to be the boy's mother. She had to be an older sister, or at most, a youthful aunt.

"What smells so good?" she asked.

"My mother's cinnamon rolls," I said. "Fresh baked. And there's hotcakes, eggs with sausage, fatback, or hash. Oh, and oatmeal."

The gentleman laughed. "That's the whole menu? No wonder it's not printed up."

My face colored. I didn't have anything against city folks, even if most of them couldn't tell a pine tree from a horse's rear end, but I didn't think they had a right to come to our town and make fun of us. Still, they might want a tour, so I smiled. My politeness paid off, too, because after they ordered, the woman said, "We have the whole day here before going on. Can your kitchen prepare a lunch basket?"

"Yes ma'am," I said. "It's going to be a fine day for a picnic." I glanced out the window as I said it, only to have my hopes plummet to my toes. Old Josie Gilbert was stumping up the street toward the café. She wore her usual ragged miner's overalls, and bulky men's boots. Her iron gray hair was pulled back severely from her tanned and wrinkled face. As usual, she carried a stack of leaflets under her arm and a determined look in her black eyes. She was sure to drive away any visitors in no time if she was campaigning—and that look in her eye told me she was.

'I'll get your order in right away," I said hastily. I hurried into the kitchen even as I heard the bell on the door signal Josie's arrival.

"That's Josie, and she's campaigning!" I complained to my mother.

"Mrs. Gilbert," my mother corrected without looking up from the eggs she was cracking into the big skillet on the stove. "Remember your manners."

"She never does," I grumbled. Mother gave me a sharp look.

"She's bad for business," I persisted. "Tell her she can't

hand out her leaflets in here, Mother. Please? She scares away the tourists."

"You're exaggerating, Pearl."

"Well she makes them uncomfortable."

"Perline Rose Barnell, she's your elder and you'll speak of her with respect. She's got the same right as anybody to say her piece. Now go serve her politely, and let me get on with my work."

I gave my mother the new order and returned to the front.

Josie had already swooped in on the tourists and they were each gazing at a leaflet with polite disinterest.

"Women have had the vote in Colorado since 1893, but that doesn't mean we can rest. We have to keep up the fight for our sisters across this great nation!"

"Honestly!" said Mrs. Crawford at the corner table. She stood. "Come along, George. I won't sit here and listen to this." George rose, and with a polite nod and thanks to me, he followed her out of the café. I watched him go, mortified that Josie had driven them away.

Indifferent to my embarrassment, Josie's voice was rising in a self-righteous lecture. "The National Women's Party intends to send a united message to Mr. Wilson in the White House. The fight for liberty isn't just overseas. It is right here at home, in your kitchens and parlors. Everywhere women are found!"

The city folks set the leaflets down on the table and glanced at each other uncomfortably. Josie barreled on.

"Our forefathers said it best—no taxation without representation. It's high time that applied to every adult citizen of this country."

I looked desperately to the old timers for help. Tom, Harry, and Orv bent over their coffee cups and pretended not to notice my look. Only Russell took pity on me.

"Sit down, Josie, and leave those poor folks alone. You're curdling the milk in their coffee," he said.

Josie turned a glare on Russell and I used the opportunity to slide a chair over to the old timers' table and fill an extra cup with coffee for her.

"Thanks a lot, Russell," Orv muttered. Russell smiled at Josie and patted the chair I'd pulled up beside him. "Come have something to eat, Josie. Eggs and bacon, perhaps?"

She scowled, but lumbered over. She had a clumsy limp that made her broad frame roll back and forth like a ship in a choppy sea. She plopped down into the chair.

"I'll have the flapjacks," she said.

"With plenty of syrup," added Orv. "Maybe it'll sweeten her up a little."

"Sweet," she grumbled. "Why is it women have to be sweet for fool men like you? Mark my words, Orv. Someday women won't just vote, we'll do everything men do, and then we'll see who's sweet."

"In the meantime, you surely do put the sufferin' in suffragette," Harry said.

Russell fought down a smile and slid the cup toward her.

"Drink your coffee and let's talk about the weather, like decent folks. I think we're in for a dry summer."

I hurried back to the kitchen to see if Mother had breakfast ready for the tourists. I carried their food carefully, smiling as I set each plate before the correct person, hoping to make up for any offense Josie might have caused.

"The man at the hotel said someone here named Pearl could give us good advice about where to go on our outing. Is that your mother?" the lady asked.

"No, ma'am, that's me," I said eagerly. I could tell by the way her eyebrows raised that she wasn't sure about taking advice from a thirteen-year-old kid.

"Annie here, would like a picnic," said the slick man. "And Frank probably wants an adventure, don't you Frank."

The boy shrugged, but I could tell he did.

"I have maps, a penny apiece, that show all the sights in the valley, and I'd be happy to take you to any of them." If, of course, Mother would let me go without Father.

"Sounds like a penny well spent," Frank said. "Do you have a penny, Robert?"

Robert pulled a coin out of his vest pocket and handed it to me.

I scurried to the kitchen to retrieve one of my maps. In the winter months, when trains were few and far between and the station master was glad for the company, I traced the old railroad land office map at the depot. Now that the tourist season was starting, I had a good supply of them.

"Let's see," Annie said, flattening the map on the table beside her plate. "What do you recommend? We have all day."

"If you want to try your hand at fishing, I'd recommend the Tarryall," I said, running my finger along the line of the river leading upstream from town.

"The only way I want to see a trout is Almandine," Robert said. Annie giggled and he looked pleased with himself.

"Where's a good spot for our picnic?" asked Frank.

"Good old Frank, always thinking with his stomach," Robert said. Frank looked embarrassed and I felt sorry for him, the odd wheel at the table.

"You might try Buckskin Creek," I said, pointing along another route. "There's a good buggy track as far as Buckskin Joe, if you like ghost towns."

"Are there real ghosts?" Frank asked eagerly. I smiled at his enthusiasm.

"It's what we call the empty mining camps," I explained. He looked mildly disappointed, so I added, "There is a cemetery at Buckskin Joe, though."

I was going to tell him more, but Robert interrupted. He was looking at the white capped peak I'd drawn behind the town, his finger on the label, "Mount Silverheels."

"So did you name your café after the mountain? Or is this such a fine culinary establishment that they named a whole mountain after your café?" he said with a grin.

Annie smiled at Robert. Frank scowled at him. I liked Frank.

"The mountain is named for the most beautiful woman ever to set foot in Park County. She saved the town of Buckskin Joe, and some say she still walks its cemetery."

"Really?" Frank said, brightening again. "That sounds promising. Go on."

So I began.

Did you **LOVE** this book?

Want to get access to great books for **FREE?**

Join

Simon & Schuster
IN THE book**loop**

where you can

✗ Read great books for FREE! ✗

• Get exclusive excerpts •

§ Chat with your friends §

Log on to join now!

∞ everloop.com/loops/in-the-book

Meet Hilary McKay's Casson Family: Cadmium, Saffron, Indigo, and Rose.

Praise for *New York T...*
bestseller *The Winte...*

"Highly reminiscent of Barbara Erskine's *Lady of Hay* and Mary Stewart's works: evocative novels that lift readers straight into another time and place to smell the sea, feel the castle walls, see history, and sense every emotion. These are marks of a fantastic storyteller."

—*RT Book Reviews*

"An emotionally poignant, gripping tale of adventure both in the past and the present with characters full of life, and conflicts that tug at the heart strings. A definite read!"

—*History Undressed*

"A creative tour de force. Sometimes an author catches lightning in a bottle, and Susanna Kearsley has done just that."

—*New York Journal of Books*

"A deeply engaging romance and a compelling historical novel... Susanna Kearsley has written a marvellous book."
—Bernard Cornwell, bestselling author of *The Burning Land*

"Kearsley's writing is touching, her imagery is vivid and her characters are deep, intense, and intriguing. *The Winter Sea* successfully tells two stories at the same time leading up to an absolutely brilliant ending."

—*Rundpinne*

"One of the most enchanting romance novels of the decade... immensely unforgettable... a literary work of art deserving of the highest praise... had me utterly enthralled."

—*Romance Fiction on Suite 101*

"Fascinating... skillful writing and research... enthralling."
—*Historical Novels Review*

"Pure magic... I found myself just sinking in to the beautiful descriptions and prose... a fantastic read."
—*Queen of Happy Endings*

"My favorite book of the year."
—*The Royal Reviews*

"The rich history and the historical aspect of this novel made it hard to put down."
—*The Romance Studio*

"A stunning, gorgeous, and heart-wrenching tale."
—*Psychotic State*

"Marvelous and flawless... A magical work of narrative bound to please all fans of historical fiction."
—*Read All Over Reviews*

"Completely captured me... a thoroughly escapist read but also a dazzling adventure... Beautiful, clear writing, a believable story line, adventure, and romance landed *The Winter Sea* on my list of favorites for 2010."
—*Bookfoolery and Babble*

"An epic story rich in historical detail."
—*In the Hammock*

"A breathtaking novel."
—*Luxury Reading*

THE
ROSE
GARDEN

SUSANNA KEARSLEY

Sourcebooks and the colophon are registered trademarks of Sourcebooks, Inc.

Published by Sourcebooks Landmark, an imprint of Sourcebooks, Inc.
P.O. Box 4410, Naperville, Illinois 60567-4410
(630) 961-3900
FAX: (630) 961-2168
www.sourcebooks.com

Library of Congress Cataloging-in-Publication Data

Kearsley, Susanna.
  The rose garden / Susanna Kearsley.
    p. cm.
  1. Time travel—Fiction. 2. Great Britain—History—George I, 1714-1727—
Fiction. I. Title.
  PR9199.3.K4112R67 2011
  813'.54—dc23

                              2011027394

                    Printed and bound in Canada
                    WC 10 9 8 7 6 5 4

For my sister, who, as always,
has gone on a step ahead,
and still dances in my memory
and my heart.

Let the new faces play what tricks they will
In the old rooms; night can outbalance day,
Our shadows rove the garden gravel still,
The living seem more shadowy than they.

—William Butler Yeats
"The New Faces"

CHAPTER 1

I LOST MY ONLY sister in the last days of November.

It's a rotten time to lose someone, when all the world is dying too and darkness comes on earlier, and when the chill rains fall it seems the very sky is weeping. Not that there's ever a good time to lose your best friend, but it seemed somehow harder to sit there and watch in that hospital room, with the white-coated specialists coming and going, and see only grey clouds beyond the hard windows that offered no warmth and no hope.

When my sister had first fallen ill, we would sometimes go out to the garden and sit side by side on the bench by the butterfly bush. We would sit a long time, saying nothing, just feeling the sun on our faces and watching the butterflies dance.

And the illness had seemed very small then—a thing she could conquer, the way she had overcome everything else fate had flung in her path. She was famous for that, for her spirit. Directors would cast her in roles that were more often given to men than to women, the rogue hero roles, and she'd carry them off with her usual flair and the audience loved it. They loved *her*. The tabloids were camped round the house through the summer, and when she went into the hospital they came there too, standing vigil around the main entrance.

But just at the end there were only the three of us there in the room: me, my sister Katrina, and her husband, Bill.

We were holding her hands, Bill and I, with our eyes on her face because neither of us could have looked at the other. And after a time there were only the two of us left, but I couldn't let go of her hand because part of me couldn't believe she was actually gone, so I sat there in dull, hollow silence until Bill stood slowly and took the hand he was still holding and laid it with care on Katrina's heart. Gently, he pressed his own hand on hers one final time, then he slipped something small off her finger and passed it to me: a gold ring, a Claddagh ring, that had belonged to our mother.

Wordlessly he held it out and wordlessly I took it, and still we couldn't meet each other's eyes. And then I saw him feel his pocket for his cigarettes and turning, he went out, and I was left alone. Entirely alone.

And at the window of the room the cold November rains slid down the glass and cast their shifting shadows in a room that could no longer hold the light.

I didn't go to her memorial service. I helped arrange it and made sure her favorite songs were sung, her favorite verses read, but when the crowds of fans and friends turned up to pay their last respects, I wasn't there to shake their hands and listen to their well-meant words of sympathy. I know there were people who thought me a coward for that, but I couldn't. My grief was a private one, too deep for sharing. And anyway, I knew it didn't matter whether I was at the church or not, because Katrina wasn't there.

She wasn't anywhere.

It seemed to me incredible a light as strong as hers could be extinguished so completely without leaving some small glow behind, the way a lamp that's been switched off will sometimes dimly shine against the darkness. I'd felt certain I would feel her presence somewhere... but I hadn't.

There were only dead leaves round the butterfly bush in the garden and flowerless shrubs round the porch with its empty swing, and when I started to pack up her closets there wasn't so much as a movement of air in the hallway behind me to let me believe that my sister, in some way, was there with me still.

So I went through the motions. I dealt with the small things that needed attention and tried to get on with my life in the way everybody was saying I should, while a great hollow loneliness grew deep inside me. Then spring came, and Bill came—turned up on my doorstep one Saturday morning without calling first, looking awkward. And holding her ashes.

I hadn't seen him since November, not in person, though because he had a film just out I'd seen him fairly often on the entertainment news.

He didn't want to come inside. He cleared his throat, a bit uncomfortably. 'I thought…' He paused and held more tightly to the plain oak box that held Katrina's ashes. 'She wanted me to scatter these.'

'I know.' My sister's wishes hadn't been a secret.

'I don't know where to do it. Don't know where to take them. I thought maybe you…' His pause this time was more a moment of decision, and he held the box towards me. 'I thought you could do a better job.'

I looked at him, and for the first time since her death, our eyes met and I saw the pain in his. He coughed. 'I don't need to be there when you do it, I've said my goodbyes. I just thought you'd know better than I would where she was the happiest. Where she belongs.'

And then he pushed the box into my hands and bent to kiss my forehead before quickly turning from my door and walking off. I wouldn't see him after that, I knew. We moved in different circles, and the bond we'd had between us was reduced now to the simple box he'd handed me.

Inside, I set it on the narrow table by my window, thinking.

Where she'd been the happiest, he'd said. There were so many places, really. I tried narrowing the choices in my mind, recalling images: the morning we had stood and watched the sun rise from the brink of the Grand Canyon, and Katrina's face had radiated wonderment as she had pointed out a small, white airplane flying far below us, and she'd said she'd never seen a place so beautiful; the time she'd made a movie in Mumbai and the director had rewarded her for days of grueling action with a weekend in Kerala on the southern coast of India, and I had flown over to join her and we'd spent our evenings walking on the black sand beach while gorgeous sunsets flamed the sky above the blue Arabian sea, and Katrina had splashed through the waves like a child, and been happy.

But then, she'd been happy wherever she went. She had danced through her life with an air of adventure and carried that happiness with her, so trying to imagine where she might have felt it the most was a difficult task, far beyond my abilities. Finally I gave up and turned my focus to the last thing Bill had said: *where she belongs.*

That should be easier, I knew. There should be one place that would rise above the others in my memory, so I closed my eyes and waited.

It was coming on to evening when I thought of it, and once I'd had the thought, it seemed so obvious to me where that place was, where I should take her.

Where both of us, once, had belonged.

CHAPTER 2

Crossing the Tamar for some reason made me feel different inside. It was only a river, yet each time I crossed it I felt I had stepped through some mystical veil that divided the world that I only existed in, from the one where I was meant to be living. It was, my mother always used to say, a kind of homecoming that only those with Cornish blood could feel, and since my blood was Cornish on both sides for several generations back, I felt it strongly.

I'd been born in Cornwall, in the north beyond the sweep of Bodmin Moor, where my film-directing father had been working on a darkly Gothic thriller, but both my parents themselves had been raised on this gentler south coast—du Maurier country—and after my father had settled into lecturing in Screen Studies at the University of Bristol, his more regulated schedule made it possible for us to cross the Tamar every summer and come back to spend our holidays with his old childhood friend George Hallett, who lived with his young and lively family in a marvelously draughty manor house set on a hill above the sea.

We'd come back every year, in fact, until I'd turned ten and my father's work had taken us away from England altogether, setting us down on a different shoreline, in Vancouver, on the western coast of Canada, where he'd become a fixture at the University of British Columbia's Centre for Cinema Studies.

I had loved it in Canada too. And of course it had been in Vancouver that my sister, newly turned eighteen, had first begun to get her acting roles—small parts at first, then larger ones that brought enough attention from the Hollywood directors who came up to film their movies in Vancouver that they'd wanted her to go down to L.A., and so she had.

I'd followed her in my own turn years later, more by accident than anything. My own career path took me into marketing, and sideways through an unexpected string of opportunities to corporate public relations, and from there, again by chance, to a PR firm that worked mainly in the entertainment industry, and so I found myself at twenty-five being transferred down from Vancouver to the office in Los Angeles.

It never was my favorite place, L.A., but shortly after I'd moved down, my parents had crossed paths with a drunk driver on a rain-drenched road back home, so after that Katrina was the only family I had left, and I was loathe to leave her.

We were close. When she was shooting somewhere, I would always find the time to visit. I was there when Bill proposed to her and there when they were married in a private ceremony to avoid the paparazzi. And she'd hired me, of course, to represent her. Just to keep it in the family, she had said. These past two years, with her success, she had become my main account.

But I had never really settled in L.A., not with apartments—I had gone through four—nor with the men I'd met and dated. I had gone through even more of those, and none had stuck, the last one fading from the picture with convenience when Katrina had grown ill.

I'd barely noticed his departure then. I didn't miss him now. I had been all but dead myself these past six months, a walking shadow, but this morning as my First Great Western train ran rattling on its rails across the Tamar I felt something deep inside me stir to life.

I was in Cornwall. And it *was* a kind of homecoming—the swiftly passing landscape with its old stone farms and hills and hedges held a warm familiarity, and when I'd changed the big train for a smaller one that ran along the wooded valley branch line leading down towards the coast, I felt an echo of the childish sense of thrilled anticipation that had signaled each beginning of those long-lost summer holidays.

The station at the line's end was a small one, plain with whitewashed walls, a blue bench set beside it and a narrow platform with a white stripe painted at its edge, and a handful of houses stacked up the green hillside behind.

Three people waited on the platform, but I only noticed one of them. I would have known him anywhere.

The last time I had seen Mark Hallett he'd just turned eighteen and I'd been ten, too young to catch his eye but not too young to be completely smitten with his dark good looks and laughing eyes. I'd followed him round like a puppy, never giving him peace, and he'd taken it in the same good-natured way he took everything else, neither making me feel like a bother nor letting it go to his head. I'd adored him.

Katrina had too, though for her it had gone a bit deeper than that. He had been her first boyfriend, her first great romance, and when we had left at the end of the summer, I'd watched both their hearts break. Hers had healed. I assumed his had too. After all, we were twenty years on and our childhoods were over, although when I stepped from the train to the platform and Mark Hallett turned from the place he'd been standing, his eyes finding mine with that shared sense of sure recognition, his smile the same as it ever was, I couldn't help feeling ten again.

'Eva.' His hug was familiar yet different. He wasn't a tall man, despite his strong West Country build, and my chin reached his shoulder, whereas in my memories I'd barely come up to his chest. But the comfort I felt in his arms hadn't changed.

'No trouble with the trains?' he asked.

'No, they were all on time.'

'A miracle.' He took my suitcase from me, though he left me with my shoulder bag, I think because he knew from what I'd told him on the phone what I'd be carrying inside it.

The station didn't even have facilities, it was so small, and the car park wasn't much more than a leveled bit of gravel with a pay phone at one side. Mark's van was easily identifiable by the 'Trelowarth Roses' logo on its side, ringed round by painted vines and leaves. He noticed me looking and smiled an apology. 'I would have brought the car, but I had to run a late order to Bodmin and there wasn't time to stop back at the house.'

'That's all right.' I liked the van. It wasn't the same one his father had driven when I'd come down here as a child, but it had the same mingling of smells inside: damp earth and faintly crushed greenery and something elusive belonging to gardens that grew by the sea. And it came with a dog too—a floppy-eared mongrel with shaggy brown fur and a feathered tail that seemed to never cease wagging, it only changed speed. It wagged crazily now as we got in the van, and the dog would have crawled right through onto the front seat and settled itself on my lap if Mark hadn't with one gentle hand pushed it back.

'This is Samson,' he told me. 'He's harmless.'

They'd always had dogs at Trelowarth. In fact they had usually had three or four running round through the fields with us children and traipsing with muddy feet through the old kitchen and out to the gardens. Mark's stepmother, Claire, had forever been washing the flagstone floors.

Scratching the dog's ears, I asked how Claire was doing.

'Much better. She's out of the plaster now, up walking round on the leg, and the doctor says give it a few weeks and she'll be as right as rain.'

'Remind me how she broke it in the first place?'

'Cleaning gutters.'

'Of course,' I said, sharing his smile because we both knew how independent Claire was, and it was no surprise that, even now that she'd moved from the manor house into the cottage, she still tried to do all the upkeep herself.

'It's a good thing,' said Mark, 'it was only the gutters, not roof slates.' The dog pushed his way in between us again and Mark nudged him back, starting the van and reversing out onto the road.

Cornish roads were like none other anywhere. Here by the coast they were narrow and twisting with steep sloping banks and high hedges that blocked any view of what might lie ahead. My father had shaved several years off my life every time he had driven down here at high speeds, simply honking the horn as we came to a corner and trusting that if anyone were approaching unseen round the bend they'd get out of the way. When I'd asked him once what would have happened if somebody coming towards us had chosen to do the same thing he was doing, to honk without slowing down, Dad had just shrugged and assured me it never would happen.

And luckily for us, it never had.

Mark drove a little less recklessly, but I nonetheless needed some kind of distraction from watching the road, so I asked him, 'Is Susan still living at home?'

Susan being his sister, a little bit younger than me.

'She is.' Mark pulled a face, but he didn't convince me. I knew they were close. 'We got rid of her once. She was living up near Bristol, but that didn't stick and now she's back, with plans to start some sort of tearoom or something to bring in the tourists. She's full of ideas, is Susan.'

'You don't want a tearoom?' I guessed from his tone.

'Let's just say I don't think there'll be too many tourists who want tea so badly they'd brave the hike up from the village to get it.'

He did have a point. We were entering the village now—Polgelly, with its huddled whitewashed houses and its twisting streets so narrow they were closed to all but local traffic and the taxis that each summer ferried tourists to and from the trains. Mark's van, as compact as it was, could barely squeeze between the buildings.

Polgelly had once been a fishing port of some renown, but with the tourist influx into Cornwall it had changed its face from practical to picturesque, an artist's haven full of shops that sold antiques and Celtic crafts, and bed & breakfast cottages with names like 'Smuggler's Rest'. The old shop near the harbor where we'd always bought our fish and chips still looked the same, as did the little fudge shop on the corner. And The Hill, of course, remained the same as ever.

From the first time I'd walked up it I had thought of it like that—*The* Hill, for surely there could be no other hill on earth that could with more perfection test the limits of endurance. It was not its height alone, nor just the angle of its slope, though both were challenging. It was that, once you started up it, there seemed not to be an end to it—the road kept rising steadily through overhanging trees on stone and earthen banks, a punishing ascent that made the muscles of your thighs begin to burn and left them shaking for some minutes when you'd finally reached the top.

Yet being children, and not knowing any better, we'd gone down it every day to play with Mark's and Susan's school friends in Polgelly, and to sit along the harbor wall to watch the fishermen at work, and in the cheerfully forgetful way that children have, we'd pushed aside all thoughts about The Hill until the time came round again for us to climb it. Mark had actually carried me the final few steps, once, which was no doubt why I'd developed such a crush on him.

This time, we had the van, but even it seemed to approach The Hill with something like reluctance, and I could have sworn I heard the engine wheezing as we climbed.

From either side the trees, still bright with new spring green, closed overtop of us and cast a dancing play of light and shadow on the windscreen, and I caught the swift familiar blur of periwinkle tangled with the darker green of ivy winding up along the verge. And then I looked ahead, expectantly, as I had always done, for my first glimpse of the brick chimneys of Trelowarth House.

The chimneys were the first things to be seen, between the trees and the steep bank of green that ran along the road—a Cornish hedge, they called it, built of stones stacked dry in the old fashion, herringbone, with vines and varied wildflowers binding them together and the trees arched close above. Then came a break in both the trees and hedge, and there, framed as impressively as ever by the view of rising fields and distant forests, was the house.

Trelowarth House had weathered centuries upon this hill, its solid grey stone walls an equal match to any storm the sea might throw at it. For all its size it had been plainly built, a two-storey 'L' set with its front squarely facing the line of the cliffs and the sea, while its longer side ran fairly close beside the road. In what might be viewed as a testament to the skills of its original builders, none of its long line of owners appeared to have felt the need to do a major renovation. The chimneys, dutifully repointed, were in the original style, and a few of the casement windows still had the odd pane of Elizabethan glass, through which the people who had lived here then might well have watched the sails of the Armada pass. The house itself did not encourage such romantic fancies. It looked stern and grey, unyielding, and the only softness to it was the stubborn vine of roses that had wound their way around and over the stone frame of the front door and waited there to bloom, as they had done in all the summers of my childhood.

Three-quarters of the way up The Hill, Mark took the sharp left turn into the graveled drive that angled right again along the fifty feet or so of turf that separated house and road. The garages themselves were in the back, in the old stables at the far edge of the leveled yard, but Mark stopped where we were, beside the house, and parked the van, and in an instant we were overrun by what appeared to be a pack of wild dogs, all leaping up and barking for attention.

'Down, you beasts,' Mark told them, getting out and going round to take my suitcase from the back.

I got out carefully myself, not because I was afraid of the dogs, but because I didn't want to step on them by accident. There were only three of them, as it turned out—a black cocker spaniel, a Labrador, and something that underneath all the dirt looked a bit like a setter—and with the little brown mongrel dog, Samson, who'd jumped out behind me, the pack was quite manageable. Once I'd patted all the heads and rumpled a few ears and scratched a side or two, the leaping changed to energetic wagging, with the four dogs weaving round Mark's legs and mine as we followed the curve of the path round the corner.

At the front of the house a small level lawn had been terraced out of the hillside, with hedges around it to block some part of the wind, and below that the steep green fields tumbled and rolled to the edge of the cliffs.

I was unprepared, as always, for my first view of the sea. From this high up the view was beautiful enough to steal my breath with such a swiftness that my rib cage almost hurt. There were the green hills folding down into their valley, with the darker smudges of the woods marked here and there with paler arcs of blackthorn blossom. There, too, was the harbor of Polgelly with its steeply stacked white houses looking small so far below us, and the headlands curving out to either side, already showing the first spreading cover of sea pink that made a softer contrast to the darkly jagged rock beneath. And past all that, as far as I could see, the endless rolling blue of water stretched away until it met the clouds.

Mark stopped when I stopped, turned to watch my face, and said, 'Not quite like California, is it?'

'No.' This ocean had a very different feel than the Pacific. It seemed somehow more alive. 'No, this is better.'

I hadn't heard anyone open the front door behind us but suddenly someone said 'Eva!' and, turning, I saw a young woman in jeans and a red sweater, her dark hair cut even shorter than Mark's. This had to be Susan, I thought, though I wouldn't have known *her* if we'd met away from Trelowarth.

She'd only been seven or eight when I'd last been here. Now she was in her late twenties, grown taller and slender, her smile wide and welcoming. 'I thought I heard the van.' Her hug was just as warm. 'Honestly, Eva, you look just the same. It's incredible. Even your hair. I always envied you your hair,' she told me. 'Mine would never grow like that.'

I didn't really think much of my hair, myself. My father had liked my hair long, so I'd left it that way. It was easy enough to take care of, no styling required, and whenever it got in the way I just tied it all back.

'Short hair suits you, though,' I said to Susan.

'Yes, well, it's not by choice.' She smoothed it with a hand and grinned. 'I tried to dye it red…'

Mark said, 'It came out purple.'

'More maroon, I'd say,' she set him straight. 'And when I tried to fix it, it got worse, so I just cut it.'

'By herself,' said Mark.

'Well, naturally.'

'I could have done as good a job as that,' he told her dryly, 'with my garden shears.'

Their banter was affectionate and utterly familiar, and I felt myself relaxing in the way one only did when in the company of friends.

Susan let Mark score that last point and shrugged as she told him, 'Just drop that suitcase here for now. Claire said to bring you both round to the cottage when you got here. She's made sandwiches.'

Mark did as he was told and then fell in behind as Susan— with the dogs bouncing round her as though they'd caught some of her energy—led the way along the front walk of the house and down the long green sweep of hill towards the sea, to the place where the old narrow coast path, trampled hard as rutted pavement by the feet of countless ramblers who came up along the clifftops from Polgelly, disappeared into the Wild Wood.

I'd given it that name the summer Claire had read me Kenneth Graeme's timeless tales of Mole and Rat and Mr. Toad. A chapter a night of *The Wind in the Willows* and never again could I enter that old sprawling tangle of woods without cocking an ear for the scurrying footsteps of small unseen creatures and feeling a touch of the magic.

I still felt it now, as I followed Mark into the dim, sudden coolness. The air changed. The light changed. The scent of the woods, dank and earthy and rich, rose around me. The woods was an old one, and where it was deepest it stretched down the hill to the edge of the cliffs, but the trees grew so thickly I lost my whole view of the sea. I was closed round in branches and leaves—oak and elder and blackthorn and ghostly pale sycamores, set amid masses of bluebells.

The coast path, which entered the woods as a narrow track, broadened a little in here so two people could walk side by side, as though those who came into these woods felt more comfortable walking that way in this place where the shadows fell thick on the ferns and the undergrowth, and the high trees had a whispering voice of their own when the wind shook their leaves. But I'd never felt fear in these woods. They were peaceful and filled with the joyously warbling songs of the birds tending hidden nests high overhead.

Susan, leading us through, turned to tell me, 'We actually do have a badger. Claire's seen it.'

If it was anything like the reclusive Mr. Badger who had ruled the Wild Wood in *The Wind and the Willows*, I didn't hold out too much hope that I'd catch a glimpse of the creature myself, but it didn't stop me looking while we walked.

I caught the sharp scent of the coal smoke from Claire's cottage chimney before we stepped into the clearing, a broad semicircular space blown with green grass that chased to the edge of the cliff, where again I could have a clear view of the sea.

I knew better than to go towards that cliff—there was a wicked drop straight down from there, all unforgiving rock and jagged stone below—but the view itself, framed by the gap in the trees with the flowers and grass in between, and the glitter of sun on the water far out where the fishing boats bobbed, was beautiful.

And facing it, set tidily against the clearing's edge, the little cottage waited for us with its walls still painted primrose-yellow underneath a roof of sagging slates.

The cottage had been rented out to tourists when I'd come here as a child, to earn a bit of extra income for Trelowarth, but apparently Claire had decided just this past year to move into it herself with all her canvases and paints, and leave the big house for her stepchildren. I couldn't really blame her. While Trelowarth House was wonderful inside, it was an ancient house with draughts and rising damp and tricky wiring, and it took a lot of work, whereas this little cottage had been put here in the twenties and was snugly made and comfortable.

There wasn't any need to knock. We just went in, the three of us, and all the dogs came with us, spilling through into the sitting room. Claire had been reading, but she set aside the paperback and came around to fold me into the third hug of warmth and welcome that I'd had this afternoon.

Claire Hallett was a woman who defied the rules of ageing. She looked just as fit approaching sixty as she'd looked those years ago. Her hair might be a little shorter and a paler shade of blonde now from its whitening, but she was still in jeans and giving off that same strong energy, that sense of capability. Her hug seemed to be offering to carry all my burdens. 'It's so good to have you here,' she said. 'We were so very sorry when we heard about Katrina.'

Then, because I think she knew that too much sympathy on top of my reunion with the three of them might lead to tears I wasn't ready yet to cry in front of anybody, she turned the talk to other things: the cottage and the decorating projects she had planned for it, and the next thing I knew we were all in the kitchen and sitting at the old unsteady table with its one leg shorter than the others, drinking Claire's strong tea and eating cheese and pickle sandwiches as though it had been months, not years, since we'd all been together.

Susan raised the subject of the tearoom she was planning. 'Mark's against it, naturally,' she told me. 'He was never one for change.'

'It's not the change,' Mark said with patience. 'It's the simple fact, my darling, that there's really no demand for it.'

'Well, we'd create one, wouldn't we? I've told you, if we opened up the gardens more to tourists, we could bring them by the busload.'

'Buses can't come through Polgelly.'

'So you'd bring them in the other way, across the high road from St Non's. The tourists go there anyway, to see the well—they could come on here afterwards, for lunch.' Her tone was certain as she turned to her stepmother. 'You're on my side, surely?'

'I'm staying out of it.' Claire leaned across both of them to pour me a fresh cup of tea. 'I've given up the running of Trelowarth to the two of you, you'll have to work it out yourselves.'

Susan rolled her eyes. 'Yes, well, you say you've given up Trelowarth, but we all know you could never—'

'If you're wanting an opinion,' Claire said lightly, 'you might think of asking Eva. That's her job, you know—promoting things and dealing with the public.'

Suddenly Susan and Mark were both looking at me, and I shook my head. 'I think I should stay out of it too.'

Mark's amusement was obvious. 'Sorry, there's no likes of that, not with Susan about. She'll be picking your brains the whole time that you're here.'

Susan said, 'You will stay for a while, won't you? Not just the weekend?'

'We'll see.'

Claire, who'd been watching me quietly, glanced at my hand. 'That's your mother's ring, isn't it?'

'Yes.' The gold Claddagh ring that Bill had slipped from Katrina's still finger and given to me in the hospital room. It had come to my mother from her Irish grandmother who'd moved across into Cornwall and who, by tradition, had passed down this small ring of gold with its crowned heart held lovingly by two gloved hands, a reminder that love was eternal.

Claire smiled, understanding, as though she knew just what had brought me here, why I had come. Reaching over, she covered my hand with her warm one and said, 'Stay as long as you like.'

CHAPTER 3

WHEN WE CAME OUT of the Wild Wood by the coast path and turned up to climb the slope of field towards Trelowarth House, the sun had sunk so low it stretched our shadows long in front of us and glittered in the windows that were watching our approach.

The dogs, having patiently waited while we had our visit with Claire, were all bouncing round Susan now. 'Feeding time,' she told us, before taking the dogs round to the back of the house. That was how we'd most often gone in, through the kitchen, but Mark had left my suitcase just inside the main front door, so I went that way with him now and in through the more formal entrance, with its short flight of steps and the vine trailing over the lintel.

As I followed Mark through and he switched on the light, I was happy to see that the house hadn't changed; to inhale the same scents of old polished wood and wool carpets and comforting mustiness, here in the spacious square hall. Once, this whole space had most likely been paneled in the same wine-dark wood as the sitting-room door on my left and the staircase that angled up just behind that to the bedrooms upstairs, but some earlier Hallett had covered the paneling over with plaster, no doubt in an effort to make the great space seem more welcoming.

Still on my left and beyond the great staircase, a narrower

corridor carried on back to the games room and the kitchen at the rear of the house, and off to my right were the doors to the dining room and the big front room.

Beside me Mark waited, my suitcase in hand. 'We weren't sure if you'd want your old room or—'

Their thoughtfulness touched me. 'Yes, please.'

He let me go first up the stairs. They were old stairs, as old as the house, running up from the hall at a perfect right angle to pause at a half landing before doubling back on themselves for the final rise up to the next floor. The stair steps themselves were of stone, worn concave at their centres by centuries of climbing feet, and the walls of both stairway and landing were still the original paneling, wood of the same dark mahogany hue as the old doors downstairs, so that while I was climbing, I couldn't help feeling I'd somehow stepped into the past.

The first floor looked rather less ancient, with carpets to cover the old floors and softly striped wallpaper brightening things. There were furnishings here that I didn't recall, but I knew my way round.

And I knew which door led to the room I had shared with Katrina. Being in the far front corner, closest to the road, it had three windows—two that looked towards the sea and one that overlooked the drive, that last one set beside the fireplace with its screen of flowered needlepoint in front.

The double bed still sat in the same place it always had, its headboard to the west wall so its footboard faced the fireplace. Katrina and I had both slept in that bed when we'd stayed here, the six years' gap between our ages making me a nuisance to her, keeping her awake by constant chattering or stealing more than my share of the covers.

I smiled faintly at the memories, even as I felt the stabbing pain of loss. I fought it back and found my voice as Mark came up behind me in the doorway, and I said, 'You've moved the pictures. The old shepherd and his wife.'

'Oh, right.' He looked above the bed, where I was looking. 'They're in the dining room, I think.'

'It's just as well. They had those eyes that always watched you.'

Mark set the suitcase by the bed and looked around in friendly silence for a moment. Then his gaze came round to me. 'How are you doing, really?'

I didn't meet his eyes directly. 'Fine. I'm fine.'

'You're not.'

'I will be. It takes time, I'm told.'

'Well, if you need to talk, you know I'm here.'

'I know.'

He touched my shoulder briefly as he passed. 'You know the house,' he said. 'Just make yourself at home, then.'

'Thanks.'

The door had a lock, but we'd never been allowed to lock the door as children and I didn't feel the need to do it now.

There were, in fact, three doors into this room. Trelowarth House was a proper smuggler's house, with doors that led from room to room as well as to the corridor, a feature that had made it unsurpassed for games of hide-and-seek. Just as the smugglers had been able to evade capture by sneaking from one room to another while the customs men were searching for them, so we children had slipped secretly between the upstairs rooms to the frustration of whoever had been 'it'.

Besides the main door to the corridor, my room had one more door farther along the same wall that connected with the bedroom just behind here on this east side of the house, a room that Claire had used for sewing, almost never giving it to guests because Uncle George's cigar smoke had often seeped in from his study beyond.

And the third door was set in the wall by the head of the bed, and led to a smaller front bedroom that had, I recalled, been used mostly for storage.

I didn't bother looking in there now. There'd be plenty of time for exploring tomorrow. Instead I sat down on the bed, making the bedsprings creak lightly as I looked around at the room from my childhood vantage point. The room looked much the same to me as it had twenty years ago. The walls were still a soft sea green, the bedspread hobnailed white and fringed, the curtains lace and insubstantial, lifting with the cool May breezes blowing through the partly open window. The wide-planked floor was bare, save for an old worn rug between the wardrobe on the two-doored wall and the small rocking chair set in the fireplace corner, and the same old white-framed mirror hung above the chest of drawers between the windows at the front.

In the mornings this was one of the first rooms to catch the light but it was late now, and the afternoon was fading into evening, and the room was full of shadows. I could have put a light on, but I didn't. I lay back instead, my hands behind my head.

I only meant to rest a moment, then wash up and go downstairs. But lying there, my face brushed by the soft sea breezes blowing in the window, feeling comfortably nostalgic in the dim, high-ceilinged room, my weariness began to weight my limbs until I couldn't move and didn't really want to.

By the time the sound of Mark's sure footsteps had gone

all the way downstairs and crossed the hall below, I was no longer listening.

❦

I realized my mistake a few hours later when a restless dream brought me back wide-eyed to wakefulness, into the dark of a house that had fallen asleep. Rolling, I turned on the bedside lamp and checked my watch and found that it was nearly midnight.

'Damn.' I'd had just enough sleep that I knew I would never drift off again, no matter how much I needed the rest. And I needed it badly. The time change and long hours of travel were taking their toll and if I didn't get back to sleep now I'd pay a steep price in the morning.

I tried to resettle myself. Getting up, I changed out of my clothes into proper pajamas and snuggled in under the blankets and switched off the light. It was no use. The minutes ticked by.

'Damn,' I said again, and giving up, I rose to rummage in my handbag.

I'd had sleeping pills prescribed for nights like these because my doctor had assured me it was normal to do battle with insomnia from time to time while grieving. I had never had to use them, but I'd brought the pills to Cornwall just in case.

I took one pill and climbed back into bed, taking care not to pull all the covers to my side, from force of long habit, and mumbling 'good night' to the place where my sister should be.

❦

The first thing I thought when I woke was, I wasn't alone.

I knew where I was. My mind had already made sense of

the signals and sorted them into awareness—the sound of the gulls and the scent of the air and the way that the sunlight speared into the room through the unshuttered windows. I heard voices talking quietly somewhere close by, not much above a whisper, the way that people talk when they don't want to wake someone who's sleeping. Mark and Susan, I assumed, but then I wasn't sure because both voices sounded male. I couldn't catch more than an odd word, fleeting, here and there: 'away' was one, and then, quite clear, 'impossible'.

The voices stopped. Began again, much closer to my head this time, and then I realized that they must be coming through the wall from the next room, the small front bedroom.

Workmen, probably. Old houses like Trelowarth always needed something done, and Mark had mentioned something when we'd been at Claire's about some sort of trouble with the wiring. My mind was alert enough now to be wary of having strange men in the next room, and rolling, I reached with my one hand to lock the connecting door set in the wall by the head of my bed.

The door handles here were the old-fashioned kind with a thumb latch, without any keyholes, but small sliding bolts had been set just above them, and this bolt shot home with a satisfyingly sturdy click that made me feel a little more secure while I got dressed.

In the corridor outside my room I met Mark, who was coming upstairs. 'Good, you're up,' he said. 'Susan just sent me to see if you were. She's got breakfast on. How did you sleep?'

'Very well, thanks.' I gave a nod towards the closed door to the spare front room and added, 'You can tell them they don't have to be so quiet, now I'm up.'

He looked at me. 'Tell whom?'

'The workmen,' I said, 'or whoever they are. In there.'

Still looking at me strangely, he opened his mouth to reply and then shut it again, as though wanting to make very sure he was right before speaking. He turned the handle of the room beside my own and pushed the door wide enough to put his head round, then said to me, certain, 'There's nobody in here.'

I looked for myself. 'But I heard them. Two men. They were talking.'

'Then they must have been outside.'

'They didn't sound like they were outside.'

'Sound plays tricks, sometimes,' he told me, 'in old houses.'

Unconvinced, I made a final study of the empty room then let him close the door.

He said, 'Come down for breakfast.'

Downstairs, Susan had a full cooked breakfast on the go, with sausage spitting in the pan and floured tomatoes sizzling beside them, eggs and toast and juice and coffee that smelled sharp and rich and heavenly and brought my eyes more fully open.

Susan, turning, waved a spatula towards the table. 'Have a seat, it's hardly ready.'

The kitchen had had a remodel since I'd last been here, and the table was a larger one than I remembered, but it occupied the same spot by the window that looked out across what used to be the stable yard, now greenly ringed with overhanging trees and with the former stable building now converted to a garage at its farther edge. I sat where I had always sat, my shoulder to the window-wall, and looked across the yard towards the terraced gardens, sheltered by their high brick walls.

The gardens were all separately enclosed and named: the Lower Garden, closest to the house; the Middle Garden; then the largest one, the Upper Garden, and my favorite of them all, the Quiet Garden, which I'd loved best for its name.

These were the legacy of Mark and Susan's great-great-grandfather, who'd returned from the Boer War with only one leg and a mind in sore need of tranquility. Nostalgia for a simpler time had driven him to cultivate traditional varieties of roses that were falling out of fashion with the rise of the more modern hybrids gaining popularity because they could bloom more than once a season.

Disdainful of these new hybrid perpetuals, he'd cared for his old-fashioned roses with a passion that he'd passed to his descendants, and through the hard work and investment of subsequent Halletts, the business had grown into one of the country's most highly regarded producers of older historic varieties. In fact, thanks to the family's obsessive caretaking, these gardens now sheltered some roses that might have been lost altogether to time were it not for Trelowarth.

The sizzling from the cooker brought my gaze back from the window and I watched while Susan turned the sausage.

'Honestly,' I said, 'you didn't have to go to all this trouble. Cereal and milk would be enough.'

Mark, who'd been pouring the coffee, came over to hand me my mug and sat down in the place just across from me. 'It's not for you,' he assured me. 'She's trying to soften me up.'

'I am not,' was Susan's protest.

Mark said, 'So I guess it's coincidence, then, that you've set your big file of plans for the tearoom out here on the table?'

'I wanted to look at them.'

'Wanted to show them to Eva, more like.'

'I did not.' Susan scraped the sausages out of the pan and, crossing to the table, set Mark's plate down, hard, in front of him.

Oblivious, he pointed at the folder with his fork. 'You've got the legends of Trelowarth and that sort of rubbish in there, don't you?'

Susan passed my plate across for me and, with her own in hand, sat down herself. 'Of course.'

'Good. So then you can reassure Eva we don't have a ghost.'

It was my turn to protest. 'I never said—'

'Why would she think there's a ghost?' Susan asked.

'She's been hearing men's voices upstairs.'

Susan told him, with feeling, 'I wish.'

Mark grinned. 'What, that we had men upstairs?'

'No, stupid. That we had a ghost. Now *that* would bring the tourists in.'

Mark told her that depended on the ghost.

Ignoring him, she asked me what the voices had been saying, and I shrugged.

'I couldn't hear.'

Mark said, 'Perhaps they came to give a warning.' Imitating a stern, ghostly voice, he went on, 'Do not build a tearoom at Trelowarth.'

'Do you see?' asked Susan, looking to me for support. 'You see the sort of thing I have to deal with.'

'And you love me anyway.' Her brother's smile was sure.

'Yes, well, lucky for you that I do. That's the only thing keeps me from planting you in the back garden alongside your roses.'

Mark took the threat lightly and turned his attention to me. 'So then, what are your plans for the day?'

I said, 'I don't know. I suppose I should take care of… what I came for.'

That sobered the mood. Mark looked down at his plate and went on eating silently, then he said quietly, 'Do you know where?'

'I was thinking,' I started, then paused for a moment, collecting myself. 'I was thinking of up by the Beacon.' He didn't react, but I still felt the need to explain, 'She would want to be somewhere where she had been happy.'

Mark gave a short nod and said, 'That's a good spot then.' And after a moment, 'You want me to come with you?'

He offered that as though it didn't matter either way, but there was something in his tone that made me ask him, 'Would you like to?'

Pushing his half-empty plate away he told me, 'Yes, I would.'

I glanced towards the clearing sky. 'We ought to wait until the sun comes out.'

'Right.' He hadn't finished with his coffee, either, but he set that down as well and stood. 'You let me know, then, when you're ready.' And with that he turned away and went to start his work.

CHAPTER 4

'H E REALLY DID LOVE her, didn't he?' Susan, standing at the sink to rinse our breakfast dishes, tipped her head to one side in a movement that was half-familiar. 'I mean, it's not as though he's been pining away all these years or anything, and he's had girlfriends since who were serious, but your sister was special, I think.'

I pushed at a small bit of egg with my knife. 'Well, she was his first love,' I said. 'At least, that's what he told her. I know he was hers. And you never forget your first love.'

'I suppose not.' She frowned. 'I don't honestly remember what they were like as a couple, I was only seven. And you and I played together more, really. Katrina and Mark always seemed so much older.' She was filling the sink now with water and dish soap, and I would have risen to help her if she hadn't motioned me down again. 'Sit. You're a guest.'

'Not that kind of a guest. I can help.'

'No, you can't,' she insisted, and from her expression she wouldn't be budged, so I did as she told me and stayed in my seat at the table while she started washing the cutlery. 'Who was *your* first love?' she asked me, and the question broke the subtle air of sadness that had settled on us; brought the light again into the room.

I smiled. 'A boy at my school in Vancouver. He played junior hockey, I spent all my weekends in freezing cold ice rinks.' Somehow it didn't have quite the same level of romance as Mark and Katrina. 'And you?'

'I'm still waiting for mine,' Susan said. 'I'm too fussy, Mark tells me. I want what my dad and Claire had.'

'God, you'll be waiting a long time for that.' Even my parents, for all their devotion to each other, hadn't been a patch on Uncle George and Claire. The Halletts had been one of those rare couples who, between them, made a little world that no one else could touch. True soul mates.

Susan ran the dishrag round a coffee mug. 'I know. Worth waiting for, though, I think. And it doesn't mean I can't have some adventures in the meantime.'

She'd been born to have adventures. Although she'd been the youngest and the smallest of the four of us, she'd been the one most likely to explore, to push the boundaries, and she'd often had the skinned knees and the bandages to prove it. From the little I had seen now of the woman she'd grown into I suspected she still had that spirit in her, that her mind still saw beyond the limits others liked to place on things.

Which made me wonder why she had come back here, to this quiet little corner of the country, and Trelowarth.

'Mark said you'd been living near Bristol,' I ventured.

She glanced at me. 'Did he?' I had the strong impression I had somehow touched a nerve without intending to, but Susan hid it with a shrug. 'Yes, well, I had my own catering business up there, did he tell you?'

He hadn't, but I took the opportunity to shift to safer ground. 'So then you should be able to make a success of your tearoom.'

'I hope so. I mean, Mark would never complain, but I know that it hasn't been easy these past few years, since Dad's investments went—' She stopped and glanced at me and quickly looked away and would have likely changed the subject if I hadn't stopped her.

'Susan.'

'Yes?'

'Trelowarth's in financial trouble?' I could read reluctance in her eyes. I asked her, 'How bad is it?'

'Bad enough. But don't tell Mark I told you or he'll plant *me* in the garden with the roses.'

I imagined a place this big must take a good deal of money to run. Apart from the house, there was all the land—not just the gardens themselves, but the fields where the roses were actually grown. Most of the regular work could be done by two men, but with Uncle George gone that meant Mark would have had to hire someone to help. They'd be busiest during the winter months, digging the bare-rooted roses and shipping them off to fill all of the orders that would have come in through the year, after which all the rest of the harvest still had to be potted and delivered to the garden centres that had always sold Trelowarth roses. But even at this time of year there was much to be done. Taking care of Trelowarth, I knew, was a full-time concern.

'Anyway,' Susan said, 'that's really why I came back. To help out where I could.'

'Hence the tearoom.'

'Exactly. My dad used to talk about having one someday. I thought if we put in a tearoom and opened the gardens for tours, it might bring in some revenue and make more people aware of our product.' She heard her own words and smiled wryly. 'I've been swotting up on marketing, can you tell?'

'Good for you, though. That's just what you should do.' My gaze found the folder of plans she had left on the table. 'You mind if I look at these?'

'No, go ahead. Only—'

'—don't tell Mark. I know.' I reached for the folder. 'Why is he so set against your tearoom?'

Susan set the final teacup on the draining board and pulled the plug to let the water out. 'I wouldn't say he's set against it, more that he's resistant, and that's just because it doesn't fit his vision of Trelowarth. Mark's a purist, like my grandfather. Change doesn't interest him.' She grinned. 'If you ask me, Mark's simply not sure about sharing our roses with strangers.'

Reading her notes while I finished my coffee, I rotated one drawing slightly to help get my bearings. 'So you'd put the tearoom over there, then,' I said, pointing at an angle out the window, past the stretch of level turf that once had been the stable yard and to the tangled greenery beyond it.

'That's right, in Dad's old greenhouse. No one uses it anymore, but it's still got all the plumbing in place and the glass is all good. I've been told that it wouldn't be hard to convert.' She came round beside me to study the plans. 'Claire's grandparents met in a tearoom, apparently. She told us the story, it's very romantic. I'll have to ask if she remembers the name of the place. We could call ours the same, put a bit of her history here too.'

This was the sort of project that my mother, with her passion for historical research, would have loved. If she'd been living still, she would have wasted little time in digging through the records to unearth the finer details of Trelowarth's past.

But when I said as much to Susan, she said only, 'She'd have bored herself to tears then. They're all deadly dull, my family, and they've been here for two hundred years, at least. I keep hoping that I'll come across a smuggler or a pirate, someone infamous, to help bring in the tourists.'

'Someone famous might work just as well.' I kept my focus on the drawings and the notes as I reminded her, 'You have a famous movie star who used to spend her summers here, remember.'

'No,' she said. 'It wouldn't feel right, trading on Katrina's name. And Mark would never go for it. You know my brother.'

Yes, I did. The years might change our outer selves, but underneath it all we stayed the same, we kept our patterns, and I knew where I should look for him when I went out a short while later with the box of ashes. In the mornings, he had always started in the highest terrace and worked down from there. I found him in the Quiet Garden, pulling weeds. His boots were caked and muddy and the wind had blown his hair and he was wearing an old denim jacket not unlike the one I held a memory of him wearing when he worked among the roses.

He stopped as I came in through the old wooden door in the high stone wall, into the roofless, still space where the wind couldn't reach with its fine salty spray from the sea that could burn through the delicate petals and leaves. When Mark saw what I'd brought with me, what I was carrying, he asked me, 'Ready, then?'

'Whenever you are.'

He tugged off his gloves, set his tools away tidily into the small corner shed, and picked up a small battered rucksack he slung on his shoulder before leading me out of the garden.

The walk to the Beacon was one of the prettier walks at Trelowarth. We went down the hill to the coast path again, through the Wild Wood as if we were going to Claire's, but we passed by the cottage and right through the clearing and into the woods again, still on the coast path. We came out the other side close to the top of the cliffs, close enough to be able to hear the harsh rush of the waves as they broke on the black rocks and shingle beneath. Here we left the path, turning our backs to the sea as we came to the fence of a broad sloping pasture where several cows lazily stood with their heads to the grass, paying no heed to either of us as we climbed up and over the stile.

Mark helped me over, then went back to walking just in front of me, head down, his thoughts turned inward. I knew why.

He'd often brought Katrina up here, that last summer. This had been their special place, a place to get away from all the adults and us younger children, to be on their own together. I'd been too young then to be my sister's confidante, too young for her to tell me what they'd talked about up here. I'd only known that when she'd been with Mark up at the Beacon, she had come back shining like a lamp had been switched on inside her, stepping lightly as the butterflies that danced around my feet now as my shoes brushed through the bluebells in the windblown grass.

And Mark, I knew, was walking with the memories.

I had memories of my own to keep me company. My mother, loving history as she did, had loved the romance of the Beacon, ancient relic of the days when there had been a chain of signal fires on hilltops all along the coast of Britain, standing ready to be lit in times of trouble. They had served a double purpose, calling everyone who saw them to come out and take up arms against the enemy, while at the same time swiftly sending warning word to London of approaching danger. In Elizabethan times, this beacon at Trelowarth had been used to pass the signal when the sails of the Armada were first spotted from the shore.

In those days, the Beacon would have been a sight to

see—a high stone table, higher than a man, much like the
Neolithic cromlechs that one still saw perched on hillsides
in this area, but with a pile of kindling wood, perhaps,
stacked on top of it in readiness. My mother's words had
painted such a clear and vivid picture of it in my mind that
when we'd come up here on picnics I had always felt the
urge to keep a sharper watch on the horizon for a stealthy
Spanish sail, and sometimes glanced from left to right along
the coast to see if I could spot another beacon fire flaring in
the distance.

I still felt a small tug of that same feeling now as we
came to the top of the field, to the level place scattered
with old weathered stones that had tumbled into a rough
circle and gave little hint of their earlier purpose, except
for the stone at the centre that lay like a low table, cracked
at one end.

The view from here was wide and unobstructed—I could
see the whole unbroken line of coast, headland to headland,
the waves beating white on the black cliffs and dark shingle
beaches, and the sea deep blue today beneath a warmly
glinting sun.

I set the box that held Katrina's ashes on the table stone
and looked at Mark, who looked at me.

And then he reached into the rucksack he had carried up
with him and brought out three small paper cups, the kind
you find near water coolers, and a dark green bottle. 'We
should do this right,' he said.

'What is that?'

'Scrumpy. When Katrina and I came up here, we always
brought a bottle with us.'

'Scrumpy?'

'Cider. With a kick.' He filled a cup and set it on the

wooden box, then poured two more and handed one to me, and raised his up as though to make a toast. 'Here's to…' he said, then faltered. 'Well, to hell with it,' he finished off, and drained the cup.

I drank mine too, and Mark poured out the third cup on the box itself before he stepped aside and gave a nod to me. 'Go on, then.'

With uncertain hands I flipped the latch that held the box shut. 'There was something I was going to read.'

Mark looked at me and waited.

'From *The Prophet*,' I explained. 'Kahlil Gibran's *The Prophet*. There's a passage about death that Katrina always liked. She read it at our parents' funeral.'

I had crammed the folded paper in a pocket, and I had to tug it out and spread it smooth against the blowing breeze.

'"For what is it to die,"' I read, '"but to stand naked in the wind and to melt into the sun? And what is it to cease breathing, but to… but to…"' And there my voice trailed off and would not carry on, and Mark reached over for the page and gently took it from my hand, and went on with the reading in his steady voice. I turned my face towards the sea and let my eyes be dazzled by the brightness of the water while Mark finished off the passage and came down to the last lines:

'"And when you have reached the mountaintop, then you shall begin to climb.

And when the earth shall claim your limbs, then shall you truly dance."'

It seemed the perfect time then, so I tipped the box and let the ashes spill.

Beside me, very quietly, Mark told them, 'Go and dance now.'

And they caught the wind and did just that, and for that fleeting instant there were three of us again upon the wide and sunlit hill, before the ashes gathered on an upward swirl of breeze that blew them westward, out across the blue and endless sparkle of the sea.

CHAPTER 5

'Do you know,' I said to Mark, 'I think I'm getting drunk.' We were still sitting on the cool ground at the summit of the hill with all the old stones of the Beacon tumbled round us, giving us some shelter from the strengthened wind that blew across the waving grass and wildflowers.

I looked down at my paper cup. 'What do you call this stuff again?'

'Scrumpy.'

'Scrumpy.' I'd have to remember that name and avoid it in future, I thought. It came on at first like common apple cider, and then suddenly you realized you were, 'Definitely getting drunk,' I said. 'You have the rest.'

Without a word he poured the bottle's dregs into his own cup and sat back and leaned his elbows on the table rock, and looked as I was looking down the hillside to the sea. Like me, he seemed to be in no great hurry to go anywhere.

As if he'd read my thoughts, he asked, 'How long till you have to go back?'

'I don't, actually.' Far over the water the tiny white speck of a gull wheeled and languidly dipped and I followed its flight with my faintly blurred gaze. 'I don't have a job or apartment, I gave them both up. It's not home for me there anymore, not since…' Letting the words trail off, I gave a shrug. 'When Bill gave me those ashes, I had to think hard, really think, about where I should scatter them. Where she belonged. And it got me to thinking where *I* belonged, now that she's gone. I have friends in L.A., but not real friends, you know? Not the kind you can really depend on. And where I was living… well, it was all right, but it just wasn't… just wasn't…'

'Home?'

'No.' It was comforting to know he understood. 'I thought I might look round here for a property to rent. A little cottage, maybe.'

'Everything around here will be full up for the summer,' was his guess. Then when he saw my disappointment he went on, 'But come the autumn you could have your pick of properties, and meantime you can stay right where you are, with us.'

'Oh, Mark, I couldn't. That would be imposing.'

'Why? We have the room,' he pointed out. 'You always used to come and stay the summer.'

His tone had taken on a stubborn edge that I recalled enough to know I wouldn't win the argument, and so I simply told him, 'Well, you'd have to let me pay you then.'

'The hell I would.'

'I have the money, Mark. I have more money than I need. I can't just sit here like a sponge and let you feed me and take care of me when…' Just in time I caught myself, remembering I wasn't meant to know about Trelowarth being in financial difficulty.

Mark glanced sideways. 'When what?'

'Nothing.'

Silence dropped between us like a stone. I felt his gaze grow keener. 'What has Susan told you?'

'Nothing.'

I had never been much good at lying and I knew it, but he didn't press the point, and after studying my face a moment longer he looked back towards the sea again and told me, 'Friends don't pay.'

There was no way of getting round that, so I took a different tack. 'Then let me pay in kind.' I paused a moment, trying through the growing haze of drink to organize my argument, both because I had only just thought of it and because all of a sudden it struck me as something that truly appealed to me, something I'd even enjoy. 'I could help Susan with her tearoom project, help her get it off the ground.'

'Oh, right. That's all I need.'

'You've seen her plans?'

'You think I've had a choice?'

I said, 'I like them.'

'Do you?' It was more a comment, really, than a question, but I answered.

'Yes. She seems to have it all in hand, she's thought it through.'

'I don't doubt that.' His mouth curved, briefly. 'She gets that from our mother. My dad was the one who had all the ideas, but Mum was the person who saw things got done.'

He'd remember his mother, of course. He'd been eleven when she died, whereas Susan had still been a baby and I'd just started nursery school. My earliest memories went no further back than his stepmother, Claire, and Claire had always been so wonderful I'd never given much thought to the woman who'd preceded her.

'My dad was rudderless when Mum died. It's a good thing he met Claire; she really set him on his course again.' Mark's eyes crinkled faintly with fondness. 'She's a different sort of woman than my mum was, though, is Claire.'

'Well, she's an artist.'

'That she is. So was your sister,' he informed me. 'Even

back when we were young, before she ever started acting, she still had that spirit in her, same as Claire. They need the space to spread their wings. Like butterflies.' He squinted at the brightness of the sea as he looked westward, where the restless wind had blown Katrina's ashes. 'Ever try to hold a butterfly? It can't be done. You damage them,' he said. 'As gentle as you try to be, you take the powder from their wings and they won't ever fly the same. It's kinder just to let them go.'

I looked at him, and asked, because I'd always wondered, 'Is that why you stopped writing to Katrina?'

'She had bigger wings than most,' he said. 'She needed room to use them, and she couldn't do that here, now, could she? Anyway, it worked out for the best. She found her husband. They seemed happy.'

'Yes, they were.'

'Then that's all right.'

We fell to silence once again and might have gone on sitting there all afternoon if overhead the clouds had not begun to thicken and to threaten rain.

Mark stood first, more steady on his feet than me, and reached a hand to help me up. 'Come on,' he said. 'We'd best head back.'

He carried the now empty box for me, walking a few steps ahead down the field. Getting over the stile in the pasture fence took a bit more concentration this time, I couldn't get my legs and hands to coordinate in quite the same way as before and I nearly flipped headfirst down into the dirt, but luckily Mark didn't see that. Recovering my balance, I followed him carefully into the woods.

It was cool in here, quiet with ferns and the thick press of trees, and all the little flowers that I hadn't noticed coming up, but that I noticed now since I was keeping such a close watch on my feet and where they landed. There were little white wildflowers close by the edge of the path, and I wanted to ask Mark their name, but I suspected that he'd just come back with something long and Latin, like he always used to do. Show Mark something as lovely as a tiny star of Bethlehem, and he would take one look at it and without blinking say it was an *Ornithogalum umbellatum*. No, it had been my mother who had given me the names of all the grasses and the flowers I had brought back from my afternoon adventures in the woods and fields. I still remembered some of the old names she'd taught me—tailor's needles, feather-bow, penny-cake, and ladies' smock.

Ladies' smock used to be easy to find at this time of the year. I was looking for some when we came to the clearing where Claire's cottage sat with its windows wide open and welcoming. We hadn't bothered stopping in to see her when we'd come through here the first time, on our way up to the Beacon, because what we had gone up there to do had been a private sort of pilgrimage for both of us. But it would never do to pass Claire's cottage twice and not stop long enough to say hello.

Mark went to knock but got no answer.

'She's gone out,' I guessed.

'Most likely.' Still, he took his own keys out and stepped inside and called out from the entryway, then had a quick look round to reassure himself she wasn't lying ill or injured somewhere. 'Gone off sketching something, probably,' he gave his final verdict as he reappeared. 'She does it all the time.' Glancing up at the sky he said, 'I ought to get her windows shut before this rain starts. You go on, I'll catch you up. No need for us both to get soaked.'

The first splat of a raindrop on my shoulder helped convince me.

I moved quickly through the trees—a little too quickly, perhaps, because before I'd made it halfway through I started feeling dizzy so I stopped and briefly closed my eyes, recovering my balance. When I opened them again the woods became a blur of green and brown and quiet shadows. Damn the Scrumpy, I thought. It was muddling my thoughts and confusing my vision.

A tree a short distance in front of me went all unfocused, dividing in two. And there suddenly seemed to be two paths as well, one I didn't remember that angled away to the cliffs. I heard footsteps coming up behind me and I turned, expecting Mark, but there was no one there.

It must have been an echo, I decided, because here was Mark just coming into view now on the path, and looking slightly blurred as well until I focused with an effort. Seeing me standing there seemed to surprise him. He turned his collar up against the damp wind shaking through the leaves and asked me, 'Something wrong?'

'No, not at all.' I stood as steadily as I was able, not wanting to let on how much the Scrumpy had affected me. 'It's just that I couldn't remember which path to take.'

He laughed at that—the first time I had heard him laugh since I'd been back, and turned me round so I could see with my own eyes the way through the trees. 'There is only the one path, you know.'

There seemed little point in arguing. I simply let him take my hand as he had done when I was small, and as we came out of the woods the rain came on in earnest and we made a breathless run for it across the rising field towards the house.

❧

The dogs had been out in the garden as well. They sat lined up like penitents in the back corridor while Claire, with mop in hand, dealt with the crisscrossing paw tracks that muddied the floor. The corridor smelt of stone and plaster, and the rubber of old boots left drying underneath the rows of hooks that held a heaped array of well-used coats and cardigans. As Mark and I came diving in the door, wet through and stamping mud from our own feet, Claire gave us both a look.

'Not one more step,' she warned us, 'till you've taken off those boots. I'm nearly finished, I don't want to have to do this over.'

As Mark bent to his laces the dogs swarmed him happily, pleased he'd come down to their level. He fended them off as he told Claire, 'You don't need to do it at all. I'll take care of it.'

But there was no breaking the long years of habit. She twisted the mop in its bucket of hot water, wringing it out and then slapping it onto the flagstones in front of the dogs. 'And you lot,' she said, as she swished past them, 'can stay where you are, till your feet dry.'

I could have sworn the dogs snickered, the way men will nudge one another and wink when their wives tell them off. Claire had noticed it too, and she gave them a withering look that made the setter and the Labrador lie down, pretending submission. The cocker spaniel and the little mongrel, Samson, stayed near Mark and would have followed him in defiance of Claire's orders if he hadn't told them both to stay. They whined a token protest, but they did as they'd been told.

Mark said, good-naturedly, '*My* feet wouldn't be wet at all, if I hadn't had to stop and close your windows.'

'Did I leave them open? Sorry.' Thanking him, she glanced towards the windows just behind him as he straightened, but they both were tightly shut.

This was the part of the house that we children had passed through most often—the workaday, less showy side of Trelowarth. The section we were in now jutted farthest back into the yard—on one side of the corridor two windows and the door faced out across the yard itself, while on the other side the laundry room and office nestled side by side, their doorways all but hidden in among the hanging coats.

I left my own boots with their heels lined up against the wall, the way Claire liked them, and led the way round past the narrow back staircase that dropped like a chute from the old servants' quarters above, and then up the one uneven step to the kitchen.

Mark brought the box with him and asked where I wanted it.

'Anywhere's fine.' It was only a box now, with nothing inside.

Claire, who'd followed behind us, asked, 'How did it go?' in a tone that, to anyone else, might have sounded as though she were asking an everyday question.

I said, 'It was perfect, thanks.'

Mark put in, 'Eva got drunk.'

'I did not.'

'Get over it, you said yourself you were.' His grin was, like his stepmother's tone of voice, designed to even out the day's emotions. 'You still are. You ought to see your eyes.'

'Well, if they're anything like yours,' I said, 'I guess I'll need some coffee.'

'Guess you will. I'll make some, shall I?' And he headed for the kettle with an amiable purpose.

I was moving much more slowly, and Claire came to take my elbow. 'What on earth were you two drinking?'

'Scrumpy.'

'Ah. Then you'll be needing to sit down, darling.'

She took me through into the big front room that we had always called the library, because of all the bookshelves, and she saw me seated next to the piano, and then Mark came, with coffee for us all, and slouched into the sofa at my side. His hair was curling as it dried, and he looked so much like the boy he'd been once that it seemed incredible to me so many years had passed since I'd last sat in here, like this. With them.

Claire's mind had been traveling on the same line. 'I feel I ought to send you straight upstairs to have a bath,' she told me.

'I don't think I'd manage the stairs, at the moment.' I leaned my head back on the cushions, then brought it back upright to stop it from spinning as Claire asked where we'd taken the ashes.

Mark answered. 'The Beacon.'

If Claire understood the full meaning of that, she gave no indication. She only said, 'Oh yes, it's lovely up there.'

'It was, today,' he said. 'Where's Sue?'

'I'm here,' said Susan, coming in. She stopped inside the doorway, looked from Mark to me. 'Are you all right?'

'I'm fine,' Mark said, 'but Eva's had too much to drink.'

I sighed. 'I have not. Anyway, you can talk. Look at the state of you.'

'I'm not the one seeing double, now am I?'

Claire's voice was calm. 'Children.'

Susan came all the way into the room and sat down on my other side, curious. 'Who's seeing double?'

Mark rolled his head sideways. 'Eva tried to convince me there were two paths in the Wild Wood.'

I couldn't argue that, but I could lay the blame where it belonged. 'It's his fault.'

Susan looked at me in sympathy. 'What was it, whisky?'

'Scrumpy.'

'God. How could you?' she asked Mark.

His shrug seemed a great effort. 'Before you rush to judgment, you should know that *after* drinking Scrumpy with me, Eva started thinking that your tearoom was a wonderful idea.'

I elbowed him. He clutched his ribs and half-laughed, 'Ow.'

'I thought it was a wonderful idea before the Scrumpy.'

Susan, looking pleased, asked, 'Did you?'

'Yes. I was just telling Mark I'd like to help you set it up. Be your PR consultant, if that would be any use to you.'

Mark said, to Claire and Susan, 'In exchange for room and board. She'll be staying with us for the summer.'

He didn't mention anything about my plans to rent a cottage nearby when the tourist season ended in the autumn, presumably because, like me, Mark knew that Claire was generous to a fault, and had she known that I was looking for a cottage she'd have instantly insisted I take hers.

As it was, she smiled approval at me warmly from her corner while beside me Susan said, delighted, 'Are you? Eva, that's wonderful. Really, it's going to be just like old times.'

Mark shot her a sideways look over my head that I took as a silent reminder that things weren't exactly the same, with Katrina not here, and because I felt Susan's self-conscious reaction I covered the moment of awkwardness with, 'So you see, I'll have plenty of time to help out with your plans for the tearoom.'

Susan gratefully said, 'I can show you the greenhouse

tomorrow. Felicity's coming to help me start clearing it out. There are things stored in there that I don't think have moved since I went off to uni.'

Claire smiled. 'Very likely before that.'

I asked, 'Who's Felicity?'

'One of my friends from the village. You'll like her, I think. Won't she, Claire?'

'Yes, we all like Felicity.' Claire looked with affection at her stepson, who was sinking ever lower on the sofa. 'You'll be fast asleep, Mark, if you sit there much longer.'

'Mm.' He closed his eyes and proved her point by drifting off immediately, breathing in a slow and even rhythm.

'Men,' said Susan, rather fondly. Then to me, 'You ought to have a nap as well. I'm sure it's been a trying day.'

It had, and she was right, except my cup of coffee had kicked in now and I wasn't feeling sleepy anymore. Instead I sat with Claire and Susan, talking of small things while Mark snored on. And when we'd finished all the coffee in the pot and Claire had started thinking about what to make for supper, I felt more awake than ever.

'I can help,' I offered.

Susan shook her head. 'No, we can do it. You just stay here and relax.'

'You've only just arrived,' said Claire, and rubbed my shoulder as she passed. 'Let us take care of you.'

The sitting room was filled with things to do, except I couldn't play piano and I didn't want to turn the television on while Mark was still asleep. Instead, I stood and stretched and went to make a study of the bookshelves, where I recognized the old and battered bindings of the local history books my mother had so loved to give to Uncle George and Claire as gifts. It had been something of a passion for her, hunting down forgotten volumes in her favorite musty shops in London, antiquarian establishments with creaking floors and crowded shelves.

I chose one book and opened it: *A History of Polgelly*, written in the 1800s by a gentleman who, from his tone, had been an ardent Methodist. He disapproved quite heartily of all that had gone on here and had nothing good to say about Trelowarth, which he said had been 'a den of godless blackguards though its current owner, Mr. Hallett, has done what he can to drive the devil from that place.'

Unfortunately, being such a devout man, the author of *A History of Polgelly* never did get round to mentioning exactly what it was those godless blackguards had been up to. Losing interest, I reshelved his cheerless book and tried another one: *Polgelly Through the Ages*.

This was better. Not as preachy, and its author was a more romantic soul who started off with ancient legends and the story of the old well at St Non's, and wove his facts with bits of poetry that made the book a pleasant read.

I was halfway through by supper, and I took it upstairs afterwards to read in bed, in hopes that it would lull me off to sleep. But once again, I found myself too restless, whether from an overdose of coffee or residual emotion from our scattering the ashes, and when midnight came and went and left me staring at the walls I took another of my sleeping pills and waited for the drowsiness to claim me.

I was in that strange, floating place, well aware I was nearly asleep and past caring, when I thought I heard the same voices I'd heard before breakfast, the barest of whispers that seemed to come straight from the wall by my head.

'Oh, knock it off,' I mumbled with my face against the pillow. 'Let me sleep.'

They didn't stop. But in the end, I didn't mind, because the one voice had a very pleasant rhythm to it, and I let it soothe me into letting go my final hold on consciousness.

CHAPTER 6

SUSAN HAD BEEN RIGHT. I really liked her friend Felicity. She was, like Susan, lively and intelligent and quick to laugh, a pretty young woman with dark hair that would have come down in a cascade of curls if she hadn't kept it bound back with elastics and a clip and tied a scarf around it, gypsy style, presumably to guard against the dust that we were raising.

'I mean, honestly,' she asked us as she lifted yet another broken snooker cue, 'why would somebody keep all these?'

'You didn't know my Dad.' Susan smiled. 'He probably had plans to make them into something useful.'

'Yes, well, I've got plans for them and all.' She chucked the cue with all the others on the growing rubbish heap outside the door. The greenhouse was a fairly modern structure. According to Susan it had been built a decade ago, when Uncle George had suddenly decided he wanted to breed roses, to create new varieties instead of only cultivating existing ones, but as with so many things that Uncle George had started with enthusiasm, it had failed to hold his interest long. His passion for hybridizing had waned when it proved to be trickier work than he'd thought it would be, and at some point he must have abandoned his efforts because it appeared that the greenhouse had been given over to storage for several years now.

We three had spent the last two hours since breakfast digging through the clutter and attempting to create a bit of order. It was challenging.

'The thing is,' said Felicity, 'your family doesn't seem to have thrown anything away. What is this, your first shoe?' She held a tiny trainer up, and Susan looked.

'More likely Mark's.' She'd found a treasure of her own. 'Come look at this,' she said, and spread the pages of a heavy album open so that we could see the photographs. The colors of the pictures had begun to change a bit with age, more reddish than they should have been, but still they showed some lovely views around Trelowarth gardens.

'This shouldn't be in here, it's going to get ruined.' Susan turned the pages reverently. 'Oh look, there's Claire.'

'That's quite the outfit,' said Felicity.

'Have a heart, it *was* the eighties. Eva, look at this. Just look.'

I looked and saw a charming picture of the Lower Garden with the roses all in bloom and beautiful. I said, 'You ought to have that one enlarged and hang it up in here.'

Susan turned towards Felicity. 'Could you do that, Fee?'

'Course I could.'

'Fee's brilliant with photography. You ought to see her pictures of the harbor,' Susan told me.

'Well, it's what the tourists want. I had some made up into note cards for the shop last summer. Couldn't keep enough of them in stock.'

I asked her, curious, 'Where is your shop?'

'Beside Penhaligon's.'

'Where Mrs. Kinneck's used to be,' said Susan. 'You remember Mrs. Kinneck, Eva? She had all those jars of sweets behind the counter, and she always gave us liquorice babies.'

I remembered.

'It's all changed, now,' Susan said. 'The old shops are all gone. Except the fudge shop—that's still there, thank God—but Mrs. Griggs is gone and Mr. Turner's.'

I asked, 'What about the little place that sold the seashells in the baskets, near the harbor?'

'It's a tearoom, now,' she told me, 'but the girl that runs it can't make scones for toffee.'

'Sue will put her out of business,' said Felicity.

Susan turned another page of photographs. 'I don't want to put anybody out of business, Fee. I'm only interested in keeping us *in* business.' She looked down at the photographs, determined. 'My father would spin in his grave if Trelowarth passed out of the family.'

Felicity held up a long piece of signboard with the name 'Trelowarth Roses' stenciled on it in blue paint. 'What's this?'

'Oh. Part of the display we used to take around to flower shows, when Dad was still keen on that sort of thing.'

I vaguely remembered the rhythm of all those shows, spread through the season from springtime to autumn, although as a child I'd been barely aware of the effort that Uncle George put into preparing for them. Looking at the neglected display, I asked, 'Doesn't Mark do shows?'

'He hasn't in years. He's a true Hallett male,' Susan said. 'You can't blast the man out of his garden unless he sees a need for it, and now he's got the Internet he rarely sees the need for being sociable. He's going to die a bachelor,' she predicted.

'Oh, I doubt it. Mark's a handsome man,' I said.

'Well, not with this hairstyle, he isn't.' Still flipping through the pages of the photograph album, she turned it so Felicity and I could see the photo of a teenaged Mark with denims and fluorescent lime green T-shirt, with his hair blow-dried and feathered like a 1980s pop star.

Felicity laughed out loud. 'And who on earth is that, behind him?'

'That,' said Susan, 'would be Claire, again. We really should take these to show her, she'll have probably forgotten they were here.'

Felicity thought it more likely that Claire had been storing the album out here in the greenhouse on purpose, to bury the evidence. 'Who would want to be reminded of those clothes?'

But it was getting near to lunchtime and my stomach was aware of it, and Claire had made it clear she was expecting us for sandwiches and tea, which at the moment seemed a very good idea.

The same thought must have struck the dogs, for as we walked downhill towards the coast path all of them fell in behind us, bouncing playfully on one another until Susan with a whistle sent them racing on ahead. The larger three dogs vanished in the woods, but scruffy Samson circled back and snuffled happily along close by my heels as Susan and Felicity forged on ahead of us.

I'd always liked the company of dogs. I'd never had one of my own. When I was younger in Vancouver we'd had two cats that my father had said firmly were the only pets we needed, and none of my apartments in L.A. would have allowed a pet, but walking now with Samson I reflected on how comforting the bond could be between a person and a dog.

Apparently he liked me too. He wagged his stumpy tail at the least word from me and seemed content himself to let the others go ahead while he stayed close beside me on the path, so when he paused to let his nose explore a patch of undergrowth, I stopped as well and waited for him. 'What's so interesting?'

Samson couldn't tell me what he smelled, of course. He

cocked his ears to catch my voice but kept his nose down, focused on the scent around the leaves. A rabbit, likely. Maybe even Susan's badger. I was going to suggest we move along when something rustled not far off, and Samson's head shot up. One sniff and he was after it, his little body plunging through the trees, and even as I drew in breath to call him back the trees themselves began to shift and move.

At least, it looked as though that's what the trees were doing. Startled by the strangeness of it, I stopped short.

The path, for some reason, appeared to have narrowed. The wind had grown suddenly warmer and sunlight was filtering down through the leaves at a new angle, dappling everything round me with shadows. And there, just in front of me, where I knew full well it hadn't been moments before, was a fork in the path.

The surprise held me motionless. That, and the uneasy knowledge that what I was looking at couldn't be real. It was only a trick of the mind. Had to be. There was only *one* path through the woods. Mark had shown me that yesterday—and anyway I'd just been looking right there, at that very spot, not half a minute earlier, and I'd seen nothing. Only trees.

The second path lay quietly in shadow, unconcerned with my refusal to believe that it was there. It curved away towards the cliffs, towards the sea, and all the ragged growth along its edges showed it hadn't just been newly made, as did the deeply sliding marks that looked like footprints left by someone walking there just after rain.

Confused, I looked along the path I knew, the only path that should have been there, but Felicity and Susan had gone on so far ahead I couldn't see them anymore. I called out to them anyway. 'Susan?'

But nobody answered.

The wind shook the branches and leaves overhead and the scenery shifted again, faintly dizzying. I closed my eyes.

Something crashed through the ferns at my side and my heart jumped straight into my throat, beating hard. Then a snuffling nose nudged my leg. Very slowly, I opened my eyes and looked down to see Samson returned from his chasing whatever it was, with a bit of twig stuck in the fur of his fast-wagging tail.

I breathed carefully. Lifted my gaze to the trees. All was just as it should be—one path through the woods, every tree in its place, and Felicity walking with Susan ahead of me.

And when my own legs stopped trembling, I followed them.

⁂

Lunch was a blur. I remembered to eat and to follow along with the table talk so I could nod when I needed to. I even joined in a couple of times. But I wasn't entirely there, and Claire noticed.

She wasn't the kind of a person to pry. Still, she took me in hand after lunch, when we'd moved with our biscuits and tea to the patio in the back garden. Claire's garden had a fairy-tale look to it, bordered as it was by the tall trees of the Wild Wood. Whatever grew here grew in shade. A trailing vine heaped tiny buds of honeysuckle all along the waist-high wall of stone built in the tight-fitted herring-bone pattern so common in this part of Cornwall, and the back of the garden was lush with soft ferns and tall spikes of something that looked darkly tropical. Yet in defiance of the shadows, Claire had set a sundial squarely at the centre of her garden in the one place where the sunlight always reached, and with a ring of upturned earth around it, ready to be planted.

When Felicity and Susan brought out the photo album once again and started flipping through its pages, Claire said, 'Eva, come and help me plant my flowers, darling.'

She fetched me a spare pair of gardening gloves and a trowel and took me across to the sundial, beneath which a varied assortment of seedlings were waiting in small plastic pots. 'Here.' She tipped out a small spindly flower of some kind, its fragile roots bound in a pressed clump of soil, and I knelt down beside her to take it. At first we said nothing. We planted the flowers together in a rhythm I remembered— scoop, set one down, tamp, tamp, mound up a basin to keep in the rainwater, reach for the next one, then scoop, set one down, tamp, tamp…

The repetition soothed me, and the sunlight caught my moving hand and glinted on the little golden Claddagh ring. 'Aunt Claire.'

'Yes?'

'Can I ask you something?'

'Certainly.'

'When Uncle George died…' No, that wasn't right. I started over. '*After* Uncle George died, did your mind ever play tricks on you?'

'What sort of tricks?'

'Well, make you think you saw things that weren't really there.'

She stopped digging with her trowel partway in the earth and glanced up again. 'Are *you* seeing things?'

'Sometimes. And hearing them.'

'You mean the voices you heard in your room. Mark did mention that yesterday.'

I mounded my basin with careful hands. 'What, did he think I was losing my mind?'

'No, of course not.' She gently pinched a dead and wilted bloom from the next plant before she set it in its hole. 'Our bodies have a lot to deal with, darling, when we're grieving. And in answer to your question, yes, my mind played tricks when I lost George. It still does, even now. I smell his aftershave, from time to time. It's been five years this spring,' she said, 'and sometimes I still feel as though he's very near.' She looked directly at me then and smiled a small and understanding smile. 'Be patient, Eva. It will all get easier.'

I'd reached the final flower. 'Yes, I know.' Scoop, set it down, tamp, tamp.

'There,' said Claire with satisfaction, dusting off her hands against her legs as she stood to inspect our work.

I rose too, and for the first time took a good look at the sundial. The stone base had graceful curved lines and the vane on its top face that marked the sun's passing was shaped like a butterfly pausing at rest with its wings folded upwards, set to cast its ever-moving shadows round a dial of Roman numerals raised in elegant relief. Around the whole top ran a poignant bit of poetry, in script:

The butterfly counts not months but moments,
And has time enough.

I traced the letters with one finger. Claire said, 'That's a lovely poem, don't you think? By Rabindranath Tagore. I've always liked his poetry. Felicity outdid herself, I think.'

'Felicity made this?'

'It's what she does,' said Claire. 'She's quite a brilliant sculptress.'

'Yes, she is.'

The bronze wing of the butterfly was casting its long shadow at the halfway point between the Roman numerals one and two, and Claire looked at her wristwatch to compare the times. 'Bang on,' she said. 'There's something to be said for the old ways.' A breeze swept singing through the branches of the trees that marked the edges of the woods around us, and she raised her face to it. 'I've always rather liked the Celtic view of life, that this world and the next one aren't so separate from each other. My grandmother believed that. She was Welsh, you know—a true Celt, through and through—and if you'd told *her* you'd heard whispers in your walls, she would have taken it in her stride,' she said, with certainty. 'She would have said you'd heard the voices of the people living at Trelowarth, sharing space with us, but in another time.'

I thought that was a rather lovely concept, and I said as much.

'I think so, too,' said Claire. 'So there, you see? Perhaps the voices you've been hearing aren't imagined ones at all.'

'You're only saying that to make me feel less crazy.'

'Is it working?'

'Sort of.' With a rueful smile I leaned into the comfort of her one-armed hug, and told her, 'Thank you.'

'You're most welcome.'

Turning, she looked back towards the patio, where Susan and Felicity were sitting with their heads bent close together over the old photos. 'Haven't you two finished laughing at my frocks, yet?'

'Hardly.' Susan called over. 'We're choosing a few to put up in the tearoom.'

'You do, and I'll take them back down.'

'Not of *you*,' Susan said with a laugh. 'Of the greenhouse.

Like this one.' She hefted the album, and rose and came over to show us.

'Oh,' Claire said. 'Well yes, that one's lovely.'

Looking at the picture of the greenhouse, with Claire's mention of her grandmother still recent in my mind, I said to Susan, 'Weren't you going to ask Claire about the tearoom where her grandparents met?'

'So I was.'

Felicity, who'd come across to join us by the sundial, didn't know the story, and asked Claire, 'Your grandparents met in a tearoom?'

'They did.'

Susan prompted, 'You have to tell the story, it's romantic. Especially the part where your grandfather takes off his clothes.'

Claire smiled. 'He did no such thing.'

'He did. He took off his shirt.'

'He was being a gentleman.'

Felicity found that amusing. 'That's what they all say.'

Claire went on, 'It had started to rain, and my grand-mother's group—she had come down to Cornwall with some of her friends, from St Davids, in Wales—they got caught in it, soaked to the skin, so they ducked into the tearoom to get warm. And my grandfather was working there that day, he was a plumber, and he saw her and was smitten.'

Susan picked up the tale. 'So he went straight over to her table and whipped off his shirt, and—'

'Nothing quite so dramatic.' Claire's wry glance was indulgent. 'He saw that she was shivering and offered her his own dry shirt. A gentleman,' she said again. 'Although, in fairness, Gran always suspected that he only did it to show off his chest. He was a well-built man.'

'What was the name of the tearoom?' asked Susan.

'The Cloutie Tree.'

Perfect for Cornwall, I thought. Cloutie trees were a Celtic tradition, most often a thorn tree that grew by a holy well, on which the faithful tied 'clouts', bits of cloth they'd first dipped in the water, to take away sickness and wounds. As the cloth wore away to the elements, the ailment supposedly healed. There was one of these trees at St Non's, in fact, not all that far from here, only the pilgrims who came to the holy well there were more likely to wish for things other than health when they tied their bright strips of cloth onto the tree. I'd once wished for a pony, myself, though I'd never received one.

'The Cloutie Tree Tearoom.' Susan tried the name herself and seemed to like it. 'I believe I'll call mine that, as well. What do you think, Claire?'

Claire looked as though her thoughts were somewhere far away. I saw her pull them back again and find a smile. 'I think it would be lovely, Susan. Very fitting.'

She touched the sundial at her side with almost wistful fingers and then turned and went to put her tools away.

It struck me as I watched her walk across the wild back garden that Claire, like me, had lost her family young. Her grandparents, her parents—they'd have all been gone, as mine had, by the time she reached her twenties, since according to my parents she had been alone when she had married Mark and Susan's father. And except for Mark and Susan, she was now alone again.

It was the way of things, I thought. We never knew what time would bring us. Looking down, I watched the shadow shift a fraction on the sundial.

Counting, not by months, but moments, as the poem said. I almost envied that bronze butterfly, content to live completely in the present, unconcerned with what had gone before. What might have been.

The memory of Claire's words of comfort rose again to fill my mind: *Be patient, Eva. It will all get easier.*

I hoped—I really hoped—that she was right.

CHAPTER 7

THE TERM "HALLUCINATION'", READ the article I'd called up on the Internet, 'is applied to false perceptions made by any of the senses, though the ones that are most commonly involved are sight and hearing.'

Shifting again in the chair at Mark's desk in the room that he used as his office, just off the back corridor, I settled in to keep reading. The article scrolled for what seemed like forever and slipped into language that probably only made sense to psychiatrists, but the subsection on 'Auditory Hallucinations' perfectly described the kind of voices I'd been hearing from my room. And while most people seeing things appeared to conjure nonexistent people and not empty paths, it was still obvious to me that what I'd seen in the Wild Wood fit the criteria for 'Visual Hallucinations'.

The causes, the article told me, were varied. If I ruled out schizophrenia, that left a list of others that included stress, depression, and fatigue. And there were several medications that apparently induced hallucinations as a side effect. Particularly sedatives.

I rummaged in my handbag on the floor beside the chair to find the sleeping pills I'd been prescribed, and entering the name on the computer searched for side-effects. Yes, there it was—right there in black and white: *Hallucinations*.

I could feel myself relax. I wasn't going mad at all, I

thought, relieved. It was the pills and nothing more. And if I didn't take them anymore then that would be the end of it, because the detailed article explained hallucinations always stopped when one removed their cause.

Outside the office in the corridor I heard the back door open and the stamp of boots and scrabbling feet of dogs. I just had time to drop the pills back in my handbag and close down my search screens, returning to the colorful display of website templates I'd been looking at before, as Mark came in and asked me, 'Any joy?'

'I don't know. Which one do you like?'

He arched an eyebrow warily. 'I thought you said the website was for Susan.'

'Well, she'll be maintaining it,' I said, 'but it's Trelowarth's image that we're putting out here, and you'll want to have some say in that. Besides,' I pointed out, 'your blog will be from the same template.'

'*My* blog?'

'You're the expert on Old Garden roses. Oh, come on.' I smiled at his expression. 'You'll have fun. You'll get to interact with all your customers.'

'I do that now. They email me their orders and I fill them.'

'Mr. Sociable.'

'And what exactly am I meant to blog about?'

I gave a shrug. 'Whatever you get up to in the garden. Or the history of the roses. Or whatever strikes your fancy. It's your blog.'

'All right then, mastermind.' He hitched a chair close to my own and sat. 'You win.' He scanned the templates. 'That one's not too bad.'

'Good. That's the one that Susan liked, as well. Now, let's talk colors…'

Mark had always been a good sport. He endured another half an hour of website-planning torture with me before he began to fidget.

'Never mind,' I said. 'I've got enough to start with. I can have this up and running for you in a week.'

'A week.' From the way he looked around I could tell that the prospect of having me taking up half his home office for that length of time gave him pause.

I reassured him, 'I don't have to work in here, if it's a problem. I can use your extra printer and the laptop, on the kitchen table.'

'No need for that. I tell you what,' he said, 'why don't you use my dad's old study? Set the printer and the laptop up in there, and you can work in peace. You won't be tripping over all my mess.'

A good solution, really. Uncle George's study was conveniently close to my own bedroom, and well across the landing from both Mark's and Susan's rooms, so I could work late if I wanted without worrying I'd keep them up. And working late was how I got myself through those first nights without the sleeping pills, which I had safely buried at the bottom of a drawer.

I was, if nothing else, productive in my work. I had the website done within a week, as promised, and when Wednesday rolled around again I'd finished with the final bits of testing and was drifting off to sleep at night without the aid of anything, and feeling more myself.

And very ready for a change of scene. It had been raining off and on for the past week, and so I hadn't really minded being cloistered in the study, but stepping out the back door now I found the morning bright and fresh and sunny, with a clean wind off the sea that swept the calling gulls along with it and cleared my cobwebbed mind.

The dogs came bounding up to greet me and raced off again to be with Mark, wherever he was working in the gardens. I considered going after them, but knew I wouldn't be much help to Mark, I'd only slow him down. Besides, now that I had the website done, I needed to discuss the next steps in our new promotion plan, and that meant finding Susan.

She was in the greenhouse with Felicity, standing just inside the door and staring at the plumber who'd arrived a few minutes before, sent by Andrews & Son from St Non's to inspect the old plumbing and give her a quote for the work to be done. I couldn't help but stare a bit myself—he was a decidedly well-built young man, so much so that Felicity, watching him study the pipes, nudged her friend and said, 'Well done you. Recreating the past with precision, aren't you?'

Susan asked, 'What?'

'Recreating Claire's Cloutie Tree Tearoom, right down to the good-looking plumber. I'd like to see *him* take his shirt off.'

'Fee!'

'What? He can't hear us. God, will you just look at that.'

I looked too and smiled a little as the plumber, seemingly completely unaware he had an audience, reached up to test the soundness of an overhead joint in the piping, a movement that showed off his broad muscled chest.

'What's his name?' asked Felicity.

Susan, equally awed, shook her head. 'I don't know. They just sent him.'

'Well, they've got my business.'

I smiled even more at Felicity's tone, but it didn't convince me. She'd been up to Trelowarth a few times this past week, enough for me to come to the conclusion that Felicity, for all her talk, was already quite hopelessly infatuated.

Mark, of course, had no idea. I could see how Felicity looked at him when he came into a room, and the way that she constantly watched him, the light in her smile when he spoke to her. But men could be so impossibly blind, I thought, just as the plumber was blind to the fact we were all of us watching him now.

'Perhaps I ought to see if he has any questions,' Susan said, all innocence, then spoilt it with a wink and crossed the greenhouse with a more purposely feminine walk than her usual breezy stride.

Felicity watched her friend go with approval. To me, she said, 'It's good to see her taking an interest in men again, after the last one.'

After Susan's sharp reaction to my mention of her time in Bristol, I hadn't pried further, but I felt safe in asking Felicity now, 'Was he awful?'

'Not at all. But he was older. Much older than Sue, and that made things quite difficult sometimes. She didn't really fit in with his friends, and he didn't fit in with hers, and... well, they came from different generations, different worlds, and sometimes that's a gap that can't be bridged. I know she tried. It was your sister's death,' she told me, 'that decided things, I think. Sue said it made her realize life was just too short, so she came home.' She glanced at me confidingly. 'Your sister's death affected everyone round here. It was a blow.'

'To me as well.'

I liked the way Felicity accepted that, not leaping in with platitudes. 'Was she your only sister?'

'Yes.'

'I can't imagine. Me, I've got three sisters and two brothers. Breed like rabbits, we do. Every time I go home for a visit it seems that I've got a new nephew or niece.'

'Where's home?' I asked her.

'Somerset.'

It surprised me she wasn't from Cornwall. She looked Cornish enough, with her dark hair and eyes and her small tidy figure set off to advantage in jeans and a form-fitting shirt and the gypsy-like scarf that today bound her curls in a long swinging ponytail. She'd picked up a bit of the accent as well, the distinctive and musical cadence of West Country speech, and I wouldn't have known that she wasn't a native.

'It's not all that far away, really,' she told me, 'though when I first came down here it seemed like a different world, like I had crossed some great divide.'

'You did,' I said. 'You crossed the Tamar.' And I told her what my mother had told me about the crossing of the river Tamar and how it affected those with Cornish blood.

'Well, I must have an ancestor from Cornwall then,' she said, 'because I definitely felt it. I was on a summer holiday with friends, and I had one more year to finish uni, and all that time the only thing I thought about was how to get back here. And in the end I just packed up and came. No plans. My parents thought I'd gone completely mad. They still do,' she said, 'but they've given up trying to cure me. I've told them, it's Cornwall. There's no way to fight it.'

I knew what she meant. There was something about this remote western corner of Britain that captured the soul and refused to let go, something ancient and wild in the moors and black cliffs and the voice of the sea that spoke always of something unseen and enchanted.

Felicity tried to express it in words. 'In Cornwall,' she told me, 'one truly feels magic could actually happen.'

❧

I thought of those words as I walked down The Hill after lunch on my way to the bank in Polgelly. There was no one but me on the road. Which was just as well, really, since there would have been little room for a car to push past me, especially once I got under the shady green canopy of the arched trees, with the steeply banked hedges of stone, turf, and tangled growth rising to block out my view of the fields at both sides. As the breeze shook the leaves overhead I remembered the strong sense of magic I'd felt here myself, as a child.

I'd been sure there were fairies concealed in the soft nodding bluebells that peered from the grass of the verge, and I'd trodden with care so as not to disturb them. Each stir of the breeze through the leaves had, to my childish ears, seemed to carry a faint lilting music, not meant for the grown-ups, that beckoned me on. I had often imagined the tunnel of trees was the doorway to fairyland, and I'd been certain that one day I'd step out the other side into some wonderful place.

It hadn't happened to me then. It didn't happen now. But still, I felt a thrilling echo of that old anticipation as I passed out of the trees and started down into Polgelly. Here, I thought, was all the magic one could need.

I felt like a child in the summer again at the first sight of the whitewashed shops and houses on the twisting streets, the rooftops stacked like toy blocks up the hills around the harbor where the gulls, drawn by the smells of fish and seaweed, circled with their plaintive cries.

The tide was out. Along the closer edges of the harbor all the smaller boats lay drunkenly tipped over on their hulls in the wet mud, still at their moorings while they waited for the sea's return.

The harbor was a classic smuggler's haven, curving like

a finger inland, shielded at its entrance by the jagged rocks along the coast. If there had been no houses here to mark the spot it would have been impossible to know there was a harbor in behind those rocks, and even as it stood it took a bit of skill and luck for any tourist who tried navigating in by sailboat.

The street that ran along the harbor wall looked very much as I'd remembered it. The bank had undergone a change of name, but it still sat on the same corner, and the same strong scents of polished floors and paperwork were there to greet me as I entered. The new accounts manager, Mr. Rowe, was a patient and thorough man who walked me through all the forms that I had to fill out. I had kept my British passport and was still a British citizen, which made things somewhat simpler.

'And you're living at Trelowarth, now, you said?'

'That's right.'

'I'll use that as your local address then. And how much money would you like me to arrange to have wired over from your bank in California?'

I said, 'All of it,' and handed him the printed details of my two American accounts. He raised his eyebrows at the sum but didn't comment. All he said was, 'Very good, I'll have this all approved and let you know when we receive your money.'

'Thank you.' With a handshake, I went out again, crossing the road to the fudge shop.

The little bell still rang as I went in, and as I crossed the threshold I felt ten years old again, transported by the sweet assault of wondrous smells too rich and varied to be numbered or identified. I bought half a pound of my old favorite flavor, mint chocolate, and took it out with me, intending to indulge in more nostalgia and enjoy it while I sat among the tourists on the sun-warmed harbor wall, but my eye was caught instead by the green chemist's sign a little farther up the winding street. Felicity had said her own shop was beside the chemist's, so I tucked the rattly paper bag of fudge into my pocket and went up to have a look.

I'd expected to find it closed, since Wednesdays were Felicity's days off and she was still up helping Susan at the greenhouse, but an 'Open' sign was hanging in the front door like an invitation, so I ventured in.

The shop had a lovely, eclectic appeal, like its owner. There were note cards in delicate pen and ink, scenes of the harbor, and wind chimes of spun glass that caught the sun, sparkling. A rainbow of silk scarves and bright Celtic jewelry in silver and gold fought for space with a jumbled display of framed paintings, a few of which were Claire's—I knew the strong sweep of her brushstrokes and the boldness of her palette and the way she brought her scenes alive with light.

Felicity's sculptures were here as well, castings in bronze that showed all of the skill of the butterfly sundial and more. My favorites were the little piskies, fairy folk of Cornwall— different versions of the same small figure, looking as though somebody had caught them in the middle of a dance.

Behind me, near the till, I heard a stool scrape and the sound of footsteps crossing the shop floor, and then a young man's voice, friendly, spoke up at my side. 'Can I help you?'

I glanced round with a shake of my head. 'I'm just looking.'

'See anything you like?' The lazy smile let me know the double meaning was intentional. He would have been about my age, nice-looking, with golden-blond hair and blue eyes that seemed oddly familiar.

I looked at him more closely and his smile grew more reproachful as he said, 'You don't remember me.'

I wasn't certain. 'Oliver?'

Surely it couldn't be Oliver, son of the woman who'd looked after Susan and Mark when their mother had died. Having come with his mother each day to Trelowarth he'd known both the house and the grounds just as well as the rest of us did. Even after Claire had married Uncle George his mother had come up to help from time to time, and when we children came down to Polgelly we had often played with Oliver.

He folded his arms on his chest, looking pleased. 'You remembered.'

'Yes, well, you don't forget boys who throw rocks at you.'

'Once,' he said. 'I threw a pebble at you *once*, and anyway as I recall you picked it up and chucked it back. And you had better aim.'

I had. I'd hit him on the forehead. Knocked him over. 'You grew up.'

'And you.' He smiled again. 'Mark didn't say that you were coming for a visit. Are you here for long?'

'I might be,' I said. 'So you work with Felicity, then?'

He corrected me. 'Only on Wednesdays. I'm closed myself, Wednesdays.' In answer to my questioning look, he said, 'I have my own Smugglers' Museum.'

'Oh? Whereabouts?'

'Down by the harbor, between the pub and the tearoom.' Oliver grinned. 'I weighed twelve stone when I started up the museum. I won't tell you what I weigh now.'

He looked fit as an athlete, to me. With his head tipped to one side, he asked, 'Do you smell chocolate?'

'It's my fudge.' I took the bag out of my pocket to show him. 'It's energy,' I told him. 'For The Hill.'

'Let's have a piece, then.'

I offered the bag and he reached in and helped himself.

'What's your excuse?' I asked. 'You live down here.'

'True.' The charm was deliberate. 'But I have a feeling I'm going to be climbing The Hill fairly often myself, in the very near future.'

CHAPTER 8

I CHEATED IN THE end. I didn't climb back to Trelowarth by the road, but went around the harbor's edge and up the coast path, up the gentler slope that rose by stages to the level of the clifftop, keeping to the bottom of the fields below Trelowarth as it wound its way towards the Wild Wood.

At the side of the path, clumps of dark spiky gorse were in bloom with their deep yellow flowers, the foxgloves were rampant, and thick drifts of sea pink spilled over the edge of the cliffs. I could hear the full roar of the sea here, the swirl of the spray crashing hard on the rocks far below where I walked, and the sullen retreat of the waves.

Most tourists avoided this stretch of the coast path. Only seasoned ramblers came this way, or people who wanted to visit the Beacon. Or those, like myself, who preferred the wilder, untouched ways, and didn't mind walking too close to the edge.

Even so, when the path reached a place where it rounded a cleft in the cliff side a little *too* closely, a quick downward glance at the white water boiling below on the rocks made me feel slightly dizzy. And when, as I straightened, the wind rose with a sudden force that rocked me on my feet, I turned my back to it and left the path for safety's sake, cutting up on a diagonal through the fields below the house.

I huddled in my jacket, head tucked down, and climbed

determinedly. I'd nearly reached the house when it occurred to me that something wasn't right.

I should have reached the lawn by now. The level hedged lawn at the front of the house where we'd always played badminton. But I hadn't. I lifted my head to see how much farther I had yet to go. And then I stopped dead in my tracks.

The lawn was gone.

And where it should have been, not fifteen feet from me, a man was standing with his back towards me, unaware. He seemed to be watching the road.

He wore a sleeveless coat of some rough brown material that flared below his waist, and the sleeves of the white shirt he wore underneath it were rolled to his elbows in working-man style. On his legs he wore tight-fitting brown trousers tucked into boots, also brown, that came up to his knees. And his hair—that was brown as well, worn long enough to be combed back and tied at his collar, the way I'd seen sailors wear their hair in period films.

He couldn't be real, I thought. Clearly he was nothing more than another hallucination. A good one, to be sure, and very vivid, but not real.

But it was frightening to know I'd lost control of my own senses so completely. I could only stand there, frozen, not quite certain what to do. And I would always in my mind replay the moment when, incredibly, he turned. And saw me too.

His eyes were not brown. They were of some lighter color, clear in their intensity against his suntanned face.

Uneasy, I stepped backwards, and he raised one hand to calm me.

'Do not fear me. I'll not harm you.' Something struck me as familiar in the cadence of his voice—a deep voice, rough around the edges.

But I *was* afraid. It made no sense for me to be, I knew, because he wasn't real; he wasn't there. Pure instinct made me take another backwards step, and then another.

'Wait,' he said, and moved as if to follow, only something very curious began to happen then. As I moved backwards and away from him, he started to dissolve and fade, becoming like a shadow I could almost see but not.

I thought I saw him stretch his hand towards me as though trying to reach out, to stop my leaving. And then all at once he was no longer there on the hillside, and in the same heart-beat I wasn't there either.

Instead I was back on the coast path again, standing all by myself at the place where it rounded a cleft in the cliff side a little too closely, and watching the water boil white on the black rocks below.

⌘

Uncle George's study, where I'd worked on the computer this past week, had been my favorite room for hiding in when we'd played hide-and-seek as children. From behind the green chair I'd been able to see all three doors—the one directly opposite that led into the corridor, and both doors that connected with the rooms to either side. The old desk had a kneehole space that had been just the size for me to crouch in, and the long and heavy drapes that hung to each side of the window were the perfect length for someone small to hide behind.

I couldn't hide there now, but it was maybe no coincidence that I had sought my refuge here this afternoon. I'd been here an hour, having raced up through the fields in record time to find, to my relief, that there was no one in the house yet—they were all still out attending to their work. Which meant nobody was here to ask me why I was now surfing through the Internet for articles on mental illness and hallucinations.

What disturbed me wasn't simply that I'd slipped out of reality so quickly and so easily, but that I could have done it so completely, and that my own sense of place and time had been so badly skewed that in my mind I could believe I'd climbed the hill and seen the man in brown, when actually I'd never left the coast path.

I could no longer blame the sleeping pills—even though the articles I'd read did say withdrawal from the drugs could have the same effect as taking them, I'd only taken two pills to begin with and I'd gone a week without them, so I doubted I was going through withdrawal. And in case the cause was stress, I'd tried removing any source of that as well, even going so far as to take off my wristwatch and put it away in the drawer with my mobile phone, both former trappings of my tightly scheduled life.

I'd done everything I could do, but this obviously wasn't something I should try to diagnose myself. I'd have to find a local doctor and explain what had been happening and see if there was any way to treat it. And I had to find out how I ought to handle any episodes I might have in the meantime.

Curled in the green chair, I scrolled through the pages and carried on reading:

Sane people know they are hallucinating. Those with mental illnesses do not.

Well *that*, at least, was one small bit of comfort. I'd been very well aware the whole time I'd been interacting with the strange man on the hill that he had not been real. And yet, it had all felt so real. The strong wind and the sun's warmth and the hardness of the ground beneath my feet…

Hallucinations can involve a multitude of senses—touch and taste and smell as well as sight and hearing—to the point where it can be all but impossible to distinguish the imagined from the real. A glass of juice, the writer said, will taste like juice, and silk will feel like silk.

I searched on for further points on 'Seeing People', and discovered it was common to imagine human figures when hallucinating, and to hear them speak, and just as common to be able to have conversations in which they responded exactly as real people would. The articles assured me that, so long as these imagined people didn't try to tell me to do questionable things, like kill somebody, they were harmless.

Our studies have shown, one psychiatrist said, that while ignoring these apparitions appears to have little effect, success can sometimes be achieved by simply telling them to go away.

Moreover…

I broke off my reading as a movement caught the corner of my eye.

I glanced up, expecting Mark or Susan, only there was no one in the doorway to the corridor. No one… and yet the doorway was not empty.

The figure of a man was passing. I could see him very faintly, like a grey transparent shadow, moving past as though he'd meant to walk right by the room. But at the doorway's edge he stopped and leaned back slightly, looking in as though he'd just seen something that he too considered out of place.

I closed my eyes and held my breath, not moving. Counted heartbeats. One. Two. Three. *It isn't real*, I told myself. My brain cells were misfiring, as the articles had just explained. There wasn't really anybody there.

And when I looked again, there wasn't.

It gave me a thrill of accomplishment, knowing I'd managed to control it that time. Maybe that was all it took, a short pause to remind myself that I was only seeing things. At least I would be able then to muddle through until I'd had a chance to see a doctor.

On the desk a small brass carriage clock whirred briefly and began to chime the hours: five o'clock. The others would be coming in quite soon, I thought, which meant I should stop sitting there and try to make myself a bit more useful to my hosts by going down and finding something I could cook them all for supper.

I stood and reached to switch off the computer, but before my hand made contact, the entire desk and what was on it wavered out of focus with the room and then dissolved.

I closed my eyes again, more firmly this time, fighting back with all I had. I heard the window rattling as though from a blast of wind and felt a brightening of light against my eyelids that surprised me into opening my eyes.

The door connecting with the spare room next to this one was now open too, and framed within it stood the man in brown.

At least, the man who had been wearing brown the last time I'd imagined him. This time, in place of the jacket, he wore a wine-red dressing gown that hung unfastened so that I could see he was still fully dressed beneath it in the plain white shirt and trousers and tall boots. It should have made him less imposing, but it didn't. With the door frame for a reference he looked taller to me here. He'd have been six foot something, easily. His shoulders blocked the open space. He didn't smile.

His voice was low and quiet, carefully controlled. 'What are you?'

I was thinking just how odd a question that was for my own hallucination to be asking when his right arm shifted slightly and I saw what he was holding in his hand. I saw the knife.

It was a dagger, small and neatly made, and fit his hand so well I only really saw the blade, but that was all it took to make me feel a twinge of fear. Irrational, I knew, because this man was my creation, my own mind had called him up from somewhere, and as all the articles had said, he would be harmless. But I started to retreat, to back away as I had done before when we had faced each other on the hillside, hoping it would have the same effect. It didn't. This time, instead of disappearing, he came after me and in two strides had crossed the room to take a firm hold of my arm with his free hand.

If the contact was a shock to me it seemed to shock him more, as though he'd been expecting that his hand would pass right through me. I was much too stunned to struggle, and besides, there was no point. His grip was far too strong, and he was far too close.

He asked again, as though the answer mattered even more, 'What are you?'

Trying to remember the advice that had been in the final article I'd read, I met his gaze with all the calmness I could muster, and replied, 'I'm real. And you are not. Now go away.'

❧

The dressing gown he'd worn was made of heavy silk, with hand-stitched seams. I knew this because he had shrugged it off a moment earlier and given it to me, with the excuse that my own clothes appeared 'ill-suited to the weather'. It did in fact feel cooler in the room than it had felt before, and more damp, and the dressing gown, although it was imaginary, seemed to make a difference, so I thanked him.

After all, I reasoned, if I had to sit here with my own hallucination, who was acting like a gentleman, I could at least be courteous. I knew the situation would correct itself in time, and for the moment it was nothing short of fascinating.

Smoothing a fold of the dressing gown, I let the weight of the dark red silk slip through my fingers and marveled again at the power the mind had to make things seem real. It was one thing to read a psychiatrist's paper on how hallucinations could deceive a person's senses. It was quite another thing to wear a dressing gown that wasn't there—to feel the fabric plainly in my hand and see the little imperfections in the stitches of the sleeve.

Even the chair I was sitting in couldn't be real, but I felt every bump of its low slatted back. There were two chairs, with curving arms, set facing one another by the window in this room that, while a vastly altered rendering of Uncle George's study, still appeared to be a masculine retreat. Between the two chairs was a little table of dark wood that held a tray of pipes for smoking, one of which sat on its own and clearly was a favorite. There were no shelves for books, but there were books stacked on the one freestanding cabinet that appeared to have a locking door, and books again at one end of the long and narrow table set against the wall, and on the table was a bottle that the man was lifting now to fill a pewter cup with something that both looked and smelled like brandy.

'I'm not going to faint,' I promised as he set it on the table.

'I did not imagine that you were.' He took the other chair and with one elbow on the table tipped the bottle over his own cup. 'But it is clear your health has been affected by the shock of your arrival, and you would be wise to guard it.'

'I haven't arrived anywhere,' I corrected him. 'You're the one who keeps turning up, and you're not even real.'

'Am I not?'

I hadn't yet adjusted to the difference that a smile made to his face. I'd been too overwhelmed before to take much notice of his looks, beyond the broader details, but now that I'd relaxed more I was very much aware he was a very handsome man, for an illusion. His hair was not plain brown, but brown with glints of gold that caught the light. Close up, I now could see that his light-colored eyes were green, so clear that at some angles they appeared transparent, and beneath the roughness of a day-old growth of beard his cheek and jaw were shaped with strength. A handsome man. But when he smiled he bordered on the irresistible.

I drank my brandy.

Thankfully, it had a taste. And even better, an effect. If I was going to have hallucinations, I decided, I would have to try to make them less distracting.

This one studied me with eyes that seemed to weigh the possibilities. 'You clearly are no ghost, and I do not believe in witches.'

'Well, I don't believe in *you*,' I told him. 'Go away.'

I might as well have swatted at a fly. He didn't vanish this time either. All he did was settle back, the cup of brandy cradled in his hand, and watch me quietly a moment as though trying to decide how he should deal with me. 'Where are you from? I only ask because your speech is strange,' he said. 'Your accent is not of this place.'

'Yours isn't either.'

'I was born and raised in London.'

'Really?'

'You do not believe me?'

'You're not real,' I reminded him. 'You can be born where you like.'

'Thank you.' Now he looked amused.

How long was this going to last? I wondered. All my previous hallucinations had been brief ones. This was going on for far too long. Maybe, I thought, if I took more charge of what was happening, controlled the situation more, I'd speed things up.

I drained my glass and told him, 'Look, I can't just sit here, I have things to do.'

He stared at me. 'You do?'

'Yes. So if you'll excuse me…'

As I stood, he stood as well as if by reflex, and when I went out he followed. Happily the corridor looked very much the same as in the real Trelowarth, and I headed for my bedroom door.

The man behind me asked, 'Where are you going?'

'To my room.' The old thumb-latched door handle actually fit in quite well with the age of the other things I was imagining, though the room itself looked a bit different inside when I opened the door. Unfazed, I stepped across the threshold, turned to face the man who wasn't really there, and told him, 'Look, you're being very nice, but really I just want to be alone so *go away*.'

I put as much force as I could into those words, but as

before he only stood and looked right back at me instead of disappearing as he was supposed to.

With a sigh I said, 'Oh, fine,' and closed the door between us.

෴

There were voices in the next room.

One was now familiar to me, but the other was a stranger's who was making no great effort to be quiet. His was not a Cornish voice. It sounded Irish, and impatient.

'Have you no sense left at all? 'Tis not your battle, and you know it.'

'And whose battle is it then?' That was the man in brown, I recognized his level tone.

'Not yours.' The Irishman was firm. 'Not mine.'

Half an hour or more had passed, or so it seemed, and I was still as deep as ever in the same hallucination, in this room that was my own, yet not my own. The walls were plaster white, not green, and where the wardrobe should have stood there was a simple washstand with a bowl and pitcher on it. Gone too were the rocking chair and chest of drawers, replaced by two low trunks and a small writing desk tucked in the window alcove by the fireplace. But the fireplace was the same one, and the wide-planked floor still creaked when I set foot on it, and the bed was where it should be. Not the same bed, to be sure. This was a larger one—a tester bed with wooden headboard and high posts and railings set with rings to hold the curtains that hung drawn back to the posts at all four corners. With the canopy above it looked like something that belonged in a museum or historic home.

I was sitting on it now. I'd heard the footsteps in the next room as the man in brown went into it, and several minutes after that a different man—the Irishman, presumably—had climbed the stairs and come along the corridor, and now the two were arguing.

The Irishman went on, 'When did the flaming Duke of Ormonde ever think to do you favors? Never, that's when. Did he think to put his hand in when they had you up to Newgate? Did he come to pay you visits?'

'Fergal.'

'Did he?'

'I am bound to him by blood.'

'Well fine,' the man named Fergal said. 'Let him go spill his own then, and leave us a bit of peace.'

A low laugh answered him. 'You will remind me not to ever cross you?'

'Sure if I'd thought you ever would, you'd have been dead before now.'

''Tis a comforting thought.'

'Jesus, you need to be thinking now. Fine if you're putting your head in a noose, that's your business. But not for those bastards.'

'I thought you were all for the king.'

'So I am. 'Tis the men he keeps around him I've no faith in. They've had nearly one full year to bring him back since Queen Anne died, and they've done nothing.' I heard footsteps cross the floor, and heard the handle of a door turn. 'Just you think on what I've said now.'

'Do you mean to roast the squabs tonight?'

I heard the footsteps pause. 'Now what the devil does that have to do with anything?'

'I think more clearly when I'm fed.'

'Is that a fact?'

'You might do well to roast an extra bird.'

'I'll roast the flock for you,' the Irishman said dryly, 'if it helps you find your sense.'

He didn't slam the door exactly, but he closed it with a force that gave his final statement emphasis. I heard his footsteps tramping down the stairs.

Now where on earth, I wondered, had I conjured *him* up from? And why was his name Fergal? I had never met a Fergal.

From the hall below, the Irishman called up the stairs, 'The constable is coming!'

Oh, terrific, I thought. *Someone else to join the party*. I'd have stayed exactly where I was, except I caught the faint sound of a horse's hooves above the wind and couldn't help but wonder if I'd actually hallucinated horses, so I rose to have a look.

I heard the floorboards in the next room creak as though somebody else were doing likewise, crossing to the window, looking out towards the road.

The horse and rider coming up The Hill had an official look—the horse a gleaming bay, the man who rode him middle-aged and wearing black clothes with a hat that slanted down to hide his face. From the next room I heard an exhaled breath that might have been annoyance, and then footfalls crossing back again, the opening and closing of the door, and steps that took the stairs by twos on their way down.

I found it strange to stand there at the window where I'd stood so often and gaze out upon a scene that looked the same yet not the same, as though an artist had gone over it again but lightly, painting trees where none had been before, erasing roofs and buildings from the village of Polgelly and retexturing the road to rutted dirt.

The rider had turned off that road now, and halted his horse at the front of the house, and was shifting as though to dismount when the front door banged below me and the man in brown—still hatless but wearing his jacket again—came in view.

With my window tight shut and the wind beating hard on the glass I heard nothing of what the men said, but they didn't shake hands, and the constable stayed in the saddle. I couldn't see anything of his face under the hat, but his gestures had an arrogance I found unpleasant, and from their body language I'd have guessed the two men didn't like each other. As the man in brown shrugged off some comment the constable made, the sun glinted on something and I saw that he'd put on more than his coat before coming outside. He had strapped on a sword belt. The sword itself hung at his left side, a deadly thing partly concealed underneath the long jacket but meant to be seen.

I was focused on that when the constable lifted his head.

He was looking up, scanning the windows. His gaze landed squarely on me and without really thinking I took a step backwards…

The room slowly melted.

And just as before on the coast path, I found myself back in the same place I'd been when the vision had started. This time I was standing at the desk in Uncle George's study, with my hand outstretched to switch off the computer, with the carriage clock in front of me still chiming off the hour.

The final chime fell ringing in the silence as I noted that the clock's hands were still pointed to the same position: five o'clock.

Incredible, I thought, that the hallucination could have taken no real time at all. Yet here I was, and there the clock was, showing me the proof.

I turned off the computer and sank gratefully into the green chair, propping both elbows on the desk for support as I lowered my head to my hands. Then in sudden confusion, I stopped.

Raised my gaze again. Stared at my sleeve. Touched it, just to be sure.

The red silk of the dressing gown ran smoothly through my fingers, still as dark as wine. And somehow now as real as I was.

CHAPTER 9

I T WAS STILL THERE the following morning, when, having
locked my bedroom door, I pulled the wardrobe open and
drew the garment on its hanger from the very back, where
I had hidden it. Not something I'd imagined, but a real,
substantial dressing gown, a little faded now and frayed a bit
around the seams, but still the same one I had worn while
I was... well, that was the problem, because now I didn't
know *what* I'd been doing.

All I knew was that whatever had occurred, it must have
happened in the blinking of an eye. The carriage clock on
Uncle George's desk could not be argued with. Even if I'd
fallen into some kind of a trance for that brief instant, and
the dressing gown had been there in the study—which it
hadn't, I was sure of it—I'd scarcely have had time to put it
on before the clock had finished chiming.

But if that wasn't what I'd done, then that would mean
that what I had experienced was real. The man in brown
was real.

I shook my head. It simply wasn't logical. I couldn't wrap
my thoughts around it. Traveling through time was something
people did in books or films. It didn't really happen. Yet the
dressing gown here in my hands, and its obvious age, seemed
to stand in denial of that line of reasoning, and I couldn't think
of how else to explain it. I'd tried. I had spent the whole night

trying hard to come up with another excuse for the dressing gown's being here, and I'd come up empty-handed, with nothing to show for the effort except a real headache in place of the fake one I'd used last night as an excuse to miss supper.

I would have skipped breakfast this morning as well if there hadn't just then been a knock at my door.

'Eva?' Susan's voice.

Thrusting the dressing gown back in the wardrobe I crossed to the door and unlocked it to open it.

'Still have the headache?' she guessed when she saw me. 'Poor you. I've made tea and some toast. You can't go without eating.' She brought the tray in with her, setting it down on the bed. 'Is there anything else I can get you?'

'No, really, this—' Looking down at the tray, I deliberately dragged my mind back from my own worries, into the here and the now. 'This is perfect. And so thoughtful. Thank you. You have to stop spoiling me.'

'Well,' Susan said, 'you're our guest.' And when she saw me start to protest, she put in, 'Besides, it's not as though you're doing nothing in return. You've spent the past week building us a website.' With a smile she said, 'That's likely how you got your headache.'

'No.' But since I couldn't very well explain how I *had* got it, I took a bite of my toast instead. Then I remembered. 'It's ready, by the way. Your website.'

'Really? Can I see it?'

I was hesitant to go back into Uncle George's study after what had happened last time, but I couldn't think of any good excuse to make. My indecision must have shown on my face because she said, 'If you're not up to it this morning—'

'No, it's fine.' I squared my shoulders slightly. 'I'm fine. I'd love for you to see it.'

She insisted that I finish off my toast first, but I brought the tea along with me and sipped it for its steadying effect as we ran through the different pages of the site.

It wasn't until later, when we'd finished with the website and we'd talked about the next step of publicity—the press release—and she'd gone off to fetch some details of the gardens' history to include in it, that it suddenly occurred to me that history might be one thing I could use to help shed light on what had happened to me yesterday.

The Irishman, as I recalled, had said a name: the Duke of Ormonde.

Though it had meant nothing to me then and didn't now, it sounded real enough. And real dukes would be mentioned in *Burke's Peerage*.

There were, in fact, two Dukes of Ormonde listed on the Internet, but since the man named Fergal had said something about Queen Anne too, I chose the second duke, who'd lived through Queen Anne's reign.

I wished my mother had been here to give me one of her amazing history lessons, but she wasn't, so I settled for the basics, starting off in 1714 with Queen Anne's death and the dispute over who should inherit the throne—her half brother James Stuart, who was Catholic and living in exile near France, or the properly Protestant German Prince George, a more distant relation. I read the accounts of how deeply divisive the politics were at the time, with the Tories who favored the rights of young James locking horns with the Whigs who supported Prince George. And I read of the riots and public unrest that had followed George's coronation as the King of all Great Britain.

Which brought me to the spring of 1715, when Jacobites—the followers of James—were plotting armed rebellion, making plans to rise in arms and bring young James himself across to claim his throne.

It seemed most people's sympathies in Cornwall had been squarely with the Tories and James Stuart, and they hadn't tried to hide the fact. And so King George's parliament, controlled by Whigs, had swiftly moved to stamp out any smolderings that might ignite the fires of a dangerous rebellion.

The Duke of Ormonde, hero of the people, had been right there in the thick of it. Three years earlier, when the mighty Duke of Marlborough had fallen out of favor, the dashing Ormonde had replaced him as commander of the British armies fighting on the Continent, and his patriotic exploits had increased his popularity to the point that the Whigs had grown uneasy. When Ormonde had taken the side of the Jacobites, the Whigs had moved against him too. He and another leading Tory, Lord Bolingbroke, had been charged with high treason, and though both men had managed to evade arrest and imprisonment by fleeing the country, Parliament had gone ahead and impeached them in their absence, stripped them of their rights and status, left them both as marked and wanted men.

I had his portrait on the monitor when Susan came back. 'Who is that?' she asked.

'James Butler, second Duke of Ormonde.' A man I'd never heard of until yesterday. A man who was as real as the red dressing gown. And how could I have even known his name, I wondered, if I hadn't traveled to the past?

'And who is he?' asked Susan.

I gave her a summary of his biography, adding, 'He played a big part in the Jacobite uprisings down here in Cornwall. Maybe I'll find he's connected somehow to Trelowarth. You never know.'

She frowned. 'I thought the Jacobites were Scottish.'

'So did I. But there were lots of them in England too, apparently.'

She leaned closer, studying the picture. 'Nice wig.'

'Yes, well, most men wore them back then.' I knew one man who didn't, or at least he hadn't worn one either time that I had met him, but I couldn't say that either. Instead I looked more closely at the portrait, searching for some small resemblance to the man in brown who'd said, about the duke, that he was 'bound to him by blood'. If they were relatives, that blood appeared to be the only thing they shared. The Duke of Ormonde's face was soft and overfed, his nose too long and large, his gaze too proud and condescending.

'What year were the uprisings?' asked Susan.

'1715.'

'Before the Halletts came here, then. Well, as you say, you never know. It would be fun to have some kind of tale to tell to tourists, and a Jacobite rebellion's always good.'

Not for the Jacobites, I thought. Things never had gone very well for them. At least the Irishman named Fergal had appeared to sense that it was not a fight worth fighting, and I couldn't help but wonder if he'd ever managed to convince the man in brown. Perhaps I'd never know.

I pushed the thought aside and settled in to work with Susan on the press release, a thing I'd done a hundred times before with other clients, so the process was predictable and calming. Susan had some good ideas.

'We should use the word "romance",' she said, 'and "lost", because they paint a sort of picture, don't they? And I think what makes Trelowarth interesting is that we have so many roses here that might otherwise have vanished, been forgotten. It makes Trelowarth like a...' Pausing as though searching for the proper phrase, she finished, 'Well, it's like a time machine. One step into the gardens takes you back a hundred years.' Her face grew bright. 'That might make a brilliant heading, don't you think? "Step back in time—come visit the old roses of Trelowarth".'

I kept my fingers steady on the keyboard as I typed. 'Yes, that's quite good.'

Step back in time. Step back in time. The words kept playing over in my mind and stayed there even after Susan had gone off again to see to something over at the greenhouse. *Back in time...*

My fingers hesitated on the keyboard. Then I opened a new window for a search and typed in: 'Time Travel'.

I didn't know what I'd expected. Strange stuff, I supposed. A lot of people writing, 'Hi, my name is Zog, I'm from the future.' But that wasn't what I found. Instead I found page after page of true science, with actual physicists—some of them famous—discussing the concept as though it were wholly respectable, even conducting experiments at universities.

Much of their dialogue, arguing theories and drawing those squiggly equations that filled half a page, was beyond me. They talked about space-time and wormholes and String Theory, extra dimensions and closed time-like curves. But not one of them said that it couldn't be done. Even the great Stephen Hawking was quoted as saying, in one of his lectures, that 'according to our present understanding' of the laws of physics, travel back in time was not impossible.

It all had to do, so I gathered, with Einstein's Theory of Relativity having proved that time and space were curved and changeable, not fixed and absolute as Isaac Newton had maintained.

There was a portrait of Sir Isaac Newton in his old age, painted sometime, it said, around 1710. He had a pleasant sort of face, but it was not his face I noticed, not his face that made me shrug away the shivers that chased lightly down my spine.

It was the simple fact that he was wearing the exact same style of dressing gown that hung now in my wardrobe. And the sight of it convinced me, even more than Stephen Hawking's words, that all the reading I had done on mental health and all my plans to see a doctor had been nothing but a wasted effort. Though it seemed incredible, I *had* gone back in time.

And that wasn't something a doctor could cure.

There were voices in the next room.

My eyes opened to the darkness with a wary sensibility and waited to adjust to the faint moonlight from outside my bedroom windows. The house had always had a lonely feel this late at night, and as a child I'd hated waking up this way, surrounded by the shadows, but tonight I only felt relieved to see that everything was in its proper place—the beds, the chair, the wardrobe. I was where I was supposed to be.

Three days had gone by since I'd traveled back into the past, and in the meantime things had been so normal I might easily have slipped back into thinking I'd imagined what had happened, if there hadn't been the dressing gown as evidence.

The voices went on talking, low and quiet, from the far side of the wall behind my head. The man in brown's voice was familiar to me now, at least in tone, and I presumed the other speaker was the Irishman. His voice was the more animated one that rose and fell as though in argument, while through it all the other answered back with level calm.

I wasn't feeling calm, myself. I knew I'd heard the voices on their own before, when nothing else had happened, but a lot had changed since then, and now the sound of them unnerved me, made me want to put a bit of space between us. Just in case.

Forcing myself into action, I got up and went to the bathroom.

There was darkness in the corridor as well, but I had walked this route enough by night to do it with a blindfold. By the light above the mirror in the bathroom I examined my face with a frown. 'You're a coward, you know.' Which was true. But I still took my time, and I waited a good fifteen minutes before going back.

The bedroom was quiet. No more voices.

Just the whisper of the night breeze through the partly opened windows. And the sound of someone breathing from the bed.

My heart began to pound so heavily it held me to the place where I was standing just inside the door. I couldn't move.

It wasn't my bed anymore. The moonlight fell on posts and curtains and the figure of a man who lay stretched out full length on top of the blankets, his hands behind his head, still clothed in breeches and the white shirt I had seen him in before. There was light enough for me to recognize the angles of his profile. I could hear him breathing evenly, asleep.

Or so I thought.

Until his voice spoke from the shadows.

'I do confess I have forgot your name.'

He'd spoken quietly, and mindful of the fact there might be other people sleeping in the house, I answered just as low. 'You never asked it.'

His head turned till he was looking right at me, though

nothing else about him moved. The moonlight gleamed behind him but I couldn't see his eyes or his expression. 'Do you have one?'

Did I have a name? I couldn't quite remember. 'Eva.'

'Eva. Is that all?'

'My name is Eva Ellen Ward.'

'A good name.' In the dark he looked at me a moment longer. 'I did fear that you had come to harm since last I saw you, Eva Ward.'

'I'm fine.'

'So I do see. And glad I am to see it, for your welfare has weighed heavy on my conscience.'

'Why is that?'

'Because I did not think to warn you not to leave the house,' he said. 'This countryside would offer little safety to a woman, and the roads around should not be lightly traveled.'

'I wasn't on the roads.'

'No?'

'No. And I didn't go outside the house.'

'So where then…? Ah,' he told me. 'You went back.'

'Yes.' I considered how to tackle this. The last time he had seen me I'd been claiming that he wasn't real and telling him to go away. He probably already thought I was crazy. But I wanted to know. 'Am I right in thinking I've just traveled back in time?'

He didn't answer right away, but after some reflection he replied, 'That would depend entirely upon where you began.'

Which seemed a logical assumption. I could see no harm in telling him the year that I'd just come from. If he registered surprise, I didn't notice. 'Yes,' he told me then. 'You have indeed come back in time by some three centuries.'

'It's 1715?'

'It is.' That did surprise him. 'How did you know the year?'

'I did some reading.'

'You can read.' It wasn't actually a question, more a challenge, I could hear it in his voice. 'A brave accomplishment for a woman, even one who voyages through time.'

'You don't believe me?'

'On the contrary. 'Tis ghosts and walking spirits that I never have believed in, so I must confess I find your tale a singular relief.' He paused in thought. 'So, have you learned to work this magic at your will?'

'And if I had,' I asked him, 'do you really think I would have turned up here, like this?'

'In my own chamber, do you mean, and in the middle of the night?' I sensed his smile but was more focused on his words.

'This is your room?'

''Tis why I chose to fall asleep in it.'

I said, 'But when I came in here the last time… when I—'

'Told me I should go away?' His tone was openly amused.

I hoped the faint light covered my embarrassment. 'You didn't tell me this was your room too.'

'An oversight on my part, I'll admit. Perhaps the shock of finding out that I did not, in fact, exist, after a lifetime of believing that I did, had some effect upon my manners.'

I was blushing now in earnest. 'Look, I'm sorry I was rude to you. I thought that I was seeing things.'

'I did not take offence,' he said. 'It did not trouble me to share my chamber then, no more than it does now.' He shifted round and sat up slowly as he swung his long legs to the floor. Somehow he looked much larger that way, sitting with his white shirt gleaming ghostlike in the pale light of the moon. There was a silent moment.

Then, 'You've changed your clothes,' he said, as though just noticing.

If he'd asked me at that moment I could not in truth have told him what clothes I *was* wearing. Glancing down myself at my plain T-shirt and pajama bottoms, I said by way of explanation, 'I was sleeping too.'

He seemed to be deciding something. 'If you are still here by day, you will need proper clothes to wear.'

I hadn't thought of that.

He stood and said, 'Wait here.' I had forgotten just how tall he was. His shoulder passed me at the level of my eyes as he went through the door connecting with the small front bedroom next to us, returning not long after with what looked to be a bulky length of fabric that he pressed into my hands. 'Take this and wear it if you will.'

I told him, 'Thank you,' and he gave a nod, still standing in the door between the two rooms, his expression too obscured by shadows to be clearly seen. He told me, 'Sleep well, Eva Ward,' and with a backwards step he closed the door between us.

There was no way I could sleep. I didn't even try. Instead I sat and faced the window near the bed, the one that had the most familiar view, and fixed my gaze on the far place where the dark sea was met by sky, and stayed there waiting till the sun began to rise.

Its first rays came, not through that window, but the ones that faced the road and flanked the fireplace. The slanting sunlight, faint at first, chased out the shadows from the corners, falling warm across the floorboards and the surface of the writing desk that sat against the wall.

It touched the fabric that I still held in my arms as well, and I could finally see it was a dress—a bodice and a separate trailing skirt, with something like a nightgown underneath them, and a pair of shoes like slippers that fell tumbling to the floor as I rose carefully and spread the clothes out on the bed to have a better look.

The gown—for that was what it was—was plain but beautiful. The bodice had a low round neck and straight three-quarter sleeves, and was stiffened at its seams with supple boning, like a corset. The skirt was plain as well but full. It ran like silk between my fingers when I touched it, and its color shifted in the light from blue to grey and back again.

It seemed so strange to think of wearing clothes like these, but then again, if I were truly stuck here in this time I couldn't very well walk round in my pajamas.

And it was easier than I'd expected, sorting out how everything went on. First came the undergarment, a simple plain chemise with rounded neck and sleeves that fit quite closely to my elbows and below that widened into tiers of lace, so when I put the bodice on, that lace peeked out from underneath the bodice's three-quarter sleeves and softened the effect. I ought to have put the skirt on, really, before the bodice, but I managed to get everything adjusted—the skirt tied round my waist and the bodice smoothed down over that, so it all looked like one piece.

Both the slippers and gown fitted me well, which surprised me. I'd thought that I might be too short or not slender enough, but the skirt brushed the floor without trailing too much and the bodice, while snug, was not tight, though I found it a bit of a challenge to fasten. It closed at the front and was held not with buttons but pins, so I pricked myself painfully trying to do it and swore out loud once in frustration. I was sliding in the last pin when the room's door was flung open and a man angrily asked, 'Who the devil are you?'

I could not have mistaken the voice of the Irishman, but his appearance surprised me. He wasn't a large man, as I had expected. He stood average height with black hair and a face that I guessed would ordinarily have been quite friendly.

It wasn't, though, just at the moment.

He glowered. 'I said, who the devil might you be?'

'I'm Eva.' It sounded inadequate, even to me, and too late I decided I shouldn't have spoken at all, since the sound of my accent had narrowed his eyes.

'Eva.' Planting himself in the doorway, he folded his arms firmly over his chest. 'Tell me, where do you come from? And how did you come to be here in this house?'

Neither question was one I could easily answer. I didn't feel safe with this man, like I had with the other one. There was anger and open distrust in his eyes, and no promise that he would behave like a gentleman. Not that I thought he would actually hurt me. I only suspected he wouldn't much care either way if he did.

I tried calming the waters. My memory raced backward in search of his name. 'Fergal. That's your name, isn't it? Fergal?'

His gaze narrowed further. 'And who told you that?'

'He did.'

'Who did?' he challenged me, moving another step into the room.

Damn, I thought. I had no clue what his name was. 'The man...'

'Which man would that be?'

'The man who lives here.'

He took one more step and the black eyebrows rose in a mocking expression. 'He told you my name?'

'Yes.'

''Tis odd, do you not think, that he'd tell you my name and not tell you his?'

I had no easy answer to that one, and so I said nothing while Fergal advanced.

'So he told you my name. And he gave you that gown, no doubt.'

Something in how he was looking at what I was wearing felt wrong, but I didn't know why. 'Yes.'

He spat the word, 'Liar.'

I lifted my chin. I was scared and confused but I still had my limits, and deep in me I felt the stir of rebellion. 'It isn't a lie.'

I'd surprised him with that. I saw his flash of hesitation and drew strength from it.

'You go and ask him,' I said bravely. 'Go and ask him where I got this gown. He'll tell you.'

'Will he, now?' His tone was still belligerent, but he had lost a little of the righteousness. He tipped his head to one side while he looked at me and thought. And then he said, 'All right then, if you've got a mind to test the devil, we'll go ask him, you and me together.'

'Fine.' I said it bravely, though I didn't really have a choice. He'd taken such a firm hold on my arm that I could not have broken free of it if I'd been fool enough to try.

The whole way down the stairs he kept on muttering his certainty, as much for his own ears as mine. 'Haven't I known him these twenty long years and he's never once done a thing yet without telling me first, and he'd be burning that gown with his own hands I think before he'd let another woman wear it in his sight, you mark me...'

On and on the tirade went, as Fergal dragged me with him through the hall into the kitchen. He apparently expected me to show the fear appropriate for somebody about to have their lie exposed, but all I really felt as we got closer to our goal was the relief of knowing I would soon be proven right. The fact that I was growing calmer by the minute didn't help his mood.

'All right then,' he repeated, when we reached the back corridor and the door leading outside. 'We'll just see who's telling tales now.'

He had thrust me through the heavy door ahead of him, so when I stopped abruptly on the threshold there was nothing he could do but stop as well and swear an oath, and it was luck alone that kept us both from going down like dominoes.

But I paid no attention. I was busy staring at the man who stood not far in front of me, my man in brown who looked as though he'd just been at the stone-built stables set beyond the sweep of yard. His boots were clumped with mud and there were straws still clinging to his sleeve. There was no welcome in his eyes. His gaze had locked with Fergal's past my shoulder in a wordless kind of warning.

And beside him, dressed in black as he had been before, the constable stood watching us as well. Or, more correctly, watching me.

'Well, now.' The constable's voice was as smooth as the fin of a shark slicing water. 'And who have we here?'

CHAPTER 10

I'D MET PEOPLE IN my life who were pure poison. I had learned to know the look of them—the way their smiles came and went and never touched their eyes, those eyes that could be so intense at times and yet revealed no soul. Such people might look normal, but inside it was as though some vital part of them was missing, and whenever I saw eyes like that I'd learned to turn and run and guard my back while I was leaving.

The instant that I looked into the cold eyes of the constable, I knew what sort of man he was. But here I couldn't turn and run. I still had Fergal standing solid at my back.

The constable came forwards slowly, sizing up this new turn of events. He looked to be in his mid-forties, not a tall man but a lean and wiry one, his long face lean as well and framed by the uncompromising curls of a white-powdered wig beneath the brim of his black hat. His gaze traveled my length from my loose-hanging hair to the hem of the gown that he too seemed to recognize. The sight of it kindled a new light of interest behind the dark eyes that returned to my face as he said, in a tone that was meant to provoke, 'Butler, you do surprise me. I would not have thought you a man to waste time with a harlot.'

'Mind your tongue, sir,' said the man in brown, his voice controlled. 'You speak of Fergal's sister, come to help us keep the house.'

I felt the slight reaction of the Irishman behind me, though he barely moved at all, and for a weighted moment I was unsure whether he would play along.

The constable was unconvinced. 'Your sister?' he asked Fergal. 'I was not aware you had one.'

There was silence as the Irishman appeared to be deciding something, then he drew himself up at my back, defensive and defiant. 'I have seven of them, ay. This one's next eldest to myself, she is.'

The constable was studying my face for a resemblance. Whether he found any I didn't know, but I doubted it. 'What is your name?' he asked.

'She cannot speak,' said Fergal, and his hard grip on my arm grew tighter, warning me to silence.

'Why is that?'

'You'd have to take that up with the Almighty, for He made her. All I know is that she never learnt the way of it.' He was a brilliant liar. In his voice I heard no hint of hesitation, and I couldn't help but admire the speed at which he'd seen the danger and defused it all at once. My voice didn't fit here. Even if I'd been able to manage an Irish accent, my patterns of speech were too modern, I would have slipped up. Now he'd saved me from having to try.

The man in brown said, 'Eva, this would be Constable Creed from the village. I do not doubt that, as he is a gentleman, he'll wish to offer his apologies and bid you welcome.'

It was a daring gamble, but he stood his ground and pulled it off. The constable's disquieting gaze took in my borrowed gown one final time before he gave an unrepentant nod and said unconvincingly, 'Mistress O'Cleary, I meant no offence. You are welcome of course to Trelowarth.' He took a step back and extended his nod to

the other two. 'Gentlemen.' And then he turned and went
out of the yard.

He left tension behind. I could feel it in the man behind
me, see it in the squaring of the shoulders of the man in
brown, who hadn't moved a step from where he stood. He
was wearing the clothes I remembered: the tight brown
trousers ending just below the knee in boots, a full white
shirt with what I thought was called a stock tied round his
neck, beneath the long brown jacket that he wore unbuttoned, hanging open. But he had shaved, his jawline clean
and strongly drawn. It made him look more civilized.

I felt the exchange of looks over my head as he said to
his friend, 'Were you wanting to see me?' The question
seemed careless enough and relaxed, but I knew from his
face he was keeping his guard up, aware that the constable
might still be listening.

Fergal no doubt was aware of that too, but he had his
own questions to ask, in his own way. He nudged me a half a
step forwards and said, 'She'd a mind to come show you the
gown and to have me tell you how she does appreciate the
gesture. 'Tis most generous.'

With a glance at Fergal's hold upon my arm, the man in
brown turned his attention to my clothes, and for a moment
in his eyes I thought I glimpsed a fleeting darkness like the
passing of a pain, but it was so swift I wasn't certain. It had
vanished by the time his eyes met mine. He said to Fergal,
'Tell your sister I am pleased she finds it to her liking, for in
truth it suits her well.'

I sensed a challenge had been made and answered, and
with what seemed like reluctance Fergal let me go. He
grumbled, 'Sure you can tell her that yourself, she's got her
ears.' And without waiting, he turned on his heel. 'Come

have your breakfasts then, and perhaps one of the pair of you can tell me what the bleeding Christ is going on.'

∾

The kitchen window had a different view than I was used to. There were no walled gardens, neatly kept and tended, to look out on—only two old apple trees that grew close by the house, both beaten by the unforgiving coastal winds into hard twisted shapes that reached towards the hill as though in search of refuge.

And the kitchen itself was a much different room. There were no fitted cupboards, no worktops, no stove, just the fireplace and stone hearth and iron hooks hung with a motley collection of pans and utensils, the purpose of most of which I didn't know.

But the table, although it was smaller and rougher, was in the same spot, pushed up under the window. And sitting there having a breakfast of dark ale and bread felt familiar enough that it calmed me a little.

Fergal had calmed a bit too, though his face betrayed his open incredulity at what he'd just been told. He filled his tankard for a second time and said, 'So you're telling me then, that you've come from the future.'

'That's right.' I didn't care if he believed me. My only defence was the truth.

He was looking at me strangely. He shifted his attention to the man in brown beside me, who'd been sitting back in silence while I'd talked. 'And you believe this?'

'I have seen it.' With his booted legs stretched out beneath the table and his folded arms across his chest, he said, 'I've seen her pass between the worlds. 'Tis not a trick.'

'It might be witchcraft.' But he said it without any true conviction.

'Other men than you and I believe in witches,' said the man in brown, and Fergal gave another nod.

'Ay. But if not witchcraft, what then?'

'Why not truth?'

'Because the two of us both know it is impossible.'

'And men once thought the sea had limits that could not be sailed beyond for fear of dragons,' was his friend's reply. He turned his head to look at me, his clear eyes thoughtful on my face. 'I would submit that she is her own proof that it is possible.'

Fergal set his tankard on the table. 'See now, all that this is doing is to make my head ache like the devil has a hammer to it, so if you'll both excuse me I have work I should be seeing to.' With a scrape he pushed his chair back and went out, and left us sitting there together by the window.

It was open, and the morning winds from off the sea were coming in by gentle gusts that crossed the sill and brushed my hands, a reassuring touch. Unseen within the tangled branches of the nearest apple tree a songbird had begun to trill, a carefree sound that seemed in contrast to my troubles.

At my side the man in brown said, 'Fergal is a good man. But he does not lightly give his trust.'

'I've noticed.' I gave my arm an absent rub, remembering.

'I give you my apologies if you were roughly handled.'

'That's all right. He thought I was a thief. Besides, he's more than made it up to me, coming up with that story for your constable.'

He gave a shrug, acknowledging the truth of that, and as he turned his head away the silence started settling between us once again.

I said, 'I didn't know your name.'

His eyes came back to me. 'I beg your pardon?'

'That's why Fergal thought I was a thief,' I said. 'Because I didn't know your name.'

A moment passed, and then with the suggestion of amusement in his voice he tossed my own words from our meeting in the bedroom last night back at me. 'You never asked me.'

Two could play that game, I thought. I met his gaze with one as steady. 'Do you have one?'

No denying the amusement now. It briefly lit his eyes inside as he said, 'Daniel Butler. At your service, mistress.'

'Thank you, Mr. Butler.'

With a gallant nod he pushed his own chair back and stood and stretched and said, 'Now, by your leave, I have some work myself I must attend to. I'd advise you keep within the house, but you may have the freedom of it.'

'Thank you.'

'Oh, and Eva?'

'Yes?'

He'd stopped within the doorway. 'I should think a woman who had slept in my own bed might properly presume to call me Daniel.' With the smile still in his eyes he left before I'd had the time to form a suitable reply.

❧

It felt so strange to walk the rooms I knew so well and find them different.

The furniture was more austere and harder in its lines, though I could sense a woman's hand had tried to soften the décor a little, likely the woman whose gown I was wearing. There were cushions on a few chairs and woven rush seats on some others, and long hanging curtains in calico prints at the sides of the windows. The downstairs hall hadn't yet been plastered over and the rich wood paneling made everything seem darker, but the rooms themselves were brightened by their carpets and their picture frames with lively prints of country life hung all round on the walls, and everywhere I looked were candles, set in sconces on the walls or shielded by glass chimneys on a table or a mantelpiece, all waiting to be lit against the darkness come the evening.

Some downstairs rooms were used for other purposes—the dining room from my own time was used here as a sitting room—but in the big front room I'd always known as the library there were still shelves and books, and in the place of the piano was a cabinet full of china cups and plates and curiosities that trembled with a tinkling sound in rhythm with my footsteps on the wide-planked floor.

Intrigued, I took a closer look.

The cups and plates and saucers were a delicate design of whorls and rosebuds on an ivory background, carefully lined up in proud display. And on the shelf below were seashells, gorgeous things of varied shapes and colors. Some I recognized from my collecting days: a knobbed murex, pink and white, the iridescent rainbow lining of an abalone, and the broad flat fan of a Japanese scallop. And set in their midst was a little glass box, hinged and shaped like a scallop-shell too, and inside was a tightly wound curl of dark hair tied with blue ribbon.

Only that, and nothing more, and yet it was enough to speak to me. It told me Daniel Butler had lost someone too, as I had.

Other footsteps shook the cabinet as they came into the room and then they stopped, and Fergal's voice behind me said, 'You'll not find anything in there of any value, save the dishes.'

'I'm not going to steal your dishes.'

Coming up beside me, he glanced at my face with

curiosity then looked down at the little shell-shaped box that held my interest.

'That was his wife's,' he told me, in a voice turned clipped and hard.

I'd guessed as much. Just as I'd guessed the dress that I was wearing had been hers as well. I smoothed it with a hand and would have turned, but Fergal's sharp eyes had caught sight of something else with my small movement.

'That's an Irish ring,' he said, and gave a nod towards the Claddagh ring I wore. 'I've seen its like in Galway.' With a narrowed gaze he asked me, 'May I?' and I put my hand within his rough one while he turned it to the light. 'I've never seen one made so small. How did you come by it?'

'It's been passed down from my grandmother,' I told him. 'She was Irish.'

'Was she, now? And where was it she came from?'

'I'm not sure.'

'No doubt from Galway, if she had a ring like this.'

I said, 'It's called a Claddagh ring. A lot of people have them.'

Fergal raised an eyebrow slightly at the name. 'A Claddagh ring? 'Tis as unlikely a name as I've heard for a token of love. Have you been to the Claddagh? No? It is the finest place to fish in all the western shore of Ireland, and yet you'll not get near it if you come there as a stranger, for the fishermen of Claddagh are a fierce breed to themselves. They'll sink your ship as soon as look at you.'

I couldn't help it. 'So are you from Claddagh then?' I asked him.

Fergal, not expecting that, stared down at me a moment. Then he smiled. 'Nah. Me, I come from County Cork, where all the men are soft and mannered, don't you know.' He let me have my hand back. 'Are you hungry, Eva Ward?'

'A little.'

'Can you cook?'

'A little.'

'Well,' he said, 'then come along with me if you've the courage to. We'll put you to the test.'

CHAPTER 11

I SAW A DIFFERENT side of Fergal in the kitchen than I'd seen before. His roughened edges smoothed a bit and what I'd seen as grumpiness revealed itself to be a dry and entertaining wit. He even smiled now and then, and from the crinkling lines that marked the outer corners of his eyes when he was smiling, I imagined that he did it much more often than he'd led me to believe. On top of which, he seemed to be completely in his element in this room of the house. He cooked with skill.

'And wasn't I sent off to sea the minute I was walking,' he replied when I remarked on it, 'and I proved myself of no great use to anyone except the ship's own cook, who taught me all I know. 'Tis why I'm better stewing fish than roasting fowl, as you'll be learning to your cost.'

I didn't recognize the type of bird that he was now preparing. There were two of them, narrow and lean. Perhaps ducks. I said, 'But you are not a ship's cook now.'

'I am at that, from time to time. Whenever Danny sails.'

'He has a ship?'

'The very best of ships.' He gave a nod. 'The *Sally*. She's away just now with Danny's brother at her helm, but when he brings her back you'll likely see her for yourself.'

I took this in. 'So who's the captain? Mr. Butler or his brother?'

Fergal's sideways look said I'd amused him. 'Well now, there's a question no man yet could answer for you. 'Tis for certain sure that neither Jack nor Danny could; they've argued it for years between their own selves. Like as not the *Sally* knows, but being such a lady as she is she goes as nicely for the one as for the other.' He skewered the birds with a long spit and set them to roast on the hearth while he dusted his hands and moved on to the vegetables.

There I could help him, at least. I could peel things and chop them and toss them together into the three-footed iron kettle in which he was making what looked to be some sort of soup, richly thickened with barley.

He shot me another glance while I was working. 'You're not a woman to complain, I'll give you that.'

'And who would I complain to?'

'Fair enough.'

'Besides,' I said, 'I'll have to practice being silent, won't I, now you've got the constable convinced that I can't talk.'

'Ay, well, I'm sorry for all that,' he said, not looking in the least bit sorry. 'But 'twas all that I could think to keep him from discovering the queer way that you talk. He'd have asked questions, to be sure.'

'No, don't be sorry. It was very gallant of you.'

'Was it, now?'

'It was. And thank you.'

With his head tipped to one side he wiped the blade of his own cutting knife to clean it, while he kept his eyes on me as though deciding something. Then he set the knife down and remarked, 'I have a thirst from all this work now. Will you have a drink of cider, Eva Ward?'

I was hesitant, remembering Mark's Scrumpy, but I knew that this was more than just the offer of a drink; it was the offer of a hand in truce. I couldn't turn it down. 'Yes, thank you.'

Which was why, when Daniel Butler finally came in from whatever chores he had been doing, he took one look at my eyes—which looked far too bright even from my side—and lifted his eyebrows.

'Take your boots from under there,' said Fergal, stopping his friend from taking a seat. 'Have you no manners at all? We've a lady among us; we'll dine at the table we're meant to be dining at.'

That turned out to be in the long room beyond the pantry that in my time was a games room but in this time had wood-paneled walls, not wallpaper, and shutters on the windows, and where Uncle George's billiard table should have been, right at the centre of the room, there stood a trestle table built of heavy oak, with ten imposing chairs.

Fergal set us three places around the one end. 'You'll pardon the dust,' he said, giving the table a wipe that whirled particles upward to dance in the light. 'We'd a girl coming up from the village to clean for us, but her da's fallen ill and she's needed at home, so we've had to make do for ourselves this last while.'

It was a big house for two men on their own. When I'd visited Trelowarth as a child there'd been a local woman, Mrs. Jenner, who had done most of the housework, and even today Mark and Susan had cleaners come in every week.

Daniel Butler took the end seat with a smile and told me, 'Do not let him stir your sympathies. He charms a girl up here with regularity, and 'tis the rare occasion that one leaves without first taking up a broom.'

'You're telling secrets, now,' said Fergal, but he winked as he went out to fetch our dinner from the kitchen.

I looked at Daniel Butler's handsome face and asked him, disbelieving, 'Fergal charms the girls up here?'

'He does. He is not always so ill-natured, as you seem to have discovered for yourself.' The smile lingered in his eyes. 'What were you drinking?'

'Cider.'

'Then you have impressed him, for the cider in our cellars here was made by his own hand, and he does guard it as a dragon guards its gold. He would not offer it to anyone he did not feel was worthy.'

'Yes, well, I'm honored but I hope he doesn't make a habit of it. Cider makes my head spin.'

'Do you have it in your own time?'

'Cider? Yes. It makes my head spin there as well.'

'So there are some things at least that are the same for you.' Beneath the lightness of his voice I thought I caught a trace of something like a scientific interest. 'I should think it must feel strange, to step into another age and find yourself so far removed from all you know. Like being shipwrecked in a foreign land.'

It was a good analogy. 'It feels like that a bit.' I hadn't really stopped to analyze it all that much. A part of me, I knew, was still adjusting to the shock of being tossed around in time, and I could only cope with every situation as it came. But now I came to think of it, it was like being washed up on the shore of some strange country not my own. Except, 'The house is still the same,' I said. 'At least, I know my way around the rooms. That helps a little. And the fact that you believe me, that helps too.' I hadn't realized how much that last fact meant to me until I'd said the words out loud.

I looked away from him and coughed to clear my throat, and changed the subject as I glanced around the room for inspiration. 'Have you lived here at Trelowarth long?'

'Twelve years. It was left me by an uncle who desired I should settle myself to a more honest trade.'

But before I could ask him, 'More honest than what?' Fergal came with an armful of plates heaped with food.

'There,' he said, as he set mine in front of me, 'best to enjoy that, I've nothing so fancy to serve you tomorrow. It's stirabouts now, till I'm next to the market.'

It was plain food, but flavorful. Fergal had basted the roast birds with honey, and seasoned the barley and vegetables with unknown spices and herbs that made everything sit on my stomach with comfortable warmth. I ate with knife and spoon, as both of them were doing, grateful for the light ale Daniel Butler offered me in place of cider. Although the small tin tumbler it was served in gave the ale a faint metallic taste, it was at least a drink that, slowly sipped, could leave me sober.

The men drank wine, a rich red wine they drank from tumblers like my own, of beaten tin. As Fergal poured the dregs into his own cup, he remarked, 'We'll soon be out of this as well. We've but a single case remaining in the cellar.'

Daniel Butler said, ''Tis good we've got your cider then.'

'The devil you do. Any man will be losing his hand if he touches those kegs.'

'Do you see?' Daniel Butler directed that comment at me, with a smile. 'Did I not say he guarded his casks like a dragon?'

'Ay, and did you think to tell her why I do that, now? Did you say what your brother did the one time that I turned my back? And didn't he have all my cider on the *Sally* and away on the next tide without so much as a farewell and by-your-leave?'

'Well, that is Jack for you.'

'Ay, steal the coins right off a dead man's eyes and do it

smiling, so he would.' But there was still a grudging admiration in his tone, from which I guessed he couldn't help but like the man they spoke of. Then he seemed to think of something. 'Jesus, Danny, he'll be coming back at any time now.'

'And?'

'Well, how the devil will you be explaining *her*?' This with a nod across the table towards me. 'You know as well as I do Jack can never keep his mouth shut, and he'll never be convinced she came the way she says she did.'

I watched while Daniel Butler weighed the options in his mind and then he gave a shrug and said, 'She is your sister, come to help us keep the house. Is that not what you said to Creed? And he believed it.'

'Did he? Sure of that then, are you?'

'No.' His eyes were thoughtful on my face. 'But Jack is not as clever as the constable. And Eva, I suspect, is rather more so. Will it bother you,' he asked, 'to play a part?'

I wasn't sure, despite his faith in me, that I could pull it off. I'd never been much good at acting, never had Katrina's gift. She would have loved this whole experience, I knew, of stepping back into another age. She'd have thrown herself into the role, would have altered her accent and gestures until Daniel Butler himself would have thought she was from his own time. She'd have had an adventure.

I smiled faintly, feeling for the thousandth time the small and pulling pain of separation and the hollow ache of being left behind. I saw his eyes grow quizzical, and so I said, 'I'll try. But I'm afraid I'm not an actress.'

'It was not my intention to suggest you were. I would not so insult you.' The apology was so swift and sincere it surprised me until I remembered that actresses had once been seen as no better than prostitutes, women who offered themselves to the public for money and couldn't be classed as respectable. I thought of the actresses I'd known and worked with, the wealth and the power of some of them, and couldn't help but reflect on how far we had come in a few hundred years. But I felt much too tired at the moment to try to explain that, and all that I said was, 'I wasn't insulted.'

Fergal feigned insult on my behalf. 'Mind how you speak to my sister, now,' he warned his friend. Then, to me, 'I'd best show you the house, so you'll know where things are.'

Daniel said, 'I can do that.'

Fergal's long look assessed him and seemed to see something he hadn't expected, because he leaned back in his chair with new interest. 'All right.'

To be honest, I paid more attention to Daniel than I did to what he was telling me as I was shown through the rooms of Trelowarth. The downstairs I'd already seen, which was a good thing because all that I managed to take in down there was that Daniel had nice hands he used when he talked, and that when he smiled it carved a shallow cleft in his right cheek. All useful things, but as we climbed the stairs I tried to focus more on my surroundings, and a little less on how his shoulders moved beneath his jacket.

Only that too wasn't altogether pointless, as it prompted me to say, 'I'm really sorry that I didn't bring your dressing gown back with me.'

He half-turned on the landing. 'What?'

'Your dressing gown. The one you loaned me.'

'Ah.' He gave a nod. 'My banyan. It is of no consequence. I'll have another made.'

But I realized that if I returned to my own time in what I was wearing right now, in this gown that had once been his wife's, that was something he couldn't replace. And I wondered if he realized it too.

If he did, he kept it to himself as he began to show me through the upstairs rooms. I had already seen his study, but he added, 'Should you wish something to read, you may take any book that you please from in here or from downstairs. You saw the shelves there?'

I assured him I had. 'Thank you.'

'Nobody else in this house has much liking for books,' he said. 'Fergal has no patience for reading, and my brother Jack would rather be the author of his own adventures. This,' he said, 'is Jack's room.' He nodded to the door of the back bedroom. 'And I'll warn you, though I love my brother dearly, you'd be wisest not to venture near this door when he's at home. 'Tis not for nothing all the mothers in Polgelly lock their daughters up for safekeeping when Jack comes into harbor.'

The warning was a light one, so I answered him in kind, 'I doubt your brother will be bothered with me, seeing as I'm sleeping in your room.'

His eyes were laughing when he looked at me. 'My brother might just take that as a challenge.'

We were so close now in the corridor I had to look a long way up. A man would have to be a fool, I thought, to challenge Daniel Butler's right to anything. It wasn't just his height or strength of build, it was the whole of him, that certain quiet sense of self-assuredness that told me he would not be on the losing side too often in a fight. Were I a man myself, I wouldn't want to test him.

I was looking at him, thinking this, when I first realized that his eyes weren't laughing anymore. And then he noticed I had noticed and he let his gaze drift upwards from my own and said, 'Tomorrow I shall find you pins, so you can dress your hair.'

'I don't know how to.'

'No?' He focused on my eyes again but briefly. 'No, of course you would not know. Well, that will be a minor thing to overcome.'

I asked, 'Where are *you* sleeping?' because suddenly it seemed like something I should know.

For an answer he crossed to the door of the room beside mine. 'Here,' he told me, as the door swung open.

This was where he and Fergal had been talking when I'd overheard them, in this narrow bedroom filled with soft light from the single window at the front. The bed here was not quite as big as the one he'd turned over to me in the room next door, but it was also high and canopied with curtains of a soft sky blue. A long lidded blanket box sat at the foot of the bed, and a chair had been placed by the window so someone could sit looking out at the view of the green hills that rolled to the changeable sea.

It was a woman's room. I didn't need to ask whose it had been because her presence was so tangible I all but saw her sitting in the chair beside the window. I imagined he did too.

I wondered how long she'd been dead but didn't like to pry, and so I turned my gaze instead towards the closed door in the wall between this room and mine. He looked as well, and said, 'I do not doubt that I could find a lock to fit that latch if it would ease your fears.'

I turned to him. 'My fears?'

'You surely have them, being far from home among strange men. And you were frightened when we met.'

'You had a knife, and you were angry,' I reminded him.

'Did it seem like anger to you? For my part, it felt like cowardice. I'd never faced a ghost.'

'Well, any ghost that saw you come at them like that would likely take off running.'

Daniel Butler smiled. He hadn't moved, and yet I felt the space between us shrinking as he said, 'But you are not a ghost.'

I shook my head.

'And I'll admit you do not seem afraid.'

I said, 'I'm not afraid at all.' The words surprised me when I said them, for I knew that they were true. I said them over, to be sure: 'I'm not afraid.'

He watched my face a moment, then he gave a nod and told me, 'Good. For that is a beginning.'

❧

Sleeping was impossible. I rolled my face into the pillow, eyes closed tightly.

I did not belong here. This was not my room and not my bed. And yet, a part of it felt right to me, and somewhere deep inside my mind a tiny voice kept speaking up to say that Daniel Butler had been wrong to tell me I was far from home.

It was a voice I couldn't quiet, and I rolled again and dragged the covers with me, staring out the open window at the moonlit sky shot through with stars that danced against the blackness of infinity. The sea had a voice tonight, rolling and whispering on the dark shore as though trying to give me advice. I ignored it at first, but when other sounds, equally furtive and low, rose to join it, I gave in and rolled from my bed, crossing barefoot to stand at the window.

I'd changed back into my pajamas, and the beautiful gown was spread out on the chair in the corner to wait for tomorrow.

Tomorrow, when I would see Daniel and Fergal, and I would be shown what to do with my hair so that Daniel could take me outside, as he'd promised, and give me a tour of the property.

From where I stood now at the front of the house I could see the broad slope of the hill rolling down to the cliffs and the sea, with the darkness of the Wild Wood pressing closer to the house and looking larger than my memory of it, shot through in places with the ghostly white of blackthorn still in bloom. The sounds continued, and I saw a stir of shadows in the woods.

They slipped out one by one and left the path to turn uphill and climb towards the house, a silent line of darkened figures, moving in the moonlight. Well, not wholly silent. I could hear the rustle of their footsteps and the heavy tread of two dark horses being led in single file behind, with bundles piled on their backs.

The floorboards in the next room creaked as Daniel Butler rose as well, and stealthily went out and down the stairs. A moment later, from my window, I could see his shadow going out to join the others and to clap the shoulder of the man in front in greeting, and to guide the line of men and horses up around behind the house.

It didn't in the least surprise me that he was a smuggler; I had guessed already from the things he'd said about his less than honest trade and from the character he'd painted of the brother who shared the command of his ship. Besides, this was Cornwall, and every house here had its smugglers.

I wondered what the men had carried up tonight then I decided that I didn't need to know. It didn't matter.

It felt colder on my feet now, standing there beside the window, so I turned away and headed back to bed.

And then I stopped.

Because the bed had started wavering. Across the blankets shadows played and shifted as the hanging curtains caught the breeze that blew in from behind me like a long, regretful sigh.

Another breath and it had faded like a swirl of smoke in wind, and I was once more in the corridor, just crossing from the bathroom and a few steps from my bedroom door, while all the house around me went on sleeping as though nothing had been changed.

CHAPTER 12

Y OU'RE QUIET THIS MORNING. You feeling all right?'
Mark had already been up and out and hard at work
for hours by the time I ventured outside. There'd been a
sharp change in the weather, and all round the flowers were
ducking in front of the wind, gusting damply and chilly for
this time of year. Even the dogs hunched their backs to it,
keeping their tails down and gathering closely around Mark
and me as we walked to the greenhouse.

The truth was, I wasn't too sure *how* I felt. I was glad to
be back. But if things had gone differently I might be taking
this same walk with Daniel right now, and not Mark, and
for some reason that left me feeling a little bit... well, a bit
cheated, though I knew that didn't make sense.

Nor was it really fair to Mark, who was still looking at
me with concern. I made an effort and met his gaze brightly.
'I'm fine.'

He seemed prepared to take me at my word. His own attention was distracted by the dogs, who had gone wild because
Felicity was coming out to meet us from the greenhouse.

Her good spirits, at least, were as buoyant as ever. Dancing
her way through the onslaught of leaping dog bodies and
wagging tails, she said, 'It took you both long enough. Wait
till you see what we've done!' As we neared the doorway to
the greenhouse she slipped in behind Mark, covering his eyes

with both her hands. 'Don't look, not yet. You either, Eva. Close your eyes.'

'Felicity, what... ow!' Mark whacked his elbow on the door frame as he tried to step through blind.

'All right. Now.' Lifting up her hands with an enthusiastic flourish, she revealed the latest triumph she and Susan had achieved. They'd painted. Everything was green and ivory, beautifully elegant and restful. For the first time, it looked less like an old green house than a tearoom in the making.

Even Mark was forced to say a heartfelt, 'Wow.'

And that one word, because it came from him, was all the benediction that Felicity had hoped for. I could see it in her eyes, her brightened smile, and once again I marveled that Mark couldn't see it for himself. She said, 'Of course there's still the floor to do and all the rest, but doesn't it look wonderful?'

It really did. I told her so.

Susan was cleaning the paintbrushes in the new sink that the plumber had just installed, but when she saw us she turned off the water and came across. 'Well, brother? What do you think?'

Mark was still looking up. 'I think maybe you might have a tearoom.'

'I told you.' But she seemed pleased too, to have won Mark's approval. 'Now all we have to do is bring the tourists in, and Eva's got a start on that already. Did she tell you that she's found a duke who might have some connection to Trelowarth?'

'Really?' Mark turned. 'Who would that be?'

'Oh,' I said. 'The Duke of Ormonde.' I'd forgotten all about him, but for the benefit of Mark and Felicity I gave an account of his career, how he'd fought against the Jacobites initially and then switched sides and tried to bring the young

King James across to take the throne when Queen Anne died. 'He was raising a rebellion right down here,' I said, 'in Cornwall, only Parliament got wind of it and voted to arrest him as a traitor, and he took off into exile.'

'A Jacobite rebellion? Here in Cornwall?' asked Felicity.

'I know,' said Susan. 'That's what I said. But it's quite romantic, don't you think?'

Mark asked, 'And how's this duke connected to Trelowarth?'

If I'd had Fergal's gift for lying I'd have answered that I'd read somewhere the Duke of Ormonde might have had a blood relation living here in 1715, but as it was I only glanced away and shrugged and said, 'I haven't really got it all worked out. I'll have to do a bit more research yet.'

Susan said, 'You should ask Oliver. Remember him?'

I nodded. 'Yes, of course. I just bumped into him Wednesday, in fact, in Felicity's shop.'

'*Did* you?' asked Felicity. 'He didn't mention that to me.'

I felt the quick surge of new interest all round.

Susan asked me, 'And what did you think of him?'

'Well...'

'He's filled out a bit, hasn't he?' Susan grinned. 'Who knew he'd grow up to look like a film star?'

Mark said, 'I should imagine Eva's seen her share of film stars, Sue.'

'Well, I'll take him if she doesn't want him. The point is,' she told me, 'if it's history you're after, he'd be a good person to go to, because he knows all sorts of obscure things. He researched a lot when he set up his smugglers' museum. If he doesn't know the exact facts you're after, he might point you in the direction to find them.'

Mark looked doubtful. 'Would he be open on a Sunday?'

Susan said, 'If the museum's closed, he only lives upstairs. I'm betting if you knocked he'd come and open up.'

'Especially,' Felicity said, teasing, 'for the right sort of a customer.'

⤫

Oliver's museum was along the harbor road, and it *was* open. The force of the wind blew me in through the door and I had to lean all of my weight on the heavy wood to make it swing shut behind me and latch.

Inside, everything smelt of the salt of the sea and the old plaster walls and the wood dust that came from the floorboards. Brass ship's lanterns hung from the dark weathered beams overhead to create the illusion the room owed its brightness to them, not the more modern pot lights set into the ceiling. The ceiling itself seemed unusually low at first, but like most very old cottages here, this one's floor had been hollowed out so that it actually sat at a level below the street outside. Once I'd gone down the two steps from the door I could stand without bumping my head.

It was rather like stepping below decks, I thought, on a ship. With the posts and the beams and the lanterns and barrels and ropes worked so cleverly into the big room's design, I almost expected the floor to roll under my feet when I walked on it.

'Eva!' He'd been in the back, either reading or working because he was wearing his glasses, but he took them off, tucking them into his shirt pocket as he came forwards to greet me.

I looked round the room. 'This is really nice, Oliver.'

'Thanks. I'm afraid I can't take all the credit, though. It was my mother's idea. She came from a smuggling family herself, and she had this collection of things she'd been gathering over the years, and she always said someone should build a museum to put them in, so…' With his hands spread, he gestured to what he had made. 'Mind you, she didn't stay to help me with it.'

I remembered his mother, a cheerfully no-nonsense woman. 'Oh? Where did she go?'

'Up to Bristol, to live with my aunt. Left me to fend for myself, so she has.'

'Well, you seem to be doing all right.'

'What, with this? The museum won't pay any bills for me.' Oliver smiled. 'It's a labor of love. No, I've got a collection of holiday cottages over St Non's way. I let them year round, and so far that's been enough to keep me in the black. I can't complain.'

'Holiday cottages? Really? You wouldn't have one sitting empty right now, would you?'

'I'm afraid not. They're all booked through September.'

'Oh.'

'Why, were you wanting one?'

'Thinking about it.' I nodded. 'I'm taking a bit of a break from my job and L.A. and… well, everything, after Katrina. You know. I was thinking I might rent a cottage round here, maybe stay for a while.'

He said, 'Choose the cottage you like, and I'll turf out the tenant.'

I smiled. 'You don't need to do that. But if one does come free in September—'

'It's yours.' He watched me looking round the room and asked, 'You want the tour?'

'Yes, please.'

He'd done a good job setting up all the exhibits so they flowed one from the other in a pattern that was logical, from the earliest days of the settlement here through the bold privateers of the Tudor age, right to the heyday of 'free-trading' in the late 1700s, when practically everyone took part in it, sometimes including the revenue men who were meant to be keeping the smugglers in check.

There'd always been trade between Cornwall and Brittany, on the French coast, and neither wars nor taxes had been able to persuade the Cornish free-traders to give up what for them was a good livelihood and, more than that, a most diverting game.

'Like cat and mouse,' was Oliver's analogy. 'Everyone knew who the smugglers were, the real job was to catch them. And then, once you'd caught them, you had to make the charges stick, because the local juries here would only let them off again. That's why some of the revenue men in the end gave it up, helped themselves to a cut of the profits, and turned a blind eye.'

I couldn't imagine the constable turning a blind eye to anything, though he had not seemed to me like a man to be easily fooled. He must surely have known what the Butlers were up to. But then again, those men I'd seen from my window had gone to great lengths to come up from the woods without anyone noticing.

'What did they smuggle in, usually?' I asked.

'Oh, brandy and tea and tobacco, French laces and silk. Anything that the government slapped a big duty on.' He hitched a barrel over and sat down while I examined a small gallery of drawings of Polgelly's famous smuggling ships.

I didn't find the one that I was looking for, and so I asked him, 'Did you ever hear of a ship called the *Sally*?'

He considered it a moment. 'No, it doesn't ring a bell. Was she a smuggler's ship?'

'I think so. She belonged to the Butlers who lived at Trelowarth.'

'The Butlers? I don't know them either. What year would this be?'

'Early 1700s,' I said, trying hard not to sound too specific, because I could already tell from his face he was going to ask me:

'And where did you come across all of this?'

I shrugged. 'I read about them somewhere on the Internet; I can't remember where. I wasn't smart enough to bookmark it.'

'The Butlers. Did it give their first names?'

'Jack and Daniel.'

'Well, I should at least remember *that*.' He grinned. 'It sounds enough like what I like to drink.' Which led him to his next idea. Glancing at the windows that were for the moment free of rain, he said, 'You've done the tour. Now let me buy you lunch.'

'That's what you do for all your tourists, is it?'

'Certainly.' His eyes, good-natured, challenged me to challenge him. 'What's it to be? Your choice—the Wellie or the tearoom?'

I was torn at that, because I'd never been inside the Wellington. It hadn't been the sort of pub you took a child into, which had only made it all the more intriguing. But I settled on, 'The tearoom, please. I'll do a bit of corporate spying while I'm here, for Susan.'

'Right,' said Oliver. 'I'll fetch my coat.'

We were the only customers for lunch, and it was clear the waitress had a crush on Oliver because she set my soup down with a lack of care that bordered on disdain. Oliver, not noticing, looked puzzled when he saw me trying not to laugh.

'What?'

'Nothing.'

'So, Felicity tells me Sue's put you to work.'

'Yes. That's what brought me down here today, actually. I was hoping I could find somebody famous in Trelowarth's past, a name that she could use to draw the tourists in.' I knew from how he looked at me he'd hit upon the obvious, as I had, so I told him, 'Yes, I know. I told her she should use Katrina's name, but Susan wasn't having it. I'll have to find her someone else.'

'A famous person in Trelowarth's past.' He wasn't sure.

'Well, there's the Duke of Ormonde, maybe.' We discussed that for a minute. He impressed me with his knowledge of the details of the Jacobite rebellion I had read about, which encouraged me to add, 'His name was Butler, right? James Butler.'

'Like your Butler brothers, you mean?' He considered this. 'It's a bit of a shot in the dark.'

'Oh, I don't know,' I told him carelessly. 'They might have been related.'

'You're determined to find Sue her famous person, aren't you?' Oliver was smiling but he sympathized. 'I know, it would be brilliant if her plans worked out. I'd hate to see the Halletts lose Trelowarth.'

In surprise I set my spoon down. 'It's as bad as that?'

He gave a nod. 'It's bad.'

'I didn't realize.'

'Never fear,' he said, 'I'll do a little research of my own and see what I can find. Even if the Duke of Ormonde didn't come this way, your Butler brothers might prove interesting enough themselves.'

'Thanks, I'd appreciate that.'

'Would you? Then you'll have to let me buy you lunch again.'

The waitress heard that part and slammed my sandwich plate down with such force the table rattled.

This time even Oliver noticed. Watching our waitress depart he said, 'She's in a bit of a mood today, isn't she?' Then catching sight of my face, he asked, 'What?' again.

It took an effort to straighten my smile as I answered him, 'Nothing. It's nothing.' But I had a feeling that lunching with Oliver anywhere here in Polgelly might turn out to be an adventure.

CHAPTER 13

CLAIRE WAS PLEASED. WE hadn't seen her for a few days, she'd been keeping to herself, and after supper I had walked out to the cottage for a visit, with the little mongrel Samson at my heels. The dog was lying in a warm contented coil now underneath the narrow table that Claire used for mixing paints in her bright studio. I'd always liked to watch her work. I liked the mingled smells of oil paint drying slowly on the canvases, and brushes left to soak in jars of turpentine, and underneath all that the fainter scent of coffee sitting somewhere in a mug and growing cold because she had forgotten it as usual when she began to paint.

I liked her paintings too. The landscapes had a quality of fantasy about them, as though she'd taken what was there in front of her and shaped it as it could have been. The Christmas cards she'd sent to us each year while both my parents were still living had been painted by her own hand, printed privately, so beautiful they'd sat out on our mantel-piece long after all the other decorations of the season had been cleared away. I wondered what had happened to them. After the death of my parents so many of those little links with the past had been lost.

Claire swept an edge of sunset color underneath a cloud and said, 'I'm glad you got to spend some time with Oliver.'

'I nearly didn't recognize him.'

'Yes, he's changed a little, hasn't he?' Her sideways glance was twinkling. 'On the inside, though, he's still the same old Oliver he ever was. Where did you go for lunch?'

'The tearoom by the harbor. And Felicity was right, the woman there can't make a scone to save her life. She'll be no competition for Susan.' Which was, I thought, as good a starting point as I was going to get for what I'd really come to talk about. I said, 'Aunt Claire?'

'Yes, darling?'

'If I ask you something, will you give an honest answer?'

The motion of her brush stopped on the canvas as she turned to me with eyes that seemed to know already what I was about to ask her. 'Always.'

'How much money would it take for Mark and Susan not to lose Trelowarth?'

She blinked and set the paintbrush down. 'However did you hear of that?'

'I'm not allowed to say.'

Claire crossed to put the brush in turpentine and slowly cleaned her hands. And then, because she'd made a promise to be honest, she explained how the investments had diminished and the taxes had increased. 'Mark's not in debt yet,' she assured me, 'but he will be this time next year if he can't turn things around.'

'I want to help,' I said.

'You are helping.'

'I mean really help. Financially. I know that Mark would never take my money, but it isn't mine,' I justified. 'Not really. It's Katrina's. And she wouldn't want to see Trelowarth struggling if her money could prevent it.' I paused long enough to glance at Claire and satisfy myself that she agreed with that before I carried on. 'I thought if I were to set up a trust, Mark and Susan could draw on the funds when they needed them, keep the place going, and know that the trust would be there for their children as well, and their grandchildren.'

I waited for Claire's arguments and braced myself against them. There was no way I could properly explain in words why this was so important to me, why it seemed so right to me that something of my sister should remain here, something tangible.

Claire looked at me a long and silent moment. 'I think,' she said finally, 'that would be a lovely legacy. Katrina would be pleased. How can I help?'

We talked it over while we moved into the kitchen from the studio, and Claire made some suggestions as she put the kettle on to boil, and by the time she'd filled the Wedgwood teapot we had worked the whole thing out between us.

'I'll go see Mr. Rowe at the bank in Polgelly tomorrow,' I said. 'He can help me get everything organized.'

Claire smiled. 'You'll have to fortify yourself then, for the climb back up afterwards. Which biscuits would you like? I've coconut or chocolate.'

As she set the biscuit tin down on the table I shook my head. 'I'll have to walk up and down The Hill ten times a day, if I keep eating these.'

'Nonsense. You're too thin as it is.'

'There's no such thing in California as "too thin".'

Claire's dry and wordless glance said much about her view of California and its fashions, but she didn't say a word. She only opened up the biscuit tin and tilted it towards me till I took one. It was coconut. I shared it with the dog, who'd come to join us with expectant eyes and wagging tail. He settled by my chair as I asked, 'Have you seen the greenhouse yet?'

'I haven't, no.'

'They've painted. It looks wonderful.' I filled her in on everything Felicity and Susan had been doing, while we sat and drank our tea.

I liked this kitchen, liked the feel of it, the cozy warmth and comfort that owed more to Claire herself than to the decorating. She changed the feeling of the rooms that she was in. She made them welcoming.

And maybe that was why I felt my sister's presence here as well, this evening. It didn't take a great stretch of imagination to picture Katrina in the empty chair just at the table's end, with her chin propped on one hand the way she'd always sat when she was following the flow of conversation.

And when we took our tea into the sitting room I felt her come along and curl herself into the sofa at my side, so that I felt no need or inclination to get up, and when Claire told me I looked tired and brought a pillow and a blanket so that I could 'rest my eyes' I didn't argue, only lay my head back happily, still feeling that Katrina was right there with me.

Perhaps she was.

But when I woke, she'd gone.

I'd slept much longer than I'd meant to. It was morning, and the smell of toast still hovered in the kitchen. Claire had left a note:

Gone walking with the dog. Help yourself to what you like.

But she had cleaned the kitchen and I didn't want to spoil its spotlessness, and having slept the whole night in my clothes I felt rumpled. My breakfast could wait, I decided, until I'd got back to Trelowarth and showered. I wrote my own note underneath Claire's, thanking her, and propped it back up on the table.

Then taking my coat, I slipped out the front door. It had rained in the night, and the leaves in the woods all held loose beads of water and when the wind chased through the branches and set them to shivering, light little showers came scattering down on my shoulders and head, and my boots slipped a bit in the mud of the path, but I didn't much mind. And as I came out the far side of the woods there was sunlight at least breaking through the clouds over my head, and Trelowarth itself standing waiting to welcome me, and Susan coming out now to walk round to the greenhouse. I'd go out myself after breakfast and help her, I thought. And then I'd go down to the bank.

When I took my next step, though, the heavens suddenly opened with a fury, and a torrent of rain blown by wind struck me full in the face out of nowhere. I struggled to regain my footing, steadying myself against the onslaught of the sudden storm, and made a dash towards the house and shelter.

The wind was like a wild thing pursuing me. It shrieked as I blew through the back door and slammed it shut behind me, and the blast of rain that followed pounded on the wood like fists demanding entry.

I had water running in my eyes. I pushed my hair back from my forehead, stripped my jacket off, and shook it out and turned to hang it on its hook with all the other coats.

Except there were no other coats. No row of hooks. No rack of boots.

The realization hit me with the same force as the storm and just as suddenly. I let my jacket drop. It made a puddle on the flagstone floor as, stepping from my muddy boots, I padded in on stockinged feet.

In the kitchen, the gnarled branches of the apple trees were scraping at the window and their dripping leaves cast ever-changing shadows in the dimness. All the dishes had been cleared away; the pots scoured clean and set to wait upon the fireless hearth that smelt of cold dead ashes. No one had been cooking here this morning.

Very quietly, I took my sodden coat and boots and stored them out of sight beneath some sacking in the little room that Fergal called the 'scullery', which looked to simply be a place for storing things and washing up, with wooden boxes, woven sacks, and empty jugs shoved up against the walls, one small scrubbed table and a tall freestanding cupboard with an iron lock.

Then slipping from the scullery I tiptoed back across the kitchen to the narrow back staircase that might let me get to the safety of 'my' room before someone saw me. I didn't have to worry about Daniel or Fergal, of course, but they weren't the only people living here, and they'd both said that Daniel's brother Jack might be returning any time. For all I knew, he might be home already.

I kept that thought in mind as I creaked lightly up the steep slope of the stairs to the first floor and crept past the closed door of the room that Daniel had informed me was his brother's. It was closed, as were the other doors up here, but I was still relieved to reach the large front corner room and shut myself inside it.

And relieved again to find the blue gown draped across the chair before the writing desk, where I had left it. This time it was easier to dress myself, though fastening the bodice with the pins still took some time and patience. But I could do nothing with my hair yet except comb my fingers through it and allow it to hang loose.

Prepared now, I sat on the bed's edge patiently and waited.

Maybe I'd come back too early in the morning. It was difficult to judge the time with dark rain sluicing down the windows, driven hard against the glass by a rough wind that rose and wailed and died again into a weeping moan. It was a lonely sound.

The minutes passed. My shoulders stiffened, unaccustomed to the damp, and I got up and paced a little in an effort to get warm. I thought for certain that my pacing would wake Daniel in the next room, but the house stayed silent. Finally, after what seemed an interminable time, I raised the courage to cross over to the door between our rooms and very gently eased it open. If he was in there asleep, I thought, I'd simply close the door again and wait.

But the blue-curtained bed was empty.

Moving cautiously past it, I knocked at the next connecting door, but that room too had no one in it. That discovery and the need for movement made me bolder, and in time I had repeated the maneuver with the other upstairs rooms, and then with those downstairs, and found that, for the moment, there was no one in the house but me.

I might have gone outside to see if they were there, but I remembered Daniel saying clearly that it was not safe for me to leave the house, and I agreed. I really didn't want to meet the constable alone.

The problem was, it had been a while now since I'd woken up at Claire's and come away without my breakfast, a decision I regretted now. It wasn't just the food—I could go hungry for a while with no real ill effects—but I had never coped too well with thirst. The more I tried ignoring it, the deeper it took hold, and if I didn't find some water soon I knew I'd get a headache.

I'd seen Fergal dipping water from a pail beside the kitchen hearth, but when I checked the pail I found it empty. I stood frowning for a moment till a blast of rain against the kitchen window gave my thoughts a jolt. Taking the pail with me, I went to open the back door and set the pail out in the rain. It took several minutes before I'd collected enough for a small drink of water, but that was enough. With my thirst partly satisfied, I put the pail back outside to get more, just in case I got thirsty again before Daniel or Fergal came back.

They'd be back soon, I thought. They had left the doors open, and surely they wouldn't have done that unless they'd been somewhere close by. In the meantime I felt sure they wouldn't begrudge me a handful of food.

And a handful of food was the most I could find in the scullery. One of the sacks held the barley that Fergal had used for his broth, but uncooked it was hard and inedible, and in the other sack there was just coarsely ground flour. I found two soft apples in one corner of an otherwise empty box under the worktable, but all the other food must have been in the tall cupboard, and that was locked.

I ate one apple, saving the other for later, and went in search of something that would help me pass the time.

It felt strange being in that house with no one else around. I wasn't used to it, and even with the wind and rain, Trelowarth had a multitude of voices—stairs that creaked with no one on them, joists that settled with a sigh, and unseen mice that scrambled through the walls with tiny furtive noises.

What had Daniel's wife done on the days he was at sea, I wondered? True, she would have likely had the house to keep and clean, and meals to make, if only for herself. And housework might have filled her waking hours with no time left for boredom. But for me this was a foreign country, really, coming from a place where I could flip a switch and instantly have music or the hourly news to chase away the loneliness.

I wondered whether Daniel's wife had ever gone upstairs, as I did now, to seek the comfort of the study where the fragrance of his pipe smoke lingered as though he were not far off. I scanned his books in search of something I might know. The books themselves were lovely things to look at, bound in half-calf leather so the scent of them alone enhanced the beauty of the room. Some had their titles stamped in gilded printing on the spine, and curious, I picked out a copy of Jonathan Swift's poems, so recently printed that I could still smell the sharp scent of fresh ink on the pages. As I read the satirical lines I was struck by the strange realization that Jonathan Swift was alive right now somewhere and walking around, maybe forming ideas for *Gulliver's Travels*, a book that he hadn't yet written.

Now I'd noticed it, several of the books in this room were by writers who would have been very much alive in 1715: Alexander Pope and William Congreve and the poet Matthew Prior. It was thrilling just to hold those books in the same form in which the authors would have held them, in what likely were the first editions published, with their covers smooth and new and all the pages crisply cut.

I wondered how the writers would react were I to tell them that a woman living in this house three hundred years from now would know their names and still be reading what they'd written.

Putting back the Swift poems I chose instead a folio of Shakespeare's plays and flipped through till I found *The Merchant of Venice*, the first play I'd ever seen on the stage, when my parents had taken Katrina and me up to Stratford as children. Katrina had always said that one performance had started it all for her, switched something on deep inside her that told her that acting was what she was meant to do, what she'd been made for.

I settled myself in the chair by the window, and passed the next hour or so quietly reading. It carried me back, as so many things did. I could almost imagine Katrina beside me, the two of us there in the dark of the theatre and lost in the magic the actors were weaving with just a few props and their voices. Of course it had helped that the young actor playing Bassanio had been so hugely good-looking that right from the opening scene, when he'd leaned on a railing directly above us bemoaning his fate, he'd commanded our sympathy.

It had likely been his fault, as much as the play's, that Katrina had taken up acting. She'd met him in person once, years later, making a film, and had been unimpressed. 'A walking ego,' she had called him, when she'd come round to my place that evening as she sometimes did after a long day's shooting, to relax.

I'd made brown sugar sandwiches, my mother's bedtime specialty, and asked her, 'Really?'

'Really. And to think, for all these years he's been a fantasy of mine. I guess it's true, you should be careful what you wish for.'

I could hear her voice within my head again now, though I didn't need the warning. I already knew it to be true. I'd just come halfway round the world myself in hopes that at Trelowarth I could touch the past and hold what I had lost a little longer, and now here I was. I'd touched the past all right, but I had missed Katrina by three hundred years, and in this strange place I felt more alone than ever.

❧

Evening came and brought the realization that I might be on my own for longer than I'd thought. I'd had to leave the study and the books with some reluctance and come back downstairs. The darkness here could not be held at bay by switching on a light, and though the house had no shortage of candles, they had to be lit to be useful. Besides, since I'd now eaten the last apple, if I didn't want to starve I'd have to find a way to somehow cook the barley. I would have to light a fire.

The iron grate inside the kitchen fireplace had a dusting of cold ashes underneath, but it already held a stack of fresh wood waiting for a flame. Except I wasn't good with fires. Not even with a modern box of matches, which I didn't have to hand, although a quick search of the crannies near the kitchen hearth produced a metal tinderbox, the kind I'd only read about in books. I knew the theory of the tinderbox: I was supposed to take the flint and steel and strike some sparks onto a small pile of the tinder, in this case a mixture of wood shavings and bits of cloth. When the sparks caught on the tinder I was then supposed to blow on them and coax them to a flame that would in turn ignite the wood stacked in the fireplace. Foolproof.

Only this was me, and after working at it for what felt like an hour I'd only managed to produce a few small sparks that flashed and smoldered and did no more than consume my precious scraps of tinder before burning out completely in a listless puff of smoke. My face was smudged, my temper frayed, my knees were stiff from kneeling at the hearth, but I'd been born too stubborn to let such a small thing beat me, so I focused all my concentration on the task and shut out everything around me that might serve as a distraction—every creak and groan the house made, and the rattle of the storm against the windows, and the wailing of the wind across the chimney-top above me.

And the door. I didn't hear it either, so the sudden heavy tread of boots behind me on the floorboards made me jump. I turned, expecting Daniel. Maybe Fergal.

It was neither.

CHAPTER 14

IN THE NEAR DARK of this room, the silent presence of the constable was something to be feared. My one advantage was that I had caught him off his guard as well—he clearly hadn't been expecting to find anyone at home.

I stood with care and tried to calm my racing heartbeat with determination.

He recovered first. 'Mistress O'Cleary.' There was no attempt to make even a mocking bow this time, no need to show respect since there was no one watching. Those cold, uncompromising eyes grew narrow as he processed this discovery. 'Have they left you here alone for these past days?' His gaze moved briefly to the hearth and back. 'And with no fire. That was unkind of them. I confess when I did not see smoke from the chimneys I was myself convinced the house was empty.'

So that was why he'd come in unannounced like this—because he'd thought he could. He'd thought there would be no one here to notice or to challenge him and that he would be able to poke round at leisure, undisturbed.

Except I'd spoilt his plans.

Now, like some reptile who could change the pattern of his skin when needed, he appeared to be adapting to this new twist of events. I saw his features lose a little of their hardness in a calculated way, and when he spoke again his voice made a deliberate stab at being civil. 'Are you having difficulty?'

It was just as well that I was scared of him, because that fear prevented me from answering for long enough that I remembered I was not supposed to have a voice. I gave a wary nod.

'Stand aside then.' He did not appear to notice that my fingers shook a little as I passed the tinderbox into his outstretched hand. It took him time as well, but in the end he made a fire that grew steadily upon the hearth and cast a welcome light and spreading warmth into the dreary room.

When he straightened, it took all my effort not to take a backwards step away from him, because he seemed too close. 'Now, how then will you thank me for my aid, when you have not the use of words?' He saw my wariness increase and seemed amused enough by it to push my panic button further, giving me a purposefully slow once-over, pausing on my loose hair. 'I can see you were preparing for your bed. Perhaps you need assistance there, as well?' He smiled at my reaction and then went another route. 'But no, some wine, I think, will be enough. A bottle of the best that Butler has and you may count your debt repaid.'

I stood a moment at a loss, until I suddenly remembered there had been wine in the dining room when we had eaten lunch there—several bottles lying dusty in a corner near the sideboard. I had no idea whether they were Daniel Butler's best or not, but that's what he'd been drinking so the wine would not be bad.

I gave a small nod to excuse myself and hustled off in that direction, hoping that the bottles would still be there. And they were. I grabbed the top one, wiped the dust off with my hand, and took it back to give to the constable, in hopes that would get rid of him.

He wasn't where I'd left him in the kitchen. Apprehensive, I stood still beside the hearth a moment, listening. He wouldn't have gone far, I knew. I'd only been a minute. But I also knew his aim in coming up here in the first place must have been to look around, and he was obviously taking full advantage of my absence.

Then I heard him. In the scullery.

My mouth went dry so suddenly I found it hard to swallow down the nervous lump that lodged itself above my heart. My jacket and my boots were in the scullery, and if he found them…

I could feel my fingers clenching round the bottle's neck so tightly that my fingernails were digging in my palm as I went through into the scullery to join him. To my great relief, I saw that he had not yet moved the sacking on the floor. His interest seemed to be directed at the pantry cupboard with its lock.

'Tell me,' he asked idly, 'does your brother always lock the food away when he does leave you on your own?' His glance towards me held no expectation of an answer, but his eyes were watchful on my face for my reaction. 'Or might there be more in here than food?'

I kept my own face neutral, trying hard not to react at all, not even when he walked towards the sacking. But he only kicked it to one side and reached for a short-handled axe that leaned against the wall behind. I hadn't even known the tool was there, myself. The constable had sharper eyes.

'We must not let you starve,' he said with mock concern. He brought the axe down with a force that broke the locked door cleanly and the cupboard swung wide open.

I hadn't been too sure, myself, what he might find inside. For all I knew there might be contraband behind the food, but after he had opened the few tins and shoved some sacks aside, he muttered something to himself and stood a moment, thinking. Then he turned his head and looked at me.

I really didn't like his eyes. They made my flesh crawl cold.

He'd thought of something, I could see it in the way his mouth began to curve. He asked me, 'Are you in the house alone?'

And how was I to answer that? He obviously knew that Daniel Butler and the rest were gone away somewhere, and if there had been anybody here with me I wouldn't have been trying on my own to light the fire. No matter how much my protective instincts warned me not to give a truthful answer, I knew full well that I wouldn't fool him if I lied. I gave a slow nod.

'Well then, I do think it would be wise were I to make a full inspection of this house and all its rooms, that I might satisfy myself as to your safety.'

There was nothing I could do to stop him anyway, but still he'd picked a clever way to word things so that neither I nor anyone could argue his intentions.

He carried the axe with him out of the scullery and when I followed he turned round and using the blade, pointed back at the kitchen. 'No mistress, wait there. I would do this alone.'

He was gone for a long time. Long enough for me to think about escaping to the stables or the woods, but with the storm outside it seemed a foolish thing to do, and anyway my fear was slowly melting into anger at his arrogant intrusion, and a part of me refused to give him any satisfaction, so I didn't run. Whatever happened, I'd at least be able to tell Daniel what the constable had done. And what he'd found.

With the wind at the window I couldn't hear what he was

doing upstairs, though. I didn't know what he was touching, defiling. It was, I thought, rather like having a rat roaming unseen behind your walls, doing its damage.

I was happy to see, when he came back down, that his hard face had the look of frustration, as though he'd been cheated. Clearly he hadn't found what he'd been looking for.

Passing the scullery door he stopped briefly to throw down the axe he was holding. It fell with a clatter and thud on the flagstones. 'Well, Mistress O'Cleary.' His tone was a challenge. I saw his gaze fall on the bottle that I was still holding. 'Would that be my wine? Give it here then.'

Heavily he sat beside me, took a small knife from his pocket, and pried out the seal and then took a long drink from the bottle itself. And another. Then wiping his mouth on his sleeve he said, 'It may be that I am approaching this wrongly. Perhaps I have only to ask, hmm?' He angled his head and his eyes fixed themselves on my own. 'Have you had any visitors here to Trelowarth of late? Any men of high birth?'

Very carefully, I shook my head.

'You would do well to tell me the truth, mistress, for I remind you that this country's laws of high treason can give no protection to those who might shelter a traitor.' His voice held a velvet contempt as he added, 'Nor even for those who would take one to bed.' His glance flicked down my length and back as he drank deep from the bottle again, and when I failed to react to the insult he said, 'Do not flatter yourself that he holds you in any regard. Do you know why he gives you that gown? To give life to a ghost. Any whore could fulfill the same purpose.'

His smile had the power to cut just as cruelly as that small knife he'd used to open the wine and that he now put back in his pocket. He stood. 'Think on that while you seek to protect him from justice. I am not myself without mercy, you'll find, but I can do nothing to help you if you put the noose round your neck by your own choice.' Setting down the bottle on the table, he said, 'Take you good care of that fire I have made for you, Mistress O'Cleary. 'Twould grieve me to see you get burnt.'

I did not stand myself nor look round as he left. The truth was that I'd started shaking too badly to stand. It was only the aftereffect of the fear I had felt while he'd been here, my body's release of the tension I'd had to hold in, and no more. But in spite of the fire that now crackled so warm on the hearth it was some time before I stopped shaking, and even when I finally stood I still felt cold inside.

The wine that he'd left on the table might have helped warm me, but I didn't want to drink from any bottle he had held. It was as though he had a poison in him that was transferred by his touch and needed to be cleaned away. I took the bottle in my hand and carried it around to the back door where I upended it above the muddy ground.

And then I tilted my face to the rain until I felt clean too.

The bucket I'd set out before was now half-full. I brought it in and locked the door, then hauled the three-legged iron kettle to the hearth and emptied most of the water into it, saving some for drinking later. I'd lost my appetite, but knowing that my hunger would return and that I needed to keep eating to survive till someone came, I sifted barley from the sack into the water and I left it there to boil while I lit a candle and went up to see what damage the constable had done.

My anger returned in full force when I saw the effects of his search. Daniel's books lay strewn across the study floor, and in the bedrooms there were drawers pulled out and mattresses askew with no attempt made to return the rooms to order. He'd had the time to search and leave no sign of it, I thought, but it was obvious he'd wanted to let Daniel know he'd been here. Why, I didn't know. If *I* felt this much anger simply looking at the things that had been tainted by the presence of the constable, it stood to reason Daniel would be furious.

Unless that was the purpose of it all, provoking Daniel to retaliate, because although I didn't know the laws of this time, surely there would be a nasty penalty for challenging the king's own loyal constable. Arrest, at least. And maybe more.

I fought my anger down and lit more candles to bring light into the rooms, and started tidying, returning books to their neat rows and righting chairs and trying hard to make things look the way they had before. I took the greatest care in the small room that had been Daniel's wife's, because to me the very thought the constable had been in here among her things seemed unforgivable, an act of violation.

And he had been here. He'd rifled through the clothing in the long box at the foot of the bed, leaving petticoat edges and sleeves hanging out. I restored them to order as best I could, smoothing the dresses in folds with as much care as if they'd belonged to Katrina. 'I'm sorry,' I told her, and closed the box gently.

And then I remembered. 'Oh, Christ,' I breathed, feeling the drop in the pit of my stomach. Because when I'd changed out of my own clothes into this gown, I had hidden my things at the bottom of one of the boxes that sat by the wall in my bedroom, and if he had taken the time to search this one, then...

'Dammit.' I yanked the door open between the two rooms and went through with a feeling of dread.

Both the boxes were closed. And the first one, the one where I'd hidden my clothes, appeared just as it had been before when I opened the lid. On the top were a few white shirts, fine to the touch, and below them two brocaded waistcoats, and then below *them* were my own things, still folded, with no indication that they'd been disturbed.

It appeared, from a glance round the room, that the constable's focus in here had been on the small writing desk, to the exclusion of everything else. He had sat at the chair, for it was in a different position than it had been earlier, and when he'd closed the lid, part of a paper had caught in the hinge.

I crossed over and opened the lid to release it, to put it back into the tidily organized pile where it had been. It was a short statement of household accounts, written in a strong and heavy hand. Nothing of interest to the constable, apparently, or else he wouldn't have looked so frustrated when he'd finished with his search.

He'd been looking for something specific, I sensed, and I could feel a bit of satisfaction knowing that he hadn't found it.

I made very certain the doors were all bolted that night, having forced down a bit of the porridge I'd made and left the rest to cool beside the hearth. It was too much to hope that there'd be anything left of the fire in the morning, in spite of my amateurish efforts to bank it, so I took one of the tall glass chimneys from the sitting room and used it at my bedside as a shield for the one candle I left burning there, in hopes I might be able to use that to start a fire on the hearth if it were necessary.

I took off the bodice and skirt of the gown that had been Daniel's wife's, but I left on the simple chemise underneath in an effort to conjure up some of her courage—for it must have taken courage to have slept in this big house with all its shadows when the men were off at sea.

When Katrina had died I'd gone through all her closets as Bill had requested, and sorted a lot of her clothes to be given to charity, but I'd kept the comfort clothes, the ones that she'd most often worn, and in those moments when I missed her most I still found putting on her favorite flowered shirt could bring her close to me.

As I drifted with eyes closed, the voice of the constable asked me again, 'Do you know why he gives you that gown? To give life to a ghost.'

I could have used that ghost for company right now, and so I huddled deeper in the blankets, hugging the borrowed chemise all the tighter around me and trying to work the same magic, alone in the dark.

Something clattered downstairs in the kitchen and brought me awake. I had slept through the sunrise, although not by much, for the shadows were still sharply angled across the floor, cast by the daylight that came through the east windows flanking the fireplace.

I sat up to listen.

And then I heard whistling and booted feet climbing the stairs, and the whistle altered from a tune into a sharper blast, the way Mark whistled up the dogs when they were running wild, and from the hall a stranger's voice called, 'Are you yet in bed? You've let the fire go nearly out. And why the devil did you lock the doors?' He had grabbed the handle of my own door now and swung it open as he talked. ''Tis hard to think that my own brother is now turning into an old...'

Then he saw me sitting up in Daniel Butler's bed, so that his last word, '...woman,' trailed away unsure.

Jack Butler—because from the look of him and what he'd said he could be no one else—shifted in the doorway to a steadier position, his expression changing gradually from pure surprise to something that reminded me of how a man might look when he had seen a friend perform a feat that he had thought impossible. With a slight shake of his head he flashed a quick lopsided smile and said, 'Good morrow to you, mistress.'

I was not supposed to talk, I knew. According to the plan that Daniel Butler had decided on with Fergal, Jack was meant to think that I was Fergal's sister too. I could still hear Fergal saying, 'Jack can never keep his mouth shut, and he'll never be convinced she came the way she says she did.' So I just nodded in reply.

'And is my brother in the house?'

I shook my head.

'Can you not speak?' He asked that jokingly, as though the situation still amused him.

When I shook my head again he looked surprised at first, since it was not the answer he'd expected, then the faintest light of envy touched his eyes. 'A woman with no voice.' He swore a cheerful oath and said, 'My brother always had the better fortune.'

He leaned one shoulder on the doorjamb, not as tall as his brother nor to my eyes as good-looking, but with an easy charm that made it plain to me why all the mothers of Polgelly locked their daughters up whenever Jack came home. 'Well then, can you cook? For on my way here I did stumble on some mutton that was longing to come join me for my dinner, though I've no idea myself what I should do with it. Do you?'

My nod was somewhat less than certain, but it satisfied him. 'Good. Then let me give you back your privacy. Unless you do intend to wear that today? No? A shame, in my opinion.' And he left me with a friendly nod and one last smile.

Alone, I closed my eyes and raised both hands to hold my forehead for support as I exhaled a sigh. I may not have been relishing the thought of spending one more day alone here at Trelowarth, and having Jack Butler around would indeed make my life that much easier, but he wasn't quite the kind of company I'd wished for. He was going to be another complication.

Dressing quickly, I went downstairs where I found the joint of mutton waiting for me in the kitchen, on the table by the window that Jack Butler had apparently come in by. He had knocked a chair down in the process, and I set it upright while I tried to figure out how people in this time cooked mutton. I had no clue. In the end the only thing that I could think of was to roast it in the same way I'd seen Fergal roasting fowl, though forcing the spit through the mutton proved harder than I would have thought, and the spit and meat together were a heavy, awkward burden to try hanging in the hearth.

But at least Jack had got the fire going again and set new wood on top of it, and in the cupboard that the constable had smashed open I found the tin of honey I'd seen Fergal use before, and if I copied Fergal's trick of basting roasting meat with honey, then I couldn't go far wrong.

And since Jack had also left a bunch of carrots on the table with the soil still clinging to them, I decided I could add them to the porridge I'd already made and thin it down to something that approximated Fergal's vegetable and barley broth, if I could find some water.

That problem solved itself a moment later when Jack Butler came in through the back door with a sloshing pair of buckets. 'We've no water in the house at all,' he said, as though I wouldn't know it. 'So I went and fetched us some.' He set the buckets down and took a seat himself, with an approving glance towards the mutton. ''Tis as well that you were here. That would have gone to waste had I attempted it.' And then he said, 'I did not mean to hurry you.'

He must have seen I didn't understand, because he made a gesture at his own head and explained. 'Your hair. You could have taken time to dress it, I would not have minded. You'll find me not so difficult,' he promised, 'as my brother.'

He was definitely chattier. Some people might have found it awkward spending time with somebody who didn't speak, but not Jack Butler. While I cooked he rocked his chair back on two legs and, shoulders to the wall, kept up a mostly single-sided conversation, asking questions that he answered for himself. 'So did he tell you all about me, then? Of course he did, or else you would have feared me as a stranger, though I doubt he would have thought I would be home before him.'

From the track his conversation took I gathered he'd concluded that his brother was still off aboard the *Sally*, which to me made perfect sense. It explained too why the constable had seemed so sure that no one would be in the house.

'And so you've been here all this time and on your own?' He would have answered that himself as well, I think, except he saw my face. He stopped. 'Have you then had a visitor?'

I nodded, once.

His chair came down, but slowly and controlled, and when he spoke again his voice had changed, no longer lightly teasing but more serious. 'A welcome one?'

I shook my head and knew from how his eyes had altered
that he didn't need to be told who, any more than he needed
to have anything spelt out for him when I showed him the
smashed cabinet lock in the scullery.

He was quick enough putting the pieces together.

'The constable came on his own? Did he search the whole
house? Did he find anything?'

Here, instead of a nod, I was happily able to shake my
head 'no'.

Jack Butler said, 'That must have spoilt his temper.' He
seemed pleased by that, until another realization crossed his
mind and he looked down at me. 'Did he then do you harm?'

I shook my head, but he had seen my moment's hesitation.

'Are you certain?' He was looking at me clinically, not
trusting what I'd told him, when I saw his face change once
again, as though he'd just this minute noticed what gown I
was wearing.

Though he obviously recognized it, he did nothing more
than raise his gaze to mine a moment before going on without
a comment, 'Good, for Daniel would have gutted him.'

I hadn't thought of that. I had forgotten that in this age
men still felt an obligation to defend a woman's honor. Having
lived so long where men were more likely to push their way
past me than open a door for me, I hadn't even considered
the fact that if I *had* been harmed, Daniel Butler might well
have responded with violence. I gave silent thanks that the
constable had only struck me with words, not his hands, even
though I felt sure that he'd wanted to.

Thinking of it now, I wasn't certain what had stopped him,
since it would have been another way to try provoking Daniel
into action, if that had in fact been what he had intended.
I remembered how the constable's dark gaze had raked my

gown. It made me wonder if he'd seen a ghost himself when he had looked at me, and she had stayed his hand.

Whatever the reason, I was thankful for it, just as I was glad I'd taken time last night to tidy up the rooms before Jack had a chance to see them, for I knew there was no chance of keeping anything from Daniel if Jack knew it. Fergal might have been exaggerating when he'd said Jack Butler couldn't keep a secret—after all, a man who made his living smuggling had to keep a secret now and then—but I could understand what Fergal had been getting at. Jack Butler liked to talk.

About himself, mainly, but he was good-natured about it and in spite of my earlier misgivings, after having been alone in the house I found him welcome company. Besides, I felt better with someone around for protection, and I had a feeling Jack Butler was good in a fight. Not as good as his brother, I guessed, because Jack seemed like someone who didn't have much self-control, but he likely fought dirtier.

Still, he was not without manners. The mutton I'd roasted came out a bit charred, and my barley and carrot broth didn't have even a bit of the flavor that Fergal's had had, but Jack ate them without a complaint, and then ate them a second time, cold, for his supper.

It was not until afterwards, when twilight settled outside on the hills and Jack lit the candles on the table and the atmosphere inside the kitchen grew close, that he showed a small flash of his mischievous nature.

'So, mistress,' he asked, 'shall I help you to bed?'

I probably wouldn't have dignified that with an answer in any event, whether spoken or otherwise, but as it turned out I didn't have to give him a reply. The answer came out of the dimness behind us, surprising us both.

''Tis a kind offer, Jack.' Daniel Butler had settled himself in the doorway that led to the corridor, arms folded over his chest. 'But I think that would be my prerogative.'

CHAPTER 15

Fergal was having none of it. Shouldering his way past Daniel Butler he said dryly, 'You can both of you behave yourselves, or do you need reminding in the way of it? My sister has the wit to see herself to bed without the aid of either of you.'

I heard Jack say in surprise, 'Your sister?' and I was aware that Fergal answered him, but the bulk of my attention was still focused on the tall man in the doorway and the warmth within his eyes.

He looked as pleased to see me there as I was glad to have him back, and if we'd been alone I would have told him so, but I could only let my smile speak for me.

'...and that will be my only warning to you, so you pay it heed and mind your manners,' Fergal finished off to Jack.

'Would I do otherwise?' Jack's voice was mild. He'd turned to look at us. 'And I do fear you may be warning the wrong Butler in this instance.'

'Ay, I've said the same to him and all,' said Fergal. He had noticed the remains of what I'd cooked, an eyebrow lifting at the blackened meat. 'Where did you find this mutton?'

'I did meet with it upon the road on my way home,' said Jack, 'and in so sad a circumstance that pity moved my hand to see it liberated.'

Fergal's sideways glance was dry. 'And what else did you liberate?'

'Only the mutton. 'Twas all I could carry.'

Daniel, lounging comfortably within the doorway, asked, 'And who now has gone hungry by your hand?'

'None but a lazy merchant who was fool enough to leave his wagon unattended while he slept.'

'You'll try your luck one time too often,' was his brother's comment. 'You are fortunate you did not meet the constable upon the road. He would have had you taken for a thief.'

Jack shrugged. 'I am well liked by juries in these parts; they would have voted me my freedom. And in any case, the constable had other things to occupy his time.' His tone had sobered. 'He was here. He searched the house.'

I saw the narrowing of Daniel's eyes as Fergal, who'd been tearing off small chunks of mutton, tasting what I'd done with it, turned round with sudden fierceness. 'Christ's blood, Jack, and did you never think to stop him?'

'I had not the opportunity, he came and went before I did arrive. Your sister could not tell me what occurred, of course, but it appears she faced him on her own, and even had she had a voice she would have had no chance of stopping him herself. He must have been in a rare temper from the treatment he did give that cupboard standing in the scullery.'

While Fergal went to check the cupboard, Daniel studied me with quiet calm, the kind of calm that sometimes silences the winds before the weather takes a turning for the worse, and it appeared to be a warning sign to Jack who quickly said, 'I asked her if the blackguard used her ill, and she assured me in her way that he did not.'

Daniel said nothing, but his eyes moved briefly past me

as behind me Fergal stepped out of the scullery and said, 'He used the axe.'

The calm of Daniel's face grew deeper, settling over his whole frame, and Fergal said, 'Jack, come and help me take a look around the stables, will you? God alone knows what he might have done out there.'

'But—'

'Shift yer arse.' The terse instruction left no room for argument, and Jack made none.

Daniel moved from the doorway to let them go past, but he waited until they'd gone out to the yard and the back door had swung shut behind them and they had moved well out of hearing before he asked quietly, 'Are you all right?'

'He didn't lay a hand on me.'

'That was not what I asked.'

'I'm fine.' I half-turned away from those steady eyes that I suspected saw more than I wanted them to. 'It rattled me a bit, that's all. I mean, I'd just come back and all of you were gone, and it was raining, and I couldn't start a fire, and then I turned around and there he was…'

'You did not let him in?'

'He let himself in. I don't think he expected to find anybody here. He seemed to know you were away.' I paused and glanced back. 'Were you off on your ship?'

'Yes.' He didn't elaborate. 'What did he do when he found you at home?'

What I told him was an edited account of what had happened, from the constable's starting the fire to his smashing the lock on the cabinet and going to search the upstairs. 'I'm fairly sure he didn't find what he was looking for,' I finished.

'No more would he. There was nothing here for him to find.' From his tone I could tell that he wasn't protesting his innocence, only saying he had better sense than to leave any evidence lying around. 'So he came back downstairs. And what then did he do?'

'Nothing, really. He drank some of the wine that I'd brought him,' I said very carefully, 'and then he left.'

'And only that.'

I nodded, and I saw a flickering of warmth behind his eyes. 'You must ask Jack to school you in the art of telling lies, for plainly you have not yet learnt the trick of it.'

I raised my chin. 'It's not a lie. He didn't touch me.'

'I am close enough acquainted with the constable to know that he has other means of doing harm.' He didn't press the point. Instead he said, as though he meant it, 'I am sorry that I was not here.'

'It's just as well you weren't. You might be up now on a charge of murder.'

'Yes, I might at that.' And with his smile the deadly calm that had been hanging round him broke and fell away. 'And do I have to call my brother out, or has he been behaving like a gentleman?'

'He's been behaving.' Mostly, I suspected, because of where he had discovered me, in Daniel's bed. Jack Butler might be reckless, but that didn't make him fool enough to trespass on what he would have believed was ground belonging to his brother.

'I would find that most unlikely,' Daniel said. 'And you forget I have the evidence of my own ears against it.'

I'd forgotten what he'd overheard as he came in—Jack's offer to escort me up to bed. And Daniel's answer. I surprised myself by blushing. I had lived so long in Hollywood I'd thought that there was nothing anymore that could embarrass me. I covered it by saying it had only been a joke. 'He was no more serious than you were.'

'Was he not?' The smile held, and in that moment while he looked at me, I swore that I could feel the air between us as though it had come alive. Perhaps it had.

But then he looked away again and everything was normal. 'You have done well with Jack. It does appear that he accepts you in your role and does believe you cannot speak.'

'Yes, well, it wasn't all that difficult. Your brother talks so much himself I doubt I could have got a word in edgeways if I'd wanted to.'

I had never heard him laugh. I liked the sound of it. He asked, 'When was it he arrived?'

'This morning. Through that window, actually. I'd locked the doors.'

'And if you should be here and on your own again, I trust you'll do the same, and keep them bolted fast till one of us returns. Nor should you hesitate to use the hole to hide from an intruder.'

'What hole?'

'The priest's hole.' With a glance at my uncomprehending face, he asked, 'Is it not used in your own time?'

I shook my head. 'We don't have any need to hide our priests.'

'No more do we. But such a hiding place does still have uses. Come.' He took a candle from the table and led me from the kitchen, through the hall and halfway up the staircase to the broad half landing with its paneled walls. 'The tale is that the building of Trelowarth happened not long since King Henry had defied the Pope and set aside his queen to marry Anne Boleyn. The times then were as troubled as our own, and men who kept to the old faith were forced to say their prayers in secret and to hide their priests whenever the King's agents came to call.' His fingers found the corners of a panel with a sureness born of practice and he gave a single push, and with a quiet click the spring gave way. A length of panel nearly my own height, hinged like a door, swung neatly outward.

In the space behind, a man could stand—or sit if he grew tired—but he couldn't do much more than that. It would be dark and close, but safe.

'You pull it shut with this, when you are in,' said Daniel, showing me the metal ring attached to the inside, 'and none will find you.'

'Have you ever had to use it?'

'On occasion.'

It would be an uncomfortable place for a man of his height, and I said so, but he only shrugged.

'I had rather stoop here for an hour than be stretched at the end of a rope.'

It was not the first time he'd implied he earned his living in a way that wasn't legal, and I called him on it. 'Is the law so merciless with free-traders?'

He took the question in his stride. 'The law, in my experience, is more strict in its word than in its practice. And the constable does line his pockets well by his arrangements with the free-traders who choose to make their harbor in Polgelly, and does please himself to look the other way while we unload our cargoes. No,' he said, ''tis not my free-trading that so concerns the constable. He would see me hang for something far more heinous in his view.'

'For treason.'

Daniel swung the panel shut with a decided click, and turned. 'Is that what he did tell you?' He seemed curious, not angry, but I didn't have the courage to repeat the words the constable had said to me, however much they resonated in my mind.

I didn't need to. Daniel said, 'And did he tell you that you would be damned yourself for comforting a traitor to the Crown?' He smiled slightly without waiting for an answer, and a hardness touched his eyes although I knew it wasn't meant for me. 'I can but guess what words he used when he did phrase that speech. I am no traitor, Eva.' With a level gaze and even voice he faced me. 'I am loyal to the rightful King of England, as my father was before me, and will be so for as long as I do live.'

I knew that he was saying he was loyal to James Stuart, still across the sea in exile, and I could have told him that there was no future in that loyalty because the Stuarts never would regain their crown, and all their dreams of restoration would be killed on battlefields and paid for with the blood of count-less Jacobites. But if I told him anything, I'd interfere with what was meant to happen, maybe change what was to come, and that might have a far more devastating consequence.

He must have seen the conflict of emotions on my face, but he misunderstood their cause. 'I promise you,' he said, 'I will let no one do you harm.'

I couldn't hold his gaze. I looked away.

I hadn't realized he was close enough to touch me, but he did. He reached out a hand to lightly take my chin and turn my face back round so that our eyes met, and he said again, more quietly, 'I promise.'

I couldn't speak.

Which probably was just as well, because at that same moment I heard Fergal coming back with Jack, and making noise enough to let us know it.

Daniel smiled and let his hand drop. 'Damn the man,' he said, without an ounce of violence. 'Even now he is developing the instincts of a brother.'

He was right. For it was Fergal, in the end, who saw me safely up the stairs that night and checked in all the corners of my room before he left me, and stood waiting in the corridor until I'd put the key into the padlock he had given me and turned it to secure the latch.

And next morning it was Fergal and not Daniel who instructed me on how to do my hair.

He brought a looking-glass and pins into my bedroom, sat me down beside the window, and with hands that were surprisingly adept and gentle, showed me how to wind the strands in curls and pin them into place.

I asked him, 'Is there anything you can't do, Fergal?'

'Likely not.' He'd moved to stand behind me and I saw him now reflected in the looking-glass that I was holding, with his head bent, concentrating. 'Though I'll have to warn you this may not be in the latest fashion. I've not done this for some years, and even then I doubt I did it well. Ann used to say I made her look more like an ill-made bird's nest than a lady.'

'Ann?'

He'd caught himself, and in the mirror his eyes briefly flicked to mine, then down again. 'Ay.'

'Daniel's wife?'

'Ay.' Silence for a moment, then, 'When she grew too ill near the end to attend to her own hair I helped her, for she was determined that he would not see her as less than she wanted to be.'

I was holding the hairpins. I fingered one thoughtfully. 'Was she ill for long?'

'Ay, for some months. It started as a cough that would not leave her, and it wasted her away, and by the summer's end we'd lost her.'

I was silent in my turn, because essentially that was how I had lost Katrina too. I knew the pain of it.

'He'll have my head for telling you,' said Fergal.

'Fergal?'

'Ay?'

'Could you... could you do my hair a little differently than you did hers?'

His hands stopped, and again his eyes met mine within the mirror for an instant and he nodded understanding. 'I was thinking that myself, I was. Come, put that glass down and I'll teach you how to do this back part, for we'll not be fooling Jack for long if I'm here in your chamber every morning doing this.'

'Where is Jack?'

'He's gone to fetch the horses back. Whenever we're away we loose the horses in the paddock at Penryth where there's a farmer who can see they're fed and watered.'

I hadn't even thought of the horses. They might have been starving in their stalls within the stable, and I wouldn't have known. But when I confessed as much Fergal just said, 'Well, you had other worries, I expect. And no harm done.'

I barely recognized myself when we had finished. All my hair had been piled up and fastened daintily, making a circlet on top of my head with a few curls escaping as though by pure chance. 'I'll never be able to do this myself.'

'Ay, you will,' Fergal told me. ''Tis nothing to facing down Constable Creed. Now then, put your pinner on your head,' he said, handing me a modest-looking cap of soft white linen, 'and we're done with this fussing and on to the next of your lessons.'

'What next lesson?'

''Tis sure any sister of mine should know how to cook mutton without setting fire to it, and at the least, how to season a stirabout. Our ma,' he informed me, straight-faced, 'would be scandalized.'

CHAPTER 16

THE *SALLY* DIDN'T LIE at anchor long. Next morning Jack was off again in his turn, and I stood with Daniel on the hill below the house and watched the sloop's white sails pass by the harbor of Polgelly far below us, heading east.

'Where is he taking her?' I asked, but Daniel only glanced at me and answered noncommittally, 'I cannot say.'

'Because you still don't trust me.'

'Because,' he said, ''tis best that you do not concern yourself with certain things.' I felt him glance at me again although I kept my own face turned towards the sea and the departing ship. 'Are all the women of your time so curious?'

'The women of my time are many things,' I told him. 'Doctors, lawyers, heads of state. We can do anything a man can do.'

I couldn't tell if he believed me. 'Heads of state? Well, we have had a queen ourselves, till lately.'

'Not only queens. I mean elected heads of state, leaders of parliaments.'

'You jest.'

'You don't believe a woman's capable?'

He seemed to give the matter thought. ''Tis not that I dismiss a woman's capability,' he said, 'nor her intelligence. 'Tis only that I would be fair amazed to see society permit it. I would think that she would find herself opposed by members of my sex and ridiculed by members of her own.'

I had to smile. 'Yes, well, that does still happen sometimes. But at least the opportunity is there. We can be anything we choose to be.'

I looked away again. The *Sally*'s sails had grown much smaller now, a little blot of white against the rolling blue of the Atlantic.

Daniel was still thinking. 'If in truth there is such freedom for the women of your time, then you must find it difficult to be here.'

I actually hadn't thought that much about it. I'd only been here for short periods, and I'd had more on my mind than my freedoms and rights. But if I were to stay here forever, I thought, he was right. It would not be an easy adjust-ment—to know that my opinions would no longer count for anything in public and that all the legal rights I'd come to take for granted were no longer mine; to be dependent for support on someone else because I could not earn my living.

Daniel watched my face a moment, then he turned his own gaze out to sea and said, 'My brother sails to Brittany.'

It was an open declaration of, not just his trust, but his respect.

I turned to look at him as he went on, 'There is a harbor there where he has friends who keep him well supplied with wine and silk and wigs for trade, and where there are young brides whose husbands are too often gone off to the fishing. 'Tis most likely more than one child in that town does bear a passing likeness to my brother.' He was smiling when his head came round. 'No doubt the women of your own time would be too wise to fall such victims to his wicked ways.'

'Oh, I don't know. There'd still be some who'd swoon.'

'But not yourself.' His tone was sure. 'My brother did remark upon the fact you seemed unmoved by all his charms.'

'Was it a blow to his confidence?'

'Likely. Though he claimed that his purpose in telling me was to set my mind at ease, for his own mind has leapt to a certain conclusion since he did discover you in my bed.'

I wasn't used to the dark light of mischief that flared in his eyes, and not knowing him well enough to know the way to respond to his flirting, I treated it lightly.

'Well, at least it won't happen again. Fergal's given me padlocks.'

'Has he now? Thoughtful man.' He'd have said something else, but a sound from the road to the back of Trelowarth distracted us both—the hard clop of a horse's hooves, coming along at a purposeful trot.

Daniel motioned me to step towards him and I didn't argue, knowing that his size and strength, together with the sword he carried, would give me protection. It was not his sword he reached for, though. Instead he took the dagger from his belt and held it as he'd held it that first day I'd faced him in the study, with the blade all but concealed within his hand.

His other arm he offered to me as the rider came in view and I could see that it was not the constable, only an ordinary man on a high-stepping grey horse. I felt relief, but Daniel didn't drop his guard. 'Stay beside me.'

As we climbed the short slope of the hill towards the house, the rider turned the grey horse off the road into the side yard, and dismounted. From that distance I could only see that he was lean and wearing a white wig beneath his hat, and that his clothes looked to be fancier than those I'd seen here so far. This impression grew stronger the closer I got to him and owed as much to the fabric his clothes had been cut from as to their design. His long jacket was dark green brocade, with an elegant sheen to it, and his high boots were so gleamingly black that they looked as if they'd hardly been worn.

But his face, when he turned, was plain-featured and didn't quite match the effect.

He ignored me completely and nodded a greeting to Daniel. 'Good morrow. I wonder if I might impose on your kindness. My horse has a shoe loose.' The accent was hard to place. Scottish, I guessed, though it held a faint trace of the Continent.

I could feel Daniel's shoulders relaxing. He said, ''Tis a dangerous road.'

'So I'm told.'

For a moment the men faced each other and waited, and then the newcomer offered his hand with a smile. 'The name is Wilson, Mr. Butler, and I do bring with me the good wishes of our mutual acquaintance.'

'I am glad to have them, Mr. Wilson.' Daniel sheathed the dagger in his belt so neatly that another person watching would have missed the motion altogether and not even known that he'd been holding it. He shook the stranger's hand and, looking up the empty road, he asked, 'You travel on your own?'

'I did arrive with my man yesterday. We took rooms at the inn at St Non's, and I charged him to stay there and wait while I came on alone to you here.' He had noticed me finally. His eyes held polite expectation as he looked at Daniel and waited.

'Forgive me,' said Daniel, as though it had been an oversight and not protective instinct that had kept him from bringing me forwards. 'Mistress Eva O'Cleary, a guest of my house.'

Wilson bowed. 'Mistress O'Cleary, your servant.'

I wasn't sure how to respond, so I did what I'd seen women do in the movies—I made a deep curtsy and hoped that was right.

To my relief, Wilson turned back to Daniel and asked, 'May I stable my horse?'

'In the back.'

There was nothing uneven at all in the horse's gait, confirming my impression that his mention of a loose shoe had been part of a script, as had Daniel's reply—like two spies trading passwords to make themselves known to each other.

I guessed too that their 'mutual friend' was most likely James Butler, the Second Duke of Ormonde, who according to the reading I'd done earlier would still be in England, waiting to learn what the House of Lords would do in answer to the charges brought against him of high treason. He would be impeached, I knew. And soon. But no one here was yet aware of that.

'How fares our friend?' asked Daniel.

Wilson, if in fact that was his name, was walking several steps ahead of us, the horse's bridle in his hand. 'He is quite well, though incidents of late have tried his patience, as you likely can imagine. It has been suggested to him he might seek to cure his restlessness with travel.'

'If he has a mind to travel he has but to say the word and I will put my ship and crew at his disposal.'

''Tis most kind,' said Wilson with a nod of thanks. 'I will be sure to tell him so when next I see him.'

Trailing silently behind, still holding Daniel's arm, I tried to remember if any of the history sources I'd read in my research had said how the Duke of Ormonde had escaped to France. I didn't think they had. Which left me wondering if he had made the crossing as a passenger aboard the *Sally*.

No doubt I was going to find out.

It was strange, knowing what I was seeing was history unfolding. How many historians would have paid money to walk in my shoes at this moment? I wondered. To be able to listen and watch while these men played their parts in a growing conspiracy, one that would lead in a few months to open rebellion?

From the glance Wilson gave me, I guessed he was finding my presence a bit of a nuisance. His next words were proof. 'Surely Mistress O'Cleary will much prefer waiting out here while you show me which stall I may use for my horse?' And directly to me he said, smiling, 'You'll not want to ruin your slippers.'

He appeared to be expecting a response from me, but Daniel stepped in smoothly.

'She has not the use of speech.'

The man named Wilson raised his eyebrows. 'Does she not? And how then was she robbed of it?'

'It is my understanding she has been afflicted since her birth.'

'Remarkable.' He looked at me as though I were a scientific specimen, and I had the impression he'd just dropped me down a few points on the scale of intelligence. 'How sad,' he said, then turned away dismissively.

I knew Daniel would have to follow, so I lifted my hand from his arm and the look he angled down at me held quiet thanks. He said, 'Please go and let your brother know that we will have a guest for dinner.'

With a nod, I went. I looked back once, but they had

gone into the stables with the horse already and the yard was empty. When I brought my head back round I saw that Fergal had come out to stand within the open doorway, hands on hips. He frowned. 'I thought I heard a horse.'

I quickened my steps, knowing I'd have to be in the house with the door shut, and able to talk without worrying Wilson would hear, before I could tell Fergal what was going on.

'Has someone come?' he asked.

I gave another nod but faintly, because something had begun to change in Fergal's face. He was looking at me strangely. With my next step I came close enough to see his eyes, to watch the question in them change to open disbelief. And then he raised his hand and crossed himself. 'Sweet Jesus.'

And before I could react, he started wavering and faded to a shadow and then vanished altogether like a breath of smoke dissolving in the air.

I stopped walking.

And suddenly I wasn't in the yard myself, but stepping out onto the open hillside from the Wild Wood, with sunlight breaking through the clouds above me and Trelowarth waiting patiently to welcome me, and Susan a small figure heading off towards the greenhouse.

I hovered in confusion for a moment before memories started swirling back—my evening spent with Claire, my sleeping over at her cottage, and my waking up to find she'd gone out before me. Coming back along the coast path through the woods, and then the sudden rain and running for the house, and...

That had happened two full days ago for me, yet here I was back in the present day, and it was plain to see no time had passed. When I looked down I saw the deep impression of my footprints in the muddy ground that led to where I stood now on the soft grass of the hill, and everything was as it had been. As it should be.

Well, perhaps not everything.

I ran my hand down one hip to make absolutely certain, and my fingers smoothed across the silken fabric of the gown I was still wearing. And beneath its linen covering my hair was still pinned up in its elaborate style. Not things that could be easily explained, I knew, if anyone should see me.

It was that one thought that shifted me to motion, forced my feet to leave the spot where they had taken root, and lead me running uphill in a hurry to be safely out of sight.

At this hour of the morning Mark should already be out and working. I could only hope that he'd be keeping to his schedule. But in case he was still finishing his breakfast in the kitchen, I went in by the front door and made a beeline for the stairs.

I'd gone halfway up before I heard a door close overhead and cheerful humming that I recognized as Claire's. There was no chance for me to make it to my room without her seeing me, and since her steps were coming down the corridor right now there likely wasn't even time for me to turn and go downstairs again. I'd never cross the hall in time.

I was panicking, pressing my back to the paneled wood wall, when the feel of that wood stirred my memory and I turned to push the panel on the landing in the way Daniel had shown me. Part of me didn't expect it to open, but it did, and just in time I slipped into the cramped and cobwebbed space and pulled the panel closed again behind me as Claire's footsteps neared the stairs.

I heard her light and even tread come down and cross the landing, passing close beside my hiding place, and without pause she carried on and down the final half flight to the hall.

❦

The dress looked different here. I spread it on my bed and touched its folds with careful fingers, for the journey across time had left it faded, and the stitching of the seams showed through in places, weakened. Fragile.

Such a lovely thing, I thought. And now I'd brought it here, and there was likely no way I could ever take it back to where it properly belonged. My own clothes, left behind in Daniel's time, were easy to replace, but this…

'I'm sorry,' I said quietly, although I knew the people the apology was meant for couldn't hear me. I found a padded hanger in my wardrobe and I hung the chemise and skirt and bodice on it, then I covered all of them with Daniel's red silk dressing gown—his 'banyan', he had called it—because somehow it seemed right to me for them to be together. They were almost too bulky to keep in the wardrobe now, and anyone who opened up the wardrobe door would see them, but for the moment it would have to do.

The slippers and hairpins were easier. Wrapped in the soft linen cap they tucked tidily into the drawer where I'd already hidden my sleeping pills, wristwatch, and phone. I'd left the watch and phone there even after I had figured out that stress was not my problem, since I didn't want to run the risk of taking either item back in time with me. Modern technology didn't belong in the past.

Nor do you, I reminded my face in the mirror.

But somehow the eyes that looked back at me didn't seem wholly convinced.

CHAPTER 17

Mark and Claire were in the kitchen when I went downstairs. Claire glanced around as I came in and said, 'Got back all right, did you? Oliver telephoned. Something about an old book he found down in his archives that mentions a smuggler who lived at Trelowarth.'

'Really?' I felt a small charge of excitement. 'That was quick.'

'You're to meet him at one, if you're interested. He said he thought it was well worth a lunch.'

Mark said, 'That's the line he's using these days, is it?' With a grin he reached to take an orange from the basket on the worktop and began to peel it. 'Good one.'

'Give it up. He's helping me do research.'

'Oh, I'm sure he is.' He tried to school his features. 'And you're sticking to your story, are you, that you spent last night at Claire's?'

I looked to her for confirmation. 'Claire?'

But she was smiling. 'Just ignore him, Eva,' she advised, and crossed between the both of us to fill a glass with water at the sink. 'He knows full well you were with me. I rang him up to let him know.'

'And a good thing she did,' Mark said. 'I was beginning to think you'd gone the way of the Grey Lady. Though it's not really proof, is it, Claire only *saying* you were with her...'

I interrupted, disregarding that last bit to ask him, 'Who's the Grey Lady?'

'You know. The one who vanished at Trelowarth. Have you never heard about her?'

'No.' I had the sudden feeling I was standing in a draught. I moved and asked him, 'When was this?'

He turned to Claire. 'When was it? You're the one who knows the story.'

She considered. 'Oh, before my parents' time. I had the story told me when I first came to Trelowarth by an old man in the village who was nearly ninety then, at least, and he had been a young man when it happened. He'd seen it with his own eyes, so he said.'

'What did he see?' I had the strange sense that I knew what was coming.

'He saw a woman disappear.' She said it very plainly, as though such a thing were possible. 'Right here, behind the house. A woman he knew well. He said one minute they were talking, and the next she went all grey and then just faded into nothingness and disappeared.'

The draught returned.

Mark saw me shiver and said, 'It's a story, Eva. People don't just disappear.' He split the orange into sections, offering a piece to me.

I took it. Forced a smile. 'I'm only thinking it might be another tale to tell the tourists, that's all.'

'Why don't you ask Oliver?' he said, his eyes all innocence. 'He's good with local history.'

Claire told him, 'Actually, I'd think it would be more the sort of question that you'd want to ask Felicity.'

'Why Felicity?'

'Well, she's keen on ghosts and folklore. She'll be in the

shop today, Eva, if you're going down to Polgelly. You ought to stop in for a chat.'

I had hit on a better idea. 'Why don't we all go? We could have fish and chips at the harbor.'

Claire shook her head. 'Susan and I have to go shop for tables and chairs,' she said, then went on in an offhand way, 'but Mark will come, I'm sure. He's always up for fish and chips.' I saw the glance Claire sent her stepson and I knew that she, like me, had noticed Felicity's feelings for Mark, even if he hadn't, and was trying to play matchmaker.

He fell for it. 'All right. I've got some work I need to finish first, though,' he said dryly, 'on my blog.'

I smiled. 'Why don't I go ahead, then? I've got banking that I need to do, and I'll collect Felicity and Oliver, and you can meet us at the harbor. One o'clock?'

With that agreed, I headed out. I wasn't sure that I was really up to lunching in Polgelly, since I wasn't quite myself yet and a part of me just wanted to lie down and rest, to find my balance and restore it after all my traveling through time. But overriding my exhaustion was the lure of learning more about the Butler brothers from the book that Oliver had found.

And I did have a bit of business to attend to at the bank. If I surprised Mr. Rowe with my request to put a trust in place, in secret, for Trelowarth, he was too much the professional to let it show. Of course, he said, it could be done. It would take time, preparing all the paperwork and seeing to the finer points, but yes, it was quite possible. And with those wheels set spinning into motion, I moved on to my next stop.

Felicity had customers. I waited by the shelves that held the little dancing pisky figures, picking up the nearest one and weighing it within my hand until she had the time to come across and say hello.

'You want to watch those,' she advised me. 'Tricky things, those piskies.'

With their pointed hats and elf-like clothes and laughing eyes they looked completely harmless, but I knew the tales of piskies and their mischief. 'I'll be careful. What is this?' I asked, and pointed to a little sign among them with the words, 'Porthallow Green' carved on it.

'Don't you know that story? Well, you know Porthallow, surely? And according to the legend there was once a boy from there sent on an errand by his master, and it was dark before he'd finished and on his way home he heard a voice at the roadside say, "I'm for Porthallow Green." And the boy thought, well, it might be good to have a bit of company, even from a stranger, so he called out, "*I'm* for Porthallow Green," and quick as a wink, there he was, on Porthallow Green, with the piskies dancing round him. Have you really never heard this one?'

I told her that I hadn't.

'Well,' she said, 'one of the piskies called out, "I'm for Seaton Beach!" and the boy thought, *well, why not?* So he said, "*I'm* for Seaton Beach," and there he was, with the piskies again. And they went on like that all night, all the way to the King of France's cellar, where they drank his wine and danced, and when the piskies brought the boy home in the morning to Porthallow Green, he still had his wine glass to prove it.' She smiled. 'Wouldn't happen today, of course. Think of the airfare I'd save if I could go and stand in a meadow and simply call, "I'm for Ibiza", and land on the beach.'

'But you'd have to rely on the piskies to bring you back home again,' I pointed out. 'They don't always.'

'True enough.'

I asked casually, 'I don't suppose you've ever heard of anybody disappearing from Trelowarth?'

As it turned out, she had never heard the story of the Grey Lady. 'When was that, do you know?'

I did the math. 'Claire said she heard it when she first came here to live, which would be nearly thirty years ago, and the man she heard it from was maybe ninety, so assume that he was twenty-five or thirty when it happened… ninety years ago?' I estimated. 'Give or take.'

'I'll have to ask around,' she said, 'but nothing would surprise me. You know Trelowarth's built right on a ley line?'

'A what?'

'Ley line. Sort of a geomagnetic conduit, if you like. A lot of ancient monuments and holy sites were built on top of ley lines. There's a line that runs clear under St Non's well and through the Beacon and Trelowarth to Cresselly Pool.' She laughed at my expression. 'I'm not making it up, honestly. Dowsers can find them, they're actually there. They've a powerful energy. All sorts of strange things can happen on ley lines.'

I certainly wasn't in any position to argue that, I thought. As I set my pisky back among his dancing brethren on the shelf, Felicity asked brightly, 'So, what are you doing down here in Polgelly?'

I turned and told her, 'Taking you to lunch.'

❧

The tide was in, the wind was fair, and many of the fishing boats had gone to take advantage of the day, to ride the sea beneath a sun that warmed my shoulders even through the fabric of my shirt and felt like summer's kiss upon my upturned face.

I felt another happy moment of nostalgia, sitting on the whitewashed harbor wall enjoying fish and chips that had been wrapped in newspaper, the old way I remembered it. The rest was well remembered too: the biting tang of vinegar, the sharpness of the salt, the sound of seagulls wheeling greedily above me while the water lapped the wall below and, farther off, the waves that crashed in rhythm at the entrance to the harbor and cast up a spray that carried on the breeze to cool my skin.

Felicity, beside me, smiled. 'You look as though you've eaten the canary.'

Mark said, 'That'll be next, at the rate she's going. Where are you putting it all, Eva?'

'I'm hungry.'

'You can chase that with a pound of fudge,' suggested Oliver, who in this group had fallen very naturally back into his old childhood pattern, teasing me to focus my attention where he wanted it—on him.

Not that he had seemed at all put out that I'd brought Mark nor that Felicity had joined us. Oliver, as I recalled, was nothing if not sociable, and with his easygoing ways he could adapt without complaint to any change of plan. But he was not about to let that steer him off his course or change his purpose.

It was clear he had his eye on me. I noticed it today more than I had at our last lunch together, noticed how he looked at me and how his smiles lingered. And a month ago I might have even welcomed the attention. After all, he was a nice guy and looked absolutely gorgeous in his plain white shirt and jeans, his blond hair golden in the midday sun and tousled by the harbor breeze. I knew most women would have thought him wonderful if they'd been in my place.

But when I looked at him today my only thought was that his face, though handsome, didn't have the same appeal as Daniel Butler's, and that Daniel's eyes in that same light would have been even greener than the sea beyond the shore.

I shrugged off Oliver's remark and smiled. 'I doubt that I'll have room for fudge when I'm done with this.'

'If I take you for a walk, you will.'

Mark said, 'I thought you called her down to see a book.'

'I did. Only found it this morning. It came in a box with some others I bought at a sale last year, and it's been gathering dust at the back of my bookshelves.'

Felicity glanced over, curious. 'What sort of book?'

'A field guide of sorts to this area—natural history with small bits of color thrown in—but it mentions some people that Eva's been after. She's trying to find Susan somebody famous who lived at Trelowarth,' he said, 'and these brothers, the Butlers, were smugglers. Infamous, not famous, but the local people loved them, so the book says. They were heroes here.'

Mark said, 'Like the Carter brothers up at Prussia Cove?'

'Exactly. But the Carters weren't in business till years afterward. They weren't even born when the Butlers were free-trading out of Polgelly.' He'd finished the last of his chips and he crumpled the wrapping of newspaper into a ball. 'I have to thank Eva for putting me on to them. I'd never heard of the Butlers, myself.'

Felicity was looking at him with the keen eyes of an old friend who would not be fooled. 'I'm surprised you found the book at all,' she said innocently, 'if it was at the back of your bookshelves.'

'Yeah, well, Eva asked me yesterday about the Butlers, and I had some time last night, so I just thought I'd look. You know.'

She smiled at him. 'Oh yes. I know.'

'Shut up.' Their banter had the easy back and forth that came with practice. 'Shouldn't you be getting back to work?'

'I've got five minutes, still. And I was hoping to take one of you big strong men back to the shop with me. I've just had an artist ship over her paintings—they're huge, and I'll need help to hang them.'

Oliver was unenthusiastic. 'Mark's got bigger muscles. And while you're off doing that,' he said, 'I'll show the book to Eva.'

Which was clearly what Felicity had wanted to begin with. I watched them go. 'She's fun.'

'She is that.' His gaze moved to me as he said, 'That was nicely maneuvered.'

'What was?'

'Your inviting Fee out to have lunch with us. And with Mark. You've noticed she's head over heels for him.'

The fact that *he'd* noticed surprised me at first, till I realized he worked with Felicity and they were obviously close. 'Yes, well,' I told him, 'I didn't do *all* the maneuvering, did I?'

He grinned. 'I've done my share of helping hang pictures. And Mark's muscles really are bigger. Besides, how do you know I wasn't maneuvering for my own benefit?'

I ate my last chip and wadded the paper with careful hands. 'Oliver...'

'What?'

'I do like you.'

'But?'

'I just don't want you to think that I'm... that is, I'm really not looking for...'

'Hey.' I could hear the faint smile in his voice. 'It's a

book, not an etching.' He rose to his feet from the harbor wall, held out his hand for the newspaper. 'Come on, let me chuck that in the bin for you, then you can come and look at what I've found.'

I wasn't fooled. He still had an agenda, but I knew there wasn't a thing I could do to discourage him. Men who had Oliver's confidence weren't to be swayed by small things like the fact I had fallen for somebody else.

I formed that thought idly enough, but it struck me with a sudden force that stopped me in my tracks. I couldn't honestly have meant that, could I? Yet I sat here in the sunshine on the harbor wall and turned the thought a thousand ways, and every way I turned it, it was true.

Oliver, who had no way of knowing that I'd just been hit by something like a thunderbolt, asked whether I was ready and I numbly told him yes, I was, and went to see the book.

He'd left it set out for me on the small working desk beside the bookshelves in the storage room of the museum, in the back beside the little kitchenette that had a kettle and some cupboards and a sink, and not much more.

The storage room itself was crowded thick with shelves and boxes, and it smelt of dust that hadn't been disturbed in quite some time. Still, there was proper light to read by, and an antique wooden captain's chair that proved to be quite comfortable.

Collecting my still-rattled thoughts, I focused my attention on the book itself.

It was an older book, with cloth-and-cardboard covers frayed and dented at the edges and the binding at the spine so badly cracked and worn that whole sections of pages, stitched together, slid and shifted when I leafed my way along to find the place that Oliver had marked.

He came to stand behind me, leaning over, pointing to the lines that were of interest. 'There, you see? Below that bit about the Cripplehorn.'

But I'd already started reading in the paragraph before that:

> *At the western limit of the beach there is a rock the locals call the Cripplehorn, which at its highest point is measured more than ninety feet and which extends beyond the cliffs to form a breakwater. Upon its eastern face two minor streams converge to form a fickle waterfall, at times a mere cascade, at times a cataract that rushes to the sand and draws a varied wealth of plant life from the rock…*

After describing all this plant life in excruciating detail, and the several types of birds that liked to nest upon the Cripplehorn, the author made a detour from his scientific facts to state:

> *The base of the cascade conceals a narrow cavern safely set above the highest tide, which in former times reportedly was favored by the Butler brothers of the nearby manor of Trelowarth for the storage of their smuggled cargoes. It is spoken still with no small pride that never once did any person of the village tell the secret of this hiding place, no matter what reward was offered by the local constable, so well regarded were the Butlers for their generosity in sharing of the wealth they gained by working in defiance of the law. Their daring exploits were later recounted in a journal that was published by the younger of the brothers as* A Life Before the Wind. *Proceeding westward, one encounters an uncommon wealth of avian diversity…*

That was all that had been written of the Butler brothers. After that the author veered off once again into his birds and plants and rock formations. I read through the paragraphs again to be sure I hadn't missed something of value then I turned round in my chair to look at Oliver. 'This journal of Jack Butler's…'

He had known that I would ask that, I could see it in his smile. 'Yes. *A Life Before the Wind*. Poetic bastard, for a pirate. I've already looked it up, but I could only find two copies referenced, both of those in library collections in the States. There may be more, though. Give me time to do some hunting.'

He'd impressed me. 'And when was it actually published?'

'1739.' He didn't hesitate. 'Printed for some bookseller in London, in the Strand.'

I'd have to look it up myself. I felt a faint sense of surprise that, of the brothers, Jack had been the one to leave behind a journal. From the little I had seen of him, he hadn't struck me as the writing type.

But then again, I'd learned in life that people could surprise me.

Mark, for instance, as we walked together up The Hill a short while afterwards, didn't tease me once about my afternoon with Oliver.

I sent a sideways glance in his direction. 'You all right?'

'I'm fine. Just thinking.'

There'd be no use asking what about, I knew. Mark rarely shared his thoughts. Instead I asked him, 'Did you know there was a cave below the Cripplehorn?'

He gave a nod. 'I used to play at pirates down there as a boy.'

'You never took me.'

'You weren't old enough. It's not an easy scramble down.

And when you did get big enough, I'd grown too old myself to play at pirates.'

'Did you take Katrina?'

'Once. She didn't really care for it. Too dark and damp. She liked the light.'

We walked a bit in silence with our thoughts, which was as well because we'd reached the steep part of The Hill where speaking started taking up more air than I could spare. But still, I found enough to ask him, 'Will you take me now?'

Mark was more fit than I was, and his words came without effort. 'What, today?'

'God, no.' I took a gulp of air to fuel the burning muscles of my thighs. 'I just meant sometime.'

'Sure. There's not much there to see, though, and the climb back up is worse than this.'

'No climb,' I said, 'is worse than this.'

He grinned. 'Suit yourself. We'll go tomorrow if you like.'

'Wednesday. Then Felicity can come along.'

Mark seemed to find that odd. 'Why would she want to?'

'You're an idiot.'

'I'm what?' He turned. 'And why am I an idiot?'

I linked my arm through his and told him fondly, 'You just are.'

And that was all the breath that I had left for talking till we'd finished with The Hill.

CHAPTER 18

I DREAMT OF HIM that night; I dreamt of Daniel Butler lying in the bed beside me, only lying there asleep and nothing more. I heard his even breathing and I felt his warmth, the shifting of his weight against the mattress as he turned. His face in sleep was not so hardened as it looked by day. The lines were there, but smoother, and the slanting shadows of his lashes crossed his tanned skin peacefully.

It seemed to me we were not at Trelowarth anymore. The room felt warmer, and the night air carried strange, exotic scents I didn't recognize. But I paid no real attention to the room or to the bed, I was so focused on the man who shared it with me at that moment.

Then as I watched his face, his eyes came slowly open and he saw me too, and smiled…

The curtains at my window stirred in answer to the cooler breezes blowing inland from the sea along the Cornish coast, and half-wakeful and half-dreaming still, I turned my own head hopefully. But nobody was there.

And in the darkness of the room it seemed the walls breathed out a sigh and I'd have sworn I heard a voice, not from the next room but from this one, and not talking now to Fergal but to me. I heard him.

'Eva.'

Not quite sure if I was sleeping or awake, I said, 'I'm here.'

No answer came except the wind, and in the silence following I found a sleep that was too deep for dreams.

∽

Next morning I was up and dressed before the sun had touched the hills. Downstairs, the dogs rose from their resting places like a wagging entourage and, since both Mark and Susan were still sleeping and my mind was full of restless thoughts that wanted clearing out, I went with all the dogs still bouncing round my heels and took a walk.

I'd had some time now to adjust to the idea that I'd fallen half in love with Daniel Butler, but I still had no idea what to do about it. Any way I tackled it, the thought was still impossible. We lived in different centuries. For all I knew, we'd never meet again. And even if we did, who was to say that he would ever feel the same for me?

He couldn't, I decided, as I led the dogs up past the greenhouse by the path the tourists would be using when they came, an older path that wound along the high stone walls of all the older gardens where the birds were warbling joyously, unseen. He couldn't love me; I was nothing like the women of his time. I was a novelty, but that would soon wear off and in the end, when people chose someone to love they chose their own kind. That was common wisdom, wasn't it?

So why, I wondered, had I chosen him?

I climbed the winding path in silence while the dogs ran round me, madly sniffing everywhere and tagging one another in the way that dogs will do. I nearly tripped on Samson twice and still I didn't know the answer. They were strange to me and new, these feelings, yet I'd never been more certain in my life of how I felt, and that alone was something I found troublesome.

Why him? I asked a second time. Why couldn't it be Oliver who made me feel this way? Why did it have to be a man I couldn't have? It wasn't fair.

'It isn't fair,' I told the dogs, but they just wagged and grinned agreement as we reached the turning in the path where I could glimpse the ruined Beacon rising as it always had above the blue Atlantic where the wind had carried off Katrina's ashes.

She hadn't stayed, I thought, so why should I? I wasn't bound here, and I'd done the thing I'd come to do, so why not simply leave? I knew it had to be this place that was affecting me, this place where strange grey ladies disappeared and ley lines ran below the ground, and if I went away then surely things would soon return to normal. I would leave and not be missed and Daniel Butler would forget me, and Trelowarth would go on the way it always had, without me.

Or at least that's what I thought, until I climbed the final few feet of the path and came out with the dogs beside the turning in the road between Polgelly and St Non's, and saw that Mark had cleared a broad and level place up here to make a car park that was wide enough for several cars, I noticed. Or a tour bus.

And standing there I realized that I couldn't leave. Not yet. I turned around again and looked back down the way that I had come, to where the glass roof of the greenhouse caught the early sunlight like a mirror, and I knew I couldn't leave till Susan had her tearoom open and I'd signed the papers for the trust to keep Trelowarth where it should be, with the Hallett family, for a good long time to come. There was nothing for it, really, but to set aside all thoughts of leaving, and resolve to stay.

And if there was another reason, one I was less willing to

acknowledge, for my choosing not to go just yet, I pushed it far back in my mind and locked it there.

⁂

I set to work the next few days on doing what I'd promised Susan I would do. I sent the early press releases out and made some phone calls to the local tour providers to convince them of Trelowarth's charms.

By Wednesday, when Felicity came up to help again, I could announce that *House & Garden* was considering a feature and that one firm operating minibuses to St Non's was eager to include us in its schedule.

Susan, who'd been trying to decide which of the trees close by the greenhouse would be best used as the 'cloutie tree', stopped looking for a moment. 'Really?'

'Really. They do tourist runs from Plymouth, so they pick their people up at their hotels and stop at St Non's on their way down to Falmouth for lunch, but they wanted a different stop on the way back where their tourists could stretch a bit, walk around, and we're conveniently right on their route. So I said we could give them a garden tour and a traditional Cornish cream tea, and they went for it.'

Susan was delighted. 'Well done you.'

'I said they could start the beginning of August, is that still all right?'

She'd told me she'd need that much time to get all her work properly done on the tearoom. She gave a firm nod. 'Yes. What do you think of this one?'

I looked upwards at the tree in question while Felicity stepped back and frowned and said, 'It ought to be a thorn.'

'Why?' I asked.

'Because most cloutie trees are thorn trees,' said Felicity.

Susan said, 'But this one's pretty.'

'No, it needs the proper energy.' Felicity held firm, and in the end we settled on the only hawthorn tree close by the greenhouse door.

'Well, I suppose,' said Susan, 'I could have Mark take down these other two beside it, so it has a little bit more presence.'

Felicity thought that would do very nicely. 'And you can put a little pond or something here beside it, for the water.'

'Water?'

'Susan,' said Felicity, 'you cannot have a cloutie tree unless it's next to water, that's tradition.'

'Ah.' Resigned, she took another look around, with hands on hips. 'Well, the pipes to the greenhouse run just over there, we could maybe tap into those somehow. I'll have to speak to Paul.'

I asked, 'Who's Paul?'

Felicity smiled knowingly. 'Her plumber. Do you know,' she said to Susan, 'I have never seen a project need more plumbing work than this one.'

Susan shrugged the teasing off. 'Is that a fact?'

'If you ask me, it's all the fault of that story Claire told us about how her grandparents met,' said Felicity. 'Good-looking plumbers who strip off whenever it rains and all that. It creates expectations.'

'Claire's grandfather didn't strip off in the rain,' Susan told her friend, amused. 'He took his shirt off, Fee, and he was only being chivalrous.'

'Yes, well, we've had a lot of rain,' Felicity remarked, 'and your Paul hasn't been chivalrous once, has he? That's all I'm saying. I'll tell you who's chivalrous,' she turned her gaze to me. 'Oliver. He's been all over these past few days, looking for leads on your smugglers.'

Susan smiled. 'Yes, well, that's men for you. You can hit them with a rock and it still doesn't put them off.'

I sent her a dry look. 'You can't possibly remember the rock throwing thing. You weren't old enough.'

'I didn't say I remembered.' She stooped to pull a straggling weed. 'Did you really knock him flat?'

'I did.'

Felicity said that was likely why he had his eye on me. 'Men always chase after the women who treat them the worst. You treat them nicely, they don't notice you.'

Her tone was light, and yet there was a wistfulness behind it that I heard and understood.

I said, as casually as I knew how, 'To change the subject, if I may, Mark said he'd take me on a field trip later, if the two of you would like to come.'

Felicity perked up. 'Oh yes? To where?'

'The cave below the Cripplehorn. I've never seen it.'

Susan frowned. 'What cave below the Cripplehorn?'

'A smuggler's cave, apparently. You've never seen it?'

She had not. Felicity was fascinated. 'When would you be going?'

'Just after lunch,' I told them, 'if the rain holds off.'

The rain held off. And after lunch the four of us, with Mark in front, trekked off on our adventure.

The dogs had howled a protest at Mark's leaving them behind, but he'd been right. We couldn't bring them. While the path along the coastal cliffs was not too hard to manage, when we neared the Cripplehorn itself the path became a challenge, slippery rocks descending in uneven steps towards the beach, with a red-lettered 'Danger' sign warning the rocks were unstable and that those who passed this way did so at their own risk. As if to drive home the point, a large red-painted box the same size as a mailbox stood next to the sign, with the words 'Cliff Rope' lettered in white on its front, a reminder that several times yearly some tourist who took this path had to be rescued.

But Mark went down with the sure steps of a mountain goat, and I went after him, carefully putting my feet in the same places he had.

Around us the black rocks rose higher and sharper, more slippery because of the spray from the sea. And the sound of the sea itself grew even louder as wind-driven waves hit the beach.

The beach would not have met the Californian definition of a beach—there was no sand in sight, just hard round rocks and pebbles worn to smoothness by the water, shifting crunchingly wherever I set foot on them, all grey and black and lighter grey with clinging strands of dark green seaweed trailed across the stones.

I'd never been down here. I stood a moment on the slipping pebbles and breathed in the sharp wet salty scents of sea and stone, and found I liked the feeling of the wind-flung mist against my face. There was no ship in sight today, but I could very easily imagine one—the *Sally*, maybe—sliding darkly past the Cripplehorn and coming in to anchor while her men cast off the smaller boat to bring her smuggled goods to shore. I raised a hand to shield my eyes and squinted at the vision while I tried to make my mind up who to give her as a captain, Jack or Daniel… who would be the taller figure moving in among the others on the deck, a silhouette against the sails…

'So,' said Felicity, as she came crunching up behind me, 'where's this cave?'

Mark pointed. 'There.'

In front of us, the waterfall that tumbled down the Cripplehorn and hit the beach below in an uneven, narrow spray was flowing fast and full today, the streams that fed it swelled by all the recent rain. At times in summer it was no more than a trickle, but today it was impressive, as though it had somehow known there would be someone to show off for.

Susan, who'd taken her time down the cliff path, caught up to the rest of us now and moved past, looking hard at the waterfall, then at her brother. 'Why didn't you show me this ages ago?'

He gave her the same answer he'd given me, sort of— that she'd been too young when he'd played here, and when she'd been old enough he'd left off playing in caves. He seemed game to recapture the fun of it now, though. It was hard to keep up with him, dodging the worst of the wet of the waterfall, balancing carefully on the slick rocks. I looked down for a moment, unsure of my footing, and when I looked up Mark had vanished.

I stopped in my tracks in surprise. 'Mark?'

His voice seemed to come from the solid rock. 'Here.'

Then I moved to the left, and I saw it. The cleft in the rock was concealed by the fact that the opening faced the sea, sideways, so when it was viewed from the front all that showed was the unbroken rock of the cliff. And from the sea no one would notice it either, because of the cascading screen of the waterfall.

Mark waited till he was sure I had seen him before he moved forwards and into the cave, and I followed. The sudden close of darkness was unsettling, but as my eyes adjusted to it I could see that it was not complete. Faint shafts of filtered light from somewhere overhead showed me the inward curving walls, the deeply worn and pitted floor that, while it lay above the tide's reach, was still flecked with shallow pools of moisture everywhere; the remnants of a row of barrels, little more than bits of wood and badly rusted metal now, that had been left to molder in the shadows.

More unsettling than the darkness was the sudden change in sound, as though I'd cupped a hollow shell against my ear and shut out everything except the rushing echo of the sea and the more stealthy and insistent dripping of dark water into unseen pools within the cave.

And then Felicity came in and broke the silence with a voice that echoed too. 'This is incredible.'

Behind me, Susan asked her brother, 'Did you bring a torch?'

'Don't need a torch,' he said. 'It spoils the effect.'

I knew what he meant. Any light, let alone the hard beam from a flashlight, would ruin the secretive feel of the cave. I could see the appeal this would have to a boy playing pirates.

Could see too why the Butlers would have chosen it to hold the goods they smuggled in from Brittany aboard the *Sally*. They'd have likely dropped her anchor round the headland at high tide and, under cover of the darkness, rowed the contraband to shore. It would have taken several men to do the work, and I remembered how the book I'd read at Oliver's had said it was a point of pride that no one in Polgelly had betrayed this cave's existence to the constable.

When he had searched the house that day, the day he'd found me there alone, the thing that he'd been looking for had probably been hidden safely down here.

I wondered what it was.

Behind me, Susan moved towards the row of barrels. 'Look at these. Your Butler brothers left these, I expect.'

Mark didn't think it likely. 'They're not old enough.

Besides, they weren't all empty when I played here. I'll lay odds that was Dad's private stash of whisky.'

'I'm surprised he let you play here,' Susan said.

'He didn't know. He would have had my hide if he'd found out.' Mark took an idle step away, and accidentally his foot kicked something out of place that scuttled with a rasp across the stone. He bent to pick it up.

I asked, 'What is it?'

'Just a bit of strapping from a barrel, I'd imagine.' He tossed it back into a corner. 'Not like the treasures we used to find.'

Felicity looked at him. 'What sort of treasures would those be, then?'

'Lots of things. Musket balls, sometimes. Old coins. I've got some of them still, in a drawer somewhere.'

Susan, who had still not quite forgiven him for keeping the cave secret from her, said to him accusingly, 'I've never seen those either.'

'Yes, well, pirates hide their treasure. They don't show it to their sisters, do they?'

'If they want to go on having meals cooked for them,' Susan said, 'they do.'

Mark's smile in that dim light was hard to see, but I could tell he knew, as I did, that when Susan set her mind to something she would not be swayed. 'I'll try to dig it up,' he promised then he paused as a faint rumble filled the cavern.

Felicity, hearing it too, announced, 'Thunder.'

'So it is,' said Mark. 'We should start back, those rocks aren't so easy to climb in the rain.'

I hung back a bit and took one final look over my shoulder as though by force of will alone I could push through the barriers of time and see the cave as Daniel would have known it. But I only saw the darkness and the dripping stone and hollow walls that told me I had come too late. Three hundred years too late.

Outside, Mark's voice called, 'Eva?'

And I turned again and stepped out of the silence through the cleft beneath the waterfall, and heard again the singing of the sea.

CHAPTER 19

Back at the house, Susan gave Mark no rest till he'd gone up to look in his room for the childhood treasures he'd claimed he still kept 'in a drawer somewhere'. In spite of his earlier vagueness, he must have known exactly where they were because it wasn't long before he came back down and set a slightly grimy biscuit tin between us at the kitchen table.

'There you are,' he said. 'My plunder.'

Susan gave it an experimental shake. 'What's in it?'

'Have a look and see.'

He put the kettle on to make the tea and watched with patience while we sorted through his 'treasures': small bits of polished glass and stone, a limpet shell, a tarnished metal button, the cork from a wine bottle, two shilling coins and a ha'penny, some woman's earring with worn plastic pearls, the promised musket balls, and underneath all that a length of rusted metal so misshapen that it wasn't recognizable as anything. Until Felicity reached out to pick it up and gently brushed the flakes away.

I stared then, as the cold chased up my spine.

Susan asked her friend, 'What's that?'

'Some kind of knife.'

She looked to Mark, who shrugged and said, 'I think I found it in behind the barrels. Don't remember.'

It was in fact a dagger, small and neatly made to fit the hand that held it so precisely that whoever faced it in a fight would only see the blade. I knew, because I'd seen it twice myself already.

Susan touched it lightly. 'What's the handle made of?'

Felicity peered at it. 'Bone, I think.'

Not bone, I could have corrected her. Shell. Some sort of shell like abalone that could show its colors in the light. But it was mostly gone and what remained was crusted thick with dirt, and there would be no way I could explain how I had known. Instead I asked her, 'May I hold it?'

It felt strange in my grasp, cold and rough, not the smooth deadly thing it had seemed when I'd seen it in Daniel's hand just a few days ago. Just a few days... Had it been only that? It seemed an age, and I wondered again at how quickly he'd come to be someone I missed when he wasn't there.

Susan said, 'It looks so old.'

And Felicity, watching me, had an idea. 'Eva, why don't you take that and show it to Oliver? He knows a lot about weapons and things. *He* could tell you how old it is. And what it's worth, even.'

Mark didn't think it would be worth much. 'Not in that state.'

But Felicity told him, 'You never know. The strangest things can fetch the highest prices sometimes.'

My fingers closed protectively around the rusted knife. 'You wouldn't sell it?'

'*That?*' Mark looked as though the very thought were ludicrous. 'Of course not.'

Susan smoothly interjected, 'And you don't mind if Eva takes it down to Oliver?'

'If that's what she wants to do.' It was a bit of a challenge, but I wasn't paying attention, not really. My own thoughts were concentrated on the unaccustomed weight of Daniel's dagger in my hand, and I was trying to remember if I'd ever seen him when he wasn't wearing it.

Except for that one time when I'd surprised him late at night in bed, I didn't think I had. For all I knew he'd had it with him then, as well—it seemed to be his favored weapon and the one he reached for first when he was faced with any threat.

What threat had Daniel faced down in that cave, I wondered, that had made him draw his dagger? And why had he lost it?

⤳

Of the older stones still standing in the overgrown church-yard, most had been so worn by weather and by time that it was difficult to read the date or name, and of the names I could read none was Butler.

The Halletts were all here—Mark's father and grand-father and his great-grandfather and varied cousins and other relations, since this little church of St Petroc's had stood its whole life within view of Trelowarth and served all the families who'd lived there by turns.

It was really no more than a chapel of ancient stone set by the side of the road that ran up from Polgelly and wound past the back of Trelowarth and on to St Non's and beyond that to Fowey.

The tale went that back in the dark, misty times lost to memory, a raiding ship from Ireland had wrecked upon the coast, and the sea and the black rocks had taken the lives of the people aboard her and spared only one man who, wanting to show thanks to God, had built with his own hands this little church upon the hill. It made a rousing legend, but there was no way of knowing what was true or if he'd ever found his way back home to Ireland, or if in fact he ever had existed.

Time was good at erasing the tangible proof that a person had lived.

Behind me the gate to the churchyard creaked open and clanged like the chime of a clock. 'Morning,' said a man's voice and, turning to answer, I saw the church sexton approaching with his wooden-handled garden shears in hand. I remembered those shears and remembered the sexton who, though he'd grown greyer, still walked with the stride of a working man. And he seemed to remember me too, though his memory had likely been helped by the fact that my coming to stay at Trelowarth would have been a subject much talked about down in the pubs in Polgelly.

'Now, Miss Ward, see, I thought it was you.' The broad smile, with its row of impossibly even teeth, took me right back again.

Feeling about five years old, I smiled back. 'Mr. Teague.'

'You're a little bit bigger than my memory of you, I'll admit, but then it's been... what? Twelve years?'

'More like twenty.'

'Never.' He pretended shock. 'You'll have me feeling ancient, so you will.'

I didn't think it likely, and I said as much. 'You look the same.'

'You'll want to have a doctor test your eyes, my dear.' But he was pleased. And then he said, as though it needed saying, 'I was sorry when I heard about your sister. Never seems right when the young ones go. I'm told you brought her back with you?'

'Yes.'

'Good for you. The dead deserve to have a peaceful place to rest. She wouldn't find that in America,' he said with the certainty of someone who'd never set foot out of Cornwall himself, looking round at the shaded green churchyard with its leaning rows of grey stones. The vicars of St Petroc's came and went, but Mr. Teague had been a fixture of this churchyard for as long as I'd been coming here—it had seemed to me that every time I'd chanced to pass this way he'd been here somewhere, with his crowbar or his mower or his old wood-handled shears, and he had always taken time to stop his work and chat a minute.

It occurred to me that Mr. Teague might be the one to ask about the Butlers, so I did. He turned the surname over in his mind and frowned a little.

'Butler. Seems to me as there might be a grave or two of that name.'

'I didn't see any.'

'Well, you wouldn't now, not if they're old as you say. Let me just fetch the book from the vestry.' Setting his shears down beside the church's side porch, he took out his great jangly key ring and opened the old arched oak door with its black iron hinges. I could have gone in with him, but I preferred to wait out in the fresh morning air with the songs of the birds spilling out from the trees and the warmth of the sun on my back. In a minute or two he returned with a small book with plain cardboard covers, the kind of book that local history societies everywhere tended to publish.

Mr. Teague turned the pages with work-calloused fingers, in search of the one that he wanted. 'In 1822,' he said, 'there was a survey done of where the graves were to that time, and the inscriptions that were readable were copied down.

Ah, yes, Butler. There be two graves here, for Butlers. In the southwest corner. Come, I'll show you where they're to.'

The churchyard's southwest corner was the closest to the road, and Mr. Teague had waged a battle here against the hawthorn hedge that had been planted at its edge along the bank. The hawthorn hedge was fighting back. It had begun to creep across the top of the flat stones set horizontal in the earth. The stones themselves, already partly hidden beneath moss and waving grass, were both so beaten and eroded by the weather I could scarcely make out any traces anywhere of letters, much less read what had been written there. But luckily, in 1822, the words themselves had still been legible.

'Says here that one,' Mr. Teague said, pointing, 'is Ann Butler, died October 20th in 1711 at the age of twenty-three. "Beloved wife", it says. And this must be her husband.'

He moved on. I held my breath for one long heartbeat without meaning to.

'Jack Butler,' Mr. Teague read from the book. The stone had split across the centre, as though something had been dropped on it. 'No dates on this one, strangely. Just an epigraph: "My God will raise me up, I trust."'

I breathed again. Jack Butler would have died an older man, I knew, because he'd lived to see his journals published nearly a quarter of a century after the time when I'd met him. And the quote from the poem by Sir Walter Raleigh, an earlier seafaring rogue, seemed quite fitting for Jack.

I asked, 'So there are no other Butlers here?'

Mr. Teague read down the list of inscriptions again. 'Not here, no. That's the lot. Were they relatives, then?'

'No, I'm doing some research for Susan's new venture.' I knew he'd have heard about *that*. 'You know, finding out who used to live at Trelowarth.'

'Well, here's the lad coming now that you ought to be asking about things like that.' Mr. Teague gave a nod to the road where a cyclist was just coming round the sharp bend at the top of The Hill from Polgelly. I recognized Oliver straightaway, even with his cycling helmet on.

'That is,' said Mr. Teague, 'if you've not already been asking him.'

I caught a sly tone in his voice that made me wonder just what else was being talked around the village pubs these days.

It hardly helped that Oliver, when he caught sight of us beside the hedge, slid to a stop beside the road and smiled a brilliant welcome. 'Morning, Eva. Mr. Teague.'

The hard climb up The Hill had left him faintly winded, and his T-shirt clung with perspiration to his chest and shoulders while the muscles of his legs beneath the biking shorts were perfectly defined.

'Oliver.' With one more knowing nod in my direction Mr. Teague said, 'Well, I'll let you two young people talk. I've got my work to do.'

I said, 'Thanks for your help.'

'It weren't much.'

As he started to go, I remembered to ask, 'Mr. Teague, could you tell me the date of Ann Butler's death one more time, please?'

His weathered fingers flipped the pages of the book again to find it—October 20th, 1711—and I thanked him for a second time and, as he headed back across the churchyard to the place he'd left his garden shears, I turned instead to Oliver. 'Do you have a pen?'

He found that amusing. 'Do I look like I have a pen?'

I glanced once again at his close-fitting T-shirt and biking shorts, and said, 'No problem,' repeating the date in my memory a few times to hold it there.

Oliver asked, 'Who's Ann Butler?'

'Daniel Butler's wife.'

'You've found out more about them, then, your Butler brothers.'

'Just a bit. That's Jack,' I said, and pointed to the broken stone. 'The younger brother.'

'So where's Daniel?'

'I don't know.' I wasn't sure exactly how I felt about not finding him. There might be peace, I thought, in knowing how he'd died, and when, and yet a part of me was happiest not knowing.

Oliver felt confident that he could track the information down, in time. 'I like a challenge.'

'So I see.' I nodded at the bike. 'You do this sort of thing for fun, then, do you?'

'Actually, today I'm off on business.'

'Business?' I know I looked as surprised as I sounded, but really, that outfit...

He grinned. 'One of my holiday cottages up St Non's way has a burst pipe. I'm meeting the plumber at ten.'

'Susan's plumber?'

'Don't know. Does she have one?'

I nodded. 'From Andrews and Son, in St Non's.'

'Then it might be. Working on the tearoom for her, is he?' At my nod, he said, 'Felicity keeps telling me I ought to come by sometime and see how that's getting on.' And then, 'She also told me yesterday you'd found a knife, or something, that you wanted me to look at?'

'Oh. Daniel's... I mean, Mark's knife. Yes.' My slip seemed not to register with Oliver.

'Maybe I'll stop in on my way back, then. Have a look. You'll be in, will you?'

I had to admit that I probably would be.

'Then I'll see you later.' With a brilliant smile of promise he set off again, the bike wheels whirring as he picked up speed along the narrow road.

And watching him, I couldn't help but wonder if the tenant of his cottage was a woman. Because if she was, then her day was about to get better than she could have hoped, having Oliver and maybe Susan's good-looking young plumber at work on that burst pipe together.

I felt another tiny twinge of guilt that I could not return the interest Oliver was showing in me. After all, I'd met him first, before I had met Daniel. But I couldn't help my feelings. *There's either a spark or there isn't*, my sister had once told me. There wasn't with Oliver. Whether I'd met Daniel Butler before him or after him, I knew it wouldn't have made any difference.

I looked down and said to Ann Butler's grave, '*You* understand, don't you?'

And I felt sure that she did.

Coming out of the churchyard, I stood for a moment, trying to decide whether I should take the more scenic path through the newly made car park and down to the house through the gardens from there or walk back the way I had come, by the road. I chose the road because it had more shade, and started walking down again beneath the arching trees.

The day was going to be a warm one. Even the birds seemed to sense it and sang their songs lazily, saving their energy. Now and then something unseen, some small animal, rustled in the green and grassy banks along the road-side and fell silent. Everything seemed to be slumbering, and there were no dogs today, bouncing out from the drive of Trelowarth to welcome me home.

The dogs were likely out wherever Mark was in the gardens. But the silence of the house did strike me odd.

And something else was wrong, as well. I couldn't put my finger on it, to begin with, and then all at once I realized I was walking on hard ground and not on gravel, as I should have been. I'd missed the sound of crunching steps, the shifting feeling underfoot. And even as that struck me, I heard someone coming whistling out the front door of the house.

It was the same tune that Jack Butler had been whistling on the morning when I'd heard him coming up the stairs, just after he'd climbed in the kitchen window. The same morning he had found me in his brother's bed. And if I had surprised him then, the jeans and T-shirt I was wearing now would raise his eyebrows even more.

I looked for somewhere I could hide myself, and quickly.

The trees by the roadside were too far away to make a run for them. I hugged the shadow of the house and moved towards the back.

Then, with relief, I heard another voice I recognized. And laughter. Daniel, I thought. Daniel out with Fergal, in the back. They'd get me safely in the house before Jack saw me.

Moving faster now and with less care, I came around the corner.

Daniel, standing at the far edge of the yard, glanced up and saw me as I stepped from shadow into sunlight. But he didn't smile or nod or show in any way that he'd acknowledged my arrival. He was careful not to. And I saw at once the reason why.

The man who stood before him wasn't Fergal.

CHAPTER 20

I T WAS NOT THE best of places I could be. I couldn't
duck back around to the side of the house because at any
minute Jack could come round that way himself and find me
there. And there was no place in the yard for me to hide.
I could do little more than freeze there, like some creature
who'd been flushed out in the open and had caught sight of
the hunter.

Daniel shifted his position very casually, to draw the man
in front of him a little further round. I recognized Mr. Wilson
from his clothes, the long coat of elegant dark green brocade
and the high-cut black boots, and the white wig beneath the
wide brim of his hat.

And then Daniel looked straight at me over the other
man's shoulder, the briefest of looks, and with a quick
darting glance and a tilt of his head made it clear I should
run for the stables.

I did. How I made it across that wide yard without losing
my footing or making a noise I would never remember. I
didn't risk looking behind me, not even when I'd reached
the stables themselves and the relative safety of their shadowed stalls smelling thickly of hay. One or two of the horses
looked over the boards at me, but it seemed they'd seen
more interesting sights than myself in their time and they
looked away, unimpressed. Scooting past all of them, I found

a stall at the end that was empty and, slipping in, pressed myself close to the rough wooden wall as the aftereffects of adrenaline set my legs trembling.

I had no idea how long I had been there before I heard Daniel come in, heard his boots on the floorboards and then his voice saying, ''Tis no trouble.' Then other boots behind his. Mr. Wilson had come in as well, protesting, 'You need not be my groom, Butler. Stand back, man. I'll do that myself.'

I tried not to breathe. Not that they would have heard me, with all of the noise Mr. Wilson was making with saddling his horse.

He said, 'He will be glad to know that he does have your loyalty.'

'When will you see him next?' asked Daniel.

'Two days hence. I'll tell him also that your ship is his if he has need of her.'

'Ay. Tell him he has but to say the word.'

The big horse grunted as the cinch was pulled and buckled, and the jangling of the bridle told me Mr. Wilson had the reins in hand.

The men were moving.

Daniel said, 'If you do chance to meet our constable upon the road, you would do well to sing the praises of King George.'

'Faith,' Mr. Wilson said, betraying his first flash of humor, 'if I meet your constable, I'll call him by his name and say the king himself did send me here to test the hospitality of those who claim to serve him. I may get myself a meal of it if nothing else.'

I'd missed the sound of Daniel's laugh. 'You may, at that. I'll see you to the road.'

When they had gone, the quiet settled round the stables once again, with nothing more than the faint snort or shuffle of a horse to break it.

I heard the booted footsteps coming back, alone this time, and let my breath go with relief. My legs still shook and I was trying to convince them it was safe for them to move when all at once the man approaching broke into a careless whistle.

For the second time, I froze in place. It wasn't Daniel after all but Jack.

He came into the stable unaware and clucked a greeting to the horses, who replied with stamping hooves.

'Now, none of that,' he told them, firm. 'I've fed you once today already, and you've no call to complain.'

His steps were turning now towards my hiding place. With nowhere left to go, I slid a little further down the wall and closed my eyes as though some sudden twist of childish logic would make me invisible if I could not see him.

'Why so nervous?'

Two thudding heartbeats passed before I realized he'd been speaking, not to me, but to the grey horse in the stall beside my own. I heard Jack's feet shift in the straw as he moved round till we were separated only by the thickness of the boards that made the wall.

He soothed the horse. ''Tis only myself, you great fool.' But he said it with affection, in the tone men use for animals when no one else is watching. Then he changed his voice again and said, 'My horse has turned fair skittish.'

I had not heard Daniel enter, but he answered from the doorway, 'Has he, now?'

His deep voice, calm and quiet, filled me with relief, but I stayed motionless against my wall and breathed in tiny, shallow breaths I hoped could not be heard.

Jack gave his horse's neck a pat and said, 'Perhaps he takes objection to the company he has been forced to keep of late. I cannot say I blame him.'

'Do you speak of Mr. Wilson or his horse?'

'Both. Though were I forced to choose the company of one above the other, I admit the horse did irritate me less.'

There was a creaking of the floor as Daniel crossed it. 'I would not have known,' he told his brother dryly, 'from the civil way you did behave while Wilson was our guest.'

'I have no time to play at politics. I do but give a man as much civility as he deserves.'

'He carried his credentials from our kinsman.'

'Then our kinsman must be wanting in his judgment, if he puts his trust in Mr. Wilson.' Jack turned and his shoulder shook the wall between us. 'Christ, can you not see it for yourself? Or has your dalliance with Fergal's sister blunted all your better sense?'

There was a pause, then Daniel said more calmly still, 'Be careful, Jack.'

But Jack did not back down. 'She is not Ann, you know that? Dress her how you will, she is not Ann.'

'I'm well aware of who she is.' It was the quiet, careful voice that I'd last heard when he'd been speaking in the kitchen after learning that I'd had to face the constable alone. The voice that seemed to warn those few who knew him that his mood was growing dangerous.

He would have known that I was somewhere in the stables, which was likely why he cut the conversation short by telling Jack, 'And it is none of your affair.'

I couldn't see the look that passed between the two men, but I felt the tension of it all the same.

'All right,' said Jack. 'I'll say no more of that. And it may be that you are in the right as well about your Mr. Wilson, but you will forgive me if I test that point myself.'

He started saddling the horse, his silence stubborn until Daniel finally asked him in more normal tones, 'Where do you mean to ride?'

'To St Non's. Wilson left his traveling companion at the inn there. I'd be interested to know how he amused himself and whom he might have met. I've no doubt the information could be had at little cost. Do you object?' He dropped that last phrase like a gauntlet.

'No.'

They said no more. The horse was saddled and led out, and Daniel stepped aside to let Jack do it, and silence settled once more over all the stalls.

He said my name then. 'Eva.'

'Here.' I straightened stiffly from the wooden wall and waited while he came to me.

His face showed no emotion when he saw where I'd been standing, but he would have known that I'd heard every word that Jack had said about me, and his own replies. And since I didn't want him thinking that I cared, I forced a smile and said, 'Should I come back another time?'

It smoothed the awkward moment over, and his smile, though slow in coming, warmed his eyes.

❧

Fergal wasn't in a mood for smiling. Slamming down the plate and cup that he'd just carried downstairs to the kitchen where we sat, he wheeled on Daniel. ''Tis hardly something you can laugh about. Have you not thought what she might have faced had she appeared like that in front of Wilson or your brother, or the constable? You've seen the way it happens, when she comes and goes. You've seen it, Danny. So have I, and I'll admit it made me fear the devil's hand, and me a man of reason.'

Daniel told him in an even voice, 'You know it is not witchcraft.'

'Ay, I know it. And you know it. But another man might not. You've seen a witch trial, have you?'

Daniel didn't answer. Fergal looked away.

'Well, I have. And it is not a sight I'd wish to see again, nor yet the evil that the mindless mob does afterwards, the way they kill the wretched—'

'She is safe with us,' said Daniel, though his interruption seemed as much a warning to his friend to hold his tongue as it did an attempt to reassure me. From his face I knew he'd thought about the danger too, before this, and if he had not entirely dismissed it he felt sure it could be managed.

'Is she, now?' asked Fergal, challenging. 'And how can you be sure?'

'Do you now doubt me?' Daniel's tone grew faintly frustrated. 'Christ, any man who saw you so belligerent would think she *was* your sister.'

They'd been talking long enough as if I wasn't in the room, and I decided it was time for me to cut between them. 'If I may?'

I felt a little like a referee as both men turned their heads to look at me.

I said, 'There's not a thing that I can do about the way I come and go or where it happens. If I could, I...' Daniel's eyes were too distracting. 'Well, I can't, that's all. But once I'm here, it seems to me the best thing I can do is to stay close to one of you, because you both know what it looks like when it happens. You would know if I was... leaving. And if someone else was with us you could maybe find a way to draw them off or stop them noticing.'

I watched them both consider this, each in his way, and Fergal gave a nod.

'Ay, so we could. Though let us hope it never comes to that.' He fixed me with a gaze that seemed to recognize I hadn't really had a proper welcome yet. 'So. Did you eat before you came or will you want a second meal?'

'A second one?'

'Ay.' The empty plate that he'd slammed down before was still in front of him, and he gave it a nudge. 'See, the first one's been eaten, I've just brought that down from your room, where you've been lying ill these past two days.'

'Oh. I see.' Of course, I realized, he and Daniel would have had to think up some excuse to give to Jack and Mr. Wilson. I felt a twist of guilt that I had put them to such trouble.

Daniel said, 'She ate it all again, I see.'

Fergal's mouth twitched. 'Ay, she has a fair appetite, so she does, even when she's feeling poorly.'

To me, Daniel said, 'And a good thing you came back before he burst all of the seams of his clothing.'

The mention of clothing drew my own attention to what I was wearing. Self-conscious, I crossed my arms over my T-shirt and faced him. 'I'm sorry, I seem to have… that is, the gown that you gave me is… well, it's…'

'I did notice,' Daniel said.

Fergal had turned away and was bent over a loaf of bread, cutting thick slices that I assumed were meant for me. He paid no attention as I looked at Daniel.

'I'm sorry,' I said.

'It was only a gown.'

No it wasn't, I thought, and his shrug didn't fool me. I wondered for a moment how he'd feel were I to tell him that I'd visited her grave—Ann's grave—and seen the grasses blowing round it in its quiet corner of the churchyard, by the stone that would be Jack's.

'You needn't look so troubled,' Daniel said. 'I do have other gowns.'

Fergal, without looking round, remarked, 'The flowered one would suit her.'

Daniel looked at me. 'It would at that.'

And so the flowered one it was. When I went upstairs after eating it was waiting on the bed, the full skirt trimmed with a broad edge of blue that matched the small sprigged flowers, like forget-me-nots, that danced across the bodice of the gown. The neckline of the bodice, low and rounded, had the same blue edge. Its simple lines were lovely.

I had trouble with my hair at first, but after two or three attempts I got it right and set the little linen cap that Fergal called a 'pinner' tidily on top. If I could trust the little looking-glass, I thought, I almost looked the part convincingly enough to leave my room.

The sound of my door opening made Daniel call along the landing from his private study. 'Eva?'

'Yes?'

'Is everything all right? Do you want help?'

I crossed the few steps to his open door and breathed the aromatic scent of pipe tobacco swirling from the room. 'No thanks, I'm fine. I...'

He was sitting in the chair where he had sat when we'd first talked in here, beside the little window with his shoulder to the wall. A book lay open in his hand but he'd stopped reading and was staring at me silently.

My voice trailed off. 'It is a lovely gown,' I said uncertainly. 'If you would rather that I didn't wear it, then—'

'It is not that.' He set his pipe down as his quiet gaze trailed up to judge the full effect: the gown, my hair. He said, 'You did your hair yourself?'

I raised a hand to check the placement of the pins. 'Did I get something wrong?'

'No.' Daniel stood and offered me the chair beside him. 'Will you join me?'

As I sat, he sat as well and closed his book, and would have tapped the ashes from his pipe except I said, 'It's all right, I don't mind you smoking.'

'Thank you.' Leaning back, he shifted round to face me properly. 'You move well in a gown. Do women wear them in your time at all? Or are you all in breeches, like men?'

'We still wear gowns sometimes. Not quite like these,' I spread my hand across the lacings of the bodice, flat across my waist, 'but we do wear them sometimes.'

'I confess I am not sure which I like best.' He smiled. 'Where have you left your other clothing?'

'In the box that's in the bedroom. Underneath your shirts.'

'They will be safe there for the moment. But you really should let Fergal have them later, he knows corners of this house where even I would fail to find what he has hidden.'

Fergal seemed to have a lot of talents, and I said so.

'Ay,' said Daniel, 'there are few to equal him. It was his own idea to tell Jack and Wilson you had fallen ill, and he did play the role of nursemaid so devotedly at times that I was half-convinced myself.'

I shared his smile. 'You've been friends for a very long time, Fergal says.'

Daniel nodded. 'We have. Twenty years, more or less.'

'You must both have been young when you met.'

It was a rather clumsy way of asking him how old he was, but Daniel didn't seem to mind. Through the smoke of his pipe his eyes smiled at mine. 'I was fifteen, and Fergal a few years above that, when both of us came near to being pressed into the navy in Plymouth.'

My mother, with her love of history, had once painted me a vivid picture of the roving groups of rough men hired to forcibly recruit or 'press' unwary locals into hard military service, coercing when they could, using violence when they wanted. The strength of Britain's navy had owed much to countless lads who'd woken up from one too many drinks to find themselves aboard a ship and far from land.

'Myself, I was too green to do much but fight with my fists,' Daniel told me, 'but Fergal is quick in his mind and his speech, and he got us both out of the way of the press gang and onto a fishing boat, and these years later he still thinks me fully incapable of taking care of myself. That, I suspect, is why he does not leave.' His smile grew more reflective as he looked at me, and then he added, 'Fergal does not easily attach himself to people, and his loyalty, once won, is won for life.'

'Then you are fortunate to have it.'

'I was not speaking of myself.' His tone was patient, like a tutor's. 'If you find that Fergal seems more out of temper, you should know 'tis not from anger, but because he has been worried for your welfare and is far too proud to tell you so.'

I was touched by the thought, and I promised to keep it in mind. 'Have I really been gone two days?'

'You have.'

I hadn't figured out the workings of traveling in time yet,

beyond the fact that I appeared to leave my own time and return to it seamlessly, so however long I spent here I went back to the same moment I had left, to find that nobody had missed me.

But the rules seemed rather different at this end of the equation.

Daniel must have seen me frowning, because narrowing his gaze against an upward waft of smoke, he asked, 'What is it?'

I explained as best I could. 'It makes no sense,' was my complaint. 'It's just not logical, it's—' Then I saw that he was laughing at me and I stopped. 'What?'

'You will forgive me, but you've come across three centuries and what concerns you most is that the times will not be matched?'

'What's wrong with that?'

'Well, if a pig came up to me one day upon the road, full dressed and wearing boots, and asked the way to Plymouth, I can promise you it would not be the color of his buttons that would interest me.'

I saw his point but couldn't help but add in my defence, 'It's only that I'd like to understand what's going on.'

'I know.' His eyes acknowledged that. 'Like yours, my mind would seek to know the science. But there are things in life that lie beyond our understanding. Why they happen, we may never learn. And yet they happen.'

In his eyes the light of laughter was now fading into something more like quiet curiosity. 'What would it change,' he asked me, 'if you understood?'

'I don't know. Likely nothing.'

'You would still be here.'

I had no argument for that, and so I didn't offer any.

Daniel's pipe was dying and he knocked the ashes from it. 'When I meet a wind I cannot fight,' he said, 'I can do naught but set my sails to let it take me where it will.'

I knew that he was right. Some forces could not be controlled, and that was just as true for hearts, I thought, as for a ship at sea. I met his gaze and said, 'I'm not much of a sailor.'

'Give it time,' was his advice. 'Mayhap you'll learn.'

CHAPTER 21

THERE WERE A LOT of other things I had to learn before that.

Fergal had decided that, to guard against the chance I might come back again one day and find myself alone as I had done before, I ought to know the workings of the house and its surroundings, from the little plot of vegetables that sheltered in a terraced garden up behind the stables to the well close by the yard where they drew water.

Leaning over the lip of the stone well, I looked at my rippled reflection below. 'Is it any good for drinking?'

'Ay, if you and I were horses, maybe. Me now, I would rather meet my thirst with ale and cider.'

I'd have happily poured him a big glass of cider to soften his mood at the moment. He'd been brusque and short-tempered, as Daniel had warned me he might be, and if I hadn't known it was his way of showing worry I'd have taken it to heart. As it was, I found it touching, even flattering, that this fierce man had taken on the role of my protector so completely.

Turning from the well, he said, 'This water will not harm you, but you're best to keep to ale for drinking, anyway. You do remember where the ale is kept?'

I answered back obediently, 'In the cask beside the cellar steps.'

'And if the ale runs dry, the cider is…?'

'To be protected at all costs,' I quipped, to see if I could make him smile.

He did, a little. But he wasn't fully satisfied until I'd answered properly and told him where the kegs of cider that he prized so much were hidden. Having done that, I asked, 'Does Jack really not know where they are?'

'He does not. And I'll thank you to leave him in ignorance.'

'But if you're away and he's here when I run out of ale…'

Fergal dryly assured me there'd be little chance that I'd run out of ale with Jack in the house. 'Even if you did he would be off down to the Spaniard with his cup and bowl, he would not need my cider. But yourself,' he said, 'you cannot leave Trelowarth without Danny or myself, so if the cider keeps you safe another day, so be it.'

Turning from the well he led me off again to what I hoped would be our final stop, because my legs were having trouble keeping up to Fergal's pace. Against the north wall of the stable block stood a small shed with a rickety roof.

'And your firewood is in here,' said Fergal, and shoved the door open to show me the tightly wedged stacks of split wood. 'Though with luck you'll not have to come all this way out for it. I'll leave a fair supply stacked in the scullery.'

When we went back to the house I discovered he'd already been hard at work in the scullery, arranging the food in the cupboard so that I'd have no trouble finding the things that I'd need to make one of his stirabouts. 'If we have cheese, which we usually do, it will be at the back in that tin there. And this,' he said, raising the lid of a small keg nearby and lifting a leathery long something out of it, 'this is salt beef. Bane of a sailor's existence, that is, but we always keep some for the *Sally*. I'll leave this lot here, then you'll need never fear you'll have nothing to eat.'

I took the length of salt-cured meat from him, feeling its strange texture, hardened like wood. 'And you *eat* this?'

'Well, not like that, no. Break your teeth if you tried. No, you boil it and soak it to draw out the salt, and then cook it with other things into a broth. Here, I'll make it for dinner and show you.'

He started off by showing me the way to use a tinderbox to light the fire, explaining as he went, and while I doubted I could match his skill, at least it let me see the steps more closely than I'd seen them when the constable had done the task. And with the fire lit Fergal kept a close eye on me while he was cooking, to see I was paying attention. I was. Fergal's hands were the hands of a hard-working man, and his knuckles were scarred from a lifetime of fighting, but he cooked as deftly as any trained chef I had seen. A true man of abilities.

'Fergal?'

Turning around with his knife in his hand he asked, 'Ay?'

'Thank you.'

'For what?'

'Taking care of me. I've never had a big brother before.'

'Have you not?'

'No. I had an older sister, but she died this past winter.'

He looked at my face for a moment. 'God rest her soul.' He crossed himself respectfully and turned back to his work.

I asked him, 'You don't honestly have seven sisters, do you?'

'When did I say that I did?'

'You told the constable.'

'Well then, it's certain I told him the truth, for I'd never tell lies to the constable.'

I couldn't help smiling. 'Me neither.'

'See then,' he said with a nod of approval, 'and did I not say that you were an O'Cleary?'

The moment of companionship sat easily between us while the kettle on the hearth steamed with the scents of salted beef and boiling cabbages and carrots, and it struck me just how comfortable I had begun to feel here, even with the things I had to learn, the things I didn't know.

'And so the people at Trelowarth,' Fergal asked me, 'are they not your family, then?'

I took a minute to explain my whole connection to the Halletts, my relationships with Mark and Claire and Susan.

Fergal listened intently, as though he were storing the facts in his memory. 'And what do they think when you vanish from their time? Where is it you tell them you've gone?'

'They never know, so I don't have to tell them anything. Things work a little differently at that end,' I explained. 'When I go back, it's like I've never been away, I step back into the same moment that I left.'

I watched him think this over. Daniel had been right about the quickness of his mind, he didn't miss much. 'But the last time you went back you were in different clothes.'

'I was.'

'And no one noticed?'

'I'd been walking on my own, there wasn't anyone to see me.' But the thought of clothes reminded me that, 'Daniel said I ought to give my other clothes to you, so you could hide them.'

'Did he, now? Well, bring them here then, and I'll see what I can do.'

And that was why, when Daniel came to join us in the kitchen several minutes later, he found Fergal deep in fascinated study of my jeans.

'You see now, Danny,' Fergal told him, barely glancing round, 'this is a work of genius, this is.' And he ran the zipper up and down to prove it. 'Look at that. I've never seen its like in all my years. And see this seam, with every stitch so even. Sure my own granny could never sew a seam like that, and she was known through all the county for her needle-work, she was.' He smoothed the fabric with his roughened hand in wonder and appreciation. 'A pair of breeches as fine as this would last a man a good while. 'Tis a shame,' he said to me, 'that you were not a larger woman, else I could take these in trade for the trouble you've caused me.'

Daniel pointed out with flawless logic that if I had been a larger woman I would not have fit into the borrowed gowns. 'Then she would have no clothes and you'd have breeches that you could not wear for fear the constable might see them.'

Fergal shrugged. 'So let him see them. I could tell him they were made for me by seamstresses in Ireland, where all the finest fashions have their start.' But he'd already started folding up the jeans. My shirt had been a plain white T-shirt, which was slightly less exciting, though I saw him take note of the tag. ''Twas made in India. So are the trade routes open still, in your time?' Without waiting for an answer, he went on, 'Myself, I've never been to India. Jamaica, now, I've sailed there twice, but never yet to India.'

I was thinking, as he said that, of the black beach in Kerala on the southern coast of India, where I had gone to visit with Katrina on her holiday from filming in Mumbai. I felt the touch of Daniel's gaze and raised my own to meet it, but I only glimpsed the speculation in his eyes before he looked away respectfully and changed the subject.

With his head tipped slightly back, he sniffed. 'What the devil are you cooking, Fergal?'

'Beef broth.'

'And what are you using in place of the beef?'

Fergal sent him a suffering glance. ''Tis salt beef, so that Eva will know what to do with it.'

'Eating it,' said Daniel, 'would not be my first suggestion.'

'Are you wanting something purposeful to do?' asked Fergal dryly. 'Because I was just saying now to Eva that we need a bit of firewood for the scullery, and if you have the time to speak your mind about my cooking, you could surely spare a bit of time for walking to the woodpile.'

Daniel smiled and looked at me. 'Will you come?'

'To the woodpile?'

'It is a chore that can be made more bearable by company.'

I yielded to the smooth persuasion of his smile and went out with him into the strong sunlight of the stable yard.

'Did Fergal show you where the well was?' Daniel asked me as we passed it.

'And the garden and where to find things in the house. He even showed me where the cider was.'

'Did he indeed?'

I nodded. 'He wanted to be sure I wouldn't die of thirst if I ran out of wine.'

'And what if you ran out of cider too? What then?'

'You wouldn't be away that long.'

'If all was well, we wouldn't, no. But many things can happen while a ship's at sea,' he said. After a moment's thought he carried on, 'There is one other place you would find wine if you had need of it, though 'tis not in the house and the only way down to it wants a sure foot and some courage.'

I gave a nod. 'The cave below the Cripplehorn, you mean. Yes, I—'

'What do you know of that?' he asked me, in a tone too casual.

I didn't see the need to lie. 'I read about it in a book, and then my friend who lives here… well, he used to play down there when he was little, so he took me down to show me what it looked like.'

'And what does it look like?'

I couldn't really tell if he believed me, but I said, 'It's mostly empty, only a few old barrels left, although I don't think they were yours.' I couldn't tell him that his dagger had been there as well. I only told him, 'If it helps, the book did say that no one ever gave away your hiding place.'

We'd nearly reached the woodpile, but he stopped and turned to face me, and his eyes held open disbelief. 'The book says that?' He clearly found the thought improbable. 'It mentions me?'

I gave a cautious nod.

'By name?'

I tried remembering exactly. 'It didn't say your name. It said "the Butler brothers of Trelowarth".' I found his gaze too steady to meet comfortably.

'And why, pray, would it mention us at all?'

I shouldn't tell him anything, I knew. And yet I couldn't bear to have him look at me like he was looking now, as though he thought I'd made the whole thing up.

I took a breath. 'Because you were such well-known smugglers. Well, that is, you *used* to be well known. The book was old.' I didn't tell him Jack would one day write a book himself. I thought that might be pushing things. 'It was really only a field guide, about birds and rocks and trees, with little bits of local history. All it said was you were smugglers and the people here respected you and that you used the cave below the Cripplehorn.'

Daniel stood a moment looking down at me, his eyes unreadable, and then he let it pass and looked deliberately to one side as though gathering his thoughts. When his eyes came back to mine, they weren't so hard.

'How did you come across this book then?' There was something gentler in his voice as well that made me more aware of just how close to one another we were standing, there in quiet shade beneath the trees that edged the stable yard.

I raised my chin and told the truth. 'I wanted to find out about you.'

'Did you? Well,' he teased, 'you should not trust the things you read in books. If there is something you would know, you've but to ask.'

The problem was, when he smiled down at me like that I found it difficult to phrase a simple question, or to speak at all. And anything I might have asked seemed unimportant suddenly.

To my relief he looked away again. With slightly narrowed eyes he judged the movement of the clouds above our heads. 'We do have time, I think, to walk awhile.'

'But shouldn't we… the firewood, I mean… and Fergal's dinner—'

'Will be every bit as inedible an hour from now. Salt beef,' he promised, 'cannot be destroyed. A single piece of it would outlast any civilization.'

And so I let him lead me past the woodpile, up the slope of field that lay beyond the stables and the ordered garden plots where Fergal grew his vegetables.

The wind blew wilder here, and whipped my skirts about my legs and made it hard to hear when Daniel spoke ahead of me. He had to turn his head to ask the question over. 'Do you ride?'

I told him that I did. Not all that well, but I could ride.

'Then I shall introduce you to my favorite mare, and

mayhap someday you may ride her,' he said. 'Come, the field's not far.'

I wasn't sure at first which field he meant. The hillside had been altered through the centuries so that I had to work to get my bearings here, and what I'd always known as garden plots with walls and hedges was now open land with long grass chased in ripples by the wind, and the dark of the woods lying off to my left. We climbed to the top of the hill where the road was. *That* still had the same shape, although it was more of a track than a proper road, rutted and grassy and curving in ways that had never made sense to me until this moment, when I saw the great tree that stood in its way.

The tree was an ancient one, oak from its shape and the way it stood spreading its limbs in defiance of any assault the winds wanted to make. The road too had run straight towards it until, clearly meeting its match in the tree; it had veered to the side and gone round it instead, curving off round the hill and away to St Non's while the tree held its ground as it had done for years, maybe hundreds of years. It looked stubbornly capable of standing there a few hundred years more, but I knew that it hadn't. This tree wasn't part of the grounds of Trelowarth that I knew. I'd never heard tell of it.

'Really?' said Daniel when I said as much to him. 'Was it cut down?'

'I don't know.' I would have to ask Oliver. He might have come across something about it, I thought, in his reading.

'There's no one round here would dare cut the Trelowarth Oak,' Daniel informed me. 'The old ways die hard in these parts, and a lone tree is still seen as sacred. An oak even more so. Ask Fergal sometime about oak trees,' he said with a smile. 'For all that he does not believe in witches, he does yet keep the old beliefs.'

The Irish and the Cornish and the Welsh were Celtic peoples, bound by their shared myths and superstitions, and I didn't doubt that Fergal's 'old beliefs' were not so different from Claire's grandmother's. I found myself curious, all of a sudden, to know just what Fergal *did* think about oak trees.

The leaves of a low branch brushed softly against my blown hair as I stepped from the field to the roadway with Daniel. The church lay behind us, sedately unchanged, though its churchyard was smaller and lonelier looking, exposed on all sides with no sheltering woods and no stone wall built round it. I stole a quick backwards glance over my shoulder, but from where we were I could not see Ann Butler's grave.

Daniel saw me look behind. 'You've naught to fear,' he said. 'The road is lightly traveled at this time of day, and I am with you.' To reassure me further he slowed his steps so they matched my own and leisurely he walked close by my shoulder.

Round the bend again, we came to a long field on level land that had been fenced and gated. Through the grass there ran a darker line that marked the cut banks of a narrow stream that crossed the paddock, passed beneath the fence and underneath a wooden bridge set in the road before it carried on its way to feed the waterfall that tumbled down the Cripplehorn.

Daniel told me, 'This is where we turn the horses out to pasture, when we are away from home.'

I'd guessed as much. The field was shaded well by trees, and with the running water and the green abundant grass it made a perfect place for horses.

'They must hate to see the stables after this,' was my remark.

'Ay, I have little doubt they curse me when I come to fetch them in.'

There was just one horse in the paddock now, a bay mare who stood against the tree line at the far end of the field and eyed us both expectantly. And she did seem to be cursing Daniel when he whistled sharply to her now. Her head came up, but she stayed obstinately in her place of comfort by the trees.

He grinned and whistled once again.

The mare stayed put, but I could hear the distant clopping of a horse's hooves responding to the call, then more hooves following and growing quickly nearer, coming briskly down the road. I turned and Daniel moved a step towards me, and although I didn't see his hand move this time to his belt, I knew he'd taken out his dagger and was waiting, just in case there might be danger.

There was no time for the two of us to move where we could not be seen. The horses were already at the turning of the road... and then they came around and crossed the little bridge in single file and we saw Jack on horseback, leading them.

Or so it seemed at first. Until I noticed that his hands were strangely still upon the horse's neck, and moments after that I saw the rope that bound them and the warning in his face as he caught sight of us.

Behind him, with an air of satisfaction, rode the constable. And with him came a shorter man whom I had never seen before and half a dozen others who began to look uncomfortable as they caught sight of Daniel standing quiet by the roadside.

Daniel took a step that brought him close in front of me, so close that I could see the dagger's blade glint in his fingers where he held it very casually below his coat's turned cuff.

And then he stepped into the road and with his other hand reached out to catch the bridle of his brother's horse and bring it to a halt. 'Well, Jack,' he said, in the same tone he might have used if he had caught his brother coming home too drunk. 'And what is this?'

CHAPTER 22

THE ANSWER CAME, NOT from Jack Butler, but the constable, who'd reined his horse up deftly just behind. "Tis an arrest. And there will be another yet, if you do not let loose that horse.'

Daniel ignored the threat. 'What is the charge?'

'This merchant here'—the constable inclined his head towards the shorter, rounder man behind him—'was cruelly robbed upon the road but several days ago, and lost a purse of silver and a joint of mutton to your brother.'

The mutton. I recalled Jack's cheerful boast about the theft, and I could feel my heart sink suddenly inside me as I glanced at the indignant, unforgiving merchant's face. He was a thick-jowled man of middle age, his waistcoat stretched across a stomach that had seen its share of hearty meals, but though he looked a fool he did not look to be a liar, and his accusations would bear weight.

Jack looked less cheerful now, avoiding Daniel's eyes, his own eyes lowered to the rope that bound his wrists together. His character was normally so reckless that I wondered why he hadn't bolted anyway and chanced his horse's speed against the constable's pursuit.

The constable was moving forwards now, aware he had his foes against the wall and wanting only to enjoy it. With his boot a mere hand's-breadth from Daniel's shoulder, he looked down in mocking sympathy. 'And will you come to see your brother hang?'

I didn't breathe the whole time Daniel stood there with his gaze locked to the constable's. The calm had settled over him so evenly it seemed the very wind had lost its nerve and ceased to blow, and for that moment even I feared it would end in violence.

But he moved at last, a slight shift of his stance and nothing more, and for some reason that small movement was enough and I could breathe again.

He said, 'Where is your warrant?'

And just like that, the tables turned. I saw it in the briefest hesitation of the constable and in the faces of the men behind him.

Daniel said, 'You surely have a warrant?'

'We are riding now,' the constable assured him, 'to obtain one from the justice of the peace. If you will kindly stand aside.'

But Daniel had already turned towards the merchant. 'Tell me, sir, where did this most distressing robbery take place and when?'

The merchant, keen to share his story, named the date, and said, ''Twas early in the morning, so it was. The sun was barely up, and I had traveled all the night in this man's company.' He stabbed a finger through the air in Jack's direction. 'Offered me protection, so he did, and said he'd ride with me a ways because he knew these parts and knew the dangers of the roads, and so I let him ride beside my wagon. And at sunrise I complained of being weary and he told me it was safe for me to sleep, that we had passed the place of greatest danger and I would no longer need his aid.'

Daniel considered this and gave a nod. 'And so you slept?'

'I did, sir. And when I awoke, I found he had repaid my

trust by making off with one fine joint of mutton and my purse, sir.'

'A bold theft, indeed,' agreed Daniel. 'And bolder to do it by daylight, when he could more easily have overcome you at night, without fear of a witness. How did he subdue you then?'

The merchant frowned. 'What?'

'Well, surely when you woke and saw him stealing your belongings, you did all you could to stop him. Did he strike you? He does look a man who might resort to violence.'

Jack, as though he thought his brother had gone mad, glanced back at Daniel with a dark expression, but it went unnoticed as the merchant's hard expression altered.

'No, he did not... that is, I was not awake...'

'Ah.' Daniel gave another nod. 'But how then did you see him take the mutton and your purse?'

The constable, a step ahead of where this line of questioning was leading, said impatiently, 'One does not need to see the thief in action to be sure that he has stolen.'

'Does one not?' asked Daniel, calm. 'I do apologize. 'Tis only that it seems to me this good man here might have been set upon by any rogue while he was sleeping, for in these parts there are many, I am sure you will agree, who would do mischief.'

The constable held his gaze. 'One or two, ay.'

'And as this merchant seems an honest man, I only seek to try his memory so that he may satisfy himself that he does not accuse the innocent.'

'The innocent?' The word all but exploded from the constable, as though he had been pushed beyond his limit.

Daniel looked at Jack. 'You will admit you rode beside this merchant's wagon through the night and that you offered him protection?'

Jack's eyes settled on his brother's, wary. 'Ay, I did.'

'And when you parted ways, was he asleep?'

'He was.' Jack caught on slowly, adding, 'I was certain we had come past all the points where we might be accosted, and as I was keen myself to get back home, I thought it safe enough to leave him there to carry on his way without me.'

Daniel turned back to the merchant. 'If you are convinced, sir, that this man did rob you, though you saw it not and could not swear an oath to it, by all means take your case before the justice of the peace.'

But he had sowed the seed of doubt. I felt a fleeting twist of sympathy for the merchant as I watched him wrestle with his own misgivings, trying to decide what he should do.

Then Daniel in one motion sheathed his dagger in his belt and drew a small bag from the lining of his coat as he went on to say, 'Whatever you decide, sir, I am sorry for the loss that you have suffered, and I would not have you leave here thinking all Polgelly men are thieves.' Holding out the soft bag, which looked weighted down with coins, he said, 'This likely will not match what has been taken from you, but perhaps it may restore your faith in those who live here.'

I watched the merchant take the purse from Daniel's hand and open it, and from his quick reaction I could tell that it contained more money than he had been robbed of. Quite a bit more, it appeared, because he closed it with a hurried gesture, squirreling it tidily away into his own coat while the constable objected, 'Careful, Butler. You do seek to interfere too much.'

'I only seek to show good Christian charity to one who is in need of it.'

'By paying him with profits from your own illegal trade.'

The merchant interjected, 'Come now, come now, sirs,

I would not be the cause of any argument between you.' Giving the front of his waistcoat a pat, he gave Jack a once-over. 'I do now confess I am not altogether convinced in my mind that this man was the culprit.'

The men who'd assembled behind and who appeared to have been drawn into the whole affair to serve and aid the constable as his reluctant deputies, reacted now with uncon-cealed relief, from which I gathered none among them had been keen on taking Jack to see the justice of the peace.

I knew little of laws in this time, but I had vague recol-lections of reading at school about children who, in Queen Victoria's day, had been sentenced to hang for the theft of a loaf of bread, and that had been more than a hundred years later than this.

Jack too breathed his relief, though his cockiness showed in the half bow he aimed at the merchant. 'I am in your debt, sir.'

'Not at all,' said the merchant. 'The fault was all mine.'

Daniel didn't allow that. 'An honest mistake, to be sure. Will you dine with us?'

'Dine with you?'

'Ay, as a show of our gratitude. My house does lie but a short distance in that direction.' He pointed, and the merchant, after brief consideration, gave a nod.

'I will, sir. Many thanks.'

The constable snorted. 'You fool. These men would play you like a fiddle, and that purse you have so lately won will be back in their hands by nightfall, mark me well.'

Which was as good as saying that the Butlers were both thieves and scoundrels, there in front of everyone, and Jack's temper flared. 'Then come and guard it for him if you have a mind to.'

It was not an invitation, really, so much as a dare. I had

the sense Jack Butler often said things without thinking first, his reckless nature making him as reckless with his words.

I watched the constable react and saw him hold back his own anger in response and slyly turn things to his own advantage. 'Very well then. I will dine with you as well. 'Tis very kind of you to offer.'

Daniel kept his own face neutral. To the other men, he said, 'I do regret we have not room enough for all of you to join us, but if you ride on now to Trelowarth House and say to Fergal that I've sent you he will find you ale to drink at least, and water for your horses.'

The men—there were five of them now I could count them—broke ranks for a moment to ride forwards, splitting to both sides of the road as they came round the standing horses of the merchant and the constable and Jack. One man, an older man, stopped briefly beside Daniel.

'Thank you, Danny.' He inclined his head, and Daniel answered with a nod.

'Peter.'

''Twas not our doing,' the man said by way of apology, as he moved on and regrouped with the others who, safely past now, heeled their horses to quicken their pace as they carried on round the bend into the trees.

The silence they left in their wake had a dangerous edge.

Only the merchant seemed unaware of it, as his gaze shifted over to me. 'Mrs. Butler,' he said with a gracious bow. 'I pray you will forgive me, as your husband has.'

The constable cut in, 'That is not Mrs. Butler.' From his tone it seemed that the suggestion had offended him, and not for the first time I found myself wondering what his connection had been to Ann Butler.

Daniel let the comment pass and made the introductions

while Jack looked at me as though he had just noticed I was there.

'You're out of bed,' said Jack with some surprise. Which wasn't the best choice of words, but as the merchant's eyebrows lifted, Daniel saved my reputation with the simple statement, 'She has been ill these past days.'

I felt the keen appraisal of the constable. 'She does look well recovered.'

Jack did not agree. Whether from chivalry or from wanting to make up for his earlier comments to Daniel about me, he swung himself with hands still bound together from the saddle, landing lightly on his feet. 'Let Eva ride my horse. It is a fair walk back, and she will tire.'

He held his wrists expectantly to Daniel, who reached once more for his dagger and with one swipe sliced the ropes.

The tension that had been between the brothers when I'd overheard them in the stables was still there, and Jack avoided Daniel's eyes and called to me instead. 'Come Eva, let me help you to the saddle.'

But when I drew near the horse the hands that took my waist and lifted me were Daniel's, sure and strong. He sat me sideways, which was terribly uncomfortable and hard on my one hip, but I held on as best I could and tried to look the part while Daniel took the horse's bridle in his hand again and started walking.

To the merchant he said, 'Where would you be bound, sir?'

'For Lostwithiel.' He explained he would be there by now except the theft had made him break his journey at St Non's to sell some of his wares to have the means to live by. While the merchant told his story I saw Daniel slide a sideways glance accusingly at Jack, who kept his own gaze fixed with studied nonchalance upon the road ahead.

'Fortunately,' said the merchant, finishing his tale, 'the landlord of the Cross & Oak is, like yourself, a man of understanding and compassion. He let me have my room for no more than my promise I would pay him, and now thanks to you I can make good upon that promise.'

He patted the bulge of the purse in his waistcoat again while the constable sent him an unimpressed look.

'You'd do well to take care where you travel,' the constable warned. 'These are dangerous times here in Cornwall.'

'Dangerous times all over, sir,' was the merchant's reply. With a nod of agreement he said, 'Everywhere the countryside is verging on unrest, and every town is plagued with troubles. I've heard little these past months that does not touch upon the young Pretender's plans for an invasion.'

The constable asked him, in a calculated tone, 'And what do you perceive to be the people's mood when they do speak of it?'

The merchant shrugged. ''Tis none of my affair, sir, for I'm neither Whig nor Tory and I take no part of politics.'

'There are some here who take too great a part in it,' the constable remarked, his eyes on Daniel.

Daniel didn't bother looking round. He said, 'There are some I can think of who would rather have a king who was not only born in England but can speak the English tongue.'

The constable's eyes narrowed. 'Such talk comes close to treason.'

'Does it?'

'Ay, and with your kinsman up before the Lords for just such an offence, I should be watching what I said if I were you.'

The merchant looked from one man to the other, settling on Daniel with surprise. 'Your kinsman? Do you mean to say you are related to His Grace the Duke of Ormonde?'

Daniel nodded. 'Distantly.'

That impressed the merchant. 'A great man, the Duke of Ormonde. Very truly a great man, and I know several who did serve in his campaigns upon the Continent who feel the same. He brought us peace.'

Again a sound of rough amusement from the constable. 'A peace that served his own needs more than ours. More than Queen Anne's. He should be vilified, not honored.'

'With respect,' the merchant said, 'those accusations—'

'Come from men of higher station than yourself and I,' the constable reminded him. 'From men who better stand to know the truth.'

Beside me, Daniel turned his head. 'And has the truth become the property of those who can afford it?'

The dark eyes of the constable held Daniel's with a challenge. 'Do you think yourself an equal to the House of Lords?'

'The House together? No, of course not. Man by man? That would depend,' said Daniel evenly, 'upon the lord.'

The constable smiled, but it wasn't a smile of amusement. 'Perhaps you'll have the chance to test yourself against them sooner than you think.'

The merchant took that as a joke and laughed. 'I see that we shall have a lively dinner conversation, sirs. 'Tis sure I do look forwards to it.'

Still wearing that reptilian smile, the constable said, 'Let us hope O'Cleary's skills will stretch to feeding all of us.'

I caught the edge of Daniel's own smile as he looked away again. 'I shouldn't worry,' he replied. 'When I left Fergal he was cooking food that would fair satisfy a sailor.'

CHAPTER 23

I WOULD HAVE PAID a lot to see the constable eat salt beef, but I didn't have the chance to. When we reached Trelowarth Daniel passed me solemnly to Fergal who, in his turn, made a show of fuss about my health and took me upstairs to my room, supposedly to rest.

He closed the door behind us quietly. 'Never mind, I've had the story from the men who came before, but in your own words tell me what you saw and what was said.'

I told him, speaking low so we would not be overheard, and Fergal nodded once or twice and cursed Jack Butler's rashness in that half-forgiving way reserved for family members who bring trouble in their wake. 'You lock the door and stay in here until myself or Danny comes to fetch you.' Giving my shoulder a pat of reassurance, he went out and waited briefly in the corridor until he'd heard me lock the door behind him.

Left alone I looked around the room and weighed my options. So far it had been a crazy day. I'd risen earlier than usual this morning in my own time, and a part of me was tempted by the bed and by the knowledge that I likely had at least an hour to spend in here alone before the merchant and the constable had finished with their dinner and were gone.

But then, I wasn't confident I *could* sleep while the constable was in the house. I felt too much on edge.

The problem was there wasn't much else I could do here while I waited. There was nothing to tidy and no books to read. I was stumped till I noticed the tinderbox set on the mantelpiece. Not that I needed a fire—it was warm in the room—but the starting of fires was a skill I still needed to work on, and practicing would at least keep me distracted from what might be happening downstairs.

This tinderbox, like the one in the kitchen, was made of plain metal and held a worn flint and a ring of hard steel on a soft pile of bits of charred cloth. Kneeling on the hearth, I tried to focus and remember what Fergal had shown me that morning, the steps that he had taken.

I still found it much harder than it should have been, and clearly I was doing something wrong, because this time I couldn't even raise a proper spark. It proved a frustrating endeavor, but it *did* help pass the time. Before I knew it, I heard footsteps in the corridor and Fergal called my name outside the door.

I set the flint and steel aside and, standing stiffly, went to let him in.

'Our visitors are gone, so you can come downstairs again when you've a mind to. Just be careful how you go, for there's a wee bit of a storm wind blowing down there at the moment.'

I could tell what he was getting at the second that I stepped onto the landing. Jack's voice, raised in anger, carried clearly up the stairs.

'Have I not told you that I'm grateful? Should I bow to you and kiss your boots as well?'

'We keep a code, Jack.' Daniel now, his own tone dangerously level. 'We have always kept a code. We do not take what is not ours.'

''Tis noble of us, surely, but—'

'You robbed a man.' He fired the accusation like an arrow, straight across his brother's argument. 'We are not thieves.'

A silence followed.

Fergal, who had no doubt heard the brothers arguing like this before, kept walking down the stairs, but I stopped halfway down, unsure, not really wanting to intrude.

Jack's voice dropped slightly, but they'd moved into the kitchen now and I could still hear every word. 'King George might not agree with that.'

'The Prince of Hanover is not my rightful king,' was Daniel's stubborn answer, 'and for that I owe him nothing, for a free trade is a fair trade. What we sell we have already bought and paid for in good faith, we have not stolen it from strangers who can ill afford the loss.' I heard him exhale with impatience. 'Have you never stopped to wonder why, in spite of Creed's advances and his bribery, not one among the people of Polgelly has betrayed us? 'Tis because they do respect us, Jack. They know that we are honest men.'

'Well, *you* are,' Jack acknowledged. 'I myself have never owned that reputation. Nor, in truth, have I considered it worth owning. Being honest cannot furnish me with all I want.'

'And will that make you happy, having everything you want?'

The answer came back with defiance. 'I will let you know.'

A hand came gently round my elbow. Fergal had come back up the few stairs to where I stood. 'Come on now, they are only talking.'

'I think they want privacy.'

He seemed amused at that. 'And can you hear them where you're standing now?' There was no need for me to answer, and he gave a knowing nod. 'If they were caring about privacy, I promise you they'd talk where they would not be heard. Besides, I think the worst is over.'

He was right. We came into the kitchen to find both the brothers in a kind of standoff, like two soldiers on opposing sides who'd used up all their ammunition but weren't ready to step off the battlefield.

They noticed Fergal's entrance more than mine.

Daniel asked him, 'Fergal, will you tell Jack there are things in this life greater than himself?'

To which Jack countered, 'Fergal, will you kindly tell my brother that I suffer from a weaker moral nature than his own and so he should not hold me to his standard?'

Fergal looked from Daniel to Jack and said dryly, 'I had rather tell the pair of you to mind that there's a lady present. And,' he said to Jack, 'if you think Danny's yelling at you for the theft alone, then you're a greater fool than I'd have known you for. He feared you would be hanged, you flaming idiot, and him not able to do aught but stand aside and watch. He'll never tell you that himself, but there's the reason.' Glancing round at Daniel he said, 'And you know it too, so you can stop pretending you're so hard.'

The fight drained out of Jack first, and he looked across at Daniel as though looking for some proof of Fergal's statement. 'Were you truly worried?'

Daniel asked him, 'Were you not?'

Jack shrugged, attempting to look brave. 'A jury would have set me free.'

'Creed did not mean to use a jury,' Daniel said, and then he raised his own broad shoulders in a shrug and added lightly, 'and finding another first mate for the *Sally* would not be a simple task.'

'First mate?' Jack grinned a challenge. 'You meant to say "captain", I'm sure.'

But the tension was broken, the unspoken bond of affection restored.

Fergal passed through into the dining room and returned with a bottle of claret and cups and, having settled both Butler brothers at the kitchen table with the bottle there between them, he got down to work cleaning up after the dinner with me as his helper.

I scraped and washed the dishes while he wiped them and returned them to their places, making sure that I was watching so I'd know the spots myself.

And all the while I listened to Jack's story of his capture in St Non's.

Jack had gone to the inn, as he'd said, to enquire after Wilson. He'd met with a friend there who'd stood him a drink. 'We did pass the time merrily,' Jack said. ''Twas then that the merchant himself must have seen me and gone out in search of a constable, and Creed being there in the town he replied. He didn't dare set a foot in the inn, though. He has better sense. Nor indeed did he take me when I stepped out into the street, for again there would be witnesses, and doubtless men among them who'd have come to my defence.'

'Where did he take you then?' asked Daniel.

'In the wood, before the mill. It is a lonely stretch of road, that, and he fell upon me in a proper ambush with a cudgel, like the coward that he is.'

'A cudgel?'

'Ay.' Jack gave the bruised back of his head a rueful rub in memory. 'You do not think I'd let myself be bound without a fight, if I were conscious, surely? No matter who it was doing the binding nor how many men he had gathered around him.'

Fergal, who'd already talked to the men who had been with the constable when they'd stopped in at the house, gave a nod and said, 'Ay, well, they would have been there from their duty to the law and not their loyalty to Creed, I'll warrant. Likely they were just as pleased as Jack was to see you there by the roadside, Danny.'

Daniel's thoughts had traveled back a few steps. Tipping the bottle of claret he emptied the dregs into his cup and turned to his brother again. 'So, your time in St Non's… was it worth all the trouble?'

Jack met his gaze squarely. 'Did I find out aught about our Mr. Wilson, you mean? Ay, I did.' With a pause for a quick drink himself, he went on, 'His true name is Maclean. And the servant he traveled with did call him "Colonel Maclean" once or twice, says my friend.'

Daniel smiled and relaxed.

'Do you not find it telling that he did not use his given name with us?'

'All who are close to this venture do guard their true names out of caution,' was Daniel's reply to his brother. 'But Colonel Maclean is a good name to have, Jack, for that is the name of the duke's private secretary.'

'So he is on our side, as he claims.'

'Ay. Indisputably.'

'I hope that you are right,' said Jack. He still looked unconvinced, but having just patched up one quarrel with his brother, he did not appear to be in any rush to start another. He set down his empty cup. 'This wine has given me a thirst for something stronger,' he confessed. 'I think I will go down to try the Spaniard's rum.'

Fergal, beside me, turned round in disbelief. 'You know that Creed will be more keen than ever for your blood now.'

'He will not try a second time today.' Jack's tone was certain. 'And the lads will gladly see me safely home again this evening.'

Daniel didn't raise an argument. But when his brother left the house, I saw his face and read the worry on it.

Silence fell again upon the kitchen, and to break it I asked, 'Who is the Spaniard?'

Fergal's eyes made that familiar crinkle at their corners. ''Tis not a who but a what,' he corrected. 'The Spaniard's Rest, down by the harbor.'

A pub, I thought, giving a nod of my own. 'Where by the harbor?' I asked.

Fergal told me, and I said, 'In my day we call it the Wellie. The Wellington.'

'What sort of name is that, then?'

How could I explain to them without revealing details of the wars that were to come—the Duke of Wellington, Napoleon, and Waterloo? I only said, 'He was a famous soldier, Arthur Wellesley, Duke of Wellington. A hundred years from now. A lot of names were changed to honor him.'

But Fergal still preferred 'The Spaniard's Rest' and said so. With a sideways look at Daniel, he said, 'And where are you off to, then?'

Daniel had stood to his full height and was stretching his shoulders a little bit wearily, his one hand moving in that automatic gesture to his belt to see his dagger was in place. 'To keep an eye on Jack.'

'He would not thank you for it, Danny.'

'Perhaps not.'

'Then sit down, you great idiot. Creed wants your own blood more than he craves Jack's, and you know it.'

Daniel's silence acknowledged the fact as he reached for his hat.

'Danny...' Fergal tried again.

'He is my brother,' Daniel said, as though that answered everything.

And Fergal, seeing that there was no winning, sighed. 'Well, take your sword, at least.'

Daniel shook his head. 'There'd be no room to draw it in the Spaniard.' But I noticed that he tucked a pistol in his belt as well before he left us, and I couldn't help but wonder just what sort of crowd went drinking at The Spaniard's Rest. A rougher clientele, I reasoned, than I would have found in the Polgelly pubs of my own time.

'They'll both wind up dead by the roadside,' was Fergal's black prediction, as he gave the fire on the hearth a savage stir with the poker, 'and Creed will come and say it is an accident, he will, and I'll be left to kill the bastard with my own two hands.'

I braved his blackened mood to ask a question. 'Fergal?'

'Ay?'

'Why does the constable want Daniel's blood?'

Fergal set the poker back in place and I could sense his hesitation, so I tried to help him.

'It can't be just the free-trading,' I said, 'because I'm sure he makes a profit from that, doesn't he?'

His mouth twitched in the way it always did when I'd amused him. 'Ay, he does.'

'So I'm assuming that it's personal.' I cleared my throat and asked him, 'Does it have to do with Ann?'

He slowly turned his head. 'Why would you think of that?' But I could see from his expression that I'd hit the mark. 'What did Creed tell you?'

'Nothing. No, it's just... oh, I don't know. The way he sometimes looks at me. He doesn't like to see me wear her clothes.'

'Well now, the only one who has a say in that is Danny,' Fergal said. 'And he's not bothered by it.'

I wasn't sure I'd have agreed with that, entirely, but instead of arguing the point I asked, 'Was he in love with her? Constable Creed, I mean.'

'Love?' Fergal's mouth twisted slightly, a grimace instead of a smile. 'Not the word I'd have used for it, no. Not what Ann would have called it herself neither. No,' he said, looking away, 'he was Ann's brother.'

That one I hadn't seen coming. 'Her brother?'

'They shared the same father, though Creed's mother died before he was grown halfway to manhood. He took little notice, they say, of his father's new wife or of Ann. Not at first. But as Ann grew, he started to take an unnatural interest.' He spat in the flames. ''Twas a kind of obsession. An evil one. Smothered her with it, he did. Couldn't bear it if she looked at anyone else.'

'And she looked at Daniel.'

'She did, ay. And Danny looked back.'

I thought about this. 'So I'm guessing the constable wasn't too pleased when they married.'

'He was not. But see, Ann had a mind of her own, and she did what she wanted. She feared Creed herself at times, but she would never have shown it.' He glanced at me, and this time there was nothing hard behind his smile. 'You share that with her, anyway—the both of you too proud to let your fear show when you feel it.'

'I'm not proud at all.' I met his gaze with honesty. 'When the constable's anywhere near me, I'm scared to death.'

Fergal's face softened. 'Well now, you needn't be. He'll have to come through myself first to get to you, and after me there's still Danny left standing, and he's not so easy to get by.'

'So long as he's not lying dead by the roadside,' I pointed out, remembering his earlier prediction.

Fergal shrugged aside the words. ''Twas only myself talking, that was. You pay it no heed now.'

I did try to take his advice.

Hours later, alone in my bed, I tried focusing on the soft sounds of the sleeping house—the scuttle of mice through the walls and the creak of the beams in the ceiling above me, and Fergal's snores rattling down the long corridor. I tried telling myself that if Fergal was so unconcerned about things that he was able to sleep, well then, I should be able to sleep too. But I couldn't shake off my worries.

The images rose in a taunting progression, dissolving to worse ones of Daniel approaching the dark shadowed trees of The Hill with his unhurried stride, to be met by an ambush as Jack had been, beaten and bound while the constable looked on with cruel satisfaction...

I turned over sharply to stop my imaginings, tugging the blankets with me as I rolled on to my side. The weather had changed, growing cooler and damp, but I'd left the windows halfway open anyway, so I'd be able to hear any noise from the road. There was no wind tonight, and instead of the rush of the leaves and the rattle of window glass, I could hear nothing right now but the hoot of an owl from the woods and the slumbering roll of the waves on the shingle below the black cliffs. Now and then something made a faint sound, some small animal maybe, that rustled the grass with its passing, and after that, silence again and that horrible still-ness that seemed to be waiting.

And when, after what felt like hours, I finally heard the shuffle of approaching footsteps, my rush of relief was short-lived. The steps sounded wrongly uneven, and in those first moments the horrible images rose once again and I half-thought that Daniel *had* met with the constable's men and was staggering wounded now up the long hill from Polgelly.

I bolted from the bed, taking the top blanket with me to wrap round my shoulders for warmth like a shawl, but by the time I reached the window he'd gone past already.

From the floor below I heard the door swing open and slam shut as though it had been kicked. And then a dreadful clattering as though he'd fallen over.

I was halfway to my own door when I heard a burst of laughter, and Jack's cheerful voice so slurred with drink I couldn't catch the words. I couldn't catch Daniel's reply, either, but the deep quiet tone of his speech reassured me and made me relax. He was only bringing Jack home. He was safe.

And the reason his footsteps had sounded unsteady outside became obvious as the men started to climb the stairs—Jack must have been so drunk that he could barely stand, and from the swearing going on I gathered it was taking a bit of work for Daniel to keep his brother upright.

'Left foot... *left* foot. There you go,' said Daniel.

Jack hushed him with an exaggerated 'shh,' and, 'do you want to wake the house?' And then he fell into another fit of laughter.

Something slammed against my door with an almighty thump and scuffle and the laughter stopped abruptly.

Daniel swore.

I pulled my door half-open and looked out into the corridor to find Jack lying senseless like a barrier in front of me and Daniel reaching down to take Jack's shoulders in a firm grip as he hauled his brother upright.

The smells of a night at the pub hadn't changed much

in three hundred years. Rank tobacco and hard liquor mingled in all the stale scents that assailed me, and Jack was so completely gone that I decided I'd be safe to speak. Keeping my voice low, I asked Daniel, 'Is he all right?'

Briefly startled, he glanced round. 'What? Oh, he's fine. You can go back to bed,' he assured me. 'I'll have him out of your way in a minute.'

I pulled my door all the way open and folded my arms in the warmth of my blanket-shawl, looking at Jack, who had slumped to the side again and would have fallen if not for his brother's strong arm. 'Are you sure he's all right? He looks sort of… well, sort of…' The word 'dead' came to mind, but I stopped short of actually saying it.

'Ay,' Daniel told me, 'I know how he looks, but there's no need to worry. I've seen him look worse.'

'If you say so.' I would have gone back in my room, but Jack's eyes had come open, and from his suspended position he stared at me, trying to focus his thoughts.

'Eva?'

Damn, I thought. He'd heard me speaking. Heard my voice.

Jack pushed clear of his brother's hands, making an effort to stand on his own, his expression incredulous. 'Eva,' he said, 'you can—'

That was the most he got out before losing his balance again. He swayed once and pitched forwards to land like a fallen log, stretched on the carpet before me, unconscious.

I stood in my doorway, not sure what to say, feeling awful I'd opened my mouth in the first place and knowing that I should have stayed in my room and just let them go by. I watched Daniel, waiting, expecting a lecture.

And after a moment he thoughtfully raised one hand, rubbing the back of his neck. Then giving a nod to his brother's prone figure, he said, 'There now, didn't I tell you I'd seen him look worse?'

Which was so far from what I had thought he would say that it caught me off guard, and I laughed without thinking.

Which caused us more trouble.

CHAPTER 24

'W<small>HAT THE BLEEDING</small> J<small>ESUS</small> are you doing?' Fergal's exasperated words shot down the passageway like shrapnel as he came towards us, shrugging on his shirt and looking none too pleased to have his sleep disturbed. 'As if a man in his condition is a sight a woman needs to see,' he chastised Daniel, firing him a dark look as he nodded at Jack's crumpled form. 'What were you thinking, Danny, dragging Eva from her bed at this hour?'

I thought of stepping in to say that I'd already been awake, but Fergal didn't look in any mood to hear it and Daniel didn't need me to defend him. He stood calm against the onslaught, bending down again to lift his brother up and sling him senseless half-across one shoulder.

Fergal studied Jack, frowning, and asked, 'Was he into the rum?'

'Ay.'

'And fighting, I see.'

I looked at Jack too. In the dark I had missed seeing how the one side of his face was all bruised.

'Well,' said Daniel, 'I would think that was for reputation more than anything. 'Twas a wound to his pride, being taken by Creed's men in daylight—he purposely looked for a fight at the Spaniard to show that he was not so weak.'

'Ay, for he's looking the picture of strength, so he is, at the moment.'

'He won the fight,' said Daniel.

'Was he standing when he did it?'

Daniel smiled at that. 'He was. He was using his feet well enough till we came up the stairs just now. Then he fell.'

Fergal assured us he'd heard it. 'The same as I heard you two laughing. And what would have happened if Jack had heard Eva?'

'He already had,' Daniel said. ''Twas an accident.'

Fergal shot a glance between us, swore beneath his breath, and raised his shoulders as though bracing for a load before the movement altered slightly to a shrug. Resigned, he told us, 'Well, there's nothing to be done for it. With luck the drink will keep it from his memory.' Stepping closer he expertly shifted Jack's weight from Daniel's back to his and said, 'I'll see him to his room myself,' and waved off Daniel's protests with, 'you've done enough already.'

There was no arguing with Fergal when he'd set his mind to something.

Daniel let him go and turned to me instead.

I said, 'I'm really sorry.'

'You did nothing wrong. And Fergal is not truly angry, he is only—'

'Worried. Yes, I know.'

I'd started shivering a little and my voice had changed because of it, and Daniel looked beyond me to the darkness of my bedroom.

With a slight frown he remarked, 'You have no fire.'

'I didn't think I'd need one when I went to bed, it only got cold afterwards, and Fergal was asleep by then, and I'm afraid I'm not too good yet with the tinderbox,' I said. 'I know the theory, but it never seems to work for me.'

'It only takes a bit of practice. Shall I show you?'

I was torn. On the one hand I was cold, and that was obvious. Not only would a fire be very welcome, but it probably would seem a little odd if, after standing here and shivering and telling him I couldn't start a fire myself, I told him not to bother. But the problem was that if I told him yes, then he would come into my room and I would have to try to act as though I weren't the least affected by it, and if I was already this nervous and aware just standing near him in the doorway, who knew what kind of a fool I might make of myself if I had to stand next to him here in my bedroom. At night. In the dark. But there really was no other answer to give, so I told him, 'Yes, please.'

Daniel must have been into the rum himself down at the Spaniard. I caught the faint scent of it on his breath as he stepped into the room, but the drink didn't seem to have had an effect on him. Free of Jack's weight he moved surely and easily, taking the tinderbox down from the mantel and crouching beside the cold hearth of my fireplace. I followed and did likewise.

Through the window on the eastern wall the moonlight cast a slanting square of pale light onto Daniel's hands, so I could see what he was doing.

Choosing a piece of charred cloth from the box he set it on the hearth and said, 'You hold the steel like this.' He slid his fingers through the oval ring until it reached his knuckles, then made a fist to secure it. 'And the flint in your other hand, and strike the two together, thusly.' Steel met stone, a sharply ringing sound, and raised a single spark that scudded sideways on the hearth and quickly died.

He held his hand out, straightening his fingers in the steel ring so that I could take it from him. 'Try it now.'

I hesitated. 'Couldn't you…?'

''Tis better learnt by doing,' he insisted, with his hand still stretched towards me, waiting.

Silently I took the steel, amazed at how that brief and sliding contact of our fingers made my insides leap. The steel itself was cold but where he'd held it I could feel faint warmth, and shifting my own grip, I tried to hold on to that small sense of shared contact while he handed me the flint.

I tried to strike the two together in the way he had, but my attempt was clumsy. Adjusting the angle at which I was striking, I tried again.

'Patience,' he said. 'It is never done quickly.'

'I'm learning that.' The edge of my frustration made my words come out more sharply than I'd meant them to, and Daniel's own tone grew indulgent, in the way an expert tries to make an amateur feel better.

'You'll soon have the way of it,' he told me. As my efforts went on he asked, 'What do you use in your own time then?'

'Matches.'

'Matches?' I'd somehow astonished him.

'What's wrong with matches?'

'Nothing, if you seek to fire a cannon, but I would not think them practical for household use.'

I paused for a moment to send him a puzzled frown. 'Sorry? I mean, what do you call a match?'

He described what a match was, in detail, and smiling I nodded with new understanding.

'We'd call that a fuse,' I said. 'No, modern matches are like...' I tried to remember what he called the match-like lengths of tightly twisted paper that they used here to transfer a flame from one source to another. Spills, that's what they were. 'Well, they're like little spills,' I told him, 'only with their ends dipped in chemicals that self-ignite when you strike them on something rough.'

'Indeed.' I'd forgotten that he had a very scientific mind that would find certain things intriguing. 'Spills that light themselves,' he mused. 'What are the chemicals you use to make this happen?'

'I don't know. I... ow!' I'd hit the flint too wildly and the steel had bashed my thumb instead. I took a breath against the sudden pain and said, 'You see? I'm hopeless.'

He fell silent for a moment while he watched me in the darkness. Then his hands reached out to close around mine calmingly. His quiet voice assured me, ''Tis not such a complicated thing.'

I couldn't have replied if I had wanted to. The breath I'd drawn had somehow lodged within my chest and I could only sit there being glad that in the dark he wouldn't see the foolish way that I'd reacted to his touch.

He carried on, 'It wants some effort, yes, and patience, but then...' Tightening his hold he moved my hands for me, his fingers curving slightly round my knuckles and the steel. '...but then, what in this life that is of any worth does not?'

I couldn't answer that one either. *Get a grip*, I urged myself, but Daniel's touch was sending all my senses into overdrive. He'd shifted closer in the dark until our shoulders almost brushed, until his words came close against my ear when he said, 'If you give them time, the flint and steel will make a spark. They cannot help but do so.'

I knew just how they were feeling. Flint and steel were not the only things in this room striking sparks off one another, though I doubted Daniel noticed the effect that he was having on me. He was only being nice, I told myself. For all that he might flirt with me from time to time by daylight, that was all it ever was with him—flirtation—and he was too much the gentleman to try the same game on with me here in the darkness of my bedroom, at this hour, with us alone.

If he was sitting close to me it was because he had to sit that close to hold my hands the way he needed to, and that touch was itself a light and helpful one, designed to show me what to do and nothing more.

I was being a terrible student, I knew. My head bent lower still, my focus narrowing more fiercely on the task as I tried shutting out the knowledge of his nearness. But it wasn't any use. Each time he breathed, the faintly mingled scents of rum and pipe tobacco warmly brushed my hair, and it occurred to me that if I turned my own head just a little bit towards him, we'd be close enough to... close enough to...

'There,' he said.

From our joined hands a shower of small sparks cascaded to the hearth, and two of them fell squarely on the piece of charred cloth kindling where they glowed like tiny eyes against the dark.

Releasing my hands, Daniel bent forwards, shielding the cloth with his cupped hands while he breathed on the growing sparks. They glowed more surely now, their reddish light cast upwards to illuminate the hard edge of his jawline. And then suddenly the light turned golden, dancing up between his fingers as though he'd created it by magic. When he took his hands away, there was a proper curling flame along the charred cloth.

'You see? 'Tis as I said. A simple thing,' he told me.

Taking up a bit of splintered wood he held it to the cloth until it caught the fire as well, before he carefully positioned it beneath a larger length of log.

I found my voice. 'And what's the trick to doing that?'

'There is no trick. 'Tis only patience, once again.'

I watched him while he crouched there by my hearth and brought the fire to life with expert and unhurried movements, shifting this bit here and that bit there and sitting back to wait for the result, his focus idle on the flames.

I found I couldn't take my eyes from him. We were no longer touching but I still could feel his hands on mine, and still my heart was beating much more loudly than it should have been.

Each bit of wood that caught the spreading fire on the hearth threw more light out to chase the shadows from our corner of the room, but I saw nothing more than Daniel's now-familiar features, nothing more than that, and I could only sit and stare like some infatuated schoolgirl.

A simple thing, he'd said, and so it was. A random meeting and a touch—that's all it took to make a spark that could, with care and time, become a flame...

'Here, try it for yourself,' said Daniel, shifting to make space for me and holding out a sturdy length of stick. 'Or do you fear to burn your fingers?'

My imagination could have read a double meaning in those words of his, but pushing those romantic fancies firmly to one side I met the challenge in his face and took the stick from Daniel's hand, and concentrated on the hearth until the fire leapt to the largest log and raised a dancing blue along its length.

Approving, Daniel turned his head to me and I could see those flames reflected in his smiling eyes.

I should have looked away. I should have smiled back and looked away, but the emotion I'd been feeling surfaced suddenly, betraying me before I could conceal it, and whatever he had been about to tell me fell forgotten in the silence as the smile in his eyes took on a faintly puzzled aspect, and then finally shuttered over into something that I couldn't read.

The large log cracked and settled on the smaller ones beneath it, and I pulled my gaze away and strove for something normal. 'So,' I said, with no idea what came after that.

After a moment Daniel filled the pause himself. 'You have your fire,' he said, and standing to his full height, stretched his shoulders.

I stood too, before he had a chance to offer me a helping hand. I didn't trust my own reactions to his touch just now. Lowering my head I mumbled 'thank you', and I would have stepped away except my foot caught in the trailing blanket I'd wrapped round me and I half-tripped as I tried to pass him.

Daniel moved to steady me—a gentlemanly gesture, just one hand around my arm, but all that did was knock me more off-balance.

'Sorry,' I said, putting out both hands from instinct.

He'd reached out as well. My fingers landed on his chest as his clamped firmly round my elbows and I closed my eyes without exactly knowing why. Maybe because I was trying to keep my composure, to behave like a twenty-first century woman instead of some swooning Victorian heroine, to not let him see just how incredibly, hopelessly, helplessly hard I was falling in love with him.

'Eva.'

Opening my eyes, I met his own and found them not quite as unreadable as they had been before.

In fact, they weren't unreadable at all.

We looked at one another for so long I started wondering if Time, instead of flinging me from place to place, had stopped completely. The air grew charged between us with a thousand things unsaid, and with a growing sense of wonderment I thought, *He feels it too. My God, he feels the same way I do.*

And he did. I sensed it in the subtle change in how he held me, in the way his fingers shifted on my arms, and all at once I felt uncertain in a way I'd never felt before. I wanted him to kiss me and I feared it at the same time without really knowing why. I felt a mix of joy and dread and everything between, as though someone had thrown a switch and scrambled all my circuits.

When his hands slid to my shoulders I believe I held my breath; and then he took hold of the edges of the blanket that had slipped and with a careful touch rewrapped me in the woolen folds, his features set in studied concentration as he crossed the blanket's ends and tucked them under.

There was an instant just before he let me go when I felt sure he meant to say something, but in the end he only gave a nod. 'Good night,' he said, his measured tone the same as it had ever been.

The doorway that connected his room to my own stood partway open and I watched him cross towards it. Halfway through with his hand on the latch he turned back to say over his shoulder, 'And Eva?'

It astonished me I had a voice at all. 'Yes?'

'Lock your door.'

With which advice he pulled it shut behind him, leaving me hugging the blanket around me and feeling a warmth that had nothing to do with the fire.

CHAPTER 25

'You're in a rare fine mood this morning.' Fergal somehow made that seem an accusation. I had found him at the far end of the yard beside the stables, chopping firewood, and although he hadn't asked to have my company I'd plunked myself down happily upon a nearby log to watch. He swung the axe so hard it cleaved the length of wood in one blow and stuck deep into the broad scarred stump beneath, so that he had to wrest it out again. As he straightened he glanced sideways at me, openly suspicious. 'What's the cause of it, I wonder?'

'I'm just happy.'

And I was. Almost ridiculously happy, in a way that couldn't be stamped out by anything. Not Fergal's grumbling nor the gnawing in my stomach that reminded me I hadn't eaten breakfast, nor the fact the sun lay hidden by a bank of cheerless cloud. The world was beautiful this morning because Daniel Butler liked me.

I'd replayed the moment several times since waking, to be sure, and every time I had replayed it I'd been more convinced it hadn't been imagined. He had liked me. And he'd wanted me. And that—to use a phrase he'd used himself—was a beginning.

So this morning seemed a miracle, no matter what the weather or the moods of those around me or the fact that Daniel wasn't even here.

He'd gone out just after daybreak. I knew because I'd been awake myself, my own mind racing, and I'd heard him walking back and forth across the creaking floorboards in the next room, heard him twice approach the locked connecting door, then stop and turn away again. And in the end he had gone out and down the stairs and in a little while I'd heard the sound of hoofbeats passing from the stables to the road, and they had faded up the hill and left the wind alone behind.

That same wind brushed my face now as I looked at Fergal. Jack had been asleep and snoring loudly when I'd passed his door upstairs on my way out, and at this distance from the house there wasn't much chance of my being overheard, but still I kept my voice as quiet as I could when I asked, 'Do you know where Daniel's gone this morning?'

'No.' The axe swung down again as Fergal shot another glance my way that held more interest than the first. 'There's no one tells me anything these days, it seems.'

The axe stuck in the stump again and this time when he yanked it free he turned the blade and ran his thumb across a small nick in the metal, frowning.

'Is it broken?' I asked.

'Sadly, no. 'Tis indestructible, this relic. It belonged to Danny's uncle and is doubly as cantankerous.'

I smiled at the thought of Fergal being bested by a thing as stubborn as himself, and then I thought of something else, and asked him, 'What was Daniel's uncle's name? Was he a Butler too?'

'A Pritchard. Why?'

'I only wondered. There aren't many Butler graves up in the churchyard, that's all, only Ann's and—' Just in time I caught myself and stopped before I gave away a bit of knowledge Fergal shouldn't have. Not that I knew how Jack had died or when, except that it would happen twenty years or more from now, but still…

Fergal, true to form, missed nothing. 'Have you walked over my grave as well?'

'Fergal.'

Setting more wood on the stump, he shrugged. 'You needn't fear. I've no great wish to know my future. No man should.' Then a thought seemed to strike him. He glanced at me sideways. 'Nor should anyone, I'm thinking, know what lies in store for someone else, for that would be a burden, would it not?' His eyes met mine with understanding. 'Take this whole rebellion now, that Danny's got himself involved in. If you were to know that it would fail and could not tell us so, I'm guessing that would cause you to be troubled in your mind.'

He knew already, I could see that. He knew as surely as I did that nothing would come of the venture.

'And,' he said, 'if that were how you felt, I'd have to tell you not to waste your worries. Anyone with any wits at all knows well enough the Duke of Ormonde cannot carry through his plans.' He turned his head away and calmly spat upon the ground, a gesture that I took to be a sign of his opinion of the duke. 'And Danny knows it too, believe me.'

'Then why does he…?'

'Why does he take part in it?' He shrugged. ''Tis how he's made and how he reasons things. To Danny, knowing that the battle will not end the way he wishes does not make it any less worthwhile to fight.' He swung the axe with forceful certainty. 'I'm only saying. What you know or do not know, you needn't let it be a burden. Things will happen as they will.' With a sweep of the axe blade he cleared the cut wood from the stump and looked round for a new length of log to be split. There was none.

'You could always cut down that one,' I suggested with a nod towards the slender, deeply leaning tree behind him. 'It looks like it's ready to fall over all on its own.'

'What, the rowan?' He glanced back himself to confirm it. 'I'll never touch that one.'

'Why not?'

''Tis the whispering tree, is the rowan. The witches' tree. Show it your axe without asking permission and you'll have bad luck all your days.'

I thought of the great ancient oak tree that stood in the way of the road in this time and had vanished somehow by my own. Daniel had told me I ought to ask Fergal sometime about oak trees and lone trees and Celtic beliefs, and since Fergal seemed talkative I asked him now.

'Well, the oak is more sacred again than the rowan,' said Fergal. 'Legend says that its roots are well bound in the otherworld, and that the tree itself serves as a doorway between the two realms of the shadows and light. Never fall asleep under a lone oak, they say, else you'll wake...' He broke off.

'Where?' I prompted him.

'Somewhere you never were meant to be.'

As though on cue the wind chased lightly through the trees that edged this corner of the stable yard, and suddenly I heard the sound of heavy rolling wheels approaching and a horse's clopping steps, and a man drove around from the side of the house in a cart being drawn by a sturdily built chestnut mare. The cart rolled to a stop just in front of us as Fergal set down his axe and stepped forwards to shake the man's hand. 'Morrow, Peter.'

'O'Cleary.' The man gave a nod and then angled it round to include me too.

Fergal said, 'You'll have met my sister yesterday, I'm thinking.'

Then I realized why the man's face seemed familiar. He'd been one of the men on the road with the constable. I remembered him best because he'd been the one who had spoken to Daniel before riding off with the others, the one who'd said, ''Twas not our doing.'

He looked as though the episode still shamed him as he gave another nod to me and said, 'Mistress O'Cleary.' Then taking a sack from the seat of the cart he told Fergal, 'I'm just off to market. I thought you could find a good use for this.'

'Did you, now?' Fergal took the sack and looked inside. 'You know me too well, Peter. Wasn't I saying this morning I fancied a conger pie?' Thanking the man, he said, 'But you've no need to be giving me anything.'

'Well.' The man looked to the side. ''Twas a bad business yesterday. And you had to make your dinner stretch to extra mouths and all because of it. I minded that you had a taste for conger.' With another nod, he wished us both good day and turned the cart around and headed off.

The sack was wet and smelt of fish, and peering in I saw the coiled body of a large, dead eel.

Fergal said, 'It may be ugly, but it makes a grand pie, conger does.'

I might have made a comment, but just then the back door opened and Jack Butler took a few unsteady steps into the daylight. He stopped as though he'd hit a wall, and then came on towards us, walking gingerly, his head held in both hands.

'Christ,' he said, with his eyes shut as though even the

sound of his own footsteps caused him pain. 'Where the devil is Daniel to?'

Fergal held back his answer until he had sauntered a few paces forwards himself to stand close beside Jack, and he spoke at full volume. 'Left this morning, didn't he, though where he's gone I couldn't say.'

'Jesus.' Gripping his temples more tightly, Jack let his eyes open a fraction and squinted at Fergal. 'You bloody old—'

'None of that now,' Fergal warned. 'Not in front of my sister.'

Jack turned his head a fraction, wincing at the movement, till he saw me too. 'Eva. Good morrow.'

As I nodded in reply I saw a flicker of remembrance cross his face. He said, 'Do you know, I had the most unlikely dream of you last night…'

I'd been dreading this, but Fergal had apparently been waiting for it. 'Did you, now? And will I have to mind you to recall your manners?'

'No, it was nothing improper.' Jack made the mistake of forgetting his hangover and the small shake of his head made him wince again. 'She was speaking.'

The Irishman shot him down there on the spot with one dry look. 'Oh, ay? In what language?'

'In English, of course. She was speaking to Daniel.'

'How hard were you hit on the head, then?' asked Fergal. 'Or was it the rum?'

'It seemed real.'

'Ay, I'm sure that it did.' Fergal's tone was indulgent. 'And I'm all the time seeing little wee men when I've drunk too much whiskey, myself.' He handed the wet sack to Jack and the younger man blanched at the smell.

'What,' he asked in a weak voice, 'is that?'

''Tis your dinner,' was Fergal's reply. 'Or it will be, when

Eva and I are done gutting it. Take it on into the house for me, will you?'

Jack turned whiter, if that could be possible, and the bruising on his face stood out sickly. 'Take it yourself, you great bastard. I'm going back up to my bed.' He threw down the bag at his tormentor's feet and with one final glare of reproach turned and headed back into the house.

Fergal grinned as I looked at him.

'What?' he asked. 'Would you deny me entertainment?' Hoisting the heavy wet sack full of eel he followed after Jack and asked me, 'Bring the axe if you can manage it.'

Which sounded to my ears more like a challenge than a mere request, and with a smile I went back to the stump to fetch the axe. For a short-handled tool it was heavier than I'd expected. It took me a moment to manage a comfortable grip on the handle, and by the time I turned and started back across the yard both Jack and Fergal were already in the house.

And then I heard the rider, coming down the hill.

I couldn't see the road from where I stood, but I could tell there was no cart this time, only a single rider, turning now to come around the house at such a leisured pace I knew it must be Daniel, and I stopped there in the stable yard and quelled the nervous flutter in my stomach as I turned my head expectantly to welcome him.

The dark bay horse stepped round the corner with a certain arrogance, well suited to the black-garbed man who rode him. I was unsure which of us was more surprised to see the other, but my fingers tightened round the handle of the axe instinctively, an action that did not escape his notice.

With a smile that bordered on a sneer he brought the horse between the house and me, and reined it to a halt. 'Mistress O'Cleary,' said the constable. 'Good morrow.'

I nodded and lowered my eyes, a false show of respect, before lifting my chin again so I could meet his gaze squarely and show him I wasn't afraid. My acting skills weren't in a league with Katrina's, I knew, but I must have pulled it off with some success because his eyebrows lifted slightly in response.

His dark gaze slid down to the axe in my hand and returned to my face, and he murmured, 'Well, well. A show of spirit, is it? Very inadvisable.' He briefly glanced towards the house, then leaning forwards in his saddle told me confidentially, 'In fact, I should be careful altogether were I in your place, lest it occur to me to use a different bait to draw your lover out. A more… attractive bait, perhaps, than I have used before?'

He slowly looked me up and down. I felt that look as though he'd put his hands upon my body, and I had to steel myself to stand there while he did it and not move.

The back door banged, and Fergal's voice called, 'Eva!'

Still I couldn't move. My legs seemed weighted to the ground.

'Eva!' Fergal's voice was firmer. 'Come to me.'

I found a little of my courage then, and with a death grip on the handle of the axe, I forced myself to move out of the shadow of the tall bay horse and step around so I could cross the stable yard to Fergal. I walked carefully and did not run, aware that Creed was watching.

More than watching—he was following, his horse's steps deliberate.

Fergal asked him, 'Have you business here?'

The constable shrugged the question aside. 'Your sister,' he told Fergal, 'wants to have a care when carrying that axe. I might mistake it for a weapon.'

'Would you, now?' The words held open insolence.

As I reached Fergal's side he held out one hand for the axe

and I gave it to him gratefully. He turned it in his fist to take a firmer grip and said to Creed, ''Tis best, then, that I carry it myself, so you'll have no mistake.'

The threat was boldly made, even for Fergal, and I held my breath beside him as the two men glared at one another. And then Fergal glanced at me and told me, 'Eva, get inside.'

Surely, I thought, he wasn't about to take on the constable? Openly fighting a man of the law wasn't something a man could just do without paying a price, and though Fergal was fierce I would never have thought him so reckless.

I hesitated, showing my uncertainty, and with impatience in his eyes he turned his head again and said more forcefully, 'You're looking pale. You need to go on in the house. Now.'

He was looking pale himself. Or rather, grey.

And then I understood.

I felt the change beginning, saw the landscape start to waver and reform, and in a kind of frozen limbo I watched Creed's head start to turn, as well, towards me.

And then suddenly the rhythm of hard hoofbeats sounded farther up the hill, and Fergal said, 'Here's Danny coming now,' and Creed, distracted, turned the other way to look towards the road.

I did run then.

I ran the few steps to the back door of the house and swung myself inside the darkened corridor in panic as the walls around me melted into fading, shifting shadows and dissolved as though they'd scattered on a breath of wind.

Time blinked. And I was walking down the shaded road outside Trelowarth House, still in the lovely flowered dress whose thin and fraying hem now brushed the gravel of the drive where I stopped, my legs now trembling much too violently to carry me.

The small dog Samson bounded with his usual exuberance around the corner of the house, tail wagging, but a few feet off he paused and laid his ears back slightly.

'It's all right,' I reassured him as I crouched and held my fingers out towards him. They were shaking, and I couldn't make them stop, just as I couldn't stop the coldness that had started creeping through my body, settling in my bones. I drew a breath and once again, but this time for myself and not the dog, I whispered, 'It's all right.'

CHAPTER 26

T HE ROOM BESIDE MY own was bright with midday
sunshine, but I still felt cold. I'd started to think I might
never feel warm again. Each time I started relaxing, the
thought of how close I had come to disaster this morning
would set off a new round of shivers.

A burst of hard wind from the sea set the windowpanes
rattling as I moved farther in, stirring dust from the floorboards with each careful step. No one knew I was in here.
The door to the passage was closed; I'd come through the
connecting door from my own bedroom, with Ann Butler's
flowered gown bunched in my arms.

This was the second of her gowns that I had taken
from the time where it belonged, and it seemed right
somehow to bring it here to hide, inside this room that had
been hers.

Against the far wall, in the space below the attic stairs,
a sloping built-in cupboard held the out-of-season clothes
that no one needed till the winter. Shoving the mass of
woven sleeves and woolly things aside, I tugged a hanger
free and slipped the flowered gown onto it carefully, then
slid the hanger back in place behind the other clothing,
where the faded blue gown and the banyan hung already,
quietly concealed.

My fingers lightly brushed the silk of Daniel's banyan,

and I closed my eyes. I felt his presence here more strongly than I had before, so strongly that it almost seemed that if I were to close my eyes and wish with all my heart, then maybe... maybe...

'So you're back.' Claire's voice, approving. Coming through the open doorway from my bedroom she asked, 'Did you have a nice walk?'

I closed the cupboard door as nonchalantly as I could and turned, my eardrums buzzing from the sudden surge of guilty blood pressure. I gave a nod and told Claire, 'Yes, I went up to the church.' It seemed an age ago to me. I cleared my throat and added, 'Mr. Teague was there. He hasn't changed.'

Claire smiled. 'He never will, you know. I've no doubt when he finally passes over he'll keep walking through that churchyard every day in spirit, keeping things in order. Was he pleased to see you? I expect he was. He likes a bit of company, does Mr. Teague.' Her keen glance swept the little room. 'God, look at all this dust. I must have words with Mark and Susan's cleaner when she comes. I'm sure that cupboard wants a clearing out as well.'

I forced a shrug. 'You're better off to leave that till the winter, aren't you? When you take the coats out and put all the summer things away.'

'Well, I suppose.' She turned her gaze on me instead. 'I don't know that I've ever seen you with your hair up, Eva. What a lovely way to do it.'

I was taken by surprise. I had forgotten. In my hurry to get safely back inside the house before somebody saw me and to change into my proper clothes, I'd overlooked my hair. Reaching up to make certain, I fingered a hairpin and said, 'It's a little bit fussy...'

'No, leave it up. You'll want to look your best for lunch.' She smiled. 'You have a visitor.'

❧

Following Claire through the door to the kitchen I heard a knife's blade striking on the cutting board and thought at first, *Oh, Fergal's cooking something,* and for that brief moment following, while my mind adjusted to the modern room instead, I felt a bit off-balance. Out of step.

Mark was sitting at the table writing idly in a notebook while Susan, standing near the sink, chopped vegetables for one of her trademark huge salads. Her attention, though, appeared to be on Oliver, who lounged against the worktop not too far from her, still in his biking shorts and fitted shirt that showed the muscles of his arms and chest in perfect definition. The wind had dried his hair so that only the bits near his temples were still slightly damp from the effort of cycling the hilly road back from St Non's.

He grinned as I came in. 'I'm back.'

'Like a bad penny,' Claire said with affection, giving him a once-over. 'Does your mother know you're dressed like that?'

'My mother bought the outfit,' he returned, his wit as quick as ever, but Susan didn't let him get away with it.

She smiled her teasing smile and asked, 'No, really. Are you on the pull or something? Trying to look all manly and athletic?'

Mark, from his seat at the table, dryly commented that wearing Lycra shorts was not the best way to look manly.

'That, dear brother,' Susan told him, 'is a matter of opinion.'

Their brief exchange of banter had been all the time I'd needed to shake off my momentary sense of being in the wrong place, at the wrong time. In Oliver's defence I said, 'He's cycled over to St Non's and back this morning.'

Mark glanced up at his friend and asked, 'Crisis with one of the cottages, was it?'

'Burst pipe,' said Oliver. 'Oh, and it *was* Susan's plumber,' he told me.

She looked at him, reddening slightly. '*My* plumber?'

'Paul, from Andrews and Son. Had the pipe fixed in no time,' said Oliver. 'So I thought I'd just drop round on my way back—'

'Conveniently at lunchtime.' Claire met the full charm of his boyish smile with motherly indulgence. She asked Susan, 'I suppose we can feed him?'

Susan thought it possible.

Oliver tried to look indignant. 'I *am* answering a summons, as it happens.'

Claire glanced at me. 'Oh yes?'

'I'm here to see Mark's knife.'

Mark raised his head. 'My what?'

'Felicity said you had some old knife...'

'Oh.' The fog cleared. 'That one. Hang on, I'll get it.'

He rose and left us for a moment while Claire counted out the cutlery for five of us and started setting places at the table. 'Oliver, what will you drink?'

'Water, please.'

I heard Fergal's voice speaking again in my mind. *Me now, I would rather meet my thirst with ale and cider, same as everyone.* It faded again, but when Claire set my own glass in front of me I was half-tempted to ask her for cider.

I didn't, of course. But it seemed so much harder this time to fit back in the slot I belonged in. Especially here in the kitchen, where I spent so much of my time in the past, I found things didn't feel right. I missed seeing Fergal's black scowl and quick smile, and Jack rocking his chair on two legs with his back to the wall and his eyes full of mischief, and Daniel… I really missed Daniel.

'Your hair looks amazing like that,' Susan said to me, mixing her salad. 'You ought to put it up more often.'

'Thanks.'

Oliver confessed he hadn't noticed. 'You didn't have it up this morning, did you, at the church?'

'No. I…' Lifting one hand, I self-consciously pushed in a hairpin more firmly. 'I felt like a change.'

Susan teased us both, 'Are you two having early morning trysts now in the church hay?'

'Right,' said Oliver. 'With Mr. Teague about? Not likely. No, your PR wizard here was scouting out the final resting places of Trelowarth's famous smuggling Butler brothers.'

Mark, returning with his treasure box in hand, said, 'Them again?'

Susan said, 'Well, it's color that we're after, Mark, and smugglers do provide it. That's what brings the tourists in.'

Mark shrugged and set the box down and we all leaned in to take a look at his assorted treasures.

Oliver was taken with the musket balls, although he made a small correction. 'If you found these in the cave, I'd think it much more likely that they came from a pistol than a musket. I can't imagine someone having room to fire a musket in that space, they'd use a pistol at close range.'

I looked at the seven small metal balls lying so deadly and still on his palm.

'Can't you tell from the size of them what sort of gun they were fired from?' I asked.

'Well, not really. Both muskets and pistols were smooth-bored, they didn't leave marks to identify, and because of how they worked, the balls and shot were smaller than the barrel of the gun. You had to leave a bit of room to wrap a bit of paper round them before loading. Standard navy issue muskets used a larger ball, but blunderbusses and some other muskets could use smaller shot, like these.' He stirred the balls round with his finger. 'But at a guess, I'd still say these came from a pistol, just because of where you found them.'

I was thinking of the pistol I'd seen Daniel tuck inside his belt last night when he'd gone down to keep an eye on Jack, down at the Spaniard. Just last night...

My eyes closed briefly on the memory as I tried to focus on what Oliver was telling us.

'I've got a matchlock pistol down at the museum that takes shot about this size.'

'A matchlock pistol?' Susan asked. 'What, do you use a match to fire it?'

'Not a match as we would think of it. A match in those days was a sort of... well, a sort of...'

'Fuse,' I said.

'Exactly.' Oliver's glance praised my research. 'A slow-burning fuse, that's right. You have been swotting up, haven't you?'

Mark took the dagger with care from the box. 'Right then, Einstein, how old would this be?'

'Wow,' said Oliver, rolling the metal balls back where they'd come from and taking the dagger with reverence. 'That's really beautiful.'

Only a man who loved history, I thought, could find beauty in something so ruined by time. He turned it so the sunlight from the window caught the small bit of the handle that remained. 'That's shell, I think.'

Score one for Oliver. I waited, frankly curious to see how close he'd come in his assessment to the truth.

He said, 'Now *this* could be a smuggler's knife.'

'Why's that?' Mark asked.

'Well, someone who spent time at sea. They all had knives this size, a multipurpose gadget, really, good for cutting rope or cutting food or eating with. You wouldn't be without one on a ship. But this,' he turned it to the light again, 'is really lovely workmanship. You see here, if I hold it just like this,' he said, and palmed the handle, 'you would barely see the blade. Whoever made this knew what he was doing.' Looking at it closely he considered Mark's first question. 'How old is it? Hard to say with this corrosion, but I'd hazard Restoration era maybe, from its shape. The 1660s, 1670s, somewhere in there.'

He'd impressed Mark. 'That's pretty precise.'

'Yes, well. I have a thing for knives, actually. Care to sell this one?' He knew what Mark's answer would be, I could tell from the smile in his eyes.

'Not much point,' Mark said, taking the knife back and tucking it safe in the box with the rest of his treasures. 'There wouldn't be much value to it, not in that condition.'

If Oliver knew what the dagger's true value was, he didn't bother to share it. Instead he gave up with a shrug that made Claire give a cluck of her tongue and come over to study a tear in his sleeve.

'You've a bad scratch under there,' she told him. 'Let me get something for it.'

'No, I'm fine,' he reassured her. 'It was just that blasted tree. You know, the one beside the greenhouse.'

'Susan's hawthorn tree.' I pulled my mind deliber-ately away from Daniel's dagger and my speculations, all unpleasant, as to how it might have ended up there in the cave below the Cripplehorn. 'She's just had all the shrubs around it cleared away.'

'Well, thanks for that,' he said to Susan, who replied, 'It's Cornish culture, idiot. We're making it a cloutie tree, just like the one at St Non's well. It's great for tourists—let them tie a little strip of fabric on a branch and make a wish, like people did back in the old days. For luck.'

'Ah.' Oliver rubbed his sore shoulder. 'You're off to a grand start then.'

As he helped himself to salad, something made me think to ask him, 'Oliver?'

'Yes?'

'Have you ever heard tell of a tree called the Trelowarth Oak? A big old oak tree that once grew at that really sharp bend in the road?'

'The Trelowarth Oak? Sure.' With a wicked grin he said, 'I actually *do* have an etching of that one if you ever want to come look at it. Up in my sitting room.'

I let that pass. 'What happened to the tree itself?'

He speared his salad. 'Methodists.'

'I'm sorry?'

'Well, the local people thought the tree was magical or something, and the Methodist minister wasn't having any of it, so he had the tree chopped down.'

'When was this?'

'The 1800s, sometime. I can look it up for you.'

Across the table Susan shook her head and said, 'What silliness. They cut the whole tree down?'

'They did. And burnt the stump and dug that out as well.'

But not the roots, I nearly said. They couldn't have destroyed the roots.

The roots that, in the Celtic legends, bound two worlds together, so the tree became a doorway...

The sound of far-off laughter caught my ear—a man's laugh—and I raised my head to look, and in that shadowed instant I could see the room begin dissolving into something else, and saw a shape like Fergal's cross to where the open hearth had been... but then I blinked and everything was back the way it had been.

'You all right?' Beside me Oliver was frowning faintly with concern. 'Got a headache or something?'

'Or something.' I picked up my own fork and gave a tight smile. 'But I'm sure it will pass.'

Another shadow swept across the window as the figure of a man went by, his footsteps falling hard along the path to the back door. A man dressed all in black.

CHAPTER 27

A COLD HAND CLENCHED my chest and made it difficult to breathe until I reassured myself that I was firmly in the present, with my friends still sitting round me, and the constable had not in fact crossed into my own time. The man who'd passed by was a stranger to me, taller than the constable and broader through the shoulders.

Oliver had seen him too, and as the first knock sounded at the back door he pushed back his chair and rose. 'I'll get it.'

From the brief exchange of voices in the corridor I gathered both men knew each other, but when Oliver came through into the kitchen he looked straight at Susan first then stepped aside. The man who followed him was ruggedly attractive in a way that made it difficult to judge his age. The only thing I could have said with certainty was that he wasn't young—his well-cut auburn hair had turned to silver at his temples and his jawline had begun to lose the chiseled definition that it would have had when he was in his thirties.

He seemed to hesitate a moment, like the rest of them. Until Claire broke the tension with a smile of welcome. 'Nigel. Good to see you.'

'Claire. Mark.' He greeted them both, gave a brief nod at me, and looked over my head. 'Susan.'

Susan didn't answer him, and when I saw her face and saw the way that she was looking at him, and the way that

Mark and Claire and Oliver were watching *her*, I finally figured out who this must be: the man she'd been with up in Bristol. Her ex-boyfriend.

Nigel's gaze stayed fixed on Susan till she found her voice.

'Hello, Nigel. What brings you to Cornwall?'

'I'm celebrating actually.' His smile was lopsided, disarming, and I watched as she responded to it with the instant understanding of someone who'd shared a longtime intimacy with this man and knew his moods and his expressions.

With a slowly spreading smile herself she guessed, 'You got the promotion.'

'I did.'

'Well, that's wonderful. Really it is. You deserve it.'

He said, 'It means moving to London, of course. Thought I'd take a run up at the weekend and start looking round for a flat. I was hoping,' he added, 'that I might persuade you to come.'

She had to steel herself. I saw her do it, saw the silent effort that it cost her to resist him as she said, 'Look, we've been through all this. And anyway, you don't need me to help you choose a flat.'

'Don't I?'

'Nigel,' Susan began, but he wouldn't be put off.

'It comes to this,' he said. 'I love you. And I'm miserable without you.'

'Nigel,' Susan tried again.

'Please, hear me out. I know you think we haven't got a future, but I think you're wrong. I want to prove it to you if you'll let me.'

Then in front of us, as though we had all disappeared and he and Susan were the only people in the room, he took a little velvet-covered ring box from his pocket.

'Nigel.' Susan's voice had lost its force and faded to a level that was just above a whisper. She looked shaken by emotion as he crossed the room towards her.

'Susan Hallett.' Like the hero in a fairy tale, he got down on one knee and pried the lid up on the ring box as he asked her, 'Will you marry me?'

∽◦∾

'It's her decision.' Mark reached a gloved hand among the thorned branches and with his shears snipped off an unwanted shoot that had sprung from the roots of a red-petaled rose. 'No one else's.'

Two hours had passed now since Nigel had turned up and made his proposal, and Susan and he had gone off for a drive to discuss things. Like Mark, I was filling the afternoon hours with work while we waited for them to come back, though I realized my efforts to photograph some of the lovely old roses now coming into bloom here in the Quiet Garden might all be for nothing if it turned out Susan answered yes and moved away to London.

'She couldn't run her tearoom then,' I said, 'and she's put so much work into it.'

Mark shrugged and let the shoot fall with the other ones discarded at his feet. 'It wouldn't be the first time a project here had been abandoned. Dad did everything in stops and starts. That's why we have a glasshouse,' he reminded me, 'and why it's sitting empty.'

I'd forgotten about Uncle George's unsuccessful foray into rose breeding. 'Well, at least he tried,' I said in his defence. 'And now you have the greenhouse.'

'So we do. And that, as well,' he added, with a nod down at the sunburst colored rose beside the one that he was tending. 'My dad's one and only hybrid.'

'Really?' Lifting my camera, I snapped off a photograph. 'What is its name? And if you tell me something Latin, Mark,' I warned as he prepared to speak, 'I swear I'll have to hit you.'

'It doesn't have a Latin name. Or any name, officially.'

'Why not?'

'Dad never gave it one. It was still being field-tested when he died.' He looked at me a moment and decided, 'I suppose that we could name it if you like. It only takes a bit of paperwork.'

'What would you call it?'

'You choose.'

I touched a leaf with gentle fingers. 'You can name them after people, can't you, roses?'

He could see it coming. 'Eva.'

'Can't you?'

'Yes.'

I raised the camera for a second time to take another picture of the fragile-looking rose that held the colors of the setting sun. 'Let's name it for Katrina then.'

I heard his silent argument and answered it.

'It's not the same,' I said, 'as using her name for publicity. You know it's not. She loved this place, she loved these gardens, and it's just a way of seeing she's remembered.'

Mark's eyes told me just how likely he considered it she'd ever be forgotten, but he thought it over. 'Right then,' he said finally. 'The Katrina Ward it is.'

The garden walls were built to block the wind and yet a dancing breeze brushed past my cheek as though Katrina were announcing her approval.

I'd been feeling her around me very strongly all this afternoon, as though she felt I needed my big sister. And I did. Above all, I needed to borrow a bit of her courage.

I still felt off-balance because of my run-in with Constable Creed in the stable yard only this morning. I knew I might not be so lucky the next time we met. Even if I managed not to disappear in front of him, he might make good his threat and come at me to get to Daniel. Odds were, if I left Trelowarth I'd remove that risk.

And yet, I'd risk another kind of pain by leaving.

If I'd wanted proof of that, I'd had it when I'd looked at Daniel last night, and he'd looked at me, and suddenly my choices had seemed more confused than ever.

Susan was facing that sort of a choice now, I thought. I'd seen the conflict in her face and heard it in her voice, and knew her heart was being pulled in two directions. And it occurred to me that there was someone else here who had faced that same choice long before myself or Susan, so I went off now in search of her advice.

I knew where I'd find Claire. I heard the lovely mellow tones of the piano long before I stepped inside the house and knew that she was in the big front room. I went in quietly. I'd always loved to watch Claire play. The music took her so completely, shaped her mood and flowed from her so easily it seemed to be her own invention, her own voice. I recognized the peaceful, almost wistful notes of Chopin, and they seemed to be so perfectly in tune with my own feelings at the moment that I didn't interrupt. Instead I focused my attention on the bookshelves, searching out with idle fingertips the worn spines of the old books that my mother had once given Uncle George.

I paused at a thick book whose title intrigued me, and was lifting it down when Claire finished her prelude, the final note drifting to silence.

I told her, 'Don't stop, that was lovely.'

'I wasn't sure I would remember it all,' she confessed with

a faint smile. 'I haven't played that one in years. Not since I was your age, in fact.'

'And when was that?' I teased her. 'Yesterday?'

Her smile grew warm at my flattery. 'Seems like it sometimes.' She looked to the window. 'Is Susan not back yet?'

'Not yet, no.'

'Oh well. One can't rush a decision like that.'

I decided that made a good opening for what I'd wanted to ask her. 'Aunt Claire?'

'Yes, darling?'

'When you met Uncle George... I mean, it must have been a change for *you* to move here. And not only geographically. You were changing your whole way of life, taking on Mark and Susan and everything. How did you... that is, when someone is making that big a decision, how...?'

'How do you know it's the right one to make?' She was watching me kindly. 'Are you asking on Susan's behalf or your own?'

Before I could answer, a door somewhere opened and closed and the sure tread of footsteps approached from the back of the hall, and we turned to the doorway as Oliver entered the front room.

On cue, from the small knowing smile on Claire's face. She greeted him with, 'Didn't we get rid of you once today?'

He'd changed his clothes at least, although the jeans and T-shirt he now wore weren't that much less revealing than the biking shorts. 'I've just had a delivery that I thought might interest Eva,' he explained, and held a small wrapped packet up to show us. 'Mark said I should come right in.' He looked around the room. 'Is Susan not back yet?'

Claire answered as I had done, 'Not yet, no.'

Oliver lifted an eyebrow. 'You don't think she'll actually

marry him, do you? I mean, he's a nice enough bloke, Nigel, but he's not right for her. I could have told her that first time I met him. They're chalk and cheese, aren't they?' He sauntered across for a look at the book I was holding. 'What's that?'

I angled the cover to show him.

He read out the title: '*The Wife's Guide for Keeping a Garden and House?*'

'Newly revised in…' I flipped to the title page, briefly consulting the date, '1692.'

'That would explain why it's falling to pieces then.'

'Only the binding. The pages are fine.'

He looked at the page I'd been reading. '"For Making a Stirabout"? What's that?'

'A stew, sort of.'

'Ah. And it doesn't concern you at all that the next item down is "A Cure Against Vomiting"?'

I cast a dry look up over my shoulder. 'It's meant to be a full instruction book for housewives. Home remedies, recipes, how to do laundry and clean things.' All useful, I thought, for a young woman setting up house at the end of the seventeenth century. Or for a woman who found herself thrust back in time to the start of the eighteenth.

Oliver said, 'If you're wanting to read something, try this instead.' And he gave me the packet.

As I took it from his hands I felt the quick touch of excitement and I knew what it must be before I'd even got the wrapper off and seen the book inside, bound in smooth leather with faded gilt letters that spelt out the title: *A Life Before the Wind*. Jack Butler's diary. 'Oh, Oliver! Wherever did you find it?'

'I have sources.'

And he must have had to pay them well. The book was

an original edition from the look of it. 'You'd really let me borrow this?'

'I wouldn't, no,' he told me, and then smiled at my reaction. 'You're to keep it. It's a gift.'

I shook my head. 'I'll buy it from you.'

'Sorry, no. A gift's a gift,' he said. 'You're stuck with it.'

I would have argued further if I hadn't been distracted by the sound of tires on gravel from the drive outside. All three of us fell silent while we listened, waiting.

One car door banged shut. And then the tires rolled off again. When Susan came to join us, she was on her own.

'I've told him no.' She stood within the doorway, looking tired. 'Our lives are just too different; it would never work.' Her weariness seemed more pronounced as she glanced round the room. 'Mark's in the gardens, I expect? I'll go and hunt him down and let him know, so he'll stop worrying.'

Oliver stepped forwards, not the charmer anymore but the dependable old friend who could be leaned on in a crisis. 'You don't need to hunt him down. I know exactly where he is. Come on, I'll take you to him.'

When they'd gone, I looked at Claire and noticed her expression, and I said, 'You're not surprised.'

'No. Nigel wasn't the right man for her.'

'Because the gap between them was too great?'

She shook her head. 'Because it wasn't meant to be.' Her eyes were wise. 'Every relationship has its own obstacles, darling. And as you said, your Uncle George and I had our share of them. As would you, if you were to meet someone here.' From her smile I assumed she meant Oliver. 'There would be practical choices you'd have to make. Where you'd live, that sort of thing. Where you'd work. And there'd be differences in lifestyle that might take some getting used to. It's one thing to spend a summer at Trelowarth or let a cottage for a while, and quite another to live all year in Polgelly,' she said knowingly. 'The social structure here is... well, you'd find it rather different from America, I'm sure. It's never easy, changing how you live.'

I gave a nod of understanding, looking down.

'But,' Claire continued, 'all of that amounts to nothing if you love him.'

As I raised my head, she met me with a smile.

'Believe me, Eva dear, if *I* was able to adapt, there's hope for anyone.'

CHAPTER 28

I HEARD THE VOICES speaking low to one another from the wall behind my bed.

'You'll need my help, I'm thinking.'

'I've enough men aboard the *Sally*.' Daniel's voice.

I drifted in that drowsy plane between sleep and full consciousness, not wanting to wake up and lose the moment.

Daniel said, 'I cannot take you.'

'So then take Jack.'

'And waste the whole night arguing which one of us will take the helm? I thank you, no. Nor can I send Jack in my place,' he went on, as though cutting off an argument, 'because the message clearly states it must be me.'

A pause, then, 'For one woman,' Fergal said, 'she can create uncommon difficulties.'

'I rather think you put it in her nature when you made her an O'Cleary.'

They were talking about *me*, I realized. And their voices were very distinct, not as muffled as they'd been before with the distance of time in between us.

Rising to awareness like a diver pushing upwards from the depths, I brushed aside the clinging fog of sleep and forced my heavy eyelids open.

It was morning, fully light, and I was lying on the linens of the big four-poster tester bed, and though the doorway to the corridor was closed, the one connecting Daniel's room to mine was open. Fergal stood square in it with his back to me.

I blinked for a moment, adjusting, and tried to remember. I'd fallen asleep in my own bed last night. I'd been reading. I'd started Jack's memoir, but after ten pages or so of his exploits I'd started to drift, and then…

'I pledged her my protection,' Daniel said, and from his voice I judged that he was standing just the other side of Fergal, in his room. 'I'll not feel easy in my mind unless I know that you are here to guard her if she should return.'

Which would have been my cue to say something had not another male voice spoken up before I had the chance to. From the next room, Jack's voice asked, 'Return from where?'

I hadn't heard his footsteps in the corridor or heard the door of Daniel's room swing open, but from Fergal's quick reaction I could only guess that Jack had somehow caught them by surprise.

'I was about to say,' said Daniel quietly, 'should she return to health.'

In my doorway Fergal shifted so he blocked the view more solidly, his shoulder all but welded to the door frame.

Jack used a phrase I'd never heard, but it must have been rude because his brother told him, 'Mind your tongue. We have a woman in the house.'

'Do we now?' The floorboards creaked as Jack stepped forwards, and I looked round frantically to find a blanket, anything to cover my modern pajamas, as he went on, 'These past days you have sent me twice on errands to do nothing of importance, and in all that time I've neither glimpsed nor heard your sister, Fergal. And yet both of you keep telling me she's here and only ill.'

'And what would either of us have to gain by saying so were it not true?' asked Daniel.

Jack came closer still. 'You see, I cannot tell you, and that troubles me. It troubles me as much as does the memory of her voice.'

The only blanket I could see lay folded out of reach across the clothespress, so instead I scrambled underneath the sheets and pulled them to my chin. The sound, though slight, caught Fergal's ear. He turned to look towards the bed as Jack asked, 'How is she this morning, then?'

My gaze stayed locked with Fergal's as I marveled once again at his ability to show no outward sign of his reactions when he wanted to conceal what he was thinking. His expression hadn't changed, though he did wait a moment before telling Jack, 'She is asleep.'

I took the hint and closed my eyes.

'She is a quiet sleeper,' Jack remarked.

'See for yourself then, if you'll not believe us.' Fergal must have stepped aside because the floorboards creaked much closer to the bed, and in the pause that followed I tried hard to concentrate on breathing lightly, evenly.

After what seemed an eternity Jack broke the silence and whispered contritely, 'I'm sorry, I—'

'Call me a liar again,' Fergal said, 'and you'll wish that you hadn't. Now out with you. Both of you. Give her some peace.'

I felt someone's fingertips trace lightly over my cheek, maybe brushing a stray bit of hair aside, and I knew whose touch it was even before Fergal said, 'Danny, both of you. Out.'

Daniel said, close above me, 'I think she looks better this morning.'

'She does, ay,' said Fergal. 'I'd not be surprised to see her up and about by the afternoon. But now she needs her rest so *out*.'

He left no room for argument, not with that tone.

The light touch left my face and I heard both the brothers retreat through the next room and, trading muffled arguments, start down the stairs. Fergal crossed to shut the connecting door firmly behind them.

I opened my eyes as he turned round to face me, his own dark eyes crinkling with laughter. 'I have to confess,' he said, low, 'I'm beginning to think that you may be a witch after all, for you do have the devil's own luck with your timing.'

Returning his smile, I felt suddenly, heart-expandingly happy in a way I hadn't felt for years, the way I'd felt when I'd awakened on those childhood summer mornings at Trelowarth with Katrina in the bed beside me and a day of new adventures spreading bright before us.

This felt so exactly like that, in fact, that for an instant I had to sit still while I took it all in, the warm familiar blend of sounds and smells and half-remembered sights that strummed a chord within me deep as instinct; wrapped me comfortingly in the certain knowledge I was *home*.

Fergal was saying, 'And more luck for you that I haven't yet eaten your breakfast, it's still on the tray.'

He had brought me a thick slice of bread spread with cheese, and a cup of cool ale. Fetching the tray from the desk in the corner, he set it on the bed and stood, arms folded, while I sat upright to eat.

'You did that very neatly,' was his comment. 'How the devil did you manage it?'

Daniel and Jack were downstairs now. I heard the occasional tramp of a boot or the swing of a door underneath us and knew it would be safe to talk if I kept my voice quiet, like Fergal's. 'I'm sorry?'

'Turning up like that, in the bed.'

'I don't know,' I said honestly. 'I just woke up, that's all.'

'This is your room in your own time, then?' Seeing my nod, he gave one of his own, as though he'd suddenly made sense of why Daniel had given me this room to sleep in.

Curious, I asked, 'How long have I been gone this time?'

'Eight bleeding days.'

'And Daniel has to go somewhere?'

'He does. And he can tell you all about that for himself, I'm thinking, once you're up and dressed.' At which he stopped, as we both noticed something obvious.

Tugging at my T-shirt sleeve, I said, 'I'm sorry, I—'

'You'll need the wardrobe of a queen if this keeps up,' he told me dryly. Leaving me a moment on my own he went next door to Daniel's room and came back in through the connecting door weighed down by the most beautiful gown I'd yet seen, of a quiet green color that shifted when catching the light like the leaves of the trees shaded deep in the woods.

I touched the fabric as he laid it on the bed beside me. And I couldn't. I just couldn't. 'Fergal, I can't wear this.'

'Why not?'

'I've lost two gowns so far. Ann's gowns. It's just not right. And if I lose another—'

Fergal cut me off. 'This was not Ann's.'

I stopped. My hand fell still against the fabric as I looked at him.

'Last week,' he said, 'Danny took the *Sally* down to Plymouth on some business. He came back with this.' He flipped one sleeve so it lay straight across the bodice. 'There are slippers to go with it.'

'For me?'

'Well, fair to say it wasn't meant for me.' Straight-faced, he said, 'The color is my favorite, but the cut would never do me justice.' Digging briefly in a pocket he produced a handful of hairpins. 'You'll need these as well, will you not?'

'Thanks.'

I would have said more but a sudden rise of voices underneath us made him lift a warning finger to his lips, until the hard slam of the front door and the crunch of footsteps outside on the path made him relax. Crossing to the window, Fergal watched whoever had just left stride off towards the road.

'That's Jack away to lick his wounds,' he said with satisfaction. 'You can come down when you're ready, then, for Danny will I'm sure have things to say to you.'

And taking up my finished tray he left me on my own to dress.

The gown was of a different design than the others. More modern, I supposed. Just as the fashions I was used to changed each year, so too the fashions of this time must have evolved as well according to the current style. The sleeves were still close-fitted to the elbow and turned back above the wrists to show the ruffles underneath, but the bodice had a different shape and cut, and fastened at the side instead of at the front, which made it difficult to manage on my own.

I'd nearly reached the point of giving up when Daniel's voice behind me asked, 'Do you need help?'

I hadn't heard him coming up the stairs. I hadn't even heard the door between our two rooms open, but the thing that marked a smuggler, I supposed, was his ability to move round without drawing much attention to himself.

He'd changed his own clothes slightly from the last time I had seen him. The leg-hugging breeches tucked into his boots weren't the brown ones he usually wore but a dark navy blue, and the full white shirt left open at his throat was new as well, and of a finer-looking linen than the ones that I remembered. But his smile was just the same.

I was foolishly pleased to see him, but after the moment we'd shared in this room after lighting the fire I also felt a new degree of nervousness.

I looked away, still fumbling with the fastening. 'It's a little bit difficult.'

Taking that as a yes, he left the doorway and came to help. His fingers gently moved my own aside and did the task with expert ease.

'It suits you well, this gown,' he said. 'I did not know for certain it would fit.'

I stood quite still beneath his touch and thanked him. 'It was very thoughtful of you.'

'And expensive. This one garment cost me a full case of brandy,' he said, 'and a dance with the seamstress's daughter.'

The lightness of his tone relaxed me slightly. 'I hope she was pretty.'

'She danced like an ox, but I reasoned a gown that was bought for the price of a dance could not help but have happiness in it.' He'd finished. 'There,' he said, and turned me round to face inspection.

I kept my gaze hard on his shirt lacings. 'You shouldn't have gone to so much trouble, you know. Once I go back to my own time it's as good as lost, just like your wife's clothes. I can't seem to find a way to bring them back.'

He gave a shrug. 'And that is why I bought you this one.'

'So I wouldn't lose any more of hers?' I said it wryly, but he didn't take it as a joke.

'I bought the gown,' he told me very carefully, 'so that you could be done with borrowed things.' His hand still rested on my waist. 'I thought it time that you had something you could know was yours alone.'

My chin came up at that, and as my gaze met his I knew he wasn't talking anymore about the gown itself. The constable had told me once that Daniel only let me wear Ann's clothes to bring her ghost to life, and even though I'd known Creed's words were poison, there'd been part of me since then that couldn't help but wonder just who Daniel really saw when he was looking at me.

Looking at the darkness of his eyes now I saw nothing but my own reflection there and felt those doubts begin to fade.

His eyes asked a brief question, asked it and searched mine to read the reply before his one hand slid slowly under my hair to the back of my neck and he lowered his head.

The kiss began simply enough.

Just a brush of his lips on my cheek, reassuring and warm. But then one of us—I think it might have been me—moved a fraction, a turn of the head and our mouths met in earnest, but he remained a gentleman, not rushing things, not taking it for granted that I had any experience.

Until I kissed him back.

The rules changed then.

Another minute more and he was holding me with both arms, which was just as well because I would have had a lot of trouble standing upright on my own. God knows I lost all track of time and Daniel must have done as well, because Fergal had to cough twice and swear once before either of us paid him any attention.

And even then all Daniel did was draw back with his forehead still resting on mine as he angled his head to the doorway.

'Yes?'

Fergal folded his arms. 'Were you coming downstairs,

then? Or would you rather wait till Jack gets back so we can all sit down and talk this through together?'

Half-amazed I had a voice, I asked them both, 'Talk what through?'

Fergal said, 'He has to take the *Sally* out tonight, by order of His Grace the Duke of Ormonde.'

Daniel exhaled, patient. 'By request, not by his order. I am asked to do a favor for my kinsman, and no more than that.'

'Without a proper crew...'

'I will have men enough.'

'And not a one of them who's fit to raise a sword to guard your back should things go wrong.'

'You are more needed here,' said Daniel.

This, I thought, was where I had come in—the two men arguing.

As Daniel straightened from me I drew one long breath to calm my pulse because it was still racing from the kiss. I tried to think. And looking up at him I said, 'You won't let Fergal come with you because you want him to stay here at Trelowarth and look after me.'

Daniel half-smiled, not dropping his hands from my waist. 'I will only be gone a short while. And I'll be in no danger.'

'Then take me along.'

He had not seen that coming. 'What?'

'Take me along,' I repeated. 'Then Fergal can come too. You can tell your crew I'm there to do the cooking, or whatever, and I'll keep out of the way, and with both you and Fergal there I'm sure that nothing will—'

He interrupted. 'No. It is impossible. On any other voyage I'd consider it, but not on this.'

'Why not?' I stood my ground. 'You said yourself there'd be no danger.'

Trapped by his own words, he looked at Fergal who was standing in the doorway fairly daring him to answer.

He was caught, and the three of us knew it. If he admitted the dangers involved in this 'favor' he'd been asked to do, then Fergal wouldn't rest until he'd found a way to go along. And if Daniel stuck to his story that there was no danger at all, then he'd have no good reason to leave me and Fergal behind.

And frankly, the idea of being left behind with Fergal in the foul mood that I knew he'd be in if he didn't get to go with Daniel wasn't that appealing to me.

Fergal, from his doorway, said, 'It seems a fair idea, Danny, taking her along. And you can tell the crew I'm there to guard her virtue.'

Daniel exhaled harder this time, giving in. 'The crew will hardly need an explanation why you're with us. I'll not need to tell them tales.'

'And who says you'd be telling tales?' He sent a pointed glance towards the pair of us, with Daniel's hands still resting on my waist, and with a final dry look turned away.

CHAPTER 29

THE EVENING BROUGHT A soft wind and a softer light that settled on the woods, where all the lilting voices of the birds and hidden creatures had been soothed to drowsy silence. Fergal, for all the heaviness of his boots, made little sound himself as he walked on ahead of me, moving in his dark clothes like a shadow through the trees. I tried to copy his stealth, but the hem of my long green gown brushed with a rustling sound over grasses and twigs and small shrubs, at one point flushing out a rabbit who leapt suddenly across my path, a startled streak of brown.

Fergal wheeled round at the small burst of noise and then seeing what it was, relaxed and motioned me to follow on more quietly.

I did my best.

This was the first time I had been along this path—the same path I had glimpsed so long ago while walking through the Wild Wood. The path that had appeared and disappeared again and which I now knew led towards the sea. The scents of salt and spray grew ever stronger as we neared the south edge of the woods, where the dimness of the tangled branches overhead gave way to sudden light.

The path angled downwards here, sharp to the right, winding down the black rocks at the edge of the cliff—a wider and less treacherous descent than the one to the shore at the foot of the Cripplehorn, but I still had to be cautious and watch where I put my feet. The flimsy slippers made my steps less confident, and the swing of the heavy gown tested my balance so that I was grateful for Fergal's strong steadying hand as he helped me along.

I was vaguely aware of tall masts and the shape of a ship, but it wasn't till we'd nearly reached the bottom of the path and I could raise my head and take a proper look that I first really saw the *Sally* riding at anchor, not far out from shore.

I'd only ever seen her that one time before, when Jack set off for Brittany, and then I had been watching from the hillside at Trelowarth and I hadn't seen her clearly, just her graceful lines retreating as she'd headed out to sea.

Now, from closer up, I saw that she was not a very large ship, maybe fifty feet or so from bow to stern, with four square gun ports set along her curved side high above the water level and two soaring masts thick-laced with rigging and collapsed sails that flapped hopefully at every breath of wind.

Moored in the lee of the sheltering headland, her hull painted black like the high cliffs behind her, she shone like a lady, her trim gleaming white.

'Ay, she's beautiful,' Fergal agreed when I said so myself. 'Built at Deptford, she was, and there's few that can equal her speed.'

I'd sailed a bit with friends in California so I knew my starboard from my port, but I didn't know much about ships of this age. Didn't know what the names of the sails were or how to tell one class of ship from another, and yet from simply standing here and looking at the *Sally* I could tell exactly why both Jack and Daniel were so keen to have her solely for themselves. She was too lovely to be shared.

Fergal gave a wave, and though I hadn't seen a man on

deck before, I saw one now who waved in answer. And another man appeared. And then another.

I stood on the pebbled shore watching them lower a boat that one man rowed across to us. Fergal lifted me over the wet of the waves at the shoreline and settled me on the hard seat without giving any explanation to the other man of who I was or what I might be doing there. The fact that I was there with Fergal seemed to be enough to mark me out of bounds.

Still, when the dinghy scraped hulls with the *Sally* and I was helped up to the ship's main deck, Fergal came after me, facing the men down and setting things out in plain terms. 'This is Eva, my sister. She's coming along. She's no voice of her own, but if any of you gives her trouble I'll hear of it, see?' He didn't threaten them with what he'd do if they *did* give me trouble, but I gathered that they knew him well enough to fill those blanks in for themselves.

The youngest of the men looked like a teenager, the oldest seemed to be approaching sixty, and they all had that rough look of men who ended their hard days at sea by drinking late into the night at quayside taverns. But to my relief, not one of them looked hard enough to get the best of Fergal in a fight.

That helped me feel less nervous as they scattered to their duties.

Fergal squinted skyward as though judging the position of the sun. 'There'll be two men to come yet,' he told me, 'and Danny. We might as well wait for them in comfort.'

I didn't really want to leave the deck. I'd never been on an old ship, and I liked how the canvas and rigging above me was creaking and fluttering, and how the deck itself shifted in time with the rise of the waves, and how the wind and the sinking sun felt on my uplifted face. But arguing with Fergal was a lost cause at the best of times, and all the more impossible out here because I couldn't use my voice, so I gave in and let him lead me down below.

There was a single deck down here, with a grated trap-door that I guessed would lead further down into the hold. What cargo might lie down there I could only imagine, but here on this deck, I could count eight brass cannon, their wheeled mounts fastened to the inner hull with ropes to curb the recoil when they fired, their muzzles resting at the gun ports to each side. Towards the rear of this main space, the sleeping quarters for the crew announced its purpose with its hammocks hanging off to either side, slung from the beams overhead so they ran in the same line, from bow to stern. Behind them was a separate space enclosing Fergal's galley and a table where the men could eat, and at the back of that there was a heavy door.

'The captain's cabin,' Fergal said. 'You'll sleep in here.' He didn't add the word 'alone' but then he didn't need to—I already knew he'd be keeping a watch on my door to see I wasn't bothered by the crew. Or by their captain.

I hid my smile and felt a twinge of sympathy for Daniel, especially after I'd entered his cabin and seen the comforts he'd be forced to do without.

There were windows here, for one thing—a broad row of them that ran across the squared wall of the stern, and two of them stood open on their casements to the fresh salt air, a definite relief from the close staleness of the cabin where the crew slept. Candleholders had been fitted to the walls with brackets, and a small carved desk of heavy wood stood off to one side underneath a shelf of charts and papers. Near the farther wall there swung a hammock that looked comfortable and wide and had been fitted with a pillow for the sleeper's head.

I'd never slept the whole night in a hammock. With my luck, I thought, I'd tip out on the floor and break my neck. I was crossing to inspect it when I heard the splash and pull of oars outside the open window as the boat went out again.

'That'll be somebody coming,' said Fergal. 'Wait here.'

He left me and went up, and in a while I heard the boat come back, the creak and bump of wood on wood as it drew up against the *Sally*, and the thump of booted feet that landed on the deck above me in a cheerful rise of voices, Daniel's own among them. I couldn't hear what he was saying, the heavy wood deck and the walls of the cabin effectively muffled his words, but his laugh carried easily in through the window.

And then he was coming downstairs.

Fergal came with him into the cabin. He didn't look pleased. 'William's cousin be damned. William's ill, sure enough, but that lad you've brought with you is never his cousin.'

Daniel gave a smiling nod to me and answered Fergal, 'No, I did not think he was.'

'Then why the devil did you let him come on board?'

'Because he told the story well enough when he did meet myself and Michael on the shore. He had the password right and all. It seemed a shame not to reward such effort. And,' he said, more serious, 'because we have an hour or so to wait yet for the tide, and if I'd left the lad on shore he would have run straight off to tell the one that sent him.'

'Creed.'

'I should imagine so, yes.'

'Creed,' said Fergal, 'cannot stop you sailing.'

'He can make a nuisance of himself or send another vessel in our wake to watch and follow us. For now, he thinks he has his spy on board in safety. Let us keep him thinking so.'

With all that settled, Daniel turned to me. 'How do you like my *Sally*?'

I replied the ship was lovely. 'But I have my doubts about the hammock.'

'Do you?' He considered it. 'It holds my own weight well enough, and I have seen a bed like that sleep more than one man on a crowded voyage, so you need not worry.'

Fergal said, 'She needn't, ay, considering that neither your own weight nor that of any other man will be in there tonight with her.'

His tone was dry, but Daniel matched it with the glance he gave his friend. 'It may be I should toss you back on shore as well, together with Creed's spy.'

'You go and try it.' Fergal, unconcerned, half-shrugged to stretch his shoulders. 'What's the plan, then?'

❧

Above me I could hear the steps and voices of the men. Hard footsteps tramped towards the stern, in my direction, and although I knew the angle of the ship's hull meant that nobody could see me from above, I still drew back a pace from caution. The footsteps stopped directly overhead.

'There he is,' Daniel's voice drifted down.

Other steps shuffled forwards to join him at the rail, and a younger man's voice complained, 'I can see no one.'

'Our passenger,' said Daniel, 'is a man much wanted in these parts. He does well to be careful and keep to the shadows until you can collect him.'

'Me?'

'Ay. Rowing would be William's job if he were here to do it, and you did say you had come to do his work.'

A doubtful pause. 'But I see no one there.'

'Nor will you, till you land the boat and call the password. Now away with you, and fetch him back so that we can be off. The tide has turned.'

I heard the scraping of the boat against the *Sally*'s side again, and as the rhythm of its splashing oars moved off, I heard another sound—a labored clanking, unfamiliar. It wasn't until the *Sally* began to turn slightly as though she were drifting that I realized what I'd heard had been the anchor being raised. From above came the creaking of ropes and the sound of the great sails unfurling to gather the wind.

The *Sally* gave a forward surge of joy. As her stern came round, my windows gave a clear view of Creed's spy, who'd nearly reached the beach. Even if the luckless lad had strength enough to turn his craft and row on back to catch us, he would have surely known there was no point to it. He'd never be allowed on board again now that his game had been discovered. Instead, as I watched, he drove the boat onto the shingle and leapt out, knee-deep in water and wading ashore with the wide flailing motions of somebody in a great hurry.

The last glimpse I had of him as we slipped out of the shadows of the headland, he was scrabbling up the rocky path towards the clifftop. Not an easy climb for someone wet and tired from rowing. Still, he could count himself fortunate, I thought, that he'd been sent off in the boat and not simply dumped over the *Sally's* side.

Fergal said much the same thing minutes later when, taking his role as my chaperone seriously, he came down below decks with Daniel. The two of them joined me at the windows in the stern.

Fergal told Daniel, 'You've only made him angry now. You should have cooled his temper with a swim.'

'And if he could not swim?'

A shrug. 'We would have one less fool to waste our time with.'

Daniel smiled. 'You are a hard man, Fergal, and I do fear what would happen to me should I ever fall from your good graces.'

'Then take care that you do not,' was the advice returned, although I caught the fleeting play of light in Fergal's eye that spoilt the sternness of his warning. He was leaning to the window, looking back at the retreating shore. 'He'll be running straight to Creed.'

This time the shrug was Daniel's. 'Let him go. There will be nothing Creed can do. There is no vessel in Polgelly harbor that can catch the *Sally* when she runs before the wind.'

I believed him. I could feel the pull and power of the ship's sails as we altered course a second time and set Polgelly squarely at our back.

Beside me Daniel straightened from the window, the top of his head nearly brushing the beams of the cabin. 'Are you troubled by sea travel?'

'Pardon?' I asked.

'Do you feel any sickness?'

'Oh. No, I'm all right.'

'Good. You will find the comforts greater here,' he told me, 'in the cabin, but I should think that you would find the journey more diverting from the quarterdeck.'

It was an invitation, and I willingly accepted it.

Above, the air smelled cleaner and the sunlight from the west had taken on that warmly golden glow that marked the final hours of the evening. We were headed south, and opposite the sinking sun, the purple of the coming night had started creeping up into the wide bowl of the sky above, where soon I knew the evening star would make its first appearance.

Watching the men work the sails and the ropes with experienced ease, I gave myself up to the sinuous rising and roll of the ship's deck beneath my feet, leaning at times to the will of the wind at an angle that tested my balance.

But I didn't mind. I was looking at Daniel for most of the time, because seeing him here on the *Sally* was proving a small revelation. It occurred to me that, though I'd seen him smile and even laugh before, I'd never seen him totally content until this moment. He looked the same person but... different. He looked so at home here, the voyager, eyes to the distant horizon, relaxed at the helm.

The same thing that made me so nervous, this whole thought of venturing into the unknown, seemed to cause him no bother. In fact, it appeared to be one of the forces that drove him. Like Tennyson's Ulysses, with his plans to bravely sail beyond the sunset, Daniel had the look of someone who would not be bound by lines on maps or dragons that were drawn there, but would set his own course to discover what lay at the end of it.

I watched him till the cooling night breeze chased me down below decks once again, where Fergal set me to helping him parcel out hard bread and ale to the men with a stew made of fish that he'd somehow prepared in a cauldron secured on a firebox of bricks in the galley.

The food was simply made and roughly eaten, but I gladly ate my share and then retired to my private cabin where, with Fergal stationed like a sentry in his galley just outside my door, I braved the swinging hammock. It embraced me like a lover's arms, and sent me off to sleep with dreams of ships and sails and distant shores that lay beyond my view.

CHAPTER 30

THEY WERE LOADING THE last of the boats. The sloped deck of the *Sally* gently rose and fell beneath me as I held the rail for balance. Even with the hanging mist I still could see the shore, the little cove curved round its sheltered bit of sea, green hills that echoed those we had just left, and small square houses stacked in cozy clusters up the slopes, with only the slight difference in the architecture telling me that we had crossed the narrow stretch of sea dividing Cornwall from the Continent and had arrived in Brittany.

The crew were hard at work still bringing up the *Sally*'s cargo. I tried purposely to keep my gaze averted so they wouldn't think me nosy, but I had already seen the bales of wool.

A true free trade, I thought. They swapped the raw materials that were, by British law, so hard to come by on the Continent, for finished goods that were considered luxuries to those back home in England, just as Daniel had explained to me.

He'd gone ashore himself on the first boat, and I'd assumed I would be coming on this final one with Fergal when the crew had finished loading it, but even as I smoothed my hands across my gown to tidy my appearance, Fergal strode across the deck and set me straight.

With a curt nod he said, 'I'll be away myself now. Time you got below.'

'What?'

'You'll be safer in the cabin,' he elaborated. 'Come.'

He took me there himself and quickly looked around to see that everything was as it should be while I grappled with the fact that they were leaving me behind, that I would not be going with them when they went ashore. I hadn't been expecting that.

I wasn't good at hiding how I felt. My own face must have held a mix of irritation and dismay, but if it did then Fergal chose not to react to it. He simply faced me, hands on hips, and asked me, 'Can you fire a pistol?'

'Pardon?'

Crossing to the desk he pulled the top drawer open just enough to show the pistol lying there. 'You'll find it primed and loaded. Do you know the way to fire it?'

'Likely not.'

'Then let me show you. Pay attention now,' he told me, as he took the pistol from the drawer and led me through the steps.

'Fergal...'

'Not that you'll be needing it.' His glance was reassuring. 'There will be only three men left aboard with you, and none of them will give you any trouble. I could trust them with my mother. Still,' he added, with a shrug, ''tis always best to think the worst of everyone, for that way you'll be seldom disappointed.'

'Fergal.'

'Ay?'

I knew the answer, but I had to ask him anyway. 'Can't I come with you?'

He half-turned and fixed me with that dead blank stare that meant I'd caught him off his guard, and then he made a great show of considering the question. 'Well, you *could*, were you a fishwife or a whore, but since you're neither you'll do best to keep here safely in the cabin,' he advised me in a dry tone that asked whether I had any sense at all. 'What sort of men would you be thinking that we are, to take a woman in to shore?'

'Well…'

'You watch from this window and see how many women from the village leave the safety of their homes to welcome *us*,' he said. 'More likely when they see the *Sally* drop her anchor they all scurry out of sight to guard their precious virtues.'

'Well,' I said, 'that's probably because they think it's Jack.'

Again I got the blank look, then his eyes began to crinkle at their corners and he grinned. 'Ay, like as not they do.' He handed me the pistol. 'Bolt that door now.'

When he'd gone, I set the pistol back in place within the drawer. It felt too dangerous to hold. Above my head I heard the heavy tramp of feet as those last crewmen bound for shore climbed down into the waiting boat, and when the splash of oars passed by I took a step back from the windows so that I was partly shielded by the curtains at their edge. I didn't want to be caught watching like a child left behind but that was how I felt.

Still, there wasn't any point in sitting, stewing in self-pity when there wasn't anything that I could do about it, other than find some way to amuse myself while everyone was gone.

The captain's cabin wasn't fitted out for entertainment. I could only see that single shelf of charts and papers on the wall beside the desk, with several books wedged in among them, and the books at first glance didn't hold too much appeal. One was mathematical, another was in Latin... the third appeared to be either *by* Alexander Pope or about him, since his name was printed on the spine, which meant it might not be too terrible. But when I tried to take it from the shelf, it was so tight against the others that it brought the book beside it out as well and sent it tumbling to the floor.

The unknown book fell both face down and fully open and I scooped it up as quickly as I could so that the pages wouldn't bend. I'd planned to simply close it and return it to the shelf, but when I turned it over in my hands I saw the scratchy lines of handwriting in black and blotted ink, and realized what I held was not a printed book.

It didn't seem to be a journal or a logbook either. There were no divisions for the dates and times, just paragraphs of writing.

Then a sudden thought occurred to me. I closed the book and opened it again at the beginning, to the words that I'd suspected I might find there, written in that same uneducated hand: 'Jack Butler, His Book'.

Jack was midway through his memoirs from the look of it. The memoirs that he'd find a way to publish later on in life, and which in turn would find their way to me three hundred years from now.

I hadn't had a chance to read much more than the first several pages of my copy of *A Life Before the Wind*, the book that Oliver had no doubt paid a shocking sum of money for. He might have saved himself the bother, I thought, smiling. I could read the whole thing now for free. After all, it wasn't really an invasion of Jack's privacy if all this was already published openly in my own time. And from my first quick glance at the initial page, it seemed that he had published it exactly as he'd written it—the words had not been changed.

With that decided, I put Alexander Pope back on the shelf instead and settled down with Jack's book in the gently swinging hammock.

It felt curious and strange to read the same exact words I had read two nights ago, the same account of Jack's and Daniel's upbringing, but this time as a manuscript. And this time I was able to go further on. The focus stayed on Jack, of course—he'd clearly set himself up as the hero of the narrative—but now and then he widened out his viewpoint to include things like,

> It was at this time that my brother Daniel, going up to London, chanced upon two men who were then being pressed into the Queen's service, and taking it upon himself to intervene, he did effect their rescue and did find himself indicted for a Trespass for his troubles. Having languished several weeks in Newgate, he was finally brought to trial, whereupon it was discovered there were none who would appear against him, and he was happily acquitted to rejoin us...

I could remember Fergal making mention of that episode when I had overheard him arguing with Daniel in the next room on the first day I had come to their Trelowarth—the Trelowarth of the past. He had been reminding Daniel that the Duke of Ormonde's battles weren't their own. 'When did the flaming Duke of Ormonde ever think to do you favors?' I recalled him saying. 'Never, that's when. Did he think to put his hand in when they had you up to Newgate? Did he come to pay you visits?'

Evidently not, although from what I'd read so far it didn't

seem the Butler brothers needed anybody's intervention. They appeared to lead charmed lives. Just reading Jack's accounts of his own captures and escapes, and the few tales he told of how both he and Daniel had outwitted Queen Anne's agents while at sea, I was ready to believe the only luck they had was good luck.

With one notable exception.

And at summer's end my brother's wife succumbed to her long illness and was laid to rest with God.

He said no more about Ann's death nor its effect upon the family, though I thought the constable came into things a little bit more often after that, a darker presence in the background of the narrative.

And the narrative, in spite of Jack's poor grammar and the challenge of his handwriting, made for some fascinating reading.

So much so that when I turned a page expecting to find more of the description of a riot that had happened just this spring at celebrations for King George's birthday, and instead found that the sentence I'd been reading simply ended there, with blankness after, I was disappointed.

Flipping ahead to make sure there was nothing more, I closed the book regretfully. Oh well, I thought. At least I had the finished version waiting for me in the present day. I'd have to be content with that.

I was starting to swing myself out of the hammock when the *Sally* lifted suddenly and rocked as though a wave had struck her broadside. As the hammock swung me back again I gripped it with my free hand, though in truth there was no danger I'd fall out. It was, as everyone had promised me, completely safe.

But that safety felt relative now.

The *Sally* rolled a second time as something blotted out the daylight from the windows at the stern, behind me. Still clinging tightly to the hammock I turned round to see another ship's hull sliding ominously past, so close that I could see the gilded scrolls of woodwork on her gun ports.

The sight brought me out of the hammock in one swift decided move, planting my feet on the unsteady floor while I tried not to panic.

I couldn't see anything out the stern windows except the dark rise of the black-painted ship and one narrow slice of the grey sea and mist-shrouded shoreline that seemed too far off now to be any help, and I felt a new sense of frustration with Daniel and Fergal for leaving me here.

I'd be safer here, would I?

It didn't appear so. The unknown ship had started a slow turn that brought her bow around to face the offshore winds. I watched her black stern swinging out away from ours until the two ships rested almost parallel to one another with the hard slap of the waves against the *Sally*'s hull the only sound of protest.

I'd expected some reaction from the three men left on board with me, but so far I'd heard nothing, not so much as one stray footfall on the upper deck. Maybe, I thought, my three would-be protectors had slipped into hiding, something they wouldn't have done unless there was a reason *to* hide.

I knew that I was speculating; knew I had no way to tell if this new ship was friend or foe, but the mere sight of that black hull sliding past with all its gun ports standing open and this strange unsettled silence that now hovered over everything inclined me to believe the worst.

Hiding wasn't exactly an option for me, I didn't know the *Sally* well enough to know where I'd be safe. At least here in the captain's cabin I had that strong, bolted door between me and whatever came. And more, I had the pistol.

It had slipped my mind initially, but now I crossed to take it from its drawer again with hands that weren't quite steady.

I had barely closed the drawer again when I heard the quiet splash of oars approaching, almost furtive... heard the creak as they were lifted, and the scrape and bump of something on the *Sally*'s starboard side.

Gripping the pistol I closed my eyes briefly, preparing myself for the obvious since there was no way to stop it.

The *Sally* was going to be boarded.

CHAPTER 31

NOT KNOWING, NOT SEEING, just hearing the sounds of the men coming over the sides was the worst part by far. I'd seen too many pirate movies and my mind was freely fitting images to what I heard above me, matching every shuffling step to some crazed killer carrying a cutlass in his hand.

So when I heard the first thump of a man's boots coming down the stairs, I had the pistol waiting, cocked the way Fergal had shown me. As the boots approached I raised the pistol higher, and when the handle of the cabin door first gave a rattle I prepared to fire.

But then the intruder did something I hadn't expected.

He knocked.

And Daniel's voice said, 'Eva? Let me in.'

The rush of relief was so great that it set loose a wave of adrenaline that made my fingers fumble on the bolt until I concentrated.

Daniel looked surprised to see the gun. 'Are you all right?' He swung the door shut firmly at his back. 'Has something happened?'

I kept my voice low, so the crew wouldn't hear. 'There's a ship.'

'Yes, I know.' Relaxing, he reached out to take the pistol from my hand. He let the hammer down with care. 'There is no need for you to worry. Did you think that I would leave you so defenceless?'

I was on the brink of saying that I hadn't thought he'd leave me in the first place, but I caught the words in time before I spoke them. It was not his fault, I knew, that social customs were the way they were; that men and women here were bound by different rules. And if I was feeling left out I had no one but myself to blame. I'd asked to come along.

I said, 'I just thought I should be prepared for anything.' And then because he didn't look entirely convinced I changed the subject while he put the pistol in its drawer. 'Did you get all your business done on shore?'

'We did. And bought ourselves a boat into the bargain, to replace the one that Creed's boy rowed away in, else we'd find it a damp walk between our mooring and the beach when we got home.'

The tramping of men up and down between decks let me know that whatever they had traded for the wool was now being unloaded and stored in the *Sally*'s deep hold. Soon the great creaking winch would start hauling the anchor up. So much, I thought, for my grand sea adventure. In no time at all we'd be finished and back at Trelowarth.

Holding in my disappointment, I crossed to the windows and focused my gaze on the black ship that had given me those few unsettling moments. 'Is that ship a free-trader too?'

Daniel leaned on the edge of his desk. 'No. She is, by her colors, a French naval frigate.' He seemed unconcerned.

'She's a much bigger ship than the *Sally*.'

His practiced eye measured the looming black hull. 'Ay, she'll be close on four hundred tons, and has thirty-two guns to our eight, and she'll be carrying at least ten men for every one of ours.'

I said, 'That's hardly reassuring.'

'On the contrary, for that description fits in every way that of the ship I have been sent to meet.'

So this wasn't an ordinary smuggling run, then. 'You're supposed to be meeting another ship here?'

'My instructions were to that effect.' Daniel tipped his head slightly as though trying to get a clear view of the French ship's rigging. 'Though I must confess they did not name the ship in question.'

The scenery of my own view through the windows at the stern began to slip a little sideways as the *Sally* caught the wind and started slowly nosing out along the grey line of the shore. We glided once again into the French ship's shadow.

Daniel must have sensed my nervousness. He said, 'This is no place for us to make an introduction, with so many watching eyes. It will be better if we seek a quieter stretch of coastline where we can heave to and see what they intend.'

Looking at that line of gilded gun ports I fought back my own misgivings. 'Yes, of course.'

He wasn't fooled. 'Are you now wishing you had stayed back at Trelowarth?'

'No.' That came out too quickly. I said it again, 'No, I'm glad I came.'

He didn't comment on that, and his silence made me turn self-consciously to find he was still leaning on his desk, arms folded, watching me with thoughtful eyes. I asked him, 'What?'

He seemed to think a moment longer, then he said, 'You will not wound me, Eva, if you speak the truth. I would have honesty between us.'

'I am being honest.'

He didn't argue that. He only straightened from the desk

and crossed to stand beside me, looking out the windows while the steadily retreating shadow of the black French frigate brightened into grey waves that broke hard upon the rocky shore to spray their mist and hide the rise of greening cliffs behind. 'It has a wild beauty all its own, the Breton coast,' he said, 'but I would doubt it could compare with India.'

My turn for silence. I thought he had missed that small slip I had made back when Fergal had noticed the tag in my T-shirt that said 'Made in India', and I'd been thinking of the time I'd spent there with Katrina, and he'd watched my face...

'You have been there,' said Daniel. He spoke the words surely, a statement of fact.

'Yes, I have.'

'And where else have you traveled?'

I scrolled through the list in my memory. 'A lot of places.'

'Is it that you think my mind so limited and narrow that I will not comprehend the truth? Is that why you conceal it?'

'No, I—'

Daniel turned his head. His eyes met mine. 'There is no map for this, no ordered rules of conduct, so we must invent them as we stumble through, and I would argue that the first rule must be honesty.'

I wasn't all that sure what he was wanting me to answer. My expression must have shown that, for he gave a tight-lipped sigh and looked away again.

'You are glad that you came,' he said. 'You, who have seen and done things I can scarcely imagine; you, who have freedoms in your time the women of mine cannot contemplate. Doubtless you thought that this voyage would be an adventure, and yet you have spent this day shut in a cabin alone and in fear for your life, and you say you are glad that you came. You'll forgive me,' he said, 'if I do not believe you.'

I understood him then. 'All right.' I took a breath. 'I didn't like being left behind when you all went ashore. I didn't expect it.'

His gaze swung back to mine. 'And I apologize. I should not have assumed that you would know you could not join us.' I could see him thinking further. 'You do understand the reasons?'

'Yes.'

'It would not have been safe.'

'I know. I really do, it's just...' I paused and tried to put it into words. 'You talk of traveling. Well, even in my own time there are countries where a woman has to live with limitations. She can't get an education or go out of doors unless her husband lets her, but that's not the way I live. And when you're used to certain freedoms, it's just very hard to lose them.'

I wasn't thinking, when I threw that last bit in, that Daniel would have firsthand knowledge from his time in Newgate prison of how losing freedom felt, until he told me slowly, 'I assure you, Eva, I do have a high regard for liberty.'

'I know you do.'

'And whatever custom may decree in public, in my family every woman has been free to speak her mind.'

'Behind closed doors.'

He smiled and said, 'I've found that there are many things more safely done behind closed doors than in the public view, by men as well as women.' Then, more serious, 'Do you think I am free to say exactly what I please and when? In truth you'd be mistaken. If I stated my opinion of the current state of politics, I'd soon be clapped in irons for treason.'

He was right, I knew. 'But even if you can't state your opinions, you can act on them.'

'Not openly. No, you and I are both confined to showing but one part of us in public and another to our friends. As for the whole of us... well, that must be reserved for those few people we are fortunate enough to love and trust.'

He glanced at me then and appeared to mistake my continuing silence for sulking, because he said, 'Would it be any comfort if I told you you'd missed nothing of importance on our trip to shore this morning? That even Fergal could not rouse himself to anything but boredom? Would that help?'

'Not much.' But still I smiled. 'Did Fergal tell you that I asked to come along?'

He clearly hadn't, from the lift of Daniel's eyebrow. 'And what did he say to that?'

I told him, and he gave a short laugh, his eyes warming. 'Well, 'tis certain you've won his affection, for had any other woman asked him, Fergal would have thought it a fine joke to tell the crew.'

I said, 'I thought he might have told you, that was all.'

The laughter faded from his eyes but left the warmth. 'I've no need of Fergal to tell me when you are unhappy. Not even he can match my knowledge of your moods, I think, or know the way to read them in your face.'

The ship rolled and I put a hand against the window for support. It was no more than that, I thought—the movement of the ship and not the words that Daniel had just said or how he'd said them, or the fact that he was standing half a step from me.

Looking up at him I said, 'I'm not unhappy.'

'Are you not?'

'It's not unhappiness. It's...' Trying to find some way to describe the confusion of emotions I was feeling, I looked past his shoulder seeking inspiration. 'Daniel?'

'Yes?'

I touched his arm and for a moment he misunderstood and stepped in closer, so my cheek was pressed against the roughness of his jacket when I gripped his arm more firmly, turning him so he could see what I was seeing.

In the *Sally*'s wake a tall black ship was following, her bowsprit spearing through the waves with predatory purpose.

He briefly tightened his embrace, his mouth brushing over my hair in a quick kiss of apology or promise before he released me altogether. 'Keep back from the windows,' he told me. 'And no matter what may happen…'

'I'll stay here,' I said.

He gave a nod. 'If there is any danger, I will come for you. I promise. Oh, and Eva? Lock—'

'The door. I know.'

The quick flash of his smile was my reward for that as he stepped out and shut the door behind him.

❦

Whatever signal passed between the French ship and our own it must have proved this was indeed the ship that Daniel thought it was, the one he had been sent to meet. He brought us hard around into the wind so that we all but stopped, and the next sound I heard was the orderly scramble of men going over the side of the *Sally* and into the boat.

I knew Daniel was with them. I caught the timbre of his voice above the now-familiar slap and splash of oars as they rowed off.

And so I settled in to wait and let myself slide down the wall till I was sitting curled against it with my legs tucked up and my head resting comfortably on my knees. I sat like that a long time, drifting idly with my thoughts, rocked

by the *Sally*'s gentle motion on the water, and at last that
combination brought my heavy eyelids down and I was
lulled to sleep.

My dreams were deep and pleasant, filled with Daniel's
smiling eyes, his touch, his voice...

'You cannot stay here,' he said quietly.

'I want to,' I replied. 'I want to stay.'

I felt him lift me then, and reaching up I linked my arms
around his neck and snuggled to his chest before the hardness
of it warned me that I was no longer dreaming.

Blinking stupidly, I looked around, or tried to. It was
night, the only light within the darkened cabin coming from a
single candle set upon the desk, the curtains drawn across the
curving sweep of windows. Daniel shifted me a little higher
on his chest. I must have been a burden with the weight of
my green gown, but he made no complaints. He only said,
'You cannot sleep here on the floor.'

I wasn't totally awake yet. 'Didn't mean to. I was waiting.'

'So I see.'

'You took a long time.'

'Ay, we had a fair lot to discuss and then the cargo to
bring over.'

They'd already transferred cargo from the French ship to
the *Sally*? I'd heard nothing. 'Did I sleep through that?'

'Apparently.' He set me on my feet but kept a light hold
on my arms as though he thought I might topple over. 'Fergal
was guarding your door for the most of it. I only came with
the final load.'

Fergal. Guarding my door. With my reason returning, I
looked at the door, which I knew I had locked. 'How did
you get in?'

He raised one hand and briefly let a brass key dangle

from his fingers. 'The captain's advantage. I've brought you some supper.'

Now that I thought of it, I hadn't eaten anything since breakfast and my stomach did feel hollow.

On the desk beside the candle lay a hunk of cheese half-wrapped in muslin, two pears and a few round buns that looked a little squashed as though he'd brought them in his pockets, which he very likely had done.

'Thank you.' Picking up a bun, I took a bite. 'It's very good. What is it?'

'French loaf.' He had crossed behind me to the bookshelf and now slid a panel just below it to the side and rummaged in the recess.

The food had a restorative effect on my senses. It struck me how quiet the ship seemed. 'Where is everybody?'

'There is one man standing above on his watch. All the rest are yet aboard the French ship by her captain's invitation, having supper with her crew.'

I raised my eyebrows. 'Even Fergal?'

'Fergal,' Daniel told me, 'has few weaknesses, I will admit, but he is very partial to French cookery, and when he did discover that this French ship in particular has lately paid a visit to the Islands of Canaries and is carrying a goodly load of strong Canary sack, that decided the matter.' He'd found what he was looking for. He straightened from the recess with a flash of silver showing in his hand and slid the panel shut.

'And what is sack?' I asked.

He answered by carefully lifting a green bottle out of his deep jacket pocket. 'This,' he said, and set the bottle down upon the desk, 'is sack.'

'And Fergal likes it, does he?'

'More than cider.' Daniel set the two small silver cups he'd taken from the cupboard in the wall down too, and easing out the bottle's cork, began to fill them. 'Will you have some?'

'Please.' It tasted like sherry but stronger.

A burst of raucous laughter drifted over from the French ship, and the distant lilt of music, and I said, 'It sounds as if you're missing all the fun.'

He raised his own cup, unconcerned. 'For my part, I would rather have your company.'

Despite the plainness of the food, that supper was the best I'd ever eaten. No fine restaurant, no expensive gourmet offering, could match the simple wonderment of sitting there with Daniel in candlelight, the ship's boards creaking to the gentle rocking of the dark sea all around us that made all the world seem, for this one evening, very far away.

We talked about our families. I didn't tell him I already knew some details of his own from reading Jack's book, and anyway it didn't matter. Daniel settled in and told the tales to me himself, and then he asked about my family so I talked about Katrina and our summers at Trelowarth and the reason I'd come back.

'And you came all that way,' he asked, 'because your sister wished to rest where she had once been happy?'

'Yes.'

'Was she not happy elsewhere?'

'Yes, of course she was. Just not in the same way. Trelowarth was—it *is*—a very special place.'

'Trelowarth,' he countered, 'is rooms gathered under a roof, nothing more.' He refilled his cup and my own. 'I would argue 'tis never the place, but the people one shares it with who are the cause of our happiest memories. That is why we find that having lived them once, we never can recapture them.'

I'd never really thought of that. But now I wondered if he

wasn't right, and if that might not be the reason why, though Claire and Mark and Susan had done all they could to make me welcome, nothing at Trelowarth in the present felt exactly as I'd hoped it would. The place was the same, but the times had moved forwards. My sister, my parents were no longer there. And the girl I had been then… well, she too was gone.

I said, 'The Moving Finger.'

Daniel looked a question at me, and I gave myself a shake and told him, 'Sorry, it's a reference from a poem, a very lovely one.' I quoted the whole stanza for his benefit:

'The Moving Finger writes; and, having writ
Moves on: nor all thy Piety nor Wit
Shall lure it back to cancel half a line,
Nor all thy Tears wash out a Word of it.'

He said, 'You're right, it is a lovely poem. I do confess I'm not familiar with it.'

'No,' I said, 'you wouldn't be. It isn't written yet. That is, the original version in Arabic, that's been around for'—I tried to remember when Omar Khayyam had lived—'well, for a few hundred years. But it won't be translated to English until the next century.'

'Rather a long time to wait.' He glanced at me as though I'd just done something that intrigued him. 'I'm surprised you thought to share it. You are usually more guarded with your knowledge of the future.'

He was right, I thought. Again I blamed the sack and told him so.

'I see.' There was a trace of mischief in his half smile as he took the bottle in his hand. 'Then let us fill our cups again,' he said, 'and you can tell me about India.'

CHAPTER 32

E VEN WITH THE FORTIFIED Canary wine relaxing me and spreading warmth through all my weary muscles, I found it near impossible to will myself to sleep.

So I lay there in my hammock watching Daniel sleep instead.

He'd had more wine than I'd had, and the day's events had been much harder on him, and he'd drifted off while he was sitting in his chair with legs outstretched beneath the desk, head falling forwards till his chin was nearly resting on his chest.

It didn't look the least bit comfortable, especially since now and then he'd jerk his head up with a sudden start and let it slowly droop again, and on the third time that he did this I felt certain that I heard a crack of protest from his neck.

I lay a moment more in silence and debated what to do. And in the end I swung myself out of the hammock and went quietly over to wake him.

I'd forgotten, from the time that I'd encountered him at night in the front bedroom of Trelowarth, just how quickly he could wake. My hand had barely touched his shoulder when his eyes came halfway open.

'Eva?'

'You're not comfortable.'

He closed his eyes again. 'I am.'

'You're not. That chair's too small,' I said. 'Let me sleep there. You take the hammock.'

'No need.' His voice had the cavalier slur of a man who'd had too much to drink and was past really caring; who'd happily sleep in a ditch if he had to.

But I cared. With a bit more persuading I managed to get him to stand. He was less steady on his feet than I'd expected, and I had to steer him to the hammock with his arm around my waist, and when he obligingly lowered his long body into it, he didn't let go but kept his arm there so that I was pulled partway into the hammock too.

I tried to straighten. 'Daniel.'

He'd already started falling back to sleep.

If he'd been sleeping deeply it would have been easy to dislodge his hold and step away, but as it was, his arm lay heavily and firmly round me, keeping me in place. And to be honest, once I'd thought about it, I was not all that inclined to step away.

He'd said a hammock held the weight of two men when it needed to. I took him at his word, and since I was already halfway in, I cast propriety aside and slipped in properly, turning a bit so my head nestled onto his shoulder. I let the rhythm of his heartbeat, strong and sure beneath my cheek, chase off my worries.

He had been right earlier when he'd suggested that I'd been expecting adventure; that I'd seen a certain romance in the notion of a smuggling run to Brittany. But the romance of the voyage could no longer mask the actual reality of what was going on, not with the cargo we now carried from the French ship we'd been sent to meet in secret by the Duke of Ormonde's orders.

I might be prepared to believe that what Daniel had taken

in trade for the wool at our first port of call had been only the usual brandy and lace, but whatever the French ship had given us now had to do with the coming rebellion. And although I knew the rebellion would fail, I had not learned yet what that would mean to the man lying next to me, or to his brother and Fergal, or even the men on this ship and their families. In the history books they likely wouldn't even rate a mention, just as Shakespeare's Henry V, having read aloud the list of noblemen who'd died at Agincourt, had then dismissed the countless others lying lifeless in the mud as 'none else of name'.

But these men were not nameless to me. Not to me, I thought, laying my hand on the chest of the man at my side in a move that was faintly protective. Daniel half-woke again, drew me more closely against him and lowered his head so his wine-scented breath warmed my temple, and went back to sleep. And in time, as the ship creaked and rocked with the wind and the waves, I slept too.

❦

When I woke to a knock at the door there was light in the cabin—a grey light that spilled round the edge of the curtains. I shifted, not wholly remembering, and felt the weight and warmth beside me.

Daniel hadn't moved much in the night. He still held me against him, my head cradled into the curve of his shoulder, his hand lying heavily over my hip. It couldn't be comfortable for him, I thought. If nothing else, he'd likely lost all circulation in his arm. Carefully I eased out of the hammock without swinging it too much and crossed to answer the door.

Fergal's face was impassive. His dark gaze briefly rested on my rumpled gown and loosened hair before it flicked beyond me to where Daniel lay asleep, and then returned without expression. 'Waken him, would you?' the Irishman told me. 'He's needed on deck.'

He turned away, not waiting for an answer and not making any comment on the way that he had found us, but I sensed his disapproval.

I tried talking to him later, as we washed the dinner plates together in the galley alcove on our own. I did it quietly. I told him, 'What you saw... it wasn't like that. Nothing happened.'

Fergal didn't answer. Didn't even glance around.

I tried again. 'I said—'

'You're not meant to be speaking.' His hard sideways glance cut me off. 'And the other is none of my business.'

I knew where the coldness was coming from; knew he was not angry but concerned, and I could only guess that his concern was not for me but for his friend. He'd have seen how losing Ann affected Daniel, and no friend would ever wish to see that twice. No matter how well Fergal liked me, I felt certain that he viewed what was developing between myself and Daniel as a road to sure disaster.

And I wasn't so convinced that he was wrong.

∽

My troubled thoughts stayed with me as the *Sally* slowly settled back into the shelter of her private mooring place below the dark woods of Trelowarth, with the black cliffs at her back.

We had slipped in on the rising tide and darkness was beginning its descent upon the pebbled shoreline, cloaking our activities from idly prying eyes. And by the time the men had off-loaded the cargo with efficient speed and silence, there was barely light left in the cabin for me to make out Fergal's features when he came below to fetch me.

'Danny's waiting at the cave,' he said.

We were the last to leave. The other members of the *Sally*'s crew had scattered to their own devices with a stealth that marked them true-born smugglers.

Fergal handed me down into the Breton rowboat that we'd brought back to replace the one we'd lost to Creed's accomplice. I could see the smashed remains of that one sitting on the beach as Fergal rowed us quietly across towards the Cripplehorn.

The constable, it seemed, had not been pleased to find his spy left on the shore. And despite Jack's claims no local jury would convict the Butler brothers, I knew better than to underestimate the constable. What Creed could do within the law and what he'd dare to do outside it were, I knew, two very different things.

The boat scraped bottom on the shingle. Fergal held it steady while I scrambled out to stand beside the waterfall, which, having passed midsummer, had thinned down to a trickle that shifted and danced down the long drop from overhead, splattering onto the already wave-wet rocks close by my feet. It was a good thing I already knew about the hidden entrance, otherwise the sudden figure stepping from what looked like solid rock might have unnerved me into jumping even higher than I did.

Daniel touched my arm. 'We'll have to put the boat up. Will you wait inside a moment?'

With a nod I sidled past him through the long cleft in the stone.

The rush of silence struck me with the same swift force that I remembered from the day I'd come down here with

Mark. The sea sounded suddenly very far off, and the lyrical dripping of water from somewhere came echoing back from the walls of wet stone.

This was not the unused and abandoned space I'd seen that day, though. The scents of the sea and the salt-dampened rocks were overlaid here with more human ones—pipe smoke and new wooden barrels and candles that had only just been extinguished, the smell of their smoke still a sharpness that lingered unseen. The one candle they had left burning sat stuck in its own melted wax on a small tin plate set on the top of a barrel—one barrel among many others that stood stacked in staggering rows down the long curving wall to my right. I couldn't tell from looking at the barrels what was in them, but I would have bet the bank it wasn't anything to drink.

More likely, I decided, they held guns or arms of some sort that were meant for the rebellion. From the articles I'd read I knew the Duke of Ormonde's plans had been to raise a loyal army in the west of England that would fight beneath his banner in support of young James Stuart, when he came across the sea to claim the throne so many in these times believed was his by right of birth.

James Stuart would come, I knew. He would land in the north, up in Scotland, and men throughout Britain would rise in his name and would pay with their lives, and their cause would be lost in the end. All for nothing, I thought. All the risks that these men were now taking to bring back these guns or whatever they were, and to hide them down here, it was all wasted effort.

I felt a sudden heavy sadness in my chest, and yet I knew that, even if I did warn Daniel of what was to come, he would do nothing differently. He stood with his king, no matter what the odds or consequences, because that was where his heart and honor told him he must stand. Fergal had explained this at the woodpile when he'd said, 'To Danny, knowing that the battle will not end the way he wishes does not make it any less worthwhile to fight.'

I heard a quiet step behind me on the stone and Daniel's head came round the corner of the entrance. 'Done,' he said. 'Would you mind fetching me that candle, Eva?'

Being closer to it, I nodded and crossed to lift it from the barrel, being careful where I put my feet upon the floor with all its slippery rocks and damply filled depressions. As I lifted up the candle on its small tin plate the flame dipped briefly sideways, dancing light across a gleaming length of metal near the barrel's bottom edge—the blade of Daniel's dagger, lying on the floor. He must have dropped it there by accident, I thought. I nearly bent to pick it up... but then I stopped myself, remembering Mark's treasure box, and Daniel's dagger buried at the bottom of it.

Here was where he'd lost it. And where Mark, in time, would find it. It was not my place to interfere.

Daniel must have seen me hesitate. 'Is everything all right?'

My fingers folded to a tight fist at my side, to stop me reaching for the dagger as I wanted to. 'I'm fine,' I said, and turning I walked back to him, the candle held in front of me. It hardly shook at all.

He took it from my hand and thanked me for it, then to my surprise he blew it out. 'I would not wish to see our work destroyed by fire,' he said, by way of explanation.

'Won't we need the light for walking home?'

Which was, I later thought, a really stupid thing to ask a smuggler who would hardly want to call attention to his presence in the woods at night. But Daniel only smiled, a smile I couldn't see but clearly felt against my lips as he bent close to lightly brush his mouth across my own—the barest kiss, because there wasn't really time for more than that with Fergal waiting just outside.

'Sometimes,' said Daniel, ''tis better to be in the dark.'

CHAPTER 33

W E SLEPT LATE THE next day. Jack was up and about before any of the rest of us. I heard him moving round the house and whistling round the kitchen on his way out to the stables. In the room beside me Daniel woke and stirred. I heard his feet thump to the floor and then the quiet movements while he dressed and went downstairs.

I thought of drifting back to sleep, but in the end I rose and dressed as well. It took a little while, and by the time I got down to the kitchen Jack was back indoors and arguing with Daniel, though this wasn't like the argument I'd heard them have before. More like a stubborn disagreement.

'Ay,' said Jack, 'I know what you were thinking, but I'm saying you were better to have let the lad come with you and then tossed him over halfway through the crossing, for that might have been an accident and no one could have called it any different.'

Daniel's level look spoke for itself, but he elaborated anyway. 'I do not murder beardless lads. Good morrow, Eva.'

With a nod I took the bucket from its hook beside the hearth and slipped between them.

Jack said, 'Beardless lads who have been shamed in front of Creed may prove more dangerous than you might yet expect.'

I would have liked to have hung about longer to hear what Jack thought Creed's unsuccessful spy might try to do to seek revenge, but being on thin ice already with Jack I knew it would be best if I kept to the things that a sister of Fergal's would logically do. And right now, that meant fetching a bucket of water to start cooking breakfast.

The well had a simple design with a winch and a rope and a hook for the bucket, but hauling the bucket up full was more work than I'd thought it would be. I was leaning my weight on the winch in an effort to speed up the process when Jack banged his way out the back door and started across the yard.

Catching sight of me, he changed direction and came over, saying curtly, 'Stand aside.' I couldn't help but think the force he threw against the winch was more from a release of temper than from any real desire to help me. The bucket all but flew up from the darkness of the well, and when he yanked the bucket from its hook it sloshed a wave of water out to protest such rough treatment.

'There.' He thrust the bucket in my hands and turned away, strode off four steps, and wheeled again to add, 'If you *do* have a voice, you might use it to persuade my brother that there is a time when men must act to aid themselves, and not for honor.'

If I could have answered back, I would have told him there'd be no point in my telling Daniel anything. He was the way he was, and there was no force that could change him.

As I'm sure Jack knew already. With a final glare he turned and carried on towards the stables while I slowly lugged the water back across the yard.

Fergal, newly awake and still yawning, met me at the kitchen door and took the bucket from my hands, following my backwards glance with his quick knowing eyes. 'Don't you worry at all about Jack, he's all bluster. He's only been penned up alone in the house these past days, and he's wanting a breath of air.'

I didn't worry about Jack, as it happened. I knew he would live to a good age. It was the other two men that I worried about.

'Breakfast,' said Fergal. 'And then I'll be leaving you here to take care of the dinner.'

'Why? Where are you going?'

'Lostwithiel.'

'Why?'

'Not your business. Now, breakfast.'

'Does it have to do with the guns you brought back?'

Fergal turned then and gave me a look. 'I do hope that I never go forwards in time, for I'd not long survive in an age filled with women so curious.' Setting the bucket down hard on the hearth he said, more firmly, 'Breakfast.'

But I knew that I was right. And when he rode off in his turn an hour later, I wished hard that he would meet with no adventures on the road.

❧

Daniel was busy upstairs with his books.

The pleasant scent of pipe tobacco met me on the landing when I went up with a mind to make my bed. Instead I went the other way along the corridor and found him in his study, deeply absorbed in a book that looked, even for this time, quite old. Glancing up from his seat by the window, he took the pipe from his mouth for a moment and asked, 'Did you want me?'

A loaded question, I decided, if I'd ever heard one. Resisting the impulse to answer it, I simply told him, 'I'll be starting dinner soon. It's fish—that's all that Fergal's left. How do you like it cooked?'

'However you desire to cook it,' was his answer with a smile. 'Did he gut them first for you, at least, before leaving?'

'He did, yes.'

'A good man.' Setting his pipe on the table beside him, he rounded his shoulders to stretch them.

I looked at the book he held. 'What are you reading?'

For an answer he turned it round, holding it open at the title page so I could read the words myself. *The Sceptical Chymist*. The 'chymist' had me stumped a moment, then, 'A book of chemistry?'

'You know the science?'

'Only what I learned in school.'

'Which was, no doubt, beyond what even the greatest of our current men of science could yet fathom.' Giving a nod to the book he said, 'This man, Robert Boyle, had a very great intellect, although he dwelt too much I think on alchemy. But when I was naught but a babe he conducted experiments dealing with fire and combustion, chemical combustion. I had hoped to find them detailed here, but this book was published before that time. Still, it makes for fascinating reading.'

'What's got you interested in chemical combustion?'

'You. Your self-igniting spills.' He flipped a page and settled back. 'It does occur to me that phosphorous might have some useful qualities, but as for the other chemical or chemicals that one might need—'

I cut him off in something close to panic. 'You can't do that.' But he could, I knew. It was the way his brain worked, turning everything he could not understand into a puzzle to be solved. A sort of game. Except, 'You can't be messing round with self-igniting matches, Daniel. They're not meant to be invented till the 1800s.'

He turned another page. 'Then if I do invent them I shall swear to keep the secret in my family until then.'

'Don't joke. You can't do this.'

'Why?' Holding his place in the book with his thumb, he closed it and faced me with an air of intellectual debate. 'What harm can there be in increasing my knowledge?'

'A great deal if that knowledge isn't something anyone should have in this time,' was my argument. 'Anything you do that you weren't meant to do could change the future, change the way that things turn out.'

'How do you know this?'

'Well, it's common knowledge. Common sense.' The first rule of time travel, really, I thought—so ingrained in society's psyche through novels and films that it took on the weight of a fact.

'But what proof do you have?' Daniel asked. 'Has a man ever done this?'

I said, 'I don't know, but—'

'Have learned men studied the matter?'

'They have theories…'

'But how are they tested?' he challenged me. 'Theories are fine things, but I do confess that my own common sense tells me there is an order to life that cannot be so easily changed by the will of one man.' He spread his hands to indicate the study. 'All of this, this life that I have lived, it has already passed and faded from the memories of the people of your own time. It is rather like that poem you did speak of, with the moving finger writing words that cannot be erased. My page is written,' he said, 'and not even I can change a line of it.'

I wasn't sure which one of us was right. I said, 'But *I'm* not meant to be here. *I* might change things.'

Daniel looked at me a moment, then he set his book aside and stood and closed the space between us with his slow deliberate steps. 'How do you know,' he asked, 'that here is not exactly where you're meant to be?'

I didn't have an answer for him, partly because my mind, as always, had lost all its power to form coherent thoughts with him so near. And partly because I wanted so badly for him to be right, even though we both knew that the thing was impossible. I shook my head and repeated those words: 'It's impossible.'

'Why is it?' His eyes gave no quarter. 'Where is your proof?'

I had no hope of winning the argument, not with him standing there looking at me like that, but I still tried. 'Where is yours?'

Daniel took my hand and held it to his heart so I could feel its beating. 'Here,' he told me quietly. His other hand came up to hold my face and tilt it up while his began a slow descent. 'And here,' he murmured, with his mouth against my own.

It was a thorough and persuasive kiss that made my senses spin until I couldn't think of any reason not to be convinced.

When he drew back, the look he slanted down at me was so intense it stopped my breath. Intense, yet somehow questioning. He held my face still warm within his hand and asked me in a slightly roughened voice, 'Would you desire more proof than that?'

I knew what he was asking, then. Knew too that I'd be complicating things beyond repair if I said yes. Because if I already found it difficult to leave him as things were, that would be nothing to the wrenching loss I'd feel when I was forced to leave him after this.

Looking up, I gave a nod and watched the question in

his eyes give way to warmth. And then he lifted me, the trailing gown and all, and he was kissing me again and we were moving from the study down the corridor towards the corner bedchamber.

The door swung open with a crash and Daniel kicked it closed again behind us, and I heard the scraping of the key turned in the lock, and we were on the bed together and to tell the truth, I wasn't much inclined to notice anything besides that for a while.

Time hung suspended. And for once, I had no question of my place in it. I was exactly where I was supposed to be, where I belonged, with Daniel Butler lying in the bed beside me. I could hear his even breathing, feel his warmth, the shifting of his weight against the mattress as he turned. His face in sleep was not so hardened as I'd seen it look. The lines were there but smoother, and the slanting shadows of his lashes crossed his tanned skin peacefully.

Then as I watched his face, his eyes came slowly open, and he saw me too and smiled.

I closed my own eyes tight to hold the moment. Until I remembered how I had come into the past from the present this last time, and quickly I opened my eyes again.

He was still there.

Misreading my relief, he asked me, 'Are you back to doubting whether I am real?'

His tone was dry, and so I kept my answer light. 'After what just happened, yes, I might be.'

'I shall choose to view that as a compliment.' The smile deepened briefly. 'Or did you intend the opposite?'

My gaze still held by his, I gave my head the slightest

shake against the softness of the pillow and replied, 'It was a compliment.'

I watched the green eyes darken in that now-familiar way, as Daniel bridged the space between us with a kiss that somehow managed the impossible and left me with an even stronger sense of longing than I'd had before.

He drew back, his expression turning serious, and let his head fall to the pillow close beside my own, his one hand sliding from my face into my hair, where he absently wound a long strand round his finger as though he were making a curl. 'I have known many women, Eva, but for all that, I have only loved but twice. I cannot say that I am well accomplished in the way of it nor that I was the very best of husbands. I do hold the things I love too closely, sometimes, and I can be contrary for nothing but the sake of it, and I know well that I am not the easiest of men to make a life with.'

I held my breath and lay there watching him, and waiting.

He was studying my hair, now loosely spiraled in his fingers. 'I have only loved but twice,' he said again. 'The first I took for granted, and now she is in her grave and gone. I would not wish...' His hand closed briefly, tightening. 'I would not wish to make the same mistake with you.'

I'd held my breath too long and had forgotten how to let it out, and when I did my head felt light. 'Did you just say you loved me?'

'Ay.' His eyes were back on mine again. 'And I would have you marry me.' He must have thought that sounded too imperious, because he caught the words and phrased them differently. 'I'm asking,' he said, gently, 'will you marry me?'

I felt my eyes fill hotly with the unexpected depth of my emotions, and I tried to blink the wetness back, to hold to that last ragged edge of reason. 'I love you too,' I said. 'But...'

Daniel waited through the moment's silence, finally prompting, 'But?'

'I'm hardly ever here. I come and go, I can't control it. You can't want to have a life like that.'

His face relaxed. ''Tis you I want.' He trailed his fingers warmly down my cheek and brushed away the single tear that had escaped my lashes. 'I care not on what terms.'

He didn't try to catch the next tear or the one that followed after that. His gaze stayed steady on my own.

'Say yes,' he said so quietly it might have been a whisper. He moved his hand against my face so that his thumb could brush across my trembling lips as lightly as a kiss. 'Say yes.'

As if there were another answer I could ever give him. 'Yes.'

I'd never seen him smile like that. I knew that for my whole life I'd remember it, as I'd remember everything about this moment—the angle of the sunlight spilling through the bedroom window and the even warmer light in Daniel's eyes.

And how his touch felt, gentle on my face.

'Whatever time we have,' he said, 'it will be time enough.'

CHAPTER 34

FERGAL STOOD BEHIND ME in the shadows of the church. We hadn't needed any witnesses. Apparently the laws had not been written yet that made them a requirement. In fact, according to Daniel, we could simply have exchanged vows on our own, there in the bedroom at Trelowarth with no priest around to hear us, and then sealed the deal by making love—which had, I admitted, seemed rather appealing to me at the time.

But he'd laughed then and gathered me close and said we had in essence already done all of that. 'The promise is the same no matter where we choose to say it, yet it seems to me more meaningful to say it in a church.'

'We'll have to wait then.'

'Why?'

'Well, because we'll need a license or they'll have to read the banns, or…' I had paused, because I'd noticed he was looking at me strangely.

'All we'll need,' he'd said, quite certain, 'is a payment that will satisfy the vicar.'

He'd been right, of course.

Finding the vicar himself had been more of a challenge, but eventually he had been traced to the house of some friends in the neighboring parish, and Fergal, returning from Lostwithiel, had headed back out to go fetch him. And that was how I came to be here, with an hour to go till sunrise, standing in the aisle of St Petroc's church by candlelight with Fergal at my shoulder and the vicar off discussing terms with Daniel in the vestry.

I felt a surge of nervousness again and smoothed the skirts of my green gown till Fergal told me, 'Quit your fussing. You look fine.'

Obedient, I stilled my hands and then, not knowing what else I should do with them, I clasped them both behind me. I whispered, 'They've been in there a long time.'

'You're meant to be my sister, and a Catholic. I'd imagine that's what's keeping them.'

'Oh.'

'You've no call to worry. For the price that Danny's offering, the vicar will be sure to keep his disapproval to himself.'

I looked away again. 'Like you.'

'What's that?'

I shook my head and murmured, 'Nothing.'

Fergal took a step around to stand where I could see him. 'Do you think I disapprove?'

'I think you care about your friend,' I told him with a shrug, 'and you don't want to see him hurt again.'

'I want,' he answered carefully, 'to see him with a woman who will love him in the way that he deserves and know the value of the man whose heart she carries.' In his voice I heard that same fierce challenge I remembered from the first time we had met, when we'd squared off across the corner bedroom with me in my borrowed gown and him as mad as blazes. 'Has he found that?'

Looking up, I met his eyes and saw that underneath the challenge lay what looked to be affection, and not sure that I

could speak around the lump of pure emotion in my throat,
I gave a nod.

'Well, then,' he said, 'why the devil would you think I'd
disapprove?'

'I'm sorry.'

'So you should be. Leaping into judgment.' There was
humor in the dark glance angled down at me. 'If I truly
disapproved, you'd not be here.'

'Where would I be, then? At the bottom of the well?'

'Most likely, ay.'

'Big scary man,' I called him, low.

He didn't hide the smile this time. But he did step back
again where he had been before, behind my shoulder, where
he could more clearly see the vestry door.

The flickering candles had burned at least half an inch
lower before Daniel came through that door with the vicar
beside him—a middle-aged man with stooped shoulders who
looked as though he wasn't fully awake. But he seemed game
enough for the task at hand.

'Have you a ring?' he asked Daniel, before we began.

Daniel looked an apology at me and started to say something but with a shake of my head I reached over and slipped
off the Claddagh ring, holding it out, and his fingers brushed
warm on my palm as he took it and handed it on to the vicar.

It was, I thought, a fitting thing to use Katrina's ring for
this. A way to feel her standing at my side, where I had always
thought she would be when I married.

With a cough the vicar set the ring with care upon the
pages of his open prayer book, ready for his blessing. 'Since
I am told she cannot speak, I'd ask Mistress O'Cleary to—'

'Her name is Ward,' said Daniel, and the vicar stopped.

'I beg your pardon?'

Daniel said, 'Her name is Eva Ellen Ward, and in this place
of God she has a voice. For surely this is not a place where
anyone should speak aught but the truth.' He held the vicar's
gaze directly. 'Nor where anyone should fear betrayal.'

The vicar paused. Then nodded slowly. 'No, indeed.' He
turned to me. 'Now, Eva Ellen Ward, is it your wish that
you be married to this man?'

I looked at Daniel, grateful for his giving me the chance
to say the words out loud. 'It is.'

'Then let us now begin.'

❧

The ring felt strange on my left hand instead of on my right.
My thumb kept seeking out its smoothness there and twisting
it around to feel the clasped hands and the heart, till Daniel
caught my hand in his and held it while we walked.

We were taking the longer way back through the
fields, having let Fergal go on ahead of us. The rising sun
had just begun to push its way above the hills that lay to
the east of Polgelly, and over the wet grass our shadows
stretched long.

He'd been right. The words we had just said to each
other had seemed much more meaningful, spoken aloud in
the church, than they would have done if we'd exchanged
our vows privately yesterday. Something of the solemnity of
the traditional service still clung to me, keeping me silent till
Daniel's hand lightly squeezed mine.

'You are lost in your thoughts. May I know them?'

'I doubt they'd make sense to you.' Turning, I showed
him a smile. 'I'm still sorting things through.'

'And what is it,' he asked, 'that needs sorting?'

'You know. How we're going to manage this.'

His turn to smile. 'The same as any other married man and woman might. How else?'

'But we,' I said, reminding him, 'are not like any other married couple, are we? We can't really make plans for our future, not like normal people can.'

'Why not?'

I answered with a dry look. 'We're lucky enough if we make plans for supper. I might disappear before then.'

'Life is always uncertain,' he said with a shrug. 'We cannot let the fear of what might happen stop us living as we choose.' His fingers twined more tightly round my own.

And then to lighten things, I said, 'At least I didn't disappear in church.'

'No, you did not.' He swung my hand a little as we walked on further, then his steps began to slow. 'You did not disappear in church,' he echoed. Stopping, he looked down at me. 'Nor when we were on the *Sally*.'

I knew his thoughts were traveling the same path mine already had and coming to the same conclusion.

'I know,' I assured him, 'I've noticed the same thing. Whatever's been happening seems to be tied to Trelowarth itself.' And I told him about the Grey Lady who'd vanished years before me.

He was thinking. 'So then if you left, it would most likely stop.'

'It's possible, yes, but I don't know for certain. It's only a theory.'

'And theories are meant to be tested, are they not?' Not waiting for an answer he went on, 'Perhaps we ought to go away for a short while, to Bristol or to Plymouth. You did say you always return to the moment you left your own time, yes? Then there is no danger. If we have guessed wrongly you'll merely go back as you would have done had we stayed here. But if we are *not* wrong…' There was no need to finish the sentence.

'We could hardly be sure,' was my argument, 'after just one trip away. There'd be no guarantee.'

'No. But we could repeat the experiment, surely. I gladly would go where I needed to go if it kept you beside me.'

I looked away briefly, in thought. We were standing where, three hundred years from now, the Quiet Garden would be coming into bloom with Mark's beloved roses, safely walled to shield them from the sea-blown weather, but just at the moment there was nothing here but a sloping field with wild-flowers speckled through the bowing grass that tumbled down towards the roof and chimneys of the house below.

I asked, 'You'd leave Trelowarth?'

'I can serve the Duke of Ormonde and the king aboard the *Sally* just as well as I could serve them from on land, mayhap a good deal better. And rebellions all must have an end.' With a faint smile he brushed back the hair from my eyes where the wind kept on blowing it. 'Ill or fair, I mean to be alive to see the end of this one. And there has been talk that if this new attempt to set King James upon his throne should flounder, he will send the Duke of Ormonde to the Spanish court for aid, and I should think the duke will need assistance there.'

'In Spain.'

'Have you been there as well?' His eyes crinkled with humor.

'Well, actually, yes.'

'Did you like it?'

I lifted my chin. 'Very much.'

'Then,' he said, 'we will take it in small steps. Beginning with Bristol.'

Sealing the bargain, he drew me in close for a quick kiss that lengthened to something more, making me hold to his waist for support, and my hand touched the top of the knife handle slung at his belt.

Drawing back in surprise, I looked down at the dagger, and Daniel's gaze followed mine. 'What is the matter?' he asked.

It was not the same knife. This one had a bone handle, a cruder design. I said only, 'You have a new knife.'

'Yes. I've mislaid my favorite, but 'tis not a matter for concern. Most likely it is somewhere on the *Sally*.'

I should tell him, I thought. I should tell him I knew where it was. But I couldn't, because if I did then it wouldn't be there in the cave for the boy Mark to find it, as he was supposed to. And if I changed that, then what else…?

'Eva?' Daniel was holding me, watching my face. Waiting.

I shook it off. 'Sorry.'

And then for the first time I realized the *way* he was watching me; noticed the look in his eyes as the landscape around us began to change, wavering.

I tried to cling more tightly to him, knowing that I couldn't, and my voice this time was no more than an anguished whisper. 'Sorry.'

Daniel's arms came more closely around me. I saw his mouth moving and knew he was telling me something. I thought he was saying he'd wait for me, but he had already started to fade and I only caught one faint word: 'Wait.'

Then the wind rose and swirled and collapsed on itself in a rush of unbearable stillness.

My eyes were shut tightly.

I kept them that way, not only because I knew if I opened them I'd only see the green walls of my empty bedroom at

Trelowarth and the empty bed that I was lying on alone, but because I felt them filling with the stinging heat of tears.

I thought I'd learned the pain of loss, but this was nothing like I'd ever felt before. I'd never in my life felt so alone.

I turned my face into the pillow just in time to catch the first sob rising from this newly hollow place inside me, and the tears came with it, swelling in behind my eyes and spilling over with a force I couldn't stop or fight.

And through it all, the thing that seemed to me the most unfair was that the birds outside my window went on singing as though it were just like any other morning.

CHAPTER 35

THAT WHOLE WEEK WAS horrible. My emotions stayed close to the surface, and I had to concentrate hard to not vent them at every small irritant. Susan had noticed I wasn't myself, but I heard her explaining to Mark it was likely a mixture of grief and fatigue.

She was right.

Her solution was, too. She kept giving me things I could do round the tearoom, unchallenging tasks that would keep my mind busy without really needing much effort. I wiped down the newly bought tables and set them at just the right angle and clipped on the tablecloths, placing a bud vase for one single rose at the centre. I sent all the glasses and cups through the new built-in dishwasher, stacking them clean in their place on the shelves.

Wednesday morning I sat with Felicity, folding the menus.

She was, if it were possible, more quiet and absorbed in thought than me, and since this seemed so foreign to her nature, I was finally stirred to push my own self-pity to the side enough to ask, 'Are you all right?'

'What?' Glancing up, she said, 'Oh, yes, I'm fine.' She focused on the menu's fold. 'I'm really fine.'

She wasn't, though. Her hands shook very slightly and I recognized the barest hint of puffiness around her eyes. She had been crying.

When the door swung open at our backs Felicity looked swiftly up, face wary and yet hopeful, then her eyes dulled. 'Hello, Paul,' she told the plumber.

'What's the problem?' he asked cheerfully, his muscled shoulders and broad chest set off to good advantage in a black T-shirt this morning. In his fitted jeans and work boots, with his handsome face, he looked like the embodiment of most young women's fantasies, and yet it seemed Felicity could barely spare a glance for him as she explained the difficulties Susan had been having with the sinks.

She clearly was preoccupied with something—or with someone—and I had a good idea what. And whom.

I found Mark working in the field. The weather had been dry this week and he'd been busy T-budding the root stock that he'd planted this past spring.

Budding was a learned skill and not everyone could do it as efficiently as Mark could. Moving doggedly along the rows of plants, he bent at each to make a shallow T-shaped cut above the root, and into that he tucked a single bud stripped from the stem of the variety of rose he wanted this one to become. Protected by a rubber patch, the tiny grafted bud would hopefully begin to take by autumn, and lie dormant through the winter months until Mark came next February with his shears to prune the whole plant back to just above the bud.

From that new stump, the bud would grow and flourish, and become a rose as lovely as the ones that were now blooming in the next field over. Some things only needed time to find their proper footing. Time and patience. Others, sometimes, needed a swift kick.

Mark glanced up as I came across the field towards him, and he gave a nod but didn't break the rhythm of his work.

'What did you do,' I asked him bluntly, 'to Felicity?'

He'd been treading lightly round me all week long, uncertain of my mood, and when he looked up now I read the caution in his gaze. 'What did she say I did?'

I told him, 'Nothing.'

'Ah.'

'You made her cry.'

He looked away and took a deeper interest in the plant that he was budding, though his tone remained a shade defensive. 'All I did was tell her that I didn't have the time to see an art show with her Saturday, in Falmouth. She had pieces she was showing there, and—'

'What the hell,' I asked him, plain, 'is wrong with you?'

'I'm sorry?' Mark had raised his head again, surprised.

'You heard. You've got this lovely, lovely girl who's totally obsessed with you, and you're too blind to see it.'

He looked down again and said, so low I nearly didn't hear it, 'I'm not blind.'

'What?'

'I'm not blind.' Emphatic, with an edge of rare impatience. 'I can see she likes me, and for what it's worth, I like her too.'

'Then why…?'

'Is this your business?'

'No.' I met his glare head-on. 'But someone needs to sort it out.'

'It's sorted.'

'I can see that. You're all angry, and she's crying, and—'

'It wouldn't work.' He threw the words down with a hard finality that left no space for argument, but my emotions were already raw and I was in a mood to argue.

'Why is that?'

'Because Felicity's an artist.'

'And?'

'She needs her freedom,' he explained. 'Like Claire.' Then, seeing I was looking unenlightened, he went on, 'When I was young, Claire used to go away for days, for weeks sometimes, to do her work. She'd up and take her canvases and off she'd go. She still does, every now and then.' He raked the hair back from his face, a gesture of control. 'I used to hate it, waking up to find she'd gone. Some men can live like that. My father could. I can't.'

'Felicity's not Claire,' I said.

'Felicity's a butterfly.' Unmoved, he pointed out, 'She's barely been down here a couple of years, who knows when she'll be off again.'

I had known Mark long enough to know his body language, and from how he held himself I knew his inner conflict was a real one, but the memory of Felicity's sad eyes spurred me to say, 'Your famous theory, yes. The butterflies. There's just one little problem with it.'

'Is there, really?' Mark was probably as close as I had ever seen him to the loss of his own temper, but he held it in. 'And what would that be?'

'It's all crap, that's what.'

'And you would know.'

My own pain tumbled over then. 'I know that life's too short to live by stupid theories,' I shot back. 'I know that if you have the luck to find someone who loves you, then you love them back, you don't care on what terms.' I used the phrase of Daniel's though it hurt my heart to say it, and because I drew some strength from just remembering those words I carried on, 'Whatever time you have with somebody who loves you, Mark, it should be…' Something caught hard in my throat and made me pause to fight it.

Still defiant, Mark asked, 'Should be what?'

I got the words out somehow, just above a whisper. 'Time enough.'

And then I turned, because I didn't want to argue anymore. Before I'd gone ten steps he called out, 'Eva?'

I glanced back. I'd never seen Mark looking so torn up inside.

'Love isn't everything,' he said.

I shook my head. 'It is, you know. It's all that matters, and I hate to see you throwing it away.'

I left him standing there, to think on that.

I'd been purposely avoiding picking up Jack's memoirs since I'd come back, even though the book still sat with patience on my bedside table, bookmarked to the place where I'd left off.

I'd read beyond that now, of course, that day I'd spent aboard the *Sally*, so there really was no harm in reading what I knew already. But I wasn't too keen anymore to learn what happened next.

It was only now, with what I'd said to Mark still nudging gently at my conscience, that I drew the curtains closed against the light of afternoon and curled up fully clothed upon my bed and reached my hand out for the memoirs.

I could always stop, I told myself. I didn't have to go beyond what I'd already experienced. It would be enough to feel this closeness for a while, not just to Daniel but to Fergal too, and Jack, whose voice came through the printed pages as though he himself were telling me the stories.

While I read I could imagine that the walls around me

were those other walls, the bed a larger bed with posts and curtains, and the room beside me not an empty one but home to an inhabitant who paced the floorboards restlessly on booted feet.

When I approached the place where the pages I'd been reading on the *Sally* had gone blank I read more carefully, prepared to put the book down. There it was—the bit that I'd read last, continued over to the facing page, and then…

I stopped, confused.

Because there was no more beyond that. Nothing written by Jack's hand, at any rate, although the person who had edited the memoirs had inserted this parenthesized apology:

Jack Butler's own account ends here. What follows is the Reverend Mr. Simon's learned lecture on the usefulness of this account in teaching moral lessons to those young men who are tempted to pursue the ways of decadence, for let them be reminded that Jack Butler, having turned his back on both his earthly king and on that other King who rules all men, did thus commit himself to suffer an untimely end; and such an end as does befit a traitor to the Crown, for it was on the very first great anniversary of the accession to the throne of that good King George the First, whom he did so despise and seek to overthrow, that he did chance to fall afoul of the lawmen of Polgelly, and while fleeing from their constable was killed by one sure pistol shot and sent thus in disgrace before his Maker.

'No.'

I didn't know I'd spoken till I heard my own voice echo in the silent room, but even as the echo died I knew it didn't matter.

Daniel had been right. The words were written there

already, printed long before my birth, and there was no amount of wishing that could change them.

❧

'Hard luck,' was Oliver's opinion of the way Jack Butler met his end. Head tilted, he tried to remember his history. 'If it happened on the anniversary of King George's accession to the throne, then that would mean he died in...'

'August. August 1st, to be exact,' I said. 'I looked it up.'

'Ah.' Leaning on the corner of the desk in Uncle George's study, Oliver angled a penetrating look down at me while I worked. It was Saturday, and he'd come up to help with cleaning windows at the greenhouse in advance of next week's opening, but somehow he had found his way in here instead. I didn't mind. His company was welcome in my current mood.

He said, 'You've really taken this to heart, haven't you? Maybe I shouldn't have found you that book.'

I couldn't reveal why the knowledge of Jack's death depressed me as much as it did. All I said was, 'It just seems unfair, his being killed like that.'

'Come have lunch,' he suggested.

'I can't. I've got this press release to finish.' Searching through the papers at the side of my computer, I let out a tight sigh of frustration. 'If I ever find my proper notes. You don't remember, offhand, what the name of that big prize was that Trelowarth won back in the 1960s, do you?'

'Sorry, no. Mark would know it, but he won't be back till late tonight.'

I glanced up. 'Back from where?'

'From Falmouth. He and Fee are at the art show.'

'Mark went with her?' I stared at him. 'You're sure?'

'Do you know,' he said, 'that's the first time I've seen you smile all day.'

'Is it? Sorry. I've just been a little out of sorts, that's all.'

'Susan might know what the name of the prize was,' he said. 'I'll go ask her. I ought to be out at the greenhouse now anyway.' Straightening, he told me, 'Sue will be happy, at least, with the way your Jack Butler died. Adds a bit of drama to her story of the smugglers for the tourists. Just as well, because I still can't find anything to tie the Duke of Ormonde and his Jacobite rebellion to this area. Mind you,' he said, 'it wasn't much of a rebellion to begin with. Never really got off the ground. The Duke of Ormonde buggered off to France before it happened. He knew Parliament had voted to impeach him and he didn't wait around to be arrested.'

I couldn't really blame him, and I said as much. And then I asked, more slowly, 'Did he go to Spain afterwards?'

'He did, yeah. Why?'

'I just wondered.' I wondered, too, whether he'd brought any kinsmen along on the voyage, to help raise support for the Jacobite cause.

Oliver remarked that, when people like the Duke of Ormonde fell, they landed firmly on their feet. 'And they always choose warm places for their exiles. Spanish women, Spanish wine, I'm sure it wasn't any hardship. It was those he left behind him here in Cornwall did the suffering.'

I didn't really want to ask him, but I had to. 'Why? What happened to them?'

'Well, they were arrested, weren't they? King George learned what they were up to, and he had them rounded up before they had a chance to rise. They had to watch King James land up in Scotland, watch him lose his battle, couldn't do a thing to help him. Some were executed, afterwards, and some transported to the colonies, and—' He broke off, looking at me. 'You all right?'

'I'm fine.' I schooled my face and looked away. 'You said King George found out what they were planning. How?'

'The Duke of Ormonde sent his private secretary down here as a messenger—a Scottish colonel, can't recall his name. McSomething anyway.'

'Maclean.'

I could have told him that the man had used the alias of Wilson, could have told him what he'd looked like, that he'd worn a dark green coat and powdered wig and high black boots, and that his horse had been a grey. I could have told him that Jack Butler hadn't liked him much; that Jack had nearly lost his life in going to St Non's to make enquiries as to Wilson's true identity, and that he'd learned that Wilson's name was actually Maclean. I'd been there when Jack had told us that, when Daniel had assured him that Maclean was 'indisputably' a man to trust. The Duke of Ormonde's secretary.

Oliver nodded. 'That's right,' he said. 'Colonel Maclean. He came down to Cornwall and met all the people preparing to fight on the side of the Jacobites, and then... hang on.' His mobile was ringing. He took it out to check the number while I looked away, and just for an instant I saw in my mind's eye a man in a dark green coat standing in the stable yard with Daniel, the both of them laughing and shaking hands.

Oliver put his phone back in his pocket.

'And then?' I made the prompt quietly.

'Then he betrayed them,' was Oliver's answer. 'He knew all the names of the people he'd met, and he gave every one of them right to King George.'

❧

It wasn't the knowledge itself that was hardest to bear, it was knowing that I could do nothing about it, that even with all that I knew I was powerless. Useless.

I'd felt this before, while Katrina had battled her illness. I hadn't been able to stop that from happening either. I hadn't been able to save her. I would have paid any price then to be able to *do* something, anything, not just stand helplessly by. And I would have paid any price now. But the truth was that, once again, I could do nothing.

I couldn't warn Daniel. I couldn't save Jack. I was trapped here in my own time and I couldn't simply leap back into theirs by force of will alone, however much I wanted to. I had to wait. And worry.

I was grateful when the day of Susan's opening arrived because it kept me moving constantly, with no real time for thinking about anything except the task at hand. Things went splendidly well—the first coach load of tourists arrived spot on time and the weather held fair, and Trelowarth looked beautiful, and the photographer sent down by *House & Garden* got the whole thing very brilliantly recorded for her magazine. The interviews with Mark and Susan went off like a dream, and when the visitors all crowded into the Cloutie Tree to sample their Cornish cream teas before leaving, their chatter was glowingly positive.

By the day's end even Mark was admitting that Susan had proved him wrong.

'Say it again,' Susan challenged him, mischievous.

Crossing the carpeted floor of the big front room, Mark sank with visible weariness into the big armchair by the piano and leaned his head back. 'You were right,' he repeated, with slow perfect diction. 'And I was…'

'Yes?'

'Less right.'

I looked up from my magazine. 'That's all you're going to get,' I said to Susan. 'And be happy with it, because it's more than *I* got.'

Mark partly opened his eyes. 'When were you right?'

I sent him a calmly superior look. 'Falmouth.'

'Oh.' His eyes closed again. 'Well, yes, all right. I was wrong about that, I'll admit it.'

Amazed, Susan said to me, 'Sorry, am I delirious, or did I just hear my brother say that he'd been wrong?' Her gaze swung, curious, to Mark. 'What have I missed?'

He said, 'None of your business.'

I knew that he'd gone out a few times since then with Felicity, and though they weren't yet what I'd call a couple, they were at least making a start on it. Susan, who knew and approved of their changing relationship, wasn't aware that I'd argued with Mark. We had kept that a private affair, between us, and we'd settled it in the same way that we'd made peace when I had been little—the day after going to Falmouth, Mark had set up the badminton net on the side lawn and brought me a racquet, and though I was rusty at playing, he'd graciously let me win two of the games. That, I knew, was the way he said sorry.

We traded glances now as Susan sighed and said, 'Fine, be like that. You can't dampen my mood, I'm too happy.'

I told her, 'You ought to be. Today was perfect.'

'Can't rest on my laurels,' she said. 'We've still got the coach tour from Cardiff tomorrow.' She turned again to look at Mark. 'By the way, you don't know what's become of Dad's display stand, do you? The one we unearthed when we cleared out the greenhouse? I thought we might salvage the sign from it if nothing else.'

'Sorry,' Mark said. 'I'm painting it.'

'Painting it? What on earth for?'

'Well, I'll need it for Southport,' he said.

Susan stared at him as though she didn't know him. 'What?'

'The Southport Flower Show. You want to read my blog more often. I announced last week that we'd be going.'

'But you never go to shows. Not anymore.'

'A man can change.' A glance at me. 'Besides, like Eva said, we need to raise our profile.'

For a moment Susan looked at him in silence, then she said, 'Right. Now I *know* I'm delirious. Eva?'

'I'll get us drinks, shall I?' Setting my magazine down as I stood, I asked, 'Is there wine in the fridge, still?'

Mark thought that there was. 'Need some help?'

'Susan's delirious, and you're knackered. I'll manage.'

I wasn't sure where Claire had got to, but the house was quiet when I crossed the hall. The kitchen door stood slightly open. Pushing it, I felt it thud on something that not only stopped its inward swing but bounced it back towards me. Damn, I thought. One of the dogs must have decided to stretch out behind the door to take a nap and now I'd clouted him, poor thing.

I heard a scuffle and a thump and then the door was yanked back open from the inside, all the way this time, and I could see the thing that had been blocking it was not a dog at all. It was the body of a man stretched out face down across the flagstone floor, his black hair wetly matted where a dark red trickle had begun to stain his collar. It was Fergal.

Shocked, I raised my gaze to find a pistol leveled steady at my chest.

I couldn't focus on the man who held it, because I'd

already looked beyond him to the hard eyes of another man who stood close by the fireplace.

'Mistress O'Cleary,' the constable said, 'do come in.'

CHAPTER 36

I COULDN'T MOVE, AT FIRST.

Not that I wanted to, really. The last thing I wanted to do was step over the threshold into that unwelcoming room. But the man with the pistol had lowered it and now reached forwards to take a rough grip on my arm with his other hand, hauling me in.

'Shut the door,' said the constable. For all his calmness, he sounded displeased. 'Mr. Hewitt?'

Someone else moved in the shadows behind him. 'Yes?'

God, I thought, how many of them were there? Trying to shake myself out of my nightmare paralysis, I took a wild look round the room and counted two more faces, making five of them in total. Small wonder Fergal hadn't stood a chance.

He lay now almost at my feet, and with relief I saw his ribs move slightly.

'Did you not,' the constable was saying, 'tell me you had searched the house?'

'I did,' the man named Hewitt protested. 'I swear I saw no one. She must have been hiding.'

The constable acknowledged this. ''Tis why they call it "searching". Would you be so kind as to go try again? With Mr. Leach's help.'

The man who'd been holding my arm turned his head, gave a nod, and let go of me, slipping from the kitchen in the wake of the disgruntled Hewitt. Left there standing by the door, I tried to show the bravest face I could, my shoulders straightening a little as the constable regarded me with shuttered eyes that took no notice of the injured man who lay between us.

Almost casually, he asked me, 'Were you hiding?'

I remembered not to talk in time and shook my head. My hands had started trembling and I curled them into fists so they would not betray my weakness.

But he seemed to see it anyway. His mouth curved into something that could not be called a smile. 'In bed then.' Spoken with a certainty supported by the way his gaze raked over my appearance, and I realized for the first time that the summer frock I'd worn all day, a loosely fitting peasant-styled frock of plain cream cotton, would to him and all the other men look like a chemise. Dressed as I was with my hair loose, I could understand why he had assumed I'd been in bed.

His sneer was more apparent when he asked, 'Were you alone?'

For an answer I lifted my chin a half inch to imply such a question was not worth my answering.

One of the men near the window-wall said, 'Mr. Creed,' and the constable's stare sliced the dark air between them.

'Yes, Mr. Pascoe? You've something to say?'

An older man moved to the edge of the firelight, his features familiar. 'I'll ask you to mind how you speak, sir. The girl's done naught to warrant such insult.'

I recognized him then. I'd seen that same mix of defiance and shame on his face when he'd ridden as one of the constable's deputies on the day Jack was arrested at St Non's, and the same unvoiced apology in his quick glance the next day when he'd stopped off in the stable yard to bring the conger eel for Fergal. Fergal hadn't called him Mr. Pascoe, though. He'd called him Peter. That implied the two of them were friends, of sorts, and meant I might have one man in this group who would defend me.

The constable had brushed aside the protest. 'It can be no insult, surely, to request the facts.' He followed my quick downward glance towards Fergal. 'You fear for your brother? A touching display, but I'll warrant he'll live long enough for his hanging.'

I wasn't so sure. He appeared to be breathing more shallowly now, and defying the constable's presence I knelt on the flagstones and stroked Fergal's hair lightly, trying to find where the injury was.

When the man Peter took a step forwards, the constable stopped him. 'No, leave her,' he warned. 'Keep your watch.'

My fingers touched the broad gash at the base of Fergal's skull and I put pressure on it, hoping that would help to slow the bleeding. They had hit him from behind, a ruthless blow with something sharp enough to leave a cut and with the weight to bring him down—a jug, it looked like, from the jagged shards of earthenware that seemed to have been kicked into the corner by the door behind me.

One shard the size of my hand pricked my knee as I shifted position to check Fergal's pulse at his throat. It was there, faint but steady.

The constable's men, Leach and Hewitt, had finished their search of the upper floors. Coming back into the kitchen, Leach said, 'No one.'

'Then we wait.' The constable relaxed in his position by the fireplace. 'I have waited long enough for this already. I can wait a little longer.'

It was the note of satisfaction in his voice that made me look in his direction, and he said, 'Ah, but perhaps you have not heard, Mistress O'Cleary, that the House of Lords has passed a law suspending those protections that did lately shield your lover. And as keeper of that law here in Polgelly I now have the right to enter any premises I choose, arrest whomever I suspect of plotting treason to the king, and see them sent to London where, I promise you, they will find no reprieve.'

My fingers slid protectively to Fergal's shoulder as Leach crossed towards us to take up his earlier position, standing guard.

As I shifted a little bit further away from him, my knee came down full onto the piece of the broken jug. I could feel it cut right through the fabric that covered my leg, but I bit my lip hard and said nothing, not wanting to draw any more attention to myself.

The men had fallen back to an uneasy silence, waiting. Listening.

It might have been a quarter of an hour before I heard the measured tramp of footsteps coming.

Leach had brought his pistol up and cocked it with an evil click to hold it aimed directly at the door to the back corridor, so that whoever stepped inside would have no hope of—

'Mr. Creed?' The voice that called from outside in the yard was more a boy's voice than a man's and wavered from exertion. 'Mr. Creed?'

The fifth man, who stood nearest to the door, looked to the constable, who nodded, and the boy was swiftly ushered in.

He was stocky and round-faced and in the firelight I saw nothing in his face that was familiar, but his voice struck a decided chord within my memory when he said, 'I know where Mr. Butler's to.'

This was, I thought, the same boy who had come aboard the *Sally* as a spy and been put off again by Daniel. The same 'beard-less lad' Jack had argued might cause us all trouble some day. Jack had clearly been right, and just as he'd predicted, the boy was now trying to prove himself worthy to Constable Creed.

'I did just like you said,' said the boy, still half-breathless, 'and kept myself close to the Spaniard, and two of the men come out talking and one of 'em said to the other that it would be best when the day was well over, for one year of King George was naught to celebrate…' Pausing, he added, 'I noted his name for you, seeing that's treason and all.'

Creed's eyes narrowed. 'Go on.'

'Well, the other replied that the king would have no more years after this, and their own work this night would help in sending him where he belonged, and they both laughed, and then the first asked was it midnight at the cave still, and the other told him ay, but both the Butler brothers would be at the cave before that. Both of them together, I did hear it plainly said,' he finished proudly.

Creed was frowning. 'And where is this cave they spoke of then?'

The man named Peter dropped his gaze and gave a faint shake of his head towards the man beside him, while the young man Hewitt shifted till he stood behind the constable and gave a careless shrug. The bully Leach appeared to miss all this and clearly didn't know about the cave below the Cripplehorn himself, but even as my hopes began to rise the boy spoke up, 'Why, I was thinking that you knew it for yourself, sir, or I would have shown you sooner. I can take you there.'

'Then do it.' Creed looked blackly at the men around him, as though he were trying to assess just how much use they'd be, but in the end he only said, 'If there be any man who is uncertain of his duty to the law, then let him tell me now, for I stand always ready to remind him.' Only silence met his challenge. 'No? Then let us waste no more time. Mr. Leach, you will remain here with O'Cleary.'

'And the girl?' Leach asked.

'She comes with us.'

This proved too much for Peter. 'Mr. Creed!'

When Creed looked round as though astonished any man would speak in such a tone to him, the older man said bluntly, 'Sir, I'll not allow it.'

At my knee I felt a movement, very faint. I braved a quick look down and saw that Fergal's hand had moved a fraction, and his fingers had begun to curl. I didn't know just how aware he was of what was going on or how much he could hear, but to be safe I slipped my hand in his and lightly squeezed to warn him not to move again.

Creed's eyes were dangerous. 'You'll not allow it?'

'No, sir. First off, she's not dressed. It isn't decent.'

This apparently had bothered Hewitt too, for he put in, 'There is a chest of women's clothes upstairs, I'll just go up and—'

'No.' Creed's voice cut sharply through the offer. 'Those clothes do not belong to her.' To Peter, he said, 'Offer her your coat then, Mr. Pascoe, if it troubles you, and let that be an end to it.'

But Peter, growing bolder, said, 'And any rate, the way down to the cave would be too rough for her, too rough for any woman in the daylight, let alone the dark.'

He hadn't realized what he'd just admitted, I felt sure, until the constable's hard features altered subtly and his voice smoothed to the tone I found most frightening.

'So, you know it, then? The way down to the Butlers' cave.'

The older man's jaw set, but he didn't answer either way. And in that silence I felt sure the constable would win; that I'd be taken with them down to wait in ambush in the cave below the Cripplehorn, and Fergal would be left here help- less on his own with Leach. And Leach's pistol.

In a panic I tried thinking. Then I felt the ragged sharp- ness of the broken wedge of earthenware still lodged beneath my knee, and very slowly and with care I inched it forwards till it rested underneath the hand I'd linked with Fergal's. No one noticed. Still more carefully, I guided it up into Fergal's palm and closed his fingers round it, pushing at his arm until his hand was tucked beneath the out flung edge of his dark coat, against his side.

Leach wouldn't see it there. But now when Fergal woke, I thought, at least he'd have a weapon. If he did wake.

He'd gone still again.

Creed said, in that same elegantly soulless voice I'd learned to fear, 'I do confess that I have never understood the loyalty these Butler men command, and yet I truly cannot help but be impressed by it.' He looked from Peter back to Hewitt and then to the silent man who stood between the window and the door. 'It is a pity there'll be no one from Polgelly on the jury to defend them when they're brought to trial, for Londoners will surely be less sympathetic to the Butlers' charms.' He turned to Leach. 'I know you'll be occupied watching O'Cleary, but were I to leave you his sister as well could you manage it?'

Leach looked me up and down, leering. 'Oh, ay, I could manage her fine, Mr. Creed.'

Peter moved again sharply in protest, and Creed's gaze swung round.

'You object to that also, Mr. Pascoe? Perhaps you'd prefer, then, to stay behind with them.'

'I would, ay.' The older man's face was distrustful, but Creed only told him, 'So be it,' and took a step backwards to clear the way.

Peter, still clearly disturbed by my state of undress, began shrugging his coat from his shoulders as he crossed the floor, and the constable reached to take hold of the back of the coat's heavy collar, as though to assist him.

And then his hold tightened, and swiftly his free arm swung forwards and drove hard at Peter's chest.

It happened so fast that at first I was not really sure what I'd seen. With a cough and a look of astonishment Peter collapsed to his knees, arms pinned back by the constable's grip on the coat.

'You may stay, as you wish,' Creed said lightly, and as he drew his arm back I could see the knife blade brightly red, a deadly thing. Peter coughed again, and Creed yanked back once with his other arm to wrench the coat completely clear, then watched without expression as the older man fell face-first to the floor and lay unmoving.

'Now, then.' In the small, shocked silence Creed, uncaring, wiped the bloodied knife blade on the coat's dark sleeve. 'Does anybody else prefer to stay behind?'

The men, including Leach, stayed silent.

'No?' The constable glanced round for confirmation. 'Then let us go.' He waved the knife from Leach to me and told him, 'Get her up.'

'You said—'

'I lied.' Creed's eyebrows rose as if to show surprise that anyone would have thought otherwise. 'If Butler has his men around him, he may need persuading to submit to his arrest.

Besides,' he added, 'if I left her here with you she might distract you from your duties, Mr. Leach.'

Leach didn't answer him out loud, but he was grumbling something underneath his breath as he reached down to roughly grab my arm and haul me to my feet.

Creed gave his knife a final close inspection. Satisfied, he tossed the coat across to me and turned away before I caught it. 'Cover yourself,' he said.

The boy who still stood just inside the door was staring dumbly at the body on the floor. If he had ever seen a murder done at all, I thought, he'd never been this close to one, because the stunned uncertainty was written plainly on his face.

The constable stopped walking just in front of him and waited. 'Well?'

The boy, misunderstanding, seemed to think that Creed was asking his advice, and answered, 'Shouldn't we... that is, sir, should we not attempt to move...?'

Creed frowned. 'Move what?' He turned his head, his own gaze following the boy's. 'Oh, that. No, leave him there. It was unfortunate that in our efforts to arrest O'Cleary he attacked and killed poor Mr. Pascoe, but we can at least console ourselves in knowing that a charge of murder added to his treason will ensure the judge assigns him an unpleasant end.' He looked back at the boy, impatient. 'Now, this cave.'

'The... yes, sir. Yes.' The boy recovered. 'I can take you there.'

'Then do so. Mr. Hewitt?'

'Sir?'

Creed shot one final glance behind him, cold and purposeful. 'Bring Butler's whore.'

CHAPTER 37

I SAW FIRE ON the hillside.

At first my mind just lumped that observation in with all the other things about the night that seemed surreal—the violent drama I'd stepped into, Fergal lying senseless on the floor, the man named Peter being killed before my eyes, and now the fact that I was being hurried by the hands of strangers over the dark field that lay between Trelowarth and the woods... why *shouldn't* there be fire on the hill as well, I wondered?

But even through the fog of shock that masked my sharper senses I could see it was no random fire, nor any strange imagining.

The Beacon had been lit.

I'd never seen it lit in my own lifetime. I had seen my parents' snapshots of the Beacon being lighted for the Silver Jubilee of Queen Elizabeth, before my birth, and Claire had sent me pictures of it burning on the eve of the Millennium, when all of Britain's ancient beacons had been set ablaze, but what the photographs had captured was a fraction of the full effect.

The sight was truly awe inspiring: flames of brilliant gold that speared the star-flecked sky and shifted shape in random sprays of sparks. At any other time I might have marveled at it, but my mind had narrowed in its focus and refused to be distracted long by anything that fell outside the needs of self-protection.

I had little memory afterwards of passing with my captors through the wood or scrambling down the jagged slickness of the rocks onto the beach—it blended into one long nightmarish descent where I was scraped by branches, cut by rocks, and finally hit the shingle with a bruised knee and the taste of my own blood upon my tongue. It wasn't serious. I'd bitten through my lip to keep from crying out when I had whacked my knee, but still the pain of it was real, and my lip swelled so much that when we'd found the entrance to the cave and stumbled in, and Creed had set the shuttered lantern that he'd carried from Trelowarth House in place on top of one wide barrel, opening its sides to let the light spill out, the man named Hewitt looked at me with pity and discomfort.

I felt pity for him too, because I knew he couldn't come to my defence the way he might have liked to. Both of us had seen what the result of that would be. I drew the stiff edges of Peter's jacket tighter round my throat against the penetrating dampness of the cave and turned away from Hewitt's gaze.

The constable was watching us. Without a word he took a long look round the shadowed cave and said, 'This is a most agreeable arrangement. Have the Butlers used it long?' He aimed the question straight at Hewitt, but it was the boy who answered.

'Why, they've always used it, sir. 'Tis common knowledge in the village. I was shown it by my father, years ago.'

'Is that a fact?' Creed took his pistol from his belt, examining its workings with an attitude of unconcern, but I could see his underlying tenseness. He looked not unlike a predator prepared to spring, and I was sure the people of Polgelly would be made to feel the depth of his displeasure with them. Taking out the knife he had just used to kill a man, he turned its point to make some small adjustment to the flintlock mechanism of his gun.

And that's when I remembered.

It was over there, I thought, just *there*, between the barrels to my left, that Daniel's own dropped dagger had been lying on the floor the last I'd seen it.

If I picked it up I knew I would be changing what was meant to happen, but then I'd already changed things once tonight by being here. A man lay dead because of me, because he'd tried to help me, and however that one act had changed the future it was done, and there was nothing I could do to change it back. All I could do was try to stay alive myself, and if I had a weapon I'd be bettering my odds.

The challenge was to find a way to get from where I stood to where I thought the dagger lay. I was deciding how to do it when my thoughts were interrupted by a noise approaching steadily outside the cave: the heavy crunch of footsteps over shingle.

Creed held one hand up to warn the men to silence and aimed his pistol at the entrance as a second sound rose up now with the shifting steps—the sound of someone whistling a careless tune I recognized.

My heart dropped. Jack.

And then in almost sickening slow motion all the things I'd seen and heard tonight slid into place like pieces of a puzzle, and I knew then why the Beacon had been lit. I could hear again the boy's voice telling Creed what he had overheard the one man tell the other as they left the Spaniard's Rest: that he'd be happy when the day was over, for a year of King George on the throne was not a thing that should be celebrated.

God, I thought, that must be it. In my time the Polgelly

folk had marked a royal jubilee by lighting up the Beacon, so it made sense the people here would do the same. Uncaring fate had brought me back on the first anniversary of King George's rule, the same day when, according to the note in Jack's unfinished memoirs, Jack 'did chance to fall afoul of the lawmen of Polgelly, and while fleeing from their constable was killed by one sure pistol shot.'

I knew what was about to happen—knew because the constable was with me, and the men who walked around us *were* the 'lawmen of Polgelly', and the night was not yet over.

Jack would die, because I'd read it on a printed page and printed pages weren't meant to be changed. Like in the lines I'd quoted on the ship to Daniel from the *Rubáiyát*, The Moving Finger had already written what must be.

But then I thought of Daniel telling Fergal, 'He's my brother,' and God help me, I just couldn't stand there silently and watch another man be killed.

As Jack was stepping through the opening into the cave, I made a sudden lunge against the constable and shouted, 'Jack, get out! Warn Daniel! Run!'

The pistol's deafening report in that confined space drowned my words and I could not be sure he heard them, and a second after that I couldn't see him for the powder smoke that seared my throat and stung my eyes and drifted like a white cloud through the cave, but as it cleared I saw the place where Jack had stood was empty.

The constable's shot had gone wide. Several feet away the boy took an unsteady step and stared at me with wonder and bewilderment, and then he touched a hand to the new spreading stain upon his chest and stumbled once again and fell.

Creed's eyes, much closer, had held wonder too at first, but by the time I met them they were freezing over into something terrifying. With the gun still in his hand he swept his arm out savagely and struck me full across my face. I felt the pain against my cheekbone and the trickling warmth of blood start down the bruised skin of my temple, but although I staggered back I didn't shame myself by falling down.

When Hewitt made a move as though to protest, Creed stopped him with the cold reminder, 'This is none of your affair. Nor yours,' he told the other man behind. 'Now go, the pair of you, and bring Jack Butler back.'

The two men hesitated, and he wheeled on them. 'I told you, go!'

And without any further argument the men edged off. I heard their footsteps scraping on the shingle, walking first, then moving off more quickly, breaking to a run.

Creed didn't move, but still I felt the space between us shrinking.

'So,' he said. 'You have a voice.'

I tried to think. I hadn't said that many words, and with the pistol's firing it was likely that he hadn't heard me clearly, so there was a fair chance that he wouldn't know I wasn't Irish, wasn't who he thought I was. And even though he knew that I could speak, my safest course now might just be to keep my mouth shut and not risk him finding out that I did not belong here.

'A clever play on Butler's part,' he said, 'and on your brother's, for it made me ill inclined to ask you questions, as they no doubt hoped it would.'

The knowledge that he still thought I was Fergal's sister would have eased my mind more if he hadn't been reloading the pistol while he talked, brushing the used powder out of the firing pan and repriming it deftly.

'But now that I have heard you speak,' he said as he took practice aim towards the entrance of the cave and idly sighted down the barrel, 'I've a mind to find out for myself how well you sing.'

I watched the pistol swing around to point at me.

He said, 'You can sing, can you not, Mistress O'Cleary? You will find it is a useful art for keeping your own head out of the hangman's noose. Come now, tell me what does Butler mean to shift from here tonight, and where will it be bound?'

Shaking my head once I took a step backwards, reminding myself he was trying to frighten me. Doing a fabulous job of it, certainly, but he had no real intention of killing me yet. He still needed me for the same reason he'd told his men earlier— Daniel would never submit to arrest without force or coercion, and I was the constable's leverage, his bargaining chip.

He wouldn't kill me yet, I told myself again, and clinging to that little fragment of uncertain courage I stepped back again and hoped he'd think I was retreating from the pistol. I knew well enough I didn't have a hope of moving out of range—I'd seen the damage his last shot had done the boy, who had been standing farther off from Creed than I was standing now—but the dagger, Daniel's dagger, was still lying on the damp stone floor somewhere between the barrels just behind me.

My thoughts had not yet focused through my fear enough to let me form a plan of what to do with it, but having any weapon seemed a better thing than having none at all, so I kept inching backwards with a single-minded purpose while Creed said, 'You do know, do you not, what does befall a woman like yourself in Newgate? And for what? The law is very clear for those who comfort traitors. In the end you will be forced to testify to what you know, and he will hang regardless, and your suffering will be for naught. Speak now, to me, and I may yet persuade the courts to show you mercy.'

The voice that answered wasn't mine. It said, 'A kind offer, but I rather doubt she'll accept it.'

I turned my head, astonished to see Jack not twenty feet from us, inside the entrance to the cave. Keeping his own pistol leveled on Creed and his gaze firmly fixed on the constable's face he remarked, 'You have given her small cause to think you'd be merciful.'

The constable shrugged. 'Men can change.'

If Jack felt fear he was hiding it well. He looked calm and completely relaxed as he took a step forwards and ordered me, 'Eva, go now.'

I heard Creed's gun, still pointed at me, give an ominous click. 'Butler, I should have thought saving yourself would outweigh any chivalrous impulses.'

Jack gave a half smile and said, 'Men can change, so I've been told.' Still coming forwards, he said again, 'Eva, go now, he'll not shoot you.'

The constable lowered his eyebrows at that. 'Will I not? And what makes you so certain?'

'Because it is not your design. You'd not even shoot me if I gave you the chance.'

'You seem very certain.' Creed's voice had an edge. 'Why not put your own pistol aside, and we'll see?'

Jack answered without stopping his advance, 'All right.'

And as I watched in horror he replaced his pistol in his belt and held his hands out slightly from his sides to plainly show he was unarmed.

Creed's pistol swung away from me to aim at Jack, and as it moved I took advantage of the fact to back away between the barrels, where I'd seen the dagger on the day we'd brought the cargo back from Brittany.

I'd nearly given up when I saw one faint edge of something metal gleaming in the lantern's light, and cautiously, my eyes still on the men, I stooped to pick it up. My hands weren't large enough to hold the dagger's blade concealed as Daniel did, but still I tried to keep it pointed straight so it was hidden by my wrist as much as possible.

Neither Jack nor Creed appeared to notice.

Jack had covered half the space between them now with his sure, certain steps, and all the while his gaze stayed steady on the constable. 'You want us dead, myself and Danny, but you will not shoot me now, for should I die by your own hand the people of Polgelly will demand to know the cause of it, and even your authority has limits in this place.' He tipped his head to one side, questioning. 'Or do you think those two men you presumably sent after me, the ones I did see running for the woods, will yet return to lend you aid?'

Creed said, 'The people of Polgelly have no choice. The laws have changed.'

'Yes, I have heard. We may be taken without benefit of warrant, may we not, and sent to London for our trials? More reason not to kill me now,' said Jack, his hands still at his sides as he came closer, 'when you could leave that pleasure to the executioner, while you stand by the gallows and enjoy the entertainment.' Without turning his head he repeated, 'Go, Eva.'

'She stays,' said the constable. 'For if you claim to know the law, then you will also know that trials do have need of evidence, and she can yet supply that.'

Jack said, 'Eva cannot testify.'

'You think I am a fool?' Creed was dismissive. 'She can speak.'

'She can. But not against my brother. Or against myself, in fact, if that would so reveal my brother's crimes.'

Jack knew. I saw it in the faint curve of his mouth before he dropped the bombshell with the satisfaction of a small boy who liked watching things explode. 'For if *you* know the law,' he said, 'then you will know no judge will have a woman as a witness at the trial of her husband.'

Creed stood thunderstruck. 'Her husband!'

'Ay, that was my own reaction, I'll confess, when Danny told me, but the vicar did assure me it was true, and for my part I now can see it was a good match wisely made.' The glance Jack sent my way held reassurance, but beneath it was full knowledge of the danger we were in. 'So you see,' he finished off, 'she'll be no use to you.'

The constable's cold eyes had taken on a colder purpose. 'Oh, I disagree,' he said. 'I can imagine quite a few ways that I might use *Mrs.* Butler, and I'll keep your brother well informed of all of them while he does rot in Newgate.'

He turned his head to leer at me, and that brief shift of focus was the chance Jack had been waiting for. Arm's length now from the constable, he closed the distance in a final surge of motion, one hand reaching for possession of the pistol.

It was over in an instant.

With the gun's report still ringing in my disbelieving ears I watched Jack stagger back and fall, and felt a sudden stinging in my eyes that wasn't from the burning whiteness of the smoke.

'No,' I whispered, blinking back the pricking blur of tears.

I'd saved him, hadn't I? I'd made a choice and changed things so this wouldn't have to happen, so he wouldn't have to die.

But he *was* dead. There was no question of it.

'No!'

I must have spoken that more strongly, for the constable glanced up and, with a twisting of his mouth, turned back and spat once with contempt on Jack's unmoving body. 'Now,' he said, preparing to reload his pistol as he'd done before, 'we've but to wait for your brave husband, have we not? I must admit I did have some misgivings as to whether he would truly hold your life so dear that he'd agree to let me take him prisoner. A mistress, after all, is but a mistress. But a *wife…*' His tone was confident and mocking at the same time, and it struck some switch inside me that I hadn't known I had.

I didn't afterwards remember when I moved or how, but in the next breath I was somehow there in front of Creed and Daniel's dagger was no longer in my hand.

He dropped the pistol with a clatter to the weeping stone and raised one hand to grasp the dagger's handle in his turn. It looked so strangely out of place there, stuck hilt-deep into the centre of his chest.

His face was angry as he yanked the short blade out and tossed it clattering aside, and looking at the rush of bright red blood that followed seemed to make him even angrier, because he raised his head and started cursing me…

The words froze on his lips.

I saw the change in his expression, saw the darkness of his glare give way to fear, and heard the horror in the word he whispered: 'Witch!'

He was already fading as his legs gave way beneath him and he dropped hard to his knees, this man who had so often fed upon the fear of others rattling out his final breath with terror in his eyes. And then he fell and his grey shadow tumbled down and thinned to nothingness.

Jack's body faded too, and all the dimness of the cave around me shuddered once and melted into the back passage of Trelowarth House, and I was standing ready to walk through the kitchen door.

Except I couldn't move.

The night had sent me back too traumatized. I couldn't seem to manage the transition; I could only stand there trembling with the tearstains on my bruised and swelling cheek, wrapped in the rough coat of a dead man that weighed heavily upon my shaking shoulders.

I'm not sure I ever would have found the will or strength to move if I had not heard footsteps clipping with a cheerful and familiar beat across the kitchen floor, though even when the heavy door swung inwards and Claire stood there in amazement at the sight of me, I couldn't think of anything to do but fling myself into her arms and cling there weeping like a child who'd just awakened from a nightmare.

CHAPTER 38

S HOCK DOES STRANGE THINGS to the mind.

My senses telescoped to focus on a few small, random details while the rest of what was going on I only grasped in fragments. Which was why I knew that Claire had seven buttons on her shirt but didn't know how we'd come halfway up the steep back stairs.

I heard somebody entering the kitchen and Mark's voice below us called me, 'Eva?'

Claire answered for me, still guiding me upwards, 'She's here with me, darling. I gave her a nasty hard whack in the face with the kitchen door, probably blackened her eye.'

A tiny voice deep in my mind argued, *That's not what happened,* but they had moved on to the subject of doctors and whether I needed one.

Claire said she wouldn't be sure till she'd had a good look at it. 'I'll let you know.'

And the next thing I knew I was soaking alone in the tub in the bathroom upstairs. On the edge of the tub sat a small dish of guest soaps, impractical things shaped like roses, six roses, quite violently pink.

Very slowly, my shaking subsided.

I wasn't in the bathroom anymore, but in my bedroom.

'There, now.' Claire was beside me again. I could feel the slight dip of the mattress as she took a seat on the edge of my bed, leaning over to tuck the sheets round me. The cool of her hand smoothed my damply hot forehead while my eyes stayed fixed on the place where a small flake of paint had been chipped from the wall near my headboard.

Claire's tone was gently undemanding. 'Do you want to talk about it?'

No.

I couldn't form the word yet, but my head moved slightly on the pillow and she understood.

'All right.' I felt her hand against my forehead for a second time, and then she left.

At least, I thought she did.

But in the middle of the night I briefly woke from fretful dreams, and rolling over in the tangle of my blankets, I was sure I caught a glimpse of someone sitting in the shadows of the corner by the fireplace, watching over me.

The house was quiet when I woke.

No laughter floating up the stairs, no whispers from the room next door, no movement but the swaying of the curtains at my windows as they sought to catch the currents of the spindrift-scented summer breeze before the wind's inconstant nature dropped them limply back to lie in wait against the window ledge.

The room felt warm. Too warm to be the morning. And the shadows were not in their proper places.

Without thinking I turned slightly on the pillow and the sudden painful pressure on my swollen cheek called back the night's dark memories in a swift, depressing rush.

I'd killed a man. I'd stabbed a man and killed him, and although he'd murdered others in his turn and would have doubtless murdered me, the fact remained that I'd done something I had always thought I'd be incapable of doing, and that wasn't such an easy thing to wrap my thoughts around.

And if my thoughts were horrible for me, I knew it would be even worse for Daniel, coming to the cave to find his brother dead. That the constable lay dead as well would be at least a minor consolation, but it wouldn't be a balance for the loss of Jack, in Daniel's view. Or mine.

I closed my eyes to shut the memories out. It didn't work. Against the blackness of my mind I saw the play of images, and I remembered everything. The only part that seemed less clear was how I'd come to be up here, in my pajamas, in my bed... then I remembered that as well and looked around for Claire.

I'd need to talk to her, I knew. I'd need to give some explanation for the state she'd found me in last night, though for the life of me I really didn't know what I could say, where I'd begin.

But knowing Claire, I wouldn't have a choice. She might be patient and prepared to wait, not rushing me, but in the end she'd want to have the answers to her questions.

Getting up and getting dressed took time. My limbs were stiff and everywhere I saw the scrapes and bruises that the night had left. The sight of my face in the mirror wasn't nearly as bad as I'd feared it would be. My eye had been left unaffected; the worst of the swelling had kept to the curve of my cheekbone and most of the bruising was up by my temple, the cut barely visible where it ran into my hairline.

In fact, if I left my hair down and allowed it to swing forwards slightly it covered up most of the damage.

The damage that showed, I corrected myself.

There was worse on the inside that, while it was simpler

to hide, would be harder to heal. But I hid it the best that I could and went downstairs, composing a speech in my mind as I went, forming lines and discarding them, finding a few that I liked and rehearsing them mentally so they'd sound normal.

I needn't have bothered. Nobody was there.

As I moved through the rooms I tried keeping my thoughts in the present day, focusing on what was actually there, but I found the lines blurring and shifting at random, and when I came into the kitchen my steps dragged a little. I didn't want to be in here, didn't want to think of everything I'd seen in here last night or to remember Fergal lying on the floor just there, the fight knocked cruelly out of him.

I thought of Fergal's dark impassive eyes and his dry wit and felt a twist of pain not knowing what had happened to him. With the sharp edge of that broken piece of pot held in his hand he would have had at least a chance against the constable's man, Leach, who'd been left to guard him. But that was only if Leach hadn't used his pistol and assuming Fergal ever had gained consciousness again.

I couldn't bear to think of Fergal dead.

And yet I knew they all were now. The world had turned and they were dead and in the ground, and there was nothing I could do about it. Daniel had been right the day he'd said to me, 'This life that I have lived, it has already passed and faded from the memories of the people of your own time...'

He'd been right, too, when he'd theorized that altering the past might prove impossible. By calling a warning to Jack as he'd entered the cave I had saved him from being shot then by the constable, but time had found another way to do what must be done, and even with my interference Jack had died the way that he'd been meant to. Even Daniel's dagger that I'd used to kill the constable had, in the end, been thrown back to the cave floor and had scuttled to the shadows to lie waiting till Mark came to find it. History hadn't changed.

At least, I didn't think it had. I only knew the present seemed to be exactly as I'd left it. It just felt a little emptier.

As if on cue, a shadow passed the window and I heard the back door open and Felicity came in, balancing a plastic washing-up tub stacked with cups and saucers while she chatted on the mobile phone held wedged against her shoulder.

'No, no,' she was saying, '*all* over the floor. Well, we've switched it off, yes, but the thing is we've got a big tour group arriving a half hour from now, and… oh, would you? Thanks, that would be wonderful, Paul. You're a prince.'

Carefully sliding the tub onto the worktop so the china didn't clink too much, she rang off and greeted me, 'Hi. I didn't wake you with the last load, did I?'

Not sure what she meant at first, I glanced towards the sink and for the first time noticed it was nearly brimful too with soaking dishes, and a second empty washing-up tub sat off to the side.

'No,' I said. 'What's going on?'

'The dishwasher's leaking. We were putting these through so they'd be good and clean for our afternoon crowd, only something went wrong in the rinse cycle and we wound up with a flood in the kitchen and lovely baked soap on the dishes.' She held up a teacup to show me and tapped the hard crystals of soap. 'Just like rock. I've been scrubbing it off.'

I grasped at the chance to do something to keep my thoughts occupied. 'Want some help?'

'Claire said to let you rest.' She looked more closely at my face. 'She really got you with that door, didn't she? How does it feel?'

I didn't correct her assumption of how I'd been injured, I only assured her it wasn't as bad as it looked. 'I'm fine, honestly.'

Working together we had both tubs restacked with clean cups and saucers in under ten minutes.

'Come on,' I said, lifting the nearest tub carefully. 'I'll help you carry these back.'

It was going to rain. The air felt unmistakably heavy and carried the scent of a summer storm underneath clouds that were gathering grey. As I followed Felicity up to the greenhouse I noticed that the thorn tree now wore flutterings of cloth strips left by some of our new tourists, and it made a proper cloutie tree beside the charming tearoom.

As we came inside, the smell of scones fresh from the oven overpowered all my other senses for a moment, and my stomach rumbled as I set my plastic tub of dishes down behind the serving counter. Susan straightened from behind the broken dishwasher and dumped a sodden rag into the bucket at her feet. She looked remarkably controlled, I thought, considering the crisis.

'Thanks,' she said, and sent a smile to both of us. 'The floor's dry now, at least. Did you get hold of Paul?'

Felicity nodded. 'I did. He'll be here in a minute, he said.'

'Right, then.' Looking around, Susan noticed my face. 'God, Eva. That must hurt. Claire said it looked pretty awful.'

'I'm fine,' I repeated. But she'd reminded me I wasn't in the clear yet, and I glanced around in my turn. 'Where is Claire?'

'She's gone up to keep an eye out for the coach, let us know what the numbers are.'

'Let's get these tables set, then,' said Felicity.

We weren't quite finished when I heard the steps crunching down the curved path from the gardens above, but it wasn't the tour group just yet—only Paul, looking as though he'd rolled straight out of bed to answer Felicity's emergency call, with his blue denim shirt hanging unbuttoned over the close-fitting T-shirt beneath.

Susan brightened. She was crouched behind the counter with him, showing him the problem, when another set of footsteps sounded briskly on the gravel and Claire came inside. 'They're here,' she said. 'Just coming down. The guide said forty-one.'

Susan stood, as did the plumber, who gave Claire a friendly nod and a good morning. He was chattier with Claire than with the rest of us. He asked, 'Where's this group from, then?'

Claire wasn't sure, but Susan told him, 'Wales. They're going on to St Non's after us.'

He said, 'Bad day for it,' and stretched his shoulders. 'Looks like rain.'

'We only have to give them tea,' said Susan cheerfully. 'They didn't want a garden tour.' Setting out plates she asked Claire, 'Forty-one, you said?'

Claire seemed oddly distracted. 'What? Oh yes, that's right.' She'd caught sight of me now. 'Eva, darling, you ought to be resting.' A motherly kind of reproach, but she said it with patience, the same sort of patience she'd shown when I'd strayed out of bounds as a child, and I felt the same need I'd so often felt then to just curl up at her side and tell her everything, because she'd understand.

But would she this time? How could anybody, even Claire, believe my story, much less understand it? She would put it down to stress or grief or even mental illness, and she'd worry...

'Here they come,' said Felicity, as the first tourists came into view on the path, and the next fifteen minutes were blissfully busy, keeping me from thinking about anything but filling and delivering the teapots—my assigned task— while the others served the scones with jam and clotted cream and Paul the plumber tried to keep his focus on the dishwasher, which couldn't have been easy since the tour group seemed to mostly be young women, not a few of whom were pretty and the bulk of whom appeared to have *their* focus fixed on Paul.

Susan and Felicity were both too deeply occupied to take much notice, but I knew Claire heard the comments and the giggling and I saw her smile a few times, then I saw her smile more knowingly in Paul's direction as it grew apparent he had eyes for one young woman in particular, a lively girl with laughing eyes who seemed to draw our plumber's gaze each time he straightened from his work, and when she went outside with friends to have them take her picture by the cloutie tree, his frequent glances followed her with interest.

Passing Claire as I returned from filling yet another teapot, I nodded at the little group of tourists by the cloutie tree and shared a conspiratorial smile. 'Susan has some competition.'

'So it seems.' She raised a hand to brush the hair back lightly from my swollen cheekbone. 'That looks rather better than I feared it would. I'm glad.'

I drew a breath. 'You didn't hit me with the door.'

'I know I didn't. But I had to tell them something, darling, didn't I?'

A laughing shriek from outside interrupted us. The rain had come at last, in a great sudden lashing downpour that was pelting on the glass roof of the tearoom like a drum roll and cascading down the windows as the small group of young women by the tree, caught unawares, made an impressive dash towards the door and tumbled through it, out of breath and dripping on the floor. Two of them had been wearing hooded raincoats and so escaped the worst of it, but the dark-haired girl Paul had been watching was soaked to the skin in her light cotton blouse.

And then Paul stood and shrugged his denim shirt off and stepped forwards, drawing all the female eyes now with his T-shirt closely sculpted to his muscled chest and shoulders and his lean flat stomach. 'Here.' He gallantly offered his shirt to the wide-eyed young woman, who took it and gave him a suddenly self-aware smile in return.

At the far edge of my vision I could see Felicity nudge Susan, and they stared together for a moment before Susan shook her head and made some comment to Felicity. No doubt she was remarking on how weird it was that history was repeating; that our plumber had done just what Claire's own grandfather had done, such a coincidence.

And then a kettle whistled to the boil and she turned back again to give it her attention, and the moment passed.

But not for me.

For me the moment stretched as though it were a string and I'd just figured out the pattern of the beads to thread upon it. Because I was watching Claire.

I saw the misting of her eyes, the strange emotion of her smile, the way she watched Paul watch the Welsh girl slide his shirt around her shoulders, and it all made sudden sense.

But still, it seemed so unbelievable that I could only clear my throat and say to Claire, 'That's just the way it happened with your grandparents.'

She turned her head and turned her smile on me, and then I knew beyond all doubt.

'My dear.' Her voice was quiet, meant for me alone, a confidence she must have felt quite sure I'd understand. 'They *are* my grandparents.'

CHAPTER 39

THE RAIN HAD STOPPED. From time to time the wind chased through the taller trees that edged the wood around Claire's small back garden, shaking leaves and letting loose a scattered showering of water droplets, sparkling as they fell like little diamonds in the spears of sunlight breaking through the branches and the ever-shifting clouds.

Claire came out with two mugs of tea and handed one to me and edged her chair around so that, like mine, it faced the little sundial with its butterfly's bronze wings forever poised for flight.

We sat there for a moment saying nothing while a bird sang somewhere, steadily, within the cooler shadows of the wood.

Then I said, 'So you knew who he was.'

'Paul? Oh yes. From the moment I saw him. And my grandmother too. Of course I wasn't *sure* I'd get to see the moment when they met, I wasn't certain of the date, but I did hope…' She glanced at me. 'I'm sorry, darling, that I haven't been more help to you this summer, but I thought it best to let you find your own way through, without my interference.'

'But you did know what was happening.'

'Of course,' she said. 'It happened much the same for me, although you travel from this time into the past, while this time *is* the past, to me.' Her gaze had settled calmly on the sundial, and she spoke as though we were discussing something very commonplace. 'The first time that I traveled back to this time, I was young, like you. Alone, like you. My parents had divorced, you see, and both of them had taken up with new people and suddenly there I was, with stepbrothers and stepsisters and our family home sold, and no place that was really my own anymore, and I began to feel a great nostalgia for the days when I'd come down here as a child, when both my grandparents were still alive and living at St Non's. When life was simpler.' Stretching out her legs, she took a sip of tea before continuing, 'I was struggling along on my own as an artist by then, no real ties or commitments to bind me to anywhere, so I came down into this part of Cornwall on holiday and spent a lovely fortnight rediscovering the place, and that of course,' she finished off, 'meant coming to Trelowarth, for a cream tea at the Cloutie Tree.'

She'd always loved to hear the story of the day her grandparents had met, and over the course of her own visits to them they'd formed a tradition of making a pilgrimage out to Trelowarth to share a cream tea.

'It wasn't the same,' she said, 'with them not there, but nonetheless it was a brilliant summer day and all the roses were in bloom and I stayed afterwards and wandered through the gardens as we'd always done. My grandmother had loved the Quiet Garden best of all, so I went up and had a little moment there, communing with her spirit. But when I was done and ready to come out again, I couldn't find the path.'

She had been more perplexed than panicked. It felt strange to lose her bearings in a place she'd known so well. Eventually, she'd found the path—not where she'd thought it ought to be, but she did find it, and began to make her way back down towards the Cloutie Tree, a bit disoriented, only to discover that the tearoom wasn't there.

'There wasn't even a greenhouse. I thought I was losing my mind,' she confessed, 'as I'm sure you'll appreciate.'

I managed a small smile. 'Yes. What did you do?'

'Well, I *did* panic then. I turned tail like a coward and ran to the house and I banged at the door until somebody answered. That was when I met your Uncle George.' Recalling that meeting, she said, 'I was lucky he didn't call in the authorities right there and then, and have them drag me off to Broadmoor. I know I must have sounded like a madwoman. But George… well, he was always kind to strays.' He'd brought Claire in and listened to her tale and made her tea.

'I'm not sure where the children were,' she said. 'Mark must have been at school, and Susan was most likely upstairs napping.'

He'd been widowed for a year by then, though at the time she hadn't known that. She'd been too caught up in her own strange predicament to notice much of anything.

I knew just how she'd felt.

'Then someone telephoned—the telephone was in the hall, I think, and George went off to answer it, and then…' She paused, as though unable to describe exactly what had happened next, before it seemed to strike her that with me, the process didn't need describing, so she simply said, 'And there I was again, back where I'd started, in the Quiet Garden.'

Everything was back where it was meant to be. The tearoom was in its place again, and she had gone inside to settle her bewildered nerves with one more pot of tea. After an hour in the Cloutie Tree amid the normal ebb and flow of patrons and inconsequential chatter, she'd convinced herself that what had happened must have been a daydream, an imagining.

But still, she'd packed her car up hastily that afternoon and cancelled her hotel and driven north across the moors to switch the subject of her paintings to the wilder-looking coastline on the other side of Cornwall, up near Boscastle.

Three months had passed before she'd found the nerve to venture back.

'I couldn't stop thinking about it,' she told me. 'I couldn't stop thinking of *him*. I'd begun to have dreams…'

It was autumn, by that time. The tourists had mostly departed, the streets of Polgelly were quiet, and up at Trelowarth the roses were reaching the end of their season, the gardens being readied for the winter.

She'd gone right up and knocked at the door of the house. 'I'd decided, you see, that the only way to get the whole episode out of my head would be to prove to myself that it couldn't have happened.' And as she'd expected, the door of Trelowarth was opened by somebody else—a man not unlike George in appearance, but with reddish hair and a leaner build. 'He was quite pleasant. I asked after George and he told me the only George Hallett he knew was his grandfather, and he'd been dead a long time.'

I felt my eyes widen. 'His grandfather? Then he was—'

'Mark's eldest,' Claire supplied. 'Stephen. A charming man. Very artistic he was, with these gardens, though all of Mark's children were artists in their own way. Something they got from their mother.'

'Felicity.'

'Yes.'

I was pleased by that.

Unseen, the wind stirred the trees at the edge of the garden and shook loose a new spray of lingering raindrops that fell near our feet and chased over the face of the sundial. The butterfly, frozen in bronze, stayed unmoving, still counting its moments.

Claire settled deeper in her chair and took another sip of tea. 'After talking to Stephen, I didn't know what to believe. What I'd seen. I only knew that there was something… something pulling me… no, pulling is perhaps too strong a word. Something inviting me to stay here. I went down into Polgelly to the pub to have some lunch. To think. And there, two tables over, was a man, a very old man, and he watched me for a little while, and then he just came over with his pint and sat right down and introduced himself.'

He'd thoroughly disarmed her with his easygoing attitude and they'd begun to talk, about her painting and her grand-parents and all that she remembered of St Non's.

'And then our talk turned to Trelowarth and the gardens and he told me that his wife had been a Hallett, and through her he had inherited a cottage on the grounds and if I wanted I could have it for the winter, do my work there. So—'

She spread her hands, and at the gesture I looked round.

'*This* cottage?'

'Yes.'

'So this was home for you in your own time, as well.'

Claire gave a nod. 'It still is, come to that. I still go back and forth, my dear. Not quite as often, anymore. The process seems to slow with age, but even so it's really not a thing one can control.'

Of course, I thought, and with a dawning sense of under-standing I recalled what Mark had told me on the day we'd argued in the field: 'When I was young,' he'd said, 'Claire used to go away for days, for weeks, sometimes, to do her work... She still does, every now and then...'

I said, 'It can't be easy, though, with Uncle George gone.'

'It was never easy.'

When all this had begun back in her own time, for the first few weeks after she'd moved her things into the cottage nothing untoward had happened. And then one day while walking in the gardens she'd heard voices, and passing the half-open door in the high wall she'd found Mark and George pruning roses.

George had smiled at her. 'Hello,' he'd said. 'You came back.'

She'd been lost after that.

But it hadn't been easy.

'It was,' she said, 'a very different life than I was used to. You think women have achieved things now, you want to wait and see what's yet to come. And then of course there were the children and their feelings to consider, and the more I fell in love with George the more it all became so very complicated.'

In the woods the bird had stopped its song. Some little creature rustled briefly in the undergrowth and then was gone, and all I heard then was the whisper of the wind among the leaves and further off the plaintive crying of a gull above the shore.

'I went away,' she told me quietly. 'I found it all too much, you see, and once I had returned to my own time I left my cottage and I went away to London.'

She had stayed away for nearly a full year.

'What brought you back?' I asked.

Her answer was a simple one. 'I loved him.'

We sat quietly together in the garden for a moment while I turned this over in my mind, and then she shook the memories off and looked at me.

'Do you feel that you can talk about it yet, my dear? I rather think your story might be more exciting than my own.'

'Oh? Why is that?'

'Because.' She reached across and lightly touched my hand. My left hand. 'Your ring is on a different finger now, and knowing you, that is no accident,' she said. 'You've taken a rare interest in the smugglers of Polgelly. And the coat you wore when you came back last night was stained with blood.' Her hand moved up to smooth the hair back from my swollen cheekbone. 'Then there's this. He didn't do that, did he?'

'Who?'

'The man you've married.'

I had always marveled at how Claire could just accept things, never doubting, taking everything in her stride, and now I finally knew the reason for it. Nothing would surprise her, I thought, after what she'd lived herself.

I shook my head and told her, 'No. He would never hit me.'

And I settled back and told her all of it, beginning where we'd started once before here in this garden, with the voices in the next room and the path that wasn't there.

It took some time to tell it properly. Enough time that we'd gone through one more pot of tea and half a plate of sandwiches before, with difficulty, haltingly, I reached the point where I had stabbed the constable.

'And good for you,' was Claire's pronouncement. 'What a bastard.'

'Yes, well let's just hope he wasn't meant to father somebody important later on.'

Claire didn't think it very likely. 'Anyway, your actions can't change history, as you said.'

'That's Daniel's theory,' I corrected her. 'He thinks

that what has happened is already cast in stone and can't be changed. That's why I couldn't stop Jack being shot and killed, no matter what I did.' That knowledge didn't make it easier to say the words. 'It was his time to die.'

Claire's quiet glance was comforting. 'He seems a very clever man, your Daniel.'

'Yes.' Which brought to mind another theory Daniel and I shared. 'Claire?'

'Yes, darling?'

'When you went away that time, and stayed away so long,' I asked, 'what happened? I mean, did you travel back in time at all?'

She shook her head. 'No. When I wasn't at Trelowarth, nothing happened.'

'And when you *were* here,' I pressed further, 'did you ever travel back in time when you were in Polgelly or St Non's?'

'No. Only here.'

I felt a twist of hope. 'So then it *is* tied to Trelowarth.'

Claire agreed that it did seem to be. 'Perhaps it has something to do with Felicity's ley lines.'

I frowned. 'But why us, though? Why are only the two of us affected? Why not Susan or Felicity or—'

'Darling, it's a mystery, and it likely will remain one. I don't know what brought your Uncle George and I together, and I doubt I ever will. He called to me, somehow,' she said. 'That's all I truly know. He called to me, or else I called to him.' The sun was setting now, the shadows growing longer on the sundial as she looked at it serenely. 'We were both a little lost, I think, and so we found each other. How does anyone find anyone?'

I didn't have the answer. I was thinking about Daniel, lonely after losing Ann, and of myself without Katrina, looking desperately for somewhere to belong. Which one of us, I wondered, had first called out to the other across time?

I watched the sundial too, and drew a breath that caught a little in the place above my heart. 'But it's so hard,' I said. 'I mean, what if I never do go back again? What if the whole thing just stops or...' My next breath caught more painfully.

I thought of Fergal, telling me he wouldn't ever want to know his future. 'Nor should anyone,' he'd told me, 'know what lies in store for someone else, for that would be a burden, would it not?' If he were here, I thought, I could have told him it was just as great a burden, sometimes, *not* to know.

I said as much to Claire. 'It's just so hard,' I said, 'not knowing what will happen.'

She looked at me, and in the fading light her eyes were filled with understanding and with sympathy. And knowledge.

And she asked me, 'Shall I tell you?'

CHAPTER 40

MR. ROWE SLID THE last of the papers across his desk
to me and sat back as discreetly as he could within
the confines of his office to wait while I read through them.

'Perfect,' I said finally. 'Thank you.'

'Not at all.' He watched me initial the pages and sign
them. 'And here,' he said, pointing to one line I'd missed.
'You are sure about this? It's a very large trust.'

'Quite sure, Mr. Rowe. It was never my money,' I tried
to explain. 'It belonged to my sister, and this is what she
would have wanted.'

'But this new arrangement leaves nothing,' he said, 'for
your personal use.'

'I have other accounts.' Which of course was a lie, but I
said it convincingly and with a smile, and he seemed reassured.

'Ah.' He gave a nod.

I signed the final page. 'There's nothing else I need to do?'

'No, nothing. From now on we'll see to everything.
Mr. Hallett and his sister and their heirs can rest assured
that the Trelowarth Trust will be well managed; they
won't have to do a thing but let us know what monies
they require and when.'

'And you'll explain this all to them? They're just off to
Southport today, but they'll be back on Tuesday.'

'Then I shall contact them on Wednesday.'

'I have a letter here, for both of them.' I drew it from my handbag. Passed it over. 'If you wouldn't mind, when you do see them, could you give them this as well?'

'Of course.' He stood when I stood. Shook my hand when I thanked him. 'It's been a great pleasure,' he said.

'And for me.'

I left the bank and stepped back out into the midday sunshine and the narrow crowded street. The mood of the tourists down here in Polgelly had subtly shifted, as though they had only just realized that summer was nearing its end and so too were their holidays. Gone were the leisurely couples and families, replaced by a purposeful horde who were actively looking for fun and impatient to find it, thronging the pavements and pushing through shops in their search for it.

People perched all down the harbor wall as always, with their newspaper-wrapped fish and chips and their rattling striped paper bags from the fudge shop, but even those people seemed restless now, keeping one eye on the time while they ate, no doubt very aware there were still many things left to do in the limited hours of the day that remained.

I knew just how they felt.

I was running a bit late myself when I wended my way through the crowd by the harbor and ducked through the door of the Wellington.

I'd never seen the inside of the pub, and the brightness disarmed me a moment. From the outside the Wellington looked every year of its age, whitewashed walls leaning slightly on ancient foundations, a little bit rough and disreputable— much as it might have looked back in the day when it went by the name of the Spaniard's Rest, when Jack had come to drink rum here and Daniel had made sure his pistol was tucked in his belt before venturing in. Knowing some of that history, I'd somehow expected the inside of the pub to look a little dark and dangerous, a den fit for smugglers and thieves.

Seeing the white stuccoed walls and the honey-warm wood of the tables and booths and the light dancing in through the multi-paned windows surprised me, so much so that Oliver, already comfortably settled in one of the booths with a view of the harbor, glanced up with a grin as I joined him.

'Not quite what you'd pictured?' he guessed.

'Not a bit.'

'I know, it disappointed me too, when my Uncle Alf brought me in here for my first legal pint,' he admitted. 'After the way all us kids had been warned off the Wellie so long, I'd expected there'd be knife marks on the tables and a band of cutthroats in the public bar, but no such luck.' Draining the dregs of the pint he'd been drinking, he levered himself from his seat and asked, 'What can I get you?'

Normally I would have had something nonalcoholic at lunch, but this wasn't a normal day. 'Half of whatever you're having, please.'

Oliver didn't question my choice, crossing over to the bar to place our order with the barman while I bent to read the menu, but when he came back and took his seat again he held my half-pint ransom. 'All right,' he asked me, curious. 'What's wrong?'

'I'm sorry?'

'First you ring me up and ask me out to lunch,' he said, 'which in itself is rather odd, you must admit. And now you're drinking in the middle of the day. Not,' he qualified, with roguish charm, 'that I'm complaining about either, mind, but it does seem a little out of character.'

I pointed at my half-pint. 'Can I have that?'

'When you tell me why you need it.' Leaning slightly back he looked me over, taking stock. 'You're either working up the nerve to proposition me,' he guessed, 'or else you're getting set to break my heart.'

'Oliver...'

'In case you're undecided, I say go with option number one, it's so much more enjoyable for everyone involved.'

I told the table, 'I won't need to rent a cottage from you after all.'

A pause. 'You're staying at Trelowarth, then?'

I shook my head.

'I see.' He took a drink himself. 'So, option number two, then.'

I said, 'Oliver.'

'What changed your mind?'

I shrugged and deflected the question because there was no way to answer it honestly. 'I thought I'd do a bit of traveling.'

'Alone, I take it?'

Glancing up, I saw he wasn't expecting an answer. The smile in his eyes, though resigned, held a trace of regret.

He said, 'Well, I *did* try.'

'You did.'

Leaning confidentially towards me he pretended to look pained. 'Was it the biking shorts? Were they too much?'

It felt good to laugh. I told him, 'No, I rather liked the biking shorts. It was just that... well, I couldn't...'

'Say no more.' He slid my glass across the table to me. 'I mean, you're not the first woman to feel a passion in my presence that's so strong she runs away from it.'

'Is that a fact?'

'It happens all the time.'

He raised his menu, feigning nonchalance, while I regarded him with fondness. How like Oliver, I thought, to try to make this whole thing easy for me, when with any other man it might have been so awkward.

On impulse I told him, 'You really are wonderful.'

He answered without looking up. 'An unfortunate side effect.'

I had to smile. 'Side effect? Of what?'

'Brain damage, actually. Somebody nailed me right here with a rock once.' He showed me the place on the side of his head and his eyes, meeting mine briefly over the top of the menu, lost their teasing light. Just for a moment. 'I've never got over it.'

And then he dropped his gaze back to the menu and said, 'Now, let's see what you're buying me.'

❧

'How did he take it?' asked Susan.

I carefully helped her maneuver the last of the show roses into the van. 'He was fine. He did get a bit drunk, though.'

'He's rather adorable when he gets drunk.' With a smile she admitted, 'I'm not sure that *I* could resist him, in that state.' Securing the roses, she took a look round. 'Is that all of them?'

'I think so, yes.'

'I do wish that you'd change your mind and come.'

'I can't.'

'But you've never been to Southport, and the flower show's quite fun. Besides, I'll need someone to play with. Fee won't have much time for me, will she?' She emphasized that with a meaningful glance past my shoulder to where Mark stood close to Felicity, talking, beside the front door. But in spite of her complaining, Susan didn't look at all put out. In fact, she looked well satisfied by how things were developing. 'Do come,' she said.

I explained that I would if I could. 'But I can't change my travel arrangements.'

'Too bad. Maybe next year, then.'

'Maybe.'

She dusted her hands on her jeans. 'Look, you've been such a help. I can't thank you enough.'

She was talking, I knew, about more than our loading the van, but I'd played such a small role in launching the tearoom that I couldn't take any credit. I said, 'It was nothing.'

'Of course it was something. I mean, our new website, and all that publicity, bringing the tour groups on board. Not to mention the trouble you went to, to find me those smugglers to spice up the brochures. And now Mark,' she said, with a nod at the van, 'doing this. It's your influence, Eva. We couldn't have done it without you.'

I wanted to say, 'Yes, you could,' but her eyes were so earnest I kept my thoughts private and hugged her instead. 'You take care of yourself.'

'And you. Don't you forget us,' she told me. 'Come back any time.'

My hug briefly tightened, and then I released her and said, 'Have a good time in Southport.'

Felicity, when it was her turn to wish me well, gave me a gift.

'I remember you liked him,' she said, as she passed me the little bronze sculpture. My pisky, the one I had held and admired in her shop on that day when she'd told me the story of Porthallow Green and the piskies who'd taken the young boy adventuring, whisking him dancing from place to place as the mood took them. The pisky looked up from the palm of my hand with his wide knowing smile.

Felicity said, 'It's insurance, to see that you'll find your way back to us. Just tell him, "I'm for Trelowarth".'

'I'll do that.' I closed my fingers round the little figure. 'Thank you.'

Mark stood and waited beside the front door as though knowing I'd want our goodbye to come last.

When it did, it was all at once harder and easier than I had thought it would be.

'Summer's end,' he said. 'Just like old times.'

'So it is.'

But it wasn't like old times, not really, and both of us knew it. Those lazy, long ago summers when the four of us children had run at our will through the gardens and roamed the Wild Wood and played laughingly all through the streets of Polgelly, those summers were gone and would not come again.

Still, the gardens remained and the roses returned, and there'd be other summers to come and new memories to make.

Mark said, 'You used to stuff your pockets full of fudge before you left.'

I smiled. 'I might still do that. What time does the fudge shop close?'

'Don't know. Just mind, if you go down the hill you have to come back up,' he told me, 'and I won't be here to carry you.'

'You've carried me enough this summer. All of you.'

'Yeah well, you needed it, I reckon.' His keen eyes were understanding. 'Better now?'

I nodded. Wanting to be honest with him, I said, 'Mark, I don't know when I'll make it back again, or even if… that is, it might be quite awhile.' I let my gaze drop to the ground between us, feeling at a loss, and Mark stepped forwards, wrapping me within his solid arms.

'It took you twenty years the last time,' he reminded me. 'However long it takes this time, it won't make any difference.'

'It's not you,' I tried to tell him. 'I love all of you, I do. I love Trelowarth. But…' I couldn't find the words.

He found them for me. 'It's not home.'

Grateful, I rested my cheek against his for a moment and shook my head.

He took a step away and stood there looking down at me, the same old Mark, the same slow smile, the comfort of his hands still so familiar on my shoulders. 'That's all right,' he said. 'I didn't really think it would be. After all, Katrina's ashes wouldn't settle at Trelowarth either.'

I'd forgotten that. I felt my smile wobble but it must have had my heart in it because he flicked a finger lightly down my cheek the way he'd done when I was small and he was feeling brotherly. 'I'm sorry that I won't be here to drive you to the station.'

'Claire can see me off.'

He gave a nod and leaned to kiss my forehead. 'You take care.'

'You too.'

It was past time for them to leave. I stayed there standing in the drive while they went off. I waved, then tucked both hands deep in my jacket's pockets as the van blurred very briefly in my vision.

From the region of my feet I heard a mournful little whine, and looking down I saw the small dog, Samson, sitting with his gaze fixed up the road where Mark had gone. He whined again and trembled slightly, and I bent to give his head a pat of reassurance.

'It's OK,' I told the dog, 'you'll see him soon.'

I felt the small bronze pisky weighing heavy in my hand,

and in a softer voice I said again, more certainly, 'You'll see him soon.'

The pisky's smile held mischief mingled with its knowing wisdom as I looked at it a moment, and I marveled again at Felicity's craftsmanship, giving this small bit of metal such life. I remembered her saying, 'In Cornwall, one truly feels magic could actually happen.' And thinking again of the legend of Porthallow Green, I held tight to my pisky and gave it a try.

Eyes closed, I said, 'I'm for Daniel Butler.'

But the wind that brushed my upturned face was all the answer I received.

Beside me, Samson whined again, and I opened my eyes. The other dogs had taken off already with the happiness of schoolchildren released from supervision, and I could see them bounding in a joyous pack along the path towards the Lower Garden.

Beyond that lay the green rise of the fields above the darker smudge of woods that tumbled down to where the black cliffs met the sea, with the wind raising ridges of white on the water as far out from land as my vision would stretch.

Above those waves the white birds wheeled and spiraled in the air and I was suddenly reminded of what Mark had said about Katrina's ashes, and I thought back to the day when we'd released them on this hill, when they had gathered in the wind and danced away.

In search of someplace else, so Mark had thought. Except I knew now in my heart that wasn't right. Not some*place*.

Someone.

And I thought I knew, at last, where she had gone.

CHAPTER 41

H E DIDN'T CALL BACK till the following morning.
I worked the times backwards: if it was nine here,
that would mean in L.A., it was one in the morning.

'Eva?'

I heard the sounds of a party around him—the clink of a
glass and an outburst of laughter and over it all the pervasive
loud beating of dance music.

'Bill, hi.' I sat at the edge of my bed. 'Thanks for getting
back.'

'I would have called you earlier, but I was on the set, and
then it got too late. I figured you'd be sleeping,' he explained.
A pause. 'How are you?'

'Fine. I'm fine. And you?'

The party sounds receded slightly as though he had
stepped away a pace or two in search of a more private
corner. 'I'm managing. You know.' Another pause. 'You're
still in Europe?'

'For the moment, yes. In Cornwall, at Trelowarth. Did
Katrina ever talk about Trelowarth?'

'Yes.' He knew where I was headed. 'That's the place, then?'

I nodded, forgetting that he couldn't see me. 'I scattered
her up in her favorite spot, up on the hill at the Beacon.'

'Good choice.'

'No, it wasn't.' I gripped the phone tighter and lowered

my head, and in a stumbling rush I told him what had happened, how the ashes had refused to settle, swirling on the wind and chasing out across the sea. 'You wanted her to be where she belonged,' I said, 'but Bill, it wasn't here.'

'Hey.' From the hoarseness of that single word I guessed what it was costing him to try to reassure me. 'Sure it was. I mean, where else—?'

'With you.' I heard my voice break, just a little, and I steadied it to tell him, 'She belonged with you.'

For several heartbeats afterwards the muted party noises were the only sounds that carried down the line. Perhaps, like me, he was imagining Katrina's ashes blowing westward over the Atlantic. Heading home.

'I just… I wanted to apologize,' I said. 'I got it wrong. You were the great love of her life, Bill. Where *you* were, that's where Katrina would have wanted most to be. That's where she should be.'

His lighter clicked, and I could hear his deep pull on the cigarette and then the long exhale. 'She still is, Eva. She's here with me every day. You didn't get it wrong.' Another pause, and I could sense that he was searching for the words that would convince me of that, grant me absolution. After half a minute more he said, 'Trelowarth's just a place, you know?'

Trelowarth, said Daniel's voice, warm in my memory, *is rooms gathered under a roof, nothing more.*

My eyes stung. 'Yes, I know.'

We left it there.

❧

I'd been afraid the day would stretch unbearably. This was still new and strange to me, this knowing what was yet to come, and thanks to Claire I knew that what was coming would not happen until dark. I'd thought the waiting might be my undoing, but the fact was there were still things left to finish, and the knowledge that I wouldn't have another chance to finish them made every hour fly faster.

It took me till that afternoon to get the files in order that I'd wanted to leave Susan, so she could take care of any future PR work herself. And when I'd switched off the computer there was still the packing left to do.

The afternoon had given way to evening almost before I had noticed, and by the time Claire came round after supper I was only just then finishing the final task of pinning up my hair.

She sat and watched me. 'I must say, you do that very neatly, Eva. Who taught you how?'

'Fergal, actually.'

'The Irishman?' She placed him with a nod. I'd told her all about the people living at Trelowarth in the past, and Claire had an efficient memory. 'It sounds as though he helped you quite a bit this summer.'

'Yes,' I said. 'He did.'

'I'm glad. It makes a world of difference, having someone to confide in.'

There was something faintly wistful in her voice that made me feel a twinge of guilt at leaving her, until I realized that I wasn't really leaving her alone.

I thought about that evening in her garden when she'd told me what the future held in store for me, and how she'd come to know it. She'd begun a little curiously in my view, by asking whether I remembered when she'd told the story of the Grey Lady who'd vanished at Trelowarth.

'Yes, of course,' I'd said.

'Do you remember when I said it happened?'

'Yes, before your parents' time, you said.' And I'd looked up at her in sudden realization.

Claire had met my eyes. 'My parents, dear, aren't born yet. Not in this time.'

'And the Grey Lady...?'

'Is you.'

She had explained it all again to me, how in the future she would meet an old man in the village who would tell her of the woman who had disappeared before his eyes when he was young. And he would know exactly who I was. He'd know my name.

She'd told me his name too, and I had tried to take it in, but even so I'd had to stop her midway through her tale to make sure I'd heard her correctly.

'And *he* was the old man you met in the pub,' I'd said, just to be certain, 'the old man you rented this cottage from.'

'Yes.'

'But you said that the cottage had come to him through his wife's family. And she'd been a Hallett.'

'That's right.' Claire had waited patiently, her gaze expectant on my face, until I'd sorted through the possibilities and reached the only answer.

'Susan.' I had been surprised at first, but then it seemed so right that I'd repeated it with pleasure. 'His wife was Susan.'

Claire had nodded. 'It was, he said, a very happy marriage. He had lost her just the year before I met him, and he clearly still adored her.'

I had thought a moment, making sense of everything. 'So you believe him, then. That I'm the Grey Lady?'

'Oh yes. He might have been a very old man when we first met,' she'd admitted, 'but there wasn't any problem with his memory. Everything he ever told me would happen did happen, my darling. And he was quite sure about this. As I said, he was there.'

'*Will* be there,' I'd corrected her vaguely. 'I haven't gone anywhere yet.'

I'd looked towards the sundial with its butterfly forever frozen on the brink of flight. Below them waved the ring of bright geraniums I'd helped Claire plant—the only mark I'd left upon Trelowarth in this time, and even that was passing. Soon the blooms would fade and nod and die and no one would remember them. 'Aunt Claire,' I'd said, asking the question she hadn't yet answered, the one that most mattered to me.

'Yes?'

'Did she ever come back, this Grey Lady who vanished?'

Claire had turned to me fully that time, and our eyes had met. 'No,' she had told me, 'she never came back.'

And I'd felt a small catch of emotion then, tight round my heart, feeling almost like hope.

I could feel it again, growing stronger as I covered my hair with the white linen pinner and turned around now to face Claire so she'd have the full effect. 'There.'

'Very nice.' Claire looked me up and down, admiring the lines of the dress. 'He chose that for you, did he? Clever man. The color's lovely.'

The green had a soothing effect on my nerves as I lifted the skirts to adjust them and took a look round to make sure I'd done everything. Both of my suitcases sat neatly packed on the furthermost bed. 'I suppose,' I said slowly, 'I'm ready.'

We each took a suitcase and carried them down the short way to the first landing, setting them down while I sprang the stiff panel that hid the old priest's hole. 'You're sure this will be OK?'

'Darling, it's been here for centuries now without anyone knowing. It's quite the safest place to leave things,' she said. 'Better than a cupboard.'

To prove it she tucked one case neatly away in the narrow dark space, taking care not to pull at the delicate fabric of Ann's faded gowns that we'd hung in here earlier, next to the coat that had been the man Peter's and Daniel's silk banyan that I'd first brought back. I slid the second case into its place and positioned Felicity's pisky on top of it, leaving him there with his all-knowing smile to watch over things as I stepped back a pace, letting the panel swing closed again.

Someday, I thought, when Trelowarth House fell to the elements, some archaeologist might stumble over those twenty-first century cases of clothes sharing space with an old bloodstained coat and the banyan and two eighteenth-century gowns and might wonder about them, and try to form theories explaining the puzzle of how they had come to be there in one place... but I'd lay odds that none of the theories would ever come close to the truth.

And the walls held their silence, no whispers this evening as I followed Claire down the staircase and through the bright kitchen and out the back door with the dogs coming too, keeping close to our heels in a tail-wagging pack, ever curious, seeking excitement.

They seemed to find it in the scents that rode the cooling night breeze blowing shoreward from the sea, and with their noses bouncing happily from air to ground and back again, they snuffed their way around the yard, some venturing with interest to the stable building doorstep, no doubt hoping that their master had returned.

I stayed with Claire and went no further than the honey-suckle vine that climbed the wall beside the kitchen window.

There was light here slanting out across the softness of the grass and casting shadows through the vine's leaves in a finely tangled net that made a pattern on my green silk gown.

I asked Claire, 'Are you sure we're not too late?'

'Darling,' she said, 'you can't possibly miss it, there's no need to worry.'

I realized she was right, that while for me the whole event had not yet taken place, in Claire's time it was something done and finished with, belonging to the past; the moving finger had already written what must happen.

But that knowledge, reassuring as it might be, didn't make me feel less nervous.

'Yes, but when—?' I left the question hanging, because just then one of the dogs raised its head and gave a shortened bark that brought the other dogs to quick attention, all their noses turned in the direction of the road.

Like them, I heard the footsteps on the gravel drive. Claire did as well.

'Quite soon, I should imagine,' was her answer as she turned to greet our visitor as he came round the corner of the house. 'Good evening, Oliver.'

And in that single moment I knew everything she'd told me had been true.

Oliver came round the side of the house and glanced up at Claire's greeting.

'Hello,' he said, fending the happily leaping dogs off with one hand as I saw him both notice my gown and, with typical nonchalance, choose not to comment beyond a quick nod and a cheerful, 'Nice frock.' He stepped closer and flashed his endearing smile. 'I thought with everyone gone off to Southport, you might be in need of some company.'

Claire said, 'I see you've brought wine.'

There was something about how she said that, some note in her voice that reminded me this was a night she herself must have waited a very long time for—this night when she'd finally be able to sit down and talk, really talk, to the man who would become her friend and confidant; the man who would one day be Susan's husband, and the man whom she would meet again some sixty years from now, when he was old and she was young.

She wouldn't know him then, of course, because for her it would be their first meeting, but Oliver would recognize *her*. On that day she walked into the pub, he would approach her, and he'd offer her the cottage, and he'd share with her the story of the Grey Lady he'd once seen disappear before his eyes, here at Trelowarth. Eventually, he'd tell her more.

He'd be as good a friend to her in her own time as he would be in this one after they sat down and talked tonight, and I was pleased to know that by my leaving I was bringing them together.

'It does make a world of difference,' Claire had told me, 'having someone to confide in.'

She would have that soon, I thought.

But for the moment Oliver was still in total ignorance of what was yet to come.

He looked down at the bottle he was holding. 'Yes, it's only the one bottle, I'm afraid, but—'

'That will do,' Claire told him, 'for a start.'

'I'm sorry?'

She didn't explain. She only reached to take the bottle from him. 'Here, you'd better let me hold that, dear.'

And just in time. The air around me had already started changing, and the breeze had stopped, and at the edges of my vision all the colors of the landscape had begun to run,

the honeysuckle vine washed grey against the stone walls of
Trelowarth House.

I had the sense of movement to the side of me and,
turning, I could see a shape that might have been a man
approaching. Unaware of me at first, he nearly passed me by
before he stopped, and I could see that it was Fergal now. I
saw the quick flash of his grin as his head lifted slightly and
although I couldn't hear him it appeared that he was calling
out to someone in the house.

Oliver's voice seemed to come from a very great distance.
'My God,' he said. 'Eva…'

Claire calmed him, 'It's all right. She's fine.'

A sudden brightness flashed behind me and I turned
instinctively towards it, blinking, watching it resolve itself
into a shape I recognized: the warm light of the open doorway
with one shadowed figure framed within it.

Daniel.

Looking at him then I knew there was no need to
wonder anymore where I belonged. There lay my home,
I thought, and all the comforts I could want, and come
the spring when all the Duke of Ormonde's plans to raise
a great rebellion in the west of England had been set aside
for schemings of a newer sort, the *Sally* would raise anchor
on the turning tide and sail towards the south, to Spain
perhaps, or the Canary Isles, where no one would remark
upon my accent and where Fergal could indulge his taste
for sack and maybe find a Spanish woman who could match
his wit and temper.

What did it matter that our lives would leave no mark
upon Trelowarth? That the path through the woods which
had led to the cliffs where the *Sally* lay moored would be
needed no longer, and little by little the years would reclaim

it, the trees growing over the trails of our feet until no one would know we had walked there at all?

I would know, and remember, and that was enough.

A breath of wind brushed past my face and brought the scent of woodsmoke with it from the kitchen hearth.

I looked back once at Oliver and Claire. Claire's cheeks were wet but she was smiling as she gave a nod and mouthed the word 'goodbye'.

I thought I heard the words 'come back' as well, but whether it was Oliver or Daniel who had spoken them I couldn't tell. My face by then was turning to the warm light of the open doorway and the man who stood within it, waiting for me.

Gaining substance by the second.

Wordlessly he stretched his hand towards me, and I saw his smile.

And with a smile, I went to him.

THE END

A NOTE FROM THE AUTHOR

Polgelly is the Cornwall of my memory. But it bears a strong resemblance to the village of Polperro, as it was when I first saw it in the summer that remains the brightest bead in all my string of childhood memories. And Trelowarth owes its heritage to Landaviddy Manor, on the hill above Polperro, where my sister and I shared a room that looked towards the sea.

I've changed the names, in part because it *is* a work of memory and in part because I've changed the landscape and the house to suit my story's needs: I've left The Hill exactly where it should be, but I've moved the cottage and the beach, and added in the Beacon and the Wild Wood and the gardens.

In my building of the latter, I'm indebted to the kind and generous help of Stewart and Rebecca Pocock, award-winning owners of both Pocock's Roses of Hampshire and The Cornish Rose Company of Mitchell, near Truro, who were constantly encouraging and patient with their guidance, as was Lara Crisp, my UK editor, who helped me prune the deadwood from my manuscript to let it take the shape that it was meant to be.

I'm thankful as well for the help of my friend, fellow writer Liz Fenwick, who from her Cornish home took time to help me get my details right.

The years stand still for no one, but I've always felt a magic in the crossing of the Tamar, and I like to think perhaps some future traveler to Polperro, having climbed The Hill, may hear a burst of laughter from the lawn of Landaviddy Manor, high above the sea, and glimpse the shadows of two sisters still at play there, in another time.

THIS TIME, THE FINAL time, it was early April, two months shy of my thirtieth birthday, and—for once—I was not lost. I still lived in London, in a tiny rented flat in Bloomsbury that I had become rooted to, in spite of an unexpectedly generous legacy left to me by my father's Aunt Helen, that same aunt we'd been visiting in Exeter all those years earlier. She'd only seen me twice, had Auntie Helen, so why she had chosen to leave me such an obscene amount of money remained a mystery. Perhaps it was because I was the only girl in a family known for its male progeny. Auntie Helen, according to my father, had been possessed of staunchly feminist views. 'A room of your own,' Tom had told me, in a decided tone. 'That's what she's left you. Haven't you read Virginia Woolf?'

It was rather more than the price of a room, actually, but I hadn't the slightest idea what to do with it. Tom had stoutly refused my offer to share the inheritance, and my parents maintained they had no need of it, being comfortably well-off themselves since my father's retirement from surgical practice. So that was that.

I had quite enough to occupy my time, as it was, having shifted careers from graphic design to illustration, a field I found both more interesting and more lucrative. By some stroke of luck I had been teamed early on with a wonderfully talented author, and our collaboration on a series of fantasy tales for children had earned me a respectable name for myself in the business, not to mention a steady living. I had just that week been commissioned to illustrate a sizeable new collection of legends and fairy tales from around the world, a project that excited me greatly and promised to keep me busily employed for the better part of a year. I was on top of the world.

Ordinarily, I'd have celebrated my good fortune with my family, but since my parents were halfway round the world on holiday and Tom was occupied with Easter services, I had settled for the next best thing and spent the weekend with friends in Bath. On the Monday morning, finding the traffic on the main road too busy for my taste, I detoured to the north and followed the gentle sweep of the Kennet River towards London.

It was a cool but perfect spring day, and the trees that lined the road were bursting into leaf with an almost tropical fervour. In honour of the season, I drove with the windows down, and the air smelt sweetly of rain and soil and growing things.

My arthritic but trustworthy Peugeot crested a small hill with a protesting wheeze. Gathering speed, I negotiated a broad curve where the road dipped down into a shallow valley before crossing over the Kennet via a narrow stone bridge. As I bumped across the bridge, I felt a faint tingling sensation sweep across the back of my neck, and my fingers tightened on the wheel in anticipation.

The most surprising thing was that I wasn't at all surprised, this time, to see the house. Somehow, I almost expected it to be there.

I slowed the car to a crawl, then pulled off the road and

stopped altogether, just opposite the long gravel drive. A large ginger cat stalked haughtily across the road without so much as glancing at me, and disappeared into the waving grass. Three times in one lifetime, I told myself, even without the cat, was definitely beyond the bounds of ordinary coincidence.

Surely, I reasoned, whoever owned the house wouldn't mind terribly if I just took a casual peek around...? As I hesitated, biting my lip, a flock of starlings rose in a beating cloud from the field beside me, gathered and wheeled once above the grey stone house, and then was gone.

For me, that was the deciding factor. Along with my mother's looks, I had also inherited the superstitious nature of her Cornish ancestors, and the starlings were a good-luck omen of my own invention. From my earliest childhood, whenever I had seen a flock of them it meant that something wonderful was about to happen. My brother Tom repeatedly tried to point out the flaw in this belief, by reminding me that starlings in the English countryside were not exactly uncommon, and that their link to my happiness could only be random at best. I remained unconvinced. I only knew that the starlings had never steered me wrong, and watching them turn now and rise above the house, I suddenly made a decision.

I grabbed my shapeless green anorak from the seat beside me and stepped out of the car, nearly tumbling into the ditch in my eagerness. I wasn't exactly dressed to go visiting, I admitted, tugging the anorak on over my jeans and rough sweater—but that couldn't be helped. I ran a hand through my hair in a hopeless attempt to smooth the short, unruly curls, but the damply blowing wind spoilt my efforts.

Now, I thought, what excuse to use? Directions? A glass of water? Trouble with the car? I glanced back at the dented and battered Peugeot and nodded. Car trouble, I decided. Anyone would believe that. Mentally rehearsing my lines, I crossed the road and started up the gravel drive. A cracked and weathered signboard bearing the words 'Strictly Private' in faded red paint hung dejectedly from a nail in a nearby tree. Undaunted, I soldiered on, hoping that my footsteps didn't sound as crunchingly loud to the people inside as they did to my own ears.

The house looked exactly as I remembered it—the same red chimneys with their clay chimney pots; the same symmetrically positioned white windows, four panes over four; the same rough-hewn grey stone walls under the steep slate roof. The only thing different was the door. I had always imagined it to be brown, but now I saw that it was clearly dark green, standing out in sharp contrast to the massive stone portal that surrounded it.

My knocking echoed heavily with a dull and hollow sound. Three times I bruised my knuckles against the heavy wood, before finally conceding that no one was coming to answer the door.

Which meant there was nobody home. And, I told myself happily, since there was nobody home, it followed that no one would be disturbed if I went round to the back of the house and looked in a few windows. Having thus rationalised my trespassing, I retraced my steps to the drive and followed it round the north side of the house.

Here the drive ended abruptly at a squat, low-slung stone building with a weedy thatched roof. Presumably this had once been the stables, but the bumper of a car protruding from one of the open stalls left no doubt as to its present use.

The view from where I stood, looking across the level farmlands and gently undulating downs, broken here and there by clusters of dark-green trees and wild shrubs, was truly beautiful. There was no yard as such, although a tumbled heap of stone a hundred feet or so behind the house looked as if it might once have been part of a boundary wall. And though I had counted three oaks, a fruit tree, and several shrubs at the front, the only bit of vegetation growing close against the back wall of the house was a solitary poplar with gnarled bark, its silvery-green branches trembling in the breeze.

There was another dark-green door here, with an old-fashioned latch, and another double row of white-painted windows. Beneath what I assumed must be the kitchen window, someone had piled a precarious stack of ancient flowerpots, their sides encrusted with thick black moss from lack of use. I stretched on tiptoe and leant closer, cupping one hand against the glass to shield my eyes against the reflected glare of the sun. It *was* a window to the kitchen, or perhaps the pantry. I could just make out a shelf of tinned goods and an old porcelain sink. I was angling my head for a better look when a man's voice spoke suddenly out of the air behind me.

'He's not there.'

It was a friendly voice, with a faintly un-English burr to it, and had come from some distance away. But I didn't register any of that immediately. I spun round, startled, and sent the pile of flowerpots crashing to the ground.

At first I could see no one, but as I stood there staring, the figure of a man detached itself from the tumbled stone wall and came across the grass towards me. He was a young man, perhaps five years my senior, dressed in rough working clothes and wearing leather gauntlets that looked oddly medieval and out of place.

'I didn't mean to frighten you,' he apologised. 'I just thought, if you're looking for Eddie, he's not there.'

He was quite close now, close enough for me to clearly see the combination of auburn hair and flint-grey eyes that is, somehow, so distinctively Scottish. He smiled, a friendly smile that matched the voice.

'Are you a friend of Eddie's?' he asked.

I shook my head.

'A relative, then.'

'No.' To my credit, I blushed a little. I had a hunch my tale of phony car trouble would not make it past those shrewd grey eyes. 'No, I don't know the owner. Will he be back soon, do you know?'

The man tilted his head to one side and gave me a long, measuring look that rather reminded me of my brother.

'I hope not,' he said evenly. 'We buried him last month.'

'Oh, I'm sorry.' I blushed deeper. 'I really am sorry.'

'No harm done.' He shrugged. 'You're just having a poke about, then?'

My face, by this time, was crimson, and I had a feeling that he was enjoying my obvious discomfort. It took a moment, but the full importance of what he'd just told me finally sank in, and I abruptly forgot my embarrassment.

I lifted my eyes quickly. 'Is the house for sale, then?'

'Aye. Did you want to have a look at it?

'I want to buy it. I've waited twenty-five years for this house.'

The man raised a russet eyebrow, and for some absurd reason I found myself babbling out the whole story of 'The House and I', to which he listened with admirable patience. I can't imagine he found it very interesting. When I'd finished my childish narrative, his level gaze met mine for a second time, and the resemblance to my brother was even more pronounced.

'Well, then,' he said solemnly, 'you'd best see Mr Ridley in the High Street. I've not got my own keys with me, or I'd show you round myself.' He stripped off one gauntlet and extended a hand in greeting. 'I'm Iain Sumner, by the way.'

'Julia Beckett.' I must have altered my expression at the sight of his hand, because he smiled again, looking down at the tiny lacerations marring his skin.

'Brambles,' he explained. 'They'd choke out my garden if I didn't thin them back. It's not painful,' he assured me, pulling the glove back on. 'I'd best be getting back to my work. Good luck with the house.'

'Thank you,' I said, but he was already out of earshot.

Five minutes later I was sitting in the offices of Ridley and Stewart, Estate Agents. I confess I don't remember much about that afternoon. I do recall a confusing blur of conversation, with Mr Ridley rambling on about legal matters, conveyances and searches and the like, but I wasn't really listening.

'You're quite certain,' Mr Ridley had asked me, 'that you don't want to view the property first?'

'I've seen it,' I'd assured him. To be honest, there seemed no need for such formalities. It was, after all, my house. My house. I was still hugging the knowledge tightly, as a child hugs a present, when I knocked on the door of the rectory of St Stephen's, Elderwel, Hampshire, that evening.

'Congratulate me, Vicar.' I beamed up at my brother's startled face. 'We're practically neighbours. I just bought a house in Wiltshire.'

READING GROUP GUIDE

1. The first known time-travel story appeared in the year 720, in a Japanese book called the *Nihongi*, and many other writers since then have explored the concept. What do you think is the reason for the enduring appeal of time-travel stories?

2. Stephen Hawking, in his essay "How to Build a Time Machine," says: "Time travel was once considered scientific heresy. I used to avoid talking about it for fear of being labeled a crank. But these days I'm not so cautious... I do believe in time travel." Does knowing that noted physicists like Hawking accept the fact of time as a fourth dimension make the whole idea of time travel seem more believable to you, or do you feel it's all a fantasy?

3. Fergal says of Daniel: "Knowing that the battle will not end the way he wishes does not make it any less worthwhile to fight." Daniel stays committed to his cause and to his kinsmen, even though it puts himself and those he loves in harm's way. Do you find this noble or naive?

4. Claire is able to meet her grandparents as young people and be present at the moment they first met. What moment

in your own family history would you like to witness if you could?

5. Katrina remains an unseen extra character throughout the story. How do you think she influences Eva's actions, and where did you sense this most strongly?

6. Eva's appearance is never described in the novel, except for the length of her hair. Did you notice this? Did it affect your ability to "see" her? Why do you think that the author chose not to describe her?

7. What do you think is likely to be the biggest challenge for Eva in her new life; the biggest adjustment she'll have to make? What would you find most difficult about living in the early eighteenth century?

8. One of the reasons that some scientists, including Hawking, think that time travel to the past is less likely to happen and more problematic than travel to the future, has to do with paradoxes and the problems they create: the chance that a time traveler might meet a former version of himself or somehow change the way the future is meant to happen. In *The Rose Garden*, Daniel dismisses this idea outright. His view is that nothing Eva does in the past can change the future, and her own experience seems to bear this out. What did you think of this departure from the usual rules of time travel? How did you feel about Daniel's belief that our lives are predestined, that what happens to us is just meant to happen?

9. In the past, Fergal steps in to become Eva's mentor and confidant. Which character do you think fills these roles in the present?

10. Even though she knew what Eva was going through, Claire purposely stayed out of things and didn't interfere. Do you think she took the right approach? Is there any way she could have made things easier for Eva? How might the story have changed if she'd been more involved?

11. The love scenes in this book (and in all of Susanna Kearsley's books) are decidedly G-rated. Do you like this approach, or do you prefer the bedroom door to be left open? Can a love story with no sex still be sexy?

12. The historical account of the attempt to raise a Jacobite rebellion force in Cornwall is true, and the events of the past story are played out against an actual historical timeline, even using some real people, like the traitorous Colonel Maclean. Does it change the way you read a story when you know that some of the events really happened? Do you find it a strength or a weakness in fiction?

13. Do you think historical fiction is a valid and useful way of learning about history? Were there any bits of history you learned from this book that you didn't know before?

14. Apart from her feelings for Daniel, why do you think Eva felt more at home in the past than the present? Did you notice any differences in the way she fit into or was treated in the two different Trelowarths?

15. At the end of the book, Eva is very certain and confident that she and Daniel will be able to build a life together in the past. Do you share her confidence? What qualities do you think she and Daniel each bring to the relationship that will help make it a success?

For additional reading group guides, please visit
www.sourcebooks.com/readingguides

ABOUT THE AUTHOR

After studying politics and international development at university, Susanna Kearsley worked as a museum curator before turning her hand to writing. Winner of the UK's Catherine Cookson Fiction prize, Susanna Kearsley's writing has been compared to Mary Stewart, Daphne du Maurier, and Diana Gabaldon. Her books have been translated into several languages, selected for the Mystery Guild, condensed for *Reader's Digest*, and optioned for film. *The Winter Sea* was a *New York Times* and *USA Today* bestseller, as well as a finalist for both a RITA award and the UK's Romantic Novel of the Year Award. She lives in Canada, near the shores of Lake Ontario.